Novellas — that satisfying midway point between short stories and novels, combining richness and limitation, length and intensity — have a fine tradition in New Zealand writing, and several of this country's most important writers have done some of their best work in this genre. This anthology — a follow-up to the same editor's *Seven New Zealand Novellas* (Reed, 2003), which was a finalist in the Montana Book Awards — groups work from nine top writers, including Janet Frame and Maurice Shadbolt in the 1960s, Ronald Hugh Morrieson and Ian Wedde in the 1970s, Keri Hulme, Russell Haley and Witi Ihimaera in the 1980s, and Mike Johnson and Chad Taylor in the 1990s.

Peter Simpson is associate professor and head of English at the University of Auckland. Born in Takaka, he has degrees from the University of Canterbury and the University of Toronto. He has taught at universities in New Zealand and Canada since the 1960s. He is the author of *Ronald Hugh Morrieson* (OUP, 1982) and *Answering Hark: McCahon/Caselberg: Painter/Poet* (Potton, 2002). He has edited several books, including most recently *Engravings on Wood* by Leo Bensemann (Holloway Press, 2004), and writes frequently for journals on New Zealand literature and art. He is also a curator and the managing editor of the University of Auckland's Holloway Press.

# NINE NEW ZEALAND NOVELLAS

Edited and with an introduction by
## Peter Simpson

REED

## Reed Publishing (NZ) Ltd

Te Karuhi tā tāpui o Reed (Aotearoa)

Established in 1907, Reed is New Zealand's largest
book publisher, with over 300 titles in print.

For details on all these books visit our website:
www.reed.co.nz

Published by Reed Books, a division of Reed Publishing (NZ) Ltd, 39 Rawene Rd, Birkenhead,
Auckland. Associated companies, branches and representatives throughout the world.

ISBN 0 7900 0992 7

© 2005 Introduction Peter Simpson

National Library of New Zealand Cataloguing-in-Publication Data

Nine New Zealand novellas / edited an with an introduction by
Peter Simpson.
ISBN 0-7900-0992-7
1. Short stories, New Zealand. 2. New Zealand fiction—20th century.
I. Simpson, Peter, 1942-
NZ823.010802—dc 22

Text design by Suzanne Wesley
Cover image courtesy of Gaffer Glass
Photography by Haruhiko Sameshima
Cover design by Sally Fullam

Printed in China

# Contents

# Introduction

*Nine New Zealand Novellas* is a companion volume to *Seven New Zealand Novellas* published by Reed in 2003. As a matter of editorial policy, none of the writers is repeated from the earlier book, though most of those included in the first book, notably Katherine Mansfield, Frank Sargeson, Maurice Duggan, Peter Wells and Elizabeth Knox, published more than one distinguished novella. Together the two volumes constitute a fairly comprehensive survey of the novella as practised by New Zealanders. In *Seven New Zealand Novellas* my purpose was partly historical; I chose works which, in addition to being excellent novellas in their own right, also represented developments in New Zealand fiction over much of the twentieth century, from Mansfield in 1918 to Wells and Knox in the 1990s. In the earlier decades, up to, say, the late 1950s, there was not a wide range to choose from, because of the paucity of works of fiction in general, but from the 1960s onwards the frequency with which the novella was practised increased markedly. This was not so much because the novella was especially favoured but because the number of practitioners of prose fiction rapidly increased and has continued to do so. Prior to the 1960s it was rare for more volumes of fiction (whether novels, novellas or short stories) to be published in a single year than could be counted on the fingers of one hand. In recent decades, however, the annual crop of books is regularly measured in the dozens. In 2004, for example, 42 works of fiction were submitted for the Montana Book Awards. A second volume of novellas, which focuses on the period since 1960, represents more adequately the richness of New Zealand fiction in this period than was possible in a single book.

Of the nine novellas included here two belong to the 1960s (Frame, Shadbolt), three to the 1970s (Morrieson, Wedde), three to the 1980s (Haley, Hulme, Ihimaera), and three to the 1990s (Johnson, Taylor). This book, therefore, provides a satisfying survey of some of the best fiction of the past four decades as well as a further demonstration of the richness of the novella form.

No single definition of the novella will cover the wide variety of fictional practice represented by these nine examples, except a very general description such as that offered by Richard Ford in 'Why Not a Novella?', the essay which introduces his anthology *The Granta Book of the American Long Story* (London, Granta Books, 1998):

> *Novella was the Latin-y sounding word long in use to refer to prose fictions of a certain, intermediate length; intermediate 'between' the modern prose forms that had achieved if not reliable definition, at least scholarly and readerly acceptance as entities — novels and short stories. (p. xi)*

Ford, who ultimately rejected the term novella in favour of 'long story', nevertheless offers an informative history of the novella form in literature. He points out that the term originates in the Latin word *novus*, meaning new or young, and that the term seems first to have been applied to literature in the fourteenth century to describe *The Decameron* by Giovanni Boccaccio, a collection of written stories supposedly recited by a group of young nobles from Florence who had fled from the plague to the Tuscan highlands, where they entertained each other with diverting and often bawdy tales. The notion of novellas being a group of stories linked by a narrative framework survived in Europe for several centuries and was followed by writers such as Cervantes in Spain and Goethe in Germany. The latter, whose influential definition of the novella was simply a story involving 'one authentic unheard-of event', instigated a period of great popularity for the novella in Germany that was carried into the twentieth century by writers such as Thomas Mann and Franz Kafka; the form was also taken up in Russia (Tolstoy, Dostoevsky, Chekhov), England (Henry James, Joseph Conrad, D.H. Lawrence), and America (Melville, Hemingway, Edith Wharton, Katherine Anne Porter).

To my knowledge there has never been in New Zealand much theoretical discussion of the novella, or the sense of there being a specific New Zealand 'tradition' of the genre, though, as I argued in the introduction to *Seven New Zealand Novellas*, it is a form that New Zealanders have utilised particularly well. The examples chosen here represent a wide variety of practice about which it is difficult to generalise, beyond the fact that all are examples of local writers messing with the 'Mister In-between' of fictional genres.

None of Janet Frame's fiction could be described as conventional in terms of its narrative construction and characterisation, but of all her writings *Snowman, Snowman* is perhaps the most radical in its departure from conventional modes. It belongs to a prolific three-year period of composition between 1959 and 1962 when she was living at 39 Grove Hill Road, Camberwell, a suburb of London. It was close to Maudsley Hospital where she had been a voluntary patient off and on between 1957 and 1959 and where she continued weekly visits with the psychiatrist Dr. R.H. Cawley, with whom she had established a trusting relationship and who succeeded in unlocking her writing again after a frustrating period during which she had written little that satisfied her. Her gratitude to Cawley for encouraging her to focus on her writing and not to concern herself with 'fitting in' to society was shown in the dedication of no fewer than seven of her books to R.H.C. As it happens, *Snowman, Snowman*, the book that included the novella, was not one of them; it was dedicated to 'John', that is, to John Money (called John Forrest in her autobiographies), the New Zealander whom she had met when she was a student in Dunedin before he moved to the United States to pursue his psychiatric career and who remained a close friend and supporter throughout her life.

In Grove Hill Road, Frame wrote the novels *Faces in the Water* (1961), *The Edge of the Alphabet* (1962), and *Scented Gardens for the Blind* (1963), and the stories that were published in a two-volume boxed set by George Braziller, her publisher in the United States, as *The Reservoir: stories and sketches* and *Snowman, Snowman: fables and fantasies* (1963). These volumes were not published in England or New Zealand. Eventually in 1966 a volume called *The Reservoir* was published in the UK and New Zealand, which included all but one of the stories in the US edition of *The Reservoir*, and 12 of the 18 pieces in *Snowman, Snowman*, though not the title piece that made up more than half the volume. The novella *Snowman, Snowman* was not published in New Zealand until it was included in *You Are Now Entering the Human Heart: Selected Stories* (Victoria University Press, 1983).

Although *Time* magazine erroneously described *Snowman, Snowman* as the thoughts of a snowman 'melting in the front yard of a middle-class New Zealand family', the setting of the novella is in fact the suburban London environment of Grove Hill Road, Camberwell, where Frame was living when she began it during the winter months of 1961. According to her biographer, Michael King, the manuscript was originally more than twice as long; she reduced it from 70,000 to 30,000 words during a visit to Cornwall that spring (Michael King, *Wrestling with the Angel*, 2000, pp. 228–29).

*Snowman, Snowman* makes no pretence at realism; it consists largely of the monologue of a snowman, in the front garden of a suburban London house, made by the thirteen-year-old Rosemary, daughter of the Dincer family, based on the family from whom Frame rented a room in Camberwell. The Snowman also enters into dialogue with a creature called the Perpetual Snowflake about the nature of snow and Time and Death and Life and other imponderables. There is no plot or narrative incident of the usual kind apart from the death of Rosemary, the Snowman's creator, in a car accident on the street. The novella is closer to poetry than to fiction in the conventional sense. It provides Frame with an unusual perspective from which to reflect philosophically and poetically on the nature of life, often with great eloquence, as in the passage with which the book begins (and with minor variations) ends:

> *Oh how I wish now that I had never conquered the earth, for people live on the earth, and animals and birds, and fish live in the sea but we do not defeat the sea for we are driven back to the sky or become what we have tried to conquer, remembering nothing except our new flowing in and out, in and out, sighing for one place, drawn to another, wild with promises to white birds and bright-red fish and beaches abandoned then longed for.* (p. 69)

*Figures in Light* belongs to the period in which Maurice Shadbolt (1932–2004) was making the transition from short story writer to novelist. He began his publishing career with two volumes of short stories, *The New Zealanders* (1959) and *Summer Fires and Winter Country* (1963); these were followed by a first novel, *Among the Cinders* (1965). His fourth publication, *The Presence of Music* (1967) was subtitled *Three Novellas*, of which the title story was the longest, followed by two shorter novellas, *The Voyagers* and *Figures in Light*. Thereafter Shadbolt concentrated on longer fiction, completing a further nine novels between 1969 and 1993. He returned to the novella with his last work of fiction — also consisting of three novellas — *Dove on the Waters* (1996). *Figures in Light* was chosen as the title story in his *Selected Stories* (1978).

## Introduction

The unifying feature of the novellas in *A Presence of Music* is that a leading character in each one is an artist — a concert pianist in the title story and a painter in both of the others. Each novella is narrated in the first person and centres on the relationship between the artist and the narrator — a lawyer in one, a journalist in the second, and a businessman (a market researcher) in the third. The conflict between the disorder and bohemianism of the artistic lifestyle and the more conventionally bourgeois way of life of the narrators is another common element in the novellas. *Figures in Light* is dedicated to the painter Pat Hanly (1932–2004), a friend and contemporary of Shadbolt's; the title is borrowed from a series of paintings Hanly painted in the mid-1960s soon after returning to New Zealand from several years in the U.K.; they are among his most successful and best-known paintings and mostly depict bodies on the beach in the brilliant light of summer. While the paintings of the artist Ruth in the novella are not a copy of Hanly's they nonetheless have qualities in common with his work, in particular a painting that Ruth had given to her brother, the narrator (who is nameless in the story but always addressed by Ruth as 'Brother mine'), as a wedding present. This painting becomes a focal point of the story, which is primarily concerned with the relationship between brother and sister. Ruth lives in Auckland, her brother in Wellington, and the difference between the two cities becomes an aspect of the contrasting lifestyles and personalities of the siblings. On a visit to Wellington Ruth expresses her dissatisfaction with her brother's conventional lifestyle by moving the picture to a different room:

*It was not a painting I had ever liked particularly, for like so much of Ruth's work it seemed to have very little to it; it lacked depth, in every sense of that word. There was a flatness, a lack of any perspective, in the scene... What I saw for the first time, though, was not detail — familiar enough — but the strange, almost unearthly light which filled the frame... Vivid, timeless and dancing, it was impossible to place, and difficult to connect with any sunrise, sunset or noon that I had ever known.... What I saw clearly was that I had somehow missed the point of the painting before; the light was the point ...* (p. 74)

What emerges during the course of the story is that the light in this painting symbolises the 'golden age' of childhood (to borrow another Hanly title) when brother and sister were intimate, so close in fact that there is a suggestion that their relationship verged on being incestuous. Ruth's dissatisfaction in life is revealed as being based on her sorrow at the loss of this intimacy with her brother, which he has betrayed by his conventional marriage. Through the death of their father and the brother's and sister's coming together over arrangements for the his funeral, they reach a kind of reconciliation so that at the end of the story, the brother, back home in Wellington, can look at his sister's picture with a new equanimity:

*The light no longer baffles me. It is perfectly obvious, perfectly familiar. That serene light flows in and out of our childhood, leaving no shadows ...* (p. 98)

Ronald Hugh Morrieson's reputation as a writer is almost entirely posthumous. He published two novels in his lifetime in Australia that were moderately successful, *The Scarecrow* (1963) and *Came a Hot Friday* (1964), but could not find a publisher either in Australia or New Zealand for his two other novels, *Predicament* and *Pallet on the Floor*. And despite the support of a number of well-known New Zealand writers who recognised his talent, such as Frank Sargeson, Dick Scott, C.K. Stead and Maurice Shadbolt, he died feeling that his literary career was a failure. The posthumous publication of *Predicament* (1974), with an introduction by Shadbolt, and *Pallet on the Floor* (1976), plus the republication of his first two novels, brought Morrieson the recognition that he sought in vain in his lifetime. Three of the four novels (all except for *Predicament*) were made into feature films, of which *Came a Hot Friday* was the most commercially and aesthetically successful.

*Pallet on the Floor* is the last and shortest of the novels, written when his health and spirits were in rapid decline. It lacks the insouciance of his other books, and its gloomy and pessimistic tone is only occasionally enlivened by mordant wit. All Morrieson's novels are crime stories of one kind or another. Here his model appears to be pulp fiction of the Carter Brown or Micky Spillane variety. Most of the characters are employed at the Kurikino freezing works and the atmosphere of death and violence spreads out from the works to the lives of the inhabitants. Rape, muggings, blackmail and multiple murders animate its cleverly managed and swiftly unfolding plot. Sam, a Pakeha, and his Maori wife Sue are delivered by the contrivance of the mortally ill McGhee (a sort of surrogate for the author) back to a 'pallet on the floor' at the pa, an outcome which Sam had earlier repudiated but which he thankfully embraces at the story's end. Unusually for Morrieson, a social theme is implied; the progression of the story seems to involve a rejection of the Pakeha lifestyle, which is identified with a joyless materialism fuelled by a slaughterhouse economy, and the embracing of a Maori lifestyle that, though sadly dilapidated and declining, is nonetheless suffused by warmth and aroha. The brevity of *Pallet on the Floor* in comparison with Morrieson's other novels may result from his illness and depression rather than any more consciously chosen aesthetic reasons (though its pulp-fiction progenitors are often brief); its brutal and rapid progress gives it the urgency of a last testament written in extremis.

Ian Wedde (born 1946) was known primarily as a poet when *Dick Seddon's Great Dive* was first published in 1976 as most of an issue of the journal *Islands*, edited by Robin Dudding. The devotion of almost a whole issue of what was then the country's leading literary magazine was indicative of the stature he held as perhaps the leading writer of his (post-war) generation. *Dick Seddon's Great Dive* was subsequently included, along with shorter stories, in a collection called *The Shirt Factory and other stories* (1981). Awarded the New Zealand Book Award for fiction in 1976, the novella was recognised on publication as one of the first substantial fictional representations of the counter-cultural scene of the late sixties and early 1970s (a world which was depicted with alienated disapprobation in Morrieson's *Pallet on the Floor*).

The novella centres on the attempt of Kate — a divorced woman around 30 years of age living in Port Chalmers near Dunedin — to reconstruct her relationship with

Chick — a bohemian drifter and substance abuser with loads of machismo and cool — which had ended with his apparent suicide (he is drowned at Bethells Beach on Auckland's west coast) some years previously. Kate, the refugee from an unsuccessful marriage, meets Chick at a typical sixties party in Auckland and impulsively begins an affair with him. At one point they hitchhike together from Auckland to Dunedin, a vividly reconstructed journey which demonstrates Wedde's outstanding narrative and descriptive skills. Other scenes involving Kate and Chick together are set in Auckland — the scene of hedonistic counter-cultural partying and subtropical beach life — and Otago, especially locations around Otago Peninsula. Chick is something of a mystery-man, both to Kate and (through her) to the reader. He is charismatic but unreliable and driven by demons which are never precisely articulated. Kate's narrative is not told consecutively but is constructed of small and larger fragments as she tries to deal with her feelings of guilt for his death and to understand the dynamics of their intense but troubled relationship. In some ways the novel parallels Kerouac's *On the Road*, since it deals with itinerant and bohemian lives. In somewhat similar fashion to Shadbolt's symbolic use of Wellington and Auckland in *Figures in Light*, Wedde, in oscillating between Auckland and Otago, develops the geographical locations as an elaborate correlative for psychological states and relationship dymamics:

*If I reconstruct his life for you it's going to have to be done like this. There's a line in his life which runs from south to north, from north to south, along which he was strung out like one of the strings of his neglected instrument* [an electric guitar]*...I found myself, in the effort of trying to discover him, stretched tight between those same poles.* (pp. 155–56)

Along with this structural metaphor is a variety of other repeated images, quotations and motifs (the Tasman and the Pacific, the colours blue, yellow and green, images of space, horizon and distance etc.), many of which have migrated from Wedde's poetry. Indeed, the skills required to make sense of this vivid and intermittently bewildering narrative are much the same as required for reading contemporary poetry: flexibility, alertness, the ability to connect up the dots and make imaginative leaps.

*Te Kaihau/The Windeater* is the title story in Keri Hulme's first volume of stories published in 1986. Many of the stories predate *the bone people* (1983), her famous Booker Prize winning novel, but the title story was one of those written after the novel. It is by far the longest story in her collection, and though relatively brief for a novella, it is given a novel-like structure by the division of the material into 29 mini-chapters each only a page or two long. The story is narrated in the first person according to a formula outlined in the first section:

*What I want to do is lay before you the unusual and irrational bits from my life because they may make a pattern in retrospect and, besides, they are the only bits that make sense to me right now.* (p. 233)

In the last section she says of the word 'windeater' that it 'becomes a woman trying to make sense of her self and her living and her world' (p. 250). These passages offer clues as to the structure and meaning of the novella.

Readers of *the bone people* will know that in her fiction Hulme mixes several of the mythologies she inherits through her mixed ethnicity, and that she is not afraid to flout the realist traditions of the novel by including elements which defy rational explanation. In that respect her fiction resembles various non-realist traditions such as South American 'magic realism' and such fantasy novels as Tolkien's *Lord of the Rings*. That is also the case with *Te Kaihau/The Windeater*. In particular it combines elements from Celtic and Maori mythology.

The life of the unnamed female narrator is surrounded by inexplicable events from beginning to end. In many episodes the narrator's life is profoundly changed by the intervention of a shape-changing presence, who is sometimes human, sometimes an insect or an animal, and sometimes supernatural. Typically, in his human form he is identified by his distinctive red-brown skin. In her infancy he speaks to her in Maori and shows her a taniwha. In later episodes he becomes her lover until she is shocked to discover he is the possessor of a feathered penis, a revelation which provokes the narrator into alcohol abuse and self-neglect. Finally she encounters him on the road as a dreadlocked rasta who leaves her with an ambiguous gift, a 'snooded sinker' she cannot get rid of; it melds itself to her arm. In the penultimate section of the story the narrator's mysterious lover, protector and nemesis is revealed to be a manifestation of the Maori trickster god Maui, the demigod who raised islands from the sea, aided humans by stealing fire and slowing the sun, but who sealed their fate by failing in his attempt to defeat the death goddess, thereby rendering human life mortal. Perhaps one way of interpreting this mysterious and absorbing narrative is that it concerns the powerful and dangerous heritage of being Maori.

*The Transfer Station* was first published as a small book in 1989 and reprinted in 2000 together with *A Spider-Web Season* as 'Two Story Sequences'. It is with the author's agreement that it is included here as a novella, the difference between a 'story sequence' — in which the stories share the same narrator, setting and general circumstances — and a novella ultimately being one of semantics. Haley has also written more conventional short story collections and novels as well as plays and poetry. He has often been depicted as one of the writers who moved New Zealand fiction away from the tradition of critical realism, though in some respects *The Transfer Station* is less radical in its departures from realism than some of his other fiction. The only element in which this sequence departs from realism is in its slightly futuristic setting. Even recognition of this depends upon a familiarity with the setting of the story. To New Zealanders the setting is familiar as the west coast of the North Island, near Auckland; the same setting, in fact, as in parts of Wedde's *Dick Seddon*. Occasional references to O'Neills (a beach near Bethells also referred to by Wedde), though, are the only explicit marker of location.

There are changes from the present reality, however. The government appears to be French-speaking and some sort of colonial takeover has taken place; English speakers, such as the narrator, present themselves as a resentful colonised minority. The transfer station of the title is a huge factory for the treatment of waste trucked from the city. Much of the native vegetation has been replaced by pines. The formerly rich oceans have been denuded of fish, partly poisoned by the outfall from the station. Such fish as are caught are diseased. There is a powerful sense of loss conveyed by the narrator, largely because of the death of his beloved wife Helen but also because of the political and environmental changes that have come about; the young people such as the pair that the narrator chums up with in the first chapter are despairing and pessimistic about the future. One of their number gets 'out of it' by throwing herself into the sea. A positive element in the story is the identification the old narrator comes to feel for the younger generation, which leads him to leave the coast in the last chapter to come to the city in search of the young women he met in the café out on the coast and who spent a night in his bach. His quest is unsuccessful, but the monarch butterfly he discovers in one of the girls' bedrooms in an abandoned house is a positive image of metamorphosis and transcendence, of 'getting out of it' in a sense other than that of suicide and existential despair.

The Halcyon Summer was first published in Witi Ihimaera's Dear Miss Mansfield (1989), a volume in which he paid tribute to Katherine Mansfield, writing in a prefatory letter:

On the occasion of the hundredth anniversary of your birth, may I offer you this small homage as a personal tribute to your life and art … Mine is but a single token of aroha and respect. (p. 9)

Ihimaera goes on to recall a breakthrough encounter with her writing:

I can remember, one sunlit afternoon in Wellington, reading 'At the Bay' again, surely, for the fourteenth time. What had simply been words suddenly sprang to life and there it all was, happening before me … It was all such a revelation to me and I leapt up and down as if I had suddenly discovered a pearl of inestimable value. (pp. 9–10)

Of the stories in Dear Miss Mansfield he writes:

They are stories in themselves, common experiences of mankind. But they found their inner compulsion in my wish to respond to your work. (p. 10)

Part One of the book consists of a novella, Maata, based on Mansfield's documented friendship with a Maori schoolgirl, Maata Mahupuku, and the legend that Mansfield had written a novel about her. Part Two, headed Variations on Stories and Themes of Katherine Mansfield, includes thirteen stories of which The Halcyon Summer is by far the longest. Ihimaera's prefatory note says:

Most of the variations have been directly based on short stories as diverse as 'The Woman at the Store', 'Her First Ball', 'The Garden Party' and 'The Doll's House'. Some have been less directly based on Katherine Mansfield's themes — like the New Age 'Pension Sketches'— or the themes of 'Prelude' or 'At the Bay'. (p. 58)

*The Halcyon Summer* belongs to the second of these categories, being very loosely connected — largely through the summer holiday theme — with *At the Bay*, together with some echoes of *Prelude*. An implicit contrast is established between the privileged circumstances of Mansfield's wealthy Burnell family with their well-appointed holiday house, and the embattled rural poverty of a Maori family threatened with dispossession of their land and rusty seaside shack.

Eleven-year-old Tama and his younger sisters are living in Gisborne around 1950. Though Maori, they are brought up in a wholly Pakeha fashion. When their parents go to Auckland, the children are sent to stay with their great aunt Nanny Puti and her large whanau in a remote East Coast seaside whare on family land north of Ruatoria. The contrasts between town and country, and Pakeha and Maori life styles are a major theme in the story:

*But Tama still didn't like the idea of going — it was all Maoris up the Coast, no Pakehas, and he and his sisters were used to Pakehas. Furthermore, Maoris wore only grass skirts and probably never even wore pyjamas to bed, and he knew that was rude.* (p.282)

The primitive living conditions — spider-infested outdoor long-drop toilets and the like — are disconcerting to the sensitive Tama who is mocked by his cousins for his stuck-up towny and Pakeha ways. Gradually, responding to the warmth and aroha of his relatives, he comes to revel in the freedom and joys of rural Maori life — harvesting crayfish from a row-boat, collecting shellfish from the reef, milking cows, going to the pictures in the local township, bathing with his cousins in a rusty tin tub, and so on. The summer idyll is progressively shadowed, though, by adult troubles which mostly go over the children's heads, though they are shocked when Nanny Puti gets rotten drunk at the pub, being unaware of the anxieties which beset her.

*Something was happening at the edge of childhood. It was just around the corner and, whatever it was, it would forever change all their lives.* (p.303)

For Tama, the halcyon summer comes to stand not only for childhood innocence but also for a time before his awakening of consciousness to the reality of Maori oppression and the threat to survival embodied in the looming dispossession of land and, more invidiously, in the willing capitulation to Pakeha values that comes with urban migration. Nostalgia, here, is tempered by emergent political awareness.

Like Shadbolt's *Figures in Light*, Mike Johnson's *Frames* comes from a volume with the subtitle *Three Novellas*. In this case the volume is called *Foreigners,* which is not one of the novellas' titles but refers to a common theme of New Zealanders abroad travelling in foreign parts. Again as with Shadbolt, there are one long and two short novellas, *Ausländer*, being about twice the length of both *The Red Key* and *Frames. Frames,* the last of the three, focuses on the dissolution of a marriage, various scenes from which are recalled and reconstructed by the narrator in a non-consecutive narrative that resembles the structure of *Dick Seddon's Great Dive.* Like

Wedde, Johnson, another poet/novelist, is fond of quoting Neruda, 'who can reclaim the personal from the political without losing the force of either'. *Frames* is set at the end of the 1980s against a background of free-market economics and rising Maori anger about the failure to honour the Treaty of Waitangi. The fractious political scene is correlative to a marriage which has slowly dissolved in bitterness in a variety of locations — Spain, Germany, Rome, North Africa, Whakatane, Waiheke Island.

To an even greater extent than Wedde's novella, Johnson's is a self-reflexive work in which the author is constantly drawing attention to the fictiveness of his narrative: 'I have decided to call your mother Monika, Eleanor, and address this to you.' (p. 306). The author is constantly digressing from his self-imposed task of writing about 'your mother', examining travel photographs, consulting the Tarot pack, listening to the radio, watching his daughter jumping on a trampoline: 'I digress, but it's always like this before the writing begins; the evasions and the indulgences.' (p. 308). The novella ends, 'Tomorrow I'll start writing', but of course in reality the story is already finished — it is the digressions and evasions that constitute the narrative. This much is suggested by the title, *Frames*, which at one level alludes to the photographs which have generated memories of scenes with Monika in different locations, and at another level refers to the act of writing as a kind of framing of reality. 'All we really have is frames … The bit that goes around the outside' (p. 329).

Chad Taylor, like Maurice Shadbolt, is primarily a novelist who worked his way up to longer forms through short stories and novellas. He began his career with a short novel *Heaven*, and the considerably shorter novella *Pack of Lies* (both 1994), followed by a collection of short stories, *The Man Who Wasn't Feeling Himself* (1995). He has since published two longer novels, *Shirker* (2000) and *Electric* (2003).

A primary challenge for the reader in *Pack of Lies* is to gauge the precise import of the title. To what extent is Catrina's first person narrative a 'pack of lies'? It is evident on even a superficial reading that Catrina — a twenty-something would-be student who has broken up with her violent and abusive boyfriend Wayne — is given to casual untruths ranging from exaggerations to outright lies when talking to police, motel-owners, friends and strangers. More seriously she lures her former flatmate and lover Babe — now pregnant to her live-in boyfriend — into an out-of-town weekend at a country motel, on the grounds that there is to be a surprise party to celebrate Babe's twenty-seventh birthday to which all their crowd will turn up. When nobody else shows up it becomes increasingly apparent to Babe (and the reader) that the party is a charade, a doomed ploy on Catrina's part to extract Babe from her domestic set-up so they can resume their former intimacy:

> *'Why did you say everyone was coming?'*
> *I thought they would.*
> *'You didn't really.'*
> *I did. We had talked about it. I thought there was going to be a party. And then all the way down here I was thinking to myself, thinking you know, these guys probably aren't gonna come. They must be busy or something, they forgot. It's typical, right? They never turn up.* (pp. 358–59)

16

As well as showing Catrina's compulsive dishonesty, this passage also illustrates Taylor's sure grasp of contemporary idiom and his adoption of the unusual device of not marking with punctuation the distinction between Catrina's conversation and her narrative voice. Some readers have found this mannered, but it contributes effectively to the uncertainty of the reality status of Catrina's narrative. Did she say that or merely think it?

And how far does this uncertainty extend? The novella opens with Catrina's having been floored by a blow to the head, serious enough as to require police intervention and hospitalisation. During the course of the narrative she offers a variety of explanations for this injury: that she was attacked by a dog, that she fell down an escalator, that she was drunk and struck her head as she fell inside her flat, that she was attacked by her former boyfriend (as the police suspect), that she was mugged by a stranger. What is the ultimate truth? Some curious repetitions and oddities in the text even raise the possibility that her whole narrative is a concussion fantasy, and that not only was the weekend party a fiction but that the whole weekend with Babe is a 'pack of lies' too.

However the reader finally resolves these intriguing conundrums, Taylor stylishly evokes the ambience of Catrina's and Babe's antipodean fin de siècle world — sleazy, amoral, transgressive, urban — and the uncertain dynamics of the relationships it engenders.

In a review of several novellas including *Pack of Lies* (*Landfall* 190, Spring 1995), Kim Worthington offers some perceptive remarks about the strengths of the novella form:

*The novella as a distinct genre...achieves a kind of double focus that draws on the characteristics of the short story and the novel—achieving both richness and limitation, length and intensity. Whereas in a novel the focus is often variable and shifting, covering a wide expanse of subjects and material, in a novella the focus remains fairly constant. Complexity is achieved through repetition, often by focusing on a single subject and limited material in the context of a number of linked motifs that develop an associated cluster of themes.* (p. 352)

Each of the novellas in this collection manifests some or all of these characteristics. Worthington also quotes from Henry James's preface to *The Lesson of the Master* in which he speaks of the delights of being freed from the arbitrary rule of word-length, 'a licence that, on the spot, opened up the millennium to the short story' and in particular to 'our ideal, the beautiful and the blest *nouvelle*'(p. 351). *Nouvelle* is the French word for novella, the term that has come to prevail for the kind of fiction James was writing about. The nine novellas displayed here bear out James' admiration for this intermediate form that has appealed so much to New Zealand writers. For all their individual differences, each in its way achieves 'richness and limitation, length and intensity'.

*Peter Simpson*

# Snowman, Snowman
## Janet Frame

## 1

People live on earth, and animals and birds; and fish live in the sea, but we do not defeat the sea, for we are driven back to the sky, or we stay, and become what we have tried to conquer, remembering nothing except our new flowing in and out, in and out, sighing for one place, drawn to another, wild with promises to white birds and bright red fish and beaches abandoned then longed for.

I never conquered the sea. I flew at midnight to the earth, and in the morning I was made into a human shape of snow.

'Snowman, Snowman,' my creator said.

Two sharp pieces of coal, fragments of old pine forest, were thrust in my face to be used for my eyes. A row of brass buttons was arranged down my belly to give me dignity and hints of fastenings. A hat was put on my head, a pipe in my mouth.

Man is indeed simplicity, I thought. Coal, brass, cloth, wood — I never dreamed.

A passing bird, a half-starved grey sparrow said to me, 'You are in prison.'

But that was not so, it is not so now. I helped to conquer the earth, but because I did not arrive here with the advance armies, I have never seen the earth except in this whiteness and softness, and although I remember a time when I was not a snowman, the habit of being a man, a creature of coal, brass, cloth, wood, has begun to persist; yet it does not seem to have deprived me of my freedom. Even in the few moments after I was born I knew how to live, and for me it is easy, it is staying in the same place without any more flying, without trespassing or falling over cliffs or being swept down to sea and swallowed by the waves; never diving or dancing; staying the same, never influenced by change as human beings are; not having to contend with the invasions of growth which perform upon human beings in the name of time and change all the eccentric acts of whitening strands of hair, shrinking pink skin to yellow leather over bones gone porous, riddled with early-nesting sleep, stopping the ears, making final settlement concerning their quota of tumult; at last bandaging the eyes injured with seeing. Partly snow, partly man, I am preserved, made safe against death, by my inheritance of snow, and this I learned from the Perpetual Snowflake on the window sill.

Let me explain. It is the window sill of the house of the Dincer family — Harry, his wife Kath, and their daughter Rosemary. I belong to them. I stand forever now in their suburban front garden looking out upon the street of the city. Rosemary created me. I have learned something of her life from the Perpetual Snowflake who has explained to me the view, the situation, the prospect of my immortality and its relation to the swiftly vanishing lives of people.

I have a strange sensation of being, a mass chill and clumsiness, a gazing through pine-forest eyes upon a white world of trees drooping with snow, the wind stirring milk-white clots and curds of my essence in street and garden, for my immortality does not mean that I contain myself within myself, I breathe my essence in a white smoke from my body and the wind carries it away to mingle it with the other flakes of the lost armies that flew with me to earth, and that still fall — see them paratrooping in clouds of silk — but they do not recognise me, they float by without acknowledging my snowman-being rooted here in the white world with my limbs half-formed by the caprice and modesty of my creator who can scarcely know the true attributes of a man, who chooses coal, buttons, hat, pipe, as his sole fuel weapon and shroud.

Am I common property? On my first day, although Rosemary Dincer made me to stand in her front garden, people in the street kept pointing to me and saying to each other, 'Look, a snowman, a snowman.'

Children came in the gate and touched me or struck me or threw stones at me, as if I belonged to them. One man looking over the hedge at me remarked, 'You won't be standing there so proudly for very long. Look at the sky!'

I looked at the sky and I felt lonely at the sight of the white whirlpool of the still-conquering armies, and I wondered if there were other snowmen, or do we exist singly and what is it that prompts people to make us?

Even Rosemary's making of me had caused her father to utter the strange observation, 'A snowman at your age! Surely not!' which called forth the reply from his wife, Rosemary's mother, 'Why not? It is not only children who make snowmen, anyone who has the chance makes a snowman, all up and down the town people are making snowmen!'

Why?

'Your time is limited, Snowman,' someone remarked, looking over the hedge at me.

'How do you like your first day on earth, Snowman? Do you feel at home? Are you learning to see with those coal-black pine-forest eyes?'

That is the Perpetual Snowflake with his questions.

'Of course I can see. Everything is outlined clearly against the snow — trees, this tree beside me in the garden, the street, cars, people, buildings, everything is whole and contained within itself. The world is a remarkable place.'

'I doubt if you will ever learn to see, Snowman. Trees, cars, streets, people, they are but the dark print upon the white page of snow. Your coal-black pine-forest eyes are no use until you are able to read the page itself, as men read books, passing beyond the visible obstructions of print to draw forth the invisible words with the warmth of their passionate breathing.'

'But my breath is ice. And I am the white page. I have no passion. Is that why I shall live forever?'

He does not answer. Perhaps he is asleep.

Two doors away a little boy began to gather the snow to mould it into the shape of a man, but he grew tired of making a snowman, with the result that he abandoned it, and it stood half-formed, eyeless, faceless, with none of the salient emblems of humanity. A few moments later the child's father appeared with a tin of rubbish, last week's relics of Christmas — paper wrappings, tinsel, discarded angels, which he emptied over the body of the snowman, and drawing matches from a box in his pocket, he lit a fire, he made a fire of the neglected snowman, and from where I stood I could see the flames rising from the snow and a smoke or mist blurring the garden, and for an age I stared with horror at the flames and I could not turn my coal-black pine-forest eyes away from them, and even from where I stood safe in the Dincer garden I could feel my cheeks burning as if they sought to attract the fire. Soon the half-formed snowman disappeared and the tinsel, the paper wrappings, the discarded angels, were transformed to black ash. I sensed an assault on my own being, but I could not discover traces of it though my cheeks were wet not with tears of rage or sadness but with a stealthy nothingness of wet as if in some way I were being drained of my life, and I knew although I could not seem to make the effort to consider the significance of it, that fire was my enemy, and that should fire flow or march against me in its crimson ranks of flame I should be helpless and without courage and my urge to escape would lead only to my swifter dissolution.

'Your first day on earth and already you consider death?'

'Oh no, oh no.'

My confidence returned. Oh the ease, the simplicity of static living! What wonders I observe with my coal-black pine-forest eyes! Is it not taken for granted that I shall live forever?

'Snowman, Snowman, a germ cell like a great sleeping beast lies curled upon the Dincer doorstep, tethered to past centuries, and every time Harry Dincer comes staggering up from the King's Arms he trips over the lead of the sleeping beast. Harry is a telephonist. He saw an advertisement in the daily paper, a picture of a man wearing headphones, listening to the world in conversation. "Ullo Marseilles, Paris, Rome," the man was saying and Harry was filled with a desire for a similar chance to eavesdrop on the world's conversations therefore he becomes a telephonist; but they have never put him on the Continental Circuit. He cannot speak the languages.

'So he goes to the King's Arms and gets drunk and staggers over the lead of the sleeping beast.'

'I can see nothing on the front doorstep but a small mat for wiping feet, and yesterday's footprints dark with mud and soot.'

'You will understand, Snowman. Tomorrow and the next day it will be clear to you.

'It is a matter of age. Of sickness, accident, time, of the assaults people make one upon the other. They are organised and trained to kill because the growth of centuries has entangled them in the habit as in a noxious weed which they are afraid to eradicate because in clearing the confusion between being and being, the thick hate-oozing stems, the blossoms feeding upon the night-flying jealousies and hungers, they face each other set in an unbearable clearing of light and proper original shade, with the sky naked in its truth, and what protection is there for them now as they crouch in fear of the new light, with none of them brave enough to stand tall, to welcome the eradication of death? Or they kill on impulse because, loving too much, they isolate the act of love and thus extend it to encompass the memorable loneliness of death; they choose to make one visit to the altar of possession, imagining that wherever and whenever they return, the scene will be unchanged. They find it has vanished, Snowman, as soon as the killing is over. And the stained glass is not pictures in beautiful compartments of colour: it is blood.

'You will understand, Snowman. Tomorrow and the next day it may be clear to you. You will learn part of the meaning of the people who made you, of the street and the city. You will know that Harry Dincer is deeper and deeper in despair because he is unable to say "'Ullo Paris, Rome, Marseilles," to communicate over thousands of miles in a foreign tongue, that although he is a telephonist with his own headphones more select and private than ears, he will never be given permission to work on other than his allotted circuit. "My headphones." He brings them from work at night and polishes them. Has skin-to-skin conversation failed him so sadly? "My headphones. I've heard famous people talking in private. Conductors of orchestras, stars of show business and television, so many stars I couldn't count them if I tried."'

'We heard rumours of stars in the sky on our journey to earth. Are people stars?'

'You will understand, Snowman, tomorrow and the next day and the next day. You will know the child who made you, and her mother, and their house and their car, their gondola shopping bags, their television sets, all of which may seem to you, a snowman, to be irritating trivialities, but when you learn to consider them it will be of their deeper layers that you think. You will have noticed how buildings emerge from the earth — houses, the shops at the corner, plants, your neighbour tree that is burdened with snow. All these things — even televisions and gondola shopping bags, are anchored to the earth or to people upon the earth, and when you find the point of anchorage, the place which most resists the ravages of the tides of forgetfulness and change, there you will also find the true meaning of the objects, their roots, those hairy tentacles which embrace the hearts of people or merely cling there, like green moss to a neglected stone that no one will ever want to overturn to observe the quick-running life beneath it.

'Tomorrow and the next day you may understand.'

'Is it necessary? I am only a snowman.'

Who is the Perpetual Snowflake? I never knew him before though our family is Snowflake. On my first day on earth I have known pride, fear, curiosity, and now sadness for I cannot ever return to the lost fields of snow that are not on the earth, that have no houses no cities no people. I cannot go back to be among my sisters and brothers far in the sky, lying in our cold white nightclothes while a calm wind ties down the corners of the sky, arranging the covers of cloud over our white sleeping bodies. I have been made Man. I am an adventure in immortality. Is it not a privilege to be made Man?

It is night now. There is a golden glow from the street light stretching its golden beak across the white street. It says no word but a quiet humming sound issues from it, as a life-signal.

I close my coal-black pine-forest eyes and sleep.

# 2

There is a clock in the city. It keeps time. That is remarkable, isn't it? When the snow came the clock stopped suddenly because the hands (which grasp) had frozen, and workmen climbed ladders to reach the clock's head, and they burned small fires day and night behind its face to warm it, with the result that it soon kept time once again. Time can be rejected, refused or kept. The chief problem is where to keep it as there is not much space on earth for invisible property. It is easier for people to put shopping into gondola shopping bags than to put time into a convenient container.

I am worried. My back aches. I have a feeling of rigidity, my roots seem so far from my head, there is no communication between them as there was on my first day on earth when I could say to myself, My one foot is in place, and know that it was so. Now I do not seem to have control of my knowing, it has floated from me like the smoky breaths floating from the people in the street when they open their mouths. The Perpetual Snowflake has confused me by trying to explain the earth when I know there is nothing to explain. The earth is covered with snow. It has always been covered with snow.

I feel so strange. He has told me that people eat dead animals and that before they choose which part to eat they mark and map the carcasses in blue or red pencil, the latitude and longitude of death. The lines are joined. Everything is named and contained and controlled. Today I seem to feel like an animal that is being killed slowly, but I have not the certainty of knowing the boundaries and labels of my own body, and if I see red marks in the snow I expect they will be not red pencil but blood. I experience the same heaviness which overcame me yesterday shortly after I was born. My head sinks deep into my shoulders, my laughter is invisible and does not show on my face or in my eyes.

I frown.

I have a feeling of anxiety because no one has yet taken my photograph, yet it seemed a promised event of importance when I heard Kath Dincer say to her husband, 'We'll take a photograph of it while it lasts. We must at all costs get a photo of the snowman!'

Large grey drops of water are running down my face.

'Mummy, the snowman's crying!'

A child walks by with her mother. They are going shopping around the corner to the greengrocer's. The little girl is tightly parcelled in woollen clothing, bright red, with a cap fitting close to her head and brown boots zipped on her feet. Her face is rosy. She belongs to the snow, all the children belong to the snow, see them sliding, scuffing, throwing snowballs, hear them shouting with their voices leaving their mouths and forming into brilliant piercing icicles suspended in the clear air!

The children dance; their footmarks have the same delicacy as those of cats, dogs, birds.

I perceive that all children are the enemies of their elders, and that the snow possesses a quality which causes all pretence of love between them to be discarded.

'Mummy, the snowman's crying!'

The little girl points to my tears which are not tears.

'Stupid, he's not crying. He's only a snowman.'

'But he's crying!'

'It's only snow, love.'

'If I hit him will he cry?'

'Don't be silly. He'll fall to pieces.'

Now that was strange. Would I fall to pieces?

'Come here won't you, I don't know what the snow does to you, you can't go into other people's gardens like that. The snowman doesn't belong to us.'

'Who does the snow belong to, Mummy?'

'Don't be silly, love, I suppose it's everybody's.'

'Then the snowman's ours!'

'Don't be silly, stupid, it belongs to the person who made him.'

Everything is very confusing. Do I belong to Rosemary Dincer because she made me, and to Kath because Rosemary belongs to Kath and to Harry because Kath belongs to Harry, and who does Harry belong to, does belonging describe a circle which starts again at Rosemary or does it extend to all people and everybody belongs to everybody else on earth? Who decides?

'What is around the corner, and in the houses, and who are the people and how do they accommodate time when he is their guest?'

'Around the corner there is a gas man, a wood louse, an empty carton, a man's ear, a desolation, a happiness, shops and people.'

'I mean what is there in its rightful order. Surely there are no ears lying on the pavement and no one is sweeping out a desolation with the night's dust from the floor of the grocer's!'

'Oh you want facts the usual way, as people arrange them through habit? You want a human focus? You prefer me to abolish the gas main and the empty carton and present the complete man instead of his Ferris wheel or a left ear; you wish to play parlour games like join the dots and name the important objects in the picture.

'It is what is known as a built-up area. With fifty square yards you have a population of hundreds. Now there are instruments to measure the sound of planes, cars and other machines, but not to measure the enormous sound of people living, their hearts beating, their digestions working or refusing to work, their throats being cleared to make way for mighty language, their joints creaking, bones grinding, hair, skin and fingernails growing, and the roller-coaster movement of their thoughts. Why, even the measurement of a man's heart beating is a wearisome business, with one person appointed as a special listener, and listening so solemnly to the wild echoes within. What hope is there of hearing a man's heart, recording the storms, the sudden darknesses and flashes of lightning, the commotions of unseen life? No one really listens to the beating of a heart. He merely listens to the listening of the stethoscope which in its turn has been eavesdropping and transmitting the most secret nameless sound which no one has ever heard distinctly, nor is anyone certain that the secret sound is not itself merely listening and transmitting another murmur which is yet more remote, and so on, to the centre, the first sound that cannot be heard apart from that other insistent murmur like the inland sea. And to think that Harry Dincer lives in despair because he is not qualified to put on his polished headphones and get in touch with Paris, Rome, Marseilles!

'People live here in the street of the city, in a constant commotion. Their lives are bustled and stirred and tasted like a big Christmas pudding packed with cheap good-luck tokens, little bells and fairy shoes that look as if they are made of silver, but they feel too heavy in the hand and they are perhaps poisonous. Life here, Snowman, is a big dark mess. Of course you are only a snowman and do not need to take account of the lives of people. See that house on the corner? The people living there have such a struggle to persuade the postman to deliver the letters addressed there, for the house is neither in one street nor in the next, and the owners are always painting heavy black numbers on the gate, and the numbers get larger each time they are painted, for it is so important for people to know where they live, and to let others know, to have their places defined and numbered. The family who live in that house have a passion for looking alike and that is quite natural for it is a family, yet the likeness is so startling that if you look from either of the two sons to his father you have the confusing impression that your eyes have telescoped time, that your glance at the son has caused him to arrive in a twinkling at middle age, to abandon his career as an apprentice accountant or an industrial designer and become his father, the homeworker, sitting in the little top floor room under the neon strip light sewing men's trousers and overcoats, with the whirr-hum of the machine penetrating the house and the sounds from the radio, Music While You Work, coming through the open window into the street; always a noise of work, an occupational murmur; it is the modern fairy tale, Snowman, it is not the old grandmother who sits in the attic spinning, but the father, the homeworker, weaving spells into overcoats.

'It is also strange that if you glance from either of the sons to his mother you experience the same feeling of the concentration of time, with the son becoming his own mother, the mother being transferred to the son. The face of mother, father, sons, has each changed from an individual right and possession to a family concern. Instead of saying proudly of mother and son, "Look, you can see the likeness," you feel a sense of uneasiness, of the massing of hidden determined forces which will destroy every obstacle in order to retain their right-of-way within the deep genetic groove.

'This family has a new car. The two boys spend Sunday mornings inside the new car, with the hood up, studying it; or sitting in the driver's seat or the back seat; standing, looking, touching. Sometimes they drive slowly round the block followed by the three West Indian children from next door, dressed in their Sunday best, bunched and frilly as daffodils.

'You are startled, Snowman? Daffodils? There's nothing to fear, Snowman. I have my own story, you know. I cannot tell the length of time I have been away from the sky and it is months or years since snow fell like this, reaped summer wheat into lily-white flour and all the cars huddled in the streets, look, like barracuda loaves of bread without any crust, only crisp snow for tasting by the saw-toothed wind, oh Snowman you need not fear daffodils for they mean nothing these days, they are forced, compelled, the pressure is put on them. People stamp and trample on everything, including other people, and everything rises dazed, dazzling, complete, from the earth. And so round and round the block the boys go in the new car, and the children follow laughing and screaming with the black eyes shining. Oh no who need be afraid of daffodils?'

Sunday morning is a separate season. In the afternoon the people watch television, that is except for the West Indian family who hold a Church Service in their upstairs rooms with their friends and relations coming from far and near, the women and children resplendent in brocades, flocked nylon, satin, the men in carefully pressed suits with bright shirts and polished shoes. They open all the windows of the room, the pianist begins to play, the congregation begins to sing, and you can hear the hymns even from where you are standing in this garden. They are not sung in a tone of weariness and complaint, as people sing when they are trying to catch up with God on the Grand March but are suffering from stones in their shoes and blisters on their feet: they are sung with gaiety and excitement as if God were outpaced, as if the congregation were arriving before him, to make everything comfortable with provisions and shelter in preparation for the long long night.

'At this time of year they sing carols: "From the Eastern Mountains Pressing On They Come." "Away in a Manger." "Oh Little Town of Bethlehem." The children from the Council Flats around the corner, the boys of twelve and thirteen set free on Sunday, with nowhere to go and nothing to do, stand outside the house mimicking the singers, adopting special piercing voices, as they mimic everything, for boys of that age, Snowman, are not people at all, they make noises like engines and lions and airplanes whenever they pass in a gang along the street, all making a noise at once, interrupting it sometimes with fragments of human language which no one listens to, and do you know, Snowman, I can never understand how without talking to one another, with only animal, machine, engine cries and disturbances of sound, these boys can yet decide so unanimously where they are going, and they swagger along in the direction of the Park or the Green or their favourite café as if one of them had said clearly in human speech, "We'll go here, eh?"

'On Sunday afternoons the man in the house opposite watches television. He comes from Barbados. He bought the house a few months ago and moved into the vacant flat on the ground floor, and at first whenever his student friends came to see him the white people occupying the top floor would lean from their window, popping back and forth like cuckoo clocks trying to arrange a regular rhythm. "Blacks," said the people on the top floor, and gave notice. Those on second floor stayed. Myra, her husband Ken, their daughter Phyllis. People have names. Ken is short and muscular with his bones arranged firmly and squarely as if to support unusual or surprising turns and somersaults of flesh — like those steel jungle-gyms in children's playgrounds which are always crowded with children swinging on them and climbing and hanging from them, their knees gripping the bars, arms dangling, faces growing redder and redder.

'People passing say warningly to each other, "Look at them. The blood will go to their head." You see, when people grow up they learn to be afraid of what is happening inside their own bodies, and they become anxious and suspicious if their blood travels suddenly from here to there, or if their hearts, tired of staying in their accustomed places, quite naturally "turn over"; and thus they are resentful of the way children seem so unconcerned when they dangle from jungle-gyms and their blood goes to their heads. Why? The adults wonder. Why can't they learn that blood going to the head is not a simple healthy matter like an impulsive excursion to the seaside?

'Myra is stout with dark hair and eyes and an ordinary face, as most faces are, with its lines and pouts and puckers and its tired middle-aged skin layered with Cake Makeup, Invisible Foundation, Fairy-Spun Face Powder. Every afternoon Myra dresses carefully and goes to the telephone box at the end of the street to make a call. To whom? I don't know, and Ken doesn't know. See the telephone box? The directory has H to K missing because last weekend some people known as *youths* tore pages from the directory and smashed the mirror on the wall and tried to wrench the telephone from its stand. People have such a hate and love for telephones. "'Ullo Paris, Rome, Marseilles. Hold the line a minute. I have got through to your heart. SOS Save our Souls."

'Snowman, I heard of a man who sent to a mail-order firm for a radio transmitting and receiving set. When he assembled the kit of tiny parts he found that he could send or receive only one message, SOS. He listened day and night, and he never found out who was sending the message or why he himself should be sending it, for he didn't need to ask for help, he was not in despair, not bankrupt or crossed in love; his life was happy.

'He got up one morning, washed, dressed, looked out of his window at the world and shot himself.'

'I am sure it is interesting. But I am only a snowman.'

'Phyllis is very thin. She wears mauve eyeshadow and mauve lipstick and the expression on her face implies that she can't understand or didn't hear clearly or interpret correctly the sound of the world about her. She works in a dusty cut-price store a threepenny bus ride away although while she was at Secondary Modern she dreamed of being a secretary, a receptionist, the manageress of a *boutique*. She spends her time amongst pieces of timber, wallpapers, paraffin cans, last year's boxed Christmas soap and cheap perfumes, dented dust-covered cans of Mulligatawny and Cream of Kidney Soup; pots, brooms, double toilet rolls; prices slashed. Even the sweets displayed in the opened boxes in the window beside the bathcubes and the plastic dishes and the free offer tube of toothpaste with shampoo riding strapped to its back, are all covered in dust. The liquorice allsorts are shrunken and crippled with age.

'On Friday nights Phyllis goes with her Indian girlfriend to the pictures or the youth club, and on Fridays when the knocker downstairs is rattled and banged and Myra opens the living-room window to see who is visiting, she has to make her observations very carefully, for usually if she looks down and sees someone with dark skin she exclaims, "Not for us! It's for upstairs or downstairs."

'But on Friday nights when the young Indian girl comes for Phyllis, Myra has to make sure to let her in, but she finds it so difficult especially on these murky winter evenings to know whether the caller has Indian skin or West Indian skin or European skin, it seems all the same when the light has gone.

'A West Indian woman and her husband live now on the top floor. He works as a conductor for London Transport. There is a new baby, Cynthia. For months the young woman, Gloria, sat up there at the window every day staring down the street, only venturing outside to shop at the grocer's or the butcher's around the corner, and then she would walk slowly and carefully, leaning backwards, with her baby safe as a coconut inside her. Then suddenly two faces appeared one day at the window, that of Gloria and of a tiny baby in a white shawl, but Gloria withdrew the bundle quickly and did not let Cynthia see out of the window for many many weeks, as if she were preparing her by first explaining to her the curious ways of people in the world. And during that time Gloria did not go out, even to the grocer's or the butcher's, but stayed inside with Cynthia, and the curtains were drawn across the window, and one evening when Gloria's husband came home from issuing tickets on the one-seven-six Catford to Willesden, Willesden to Catford, he brought a bundle of lace which Gloria made into curtains, and now there were two pairs of curtains to protect Cynthia and her mother from the world, and though it was summer with the world banging singing screaming echoing and the voices and radios loud in the street and the cars hooting and dogs barking and jet planes shuddering the sky, there was no sound at all from the room with the double curtains, and the window stayed shut, and no faces looked out. The husband went to work in the morning and came home at night. The district nurse called sometimes, propping her bicycle against the fence, staying ten or fifteen minutes in the house, then coming out, saying nothing, going immediately to her bicycle, unlocking it, putting her bag in the basket over the handle bars, cycling down the road, disappearing round the corner, and who knows if she did not then reach the edge of the world and drop into darkness with the shining steel spokes of the back wheel of her bicycle spinning blindly like a star?

'Suddenly one day the double curtains were drawn aside. There were two faces at the window, Gloria, and her baby sitting up in the cot which had been moved to the window. Gloria took the tiny black hand, held it high, and waved it merrily at the world.

'Cynthia knew now, you see. All the while, in the secretive room behind the double curtains, her mother had been teaching her, preparing her, and now everything was arranged for Cynthia to consider the world outside. If you look up there now, Snowman, you will see the baby's face staring from the window. She still hasn't learned to wave by herself, but she laughs and cries at what she sees, and this morning with you here in the garden, and with the world all sheet and tablecloth and napkin, she cannot understand, she does not know that if she came outside to tread on the snowy tablecloth she would leave footprints in common with all other creatures living or dead who touch the snow: birds, cats, branches of trees, people, the old man with the shovel, the child with the stones and the snowballs, and Cynthia's own father on his way to work with the one-seven-six to Willesden.'

It has begun to snow again. Reinforcements. I am feeling safe though my newest white coat obscures my sight. Children keep running into the garden and stealing from me — one has taken a brass button; or they prop me up with more snow as if I were in danger of falling. Sometimes they make strange menacing remarks about what will happen to me *after*. After what? Am I the only snowman in the world now?

'Others are appearing in the city. Perhaps they are your distant relations. Some are seven feet tall and others are only three feet tall. Some wear uniforms and carry weapons such as swords, umbrellas, sticks, newspapers. And all have been made by children or by those whom others regard as children. Living in the house by the telephone box there is a middle-aged woman who is four feet high and has the understanding of a child. She is employed to clean the house belonging to the Indian doctor and it is she who every morning polishes the brass plate outside his door and erases the rude remarks A WOG LIVES HERE, GO HOME BLACK, with a drop of Cleanic upon a bright yellow cloth. It is marvellous, Snowman, the way Cleanic can remove all trace of an overnight scar; it ought to be more used by human beings when they suffer attacks from those who love them so much that they must write their love as insults upon the heart of the loved. Have human beings hearts of brass?

'Snowman, Snowman, after the woman whose real name is Dora but whom everybody calls Tiny, had polished away the insults, and had cleaned the surgery and the other rooms in the house and had shopped at the grocer's for her mother, and had walked home up the road, carrying her little bag of private possessions and family food, she went outside to the back garden of her home and made a snowman. She made him exactly her own size, to fit, eye level with eye, mouth with mouth and heart with heart. The two matched perfectly.

'Then as soon as she had finished making him she stared at him with her head on one side and a serious expression on her face. She decided to push him over and get rid of him. No. She decided to keep him there in the garden forever. So she laid a ring of pebbles around him as a sign that he belonged to her and no one was to touch him, and she went inside to her lunch. In the afternoon on her way to work she stopped everyone she met and explained that she had made a snowman.

'"I made a snowman. He's mine."

'No one disputed that. Apparently if you make a snowman he belongs to you, and although children might pluck out his eyes and carry off his bright buttons and plunge his hat over his head so that he cannot see, no one will try to steal the whole snowman because he belongs to the person who made him.

'Later in the afternoon when Tiny returned from work she became angry with her snowman, at the way he stood in the garden, not speaking or smiling or moving, just submitting to the perpetual collision of fresh flakes upon his body. Tiny's anger increased. She began to cry, not simple crying with tears running down her cheeks but a moaning complaining cry without tears. Then seizing the garden shovel which had helped her to make her snowman, Tiny battered the snowman over the head, and his eyes fell out, his body broke in two, he sank within the charmed pebbled circle, making no protest, soundlessly. Tiny put away the shovel in the correct place in the garden shed and she went inside to watch television while she knitted the palm of the right hand of the gloves she is making to protect herself from the everlasting cold.

'Another of your relations was a three-inch-high snowman standing upon a cake in a shop window. He wore a red woollen cap, smoked a red pipe, and of course wore buttons, little red round ones placed in a row down his fat belly. I believe that he was different from your other relations because no one saw him being made and when people passed him they did not make the remarks which you find so fearful — about the day *after* or "what will happen soon," or "let him wait a few days and he won't be so proud." He was taken from the shop, shut in a dark box, carried to a strange room and placed in the centre of a table laden with food. The room was hung with decorations, glittering trees and lights and angels, in fact it was such a dazzle that the snowman may have imagined that he had arrived in heaven except that the angel at the top of the tree gave him no welcoming smile, her face seemed made so that she could not smile, it was a face with a small split of red like a cut, while the lights twinkling round her gave her skin a yellow colour blotched with shadow which made her two tiny black specks of eyes look like mouse dirt dropped in porridge, and that is no way for an angel to appear; therefore your distant relation couldn't have arrived in heaven, though it may have been a matter of opinion, as the people in the room were in the happiest mood, snatching kisses from one another, drinking sparkling wine, unwrapping presents given as a sign of their love. Snowman, it was a typical scene of human happiness.

'Now a snowman, though he is made of snow, is in some respects human. Imagine the feelings of a snowman when he observes that when people are in their happiest mood they are likely to seize and devour each other. I do not mean to make you afraid when I tell you that one of the guests walked over to the table, grasped your distant relation, and treating him as if he were an article of food, began to bite, chew and swallow him, while the party continued as if nothing unusual had happened. And later, when the rejoicing was over, the men took their women to bed and because they were again so happy they seized and devoured each other and the eating continued all night yet nobody disappeared like your poor three-inch-high snowman. It seems that people who have lived on the earth for so many centuries have used much of their cunning to discover this marvellously secret way of concealing the fact that they are continuously eating and being eaten by those whom they love.'

Why should I be afraid? There are grey envelopes flapping in the sky and the trees are writing their destinations against the sky, and pinned to the corners of the clouds are the red-footed storks so eager to be flying south to sit upon a golden pyramid and sharpen their beaks on the golden stone. I remember this, though I am only a snowman. I like to look up at the sky. And then I look out at the street and think of what the Perpetual Snowflake has told me of the people, and I wonder to myself, Where are the heroes driving through the streets in their chariots? I thought the earth was filled with heroes, with happiness, and so it is, oh yes, I have a feeling of happiness, there's just a soft settling of new snow brushing my cheeks, and white fellow-snowflakes disguised as dragonflies tickling my nose, and a passing child had made two hands for me and enclosed them in furry red and yellow mittens. Each day I live someone adds to me or subtracts from me, therefore perhaps I am more human than I realise? Then I must be happy, as human beings are, for in spite of the story of the three-inch-high snowman and the Christmas party, it cannot be true that people eat each other. They eat only vegetables and fruit and other animals who do not speak their language, and birds, and fish. People do not drink each other's blood. They drink wine, beer, milk, tea, coffee.

'Snowman, Snowman, there is a great gale of fear blowing in the snowflakes, for when it snows the earth is obscured and people are unaware of the divisions between street and pavement and they become afraid for they have always known where to walk. The obliteration of the earth enhances the need to touch it, to feel the shape of it, to be guided by it, knowing its hard and soft places, its corners, hollows, ravines, hills brushed by stars, valleys with lion-winds raging with their golden manes indistinguishable from the mountain grass, oh Snowman, all recognition has been wounded.'

'I am only a snowman. I am surely and permanently anchored in a small suburban front garden. Here is Rosemary Dincer, my creator. I belong to her. Why is she crying?'

'She went to the Modern Jazz club where she met a University student on holiday who promised to ring her and make a date but when he rang her mother answered the phone and said, "Do you know how old she is, she's only thirteen," and he said, "Oh. Tell her I'm sorry." And that was the end.'

'The end? Do people cry when it is the end?'

'People do not cry because it is the end. They cry because the end does not correspond with their imagination of it. Their first choice is always their own imagining; they refuse to be deterred by warnings; they say I choose this because although the price is high the thing itself is more precious, durable and beautiful. The light of imagined events is always so arranged that the customers do not see the flaws in what they have chosen to buy with their dreams. Rosemary brought so much happiness from her meeting with the University student and from the cinema date which followed, and then the concert, and then the excursion up the river, her visit to his home, his visit to her home. … Now it is the end.'

'I thought the end was death. Is Rosemary dead?'

'Rosemary is not dead. There are other places where people may find the end: the edges of cliffs, the corners of streets, the lines of boundaries, the conjunctions of sentences, the disappearance — I should say the melting — of dreams. There is the view which suddenly comes to an end not because it is the end but because an obstacle stands or takes root there and will not be displaced. Rosemary's age is blocking the path of her dreaming. There are other powers which produce and arrange obstacles. Daylight, Time, Chance, Fear, the sudden closing of two blades of scissors, crocuses, a broken wall with grass growing through the cracks — like the wall over the road which the man who bought the house takes care to inspect each evening, peering into the joints of the brick for signs of decay. On his first morning as a tenant he heard two housewives talking outside: "A coloured man has bought this house. It will go to rack and ruin."

'Rack and ruin, Snowman, is a sleepy quiescent stage before death; it allows waiting weeds and insects to nest and flourish, and the once solid bricks to move, shudder, breathe decay, split, crumble and fall.

'After one energetic day of trowelling damp concrete into the crack in the brick the man gave up. He had grown wise. A woman passed him with her face going to rack and ruin and no amount of trowelling could have hidden the decay. So why should he care what people were thinking? If some people thought of his race as a forerunner of death, well let them. It was flattering, in a way, for death is impersonal in these matters whether it is a question of the decay of a brick wall or of a human face.'

'But snowmen do not decay? A fresh overnight fall of snow and we are new. Is Rosemary dying then?'

'It is a human habit to provide remedies for grief because even if tears are a common and unusual sign of unhappiness they must never be allowed to become emissaries of death, to claim more than brief significance. "Things" are the remedy most used by people to cure grief, disappointment, discomfort, celebration by tears and laughter, in order to return to a deathless Eden — a level of uncluttered garden — vegetable state with drops of dew shining like mirrors between the separate lives, with the sun cradled in the leaves, the misty morning webs and traps making the air glimmer with deceiving lightness, with the earth safe and solid underfoot.'

'Safe and solid underfoot?'

'You have never seen it that way, Snowman. Snow is a mass camouflage. No people would accept a government which performed the world-wide deceptions of snow; or perhaps they would be unable to resist the comfort of its beautiful treachery? I have seen the earth before and after snow. You may see it too when you become an old-fashioned Perpetual Snowflake talking to next year's old-fashioned snowman.

'But I was telling you of remedies. "Things" are an effective and popular remedy. Most people begin using them very early in their lives. I don't know how it began and I'm not going to travel back until I reach the beginning, not simply for your sake, Snowman, for I may discover the real nature of the beginning, and that may frighten me, and you. Besides, I may not recognise it when I reach it, for the beginning like the end is never labelled. What should I do if I reached the beginning and thought that I had arrived at the end? What should I do? Both the beginning and the end demand such drastic action that I should be forced to decide immediately, and what if I made a mistake? There are responsibilities which even I am not prepared to face.

'Now Rosemary's life is full of things. A tape recorder, a piano, plenty of clothes — winkle-picker shoes, a white raincoat, slacks, chunky jerseys; a duffle bag, a school case with her initials in gold upon it; a share in the family car, television, a caravan in Sussex. She is given pocket money each week. Next year she will go for a skiing holiday on the Continent. The difficulty of things or objects as remedies is that the supply of them depends upon income and that is not earned according to the tally of grief. There may be a time when there is no money left, and no more things, and no more remedies, and the tears will keep running down little girls' cheeks for ever and ever, or until the little girls grow up and trowel cement upon their faces to hide the rack and ruin.

'Tonight Harry and Kath will decide what to give Rosemary in order that she may be able to bear the disappointment of being too young. I myself do not know what happens inside people when they long for the companionship and adventure of another, and are given instead a box of chocolates with separate handmade centres, or a new dress or the top of the pops gramophone record. I suppose they get used to the comfort of things, and may even approach the state of holding a thrilling conversation with one of the handmade centres. Things are really much more convenient to human beings than their own kind; things can be thrown out when they are not wanted; they can be destroyed, torn to pieces or burned without questionings of conscience; the only effective way of destroying people is to equate them with things — handmade centres or the cheap song embedded in the groove.'

A blackbird shadow came across my face. There was the sudden heavy sigh of snow when the tree by the hedge moved in the wind, a white soft dollop of a melted sigh that shifted along the branch, fell to the earth, and vanished in the concealing softness.

Now it is night, deep blue with butterscotch light under the clear folded sky, and the giants are trampling the snow, walking with two or three swift paces across the earth, for it is night, and fairy tales have come to rest, and now I will sleep. Is it the fault of my coal-black pine-forest eyes that I dream of white squirrels brushing their tails over me, or is it only the wind blowing down the reinforcements of snowflakes, the new armies that will keep control of the earth and conceal the truth forever?

# 3

'Children are ripe for smiling. Those living in the Council Flats around the corner have sallow faces and streaky hair and their clothes have chopped hems, but they go hand in hand, Snowman, hitting each other and grasping and hugging and then suddenly running away. You will not know how it feels to be a child walking with your elder sister and to have your elder sister suddenly begins to run and run until she disappears around the corner leaving you alone in the street with the buildings so tall beside you and fierce dogs with black noses parading up and down, and cars and lorries growling by, and stern-looking women in purple hats and blue aprons, out sweeping their share of pavement, and telling you to mind, mind, and what else are you doing but minding? People learn the technique of vanishing when they are so young. They rock into and out of sight and when they are gone, when you cannot see them, then perhaps they are dead or drowned in the rain barrel. Vanishing is always magic. Now you see me, now you don't, people say, laughing, and their laughter is cruel.

'"Has my sister gone away forever?" the little girl thinks. "Or is she just around the corner, up the street where I cannot see her?"

'How can she know?

'People vanish and never return, people vanish and return, but each vanishing brings unhappiness. And then when people finally vanish, when they are dead, they are brought determinedly within sight, captured, enclosed, while everyone persists in saying that they are gone and will never return. It is very confusing and contradictory, Snowman.'


Another morning. My overcoat changed, clean and white, the snow blinked from my eyes. I am pleased that the technique of vanishing does not concern me. I am so permanently established here that I would not believe vanishing was possible if I did not observe it happening each day — around corners, into the sky, behind doors, gates, hedges; the smiles, greetings, alarm, anger, vanish from faces; even the visiting wind wearing his cloak of snow, a generous gift from the night sky, has played vanishing tricks with yesterday's carpet and all the footprints, ridges, patterns impressed upon it. The morning earth is freshly decked from floor to ceiling with new white upholstery, white cushions, covers, wall hangings, the earth is a vast white room with the wind and his brothers lounging in every deep chair, drinking snow-tasting tea out of the grey and white china clouds. It is very civilized and ceremonious, I am sure.

'Just think. In a few days it will have vanished, we'll never know it was there.'

That is a passer-by speaking. What does he mean? Who are people to make such menacing remarks about snow?

'That man lives across the road with his wife, his daughter, his mother-in-law and her husband. People live in clusters like poisonous berries. The mother-in-law is the head of the house because she wears a purple hat and a blue apron and sweeps their share of the pavement and carefully closes the gate when the postman and the milkman have left it open. She makes strangled cries to children in danger in the street. Her face is almost overshadowed now by the thrusting bone-shape which will command it when it is a mean-nosed skeleton with dark worked-out mines for eyes. It is strange to think that she resembles most of the other middle-aged women in the street, yet they are not related, but all possess domineering bones impatient to be rid of the tired webbing flesh with its yellow-ochre tint which appeared gradually as the cloudy colours of time were poured into the smooth golden morning mixture; people do not stay young, milky, and dandelion.

'Mrs Wilbur belongs to the Church and for Jumble Sales, Special Evenings, Harvest and Christmas Festivals, she displays a poster inside her front window, ALL ARE WELCOME. She goes to church for the company of God and of people, for the socials and meetings and "drives". In the evening she watches television with her husband, and during the day she has her shopping and cleaning and polishing, and her granddaughter Linda to look after while her mother, Dorothy, goes into town. Yet I don't think I answer your question, Snowman. Who are these people? Their being is more elusive than separate handmade centres or the pop song swatted like a fly into the surface of the record. The young couple have a son who boards at a special school and is home during the holidays. He is Mark, that is, a strain or blot or saint. He is always afraid that his mother will vanish, and he screams for long periods in the day and the night, and when she takes him to the shops his cry is Carry me, Carry me, but Dorothy is sharp and stern for the people at the special school have told her to treat Mark as if he were an ordinary child of seven, not to give him cause to believe that he is different, not to "give in" to him — giving in is a kind of balloon collapse where people see their power escaping from them into the air and being seized by others who have no right to it — but to accept him "as he is", to be calm, casual, unobtrusively loving.

'"I can't carry you. You're seven! I mean, you can walk, Mark love, it's only to the shops and back."

'"Carry me, carry me!"

'"Don't be silly. Take my hand."

'"Carry me, carry me, carry me!"

'At the sound of the little boy's cries people living near open their windows and front doors and look out.

'"It's Mark Wilbur."

'They say his name aloud, pleased with the certainty of it, for if he is Mark Wilbur then he can't be any of their own children, can he, the ones who go cheerfully to school each morning, who can speak intelligibly, who play with other children and stand up for their share of everything, who will perhaps (like Rosemary) pass their eleven-plus and go to grammar school.

'"It's Mark Wilbur. Home for the holidays. The little girl is rather sweet isn't she?"

'That is Linda, four. One numbers people for so long then one ceases to number them, but when people die they are always given their correct numbers. Ron Smith, forty-four, suffered a heart attack. Peter Lyon, seventeen, was in collision with a van driven by Herbert Kelly, fifty-five. It is a kind of code, a time-attention and bribery. Linda has fluffy brown hair. She wears billowy clothes and velvet hair ribbons. She is allowed to help grandma put out the empty milk bottles in the morning although she cannot quite reach the window sill where grandma places them, beyond the contamination of the street. Linda is so good. She behaves. When Mark is home he smashes the milk bottles deliberately. Actions which are carried out deliberately are so hard to forgive, even by a mother who knows her child is different. And grandma busy dusting or sweeping in her purple hat and blue apron, does not always understand.

'"I was looking out the window, Dorothy, dusting the sill, and I saw him snatch the milk bottle from Linda and smash it. He did it deliberately." Dorothy is silent. There is no defence for deliberate misbehaviour, therefore she slaps Mark across the ears or the face while Linda watches smiling, feeling so good and well-mannered in her billowy dress and velvet hair ribbon. Mark begins to scream. He will not stop screaming. His mother drags him inside. The people close their front doors and windows.

'"She'll be glad when he goes back to that special school."

'"Carry me, carry me!"

'You must admit, Snowman, that there is something to be said for riding in a chariot, and who can blame the child for insisting upon what is perhaps the first right of his life? Yet now he must wait so many years before anyone will again carry him, and then what a solemn expensive duty it will be! I think that if I were human I should want to be carried, like Mark Wilbur. Every morning Mark's father climbs into his vermilion car that is balanced like a clot of blood upon the snow, and he addresses the car, "Carry me, carry me," and no one punishes him or tells him not to be ridiculous, that he is old enough to carry himself.

'And when people are asleep they cry "Carry me, carry me" to their dreams and their dreams carry them and no one complains, for dreams are secret. Yet for the real pomp and pleasure, the final satisfaction of their lifelong desire, people must wait until they are dead.

'Carry me. It is the prerogative of the dead, Snowman. You know, don't you, what has happened in the house two doors away on this side of the street? Are you too busy being flattered by the children who lick your hand to see what you taste like and find you taste like soot — how can snow taste like soot?'

'I am no more than a snowman. People are not my concern, I do not even know my creator. All I know is that she is thirteen, goes to Grammar School, and fell in love with a University student who wore a long striped scarf. Her father is a telephonist who cannot get through to Paris, Rome, Marseilles. Her mother has a blouse shop, subscribes to the *Amateur Gardener* and the annual *Flower Arrangement Calendar* and has two geraniums growing in pots outside the back door.'

'If you know as much as that, Snowman, then you easily complete the picture, play the human game with the human focus. I wanted to tell you that Sarah Inchman is dead; she died one night and you never knew because you are not yet able to read the signs or join the dots.'

'Why should I? I am only a snowman. I shall live for ever. I do not care if Sarah Inchman is dead. What were the signs which my coal-black pine-forest eyes refused to interpret?'

'The other day the doctor made two visits to the house, the second visit outside his normal hours, and when he was leaving Thomas Inchman came to the door with him and walked bareheaded through the snow to the car. You ask what is strange about that? When Thomas Inchman stands bareheaded and without an overcoat or gloves far from his front door and in the freezing air with snow on the ground and threats of snow in the sky, then it is a sign that he is in distress. He seemed more helpless perhaps because he is going bald and the blue light cast upon his head from the sky and the snow seemed to draw the blue veins nearer his scalp so that his head seemed fragile and in great danger like a baby's head with the fontanel not closed and no one to protect it. He stood there beyond the time it would usually take for him to say, "Thank you, Doctor," and for the doctor to answer, "Right. Call me if there's a change for the worse." While Thomas Inchman seemed helpless in the blue light the doctor seemed self-possessed; he wore a heavy tweed overcoat and a warm brown hat made of furry material and his gloves were fur-lined and his Indian skin showed warm and brown and alive and his hands held the rich brown leather briefcase in a secure grip. He drew up the collar of his overcoat as if enticing the forces of life closer to him, and he smiled sympathetically at Thomas Inchman, yet at the same time there was a flash of triumph in his glance. He climbed into his car, started the engine, and was away with the powerful car moving effortlessly through the snowy street where only the same morning other cars had been abandoned.

'When the doctor had visited for the third time and Thomas had once again watched him drive away, he returned to the house and drew the curtains in the ground-floor front room, not closing them casually with gaps of light shining between them but sealing them as if they were made of an impenetrable metal which only a desperate strength would cleave in order to admit the murky snow-filled daylight.

'People passing in the street may not have realized that Sarah Inchman was dead, but if they had stopped to take notice they would have sensed the disorganization of the household. Robert's car stood outside. Robert is the son. Robert came home only at weekends. Why was he home now, in daylight when people who should be at work were at work and the only movement of traffic was of heavy lorries trying to get through to Peckham, of salesmen passing with their cars stacked with samples, rag-and-bone men on their rounds, men from the Water Board making their strange probing inspections through the snowfall. All these were legitimate travellers but not sons arriving home in broad daylight when their usual practice was to come on Friday evening after dark.

'If you did not guess, Snowman, by seeing Robert's car, you would surely have known if you had seen Robert, for the wind was bitterly cold, the flakes were falling, and Robert was clad in a heavy overcoat, and why should he not be? When the doctor drew his overcoat closer to his body he was confidently enticing the forces of life; when Robert turned up the collar of *his* coat he seemed to be trying to repel the forces of death, his coat seemed to be worn with no thought for outward weather, and his reliance upon it was not born of his need to escape from the snow. With the collar turned up, all the buttons buttoned, the lapels drawn close together, he had a total appearance of helplessness. The coat was black-and-white-checked tweed. Woven with snowflakes? The enemy had penetrated the wave and lay snug on Robert's back.

'Yesterday Thomas Inchman kept coming to the front door of his home, walking out, still not dressed for the weather, and peering up and down the street, as if he were waiting for someone. His son came and went, came and went, shuttling his car back and forth from here to there with a restlessness brought on by grief. If you had observed all these incidents, and the house with the feverish hanging light shaped like a crystal ball burning behind the impenetrable curtains, and if you had not divined the nearness of death, surely you would have know when darkness fell (like an axe) and a sprightly little black van drew up outside the Inchman house. The writing on the side of the van was almost concealed in the gloom of night.

'Funeral Service And Furnishings.

'In this part of the world, Snowman, dying is meant to be a discreet matter like taking tea but the untidiness of death makes itself visible in the clothes of the bereaved, in the daily routine — yesterday's milk not opened or even collected, the television silent, the beds unmade. In spite of people's desire for death to be a neat occasion — what is neater than dying? — there are always slovenly obtrusions which mar the effect.

'The funeral will be held tomorrow. Everything will be in order. The undertaker in the sprightly black van will have arranged everything. All is quiet now in the Inchman house. There was a time when members of the family died and were abandoned, and their relatives packed their bundles and fled over the plain or desert to reach the friendly oasis by nightfall, where, seeming to forget the dead, the little group would make their meal and then huddle together looking up at the stars that were wild beasts — lions, bears, wolves — prowling the shifting cloudfields where even the white grass and trees never stay and the cities of fire are trampled by the restless sparking hoofs. And the family would fall asleep and in the morning they did not weep for the dead for the dead had no share in the living but were alone, already becoming a part of the plain or the desert with the shadows of the wings of the vultures wheeling over the earth like great broad blades of a windmill set in motion by winds blowing from beyond the frontiers of death to draw new forces of life from the mingled grass and sand and dead human flesh.

'The dead are not abandoned here, Snowman. It is not the fashion to abandon them until it is certain that they are decently covered and imprisoned. Yet the urge to escape from them is always overwhelming. Sarah Inchman has been taken to the chapel mortuary. Thomas and Robert have gone to stay with Sarah's niece and her family in Lewisham. If you looked carefully inside the house you would notice the telltale marks of flight, of haste, which would differ only in surface detail from the traces left by the bereaved tribe in the desert or the plain; you would sense the same underlying urgency to escape from the presence and the place of the dead.'

'But I am only a snowman. Death is no concern of mine, but the world grows more depressing each day that I live. Why should I who am destined to live forever be troubled by the finality which touches every human being? I am only a snowman with a head and belly full of snow. I have no means of wandering in plains and deserts or in the rooms of houses where the dead have lain. I am pleasurably heavy and sleepy, I will forget death, I am in a blue daze, tasted by rosy children, my limbs amputated and replaced by mischievous schoolboys. Soon I shall be photographed. Life is soft white bliss and the snow is falling away from my face with my laughter.'

# 4

'It is night. Here in the city the light has blue shadows under its eyes and stays up late and wanders restlessly from street to street picking up the shadows standing lonely on corners and in alleyways. The eyes of city light are bloodshot with watching. People depend so much upon the light to reveal to them the shadows and the dust which they have been careless in not sweeping away or laying shrouds against, and other people's faces which demand the most brilliant searchlight beams in order that their identity may be established. When you are walking in the street it is so important to know who passes close to you. When you are sitting at night in the same room or sleeping in bed side by side it is important to be able to recognise your companion. There are many strangers about, Snowman. Who knows? And there is also death by accident or intention in the dark. In the streets of the city they have built arcs of light which shine like gorse bushes in bloom, seen through the red haze of a bush fire; the street lights burst upon the street beneath them in thorns and blooms and twigs or red-and-gold light that stabs and changes — like a drug administered — the aspect of all colour. Tonight, Snowman, you are not snow, you are sunset; sunset and dragons.'

'It is the first time you have mentioned the sun.'

'Your nature as a snowman will reveal the sun to you soon enough. Let us talk of the night and the dragon-light which shines on you. Yet it is no use, Snowman, when events happen they appropriate the time to themselves, stealing days, months, years when a few minutes would be enough to satisfy them but there is no stopping them — what are we to do?'

'I need do nothing. I am only a snowman. It is people who are in danger.'

'One might say that a person takes a few seconds to die, and there can be no objection if someone wishes to claim a few seconds from the store of time, one might almost say it is a reward for dying, to sleep at last with a few seconds gathered like a posy of flowers upon one's breast, but the notion is false and people realize it, for it is death which takes the few seconds, and once death takes a handful of time there is no amount of minutes, days, years which will satisfy his greed; in the end he takes a lifetime. I wanted to talk to you about the night and the street lights, but I notice that the death of Sarah Inchman is at large prowling for more time, turning our attention to the Inchman house as surely as the wind turns the weather vane. Robert has come home tonight. He is aware of the prowling death of his mother, therefore he has secured the windows and fastened the chains across the front and back doors. He is sitting by the fire to read his book of science fiction but he is thinking about his mother and her clothes. What will he do about her clothes?

'Dr Merriman held up the globe of the world in all its blues browns greens reds and spun it lightly with his fingers. He withdrew his hand. The world continued spinning, faster and faster. Dr Merriman smiles. My God, he thought. He knew and the others in the room knew. The holtrime, the wentwail, the sturgescene had …

'Why were her clothes such a drab colour? The clothes of the one or two women he had brought home had been as bright as bird-of-paradise plumage, and his mother's clothes too had seemed full of colour. Where were all the blues and greens and pinks that she wore in the weekend when he came home? Why could he not find the bright clothes she had worn? Had he dreamed them? If that was so then was he also enchanted in looking at the rest of the world?

> *The fenew is cardled. The blutheon millow*
> *clane or hoven. In all the dolis gurnt plange*
> *dernrhiken ristovely; Kentage, merl,*
> *the fenew is cardled, onderl,*
> *pler with dallow,*
> *dimt, in amly wurl.*

'Why was it that as soon as his mother died her clothes seemed drab, brittle, that burnt brown colour like beetle shells found in the grass in September?

'Like a collapsed armour?'

'The fenew is cardled. Dr Merriman twirled the hollow globe faster and faster.

'That is science fiction, Snowman. Soon there will be a visitor from outer space.'

'But I am such a visitor or am I old-fashioned?'

'No, Snowman, you are just as modern as the little green man with black horns. But now that the death of Sarah Inchman has ceased her prowling and has entered her son's thoughts for the profit to be had from his dreams, we can talk once again of the night and the street lights, but most of the people in the street are asleep now, and the lights in the houses have gone out and there is no more gunfire from the television sets. The fresh evening fall of snow, like a cat set before a saucer of milk, has lapped up all the wheel and foot marks and the street has a sunken smooth appearance and with few cars and people braving the snowfall only the wind and the wandering animals and the deaths in search of extra time have the pleasure of making patterns on the snow, while you, Snowman, are growing plumper and plumper and your brass buttons are covered with new snow and your coal-black pine-forest eyes are hooded with snowy brows.

'What a drifting careless life of snowflakes flying heedlessly without effort or decision. And I am remembering as a snowflake myself the time when I too was a visitor from beyond the earth. I remember how some of my companions alighted upon a cold stone doorstep and they seemed to vanish into it, while others died before they arrived on earth. There was a movement of their bodies, a sparkle through the white shadow of their secret crystal skeleton, a sudden falling away of their flesh, now a sweetness, now a trace of salt in the air as the released bones crinkled, snapped starlike, disappeared. I remember — but Memory like Death has a way of seizing time. Do not be alarmed, Snowman, if soon the snow changes colour. Now it lies with breathing space for each flake, but within the next few days the flakes may be churned together, one may smother its neighbour while a grey or black liquid oozes from their bodies, and people will say it is the snow bleeding in its true colour, black blood.

'I am warning you what to expect, for this evening I feel the touch of a wind that is an enemy of snow, that does not breathe the penetrating freezing breath which is the delight of snowflakes. Tonight there is a warm wind blowing from the south from the world where the olive trees grow, their grey shadows falling like flakes upon the grey stone, where the red earth crumbles like the hot ashes of a fire, and yellow flowers bloom in the dried river beds; where the eucalyptus trees lean above the stone fountain and the soft dust stirs about the feet of the people walking; a world of salt marshes, hills of salt, beanflowers, almond blossom, tiny pine trees with sticky purple flowers and small syrup-oozing cones; spotted poisonous toadstools that collapse when you touch them, clouding your face with a yellow mist, toadstools with tall extravagant stems the result of spurted growth which makes people afraid for they cannot accept the outrage of such furious vegetable growth, believing it should happen only in fairy tales. And when their own children growing up, change and develop as if overnight, people utter such cries of panic, "He's growing too fast, he'll outgrow his strength, it's not healthy, it's dangerous!"

'I feel the warm wind, Snowman, although it has not yet reached us here in the street of the city. It is fresh from blowing beneath blue seas above blue skies filled with shadowy houses and people and trees and fishing boats that, like people, make their coughing sounds at morning, cough-chug, cough-chug. There is herb-smell in the wind, and the sound of new green frogs, the population explosion of ponds.

'And the sad-looking cow with the rubbed scabbed shoulders and the too-small tethering-rope, has calved and swings and rocks her udder like a bagful of sea.

'It is all in the warm wind blowing from the south. Even if you pleaded with me, Snowman, I should not be able to delay its arrival here. People plant trees against the wind yet it always sneaks in twos and threes of breath through the gaps in the branches and between and beneath the leaves. People have found no way to refuse the wind's gift of blowing; they have discovered only how to establish its direction and force and how to adjust their lives, like sails, to let the wind carry them to the place they most desire to reach before dark. Oh Snowman I have desired to reach so many places! As a Perpetual Snowflake I am powerless and diminished. You never saw me in the height of my life when a thousand snowflakes leaned upon me and found shelter near me. How quiet it is now, you can hear only the city murmur that is not the sound of people but a murmuring like the sea washing the land.

'People live on earth, and animals and birds; and fish live in the sea but we do not defeat the sea for we are driven back to the sky or we stay.

'It is a question of reptiles hatching deep in the warm sand; of flayed shredded brown weed; crushed spiral houses and tall blue-bearded shells; and an old mapped tortoise in the Galapagos Islands that woke one morning to find himself famous. The embezzlements of living — that is the sound of the sea and of the city …'

'White flying squirrels brushing my face …'

'You are dreaming, Snowman.'

# 5

'I have learned to recognise the people in the street. I know the milkman, and the meter reader, and the window cleaner, and the postman who is limping with his sore foot. "I'll have to go on the National Health," he said, "or visit the Board." What does he mean?'

'The Board is not part of a forest but is a room with rows of seats facing a counter which has been divided into cubicles the average height of a person sitting. If you wish to claim a grant from the Board you go to one of these cubicles and answer questions about your income, property, age, occupation, and so on. You will understand, Snowman, that the cubicles have been constructed to ensure privacy, and it seems to have been calculated that personal secrets do not rise above the head of those who possess them, not like warm air which travels to the ceiling or like smell which penetrates the air and the walls and furniture and clothing; it has been assumed that personal secrets have a discretion of their own, that they will roam within the cubicle but never dream of escaping. Nevertheless the people who are being interviewed have not so much trust in their own secrets, for they whisper the details, glancing around them for fear something has escaped.

'"Speak up please, no one can hear you. You're in a cubicle to ensure privacy."

'The whispering continues.

'That is the Board, Snowman. It can be of little interest to you for it is no relation to a pine forest and it is not more ancient than coal, it is a way of getting money when you have no work, and incidentally of stabling and training secrets so that they do not rise above a man's head.

'Now here is the rag-and-bone man, the totter, sitting in his chair-sized cart surrounded by old striped mattresses stained with rust and blood, by twisted bed ends, fireplaces wrenched at last from their cavern in the wall to make room for the gas or electric heater, blackened fenders, iron bars, bundles of rags. The totter's piebald horse jerks to a stop, the driver rings his brass bell like a priest summoning the communion of refuse; then he cries out but you cannot understand what he has said for surely the purpose of his cry is to distort its meaning and arouse fear in those who are listening. "What is he saying?" they wonder. "Is it Bring Out Your Dead? Any old Rags? Old Rags, Old-Ways, Old-Ways, Gold Rags Rays Racks God-racks All Ways? And why does he never mention the bones?"

'There is his brother walking up and down the street to collect the refuse in his sack. The two look like twins and the small lithe horse with its coat of grey and white seems like a third member of the family. One might imagine that the three are interchangeable and that from time to time the brothers take their turns between the shafts of the cart.

'Now they have disappeared around the corner. When it snows people do not put out their old clothes and bedsteads and extracted fireplaces with the roots of the wall still clinging to them. People in snowstorms have other matters to think of; snow fills people's minds and the world, there is no room for nameless iron bars or mattresses stained with the residue of sleep and love when the concern is the residue of sky. Look at the earth now with its fat layers of wadding, the padded gates and fences with not an iron bone protruding, and the heavy-headed roofs that will soon discard their weight of snow when the fitted grey slates of their skulls begin to shift and slide. The pipes are frozen in the houses. The water has stopped in its tracks. I fear that the black blood is beginning to flow. Look, there's a blackbird sitting on an iced twig, singing!'

'I am afraid, though I am only a snowman.'

I slept and woke. I tried to think of the pleasures of being a snowman, to anticipate the delight of being photographed, but I could not ignore the small trickle of black blood flowing through the hedge into the cutter. People passing noticed it and remarked upon it, pointing to it and speaking in tones of excitement and dismay which left me unable to tell whether they were announcing disaster or victory. I was standing staring with my coal-black pine-forest eyes when I saw a woman walking from house to house with a basket of flowers and I shuddered and bowed my head for I knew they were daffodils.

'Look, Snowman, at the children crowding around her, screaming with pleasure, even the little Italian children from next door who cannot yet speak the language of this country although Salvatore can say Hello, Goodbye, and Milk. "Milk mama, milk." He can say bread too which was once yellow in a field, like daffodils, but you need not be too afraid, Snowman, for perhaps they are not real daffodils; it will be many weeks before daffodils can calculate the arrival of their moment and take their place in the dance. Snowdrops are in bud, but snowdrops are made of snow.'

'Why does everyone seem so pleased at the sight of the daffodils? Listen!'

'Lovely daffodils, early daffodils, bring yourself good luck and buy a bunch of lovely daffodils from a Gypsy.'

'Some will buy the flowers because they rely on their personal sense of time and will not wait until it agrees with the season, and it is those people who can experience spring in winter which may be agreeable, I do not know, yet it is the same people who will dread seeing others surrounded by daffodils with crowns of violets in their hair, while their own hearts are heavy with snow and their eyes cannot keep from gazing at the never-ending shroud wrapped about the world and the dark tomb waiting to admit the dead. All who believe in daffodils while snow falls around them are living uneasily beating lives, their rhythm is the lost note which cannot or will not join the chord because although it will gain security and strength by being with other notes it will at the same time forget the sound of itself, and therefore it stays alone in strange hollow places where there is no other music. The loneliness is the price and the reward.'

'Who are the gypsies to sell early daffodils, real or artificial, when there is snow on the ground, when snowmen are in charge of the earth?'

'The gypsies are all people who are out of step with usual time and place, and it is they who are a nuisance, an uneasiness to those who set their hearts by the clock, who stay and divide each day by twenty-four hours and get no surprising untidy scrawl of blossom in the remainder column; for primroses push their way through rusting iron, and new grass is a carpenter's tool, hammer, chisel, axehead, and snowdrops are the first white steel pylons erected to carry the message.

'Gypsies come and go and baffle like the delinquent swarm of bees that does not keep to the seasonal rhyme or rhythm but follows its own signals and smokes itself out of the secret hollow trees.'

Although the gypsy seemed in the distance to be an old woman, when she came nearer I saw that she was young. I am learning to guess ages in people, and lately I have longed for a sign that time is noticing me, and each night I have considered every inch of my body, saying to myself, 'Has time been here, here — how shall I know?' I stared at a baby in its pram yesterday. Then I looked away at the sky or the street or the shifting ledge of snow on the branch of the tree, and when I looked again at the baby I saw that is red fur cap now framed the face of its mother, and beyond that face like a shadow which is given a shape in darkness by a vivid beam of light shining upon it, was the face of the mother's mother, and then her mother before that, and if I had stared long enough I should have seen the dark space where the first signs of life were imprinted. I am envious of people and their association with time, of the way they can look into each other's eyes and see backward to the first empty darkness or forward to the final sun-blistered collage of light. How does a mere snowman recognise the effect of time upon himself?

The gypsy passed close to me and looked at me.

'When snow falls,' she said, 'there is always a snowman.'

A daffodil dropped from her basket and she did not see it fall, and I thought, that is strange, it is only when people are walking to hell that they can afford to drop flowers in their path. A child picked up the daffodil and stuck it in my hat. I slept with a daffodil in my hat — how brave of me! I could not smell it and it was stiff and shiny and it hurt where the stem thrust into my head. Rosemary was on her way home from school.

'Oh, a daffodil in the snowman's hat!'

She ran to me, withdrew the daffodil, and sniffed it.

'Plastic,' she said. 'They're everywhere.'

I looked about me to see if she spoke the truth but I could see no others in the street or in the sky. When the daffodils come will they be everywhere?

The woman next door looked over the fence.

'Plastic,' she echoed. 'But they're useful for wall vases or the back of the car. They melt, though, if you put them near the fire.'

I remembered vividly the snowman with a fire burning in his head, and the way he sank into the earth and disappeared. Was that death? Had Sarah Inchman died because she leaned too close to a fire?

'What are the signs of death?'

'The signs of death are without nobility or dignity or beauty, they are as shameful as the assenting chalk marks on the rust-red sides of a loaded cattle-truck after men have learned that a cattle-truck will hold more people than cattle, that it will accommodate the whole human race in its journey to the desert over drains and dust and broken stones and dandelions where the milk is sucked by little black flies, while babies with their bones pushing like soft white mushrooms through their flesh, and grown men and women with their bones rising like sharpened axes know nothing of the thin blue trickle of milk flowing through the stem of the dandelion.'

'Dandelion milk, mushrooms?'

'People must share the world and the streams which flow through it but if the dead have lain in the streams then to drink from them is death.

'Look at the icicle, Snowman, look above your head at the melting icicle!'

I saw the glistening silver rod wedged between the snow-covered slates of the roof and the spouting slowly begin to move, with its spine breaking, to shudder and writhe while its sharp point which as a weapon might have plunged and driven through my heart, began to disappear and drops of water fell upon the path to mingle with the stream of black blood which was growing wider and swifter and now was surging out into the street, so that even the curious frightened people staring at it were forced to acknowledge the fact of the wound.

Harry Dincer came to his front door. He held a shovel which he thrust before him as if he were angry. I imagined that he had come to help me win some obscure battle, that because his daughter Rosemary had created me, he felt obliged to protect me.

His face was flushed, his eyes were streaked with red; he had been down at the King's Arms again drinking away his despair at never being able to say 'Ullo Rome, Paris, Marseilles. He plunged the shovel into the snow and began to clear great masses of snow not caring how he mishandled or crushed it, lurching it forward along the path and into the street to the gutter where it was heaped in a grey sweating mound, like a new grave.

'But you have never seen a grave, Snowman. Sarah Inchman's grave is new, in a Garden of Rest where plastic flowers in shaded alcoves await the fire. The funeral was conducted by tall men in tall black hats and the wreaths were arranged high on the roof of the polished black car — all as a pretence of being able to see into the sky, the conjurer's approach, Snowman, to the magic moment when the jaw drops and the accusing eyes are quickly pressed shut in case they spy and tell. Children sometimes joke to a tall man, "Is it cold up there?" You, Snowman, who came from the sky, you know how often during the festivals of death you must have seen the polished black chimney pots parading among the clouds and the brittle stars to get a peep at the other world.'

When Harry Dincer finished the attack with his shovel he came over to me and I thought for a moment that he would demolish me also. I had no way of defending myself.

'Our snowman,' he said. 'I forgot about you. It won't be long now will it? We'll take your photo as soon as we can, while we have the chance.'

He looked at the sky.

'More snow today,' he said wisely.

'Hi Harry!'

That was the man next door who also works in the telephone exchange but who is allowed on the Continental Circuit and can get through to Rome, Paris, Marseilles almost any time he cares to.

'Hi Max. Never known it to last so long have you?'

'Looks like more tonight, what's up with the weather? Last winter was mild as mild. You been working hard?'

Harry was silent for a few minutes. 'Ullo Rome Paris Marseilles.

'Couldn't sleep,' he said. 'Racket next door. Thought I'd clear my share of snow.'

'I wonder what the Council think they're doing, drifts everywhere.'

'How's the job Max?' Harry tried not to show his envy. 'Still on the Continental Circuit?'

'Sure.'

Harry's eyes filled with longing. Anyone could have told what he was thinking: What really happened when you put on the headphones and began to talk in a different language? To people so far away? And why did they keep showing that advertisement in the newspapers, 'Ullo Rome, Paris, Marseilles, men up to fifty-nine with or without experience. Why fifty-nine? What happened when you were sixty that gave you no hope of ever getting through to Rome, Paris, Marseilles? Max was fifteen years younger than Harry — thirty-seven — and the bald patch on the back of his head was so carefully darned with crisscross strands of hair that you didn't notice it unless you took special care to see it.

'You are learning, Snowman.'

Harry made a sudden wrench with his shovel, but I need not have been afraid for he did not attack me.

'See you Max,' he called, and went inside.

It snowed and I slept.

# 6

'There is talk of simplicity. Snow has made the world simple as deceit is simple, a soft mask concealing the intention and truth of hills and plains and cities, the toil and thrust and rock and stone and grass growing like green ribs to accommodate the sky's breath. A dust-sheet on the restless furniture of the world. You ought to be proud, Snowman, to have so changed the face of the earth, to have reduced it to such a terrible simplicity that people are blinded if they gaze upon it.'

Another morning. I am used to morning, to watching the light stealing red-rimmed through the smoke above the chimneys and the white walls of the buildings. I am used to children snatching my arms and my buttons or pipe and replacing them; to the sinister remarks made by people who stop to stare at me. I am used to the comings and goings of the Dincer family. I wonder if Rosemary has forgotten her grieving over the University student.

'Oh, that disappointment about her age?'

'Disappointment! But you said it was the end, you said it was a kind of death!'

'Language wanes, Snowman. Feelings wane. Death comes to be no more than a disappointment, and grief over events must be strictly rationed and the size of the ration is controlled by distance in time and space — the attentions of the heart are measured by the pacing of the feet and the movements of the hands of the clock. The massacre of a race of people is only on the level of a disappointment if it is beyond the range of the stay-at-home feet controlled by the stay-at-home heart beating in time with the familiar clock. When a man puts a telescope to his snow-blinded eye he can see streams of oil flowing and fields of wheat trampled by cloud-shadows driven by the wind, but he can't see the tiny distant ration of his own Care. But no, wait, what is that fluttering speck in his snow-blinded eye? It is a fly, disappointment and death, Care and Love crawling close to his own skin, the source of their lifeblood. Why should they travel to face the flood and the earthquake, the dark camp where the children's bones push soft as mushrooms through their flesh, and the men and women sharpen their gaunt axes upon the human stone?'

'Now Rosemary is walking sedately home from school. Her manner of walking comes easily to her for she has practised it during the years she was at Primary School, and now when she walks as a Grammar School girl she is preparing for the time when she will be a University student. As she walks she flings her long striped University scarf over her shoulder. Don't believe that people live in the present, Snowman. There is haste for tomorrow and the need to know how to behave when tomorrow comes. Walking like a University student is simple; and dressing like one; and later living and behaving like a wife, a mother, a career woman; knowing the clothes to wear, the smile to adopt, the opinions to discuss and agree or disagree with, the people to make happy or unhappy from the limited ration of Love and Care. But what is the correct behaviour for Death? Whom will Rosemary imitate in order to die? There is no clue for her except in her own sleep and dreams, for one imitates one's own death, and when the time comes Rosemary cannot borrow her grandmother's way of dying or her grandfather's or her Uncle Phil's or Sarah Inchman's.

'Now Rosemary is outside the gate. She sees Doris, a girl of her own age, walking on the opposite side of the road. As they go to different Grammar Schools and are not yet used to the strangeness, they like to spend their after-school hours, weekends, and holidays working delicate but swiftly fading patterns into their former Primary School friendship by embroidering their anxieties and new experiences. Now they call out and wave and smile at each other, and forgetting her Grammar School dignity Rosemary runs to talk to Doris. Her feet crunch upon the hardened snow. She slips and falls in an ice-filled trough of snow. The heavy lorry has no time to swerve or stop.

'And that, Snowman, is death.

'See how there is no concentration, no tension, only diffuseness, untidiness. There is no rigid drop of death congealed upon the surface of living, no stain that one may point to and try to erase. It is this elusiveness of death, the vacuum created when it happens that cause details, incidents, emotions of living people to flood in filling the emptiness and crowding the untidiness with a further disarray. From up and down the street, from beyond, around corners, out of front and back doors people come running toward the scene all with their contribution of irrelevance. One woman has a tea towel in her hand, another a shopping bag, the man over the road is still holding his half-sewn overcoat, the school children carry their cases and satchels. In a way they seem like refugees from the vague unimportant outer circle trying to reach a clarity and significance at the dark still centre. But where is the centre, the perfect stain of the moment? They cannot find it. Curtains are drawn aside. Those who have not chosen to join the crowd are staring from their windows, and one has telephoned 999 which is easier to contact than Paris, Rome, or Marseilles. Police ambulance fire. The lorry driver is sitting in the snow, quietly and sadly, as if his home were the snow and the snow were his doorstep where he sits in the evening looking out upon the world. The spectators seem to realize the driver's right to that small area of snow, for they avoid it and make detours about it. But the walls of the lorry driver's white house are made of glass and he can see out and the people can see in and their eyes are full of pity. They say, "What will we do, What will we do?"

'One man from the crowd is standing on guard beside Rosemary. He has felt for her pulse. He has placed his hand on her forehead, not because it will help or explain her condition but because his mother used to touch his own forehead when he was a child and felt sick. Everyone is staring at him, trying to read the expression on his face.

'Listen, Snowman.'

Like a dog yelping, I thought it was a dog and then I saw the navy coat and her in a heap.

They've rung for the ambulance.

Who rang?

I don't know. Someone, I don't know.

Is the ambulance coming?

I think so, someone rang for it.

Has someone called the ambulance?

Is there someone seeing to everything?

I suppose so, I should think so, definitely so.

I suppose the ambulance is on its way?

More than likely. Someone will have rung for it.

They're waiting for the ambulance. It shouldn't be long.

Did someone ring for it?

I think so, someone rang for it.

Who rang for it?

Someone who saw it happen.

Did you see it?

No, I was just turning the corner when I head the screeching noise and a funny thing I was thinking how slippery the snow was just there …

There? Yes, just there, and someone screamed.

Look at the lorry driver.

Yes, just sitting there.

He's ill with shock. They've been trying to get him to move but he won't.

He just stays there.

Her parents are at work aren't they? Her mother runs that little blouse shop down at the Green.

I believe so. Maisy's.

There's someone coming, it looks like an ambulance.

I think it is. Someone rang for it, someone over there.

I suppose it was the man who's standing near her.

Did he ring for the ambulance?

Someone said it was him. They say he says she's dead.

The girl Dincer isn't it?

Yes, she goes to Grammar School, her mother keeps the blouse shop down at the Green.

Daisy's?

No, Maisy's. She owns it with her sister.

Didn't her father sell you that old television that never went?

It was the tubes, and such a lot of interference.

We had a man in two weeks ago, I'm getting tired of it.

Look the lorry driver's getting up. Someone's helping him into that house. I wonder how he'll face her parents?

I can hear a bell ringing. It's the ambulance. It's taken ages.

Someone must have rung for it.

I think someone did.

There the Dincer car with Mrs Dincer driving.

And here's the ambulance. Look they're getting out the stretcher. Look, the man's shaking his head.

Isn't it awful with everyone staring, like a circus. They should tell everybody to go away, some people have no respect for privacy.

Look he's shaking his head again.

They're covering up her face. I guessed it. She must be dead.

There's a blanket over her face.

Did they say she was dead?

Someone said. They said that man said who put that coat over her to start with.

Look he's talking to the Dincers. I wont be able to walk past there today or ever.

There's blood on the snow. It's a funny green colour. The police make a fuss don't they, they have to.

They're clearing the snow, putting things in order.

All the same I can't walk past there.

Did the Dincers go in the ambulance with her?

I didn't see. More than likely. I wonder who rang for the ambulance.

Someone must have rung.

They've taken the lorry driver to hospital too.

Why have the police put lanterns there, as if it's night?

They always do. It's dark early but in a few weeks the days will be longer, have you decided about this year?

No, we're waiting, though they say book early but there's always room when the time comes.

I wouldn't be too sure though. It's their only daughter too.

She goes to Grammar School.

Did they really say she was dead?

It looks like it. You could tell really though couldn't you? Who was that man in the brown coat who took charge? He doesn't live in the street.

He looks like a foreigner. A total stranger.

He had his wits about him. Did you see it happen?

No, I was just coming around the corner when I head the scream.

They say she ran over to meet her friend, the girl Miller. Doris Miller. They've taken her away too.

Have they?

Yes, that woman who rang for the ambulance took her inside.

Did that woman ring for the ambulance? I thought it was the man in the corner house. I had the impression it was him.

Him? No, it was the woman. They say she rang for the ambulance. And then she was out there talking to the ambulance men as if she'd rung.

Then she must have. She'd ring 999 I suppose and they'd get through. I suppose that's how the police came.

Are they leaving the lanterns there? It's not dark.

It will be. The snow makes it darker. I've never known it to snow for so long, not in the city, all night and all day and the Council have had to bring in casual labour to deal with it.

Yes, men with beards and tramps. Hear the bell?

Yes, perhaps it's the ambulance on the way to King's.

No, it will have got there ages ago, it must be another ambulance.

Perhaps there's been another accident.

More than likely. They shouldn't have these heavy lorries in the snow.

It was stupid of her to run across of course. She wasn't exactly a child. She goes to Grammar School.

Her mother has that blouse shop down at the Green.

Maisy's?

No, Daisy's.

The police must have rung for her.

Or the hospital when someone rang for the ambulance.

Who rang for the ambulance?

Wasn't it that man who was standing near her, the one who took charge. I've never seen him before.

A perfect stranger.

Well someone rang anyway. Her father's a telephonist. They'd get through to him quick enough.

Yes they'd ring the exchange.

The ambulance people?

No, the police or the woman who rang the ambulance.

Didn't the man ring?

Well someone rang anyway but I don't suppose they could do anything for her.

I saw the man shaking his head.

They put a blanket over her face, one of those grey blankets.

They shouldn't have done that in full view. It let us know she was dead, they shouldn't have let everybody see she was dead, they should have taken her in the back of the ambulance as if she were ill or something and would recover.

I don't suppose they thought at the time.

But it let everybody know she was dead, and it makes things worse to know. It would have been better to read about it afterward in the paper, as if she had died in hospital.

But they couldn't keep it from people, they couldn't keep it from the parents, not with them standing there.

It doesn't seem right though. To think she was lying there dead all the time!

I couldn't go past there.

They're measuring. Why are they measuring?

It's to do with the inquiry.

They'll want witnesses.

Yes, they'll ask over the BBC. You hear them in the morning before the eight o'clock news.

Well I didn't see it thank goodness.

Neither did I, I was just turning the corner. I heard it though.

Don't.

Whoever rang the ambulance must have seen it for them to ring the ambulance.

Yes, I wonder who rang the ambulance?

I am only a snowman. What must a snowman do? I will sleep; there is news of other seasons.

# 7

'I saw a fiercely burning light flying beyond the clouds, and the shadow of it passed across my body, and tears ran down my cheeks. I shivered, and my flesh seemed to drop from me and soak into the snow at my feet, and then I think I fell asleep for two days, and when I woke it was morning. Just as I was waking a wind shook loose one of my coal-black pine-forest eyes and blew it onto the pavement where a black cat sneaked up to it, pounced at it and sent it flying under the hedge into the deep snow and there it lay until a little dog bounded along, scratched at the snow and finding my coal-black pine-forest eye he put it in his mouth where it was held prisoner until the little dog ran home to his owner and dropped my coal-black pine-forest eye at his feet.

'Coal, good boy,' she exclaimed, and taking it into her sitting-room she placed it upon an interesting mount of other coal-black pine-forest eyes. You have not explained what happened then, Perpetual Snowflake. I do not find my partial loss of sight very distressing; one coal-black pine-forest eye will serve me as well as two.

'While I was asleep I dreamed I was a snowflake again, a tiny flat Peter-Paul tissue of snow with zigzags of air, like melting lace, binding the edges of my body, and I was tucked up in the sky under a soft blanket of cloud and there was no thought of conquering the earth or the sea and no idea that I would ever be a snowman witnessing the comings and goings of people upon their curiously snow-white earth.'

'Yes, you slept, Snowman, for two days. If you were being affected by time you would discover that as you grew older you would spend more of your life sleeping. I believe time is affecting you, Snowman, accumulating like layers of snowstorms upon your life. People long to shut their eyes. They yawn. They shade their faces from the snow. In old age they curl up like leaves and sleep beneath drifts of snow and have no care.

'But I had meant to tell you that you have been photographed, you have had what they call your "likeness" taken.'

'My likeness? Taken?'

'Oh there is only one of you, no part of you has been stolen, although keeping alive is a matter of greed more than of loneliness. There is one of each creature because that creature devours all others, it roams through the world with its magnetic mouth seizing the tiny filed brightnesses which are the commencement of others of its kind. You think that you observe other creatures — you have seen many people in the street, little dogs, birds flying or perched here on your tree (your tree!) with their feet plodged in a smooth spreading of snowflake sauce. But if you observe with your invisible eye you will know that to each creature there is only one — himself. The wind blowing from life and death puffs one being to the size of the world. The sky fits him like a skin, and the surface of the earth is only as wide as the soles of his feet or the grasp of his claws, and his wing-span is east and west, north and south, and his head is forever burned by the neighbouring flames of the sun. Strangely enough, Snowman, this proud lonely greed is a condition of love as well as of hate, for the self does not know where to stop, it devours friend and enemy.'

'But I am only a snowman. I have been photographed. Has it changed me to have had my likeness taken?'

'A snowman, and afraid of change!'

'While you were asleep Rosemary was buried, and yesterday, the day of the funeral, Harry looked out of the window and catching sight of you he exclaimed to his wife, "We never took a photo of it. We promised to make a photo of it while it lasted. I think we ought to take a snap of it now, Kath. Before the warm weather comes and there is a thaw."

'"Yes, the snow's going," Kath said. "Be quick, Harry, we don't want to be seen taking photos at a time like this, it will make people wonder."

'"If we don't take it now it will never get taken, you know how snowmen vanish, one moment they're in front of you large as life the next moment they've vanished."

'Harry found his camera, came into the garden, focused, clicked the shutter, and your photograph was taken. I assure you it won't hurt you, Snowman. It's just a flat impression of you, not as important as the shadow which remains by your side here in the garden and which changes its shape according to the light in the sky, now it grows corpulent with morning, now it braves the decapitations of noon and ends a starved evening shape with its fingers clawing at the sky.'

As he spoke of the sky I looked up and with my one coal-black pine-forest eye I saw such a dazzle and it was an icicle starred like a frozen wand and I could see a pink and light and deep-blue world enclosed in it, and all the colours of the rainbow were gathered inside, knocking on the glass walls to get free, and then I heard a sharp crack, a sun-groan, and the colours burst suddenly from the icicle and water ran down my face onto my shoulders and down my body to my feet where it changed to black blood.

'What does it mean? Is it a sign because I have been photographed?'

'You need not be afraid of having had your photo taken. The photo failed. It did not come out.'

'It did not come out?'

'No, it was misty and blurred, and everything which was not covered with snow appeared white in the photograph while everything white, including yourself, showed as a black shape encircled by a jagged rim of pale light. Solid brick, wood and stone were rendered unsubstantial, became part of a landscape of nothingness, while everything covered with snow — you and your fellow snowflakes who are so sensitive to the prospect of daffodils and fire and sun and warm winds from the south, who are unable to resist even the lightest breath of wind, all that is fragile became strong and bold, as certain as stone and steel, capable of withstanding ordeal by season and sun. That was your photograph, Snowman. It was a failure, it did not "turn out", and yet your photo was "taken" and no one will ever be able to explain the nature of what the camera discovered with you to represent your body as a pillar of black stone in a garden where the branches of a black sword were growing from the earth beneath a sky full of prowling glossy black tomcat clouds; where the solid buildings melted into nothingness, doors, fences, gates, cars, including ambulances, and people dancing or resting or dead, all dissolving before the light-bribing eye of the camera. I hope you are not disturbed when I tell you that your photograph suffered the humiliation of most projects that fail — projects of light, conscience, time, discovery — it was burned quickly on the fire. It flared and crumpled enveloped in a translucent white flame which changed the photo from a cloud of light to a black brittle substance curled at the edges like a stale crust thrown out for the drooling mumbling pigeons — hear them? — that have lost the desire to fly and only potter about in people's heads making white messages in the attics of thought.

'But I wonder, Snowman, I can't tell you precisely what you lost through the burning of your photograph. I have said it is so necessary to be careful in one's observations, to question the actions of people because they do prefer most of all to be comfortable whether in the matter of truth or of toilet. And projects are considered failures because it might take too much time and energy to prove they are successes. Would you rather have an image of yourself as black stone (it might even be marble!) or as white nothingness? I myself am impressed by this bewitching process which extracts stone from snow, swords and knives from trees, and sets the sky wailing with old dark toms padding in and out of the winds that are huddled and tangled, like thorn hedges, about the borders of night.'

'How will the point of view of the photograph affect the death of Rosemary? She did not melt or change to snow, at least not when I looked at her with my coal-black pine-forest eyes. Is there a means of photographing death which changes it to life, as objects are changed in the photograph?'

'But the objects were not changed, Snowman. You are still a snowman. It was the view of them — have you ever heard people speak of a view? When they choose where to live they often say, "It must have a good view." People like to look at the sea, it flashes and shuffles the silver cards, it winks with enticement, with light, with promise. It deals out peace and speckled flowers pink and blue and rakes in the losses, deep deep, and the losses are secret and no one ever learns the extent of them.'

'I know of the sea. People live on earth, and animals and birds, and fish live in the sea but we do not defeat the sea for we are driven back to the sky or we stay and become what we have tried to conquer ...'

'That is true, Snowman. The victor has a habit of assuming the identity of those he has vanquished. It is a habit of people also, and animals and birds and bright red fish.'

'Do I understand the sea because I have arrived on land? Is that a focus where the true balance of knowing is brought into view?'

'You forget or you do not realize, Snowman, that most photographs "turn out", that is, most objects appear as they appear to everyone everywhere. The moment when the picture seems to fail or where the process is arrested before the picture is developed is one of the most exciting moments in the life a human being. The damp blurred distorted film, the unexpected "failed" view of the familiar, bring the danger of happiness, and you may know that happiness is a great danger in the lives of people, and that they are prepared from birth to fight and overcome it, to protect themselves from it with shields, hoods, specially fitted secret claws and stings.

'Rosemary is dead. Her death is no real concern of ours because we are made of snow, but if we were flesh and blood we might be tempted to colour and retouch her death and place it beside other events instead of giving it a startling isolation upon a blank page.

'No photograph can alter the fact of Rosemary's death but it is likely that the focus of Kath and Harry has been altered. Violent happenings, sudden griefs upset the development of the scene often subjecting it to so much violent overexposure that the result is a view of nothingness. If this happens in the Dincer family, Harry will feel his body falling apart, like straw, or shredded like the weave of sacking. His hair will change to white cotton floating away on the wind and when he clenches his fist the flesh of his hand will melt. He will be a true snowman. The same changes will occur in his wife. Nothing will finally become nothing. And then when all creatures and objects are cleaned of their parasitical identity, why, then the rhymes will have reason. If all the world were paper, if all the seas were ink, if all the trees were bread and cheese — what a marvellous freedom of view that would be, Snowman!

'Kath and Harry may experience a little of this changed world but it is likely that their landscape will emerge in conventional form with death as a recognizable creature, perhaps a member of the family, and with the space in the snow scattered there to make it seem as if nothing had happened, as in those photographs which are arranged and retouched with people blotted from the scene if their presence is likely to cause embarrassment to themselves or to others. Memory is quite a useful agent for retouching scenes made complicated or dangerous by grief or happiness, and when people have photographs of others whose eyes reveal too much love or hate it is a convenient trick to make them unrecognisable by concealing their eyes with a strip of tape, as in official photographs of people in prison or in places for the insane. People with too much emotion in their eyes are usually prisoners under sentence and often halfway to losing their reason.'

'Snowman, Snowman, the sheet of snow is wearing thin. Were the season a good housewife she would halve the snow and "turn" it to give the worn places a rest from wear, and she would darn the holes with tiny snow-stitches, and then once again spread the sheet over the earth and the snow would appear brand-new; but the season is not a thrifty housewife; the snow is wearing thin, and there is no one to change top to bottom or inside to outside. Grass is poking through the holes in the material; the flannelette has lost its fleecy lining. The linen is dirty, for the season has slept too long in it. During the next few days if you look high in the sky you will see the first white cleaned clouds being unparcelled and set adrift. Are you afraid to look now in the sky? Remember, Snowman, although your photograph did not turn out, they have the negative of you where your appearance is very strange because neither you nor your shadow can be identified unless the negative is held up to the light; therefore you are preserved, for a time. I think you are beginning to understand that when a positive and not a negative snowman faces the light the result may mean death. Is that why you are afraid to look high in the sky?'

'But I am only a snowman. Why should I be concerned about death? It happens only to people — to old women and to Grammar School girls attacked by lorries. Yet I confess that I am afraid. It is strange that people do not last, that they change, not as snowmen change with their flesh peeling from their body and being replaced with new snowfall but a change which like a touch of iron that has been dipped in burning time and is itself impervious to the force and fury of years, brands the visible human body and no less indelibly the secret individual life which accompanies it. As a snowman, have I thoughts inside my head? What does the inside of my head resemble? Is it like a white barn with rafters, and white mice scampering along the beams and nesting in the corners? What is my head? Is it a stone?

'Yes, it is a stone. While Rosemary was making you she found a large white stone upon which she packed layers of snowflakes; that is your head. Does it help to know what your head is made of? To know that before the city was conquered by the snowstorm your head stood bald and white on top of a gatepost? Your head was a decoration polished in its circular shape because people admired it that way. It must not make you depressed to learn that your head has been used as an ornament, for it is a custom common among human beings and often persists after their flesh and face and hair and eyes have been added, and no one would guess that a smooth white circular stone was hidden inside.

'I cannot tell you the exact moment when you were born, Snowman. I cannot say, When your right hand was made, then you became a snowman. Or, As soon as your stone head was covered with flakes, then you were a snowman. Or that you have been living since Rosemary had the idea of making you. It is the habit of people to look at the beginning of life in order to determine the moment of birth, but as a Perpetual Snowflake I am not so prejudiced, I know that seed is shed also at the moment of death, and that many people are still not born although they possess bodies with limbs in place and heads with thoughts in place.

'Look at the gap in the sky! It is the sun!'

# 8

When I looked up at the sky I could see nothing. Yet I felt my body shuddering and the familiar tears ran down my cheeks, and then in a sudden gust of wind something whirled about me, up and down, then out the gate, onto the pavement, into the pool of black blood, then toward me again, round and round my feet and then up to my head where flip-flop-flap it settled and the gust of wind vanished. I was grateful for the shelter upon my head because I was afraid to look too long at the sky in case I saw the sun, though I scarcely knew how I should recognize it.

'My head is protected now. I have shelter. I cannot even see the sky now.'

'You are not the only one to seek shelter from a newspaper; it is common practice. People use it to protect themselves from the weather, others use it to hide from history or time or any of those inconvenient abstractions which man would destroy if only they had a visible shape for him to seize and defeat. Oh these abstractions, Snowman, they are among the most intrusive companions. They are never satisfied unless they have built a nest on the tip of a man's tongue, in the keys of his typewriter, in the hollow of his pen-nib — all favourite places for abstractions to breed and overpopulate the world of words. Even in my talking to you I cannot help mentioning them. Time, I say. Time, History, change. But Time is surely an abstraction, I think he is a senile creature who is blind because his eyes have been gouged out by an historic fire; his flesh is covered with fur and he licks the hours and swallows them and they form a choking ball inside him. Then Time dies. Time. Death. It is no use, Snowman. The proper place for abstractions is in a region of the mind which must be entered in nakedness of thought. Certain abstractions are powerful and may be lethal yet the way to approach them is not to carry weapons of personification but to act as soldiers do when they surrender, to discard all the known means of defence and retaliation and walk naked toward the hostile territory. Surprising things may happen then, Snowman. We may see abstractions in their truth.

'Truth, death, time, it is no use. How grateful I am that we are made of snow! People need to burn off the old words in the way that a farmer destroys the virgin bush to put the land to new use with controlled sowing and harvesting. I will not say, though, that all such farmers are successful. Their enthusiasm wanes, the crops fail, noxious weeds take the place of the former harmless ones, there are downpours, droughts. And there are always the earliest settlers who yearn for the time when the land was covered with familiar bush and the streams were not dammed to create inexplicable hydro works, and the tall known trees were starred with centuries-old white clematis. But Snowman, Snowman, perhaps words do not matter when it is only a question of surviving for one season. Then the word *Help* is vocabulary enough. Snowmen and Perpetual Snowflakes have no need of words. Snowman, Snowman, look at the gap in the sky. It is the sun.'

'I can see nothing while I wear this torn newspaper over my head. I can see only words in print as you have explained to me. Not *Help help*, but said Mrs Frank

Wilkinson in charge of the unit I suppose they have seen some deaf and dumb people on buses and in the street and felt sorry that nobody could talk to them the boys admitted breaking into a prefab for food my girlfriend is a nurse and he made her stand in the snow waiting for me to come home before he would let her in made as new suspects arson her behaviour seemed quite out of character the role of the church is to provide this not to bribe them into attending they want real religion choice of two modern suites for happy holidays licensed bar dancing but guilty are you hard of hearing your lovers' dream home gas death two sides to him you've had your last chance I'm going to sentence you snowdrops are flowering the crocuses are showing in some places so get ready for spring planting if digging hasn't been done get it over quickly leave large lumps for the weather to work on we can still expect frost and snow fire destroys home heater blaze carpet linoleum were destroyed he woke to the smell of burning planned with you in mind luxury in the sun on the sands by the sea the summer of your dreams stretch lack threads or the new nylon web over primula or polyanthus buds before the birds get at them planting can start soon for fruit trees fruit bushes roses he's finished his lunch when someone rang to tell him it's your shop on fire an unknown young boy discovered the fire he was walking past the shop when he thought he saw smoke or steam in the window monster sale end of season ...'

I was beginning to wish that I did not know how to read my newspaper shelter. It seemed full of references to fire and sun and spring, and I thought it strange that human beings should also be afraid of fire and sun and spring, so afraid that they had to keep writing of them in newspapers in order to dilute their fear. Two sides to him? What did it mean? And the picture of the sun puzzled me. I could see the caption clearly — FOLLOW THE SUN — and at first I was foolish enough to believe that if I looked at a picture of the sun it would have the same effect upon me as if I looked at the sun itself. The sun was portrayed as a semicircle with tentacles growing from it, and a wide smiling mouth. What had I been afraid of? So this was the sun, the picture of benevolence; it had not even eyes to see me. Perhaps the smile was too wide giving its face a suggestion of falseness but there seemed to be no doubt about the sun's kind nature.

'Do these newspaper shelters often happen to snowmen?'

'You are a fool of course. As self-centred as any human being. You imagine that newspapers are printed to shelter you from the sun.'

'I don't need shelter from the sun. I have seen its kind face.'

'It is worse, Snowman, when you are deceived by your own deceit. Newspapers do make convenient shelters for snowmen; also for cooked fish, dog-meat, and they are useful as blankets for tramps; they protect people from the hot and cold weather; they deaden sound; they are the body and tail of kites, and are made into little dishes with flour-and-water paste; they are the heads of puppets, the bed for the cat to have kittens on; they are wrappers, concealers, warmers; also they bring news, even from Rome, Paris, Marseilles.

'Now a gust of wind is blowing near you, Snowman, and for your sake I hope it does not remove your newspaper shelter for when the sun shines it leans close to the earth and the snow is drawn from the earth like white milk from a white breast and when all the snow has vanished and the sun is satisfied the earth lies dry, wrinkled, folded with a dull brown stain spreading through its skin, but you will never see so much, Snowman, nor the change that follows, it is other seasons.'

The gust of wind came near me but it did not blow away my newspaper shelter, and toward evening the tears stopped flowing down my cheeks and a cloud of snow fell from the sky but I could see nothing until a blackbird, going home, stopped to rest on the tree, and seeing me standing forlorn, thin, blind, with the world's news clinging to my stone skull, he flew down and pecked at the newspaper, just a slight stab with his beak, tearing a hole in the paper so that once more I could look at the world with my coal-black pine-forest eye. The blackbird had pierced the word *snowdrops*. When I looked out through the gap in *snowdrops* I could see the blackbird disappearing over the roofs of the buildings and thus I could not ask him whether it was joy or sorrow which had impelled him to stab the chosen word.

Tonight I shall sleep deeply. I feel safe. More snow-armies are arriving upon the earth and all will be as it was on my first day. Snow repairs, cushions, conceals; knives have no blades, mountains have no swords, the yellow earth-cat has white padded claws, and it is people only, those bone-and-flesh scissors snapping in the street, refusing the overcoat of snow which their shadows wear, sneaking faithfully beside them, it is people who change and die. People and birds.

There is a sound at my feet. Something has fallen from the sky. It is not a snowflake, it is a blackbird and it is dead, I know, for I have learned the dispositions of death. Its beak is half-open and quite still and no living blackbird has such a thrust of beak unless it is taking food or attacking the enemy. Its feathers are ruffled about its neck, its body is huddled, and no living blackbird has such an appearance except in a tree in the wind and rain and now that the snow-armies have arrived for the night the wind does not blow, the tree is still, and there is no rain — but what is rain? How quickly I have learned to gather the clues of death! The bird's claws have as much grasping power now as loose pieces of string. Death has stolen the black sheen of his feathery overcoat and there are two round white pieces of skin like tiny portholes fitted and closed over his once bright watchful eyes. There is a snowdrop lying beside him; its neck is twisted and a green liquid oozes from the crushed stem.

'Snowman, Snowman, there is a gap in the sky.'

My sleep is disturbed tonight. I think I must have dozed several times. My newspaper shelter keeps flapping against my face, it seems to have lodged forever upon my head, and I do not really care to harbour or be protected for too long by stale news two sides to him you've had your last chance I'm going to sentence you snowdrops are flowering and crocuses are showing in some places so get ready for spring an unknown boy discovered the fire he was walking past the shop when he thought he saw smoke or steam in the window nobody could talk to them he felt sorry for them because nobody could talk to them they were deaf and dumb.

Stale news. Yet how can I tell whether news if fresh or stale? When the Perpetual

Snowflake talks to me of people he brings centuries-old news that is fresh to me, and the stale news of the prompt arrival of each morning brings with it the excitement of fresh news.

A prowling cat has torn the dead blackbird to pieces and eaten him. It is so dark now. I think I will sleep but I am afraid, why am I afraid, I am only a snowman, your last chance I'm going to sentence you two sides to him snowdrops are flowering and crocuses are showing in some places luxury in the sun on the sand by the sea but we do not defeat the sea for we are driven back to the sky or we stay and become what we have tried to conquer, remembering nothing except our new flowing in and out in and out, sighing for one place, drawn to another, wild with promises to white birds and bright red fish and beaches abandoned then longed for.

'Snowman, Snowman.'

Man is simplicity itself. Coal, brass, cloth, wood.

I never dreamed.

# 9

I believe the armies of snow have deserted me. There are wars of which I know nothing — the wounded and the dead are lying everywhere yet no reinforcements arrive from the sky which I can almost see if I stare through the tiny hole in my newspaper shelter. The clouds are no longer battleships.

'Battleships sail with their crews up and down on the sea and wave golden flags and below deck in the dark places of the ship they fill torpedoes with striped sweets, they press buttons which open snow-white umbrellas above the sea, and certainly it is all most beautiful. Snowman, and artistic, the candy floss of death licked by small boys from the hate and fear blossoming on the tall wooden sticks. Splinter crack, the cost. And the white wood with the sap dried. And the heads of trees hustling rumours out of the long-distance wind on its everlasting runabout ticket got cheap the endless circular limits of life.

'I cannot stare so often now at the clouds but I think I see a streak of red which all knowledgeable people on earth will say is blood from a wound but I cannot tell nor do I know if it is fire I am tired of blood and fire what is it? I find that I can scarcely breathe. I wish the reinforcements would arrive. What is the use of conquering the earth with snow if the earth does not stay conquered? Oh there are so many rumours everywhere, there's a gossiping trickle of black blood in the gutter, and through the tiny hole in my newspaper shelter I can see swellings on the twigs and branches of the tree. It must be suffering from a disease; perhaps it is dying. People, birds, trees, everything on earth seems to die. I suppose that before many days have passed everyone in the street will have died and how strange it is to think that I have not yet been told about everyone, that they will die and I shall not have known them, and it will not matter because I am only a snowman. But are knowing and being known the two triumphs which the dead carry with them to their graves, the dead who drop like parachutists to the darkness of memory and survive there because they are buckled and strapped to the white imperishable strength of having known and been known, of having made the leap to darkness surrounded and carried by the woven threads of people whom they greeted, abused, loved, murdered, or heard news from even at a great distance, a voice speaking from Rome, Paris, Marseilles or from the forbidden interior where the ticking sawdust desert is wound and whirled and as you have said, Perpetual Snowflake, men die of thirst with their mouth an O like a spokeless wheel full of the dust and sand and red earth, while tall cactus palms extend their greeting and parry at the sky as if they wore great spiked green boxing-gloves in the whirlwind.'

'There's little more to tell you, Snowman, of the people in the street of the city. You are only a snowman. It is all the same story, in the end. Widows have husbands living, the spinsters are married, the childless have borne children. Rosemary is not dead. She still sleeps late in the morning until her mother climbs the stairs to her bedroom on the top floor (decorated in red for her thirteenth birthday). "Rosemary if you don't get up you'll be late for school." "All right, I'm coming, have I got a clean pair of stockings?" "Yes but hurry." Kath, Harry and Rosemary still drive together in the polished green car which Harry cleans very weekend by removing the little rubber mats and the covers from the covers from the covers of the car seats, shaking everything up and down as if making signals, but that is absurd for you cannot make signals in that way just as you cannot rid the newspaper of its news by shaking it. Snowman, I am not describing a world where a spell has been cast over people forcing them to stay forever within the same moment of time. You saw Rosemary die. Yet she is alive, she goes to school each day, she still dreams of her University student and his long striped scarf. And yet she is also a member of the docile dead who have not yet learned to rebel.

'The idea of rebellion arises in the dead during the first night when they or their ashes lie in their grave and the rain falls all night upon the earth, and the acceptable dampness and darkness where plants thrust and stir and roots are spread with secret buoyancy and warmth like long hair laid softly upon a pillow, change to an uncomfortable wetness with the earth massed in soaking clods knocking and thudding upon the coffin until the rain leaks through to the padded satin, staining it brown, and the stitches decay in the carefully embroidered red-and-white roses, and the ashes and the body whisper with rain and the flesh sinks to accommodate lakes and seas of rain and to make a home for the fugitive creatures which crawl upon the sea bed and are sometimes as brilliantly coloured as earth-flowers; and the pools make rainbows, even in the dark. Or so I believe, Snowman. The first night of rain is the loneliest night the dead will ever endure.

'It is on that night that they rebel, and they never forget their moment of rebellion. They are satisfied no longer to be the calm docile dead with their eyes carefully closed and their hands in the attitude of willing surrender; their toes tied to keep up the orderly lifeless pretence. Rain is terrible, Snowman, the way it affects the dead. A night of ceaseless rain on earth is a night of loneliness for human beings who are alive; they draw their curtains — if they possess curtains, if they possess a home. They huddle together touching skin to skin. Or if they are alone and have no one the rag or dress or shirt which they wear is soaked with rain and clings to their skin; it is a time for clinging and touching. The bare feet sink in the earth and the earth grips them, making a hollow place for them. Birds hide beneath a verandah of leaves, perch on the edge of their nest or sit cosily within it and look out, like early settlers sitting on their homestead porch, at the misty frontier of waterfalls.

'How dark it is, Snowman, when rain falls at night, and how lonely for creatures — beasts and men — who are without shelter! It is worse than cold or thunder and lightning, for though cold cuts the flesh with an axe made of ice, it knows its boundary, it keeps its place in the wound even when it strikes completely through flesh and bone. Thunder and lightning are fearsome to people with homes and people without homes, to those who are loved and those who are unloved, but heartbeats are just as terrifying. What cause have the dead to rebel when their bodies lie night after night in quietness with no sound of knocking, of thunder wanting to get in or heartbeats wanting to get out?

'Until it rains at night. Rain penetrates, the stain of it spreads, it sinks deeper, deeper until it arrives at the dead. But you have never seen rain, Snowman, and as one of the dead Rosemary does not yet know it. Perhaps tomorrow or the next night it may rain, and the rain will continue through the night and Rosemary will lie where she has been buried as one of the dead, and the rain will treat her as earth, making pools in her where little fish swim and insects burrow and skate and new streams form and flow from her body to the clay and back again with circular inclusion flesh clay flesh, and for a while she will submit to the rain, and then suddenly it will be time to rebel both against the living and against her companion dead, and she will rise from her grave and with sympathy for no one but herself and her darkness and loneliness she will teach the living through dreams, nightmares, fantasies, the true discomforts of death.'

'I do not understand. Why is not everyone weeping? Although you have told me of some of the people in the street of the city I cannot remember them or distinguish one from the other. I only know they live in colonies and grow to look alike, but you have said that berries live in colonies and that holly leaves are webbed like bats' wings and the berries are drops of blood at their vampire mouth.'

'I wish you might be, Snowman, when the news arrives.'

'Which news? The news has arrived. You see I am wearing it as a protections against the sky.'

'Not every snowman has the privilege of looking through a gap in a snowdrop.'

I think I have listened to the Perpetual Snowflake for long enough. Since he spoke of the gap in the sky and the sun I have not trusted him. I have become impatient of his stories of the street of the city, and placed here with my feet growing securely in the earth I have no means of deciding whether he has told me the truth. How do I know there are deserts where men die of thirst? The earth is covered with snow; it shall always be covered with snow.

Who is the Perpetual Snowflake? Who is he?

'The wind from the south is blowing and you are disturbed by it, but soon, Snowman, you must have the courage to look up in the sky. There is news of other seasons.'

I wait for the night to come bringing more snow, more and more snow to cover the bare places in the street and on the buildings. The snow has melted from the tree, there is a cancer upon the branches, small swellings that will burst and cause the tree to die. The world is gloom and doom where the only survivors are snowmen. Our limbs are not afflicted with cancers from which burst tiny spears of green disease; our life is not a running sore of sap sealing our eyes and ears from the reality behind the deception. Even though stray newspapers force our gaze to pierce the word and not the perilous flower, we learn enough of life in the street of the city to wish that we were wholly snow, that no one had ever called us Snow-Man.

Even my own creator is dead and her father runs back and forth with his polished earphones trying to get in touch with foreign places but no one listens to him for he cannot make the correct signal. I pity the dead and the living people who possess the gift of sight and hearing and are forbidden to use them, who are born to dance but must be propelled from restricting wall to wall in wheelchairs of their own making. Surely the human eye can see beyond the range of telescopes, and the ear hear the sun growing to the height of day tall against the dark dwarfed hours. I talk of the sun but I do not believe in it. Snow is everlasting. I am a snowman. I feel that tonight and tonight and tonight I shall sleep my deep white sleep surrounded by the calm habitual cold air, soft stirring from corner to corner of the world of the white spiders weaving their webs to shroud the trapped earth forever with snow.

Yet it seems that I have caught the human habit of deception. Here is a little boy, the Italian Salvatore with hair like black paste. He is out late. I think he is going down to the shops to get some cigarettes for his father and chocolates for his mother and his two small sisters. From the downstairs front room where they live next door to me there is a noise like a market all day, a sound like bargaining and what pleasant bargains they must be, for everyone laughs and seems happy, and then the little girl cries because it is the end of the world, she can see it coming toward her like a terrible dream and it will not stop although she puts up her hands to protect herself oh oh it is the end of the world my lolly on the stick has dropped from its wrapper. When the father is working as a waiter in the West End Salvatore acts as father. He goes shopping. Now he hurries out the door, slithering in the snow at the edge of the pavement. He looks left and right, waits a long time, then he runs across and as he runs he is flapping his right hand against his backside and his legs are galloping and away he goes to the shops. He is a horse galloping through the snow, faster and faster, driving himself gee-up gee-up, and his black paste hair hangs like a mane over his left eye, and he tosses his head, and he snorts with his nose and mouth wrinkled up; away, away he is galloping. His olive skin steams with sweat, he is driven on and on. Suddenly he stoops to the snow, picks up a handful and clamps it in a cold mass in his mouth, drawing his breath sharply. There is the old woman who sweeps the pavement with her silver broom. She scolds him.

'Don't eat snow. It's dirty, it's only dirty water, you'll catch a disease.'

Salvatore thinks, I am eating snow, not dirty water. Besides, I am a horse.

He gives a snort, kicks his legs, taps himself smartly on the rump, and is away flying through the sky.

Five minutes later he is home, outside the window, banging upon the pane, 'Mama, Mama,' to be taken out of the cold into the warm haggling family market that is golden like oranges and yellow and black like ripe bananas.

As I watch Salvatore I think that perhaps people do live forever, their lives are a precious deception which lasts forever. Who dies then? Do snowmen die?

Although I have waited long this evening the reinforcements have not arrived from the sky. I hear something growing, a commotion of roots; it is a disease affecting the earth. I am a mountain, so strong. I am a lamppost with light burning in my head. I am a dragon. I am only a snowman. Now a wind is stirring the sleeping snow; I try to believe that the white mist created by the wind is the reinforcement of flakes from the sky but unlike human beings I am not practised in deception. I know that I am surrounded by tired snow disturbed from sleep and bleeding from its wounds of light. I wish I had the belief of Salvatore that what lies about me is clean white snow, the proper food of creatures who gallop and fly through the clouds in the sky, but again I remain undeceived, the old woman with the silver broom has been whispering in my ear.

The wind has suddenly blown away my newspaper shelter. I can see. But it is too dark now and the street lights are switched on and the cats are lifting the lids of the dustbins and prowling secure and magnificent through their world, the narrow whisker-lane with smells sprouting in the hedgerows.

'It is not true, Snowman, that before people die they experience a flashing vision of their whole lives. It is a myth someone has dreamed in order to soothe the living, to give them the longed-for opportunity to repeat their lives without effort, without trying in vain to dredge the few lost keepsakes of their memory that have perhaps sunk too deep to be shifted, that may not ever be recovered when the energies are so weakened and the sight is failing and the ears are about to be stopped with the black wax of darkness, and the claws that grew as weapons upon the hands have dried and snapped and are no use for scratching and scrabbling in the darkness of the pool. There was never room either during life or before death for the salvage of so much memory.

'When a man is dying he is afraid or is suffering pain or faith and his thought is of the room where he lies and of the people near him, of their shapes and the flapping of their clothes against their bodies. He does not waste the precious moments thinking, When I was a child: when I was a child I flew kites of gull-wide span; I bounced a rubber ball and watched the shadow of it moving like grey sun-bound elastic across the pavement, and my hands were long gloves of grey shadow; I fished in streams and followed them to their source; I stayed away from school, secretly, and was surprised that I did not know how to use the enormous day which the sun and I together were taking care of, with a promise to use it fast until its mass had become threadbare and glowing with night; the sun and I hacked at the hours, but only the sun made any impression and I was lost against the size of the time, and was glad to give up my task and go home; yet I remember that I learned too quickly to sharpen the huge axe of my needs and desires, and too soon without the help of the sun I reduced each day to darkness.

'No, Snowman, dying is a time of greed. There is no leisurely arranging of food upon one's plate when the plate is nearly empty and when what lies there may also be out of reach.'

'Why do you tell me this? I am tired of death. I am not even sure that I believe that people die, not when I see a small boy changing into a horse, galloping through the snow and flying up into the sky while everyone around him thinks that he is still a small boy; not when he tastes a handful of snow and relishes the freshness of it while the old woman with the purple hat and the blue apron and the silver broom whispers in the ears of everyone that new snow is dirty water.

I have been sleeping and now it is morning. The light is sharper than usual, piercing my coal-black pine-forest eye until it seems to threaten to steal my sight. It is a gorse bush of light, ablaze with golden flowers and thorns dusted in yellow pollen. It is dazzling me, there is a white mist rising from me, the world seems filled with a white glare with the golden bush growing upside down from the sky to meet the earth. Am I only shadow beneath the sea? Or are the sky, the sea, and the golden bush the shadows of my self? It is all the catkin dust in the world swept into a heap in the sky, it is a golden puffball of cloud trampled on my morning with the dust rising and floating and settling upon the earth and the snow, and blown through the air again into the sky. The world is suddenly too old and walked-upon, it is mildewed with gold, soft with gold moss, it has been out in all weathers for too many days and no one has cared to shelter it.

Now the light is dropping bright and sharp and smooth as yellow acorns. They make no sound on the snow.

For so long the snow has lain, the light has settled and been still, and now here is the sun to skim the cream, the top of the light, and spill it everywhere, and the morning laps it up with the wind and the clouds moving their greedy tongues through the sky. The light pours and spills and the first flies are in the air, gummed with sleep.

Oh, oh the sun, see it is a whirling flypaper with the people like new flies clinging to it and drowsy with its dazzle and the syrupy taste of it. But the sun is poison, why don't they realize that the sun will cause them to die? Now people are saying At last, At last. What do they mean? People are opening their front doors and looking out at the street. They are smiling, they are waving; what are they saying to each other?

'I knew it would be soon, not last week or even yesterday but I had an idea today would be the time, I knew it when I looked at the gap in the sky yesterday. Did you see the gap in the sky, did you look in the sky? It is all finished now isn't it, it has never seemed so long, it seems to have been lying here for months and months when it has only been a few days yet it has seemed so long, I thought it would last forever, the way it kept falling and drifting and no sweeping had any effect upon it, and even the traffic did not seem to shift it, for every morning the cars were white and the street and the pavement were without foot or wheel mark or even the mark of a bird or a cat or dog, or even the sing of that death, you heart of the death in the street, no marks only the tracks of the wind that cold wind blowing from the ice, from the north, is it Greenland or Iceland or Spitzbergen, one of those places whose names when you pronounce them are sharp with icicles for consonants and lakes of blue ice for vowels, is it, is it really, did you say Iceland is a sunny place, I had always believed, I had always believed, but it must have an Arctic climate it can't have green fields and warm days and the sun if it is up there within the Arctic Circle, did you ever read those haunting tales of the Northern Gods, of Balder the beautiful is dead is dead — the voice passed like the mournful cry of sunward-sailing cranes — that's poetry we had poetry at school once or twice — Faster than fairies faster than witches bridges and houses hedges and ditches, "From a Railroad Carriage" — but it's not, true Iceland's not warm and green, I don't believe it, look at that little boy at the gate slapping his legs and galloping as if he were a horse. A cocky little chap. Look at him. Thinks he's a horse. The children won't like it now it's all over will they? There's been no keeping them inside even when it's been cold enough to change them into icebergs but the worst is to come we've seen one death a night or two of frost and the streets will be treacherous, and it was really so pretty in a way, I used to think so didn't you. Snowmen and snowballs and tasting it, like eating white clay or frozen flour and dew mixed, and it tasted of nothing really, so much of nothing that you could imagine special flavours to it, only the sweetness sourness bitterness which you have put there yourself. Snow is a responsibility don't you think? Having no colour too; you have to mix your own colours in it and then it is the most personal weather, it is *you*. We were taught to draw snow at school. We made the grey sky with black and white, Chinese or Ivory white, Indian black, a little water, a wash on white paper and the sky was prepared for the snow to fall but we didn't draw the earth because with the snow there the earth had vanished although sometimes we made threads of grass spiking through the white — didn't snow really taste like grass and roots? And wasn't it always an ingredient of nightmares — don't you remember the times you were lost in a snowstorm in the mountains and the snow was in deep drifts around you and still falling and you were so helpless and so much in despair until you saw the light in the distance, the lantern swaying, and then suddenly your forehead was being licked by the warm tongue of a St Bernard dog and a flask was being uncorked and thrust between your teeth — don't you remember?'

'Snowman, Snowman, the privacy of snow is the privacy of death. Children do not care. They gallop like horses through the streets and fly into the sky.'

While I listen to the people talking I am thinking, It is a great mystery indeed the way they talk of snow, of me. How proud I am! One said, pointing to me, 'Look at him, he has been here ever since it started, every day on my way to catch the bus at the corner I have passed him standing there. The Dincer girl made him. Rosemary Dincer. And now she's dead, and look at him standing there as if he will last forever, as if, when all the people in the world are dead, struck down by their own brewed secret weather, the only man remaining will be a snowman. Did you ever play that game at school, where someone shouted *No Man Standing*, and immediately everyone lay on the ground as if dead and the last person to be standing was counted out and dismissed from the game? What if the last person standing turned out to be a snowman? He seems to think he may have that honour or disgrace, just look at him there so proud with his piece of coal for an eye and the brass buttons in a row down his belly. I believe they photographed him but they say it was too late for the Dincer girl to see the photo but then photos are always too late don't you think? I mean they are *after* the moment, and it used to depend on the sun didn't it, the direction of the sun and the shadow when you took the photo but somehow it doesn't seem to matter now, the sun has no real say in it, why, you can take photos inside with those tiny bulbs that burst in a flash and nearly blind you, certainly it is out of fashion to rely on the sun but there it is, look, look, oh I wish I were living in one of those places where oranges grow, I have seen pictures of such places. One day in summer I will go to France for the day, early morning and home at night. One day in summer I will go — somewhere — out of town where the sky is a blue water-race going so fast above me that it makes me dizzy, look, it isn't even blue today yet there's the sun, look up at the sky, at the gap between the clouds. Goodbye, Snowman!'

They have passed the gate now. They are walking up and down the street. More people have come out, and some are laughing and some are warning each other of the 'treacherous' snow. And all look at me with pity and contempt. Why? Why do they keep saying, One day in Spring, One day in Summer, one day soon …?

I have hunched my shoulders and bowed my head. One of the children passing said, 'Look he's a dirty old polar bear, the kind they keep in a cage with a pond made of concrete and the rocks painted blue and white to cheat him into believing they are ice, he's just a dirty polar bear, gosh it must be beaut to be a real polar bear coming up through the ice with a block of iceberg balanced on your nose!'

'Look at the snowman! Hey, you've taken his arm!'

'I didn't. It came away in my hand. Like this, see!'

'You've taken the other arm. You'll cop it. It doesn't belong to us.'

'But it's no good any more, it's melting. Snowmen don't last forever. I bet if I gave it a big push that would be the end of it.'

'You'll cop it if you do. Quick, we'll be in for it if someone catches us.'

'Want me to knock off his head? I bet I could first go!'

Fortunately they have decided not to knock off my head and they have gone up the street, with that loitering lumbering walk of small boys — they are more like polar bears than I; perhaps they have changed into polar bears because they keep talking of them and imitating their roars and one put his head in the air with his nose trying to touch the sky. He balances a block of ice upon his nose, and that is a feat which I myself would be proud to accomplish yet all a passer-by can say to him is, 'Look where you're going, clumsy, you don't want to get yourself a broken arm or leg,' speaking with the certainty which adults seem to possess when they imagine they can divine the wishes of children.

The boy looks contemptuously at the woman who tells him in a sharper tone, 'You don't want to land up in hospital.'

The little boy is wondering, How does she know I don't? Everybody but me has had a broken arm or leg and been in hospital with dishes of bananas and toffees in coloured paper beside them for helping themselves any time, and people from the BBC coming with a microphone Now little man and how old are you, how long have you been in hospital, what's your favourite subject at school and what record would you like us to play for you? Everyone in the world has been in hospital and had played for them 'My Old Man's A Dustman He Wears A Dustman's Hat he wears gorblimey trousers and he lives in a Council Flat,' or 'There's a hole in my bucket dear Henry dear Henry,' or 'There was an old woman who swallowed a fly oh my she swallowed a fly perhaps she'll die.' Everyone in the world except me. And there's this stupid woman telling me I don't want to have a broken arm or leg! Gosh! Some people!

The two boys look at each other and at the woman and to me their thoughts are clear as this bright light surrounding me.

They stare at the woman and they burst out laughing, saying in unison, 'Oh my Oh my she's swallowed a fly, perhaps she'll die!'

They look at each other, mirthfully aghast at the suggestion, 'Perhaps she'll die!'

In spite of their laughter echoing merrily around the street, I have an increasing sense of deep gloom. It is fine for the children to be content with being polar bears or horses stabled among the clouds champing the fields of sky, lifting their heads, putting out their tongues, seizing between their teeth a cluster of the million burning straws protruding from the sun. And they are content to break their arms and legs, snap, like striped rock, and to fill the snowy air with sharp menacing cries, being birds now with the quills of their shining black wings digging between their shoulder blades. As yet they are not used to the idea of dying; they have not yet set a place for death at their table in order that it may share their meals, or warmed a hollow in their bed for it to lie there at night with its arm around them, protecting them from the dreams by the living.

But why should I mourn the death of creatures on earth? I am only a snowman. I have no arms to fold across my body or hands to clasp as if in prayer. I am only a snowman. My body seems to be sinking slowly into the earth and I am weeping ceaselessly now and I do not know why, and there is a heaviness upon my shoulders as if an unfamiliar burden had been placed there, but where shall I carry the burden, to whom shall I deliver it, when I cannot move and I am planted forever in this garden? When we flew from the sky we stopped the mouth of the earth, filling it with snow, and all the sound the earth has made has been the distant muffled murmur like streams turning in a long wave of sleep, but now there are sharp subterranean cries, articulate demands which reach up through the snow. The sky, the morning, the light, the sun pay attention. Oh I never heard so much sound in my life, and underneath a hush and white steam rising and blurred creatures moving to and fro, meeting and parting. It seems as if the world were on fire.

Where shall I take my burden? Who has put it upon me? I am only a snowman. I cannot bear the weight for much longer. My body sinks deeper into the earth. I have grown thin with the perplexities of being, of merely standing here in a garden in a street of the city. How much more terrible if I were human, moving, travelling, compelled to catalogue the objects of the world in order that I may have remedies for the distress of living; comparing, creating, destroying; putting all into the picture the birthplace the home the first garden tree house street city. And then to die, to submit to the long night of rain, to become a garden pool reflecting and enclosing the face of darkness.

I am a snowman. My flesh is wasting. If I were wholly human I might deceive myself, I might change to any shape which I cared to name and thus live forever; I might imagine that I am not alone, that I can get in touch with everyone else in the world — in Rome, Paris, Marseilles — although I do not understand the language, although when I tried to learn the alphabet of it I found myself lost among columns and archways of letters with my voice only a small echoless whisper. But I am not wholly human. I am a snowman. Surely I shall live forever!

My flesh is wasting. I cannot deceive myself. I have no treasurehouse of time of imagination to provide for my survival after death.

Death? But I am a snowman. I live forever. I am growing thin, I am sinking into the earth, soon I shall be bowed upon my knees. The burden is still upon me driving me deeper to the earth. Another small boy passed me just a moment ago and struck me across the head, knocking off the top of my head, and I begin to be more afraid for my thoughts are exposed to the sun which is probing all my secrets, and a white smoke rises from my head, there's something burning, there is no help for it now, I must influence the sun, I must turn my coal-black pine-forest eye toward the sky, to the widening gap in the clouds, and face the sun. I am brave.

'Do you not think I am brave, Perpetual Snowflake?'

He does not answer. I cannot call in a loud voice for I have no voice. The burden is too much, I cannot bear it, I am down to my knees in the earth, all the creatures arriving in time for spring are piling their luggage upon my shoulders, they think I am a snow-porter, a snow-camel, perhaps it is their responsibilities and not their luggage, or the heaviness of their hearts because they know they shall die whereas I, a snowman, remain forever alive and free.

There is a curtain of fire blowing in a great gale of flame. The pine forest is burning, the pine cones are crackling and sparkling as they are used to doing only when they are ripe and it is time for them to spill their seeds. I have been so afraid of fire. I did not know that I contained it within the sight of my eyes and that when I gazed upon the sun the dreaded fire would originate from myself, that as a snowman I have been deceiving myself into believing I am made wholly of snow when all my life I have carried fire. Is my burden after all the burden of my own fire?

I am weeping now, my cheeks are touched with a red glow, like blood. People looking at me might imagine that I am human. Am I human? Are all other creatures snowmen?

There is no time to think of it, there is no time. I am going to sleep now, and the wall of the sky is patterned with snowdrops, the complete flower and not the broken word or promise.

'Who are you?'

'I am the Perpetual Snowflake.'

'Why do you talk to me? Are you here to explain the world to me because I am only a snowman? I should like to know the place where I am to live for ever and ever. Tell me.'

I told him. Sometimes I thought of telling him my own story, of when I too was a snowman in a garden in a street in a city, and how I at last faced the sun and was burned by my own fire until all that remained of me was this small Perpetual Snowflake; how another winter came and I watched the children once again making snowmen and flying like horses through the sky. But I kept silent about my life. I do not want to remember the day when I died and yet did not die, for as almost the only snowflake left on that spring morning I whirled suddenly into the air meeting the Perpetual Snowflake who had guided me in my life, and there followed a battle between us two tiny snow-tissues that were so thin the wind could look through us and shadows could signal to each other through our bodies. I survived the battle. I died once yet I survive. I wait for spring, the sun and the snowdrops and the daffodils, with as much fear as when I was a snowman. How is it that I fear death yet I have died? Or is the human deception true, and death is only a dream, is it death that dies?

Oh how I wish now that I had never conquered the earth, for people live on the earth, and animals and birds, and fish live in the sea but we do not defeat the sea for we are driven back to the sky or become what we have tried to conquer, remembering nothing except our new flowing in and out, in and out, sighing for one place, drawn to another, wild with promises to white birds and bright-red fish and beaches abandoned then longed for.

'Snowman, Snowman!'

Man is indeed simplicity. Coal, brass, cloth, wood — I never dreamed.

# Figures in Light

*for Pat Hanly*

## Maurice Shadbolt

## 1

I do not see my sister often. Strange, for we were intimate as children. Or perhaps not so strange, perhaps that is the reason. We didn't grow apart; we fell apart. I had little use for her friends, when we were students, and she had little use for mine. I started university only a year behind her, but the gap was sufficient: she was already established among friends of her own temperament and inclination, and the gap soon widened. Since then, I've seen less and less of her.

Once I marvelled that children of the same parents could be so different. Nowadays, of course, we live in cities some four hundred miles apart. It is true that there is seldom a year in which we do not see each other, but in this case 'see' is the critical word. I cannot honestly say that we converse. She asks after my children, I ask after her life: there is no real exchange. I no longer, for example, ask why she has no husband, no children. No more than I would pose such a question to a total stranger. On the other hand, I am not suggesting that my sister is a total stranger to me. I think I understand her rather better than she will ever allow. Perhaps I deceive myself, but I do not think so. That tall, sullen, untidy woman is not really so remote from the elder sister I worshipped, to put it mildly, through childhood into adolescence.

The failure, then, is not one of understanding, at least not on my side. Yet when I try to define some other point of failure, I know beforehand that I cannot do it. And if I cannot define failure in myself, I can scarcely impute it to her; it surely cannot all be hers. And if we do not share the failure, where then must we look? Where? Questions like that ring in my head on sleepless nights; I slide soundless from beneath the bedcovers, careful not to disturb my sleeping wife, and brew black coffee in the kitchen until the multiplying questions, at first churning wildly, collapse exhausted in my brain. Unhappiness is not uppermost of my emotions when I return to bed beside my wife, or when I wake heavily in the morning. It is more perplexity — if one can call perplexity an emotion, as I certainly do. For I am sure that my sister is unhappy, but why? And I know that I should help her, or should be able to help her, but how?

If I feel baffled and helpless, it is at least in part because I have gone through the usual motions. We once, my wife and I, invited Ruth — my sister — to stay with us. I imagine my idea was to help Ruth feel part of a family again; aside from our father, who has since died, I have been her only close relative. But her visit was not a success. My wife, Helen, usually so understanding in so many things, was troubled by Ruth's presence in the house. That was clear from the beginning; and, since I could exact nothing by way of confession from Helen, and perhaps offer some explanation to clear the air, there was very little I could do about it.

There was no real unpleasantness. It was all a matter of discomfort. Ruth was uncomfortable in our house; Helen was uncomfortable with Ruth. Caught between, I was uncomfortable for them both; uncomfortable, and for a while unreasonably though quietly angered. For our house, of all houses, warm and carpeted and cushioned, and sheltered by a remnant of native bush high above the city, seemed designed to contain every possible situation with some degree of comfort; my actual physical security seemed threatened, along with my peace of mind, as if the solid scenic windows in the living room had split, allowing frosty winds off the mountains entrance to our lives. The mountains are literal; on clear days it is possible to see them from our windows, across the rough water of the Cook Strait. In the steeply descending foreground there are treeferns which toss their fronds in the wind against the tall trunks of spiky cabbage trees; in the middle distance, the oval harbour busy with shipping and the city of Wellington tight-packed beneath bleak hills and eroded gullies which freak with shadow in the late sunlight; beyond are the peaks of the South Island, blue and remote in summer, often white and close in winter.

Ruth spent a great deal of her time flopped in a basket chair before the wide windows. As quiet and sleepy as a cat, her eyes dreamy with distance, her long loose body apparently empty of all tension, she seems in my memory of her visit to have spent all her time there. Her half-brushed hair fell untidily over the hand which propped her head; she seldom changed out of her check woollen shirt and jeans during her stay, and rarely left the house at all, though the fact that she had business in Wellington, some plan for a future exhibition in the city, was part of my excuse for inviting her to stay. Apparently it was all quickly settled, in a single afternoon, and the city as such had no further attraction for her.

I imagined that she missed some excitement or vivid interest which was part of her daily life in the north; though I had never known that life well, this appeared a reasonable supposition. On the other hand she seemed content — with our remarkable view. Common sense tells me, though, that she couldn't have been all the time in that chair with the city and harbour, hills and mountains for company. For the one small success of her visit was the pleasure she took in the children. I was about to say surprising pleasure, but in retrospect I see there was nothing surprising about it at all. With our children Ruth established a satisfying relationship, one which was impossible with the adults of the family, Helen and myself. She told them stories; she walked them up the patchily pine-clad hill behind the house on fine days, and romped with them on the needles among the trees. There was no doubt of Aunt Ruth's popularity. The children asked about her for a long time afterwards. I saw clearly that Helen did not like it. It was as if Ruth had left infection in the house, as in a way she had.

Certainly things took time to settle after she left, and comfort was slow to return. Nothing was said. Helen has never once raised the subject of Ruth with me and, though I've tried fitfully, I've never yet persuaded her to talk about my sister, so I have been unable to get to the bottom of her dislike or distaste, whatever it is.

'Your sister,' she once said, 'is an exceptional girl.'

Which is the nearest she has ever come to passing judgement. Well, perhaps not quite. Judgement of a kind was passed a month or two after Ruth's visit. I came home from the office one evening to find a decisive change in the living room. The paintings were rearranged, and one had vanished altogether, to find a new place on the wall of the small spare bedroom (Ruth's, when she stayed) which I use, when the children are at large in the house, as a study; with the idea of escaping my job in market research for something more stable in the university or civil service I am taking a second, part-time degree, which means I need a certain minimum of peace and quiet at home.

Anyway the painting was the one Ruth had given us when we married. Surprised, for things like this seldom happen in our house without prolonged consultation, I made some comment.

'You need to change paintings round now and again,' was all Helen said. 'Otherwise you stop seeing them. Everyone knows that.'

This was of course, perfectly true. The subject was dropped. The infection Ruth had left behind her was still at work. As I took my glass of sherry behind the evening paper I wondered what it was that so much troubled Helen. Perhaps there had been some argument with Ruth, when I was out of the house, and about which I was still ignorant? Hardly likely. There would have been some echo. No: the whole thing seemed impossible, beyond explanation. The two did not get along, and that was that. It was odd, even so because I should have thought them extremely compatible. Helen herself was by no means a conventional girl and that, I admit, was part — a large part — of her appeal at the time I married her. If Ruth had been with me at the time I was first involved with Helen, I am sure she would have approved. Even to the extent of nudging me and urging, 'Yes, her. Don't hesitate, you idiot. She's the one for you.' Now that I have said this it seems to me, quite uncannily, that Ruth *was* at my side at the time, and did nudge me and say those words. But it is absurd. Ruth was never near me in those days, no more than she has been since; she came to the wedding, a rather sullen stranger among Helen's friends and mine, and departed in the middle of the wedding breakfast — without a word, and while I was on my feet fumbling with a speech. My words crumbled, my voice faltered; there was one prolonged, horribly blank moment — or minute — while I stood there foolishly, my mouth open, staring at the empty seat at the long, festive table. I seemed to be struggling up out of some slippery pit to find myself, and my voice, again. Which, after a time, I did. Was that Helen's grievance, then, that incident at the wedding breakfast? We never talked of that, either; as I recall the incident was lost, forgotten, in all the change and commotion of the time. Could it be, though, that Helen had never forgotten or forgiven that ungraceful and unexplained departure? We should have talked of it, we should have talked freely of Ruth from the beginning. The fault is mine. I see that now.

I should never have allowed Ruth, or some notion of Ruth, to become an irritation in our lives.

I think it is safe to say that ours is a comfortable marriage. With Helen I have felt a degree of security which I once thought impossible in my life; it pleases me to think that my children will live and breathe this security in the house as they grow. Perhaps Helen saw, from the beginning, exactly what I needed; if so, she was more perceptive than I would have thought at the time I married her. She was lively, flighty, scatty. I plodded in her wake. From coffee bar to rehearsal (she did a good deal of acting before we married) to parties, rather rowdy and jammed with people of whom I scarcely approved; I didn't conceal this from Helen, any more than I had ever concealed my disapproval of Ruth's erratic friends — for they were much the same, at least similarly casual to the point of being downright destructive in their personal lives. (I may be too harsh; my attitude may be too coloured by first impressions. Nowadays I can recognize that they, as the first real friends Ruth ever made, signalled the possibility of change in both our lives; perhaps I would have resented them whoever they were.) In this sense it is true that Helen's circumstances, before we married, were not so unlike Ruth's. But it is not fair to myself, or to Helen, to make too much of similarities. Or to Ruth, either. Where Helen was always slightly diffident, Ruther was impertinent and thrusting. After all, Ruth is herself and has always been. The woman is not so different from the girl, or from the child. Perhaps — and this is the terrible, frightening thing — she will never change.

So that evening, months after Ruth's departure, I stood puzzled before the painting which now hung in my study. Helen, of course, was right. Paintings obviously did need to be changed around regularly, seen in a new context. For I had stopped seeing this one a long time before. That night I looked at it, really looked at it, for the first time in years. The children murmured sleepily in their bedroom, Helen chattered about in the kitchen, and I stood frowning before a painting I seemed never really to have seen before.

It was not a painting I had ever liked particularly, for like so much of Ruth's work it seemed to have very little to it; it lacked depth, in every sense of that word. There was a flatness, a lack of any perspective, in the scene — a fragment of seacoast, rocks and water and lumpy hills vaguely crowded and barely separable, a red dinghy drawn up on pale sand; it could have been, and possibly was, a memory of one of the many places where we spent our childhood. What I saw for the first time, though, was not detail — familiar enough — but the strange, almost unearthly light which filled the frame: I could have sworn that it had not been there before; that it was something which had sprung magically from oil and canvas as it aged. Vivid, timeless and dancing, it was impossible to place, and difficult to connect with any sunrise, sunset or noon that I had ever known. On the other hand, and this was perplexing, the flawless light seemed not at all unfamiliar to me; there was a tinkle of response, coming and going faintly, in some distant delta of my mind. I listened, but heard no more. What I saw clearly was that I had somehow missed the point of the painting before; the light was the point. And the detail, into which I had earlier peered without success, seeing no depth or perspective, was in fact there only to give the light depth and perspective;

or at least to indicate that the light was of this time, this place. Yet the light itself, its source, still escaped explanation. I stood there puzzling until the children quietened, and Helen called me to dinner. Looking at my small blonde wife across the table, observing her tired and rather harassed face, I resisted an impulse to thank her for having shifted Ruth's painting: she might have sensed irony, which I certainly did not intend. For a while we ate in uncustomary silence. Then, as if each stirred by guilt, we spoke simultaneously — I of the office, she of her family. The family won, naturally; or perhaps I should say unnaturally. Never having known normal family life until I married, the intrigues of Helen's family, even the most trivial, still fascinate me; with some wealth and little common sense, it has more intrigues than most. Helen had just had, that day, a telephone clash with her mother and another, for good measure, with an unmarried sister who was running wild with a bass-player in a jazz band.

'Be tolerant,' I advised.

'Tolerant?' she cried. 'That's just the wishy-washy sort of thing I'd expect you to say. That bitch thinks she can get away with anything.'

'Perhaps she can,' I suggested. 'Anyway let her find out. You can't affect the issue.'

'God,' she said, 'sometimes you're hopeless. You just don't want to see.'

'She'll settle down,' I predicted with confidence. 'Just give her time. After all, you had your fling. Why shouldn't she have hers?'

'It's different,' she said. 'That's why. Besides, she's been carrying on like this for years. If she's not careful she'll finish up like — ' She hesitated.

'Yes?'

'Well, if you must know — like that sister of yours.'

'Like Ruth? But Ruth's different.'

'Of course. She has to be, doesn't she?'

But, as usual, Helen was content to leave it at that: she had no wish to make a frontal attack. The main thing was that she reduced me to silence. Perhaps that is the only way I can defend Ruth, by way of silence. It was unusual for Ruth to lurch into our domestic conversation, and interesting to observe the fact that she had that night in particular; it confirmed all I felt about the shifting of the painting.

When Helen called me in my office early next morning to say there was a message, a telegram, from Ruth, I was not as surprised as I should have been; my sister seemed once again central in my life. Yet this was one of the few communications I'd had from her in my married life, certainly the first urgent one.

'Yes?' I said.

'It arrived a few minutes ago,' Helen said irrelevantly. 'I would have redirected it, but I thought you might be out of your office. So I took it down over the phone.'

She sounded strained and nervous.

'All right,' I said, impatient. 'So what is it, what does it say?'

'It's your father,' Helen said.

It seemed my father was dead. *Our* father, Ruth's and mine. After I replaced the receiver I sat in my office a few minutes longer, trying to feel things I did not feel. I could summon up regret but no grief; it obstinately refused to rise to the occasion. I suppose I am still a stranger to real grief: my mother died when I was young, too young to know or remember, and I have had no other close bereavement. It was, I thought, useless to pretend that my father had been anything but remote to me, to either of us. It wasn't that he denied us affection, in his way. It was just that patience and sympathy for the young, and any real love, were missing; we were a sad encumbrance, constantly reminding him of the love of which he had been robbed, and which he no longer wished to remember. He appears to have turned in upon himself, to have become remote from the world entirely, after our mother's death. It might have been easier for all three of us if we had put down roots there and then; but he was apparently unable to do this, and in any case it was partly in the nature of his work — he was an engineer, a man licensed to tug the earth apart — to travel from place to place, job to job. Even so, there was something frantic in his wandering: I imagine that often he must have walked off projects half finished. It was as if he were determined to bury all memory beneath the tumbling soil and rock of landscape after landscape. There was never any question of his marrying again, and he had few friends. At some stage in my childhood I overhead a conversation with one of the few who remained.

'You can't mourn her for ever,' this friend said. 'It's not right. You've got to snap out of it. You owe it to yourself.'

'I owe nothing to myself,' my father said. 'Nothing.'

'Well, to your kids, then.'

'Am I in debt to them?' he demanded. 'I do my best.'

That was undeniable. He did his best. When he had seen us both through school and packed us off to university, his relief was perceptible. And when we were independent in every sense, he turned from engineering to work menial and manual. Eventually he became the odd-job man of the tiny seaside community into which he retired. There is something awe-inspiring and humbling about a grief which can persist across the years and blight a lifetime. Love, like happiness, is something which can best be defined in its absence; I should be grateful to my father, then, for having in his life taught me the meaning of both, even if his death could teach me nothing of grief.

So our childhood, at least in appearance, was an unsettled one, with its spasmodic shifts from place to place. In this I suppose we were only a little more extreme than most New Zealanders, an itinerant people always pulling themselves up to see how deep their roots have grown; the shallowness of growth can't entirely be explained by the fact that our seed falls in hardened ruts rather than on virgin ground.

When I was young, Ruth was the only constant and settling factor in my life: housekeepers, tired and bulky middle-aged women, flicker faintly across my memory; towns, valleys, rivers, bush and beaches; and my father's haunted face looms now and again. I seldom have the impression that he was even with us physically, though in truth he was never far away. But this doesn't mean our childhood was miserable. It was never that: it was always exciting and full of promise. Perhaps because no adult, and almost no other children, intruded upon our shared imagination. As children we were seldom in one place long enough to make real friends. Our imagination was our world: each move, each new scene, was grist to the mill and fuel to the fire. There was never loss of continuity. Ridiculously, some people called us lonely children. We were never that; we had each other. It rarely struck us that this might end, any more than it struck us that childhood would end. 'Always' and 'for ever' were favourite words in Ruth's vocabulary, and thus in mine too.

'Do you think this summer will go on for always?' I remember asking — perhaps one day when we lay naked and browning in deep dry grass by a riverside, tall trees and taller hills around us, and cicadas singing thick in the afternoon heat. 'I mean, do you think it would if we wished hard enough?'

'If we really want it to,' she said, 'it will go on for ever. In our minds, I mean. That way we can stay warm in winter. Just remembering.'

She was perhaps sixteen then, large and long-limbed, and her answers just a step ahead of my questions in sophistication. But she wasn't impatient with me; that didn't come till later. Possibly that was the last year we were really ourselves. Like summer, childhood had an end, even if we might later warm ourselves with the memory.

Something of all this raced through my mind while I sat at my desk looking at the telephone. I picked it up again, booked a seat on an afternoon flight to Auckland, and then went home to pack. It was May, with Wellington's winds already wintry; my work wasn't pressing, and since it was the middle of university vacation I should miss no lectures. There was nothing to stop me staying away as long as was needed. 'All the same,' I explained to Helen, 'I shouldn't be away too long. There can't be much to tidy up. I imagine his affairs are pretty simple and straightforward. But obviously I can't leave it all to Ruth. She just wouldn't be interested. After the funeral I'll stay till everything's tidy. It'll save another trip later.'

There was concern in Helen's face. 'Are you sure —' she began.

I'm sure it'll be all right,' I told her. 'There's no need for you to come along too. After all, there will probably only be Ruth and myself at the funeral. And you hardly knew him anyway.'

Though I made my coolness plain, Helen insisted on treating me as if I were shrunken with grief. While waiting for my flight number to be called at the airport she gave me a comforting huge and an earnest kiss, then placed the palm of her hand gently against my cheek and said, 'Look after yourself, darling. And don't —'

She hesitated.

'Don't what?' I asked.

'Well, don't stay away too long. Remember we want you back.'

'But of course I'll be back. What on earth are you worried about?'

Her smile trembled. 'Nothing,' she said finally. 'I'm just being silly. You know me.'

For a moment I wondered if I did.

Our actual farewell, when the call came from my plane, was more sedate: a quick passionless peck and I walked across the tarmac. I might have been off on a business trip.

I'd sent a telegram ahead to Ruth, and she was waiting for me when I arrived after the flight at the airways terminal in Auckland. In her habitual jeans and sweater, with a duffel-bag slung over her shoulder, she was conspicuous, at some distance, among sleekly clad citizens of that city. She looked subdued, and was silent as she placed a welcoming hand on my arm. We walked together to the baggage counter.

'What are you planning to do?' she asked.

'There's only one thing we can do. Rent a car and get up there as soon as we can to make arrangements for the funeral.'

My father had lived some seventy or eighty miles north of Auckland all his retirement; a rough road in the later stages meant we had more than a two-hour journey ahead.

'Someone up there is making arrangements. A friend, the one that rang me up. A Mr Slegel.'

'Well, that's something. It hadn't even struck me that there might be a friend to do all that. Knowing Dad.'

'It was all sudden. No sickness, nothing. He died in his sleep.'

I felt guilty: I realized I should have asked about that in the first place. The fact that he was dead had been sufficient for me.

'I see,' I said. 'Well, I'm glad it was easy.'

Ruth was quiet.

'Come on,' I said. 'Let's see about that car. We'd better get moving if we want to be there tonight.'

The car was quickly procured.

'We've still a couple of hours of daylight,' Ruth observed. 'Let's run home to my place. You can straighten yourself up with some coffee while I fetch out some clothes for the funeral. That's going to be a job. To find something to wear, I mean.'

I made no comment, and concentrated on getting through Auckland's dense and noisy traffic. Ruth lives just outside the central city area, in a flat off Parnell Rise. It is part of a decrepit house among ugly warehouses, but overlooking the city and sea and sidelong to the sun. The front part of the house swarms with two large families of Samoans. The back part is Ruth's. It doesn't seem to me an ideal situation for her. But she insists that she likes the noise, the life around. Her flat consists of a small and cluttered kitchen-living room and a combined workroom and bedroom.

'Brother mine,' she instructed, 'park yourself in a seat while I get you coffee.'

'Don't worry about that. Hurry up and find those clothes you're talking about.'

'It was only ten days ago I went up to see him,' she said.

'Him?'

'Dad. A friend ran me up there in his car for the weekend.'

'I didn't think you saw him often.'

'I didn't. Not until recently, at least. But I seem to have got up there to see him every two or three weeks lately.'

'Since your trip to Wellington, you mean?'

'I'm vague about dates. I suppose it is since then. I saw a lot more of him than usual, anyway.'

I sat puzzled. I supposed I had seen my father, on average, once every year or two; Ruth, who lived so much nearer him, hadn't seen him much more often. Why the change?

'Did he have very much to say?' I asked.

'No more than usual.'

'Then why the sudden interest in the old man?'

'I don't know,' she said, clicking switches and planting the coffee percolator on the stove. 'Perhaps I had a premonition. I just felt like seeing a little more of him, that's all.'

'Did you have something you felt you wanted to talk to him about? Was that it, then?'

'Not really,' she said, and disappeared into the bedroom to look for clothes. More puzzled than ever, I sat at the bare board table in her kitchen, looking out of a dusty window at the haze on the Waitemata harbour and the neat blue crater of Rangitoto rising beyond. I thought briefly of the bleak landscapes visible from our window above Wellington, and Ruth's obvious enjoyment of them. There man still perched precariously on an island's spiny edge; here where everything was so much gentler, so much milder, man overwhelmed. Even the hills were shaped by ancient Maori settlement, and now pale houses were scattered in clumps of green around; native trees, tropical palms, and Norfolk Island pines planted back in missionary times. One could still feel warmth in the May sun; summer was never too far away. It never seemed far away in childhood either, for this was more my part of the country. For the sake of a career, for the sake of my family, I'd gone among colder hills.

No matter how I tried, though, I couldn't get it out of my mind that Ruth's belated interest in her father had something to do with the failure of her visit to Wellington. And more, with some failure of my own. But how had I failed her, and why should she have turned to him?

The percolator began working. Ruth appeared, still in jeans and sweater, swinging her duffel-bag. 'I thought you were getting dressed,' I said.

'No point in that. Not till the funeral tomorrow. And there's the car trip ahead. I always feel sticky after a car trip, don't you? Nothing seems clean. I've got all I want here.' She slapped the duffel-bag. 'Clothes for tomorrow, toothbrush for tonight. How's the coffee?'

She poured from the percolator into two chipped cups. 'Brother mine —' she began.

'Why do you keep saying that?'

'Saying what?'

'Brother mine. It's something you haven't said for years. It sounds quite odd now.'

'I didn't realise. Sorry. If it upsets you, I mean.'

'It doesn't upset me. I said it sounds odd. After all this time.'

'Does it? Well, now. Fancy that.'

'It would sound just as strange if I began calling you "sister mine" again.'

'Would it? I hadn't realized.' She passed me the coffee. 'Stir with the spoon in the sugar bowl.'

'You're not offended?' I asked. 'I mean, I was just pointing the fact out.'

'Why should I be offended?'

There was a silence between us as we sipped the coffee. I was till trying to adjust to the ground again, after the flight, and after being torn so abruptly from my life in Wellington.

'I must say,' I said after a while, 'that we don't look a particularly grief-stricken pair. But it's no use pretending, is it? We hardly knew him, really.'

'I think I was getting to know him,' she said slowly, as if measuring each word for weight. 'I feel I was, anyway. I think it was a question of approaching him on his own terms. And not expecting him to be other than what he was. Which we always did. We wanted a father like other fathers. Wouldn't you agree?'

'But even then — ' I began, and faltered. I remembered my own visits on holidays, with Helen and the children. I had hoped grandchildren, the idea of grandchildren, might produce some response from him. He was kindly enough, true; he picked them fruit from his garden, patted them on the head, walked with them down to the beach near his cottage. But there was something missing all the same. I felt that, as far as he was concerned, they could have been any children. Just as Helen, say, could have been any woman; not a daughter-in-law. 'I think you're simplifying,' I went on. 'I think there was a little more to it than that. After all, fathers don't come in a special mould. They're not all alike, I mean. Speaking as one myself.'

'Well,' she sighed. 'Perhaps I'm wrong about that. But I feel I was getting to know him, all the same.'

'In what way?'

'I told you. In his way.'

I was perplexed and unreasonably irritated, as if I had just found her cheating me of something.

'We must talk some more about this,' I said, and rose. 'It's time we were moving.'

We used the last of the daylight on the journey and travelled the last twenty or thirty miles from the headlights flashing over fern, gorse and rutted road; inland places had the chill of coming frost, but the air was warmer as we neared the sea. Ruth smoked steadily and had little to say.

'Where to?' I asked, as we drove into the settlement. Drawn-up boats and ramshackle cottages, deserted by their summer residents, rose pale in the headlights. Few windows were lit up anywhere.

'His place, I suppose,' Ruth said. 'I mean we'll have to spend the night somewhere.'

'I was thinking in terms of a motel,' I said. 'Something like that.'

'Why pay money? His place is there. And it's ours now, anyway.'

'That hadn't struck me, I admit. I mean, it doesn't seem right that his place should be ours. But what about —' I hesitated.

'The body, you mean? An undertaker's looking after it all. That's what Mr Slegel said. The man who rang me up. He found the body early this morning and he told me everything was being taken care of. He must have told me that at least four times. It seems he expected to spend the morning fishing with Dad.'

More boats, more darkened cottages. Above the engine noise we could hear the sea, the beat of surf, off to our right. A couple of shops floated through the headlights, then pale sandhills and marram grass.

'You sure we'll be able to get into the place?' The more I thought of it, the less I liked the idea of spending the night in my father's house.

'Mr Slegel said everything would be taken care of.'

Lights were even fewer at the north end of the beach. I slowed the car and changed into low gear as the road deteriorated. The last few yards were very bumpy. When we reached the beginning of my father's drive I was startled to see lights burning beyond his sub-tropical jungle of banana trees, passion fruit and paw-paw.

'Someone in occupation,' I said.

'Probably Mr Slegel. Waiting for us.'

'Who is he, anyway? Never heard of him.'

'A friend. I told you. Probably Dad's only friend. A German Jewish refugee, retired now. He got out of Germany with his wife just before the war. But his wife insisted on going back to fetch some relative. He never saw her again. She died in Auschwitz, Belsen, one of those places. He was interned himself as an enemy alien for a while. He bought himself a place here with compensation from the West German government. Dad told me the whole story.'

'I'm surprised he could get so interested in someone else. I really am.'

'You're bitter, brother. Too bitter. Don't let it rankle. Not now.'

'All right,' I said. 'Any further instructions?' On that note I stopped the car. We climbed out and made our way along the winding, rising path to the house. The place was at the extremity of the beach, against a hillside and above rocks washed by surf. In this sheltered place, on volcanic soil, his plants had flourished. We ducked beneath banana leaves heavy with dew on our way up to the house. The surf was very loud now.

A waiting figure filled the doorway and, when we approached, a hand thrust roughly into mine. 'Slegel,' a thick voice said. 'I though you would be here tonight.' He guided us through the door.

The inside of the house was warm. Logs blazed in the fireplace. 'You have eaten this night?' Mr Slegel said with concern.

'We had a bite on the way, thanks.' We hadn't really eaten, apart from a toasted sandwich with coffee at a roadside stop, but I didn't want to put him to any more trouble. It was obvious he'd slaved to get the place ready for us. Everything was prepared, neat and comfortable. Miraculously he seemed even to have tidied away the idea of death. The only thing missing, really, was my father himself. I half expected him to walk out of the bedroom to greet us, and then to sit with us before the log fire.

'So long as you are all right,' Mr Slegel said. 'That is the main thing. Anyway, if you want more, your sister knows where to find food in this house. There is a fish in the refrigerator which your father caught yesterday, a twelve-pound snapper of which he was proud. His last. I weighed it for him.'

He hesitated, a heavy and rather clumsy man who apparently found even the shortest speech an effort. It was then I realized, having just grown used to the light, that his eyes were red and puffy and still faintly damp. He'd wept as he waited for us. Perhaps wept all day. I cringed from this grief of a stranger, and perhaps Ruth did too, as we stood there fresh-eyed from the city.

'Your father was good friend to me, so good I can never tell. Life is not worth so much to me today. Perhaps tomorrow we will talk more. For is not the time, this night. Main thing now is that you are comfortable. In the morning we will speak again.'

Before I could reply, thank him for everything, he ducked out of the door.

'Well,' I said, and Ruth and I were left looking at each other. Ruth moved slowly towards the fire and warmed her hands.

'I think he was rather like Dad,' she observed finally. 'I mean they were much of a muchness, lonely here, and they got along together. They kept to themselves. I don't think they even talked much between themselves. They just liked to be with each other.'

''I see.'

She looked into the fire for a while. 'He'll miss Dad,' she added.

'Obviously.'

'Hungry?'

'I suppose I am. It's been a long day. Everything's starting to catch up with me. I mean, a lot has happened in the last twelve hours or so. I think I must have eaten, at some stage, but it's hard to remember.'

'I'll get something,' she said, and turned from the fire.

I looked at her. My voice seemed to strain across the stillness and quiet of the house. 'I suppose this is an event,' I said. 'Back in my father's house, and my sister cooking for me again. How long has it been?'

Ruth sighed as she went through to the kitchen. 'Let's not count the years,' she called over her shoulder. 'Just for once.'

I took her place before the fire and tossed a couple of fresh logs into the grate. Mr Slegel had left us plenty of wood. Then I relaxed in a chair. I felt my father's presence more strongly than ever: our old familiar furniture; his books; the photograph of the fragile stranger who was my mother, on the mantelpiece. Though I had never actually lived in this house, it could have been any one of a dozen places I had known in childhood. Ruth was right: there was no point in counting the years. For it was as if the years had been banished. My father could have been out on a job, late, while Ruth and I fended for ourselves, as we often did, in the absence of regular housekeepers.

The fire crackled; I was lost in the thought.

Ruth appeared from the kitchen. I looked at her, she looked at me. For a moment she said nothing. Then she asked, 'Why are you looking at me like that?'

'Like what?'

'So strangely.'

'Things are strange all of a sudden. I can't help it.' I was as if Helen had never existed, nor my children; as if I didn't have a warm house, warmth of any kind, waiting five hundred miles away. All my adult life seemed to crumble and vanish. 'Don't you feel it too?'

'In the sense that Dad is gone,' she said, 'yes.'

'No,' I began. 'I mean — ' But I faltered and finished, 'It's too difficult to explain. Just now, anyway. What were you going to say?'

'I came to ask whether you'd like meat, or that fish Dad left.'

'What do you think?'

'I think I'd prefer to leave the fish. If you would. Perhaps Mr Slegel might like it. Not that there's anything wrong with it. It's just that —'

'I know,' I said.

Ruth went back to prepare the meal, humming softly to herself. My insecurity ebbed slowly; I felt the return of older warmth, older certainties. As a child I had often been utterly dependent on Ruth, on her judgement. She had stood between me and the world. Her presence at the funeral would make it all so much easier. Perhaps she would even know what to say to Mr Slegel.

'How about a drink?' Ruth called. 'I couldn't rely on Dad having anything, so I put a bottle of sherry in my duffel-bag. You might get it out of the car.'

I went out into the chilly evening. The surf was noisy, the stars bright. A light wind rattled the damp foliage in the garden. I paused beside the car and looked back to the lighted house. It seemed to me now that the place strangely enclosed all the half-forgotten perplexities and mysteries of my life: if I was still alien, it was because I felt alien to myself. I fetched our bags from the boot of the car and carried them inside.

I uncorked the bottle and poured the wine. Ruth came to sit beside the fire while the food cooked. We raised our glasses.

'I'm not sure what we can toast,' I said, 'except Dad's memory.'

'To us, then,' Ruth said decisively. 'To our future. That's simpler.'

The sherry was cheap and faintly metallic. It soothed, though, and warmed. Ruth kicked off her shoes and placed her bare feet close to the fire.

'So Dad's brought us under the same roof again,' I observed.

'I was under your roof a few months ago,' she said.

'That doesn't count somehow.'

'All right, so that doesn't count. What does count?'

I shrugged.

'My dear sweet brother,' she said, 'I don't expect some gnomic utterance. Just a simple answer. What does count with you?'

'Doing my best, I suppose. Doing my best, in every sense.'

'You think you've done it?'

'How would I know?'

'Don't be so coy. Really, you're very pleased with yourself, aren't you? And proud of your good safe job, your pleasantly tamed wife, your happy family? Isn't that so?'

'Well, I suppose I've reason to be. Proud, I mean. I refuse to be ashamed, anyway.'

'Good Lord,' she said. 'Who's asking you to be ashamed?'

She padded barefoot back to the kitchen and began serving the food. I set the table for the meal: that had always been my job. Then I fetched and refilled my glass and leaned in the kitchen doorway, watching Ruth set out the food on plates. I realized I was still a little afraid of her. My elder sister had always seemed to know best.

'What do you want me to do?' I challenge.

'To be yourself for a change. To be a little less stuffy.' She looked at me sharply; her hair drifted lightly over her vivid eyes. 'To be a little less bloody pompous.'

'Fair enough,' I said. 'So what am I supposed to do now? Run round in jeans? Be a thirty-two-year-old beatnik?'

An oblique attack seemed to me the best form of defence. But she didn't bite.

'Anything,' she said, 'anything but the way you are now. You were such a bright-eyed kid. Sorry, but I can't help remembering.'

'And I can't help feeling you're unfair,' I said. 'There should be room for all kinds in this world. And if there's not room for your kind, and my kind, then it's a poor look-out. That's all I can say.'

'You enjoyed life,' she went on. 'You really did.'

'How do you know I don't still enjoy it?'

'How could you?' She shrugged. 'That house of yours, it's a living death. Really. No honest emotion could survive there five minutes. It's the kids I feel sorry for most of all, though. They just haven't a chance.'

She couldn't have surprised me more if she had struck me across the face.

'What do you want them to have? A childhood like ours? Is that it?'

'They could do worse. A lot worse. All things considered.' She gave me another sharp glance, then took up the two steaming plates of food and carried them through to the living-room table. As we sat down, she added, 'We didn't do badly. We were pretty lucky, in fact. Not many have a childhood as rich as ours, and you ought to know that by now.'

'I've thought about it,' I confessed.

'We ought to be grateful to Dad.'

'For ignoring us?'

'For leaving us alone.'

'What's the difference?'

'The difference between oversight and insight. I've only come to understand some things lately. As I've come to understand Dad himself. It's true that he was stunned when our mother died. And it's true that he didn't seem to know we were around for a while. But when he tried to acknowledge our existence again, he found that we didn't acknowledge his any more. We didn't need him. We'd grown self-sufficient in the meantime. And he seemed to think we were better for it. So he withdrew, and left us alone. Deliberately. It might have cost him a lot, for all we know.'

We began to eat in silence. The surf seemed to move closer to the house.

'That may be so,' I said reasonably, trying to sum up, 'but I still think there's a certain failure of imagination on your part if you think my kids are unhappy. You think everyone should be like we were.'

She didn't acknowledge the point. 'Then there's your wife,' she said.

'Helen? She's happy enough.'

'That shows a considerably greater failure of imagination on your part. A more insecure girl I've never seen.'

This time Ruth had gone too far.

'That's bloody ridiculous,' I said, 'and you know it. A sense of security is the one thing that Helen has got. She has precious few worries — with the house, or with the kids. I've seen to that. I've worked for it.'

'I'm not talking about that kind of security.'

'Then pray tell me what you are talking about.'

'She's not secure in herself, in her own mind. Don't ask me why. It's an impertinence to explain someone else's discontent. I felt it as soon as I walked into your house. In fact I was on the receiving end. She took it out on me. For a while, there, I was kind of whipping-boy. I don't suppose you noticed that Helen and I didn't get along.'

That assumption irritated me even more. 'I'm not altogether blind,' I said.

'Well, then,' she went on, 'if you saw she wasn't easy in mind, you might have wondered why. After all, she is your wife; the subject must have some interest for you.'

'I did wonder why. I've tried to talk to her. Without much success, I admit. But I have tried.'

'Great. So you've tried. And, having failed, did you draw the only possible conclusion?'

'I concluded that she didn't like you much.'

'That's a fact, not a conclusion. You didn't go very far, did you? Or were you afraid to go too far? The only possible conclusion, it seemed to me, was that she was jealous.'

'Jealous?' The word, usually so hard and angular, suddenly became rubbery and meaningless; it seemed to slither away from me. 'What in God's name has Helen got to be jealous about? Why should she be jealous of you?'

Ruth shrugged. 'I suppose I could list any number of reasons — none of them good ones, mind you. But then people are seldom jealous for good reasons, are they?'

'Go on, then.'

'Well, one could simply be that I'm your sister and in this situation a kind of mother-in-law. That I belong to part of your life, a good part of it, which is still much of a mystery to her and which she resents not possessing too. But that's only half a reason, isn't it? It doesn't explain anything really. The real question is why she, or any human being, should crave total possession of another, when it's so impossible.'

'Perhaps life's like that. Perhaps love's like that. And perhaps you wouldn't know.'

She took that coolly.

'We can always fall back on love, can't we?' she observed with a faint smile. 'The best whipping-boy of all.'

'All right,' I said. 'Anything else?'

'Another thing could be that she feels she's missing something. Something she imagines I've got, because I haven't married, and she lacks because she has. She may resent being tied to house and children, and may resent even more a woman who is not tied down. Can't you see?'

'No,' I said stubbornly. 'It's no use bringing the children into it. Helen's perfectly happy with the children.'

'But you admit she wasn't easy in mind —'

'That may just be you. You're an upsetting influence.'

'All right. Please yourself.'

The meal moved to its end in prickly silence. I found myself remembering the incident of Ruth's painting: the way it had vanished, after so long a time, from the wall of the living room. I decided to say nothing about it. I would interpret the incident for myself; I wasn't going to supply Ruth with ammunition.

Afterwards we sat for a while in front of the fire. Towards the end of the evening, since Ruth was taking my father's room and bed, she made up a bed for me on the couch in the living room. By that time the long day had caught up with me, and I was hazy with exhaustion. Ruth made herself a last cup of coffee and stood sipping it before the diminished fire. I lay flopped in a chair. She lit herself a cigarette, and flipped the packet into my lap.

'Thanks,' I said. 'I've stopped, but I still like one now and again, when the occasion demands. It certainly does demand today.'

The cigarette, though, only complemented my sense of strangeness; I felt a little giddy. I looked at Ruth, half silhouetted against the firelight, and realized what a lean and handsome woman she had become. It had always been difficult for me to see Ruth other than as a sister. But men must surely have found her disconcertingly attractive. In figure and manner there was an animal economy, a natural elegance of movement at odds with the erratic life she led. They must have been drawn to her. Suddenly, with a faint twinge, I was sure they had. There must have been many men, many, who had sought purchase on those firm breasts and thighs. But what had happened to them? Had there never been one who meant more than others?

'Ruth,' I said suddenly, startling myself, 'why haven't you settled down?'

'I'm perfectly settled, thanks.'

'But your life, its so untidy.'

'As far as I'm concerned, it's perfectly tidy. Everything in its proper place.'

'It's never seemed that way to me.'

'That's because you're not living my life.'

I suppose that a stupid question had, after all, deserved a stupid answer. I blamed my own reluctance to be direct.

'Well, marriage, then,' I said. 'Marriage and children. Hasn't that ever appealed to you? Tempted you?'

'Once it might have.' She shook her head. 'I really don't know now. I really don't know at all.'

I felt close to her again, for the first time that evening; her answer was disturbingly honest. As if scrub and undergrowth had parted to reveal a tall, clean-limbed tree.

'You mean you put temptation behind you?'

'It put itself behind me. Suddenly it wasn't there any more. It just wasn't an issue.'

'I see,' I said, and brooded.

'Well,' she said, 'I suppose we've another big day tomorrow.' She washed the coffee cups, said goodnight, and went off to her bedroom.

Though I was probably even more tired, I remained some time longer in the chair before the fire, still puzzling. Eventually I rose.

'Ruth,' I called. 'Just one more thing. Something I've always meant to ask you, but never have.'

The bedroom door was open. I went to stand beside it. In an undergarment luminously pale against her very brown skin, Ruth was in the act of climbing into bed.

'Yes?' she said.

'Why did you walk out on my wedding breakfast? You remember?'

'Of course I remember. I walked out because I just couldn't stand it.'

'Couldn't stand what?'

'If you must know, I couldn't stand watching my brother make a clumsy clown of himself, before a lot of drunken idiots. I don't care if they were your wife's relatives, I don't care if it was expected of you. I just couldn't stand it, that's all.'

'You were disappointed in me, then?'

'Since you've said it, yes.'

'Well,' I said, 'I suppose I've always known that, in a way.' I hesitated, and realized there was nothing more I could say. 'Goodnight, then. See you in the morning.'

'Goodnight, brother mine.'

I shut her door, and began the long night. Though I was tired and the couch comfortable, my body twisted painfully in search of sleep; after an hour of restless turning I was as far from it as ever. I blamed the strangeness of everything. The strangeness of our arrival, the lights burning eerily beyond the trees in a dead man's house, the weeping stranger at the door; the strangeness of being in my father's house again, beneath the same roof as my sister, alone with Ruth for the first time in years.

And there was the unfamiliar thud of surf outside.

I realized I should have rung Helen. Her voice would have reassured me and I mightn't have felt so vulnerable. And I might have had some sense of continuity instead of a sense of a widening crack down the middle of my life. I felt gusts of doubt, and doors creaked open on strange places in my mind. My father's face danced dimly before my closed yes, then Ruth's; finally the puffy-eyed Mr Slegel's. All seemed, in some way, accusing. It was absurd.

Then Ruth again, but younger and different. She was slight and lean in a swimming costume and running ahead of me down to the sea. The water was silver, the early sunlight vivid on sand-dunes and stumps of bleached driftwood. Ruth plunged down from the dunes, skidding, laughing. She looked back at me and cried, 'Come on, slow-coach.' Breathless, I followed. We skimmed like gulls together over the sand.

There was a savage and piercing pain in my foot. I cried out and tumbled forward. Ruth was suddenly beside me, tender with concern.

'Why don't they leave us alone?' she said angrily. She was biting her lip and weeping. 'Why don't they?'

My foot was sliced open, and my blood bright on the sand. When Ruth lifted my head I saw for the first time the ugly half-buried glass of a broken beer-bottle.

She bandaged my food with a torn strip of towel, and leaning on her shoulder, I hobbled home.

Restless on that couch the night after my father's death, twenty years later, I could still feel the shredding glass in my flesh. I could still twitch with the agony of it, yet feel at peace with Ruth's gentle hands and tender voice.

It was no use. Sleep was hours away.

I rose, switched on the light, and heaped some fresh wood on the fire. Then I heated the coffee and helped myself to another of Ruth's cigarettes.

Remembering how we had bickered so fretfully all evening, seeking to wound in tender places, I wanted to cry to her shut bedroom door, 'Look what they've done to us, sister mine. Just look what they've done to us.'

But I didn't. Instead, wide awake and tense, I hunted along my father's bookshelves for something to read, something to pass the night. But it was hard to find anything appealing. It wasn't really the time to begin an exploration of my father's collected classics, or to examine the works of Karl Marx, Daniel De Leon or Edward Bellamy; socialism had flowed strongly in my father's thought and speech when he was younger, when he could still see all mankind's problems as moral and economic. After my mother's death, an event which may have given his views some cosmic qualification, his interest and involvement in the affairs of men became more academic: Trotsky's *Revolution Betrayed* stood alongside Winwood Read's *Martyrdom of Man*; Koestler and Deutscher beside William Morris and Thomas Paine. Certainly he didn't argue or attend meetings any longer. His views became so much his own they were vague even to his children. And now — as I passed over a two-volume work on ancient Egypt, Gibbon's *Decline and Fall* — his books served still to conceal rather than reveal the man. I could not associate them with the father I knew.

Was that my fault? Should I, like Ruth, perhaps like Mr Slegel, have made more effort? My frustration at not finding something ephemeral to read merged into something larger. Even at this late stage, it seemed, I would never be able to see him clear. I would never be able to assign him a place in my mind and say: Yes, that is, that was, my father. He would always perplex me.

And there wasn't even a magazine. In the cold night foliage from warmer climates rubbed and rustled against the house, as if craving the heat within. I sat by the fire, drank coffee, listened to the surf, and smoked more of Ruth's cigarettes. It was clearly too late to search out my father, set him straight in my mind. But what had he made of us, Ruth and myself? In one way, at least, we must have disappointed him, for neither of us had taken more than a mild interest in things political; we were like passengers insulated in a ship, trapped placidly, listening now and then to faint and distant storm surges. Yet in our different ways we were children of a world he and men like him had made as surely as we were children of a country he had made: he had seen society tugged apart as well as landscape; in his lifetime the socialist idea may have faltered here and failed there, may have been stalemated by its own successes, may in desperation have assumed grotesque and fearful shapes, but nothing had been left unchanged by it, no country and no person. Had there been satisfaction in this for him? It was unlikely. I could see that, easily enough, but what I could still not see was how Ruth and I, in our separate lives, must have appeared to him. Had he been amazed that we should remain indifferent to his late urgencies, or had he been able to make some imaginative and compassionate leap into our world? For actually we weren't so much indifferent as perplexed and powerless, seekers of refuge. Had that been at all plain to him?

I would, of course, never know. An hour or two later I put out the light and tried sleeping again.

I must have slept — for a time, at least — before I became aware once more of the surf's din. The darkness was perhaps less dense beyond the windows, but dawn still some way off. Then I became aware of what had woken me: the light was on in the kitchen, and I heard Ruth moving round there. I could smell cigarette-smoke, as if she'd just been standing beside my couch.

'You're up early,' I called.

'I couldn't sleep.'

'You too.'

'Coffee?'

'Thanks.'

A minute or two later she came to sit beside me on the couch. We sipped our coffee in silence. 'I suppose I must have slept for a couple of hours,' she said blearily, pulling up the lapels of my father's dressing-gown against the morning child. 'Then something woke me — a tree scratching on the window — and I couldn't go back off again. I seem to have been awake, thinking, for hours. I'm sorry if I was unpleasant to you last night.'

'You weren't unpleasant. Just blunt.'

She seemed pained, uncertain of herself. She fidgeted a new cigarette out of a flattened packet, lit it, and then ran a vague hand through the hair which streamed over her eyes.

'I seem to remember being unpleasant, all the same. It wasn't a particularly nice way to behave on the night after Dad died. I'm sorry if I hurt your feelings. I didn't mean it. All that stuff about the wedding breakfast —'

'It was true enough, wasn't it?'

'Half true. Let me put it that way.'

'What's the other half, then?'

'You're being difficult.'

'Come on. Otherwise I will be hurt, after all.'

'Let's face it, then. We were pretty close as children.'

'That's no news.'

'No, when I say pretty close, I mean pretty close. I mean pretty incestuous, in fact. If I have to spell it out.'

'Well, I wouldn't go so far as to say that.'

'I would.'

I shrugged. 'Please yourself. Perhaps I'd better have one of those cigarettes too.'

'I think it's best to be honest with ourselves. I mean, it's easier that way. My trouble is, I've never been able to make up my mind just where incestuous regard ends and sisterly concern begins. You see?'

'No. Not really.'

'Naturally you could object that you've not seen sisterly concern much in evidence lately, anyway. Fair enough. Blame that on my suspicion of the first. My suspicion of myself.'

'Ruth, you're taking yourself much too seriously.'

'I have to, you see. So when I look back on something like your wedding breakfast

I wonder if I haven't just been concealing the whole truth from myself. About why I walked out, I mean.' She paused. 'I suppose Helen is so right to be suspicious. I don't blame her.'

'Now you're trying to dramatise everything.'

'Trying? I didn't think I had to try.' She laughed bitterly. 'We're adults now, for God's sake.'

The windows were brightening to pale grey. Ruth sighed, rose, and carried out empty cups back to the kitchen.

'Ruth,' I called after her, 'there was nothing wrong with our childhood, with us. Nothing unnatural.'

'No. That's just it, I suppose. That's just it.' She ran a tap, washed the cups, and then walked past my couch on the way back to the bedroom. 'Feel like a walk? I'm going to have a look at the sea while I've still got a chance today.'

I swung my feet gingerly to the floor and dressed quickly. Ruth didn't take long either. Then we let ourselves out of the cottage into the keen morning. Dew dripped slowly from frond and leaf; the sea in the east was pale and bright. The air was perfectly still. Below us, the land sloped sharply to rocks patchily black with mussels and tangled with shiny kelp: the tide was out. The beach began with a wide curve into the land and then swept away in a straight line until it was lost in spray-haze and distance. Banked up behind the beach were silky white dunes. Islands floated upon the first light of day. The sky was clear.

'A pleasant enough day for a funeral,' I observed. 'Even if I can think of better uses for it.'

Ruth walked slowly and silently ahead of me. It required some effort to walk slowly down that slope to the sea. A yellow scarf trailed about her neck and her hands were thrust deep in the slit-pockets of her windbreaker. She held herself very erect, as if deliberately pacing out the correct distance to the beach. For myself, it was all I could do to keep from breaking into a jog-trot and hurtling past her on the way to the sand. Once we would have careered down this slope in an instant, skimmed over the beach, thrown ourselves into even this wintry sea. We had never walked together so sedately before.

We reached the sand by way of the rocks at the end of the beach. It was a slight scramble, and the surf kicked spray over us. The razor-ridged rocks were slippery, and once Ruth lost her poise and teetered dangerously above a deep crevice filled with foam. I grabbed her hand and helped her the rest of the way.

'Thanks, brother mine,' she said, when we reached the actual beach safely.

We separated again, and trod the sand carefully, almost tenderly, a yard to two apart, as if there were glass underfoot; as if our feet were unshod.

The sea was green and uninviting, the spray fresh on our faces. The sand squeaked underfoot as we walked in silence. Once more Ruth seemed to be pacing out the distance between one point and another. At length she paused beside an amputated tree-trunk which some spring tide had flung into the dunes with such force that it had actually pierced the hirsute cover of marram grass, between bulging flanks of sand.

'Let's just sit here,' she said. 'And watch the sunrise.'

We hadn't long to wait. The cold silver of sea and sky vanished; there was spurt after spurt of colour above a reddened sea. Before long the light, diluted to pale yellow, was touching our faces with a faint promise of warmth. Lean gulls swayed above the rising tide.

'It's nice to know it's still there,' Ruth observed. 'The sun, I mean. It's about the only thing you can rely on.'

But she shivered, all the same.

'The only bloody thing,' she went on, 'and even then only sometimes.'

She hunched forward, hair falling over her face, and with a stick began drawing in the sand. Once she looked back up at our father's house, perched at the end of the beach.

'It'd be nice to stay here, though,' she said. 'Everything unimportant stripped away. Why don't we?'

'You're not serious.'

'I couldn't be, could I?' She paused. 'Just the same,' she added dreamily.

'Ruth, please —'

'Oh, of course I'm not bloody serious. Don't panic.' She stood up. 'Let's go back. We've had our free time for today, children. Now back to the business of life. Or isn't it death?'

She gave me her hand, and pulled me to my feet. We faced each other for a moment. Her eyes searched mine.

'You forgive me, don't you?'

'For what?'

'Everything.'

'In that case,' I said, 'there's nothing to forgive.'

She laid her head silently on my shoulder, then lifted it again. We walked back to the house. On our way we gathered enough mussels for breakfast.

The funeral was straightforward and almost painless. A retired clergyman, for whom my father had done odd jobs, conducted the service. He made brief reference to my father's professed agnosticism, dismissing this as although irrelevant. With the exception of Mr Slegel, all the faces at the graveside were strange; there were about twenty people present, all from the village. Only Mr Slegel wept. Ruth all but wept, I suppose; as the coffin dipped into the earth she shivered, and I slid an arm about her waist. When the service ended, I helped her along a muddy track to the car. Then I went to thank the clergyman, and shake hands with all the pleasant strangers who had attended my father's funeral. It wasn't as difficult as I expected to say the right things, since they had very little to say themselves: none of them had really known my father well. But when I looked for Mr Slegel, he had gone. I went back to the car and sat in silence beside Ruth. She lit a cigarette, and placed it between my fingers.

'So that's the end of it,' I said at last.

'The end of what?' she asked softly.

'Of something. Of him, of us, of whatever we were to each other and whatever we weren't.' I paused. 'Listen, Ruth,' I added, 'I've been thinking about things this morning. It would save a whole lot of trouble if you took over Dad's place.'

'You're not serious.'

'I am. Perfectly serious. Otherwise we'd only have the problem of selling it and dividing the proceeds between us. It's hardly worth it. I doubt if Dad's got any other asset to speak of. Another thing, I'm quite settled. I've got a house, all the security I want. You haven't. With a place like that, even if you use it only as a weekend cottage. A holiday place or a workplace, and let it to other people when you don't need it, you'll have some stability.

'And you won't need to worry about me?' she said shrewdly.

'If you put it like that, yes. I'd worry less about you, anyway.'

'All right,' she said. 'I'll think about it. And just what is Helen going to think about your brotherly generosity?'

'She can think what she likes. It's my business. In any case she should be able to see that it will solve a lot of problems. About what to do with all Dad's possessions — his library, for example. I can put the whole thing in the hands of an Auckland lawyer and fly straight home to Wellington.'

'Ah,' Ruth said, 'I see. The truth, at last. You want to fly straight home.'

In the distance a solitary gravedigger was heaping the last clay on my father's coffin. It was just noon and there was warmth in the day: the wintry sun was gentle on the small cemetery, the straw-coloured grass, the headstones gripped by convolvulus. Beyond a line of peeling bluegums the sea was very blue.

'Why not? There's no point in spending more time away in the north than I need to.'

'Are you tired, brother? Are you tired, depressed, miserable, uneasy, in fact bloody awful? Try Wife, then. Try Wife, the friendly all-purpose remedy. Back again in standard sizes or in our special flip-top box. Watch for the trademark and beware of substitutes. Obtainable today from —'

'For God's sake,' I said.

'Superior to all other brand names,' she went on. 'Get with it, be in the swim. Tests show that nine out of every ten men prefer Wife. And the others are probably homosexuals anyway.'

'Shut up.'

But she was weeping; she had her face buried in her arms. I put the car into gear and drove back through the village to the house. Ruth went quickly inside, through to the bathroom, to wash her face and brush her hair. I fell heavily into a chair and looked beyond green growth to the sea. After a while she reappeared.

'Sorry about all that,' she said calmly. 'I didn't mean it.'

'I know. You never do.'

'True enough,' she agreed. 'I never do.'

She went into the bedroom to change. Then we packed, tidied, and ate a quick lunch. Ruth defrosted the refrigerator and removed the fish for Mr Slegel. As we moved to the door, I paused and said, 'Well, there you are. It's all here, all yours, if you want it.'

'Yes,' she said. 'All right.'

'All right?'

'I'll take the place over. And if you and Helen and the kids ever want a holiday here, I'll move out — if I'm in residence, which probably I won't be, often. It might give us some sense of continuity after all. If there's something to be salvaged, I supposed that's it — some sense of the importance and relevance of the past. We may need that more and more. I don't mean just us. I mean people in general. If your children are ever going to have a sense of continuity, a sense of family, we might as well start here as anywhere, if we're going to start at all.'

'And your children?' I said.

Ruth shrugged, and we went out of the door together.

I am in my home. It is evening. The lights of Wellington glitter far below my study window. In another room the television has just been silenced and now Helen is reading to the children. I am familiar with the story she is reading them. It is a comical, clumsy, well-meaning elephant. Whatever he touches, he seems to damage. When he tried to play with other animals, he inadvertently hurts them. But — since this is a story for children — he manages to do the right thing in the end; it all ends happily. I can see myself briefly in the story, at least my clumsiness. Have I done the right thing in the end? The fact is, I've tried to buy off my sister; tried to buy her off my conscience. I may actually have done the right thing by Ruth. As for myself, I cannot tell. I just wish I felt happier in mind.

Before we left the village we sought out Mr Slegel, thanked him for everything, and presented him with that fish we hadn't been able to bring ourselves to eat. He was delighted to know that Ruth would be returning to the house regularly, and promised to look after the place for her, and tend the garden.

'Your father,' he told us, 'was a good man, good and gentle. And I can see, for it is easy to see, that he had two fine children of which he was proud. I know that always he dreamed of only the best things for his children.'

Was that the truth? Or was he just saying that for something to say? I couldn't be sure. It left me uneasy.

'I think,' he went on with a sad smile, 'that he would have liked the house kept. It would have done him good to know that he had not made a home there for nothing — not just for himself, but for his children too.'

I was glad to say goodbye to Mr Slegel, for he disturbed me — I felt drawn to him; I supposed that was the simple truth of the matter. I felt drawn to him as I had never been to my father. And I was sure that it was my fault, not my father's.

It was too late in the day to see a lawyer and catch a plane home when we got to Auckland. I spent the night with Ruth — again an improvised bed on a couch, this time in her untidy kitchen. She had greater assurance on home ground again. We talked of her work, which sells moderately well in Auckland galleries, and I looked over some of her newer paintings. I was interested to see again, in painting after painting, that curious light which had perplexed me. I was about to remark on it when there was a noise, then knocking, at her door.

'Oh God' she said. 'Visitors. I was afraid I'd have them tonight. I just had a feeling.'

Four friends, three men and a girl, swamped us. They planted a dozen bottles of beer on the floor and arrayed themselves around Ruth's bedroom-studio. With glasses supplied by Ruth, they quickly set about emptying the bottles. They all seemed to know Ruth well: I had the impression that they might be as close to her as anyone she knew. They examined me without great curiosity when I was introduced, and went on talking to Ruth. She didn't explain my presence, or mention the death in the family, until the beer was gone and the gossip exhausted.

'It's midnight,' she said wearily. 'And my brother and I have had a funeral today.'

Even that didn't particularly shake them. It simply caused a new outbreak of talk, and they didn't leave for another hour or more. Since I had little to say for myself, I had more than enough time, that evening, to sort them out as individuals; it helped keep me awake. A lean young man with thin bristly moustache, apparently some kind of writer or journalist, certainly an art critic, treated Ruth with particular deference: I guessed he was having, or had had, an affair with my sister; Ruth seemed edgily polite when she spoke to him, so I imagined the affair was a thing of the past. The other two men were bearded, and wore tight jeans; they were difficult to separate until I learned that one with dark hair was a sculptor, one with brown an artist. The girl, who in some ways might have been Ruth ten or twelve years younger, remained totally in the background and anonymous. Small and fair and frail, she curled into a corner where she smiled mysteriously to herself now and again. She gave me the impression she had heard most of the conversation before. Perhaps she had. Aside from gossip and character dissection, it mostly concerned the founding of an art magazine.

'Money,' the lean young critic said. 'Lots of lovely money. That's all we need. With a wealthy backer we could go ahead tomorrow.' He swung round on me abruptly. 'You know anyone in Wellington?'

'Me?' I shook my head.

'It's no use looking south, anyway,' the sculptor intervened. 'The further south you go, the more barbarous this country gets. God help us, they're still assimilating French impressionism down there.'

'It's not enlightenment we're looking for,' observed the artist. 'But cash. And plenty of it.'

'Mind you,' said the critic, 'I feel sure we could pull in enough money to cover expenses on prestige advertising. Once we got started. It's just a question of getting started. There's money around all right. If only we could get our hands on it.'

'You would receive a regular salary as editor, of course,' Ruth said.

'Naturally. The thing should be done professionally, or not at all.'

'Wait till we're all rich, then,' Ruth said, 'and we'll all put money up for your magazine.'

'No,' said the critic. 'The point is that it's got to be done now. To create the climate, can't you see? To give you people a place in the sun. Damn it, I want to make you rich.'

Wherever the conversation travelled, it always seemed to circle back to the same point: money, or the lack of it. Even some new exhibition was discussed in terms of inflated prices which had or hadn't been paid; I didn't quite get the drift of what was said, because by that time I was too depressed to listen — but quite unreasonably depressed, it seemed to me. After all, there was no good reason why artists shouldn't worry about money as much as other people. In fact I — a philistine in their eyes, I supposed — should have been relieved and impressed to know they were much the same as other people. That they weren't so unworldly as one might expect. Had I needed to imagine, for my own peace of mind, that Ruth existed on a different plane from the rest of us? Well, there it was: prices, patrons, dealers, prestige advertisers; my life in the actual world of commerce began to seem positively academic and monastic. Had I needed to imagine also that Ruth lived in an interesting world, with exciting friends? Well, there it was, or there they were: the critic, artist and sculptor, and muse for good measure. As people they didn't exactly dazzle me.

When Ruth finally revealed that it was our father we had just buried that day, appropriate things were said and apologies made. Someone launched into an account of a strange funeral *he* had recently attended while Ruth, in despair, made black coffee to hasten the evening to its end. In my melancholy I felt the bleakness of Ruth's flat as a grey oppression; in my tiredness the electric bulk above our heads seemed to become dimmer and dimmer, and the figures around me more and more shadowy and remote. Voices rose and merged into one long monotonous and meaningless sound.

The next thing, Ruth's hand was on my cheek. The room was empty. The visitors had vanished.

'Hello there,' she was saying gently.

'Sorry,' I said. 'I've disgraced you. Falling asleep like that.'

'Don't be silly. It was all I could do to stay awake myself. Besides, it worked wonderfully well. I mean as soon as they saw you were asleep they all cleared out.'

'These people,' I said, 'they're really friends of yours?'

'Yes,' she said. 'Why not?'

'No reason. I just wondered. I mean I couldn't really make up my mind whether they were good friends or not. Though I supposed they must be.'

'They're good friends, all right. As good as I'll ever have, I suppose. And they're very loyal.'

'I see. Well, time for bed, I guess.'

'Something worrying you, brother?'

'Not especially.

'Come on. Tell me.'

'It's nothing I can tell.'

'But something's worrying you. What is it?'

'I suppose I'm worried about dying. That's all.'

'Dying? What on earth —' She knelt beside my chair, took my hand affectionately, and looked into my eyes with concern. 'Is something the matter? Really?'

'No. I just had a sudden vision of myself dead. You too. That's all. No reason. Except the funeral — and that's not it really. I'm just tired. Perhaps that's why I need —' I shook my head helplessly. Then I knew what I needed. I needed to get home, the sooner the better. 'I need sleep badly.'

'That's no problem. I've just made your bed up on the couch.'

'Sorry. Rather a morbid way to end an evening.'

'But natural enough, considering. The shock about Dad is just filtering through to you, that's all. It's just starting to register.'

'No,' I said. 'It's something different, something more. I can't explain it.' I stood up, as if to shift the weight of my depression. 'Ruth,' I went on, 'you will look after yourself, won't you?'

'What do you say that for?'

'In case I forget to say it when I rush off in the morning. You will, won't you?'

'Of course. But why?'

'You mean a lot to me, that's all I'm trying to say. Without you, I wouldn't have any past, and I mightn't even be able to weigh my future. Without you I wouldn't be myself. That's probably what I mean. I'm not saying it very well, I'm too tired. Sorry.'

'Brother mine,' she said, and smiled. 'I think you've said it very well.' She reached up and ran a hand through my hair. Then she kissed me lightly on the cheek. 'Sleep well tonight.'

She started to turn away, but I didn't allow her to escape. Without considering why I pulled her head clumsily against my chest and held it there. Her body, her shoulders, breasts and thighs, rested inert and almost weightless against me. Yet she lived, and breathed, and possessed warmth; it seemed I needed to know that, to be reassured. Then, as if to confirm it even more, something like a sigh or a shudder shook her body. It seemed she needed reassurance too. I lifted her head and covered her lips with mine. I was sure I could still taste salt on her lips and smell sea in her hair, something of the lost day and lost summers, and I had a sense of wintry space around us.

Again her body shook. Abruptly she pushed herself away, and held me at arm's length.

'If that,' she said, 'was all I wanted, don't you think I could have got it long ago?'

Her eyes were strange, her smile thin.

'You would have been easy,' she went on. 'Dead easy. After all, I've slept with enough men. A brother here or there wouldn't make a great deal of difference.'

Astonished, I realized at last that she was trying to be brutal. It was just that for once she wasn't very good at it.

'No,' I said. 'I suppose not.'

She relented. Her hand gripped my arm tightly.

'Now turn around,' she said, 'and don't look back. Sleep well tonight and hurry home to your wife and children tomorrow. But don't look back. Don't ever look back, ever again.'

'That's your privilege?' I said.

'Mine,' she agreed. 'Goodnight, brother mine.'

The couch in the kitchen wasn't particularly comfortable. I sat on it for a while, before I tried sleeping, and smoked a cigarette in the dark and looked out Ruth's window at the lights trembling on the harbour; the fact was that I was wide awake again, at least in thought. My mind and body were fighting in separate directions. I remembered the cold beach that morning, Ruth walking silently on the sand; then the coffin descending into a dry clay hole, and Mr Slegel's stricken face.

I put my head down on the pillow but it was no use. My mind continued to race in a fever; it unreeled image after image of its own accord, as if it was searching for something. Then, as its progress steadied, as the images became less frightening, I began to understand that it was really travelling in the same direction as my exhausted body. It was collaborating, after all. Now I was wandering with Ruth, along a rocky creek, beneath huge fern; now pulling at the oars of a dinghy, while Ruth trailed a line from the stern; now lowering my rifle and bending to lift a shot rabbit from the tussock while Ruth hid her eyes; now swimming beside her in sunlit water, and the wild spray danced silvery from our bodies. Then I came, as I knew I would, to that beach: Ruth leapt ahead of me over the sand dunes, skidding and laughing and calling back. I plunged after her, down on to the beach. I prepared myself for the impact of that half-buried glass; I could not avoid it. Tensed, I knew exactly the pain to expect; exactly the moment to call out to Ruth. The colours of the world swam gently in the hazy early light. Then, miraculously, I was still running. Running on, after Ruth , over unblemished sand, and diving with her into cool water.

Light was in my eyes, and it was morning; Ruth was in the kitchen, cooking an omelette over a primus. 'I can't let you go home to Wellington half-fed,' she announced. Half an hour later, dressed and shaved, I set out to find my life again.

*

The house is quiet now. The clumsy elephant has made his peace with the world, the children are asleep; and Helen, whom I can hear now and then as she moved quietly about the kitchen, is preparing dinner. She has just, without saying a word, set a glass of sherry on the desk beside me. Ruth is in another city, four hundred miles away; but she might as well be in another country. I find it hard to imagine what she might be doing at this moment; possibly eating, or preparing to go out, or waiting for friends to call. For she could, I suppose, be anticipating an evening with friends like the one I remember enduring. That is her way; fair enough. She finds my way a living death, I find hers intolerably bleak. We do not share much in our lives, except the past; but that, when fanned in memory, can still glow so as to make a present seem lustreless and the future drably predictable. Of course I understand that the logic of that past dictates that she should be as she is, and that I should be as I am; we really have had no chance for escape. It is not a matter for regret, nor even for speculation. For Ruth was, of course, wrong when she said we were self-sufficient as children: she was speaking only for herself. Without Ruth I was always incomplete; as incomplete, say, as I am without Helen now. Perhaps that is something Ruth cannot understand. And yet ...

Love; she tried to make that an explanation. It wasn't good enough, really. For it explained everything and nothing. This is the paradox I still contemplate on sleepless nights when I rise disturbed from my marriage bed and sit solitary with black coffee in the kitchen.

Again I wonder what she is doing at this moment. At last I find a satisfying picture. She is at home, in my father's house, at the beginning of a lonely evening. She is settling down to work she has neglected, painting her way slowly and thoughtfully into a new scene. Of course; that must be it. To imagine her at work reassures me. My eyes flick up to the painting above my desk — the red dinghy on pale sand, and that strange haunting light. The light no longer baffles me. It is perfectly obvious, perfectly familiar. That serene light flows in and out of our childhood, leaving no shadows: could there ever be glass beneath that sand? All things melt beneath it — even the dinghy is insubstantial, a brittle stick to fuel the incandescence, as it speaks of this time and this place; every time and every place. Unreal? Of course. As unreal as her belated explanation of love, her romantic's rationalization. She is in love not with me, but with what we were and can never be again. More than that, she is in love with what we never were. But who am I to say? That light speaks eloquently where she and I cannot.

I do not see my sister often. But I recall that once, confused travellers at a junction, we met, or almost met, before we fell back into our separate journeys towards —

Well, where else? Towards the extinction of light.

# Pallet on the Floor
## Ronald Hugh Morrieson

### Chapter One

As the sun was westering and the dripping grey clay faces of the cliffs out at the heads of the Kurikino River became deeply shadowed in places and glorified by a crimson glow in others, Sue Jamieson opened the kitchen door of the cottage where she lived with her husband Sam.

Careful not to step on any of the more rotten boards in the floor, she went over and leaned on the railing of the veranda. Whenever she did this she was cautious lest the railing collapsed and pitched her out on to the steep slope where the cottage had been built nearly a century before. Trunks and tangled branches would have stopped her rolling far, she knew, but she didn't want it to happen all the same.

Uppermost in her mind was the safety of the child in her womb.

The path to the gate was a trap in wet weather; hard to get down when slippery and harder still to get up. One summer, Sue had dug out a rough flight of steps and made the going much easier. Several times she had tried with an axe to fell the trees and shrubs, mostly weeds or self-sown plants, which smothered the section, but digging out the roots was too much for her. It seemed to Sue the trees and shrubs grew faster than she could cut them down. She consoled herself by making jam out of crab apples, blackberries, the yellow poroporo berries and the fruit of the japonica plants. When the trees and shrubs were blossoming they made a colourful spectacle, but it was getting completely out of hand. The view which now confronted her, right to the eliagnus hedge which bordered the property, was a wilderness.

Sue never proposed to Sam that he should clean the place up. He had inherited the cottage from his grandmother. At the time he had begun courting her, Sue had been sleeping on a flaxen mat out at Wainongoro Pa, once a fort, now just a Maori village situated above a bend in the river. Also, she took into account that in the height of the season, he worked long hours — sometimes from four o'clock in the morning until midnight — in the freezing chambers of the big slaughterhouse across the bridge at the foot of the hill. At times like those he earned big money, but they had nothing to show for it.

Every late autumn as the slack season approached Sam would say, without fail, 'Look, kid, as soon as the gun goes off at the Works I'm gunna get stuck right in and clean up this section. I'm gunna mow down those confounded poroporo trees. They breed like rabbits. I'll get a slasher and belt that hedge back. Yes, I'll clean this place up if I have to get half the guys at the Works to help me.'

Sam always declared this after he had spent the evening at Amos Blennerhasset's. Amos Blennerhasset was the proprietor of the 'Brian Boru', the only hotel in Kurikino.

Sam never mentioned these good intentions if some of his friends had come home with him to drink beer and eat cheese on salty biscuits. He only said it when just Sue and himself were sitting at the kitchen table, late at night.

'Well, Sam, I think that's a good idea and I'll help all I can.'

'It's not work for a woman, Sue. It's a man's job.'

The lanky Sam would put his glass down and, raising a thin arm, would reiterate, 'A man's job.'

Sue, treading carefully, went back into the kitchen. She left the door ajar because it was a stifling hot night for the start of winter and the room was small. She groped for the light switch and then sat down at the table. She rolled a cigarette and lit it.

'I wish I had gone to the "Brian Boru" when Sam asked me. If I'd know it was going to be as stinking hot as this I'd be up there right now with a jug of shandy squash.' She was used to being lonely at night and her own whispered thoughts were company.

'Silly old Sam. Ordering a whole cord of firewood just because it's cheaper now than in real winter time. The gun'll go off at the Works and we'll be lucky to pay for it. Hell, there's enough firewood round this section to keep us warm. Let alone the driftwood along the river. And why order it off Jack Voot? Of all people!'

She blinked her eyes to stop her loyal, affectionate mind from answering. She knew the answer.

Apart from Voot once being Sam's rival for Sue's hand there had been a nasty incident. It had been over the ill-treatment of a lamb. Ever since, Sam had walked in fear of Voot.

Sam was soft-hearted. As a boy he had owned a pet lamb called 'Moobaa' because it made plaintive sounds like a calf. Somehow his departed mother and his old sheep were one person in Sam's heart. He felt that all animals knew him to be a friend. In the trucks and pens they seemed to look at him pleadingly as if they were saying, 'Where we all going, Mister Sam?' He hated to hear the bobby calves mooing with thirst and hunger as they rolled down the hill past the cottage. He was not fitted to be a freezing worker.

His father had said to him, 'Sammy boy, you'll never make a farmer unless you don't take these animals so seriously. Damn it, even the wild ducks come here in the. shooting season as if they knew they were safe with you around. You've got it from me, I suppose, but I've had to get over it. You'd have names for every cow and calf on the farm. I don't like to see the bobby calves or some old ewes I've know for years hauled off to the Works any more than you do. As for the lambs, it breaks my heart but if there's no feed what can I do? You'll have to snap out of it.'

If anything, Sam became more sentimental than ever, Voot had brought an articulator jammed with lambs to the Works. The truck was standing by the stock-yards. One little woolly fellow had a leg poked out through the slats. It looked broken.

Sam had tired to free it. Voot had come back. 'This isn't good enough,' Sam hooted. 'It's overloaded to hell. You're scum to treat poor little things this way.'

'What did you say?' ground out Voot. Sam had not been long married to Sue and an excuse to beat up Sam suited Voot fine. He advanced on him.

'Don't hit that man,' said O'Keefe in his easy drawling brogue. He was only a slender five-foot-ten man, but he strolled everywhere with one invincible companion — the legend of his fighting past: he had been a professional prize-fighter.

'If you're in a mood to hit someone, what's wrong with me?'

Voot glared at him for a tense moment and then spun away. There was quite a gathering to witness this incident and Voot loathed Sam the more. By evening every man at the Works from Grimshaw down would have heard of Voot's cowardice. Sam had related the episode to Sue without stressing his own fear, but she knew.

And then, some five months later, O'Keefe was dead. Just like that. Just walking across the bridge and he dropped like a stone. Some said it was a stroke; some, a heart attack. But, whatever it was, O'Keefe whom Sam had worshipped, made a friend of, invited to his home, was dead.

He had gone fishing for flounder with Sam. He had hunted for pauas and mussels with Sue. He had taught Sam never to hit a rough house fighter in the jaw, but in the solar plexus while looking in his eyes nevertheless.

With Sue three months pregnant at last, Sam had never been happier in all the sad years following his mother's death. But the passing of his friend hit him hard.

'O'Keefe is dead,' cried the gulls wheeling over the mud flats. 'O'Keefe is dead.'

Sue had taken it badly too. 'He was the nicest man,' she had said.

This evening, some four months after O'Keefe's death, she mumbled. 'Can't be bothered putting the billy on. 'Sides, it's that hot! God! It's hot! Good mind to get myself a bottle of the home brew.'

She knew that if Sam came home with McGhee, Entwistle and the Remittance Man, and maybe 'Gigglejuice' Saunders, she would hear them talking as they came up the curved path through the overgrown section. She calculated it would be an hour at least before he came home. She pulled her frock over her head, hung it over the back of the chair, and brushed dark locks of hair away from her tawny eyes.

'Boy, that's better.'

She knew she would have plenty of warning to be properly dressed if visitors came or, for that matter, only Sam on his own, because he always cursed and swore finding his way up the path.

Barefooted, in panties only, the nipples of her small firm breasts straight as gun barrels, the dusky Sue rolled another cigarette. She was still shapely, although her condition was obvious.

But with her frock over her ears she had not heard a heavy truck coming down the hill and rolling to a stop on the wrong side of the road down by the gate.

## Chapter Two

In the big back bar of the 'Brian Boru' the old open fireplace had been blocked off and, around the walls, ready for the cold weather, infra-red heaters had been installed. The heat now bounced off the high ceiling and beat down on the drinkers instead of going up the chimney as God had intended. Late imbibers caught a chill when they went outside.

The ornate ceiling had been plastered with a flat, blackboard paint and so had the top six feet of the walls, thus reducing the original sixteen-foot stud to ten. It was an illusion created by a giant spider's web of white nylon cord strung tautly across the big room. Below this, lightly stained wallboards concealed old wall-paper.

The oval bar had been replaced by a short counter, one end of which was railed off by curved chromium pipes to provide a counter for jug service.

Gone were the days when there were packets of tobacco and cigarettes of many brands stacked up on the shelves. Nowadays, it was necessary to go out into the draughty hallway, which had not been modernised, and insert a coin into a machine. The change was under the cellophane wrapping and rolled all over the floor when the pack was opened. With each new budget the change was less. Then with the advent of decimal coinage the first batch of these machines became obsolete and had to be either converted or replaced. There was no choice of brand at the 'Brian Boru'.

One night when Sam Jamieson had run out of tobacco he told Amos Blennerhasset, 'I'll go to another pub.'

Amos Blennerhasset, who was the only licensed publican within a ten-mile radius, had merely smacked Sam on the shoulder and laughed. But many of his customers, most of them freezing workers, were getting their own back by dropping the unstubbed butts of cigarettes on the new body carpet. With every innovation which displeased the workers, who spend the bulk of the contents of their pay envelopes over the bar, the hotel's supply of fillet steak and smallgoods stolen from the Works diminished. In the days of bare floors and the roaring open fire, Amos Blennerhasset had been given whole pigs and hams. There were still some crawlers, but Sam was not one of them. He was a man of principle. Any meat he slipped under his overalls went home to his beloved Sue.

Sam looked up at the mirror behind the bar in quest of his adolescent, fancied resemblance to the actor, the late Gary Cooper. He was inclined to think that the reflection of his lined features above the bottles stacked along the shelf still entitled him to this conceit. None of the young fry of today recalled Gary Cooper, he reflected bitterly.

Sam tilted his hat back and was about to drink his beer when he caught sight in the mirror of the short but broad shouldered Joe Voot leaving one of the jug tables known as 'leaners' and heading for the back door. That he was not just going to the Men's as the Remittance Man, Entwistle and McGhee had done a few minutes earlier was plain to Sam when he overhead Joe Voot say, in the surly Voot voice, 'See yuh' to his brother Jack who was the only other drinker at the leaner.

Sam had consumed enough alcohol now to approach Jack Voot. Inwardly he was terrified of the hulking bad tempered six-foot-one truck driver who weighed a good two hundred and fifty seven pounds and was ten years younger than him. He had been the logical winner in contending for Sue's hand, but she had preferred Sam.

The flame of hate had been fanned the day O'Keefe had ridiculed him into a show of cowardice.

Jack Voot loathed Sam and still eyed Sue hungrily. He could have broken Sam like a twig. And Sam knew it.

There were three empty stools at the bar where McGhee, Entwistle and the Remittance Man had been sitting and would return to at any moment. 'Gigglejuice' Saunders on the fifth stool didn't count. He was chuckling away to himself and dribbling into his glass of cheap sherry.

Sam sauntered off across the room to where Jack Voot was pouring beer from a jug into a glass. His nonchalant approach complete with a faint debonair smile was ruined when he pushed his hat still further back and it fell off. He grabbed it and went up to a sneering Jack Voot. Voot's sleeves were rolled up and a glimpse of his biceps was enough to indicate the strength of the man.

'Well, hello, Jack,' Sam said breezily. 'Guess you didn't forget that cord of firewood. Maybe hot tonight, but we'll have the usual hard June and July, I s'pose.'

Voot looked him up and down. 'Yeah,' he said slowly and thickly, 'there'll be more sweaty crutches than runny noses around tonight.'

Sam laughed appreciatively.

Voot did not smile. Sam was by a fraction the taller man, but Voot was half as heavy again.

'Can I buy you a drink, Jack?' Sam said.

'No, I've got this jug to finish. Then I'll hit the track. I see your mates coming back. Buy them a drink. I might even load off your wood at your old dump tonight.'

'Gee, Jack, I don't want you to go out of your way like that.'

Voot didn't answer. He glowered into his glass.

'Well,' Sam said, 'see you, Jack.'

Re-crossing the room to rejoin his friends he could sense Voot's glare, a ray of contempt and dislike.

Sam despised himself for kow-towing to the man. It was cowardice, he knew, and Sue knew it too. Although she had never said a word, Sam had long ago realised her awareness of his weakness.

He was not a fighting man, but in his day-dreams — and he was a born dreamer — he had thrashed Voot many times. Knowing the impracticability of an honest physical victory, his mind had dwelt on strange and vicious tactics.

In the mirror, he saw Voot staggering to the back door.

He had not been frightened of Jack Voot when they had been rivals in the courtship of Sue. Voot had not been invited to the wedding.

Sam had invited all his fellow-workers in the freezing chambers who had dubbed in for one impressive present, a radiogram decided upon at a secret meeting. They had turned up in their best bib and tucker, but some still wearing the boots issued by the company. They had all stood in respectful silence when Mohi Te Kiri, standing as erect as he had seventy years before when he was a young warrior, but allowing his elbow to be held by his grand-daughter Amiria, entered slowly and with great dignity. His son, big strapping Manu, was beside him also. Sue, in her wedding frock, had gently taken Te Kiri's other arm. He was impeccably dressed in a dark suit and white shirt with old-fashioned wing-collar. Chin and cheeks of the haughty aquiline features were tattooed with elaborate scrolls denoting his proud lineage.

Sam approached the old chief and clasped his hand. The two men were of a height. Sam in the traditional custom leaned forward and pressed his nose against Te Kiri's. It was something he had never done before. Te Kiri freed his arm from Amiria and placed a hand on Sam's shoulder. He saw the tears in Sam's eyes and spoke a sentence in Maori.

'Father says,' Manu translated, 'never fear again. You now have powerful friends.'

All Sue's friends at the pa located above the bend where the Kurikino River was joined by its tributary, the Wainongoro, came in on the trays of cut-down Chevvies and Fords; some of the elders, like Te Kiri, in huge but rusted sedans. All, with the exception of the more august vehicles, broke down outside the 'Brian Boru'. These dark-skinned happy people bore with them gifts of flowers as well as sacks of potatoes and whole pigs to be roasted later hangi style, near the mouth of the river, while the grass-skirted Maori girls danced with pois.

Even the Reverend Gallagher had showed signs of intoxication as the sun sank. The casks had been propped on driftwood. The tea was brewed in big billies over burning driftwood. Sam remembered the fragrance of that smoked tea, drunk from a chipped cup, with the smell of the river and the tang of the sea and the lupins on the sand-hills in his nostrils. And the exquisite taste of his tobacco when he reclined! Sam's eyes sometimes filled with tears when he thought of Mohi Te Kiri's words.

Reseating himself on his stool at the bar beside McGhee, Sam recalled Manu saying, 'Powerful friends.'

## Chapter Three

Sue's long eyelashes flicked open when she heard a loud noise on the old veranda. She thought she must have been dreaming and looked around to make sure she had not left the butt of her cigarette burning. Then the sound came again, but this time it was not a crash she remembered but a wrenching noise.

'Sam!' she cried, quite certain one of the rotten boards in the veranda flooring had finally given way. Forgetting her frock over the back of her chair and that she was as near naked as one can get, she rushed to the half-open door. Beneath her flimsy semi-transparent tight panties her abundant pubic growth of hair bulged. Above her panties her stomach protruded.

She knew immediately that the massive figure, who had now extricated his leg from the broken board, was not that of Sam.

Although Sue's skin was just dusky the nipples of her breasts were as black as gunpowder. She clasped her hands over them.

Recognising Jack Voot as he lurched into the kitchen, she rushed back to the chair over which her frock was hanging and inadvertently overturned it.

Before she could don the frock Voot's powerful arms were around her. She attempted to scratch his face but he seized a wrist. Then he scooped her up in his arms.

'I've always wanted you, baby. Now you're mine.'

'Sam will kill you for this,' Sue said, beginning to cry.

'That gutless wonder! He couldn't kill a chook.'

'No, maybe not, but all the men in Kurikino are gong to. Don't you hurt me, you brute, I'm going to have a baby. Sam isn't allowed to touch me.'

Sue knew it was no good screaming out on the lonely hill. She could only hope and pray that Sam would come home with all his friends.

Jack Voot, effortlessly carrying the struggling Sue, lurched across the kitchen and booted the half-open bedroom door. She tried again to claw him but to no avail. He threw the sobbing Sue on the bed and pounced upon her. He inserted the toe of a great clumsy boot into the elastic of her panties and pushed them down.

'Sam will kill you for this,' Sue moaned. 'Watch my stomach, you beast!'

Voot laughed; a drunken sneering laugh.

## Chapter Four

The Remittance Man sat on the stool next to Sam. Basil Beaumont-Foster had not chosen Kurikino as his home town any more than the town had chosen its name. *Kurikino* means 'Bad Dog', and a boot had played the same part in the Remittance Man's life as the legend of the monstrous killer dog which the Maoris were said to have hunted and finally destroyed in the valley had played in the naming of the town and the river.

When he had first appeared in Kurikino, in his educated blue-blooded, down-to-the-uppers, shoes, mumbling to himself (but in a frightfully well modulated mumble) it was because the guard had booted him off the train, bottle and all, and left him to walk into the little township which dominated the wilderness of sand and lupin near the river-mouth. At that time, some years before, no one had heard of him in those parts, nor of the dubious Beaumont-Foster carburettor.

Now he worked in the same gang as Sam in the freezing chamber.

Next in line at the bar, not sitting on his stool, but leaning on it with a knee and both hands except when one was busy with his glass, was the thin, gingery, freckle-faced Entwistle. Unlike the others, 'Tinny' Entwistle worked in the fellmongery. As for McGhee it was hard to say where he would be working in the new season. As usual near the end of the season, McGhee had been sacked. Or engineered to be sacked. It seemed to be an arrangement between himself and whoever happened to be his foreman. But it could be guaranteed that in the next season he would be reinstated somewhere or other. He was a permanent staff man, but apparently was determined to enjoy the periodic long holiday. He had worked in every department except the office, from one end of the great slaughter-house to the other. Now well in his fifties, he had worked for no other firm since he was a boy. The management never took the key of his hut in the compound away from him. His father had a ramshackle shop-cum-dwelling in the main street which passed as a bicycle shop, but McGhee senior was generally known as 'Mr Fixit': he would try his hand at anything. McGhee stayed on down at the compound even when sacked. It was rumoured that Grimshaw, the general manager, had once looked out the window of his office and, glimpsing McGhee, had thrown up his hands and exclaimed, 'Do we *have* to employ that man?'

Apparently they did. He was part of the scenery.

And what a part! The entire five-food-nine or ten of the man, right from the ancient tennis shoes to the cap which advertised a brand of spark plug and seemed to be always perched on his pine-cone of a head, was remarkable. In fact his fellow workers were often heard to exclaim on his approach, 'My God, it's McGhee!' His legs, encased in shapeless denim trousers, were thin and knock-kneed. His shoulders sloped preposterously, hardly existed, were just a continuation of the ribs under his jersey which, in front, curved inwards following the concave stomach right to his backbone — or so it seemed. His chin receded and took refuge in the long, wrinkled skinny throat where two folds of skin like the sides of a mitre-box guarded the prominent Adam's apple. Just as prominent were two shiny bumps, one on either side of his forehead. In contrast to his overall emaciation his nose was large and fleshy and his lips full. McGhee's rimless spectacles were the unfathomable cowls of a mysterious mind.

The squat 'Gigglejuice' Saunders, chuckling into his glass, was on the left at the end of this school of drinkers. He spent all his pension on cheap wine. He did no work unless we are to count as work the stacking of crates and the washing and rinsing of bottles for which Amos Blennerhasset rewarded him with a bed in an outhouse and permission to knock up a meal in the kitchen.

The screened doors into this kitchen from the backyard were open from early in the morning until just after ten o'clock at night, except on Sundays when the kitchen was locked as soon as tea was over. This could mean anytime because everything revolved around Amos Blennerhasset who was a golf fanatic. In the old days of six o'clock closing Amos Blennerhasset had served drink until sometimes as late as midnight, and for turning a blind eye to this illegal trading Cop Larkman had accepted graft. But Sunday has always been sacred. The drinkers knew well to stock up with beer at home for their Sunday pick-me-up. The publican played golf throughout the week as well, leaving his barmen in charge. Since the introduction of ten o'clock closing he did no after-hours serving or any sort of backdoor trading. Consequently there was no rake-off for Cop Larkman. Amos Blennerhasset had found himself just as well off financially and better physically. At one time a barman had been paid to serve drinks to shift workers at the Freezing Works as early as four o'clock in the morning. Now the doors opened at 11 a.m. sharp and closed a few minutes after ten each night.

Cop Larkman had been recently promoted to sergeant but was still referred to by derisive Kurikinoites as 'The Marshal' because of the wide brimmed hats he wore, the old open Chrysler which he drove and boasted of, and his obvious film and cheap fiction blown-up image of himself as a G-man, big city sleuth or sheriff. He scowled around the empty but still lit kitchen. No graft to-night. In twenty minutes Amos Blennerhasset would be closing up. Urging Blennerhasset to apply to be made a tavern keeper only met with the reply that as the only licensed guest house in the town the 'Brian Boru' didn't have a show with the Licensing Committee. This was probably correct, but the real truth was that things the way they were suited the publican fine.

The sergeant had only just refrained from coming out in the open and positively pleading with the publican to go back to his old ways, but he had known it would hardly tone in with his promotion and the fact that he now had a newly appointed constable working under him. It was no longer a sole charge town. Sergeant Larkman liked having young Mellow to bully around, but he disliked intensely the way his 'staff' always seemed to find some excuse to come to his office just as a bus was due and prospective passengers were lined up on seats at the bus stop directly opposite the police station. Some of the womenfolk had been known to pull up their stockings and even apart from such windfalls it was the day of the mini skirt ...

The pink and white mild-mannered young constable with his mincing manner had already been branded as 'fruit' or a 'queer' by the rough and ready Kurikinoites only too ready to work a local character into a bawdy jest.

If anything could have lifted the scowl of the sergeant standing in the kitchen of the 'Brian Boru' it was the squeal of the tyres of a car being turned recklessly, probably on two wheels, into the 'Strip', as Kurikino's small shopping stretch was known. Actually it was a few hundred yards of what was officially the Beach Road. To leap into his old supercharged Chrysler roadster, pursue and flag down some larrikins would have been a labour of love, but before he could even move, the sound of a siren drifted to his ears and his scowl returned in full force. Everything had gone to rack and ruin he reflected. As well as that sissy, Mellow, which wasn't so bad, Kurikino had been given a traffic cop. Henderson, supplied with a late model black Zephyr equipped with a revolving red dome light in the roof.

'As if the Chrysler couldn't lick that hunk of time,' he gritted. Now his was a real car, a fair dinkum sleeper, he thought, and more rakish in appearance too for all its age. However, it didn't alter the fact that girls were to be seen daily in the new Zephyr with the rather dashing looking young Henderson, and the sergeant doubted mightily whether they were being examined for a driver's licence. 'More likely a rider's licence,' he sneered. Well, the night had nothing to offer him now but the running of his torch beam around the premises of the bank which harboured the payroll due at the Freezing Works tomorrow. True, with his pistol and in his Chrysler, he would escort the taxi delivering the money, but the feeling of importance and the novelty of this weekly occasion had long since worn off, and he was forever hoping against hope that someone would pluck up enough courage to blow the safe. He knew full well that nobody would choose an end-of-season night with the staff reduced to old hands and the permanent staff but, swinging his torch, he left the kitchen.

McGhee had just been on the point of going to the kitchen to get two spoons when Sam had stopped him.

'Don't feel like no dancing to-night,' he said. 'What say we go down to my burg and scoff some home-brew. Sue'll find some biscuits and that cheese we like.'

'If that's on the cards, let's get a few flagons,' said Entwistle quickly. 'After all the eagle shits tomorrow.' This was freezing workers' slang for pay-day.

Entwistle was one guest who never made any polite pretence of liking Sam's product. He screwed up his face and shuddered with every swallow. Actually 'Gigglejuice' Saunders, who didn't care or even know what he was drinking, providing it was of an alcoholic nature, was the only person not to give the faintest of grimaces upon imbibing. All, with his exception, now ordered and were served a flagon.

Sam was a devoted tap-dancer, and in the old bare floor days had really drummed out a rhythmic beat. Now, even in his boots, he felt muffled and defeated by the body carpet. The act they had built up and put on when the booze got hold of them had lost much of its enjoyment for him. It was too much like hard work, even with McGhee banging his spoon and 'Gigglejuice' Saunders letting his loose false teeth fall up and down and click like castanets. The Remittance Man had a good baritone voice and Entwistle could fake up an obligato lapsing into string bass effects when inspiration failed him. People had often clustered around the slide into the other bar to watch and grin, and drinkers around tables in the bar marked 'Ladies and Escorts' giggled through their open door when Sam tapped his way through old numbers like 'You Must Have Been a Beautiful Baby', 'It Had to be You', 'Margie' and 'Bye Bye Blues'. Now there was a juke box in the bar through the wall and a very different type of rhythm and singing seemed to be the rage. To the younger fry in the front bar, Sam's gang were squares; a sort of comedy team.

Sam's dancing mistress had beaten the Army Medical Board to it by telling Sam that because of his flat feet he would never really be any good. Still, it was no act without Sam.

'Feel like leaving a bit early tonight, dunno why,' said Sam. 'How's about you guys?'

'At this stage of proceedings,' said the Remittance Man, 'Ai should invite you all to mai home. Unfortunately Ai have no home.'

'Nev' mind,' said Sam. 'I have.'

So it was that they filed out into the backyard earlier than usual that night, without having to hear Amos Blennerhasset shouting, 'Now c'mon you alkies, home to bed and into mum or something.'

A lone figure left the 'Ladies and Escorts' bar and followed them into the darkness of the yard.

'I want to talk to you, Sam,' Miriam Breen said.

'That sheila's got a crush on you, Sam,' Entwistle had observed one night when Sam had rejoined his friends at the bar after Miriam Breen had called him aside.

'A trifle enamoured Ai should say,' commented Beaumont-Foster.

'Longest word I know's corrugated iron,' put in Entwistle. 'But if you mean what I think you do she's got a crush on Sam.'

'Aw' bunkum,' said Sam again, although he knew it was true. Ever since they had both gone to the old reel class, Miriam Breen, then Miriam Pitts, had made no secret of her infatuation with Sam. Sam had made matters worse by taking her home after several dances, kissing her goodnight, even, on one daring occasion, putting his hand under her frock which, despite her giggle of delight, had only achieved the time honoured slap across the face.

'You just wait 'till we're married, young Sammy Jamieson,' Miriam had said. 'Then you'll get all you're looking for. I'm marrying in white I am, and looking my own height too.'

It was the first time Sam had been proposed to. Maybe it gave his ego a boost because within months he had picked up Sue. Apart from the passing drunken sexual urge, Miriam did not appeal to him, and he thought that being cool and distant and finally getting around with Sue would have made this plain to her, but he guessed there was no one more furious anywhere the day he got married.

Sam nearly fell over when Sue accepted his hand. She was only nineteen against his thirty-one. Miriam was twenty-nine. A few months after Sam and Sue had moved into Granny's old cottage as man and wife, Miriam had married Jack Breen who was in Sam's age bracket. Breen was a no-hoper who drove for the Voots. The Voots were not only livestock transporters but had access right, granted by the Maoris, to a metal quarry out by Wainongoro Pa. It was driving out here that Jack Voot had first seen Sue and had been smitten. He was the youngest of the family. They were a tough bunch. Old Manson Voot, the hunchbacked father, had founded the fleet of trucks and later his sons had taken over. There was Sydney, Joseph, Michael and Jack, in that order. They employed Breen, who was all right behind the wheel, but drunk the rest of the time.

Since her marriage, Miriam had degenerated. She still carried a torch for Sam who was now pushing forty years of age. Once she had nearly succeeded in breaking up his marriage.

## Chapter Five

Yes, Miriam had nearly managed to split Sue and Sam up. It had occurred when Sue was four and a half months pregnant. Apparently Sue had confided in Miriam when they had ended up at the Harrowville races together. She had no idea of Miriam's hatred. They had travelled on the bus together and from then on picked horses and gone to the bar together. In the end they had parted brass rags. Miriam had accused Sue of cheating her.

Sue told Sam of the incident.

'Never take bets to put on for no one,' Sam advised her belatedly.

'Anyone ever asks me to back a horse for them I wriggle out of it. Anything can go wrong. You might forget, you might get shut out like you were. Then the thing wins and they think you've got the money. No, kid, it's a mug's game. Don't have it on again.'

Breen approached Sam in the bar.

'That missus of yours better fork up that money she robbed my missus of. Seventy-nine dollars that thing paid and they were half-and-half. She couldn't afford a day at the gallops anyway. Then she gets downright robbed. You better tell her if she doesn't pay up there'll be trouble.'

'Look, Jack,' Sam said. 'I've washed my hands of the whole business. I wasn't there and neither was you. Sue says there was a queue a mile long and the bell left off ringing just as she got there. I tell you she wouldn't do a thing like pocket the money. She was mad as hell herself at not getting it on. That's what she says and it's good enough for me.'

'Well, it's not good enough for me. You just tell her to get that forty dollars together.'

Then one Saturday afternoon, Miriam herself baled me up in the T.A.B. She was thirty-seven years old by now and the mini-skirt she wore was unkind to her figure. Sam winced remembering his attempt to seduce her.

'Now how about giving me the money to put on for you,' she said. 'How'd you feel if it won, but I said I hadn't backed it? How would you like to feel diddled?'

'Oh, not that business again surely,' said Sam. 'I'm sick and tired of hearing about it.'

'Maybe you are, but I'm going to tell you something that might change your mind about your pure innocent little wife. Going to have a kid, isn't she? After all this time. And silly old Sam thinks he's a daddy.'

'What the hell do you mean?'

'I mean what I'm telling you. Your mate that dropped dead a few weeks ago knew more about that kid than you did.'

'Who do you mean?' cried Sam.

'Who do I mean?' scoffed Miriam. 'A blind man could see it. You pal up with O'Keefe. Now she's up the duff. Didn't those two go hunting the beach and the river often as they could. Nice sand-hills out there, Sam. He was a lady killer, that O'Keefe.'

'He'd kill you for saying a thing like this,' cried Sam hotly. 'He was a fine guy and my mate. Sue thought the world of him too.'

'Sure, sure. Enough to lie on her back with her legs open. Don't bluff me. You've got yourself bluffed and she's bluffed you too, but don't try it on Miriam. You work out a few dates and see how things add up.'

'O'Keefe wasn't even interested in womenfolk. Never ever heard him tell a dirty story. He used to look disgusted when other guys talked filthy-like.'

'You show me a man that isn't interested,' jeered Miriam. 'You think it over. And before you boot her out get my dough.'

Sam drank steadily all afternoon. He tried to shut Miriam's malicious talk out of his mind but she had planted a seed of doubt. Sue was six months pregnant. They had been married eight years. Why now, when the first ecstatic lovemaking had become a mere taken-for-granted business? He had chummed up with O'Keefe eight months ago. Aw baloney, he thought angrily, and drank deep. Unfortunately the nagging doubt could swim.

He arrived home on staggering feet after ten o'clock that night. Sue never growled, but sometimes she reproached him gently.

'You should have been home for tea, Sam. Hope you're not too full to eat and you don't just tumble into bed like you do some nights. The moon's full and I went out paua hunting on the rocks this low tide. Boy, I've never seen the tide so far out. I loaded my bucket. If only O'Keefe could have been out with me I'd have picked some for him. He loved hunting around for shellfish. He told me the Irish were like the Maoris that way and that's why most of them had good heads of hair. Brendon had a slick head of hair.'

'Pretty slick all ways if you ask me,' said Sam, lowering at the table.

'Sure was the fightingest man.'

'Sure you don't mean the — man,' Sam said using a word he had always respected Sue too much to employ.

'Sam!' she cried. 'What an awful thing to say! Now, I've beaten a few pauas with the rolling-pin. Shall I fry them in the pan with a little butter? I've boiled some onions and the white sauce is all ready.'

'Leave it for a minute or two,' said Sam. 'I'll try the new brew.'

'Oh, Sam, don't you think you've had enough? You know we put extra sugar in this lot. It's bound to be strong and you're rocking now.'

'You just give me a bottle. No, I'll get it myself. I like to be a bit independent in muh own home.'

He lurched over to the cupboard and returned with two bottles. He decanted one into a jug. 'It's beauty clear.' He drank. 'And good. Kick like a horse. Feel the heat in my guts straightaway.'

'I'll try one,' said Sue, and reached for the jug. As if some devil had control of him Sam slapped her hand away.

'What's the idea?' she said.

'You know.'

'I'm damned if I do. I just want a glass. I helped you to make it, didn't I?'

'Yeah, sure,' said the devil that had taken Sam over, 'but you've got something in your belly that I didn't help you to make.'

'Sam, I just don't understand you tonight.'

'Yeah, out in the sand-hills. With O'Keefe. **My buddy**. And now you're gunna have a baby. With a mixture of Irish and Maori it should have good hair. Sue *De Soto*. Your mother had the morals of an alley cat. That's no more my baby than the full moon.'

'If you're saying what you seem to be saying,' said Sue very calmly, 'you seem to be saying I'm carrying O'Keefe's baby and not yours.'

'That's just what I am bloody well saying,' yelled the devil within Sam. Sam could no more stop the blurred words tumbling out than he could stop the tide.

'Now look, Sam.' Said Sue. 'You're loaded to the ears to-night. Drink your beer if that's what you want and in the morning you'll have gotten over this crazy notion. The shellfish'll keep. Let's have a good bye-bye, eh?'

'Anything to stall me off,' raged the devil. 'That'll be the day when I doss down with a sheila that's put it across me. I'll go down to the huts to-night.'

Sue had tears in her eyes. She rubbed them away with her knuckles.

'O'Keefe never even put a hand on me. He was a gentleman. But I can see it's no good to talk. No need for you to go to the huts. It's your home just like this is your baby. No, Sam, your slut of a wife will go back to her people.'

She went into the bedroom. Sam drank moodily, regretting his drunken outburst. He should have waited at least until the child arrived. It might be the living image of him. Well, he would, up to a point apologise. Anything for a peaceful night.

Sue came out carrying her old guitar that had the top string missing. Maori blood or not she was white faced.

'I took a dollar for a taxi out of the tin,' she said. Don't worry, I'll send it to you. Sue *De Soto* pays her bills.'

'Look here, Sue,' said Sam. 'I'm raving on a bit to-night. Let me think this out.'

'There's nothing to think out. You don't trust me and that's it. Love and trust should go together. You've shocked me tonight. Well, I might slip in for one or two things, but for tonight, goodbye, Sam.'

'Sue,' said Sam — but the door had closed after her.

Sam sat there for some time drinking and smoking until the silence wrapped him up like cotton wool.

There was a knock on the door. Sam started up. Rage, hope, mingled with self-pity, arose in him. He lurched to the door. The Remittance Man, owlishly drunk, peered at him.

'Saw your light, Sam.'

'Have a drink,' said Sam, hungry for company. Anything rather than this feeling of desolation.

'Lesh go party. Was there myself but having no mates drove me out. You and I go, eh? Saturday night 'do' at Jimmy Edwards.'

'Right,' said Sam.

Together they blundered off back up the hill. Jimmy Edwards worked in the yard gang. He lived in a ramshackle house behind the Ho Chongs who owned a fruit and greengrocery shop on the main street and also the house. The first people Sam and the Remittance Man met were two of the young Ho Chong girls with glasses of beer in their hands. Someone was strumming a guitar. The young folks seemed to have selected the back of the house to kick up their heels and shout and sing, while the middle-aged had congregated in the sitting room which backed on to the Ho Chong shop. The yeah manning and yah yahing at the back was the music Sam detested. A couple were jiving. The girl was pretty and could dance but she wasn't in the same street as Sue. Thoroughly wretched he watched. The singing in the sitting room was of old songs but with bawdy lyrics invented.

Basil and Sam found themselves in the pantry. In the sink was a lonely saveloy splashed with brownish tomato sauce. There was a flagon of beer on the sink bench and they drank it all up. They decided to try the company in the front room. Here they consumed more glasses of beer. They each ate a saveloy wrapped in bread and butter. Soon they were both bored stiff.

'Goin' home,' Sam muttered. 'Full as a bull. The grog's flat.'

'Yes, I have partaken, hick, my fill.'

> Now this is number one,
> Oh, boy we're having fun.
> Roll me over in the clover,
> Do it again.
> Roll me OV-vah in the CLO-vah,
> Roll me over, lay me down,
> And do it again.

Outside, crossing the lawn, Basil and Sam grabbed hold of each other for support.

*Now this is number three.*
*Oh, boy, but you'll do me.*
*Roll me over in the clover,*
*Do it again.*
*Roll me OV-vah in the CLO-vah,*
*Roll me over, lay me down,*
*And do it again.*

They groped their way along the 'Strip'. At the top of the hill Sam shook his fist at the statue of Tiddly Tom.

'You drunken old hypocrite,' he yelled.

'Qui'ri', Sam,' Basil sobbed, hugging Sam around the shoulders. 'Qui'ri'.'

In the grey light of dawn, Sam reached a long thin arm across the bed to embrace Sue. Nobody there. It all came back to him. He sat on the side of the bed, throbbing head in hands. 'I must've been crazy,' he muttered. 'Booze, that's all it was. That bitch Miriam Breen! Other men's wives go out to dances and parties and things. What's Manu Te Kiri going to think? Powerful friends. Now I've got powerful enemies? And I'm alone in the world. What say the baby is mine? Oh Mummy, Mummy, tell me what to do.'

After a trip to the outhouse Sam opened a bottle of his home-brew. He took his tranquillisers. He knew, because Doctor Maddison had warned him, that they were incompatible with alcohol, but he was past caring. Could Doctor Maddison help him in anyway, he wondered?

He was starving hungry but the thought of paua Sue had prepared for their happy meal sickened him. He kept on drinking and rolling cigarettes. Alone. 'Couldn't have anything happen to our Sammy when he's married the prettiest colleen in Kurikino,' O'Keefe had said to him apropos of his stepping in when Voot had threatened Sam. Sam sobbed. He must get her back.

Sam looked at his watch. Time for work. They had one morning overtime this Sunday at double pay, but Sam shrugged his shoulders. The idea of slogging away in the cold and gloom with this on his mind depressed him dreadfully.

He walked slowly up to the deserted 'Strip'. He window-shopped miserably until it was after nine and then he rang Doctor Maddison.

'Doctor, I know it's Sunday but it's very important. Do you think you could see me for a moment? It's Sam Jamieson speaking.'

'Well, if it's important, come on around. I've had breakfast. Just pop in as soon as you can, Sam. You'll probably find me in the garden. You might not know me in my old clothes.

Sure enough, Doc Maddison was in the front garden. He stuck his fork in the ground and led Sam inside to his surgery.

'Hope you're not shocked at me working on the Sabbath, Sam. But the better the day the better the deed y'know. Now what's the trouble?'

'Doctor, it's not like one of my usual calls. I don't know whether you can help me or not. Doctor, Sue and I have parted and there's no more sick-at-heart guy in this town than I am.'

'Parted!' exclaimed Doctor Maddison. 'But in a month or two you'll be having a family. The girl was here last week and in fine fettle.'

'I know,' said Sam despondently. 'So was I. These new tablets you give me are the answer. Now this comes along. I've reason to believe the baby's not mine. It's rocked me. Doctor, is there any way of finding out?'

Doctor Maddison looked at him hard. In that look was the disapproval of the whole world, Sam felt.

'You talk of reason to believe. You want pretty sound reason to believe a thing like this about somebody who's devoted to you. Can't prove anything anyway. Blood tests are iffy and anyway we'd have to have the guilty party and the baby for blood grouping. And, as the old Scottish song says, 'As Yet There's no Chicks in Cockpen.' I'm afraid you've made a mess of things unless you had damn good reason. Any name mentioned?'

'It only makes it worse. My old mate, O'Keefe.'

The doctor stared at Sam. 'You mean Brendon O'Keefe who dropped dead with a coronary?'

'Yeah,' said Sam, 'and it all adds up.'

'Well, I'll tell you something. It doesn't add up more than two and two make ten. Now I *can* help you. I shouldn't be telling you this and I want you to keep it under your hat, but for Mrs Jamieson's and the baby's sake I will tell you. You'd better learn to trust a girl like that. You're a lucky man to have her. She talks about you as if you were the only man the sun shone on.'

'What, Doctor,' Sam said urgently, 'what is it?'

'As I said,' the doctor replied. 'I shouldn't tell you this, but I will. O'Keefe was operated on by me for appendicitis some years ago which is how I just happen to know. When just a boy he fell astride a picket fence and they operated. They took one of them out if you must know. He was next door to a eunuch. Couldn't have fathered a child for all the tea in China. Doubt if he was capable of intercourse. Doubt if he even thought of it. In all other respects he was a beautifully built man, but that part was missing. So I have put your silly ideas at rest.'

'You mean,' gasped Sam. 'You mean …'

'That's what I mean,' said the doctor.

'Doctor,' Sam nearly sobbed, 'you've brought back my happiness. Will you do me one last favour. Ring me a cab.'

'The better the day the better the deed,' said the doctor, dialling.

'Great day,' the cab driver said. 'Where to?'

'The pa at Bad Dog Bend. I'll let you know whether it's a great day or not later.'

The last time he had travelled this road he and Sue had attended the tangi following Mohi Te Kiri's funeral.

Manu Te Kiri was sitting on the step of a whare. On one side was Sue with her guitar; on the other side his daughter, Amiria. Because Sue was Mohi Te Kiri's adopted daughter the relationship between the two girls eluded the Maoris. They were cousins.

Nearly everyone at the pa was addressed as 'cousy'. If the connection was too obscure altogether, 'E hoa', which meant 'friend', was near enough.

'Sue,' cried Sam climbing out of the taxi. She approached him slowly, carrying her guitar.

'Sue,' cried Sam. He didn't care what the taxi driver or anyone thought. He sank down on his knees. 'Come back to me, Sue. I was drunk as all hell last night and didn't know what I was talking about.'

She said nothing.

'Please, Sue, please,' he pleaded.

Manu had joined them. He looked immense. 'You want a box on the ears, Jamieson,' he growled. 'The girl's cried all night.'

'I was drunk, Manu,' groaned Sam. 'Give us one more chance. I'll chuck myself in the river without Sue.'

Manu suddenly grinned. 'Go with him, Sue. He means it. He won't be the first or the last to get crazy ideas when he's full.'

Sam scrambled up. He seized Manu's hand. It was a speechless handshake.

Sam joined Sue, still clutching her guitar, in the back seat.

'Told you it was a great day,' said the driver. 'Where to?'

'Tiddly Tom's Hill. Last house on the right.'

They travelled in silence. Then Sam reached out his right hand. After a moment Sue took his hand in hers.

Sam exulted to himself: the three of them, himself, Sue and his baby — *his* baby.

## Chapter Six

This night in the backyard of the 'Brian Boru' Sam inwardly groaned when Miriam said she wanted to talk to him. She was forever making excuses for conversation. 'Gigglejuice' had not accompanied them. It was possible he was not even aware of their departure. The Remittance Man, McGhee and Entwistle, each carrying a flagon, moved off in the direction of the alley leading to the 'Strip'.

'Now, look here, Sam,' Miriam said. 'That dago bitch, Sue, put it across me at the Harrowville races and you know it. She wasn't shut out of no tote. That paid a good divvy that nag we picked and she went off to back. Sue southed my share that's what. I got twenty quid owing to me. Jack does up all our dough on booze and I need it. You know I got to baby-sit and do some housework when I can get it and it just isn't fair.'

'Aw hell, Miriam,' said Sam wearily. 'How often do I have to tell you Sue was broke to the wide that night she got home? She was in a long queue and she got shut out right enough. She wasn't very happy either, but you accusing her like this is the last straw. I wanted a drink that night and I went through her bag. She didn't have two bob to rub together.'

'As if the crafty bitch would have it in her bag,' Miriam scoffed. 'All these tarpots are too cunning to turn their backs on themselves. And half-castes are the worst of the lot. Who was she before Mohi Te Kiri adopted her? Sue De Soto! That's all they know about her father. Some fly-by-night salesman in a flash new De Soto. Not even his own car, but it got him a shag.'

'Aw hell,' said Sam. 'That's all water under the bridge. None of us ask to get put on this earth.'

'If you didn't grog on regardless you could fix me up yourself. You got a good job. You and that phoney Beaumont-Foster character and that half-wit giglamp 'Spud' McGhee. What can you see in them that's so wonderful?'

'They're my mates,' said Sam staunchly. 'And I better get after them.'

Flagon tucked under armpit he set off. Miriam tapped along too.

'Why you had to marry that bitch I'll never know. They all go back to the mat in the end. What's bred in the bone comes out in the flesh. And that's where you'll end up too. Eating dried shark and sleeping on a mat. Water finds its own level. And you'll be dragged down with it. Back to the mat. I've seen it time and again.'

'You'll never see it with me or Sue. Anyway you're all up the shoot. Every day the Maoris are leaving their whares and getting themselves houses in town.'

'So they're going the pakeha way now. But you'll see. Back they'll go to their old slap-happy ways. Getting a bellyful and then dossing down on the mat.'

'Well, whadda hell if they do, so long as they're happy? This is only a rate race. Slogging away day after day like a bastard for the Tax Department. And when you're too old for work you're broke if you haven't saved every bawbee and lived miserable when you're young enough to enjoy yourself. More you get in this world more you got to leave. Maybe the old Maori had the right idea. We can't all live in flash homes and have white collar jobs. And how many of *them* are happy? Paying off the latest model car and the rest going on their wife's back. Talking about our wonderful world! Just money, money, money. It's just work, work, work. Until you're dead, seems to me. Often walked along the railway siding at the Works and wondered if the seagulls hoverin' over the river wasn't better off than me. Don't have to punch no clock or live by the sound of that hooter. Still you'll never see Sam Jamieson on no mat.'

'She's getting in amongst you, though,' cried Miriam as they emerged on the 'Strip'.

Sam said nothing. Sue often did suggest going back to Bad Dog Bend. Mohi Te Kiri, who had adopted her, had passed on, but there was still Manu and they would be given a roof over their heads without question. However, this suggestion was only mooted after Sam had complained bitterly about some aspects of life as they knew it: the steepness of the slope on which the cottage was built and the almost insurmountable task of putting it in order: the exigency of repairing the little old two-roomed dwelling itself which was falling to pieces around them.

'Why they built a veranda and not another room's got me beat,' Sam would say. 'Can't risk walkin' over it. Too late to shut out the weather now. Anyhow the whole roof leaks like a sieve. Fire smokes. Fixing things up would cost a packet. Don't know where to start.'

'Well, at least you can't say things like that about the buildings out at Bad Dog Bend,' was Sue's answer.

'No, but now the old Maoris are dying out, half those dumps are empty. Rats helter-skeltering all over the place. The Wainongoro Pa might still be big, but it's on the way out.'

Sam was right. Like the language itself the traditional way of living a simple communal life was dying. The bulk of the younger generation scorned it, wanted more from life, were drifting to the towns and cities. This meant paying for rent and food and in most cases it meant trouble with the police. Not in this without their pakeha counterparts, they wore outrageous clothes and some of the males cultivated shoulder-length hair. In many ways their fashion in dress was the European fashion of centuries earlier, but now it was contributing to earning a bad name. They clustered around juke boxes listening to the ghastly beat and the singing by pop singers, their idols, of the short-lived numbers in vogue: drank and wrecked things; fought, hunted for trouble in packs: were sacked from their jobs. Some of them were steady enough. Whether time would bring the others to their senses was anybody's guess. A minority lived on at the old pas, even marrying and raising families. There were still children to be seen playing in front of whares and on the marae. Quite a few went to work on motor bicycles, but Kurikino Motors still ran buses from the pa to the Freezing Works and to take youngsters to school.

For the middle-aged it was becoming the day of the house in town. Still a hard old school of thought was self supporting, fishing the Kurikino and the Wainongoro rivers and spearing eels in the creeks, growing vegetables, killing their own meat, raising money in weird and wonderful ways to buy barrels of beer on Saturday, and taking them back on the trays of museum-piece trucks. When one had money, they all had money. They cooked pork and mutton hangi style and big stews in pots over driftwood burning in open fires. But just as the elders had brought about a colour-bar even in New Zealand by sticking to ways not acceptable to a money-dominated civilisation thrust upon them virtually overnight, so was the new generation building barriers by being only too ready to join in the defiant ways of a world gone crazy.

'You could fish the rivers and work when you felt like it in the kumara gardens,' said Sue when Sam moaned about his job. All these years of faithful work and no indication of being made a leading hand: Grimshaw not even speaking if they passed in the street: dragging himself across the bridge when the warning whistle of the great chimney stack known as 'His Master's Voice' drifted over the misty river; hastening along the railway track among the fennel and ice-plant and, his heart pumping like a German band, up the stairs to the 'donko' to wrap the sacking known as 'sneakers' around his boots; going down those same old slippery stairs from one of the freezing chambers to the cavernous cool rooms; stacking carcasses; tossing cartons of export meat on to conveyor belts; himself travelling along the conveyor belt to the next job with the icicles like stalactites on the roof nearly ripping off his balaclava; loading railways trucks on the siding until his arms nearly fell off; sewing beasts into sacks with numb fingers. And the monotony and gloom of it all, year in, year out. Then he would remember that the money was good, the meat he stole was the best, the men were a happy-go-lucky bunch; it was his life.

'But I still ain't sleeping on no mat,' he would say stubbornly in the end. 'And you're not going back to it either, say what they like.' And Sue would say no more until the next outburst.

Miriam and Sam walked along the 'Strip' in silence, the lanky Sam shortening his stride because he could not find it in his heart to outpace Miriam and downright leave her behind. The trio of his cronies had reached the top of Tiddly Tom's Hill leading down to the bridge with his own place near the bottom of the hill on the right. At the top of the hill on a pedestal was a statue in memory of Thomas Tiddleton, an early wealthy settler who had done much for the town. Unfortunately the sculptor, hired from out of town, had nearly worn a track to the 'Brian Boru' and the statue had a distinct list to starboard, while the extended hand, presumably indicative of presenting his all to the people, was bent at the elbow in manner most suggestive of clutching a glass.

When they themselves passed the statue, Miriam said, 'We'da been so happy if we'd settled down together, Sam. We could have had fun and got something outa living in this poke-in-the-arse burg. It's not too late now. Lots of people start a new life. It's all very well talking, but being shacked up with a Maori tart drags you down and you don't get invited places. The only way to get anywhere in this world is to know and mix with the right people. I didn't like even sitting with that Sue De Soto of yours in the bus to the Harrowville races. Come to think of it, it was our seat number that made us pick that outsider she cheated me on.'

Ahead of them, Beaumont-Foster had burst into song.

'I tell you she didn't cheat you,' Sam said irritably. 'And we've led a happy life together. You shouldn't be moaning. You got Jack haven't you?'

'Jack!' Miriam cried. 'With his backside out of his pants. And too full of grog to even know what he's talking about. Might as well sleep with a teddy bear for all the love I'm getting. Better. At least it wouldn't smell and snore. Puh! Half a gallon of wine for breakfast, I'd be just as well off if I was married to "Gigglejuice" Saunders.' Suddenly she grabbed his arm and he stopped or he would have dropped his flagon. 'Gis a kiss, Sam. Miriam's so lonely.'

He put his free arm half-heartedly around her and they kissed. She was certainly a changed woman. She rubbed her body against him. '*My*, but you're passionate, Sam,' she breathed. She pressed hard against him. He felt his flagon slipping and lowered it to the road. They kissed again.

'I don't care what you do,' she said huskily. 'I reckon I'd be happy if we put one over that Sue and Jack.' He began to tell her she must be crazy, but she wriggled hysterically against him.

'Right here on Tiddly Tom's Hill,' she said intensely, pressing still harder against him. He began to stumble backwards but she clung to him, one of her feet upsetting the flagon which began to roll down the hill.

Entwistle came pounding up the hill passing it as it gathered momentum.

'Sam,' he yelled. 'C'mon, c'mon! Jack Voot's gone mad and he's knocking the boys around.' He turned and raced off back downhill.

'Hell,' said Sam. 'Better see what's going on.' He loped off after Entwistle.

## Chapter Seven

'For God's sake, keep still and shut up,' Voot snarled. Sue, pinned beneath him kept wriggling about, groaning breathlessly and occasionally shouting out.

Voot had never thought his manhood would desert him, particularly astride a wench like Sue for whom he had always hungered and whom he had enjoyed countless times vicariously, but a combination of tension and a skinful of booze had robbed him of the ability. At last a panting Sue lay still and he could feel his vigour returning. Unbeknown to him, Sue had flung her right arm wide and was groping around the bedside table. Just as he was effecting an entry, a bottle half-full of home-brew smashed down on the back of his head. She made a gigantic heave and, heavy man that he was, tossed him half-stunned out of the bed. He struck his head against the table. The naked Sue rolled across and rose upright on the other side of the bed. She reached beneath it, grasped the edge, and with a superhuman effort heaved it upright and pushed. The bed struck a cursing groggy Voot as he was scrambling up. Back he went, clean through the window, out on to the veranda. He hung by his knees to the sill and again his head struck wood.

Sue made a dive for the kitchen, pulling up her panties on the way, which involved one stop to insert a leg. In the kitchen she dragged on her frock. Escape from the cottage was her only thought, but she heard Voot stumbling along the veranda. There was a bolt on the kitchen door and hurling herself across the room she rammed it home. Voot tried it and then put the boot in. A lower panel splintered. He charged it several times with his massive shoulder and the door collapsed inwards, hinges, bolt and all.

Sue thought of the tomahawk Sam kept by the fireplace to chop kindling wood. She swooped on it.

'Come near me,' she screamed, 'And I'll split your skull. Get on home and I won't tell the Marshal.'

Voot, dizzy and inflamed with fury and passion, advanced upon her. His lips curled over the words, 'You bitch.'

He seized the slender wrist as she swiped and the little axe went flying. She brought her knee up hard into his genitals and wrenched herself loose as he doubled up. Now she moved around the table keeping it between herself and the enraged Voot. Suddenly she pushed the table against him and he fell back with a jar into the fireplace. Sue groping around, espied the tomahawk again and, seizing it, brandished it.

'If you're not dead, you'll end up behind bars for this night's work,' she yelled. 'Sam, Sam! Bring Lord Muck too.'

From the road came the sounds of song.

> Vi-ve la, Vi-ve la, Vi-ve l'a-mour
> Vi-ve la, Vi-ve la, Vi-ve l'a-mour
> Vive l'amour, Vi-ve l'a-mour
> Vi-ve la com-pa-gnie.

Voot stumbled out the doorway, only for one leg to vanish through the rotten old veranda flooring again. Using atrocious language, he extricated himself. 'The place is as rotten as you are,' he frothed. He wrapped his arms around a post as rotten as the board which had given way beneath him on one side of the steps and wrenched it loose. Then he wrenched at the post on the other side. The roof sagged down. The chimney, previously cracked in an earthquake, collapsed. A shower of bricks cascaded on to the ancient iron of the lean-to roof. He blundered down the path.

Sue, imprisoned in the kitchen, looked round desperately. Her only escape was through the back window. It refused to push up. Grabbing up the axe again, she smashed out the glass and scrambled through, cutting her leg and ending up in a tangle of shrubs.

## Chapter Eight

As soon as Henderson's siren was heard, the battered Ford V8 with its louts and their girl friends, one of whom was strumming a ukulele, slowed up and the yahing and yeah-manning ceased. Past the statue and half-a-mile along the beach road the traffic officer passed them and both cars pulled in at the side of the road. Henderson came back to them.

'You shoving this bomb along, aren't you?' he said through the open window to the youth at the wheel. 'What's all the hurry? Another car coming along when you came around that bend and there would have been a good prang.'

'Sorry Sir,' said the driver. 'Must have been going a bit faster'n I thought. The light's gone out on the dash. The old man just loaned me the car.'

'Who's your father?'

'Hurley, the shoe repairer.'

'Well he's got a straight out exhaust. That's not allowed. Come around and listen to it.' Henderson could smell beer and he wanted to see the driver walk. When they crouched down by the bubbling exhaust pipe it began to sizzle.

'Tell your mates not to pour out beer through the floor-boards. Let's see your driving licence and Warrant of Fitness.'

These were duly produced.

'Well, I'll let you off with a warning this time,' said Henderson when they had gone around the front. He scribbled out a ticket by the light of the headlamps. 'But go easy on that gas pedal.'

The only person Henderson had to slow down for when he reached the 'Strip' was the Marshal, who, disappointed as usual, was jaywalking from the bank to the roadster. The traffic officer pulled up at the kerb outside a brightly lit but deserted cafeteria. Even the juke box was silent. There were voices, but they were from a television set. Soon, when the 'Brian Boru' and the cinema closed there would be customers aplenty. Then Henderson planned to enter and, over a cup of tea, ineffectively fend off Maori girls trying to grab his peaked cap. Usually a particularly pretty girl called Veronica someone or other was the successful one to wear it, survey herself in the mirror, and pretend to take the other skylarking girls' names.

The open Chrysler drew up alongside. 'You on patrol all night?' the Marshal asked gruffly.

'Like to keep an eye on that late pub traffic,' explained Henderson. 'I'll pick one of them up one night.'

The Chrysler drove off. 'What a cushy job,' muttered the Marshal. 'Pick up some Maori sheila more likely.'

Sure enough Veronica turned up at the cafeteria and grabbed his cap. This night he pursued her and holding her with one arm around her warm breasts retrieved it.

'Let's go for a ride in that swanky car,' she whispered over her shoulder.

'O.K.' said Henderson. 'But you go first. I'll get a couple of pies.'

When they turned off at the statue and down the hill the girl asked, 'What's wrong with the beach?'

'No place to be seen this hour of night. 'Sides I got reason to think there's a party down there now. No, if we head behind the station somewhere people'll think I'm keeping an eye on railway passengers. The railcar's due now. Hey! What's that truck doing in the middle of the bridge?'

The twin lights of a big, stationary truck glared at them. Men pranced right and left as he braked behind it.

## Chapter Nine

Sue actually reached the street first. Jack Voot had missed his footing on the dug-out dirt steps and fallen some distance until the path swerved to the gate where he somersaulted into the undergrowth beneath a poroporo and a karaka tree. He was just foundering out when Sue hopped past. The gate was open.

> Let ev-'ry good fel-low now join in a song.
> Vi-ve la com-pa-gnie.
> A friend on the left and a friend on the right.
> Vi-ve la …

'Basil!' Sue screamed. 'You others. Jack Voot's gone mad. He tried to rape me. He's wrecked …'

Voot seized her around the throat and bent her backwards in a stranglehold. Spindle-shanked McGhee was the first to grasp the situation. He ran forward and then stood still behind Voot. With coolness and calculation he smashed his flagon over Voot's head. Sue slumped to the ground. When Voot turned and charged McGhee he stopped the jagged broken flagon in his face, but McGhee still ended up in the hedge, doubled over, with a bleeding Voot pummelling the spark-plug cap. Beaumont-Foster grabbed him around the neck with a crooked right arm to prise him loose. Entwistle put down his flagon and headed up the hill yelling for Sam.

When they arrived back the situation was reversed with the Remittance Man on the footpath, Voot on top and McGhee on Voot's back. McGhee was rabbit-punching the nape of Voot's neck. Voot arose and hurled McGhee into the gutter. Entwistle rushed Voot only to join McGhee in the gutter. Voot was tottering.

'Get the Marshal,' croaked Sue, still on the ground. 'He tried to rape me. He's wrecked the cottage.'

Entwistle's flagon was at Sam's feet. He picked it up. It was like a dream. In day-dreams he had tangled successfully with Voot, but these had never deluded him into thinking of victory over the powerful man without resorting to vicious tactics. Sam smashed the base of the flagon on the tray of the truck, letting the beer gush down at his feet. It was as if he had done all this before. Voot kicked McGhee back into the gutter and jumped over it. He advanced on Sam. Sam stabbed the flagon into Voot's face. The jagged glass blinded Voot who fell to his knees, hands to eyes. Sam brought the toe of a boot viciously into Voot's Adam's apple. Voot regained his feet only to fall forward. He lay still. The men and Sue gathered around him.

'He's dead,' said Sam.

McGhee, whose spark-plug cap was apparently glued to his head, crouched over the inert figure and took his pulse. Voot wriggled once and then uttered a strange gurgling sound. After a while McGhee said, 'I'm not saying he is and I'm not saying he ain't but he could be. Hoh yes.'

'Turn him over,' said Beaumont-Foster. All of them, with the exception of Sue, who stood wringing her hands, turned the heavy figure on its back. There was no doubt about it.'

'He has shuffled off this mortal coil,' said the Remittance Man, breathing heavily.

'Get the police,' sobbed Sue. 'He tried to rape me. He was mad drunk. He might've killed me. He's wrecked the cottage. Who's going to pay for that?'

'It's all we can do,' said Sam. 'Come on. Let's get the Marshal.'

McGhee stopped him. Insignificant as he looked he suddenly exuded authority. 'It's no good. Four to one and we've used every dirty trick in the book. If the police believe us we've got the other Voots to think of. You know that bad bunch. We've got to keep out of this. Give me a hand to get him behind the wheel.'

'But ...' began Entwistle.

'The tide's in,' said McGhee. 'That river's deep. Everyone in town knows he's grogged to the eyeballs. There's no ramp at the end of the path. He'll go straight into the river. Let's stick some broken flagons in the cab. I'll start the motor and turn on the lights. We'll have to shift while we've got the hill to ourselves. One shove and it'll start rolling over that gap. She'll go. It's steep there.'

When they had bundled the cut and bleeding Voot behind the wheel, McGhee started the motor and turned on the lights. He threw in a broken flagon.

'She's in neutral,' said McGhee. 'But he could have just been coasting down the hill. Let's get shoving.'

One good push from the four men and the truck picked up speed downhill. Only one thing went wrong — but it was a disaster. The wheels were not facing straight ahead and the truck veered off, missing the gap and ending up half-way along the bridge.

'Now we're stuffed,' cried Entwistle. 'I knew it was a mad idea.'

'I'll fix it,' gritted McGhee. 'I'll drive the bitch of a thing back and this time there'll be no mistakes.'

They pounded towards the bridge.

'Haul him over,' panted McGhee. 'I'll have to get behind that wheel.'

But behind them a black car with a winking red dome-light drew up and lit them up. Henderson sprang out.

If it had been anyone else, thought Sam. One of our mates. But now we're done. And Sue, in the gateway, was sick with the same feeling.

## Chapter Ten

They had all forgotten Miriam Breen standing in close to the eliagnus hedge. She had seen everything and heard everything. There was a street lamp nearly at Sam's gate. The next was at the turn-off on the bridge which the truck had been planned not to negotiate.

'Murder,' she said to herself. 'And I said nothing ever happened in this poke-in-the-arse dump. Tried to rape her, ha ha! Tripped him up and beat him to the floor more like it.'

When the truck veered on to the bridge, she thought exultingly; 'They've had it now. They've had it. One person down the hill and they're gonners.'

She saw the men pelting after the truck. She thought, 'There's nothing they can do. The traffic'll start any minute. And, by God! here's someone now. And of all things it's that traffic cop fellow.'

She crouched back further in the hedge as Sue did in her gateway.

'Now, what's going on?' rapped Henderson.

'We're comin' back from the pub,' said McGhee. 'Gunna have supper at Sam's here. Well, y'know the footpath is all roots and things and we're walking at the side of the road. This guy in the truck nearly mowed us down. He was all over the place. When he stopped on the bridge we come up to him. It's Jack Voot, real shickered. Looks like he's out the monk.'

'Christ,' said Henderson, shining a torch beam on Voot slumped over the wheel. 'He's a case all right. Where does this fellow live?'

'Well now. That's got me beat,' said McGhee. 'Other side of town. Out of his mind, I guess. 'Less he's got some mate over the bridge he was gunna see.'

'Well, we've got to get him up to the station. I'll get a doctor. Told me he was dead I'd believe you.'

'Just passed out under the influence of alcohol,' said the Remittance Man.

'And who are you?'

'Beaumont-Foster. Basil Beaumont-Foster. Like McGhee and Entwistle here my address is the Freezing Works.'

'And you?' said Henderson turning on Sam, whose knees were trembling.

'Sam Jamieson. I live on the hill there.'

He couldn't see any way out of it. They had murdered Voot and as soon as the police had seen his gashed face and pronounced him dead their goose was cooked. No use shouting rape now, thanks to McGhee. They had burnt their boats.

'Well,' said Henderson. 'Let's get him to my car.'

From the distance drifted the sigh of the wind-horn on the diesel railcar bound for Kurikino and all points south.

'Tell you what,' said McGhee. 'I'll go across the bridge in the truck, turn around, and drive him to the cop-shop. I drove a heavy duty for the Works one season.'

Henderson didn't really want to advertise Veronica. 'Right,' he rapped. 'I'll back up, turn around, and you follow me.'

McGhee opened the door of the truck and with a foot shoved Voot across the seat. He sprang behind the wheel. Next thing the truck was under way.

Again sounded the sigh of the diesel. Bells began to clang and red lights to flash at the other end of the bridge.

'Hope the fool brakes,' said Henderson. He made his way back to his own car. 'Listen,' he told Veronica. 'As soon as we hit town, do the disappearing trick.'

The truck rolled to a standstill sure enough but, to those watching, the cab seemed to be on the railway line. The wind-horn sounded again and then the Westinghouse brakes screamed. A figure plunged out of the truck on the driver's side. There was an almighty crash and the truck spun around side on. Sam, Beaumont-Foster and Entwistle began to run. Henderson drove after them. 'The idiot!' he shouted. The freezing workers leapt on to the narrow footpath as he passed them.

What was left of the engine and cab was in splinter.

'What the devil happened?' cried Henderson.

'He came to and grabbed muh arm,' mumbled McGhee. 'I was pulling up but muh foot slipped off the brake. I just got clear.'

'Christ,' said Henderson. 'What a mess!'

They scrambled over the tray of the truck. A railwayman in a peaked cap like Henderson's and McGhee's came up to them. The railcar was pulled up panting half-way between the bridge and the station.

'Anyone hurt?' said McGhee.

'Not so far as we can tell. A few suitcases on the rack fell on people's heads, that's all. But the truck driver! They'll pack him into a match box.'

Sam felt sick, but it dawned on him they were in the clear.

'You trying to tell me that man came to?' demanded Henderson.

'Yes. And grabbed muh arm. I'm lucky to be here.'

Sam stared at the inscrutable McGhee. Henderson and the railwayman began to walk along the line. Now cars were mounting up behind the wrecked truck which blocked the bridge. People were calling out.

'What the hell?'

'What's going on around here?'

Sam tried to roll a cigarette, but his fingers were shaking too much.

'Have a tailor-made old boy,' said Beaumont-Foster. 'After all, it's moments like these you need minties. Have one too, Spud. Ill as it behoves me I can hardly credit Voot's miraculous revival. If my suspicions are correct I feel you deserve one.'

'Ain't saying they ain't, ain't saying they are,' said McGhee.

'Let's get back to the cottage,' said Sam. 'If anyone ever needed a drink it's me.'

He was the last to cross the tray of the truck. As he scrambled down the other side, blinded by the lights of the patrol car, people gathered around besieging him with questions.

'Voot hit the railcar,' mumbled Sam, and followed his friends.

A figure scrambled after him.

'Not so fast, Sammy boy,' said Miriam Breen.

## Chapter Eleven

There was a stream of cars across the bridge by now. To complicate matters a towing van from Kurikino Motors, presumably rung from the station, arrived but was unable to proceed. A tortuous backing off process of all the cars, led by the salvage vehicle began with much shouting of directions and scurrying of people back to their vehicles. Henderson reappeared and began to walk along the cortege.

'Look, Miriam,' said Sam. 'There's been enough fun and games tonight. I'm all toshed out. My one idea is to get home and suck down a home-brew.'

'Well now, is that so? Now what say my idea is to tell the police that people don't kick the bucket twice in the one night?'

'What're you talkin' about?' Sam queried uneasily.

'You got a fair idea what I'm talking about. I saw that fight, smashing flagons over Voot's head and putting the boot in. I heard every word you said. Tried to shove the truck in the river, didn't you? I didn't think Spud McGhee had the guts to plant the truck over the line, but he did it to save your bacon. You're all gone a million.'

She leaned back against the parapet of the bridge.

'You must be crazy,' said Sam.

'Oh, Sam.' Miriam said in a disgusted way. 'Weren't we together when Entwistle yelled out for you? What do you think I did when you took off? Just stood there? I followed you down, that's what, and I heard and saw the works. Voot was dead as a doornail.'

Sam looked cautiously around. 'Look, Miriam, the man attacked us. You saw him in the pub and knew what a skinful he had. According to Sue he tried to rape her.'

'Rape her my backside,' said Miriam crudely. 'You just came home a bit early for them, that's all. What would Voot be there for if he didn't know he was welcome? But Sam has to leave early with his drunken mates this one night. For all you know they've been putting it across you all along. Never saw a dago yet you could trust.'

'You're all to hell. The girl was upset and I better get back to her.'

'She's going to be a damn sight more upset when you and McGhee and Co. go to jail for a long time. Where will she be when you come out? A grey-haired old tarpot back on the mat. You killed that man and then tried to cover up. McGhee could've wrecked that railcar. They'll throw the book at him. And all of you. This is murder. The old Marshal'll run around in circles. Murder in this poke-in-the-arse burg. And little me can prove it. I'm a key witness.'

'Oh Miriam!' cried Sam. 'You wouldn't do that to me, would you?'

'Who says I wouldn't?' Her eyes gleamed. 'Voot was a fine man. Now he's double-dead. Nothing'll please me more than to see that Sue gets what's coming to her.'

'You better think again,' said Sam. 'There's four of us to say it happened the way we told the traffic cop.'

'And who do you think they're going to believe?' scoffed Miriam. 'They know he lives off the main street. They know I live on Eastwind Quay and would be heading this way. There's stacks of people at the "Brian Boru" that know I followed you out. Detectives will find traces of that scrap where you smashed bottles and everything. I'll bet there's blood there. And what if you did fluke your way out of it? I tell Jack and he tells the Voots. They'll kick you to death around some dark corner. You know what they did to Brian Crombie and he'd make two of any of you. Kicked his head in. You've got it coming all ways.'

Sam remembered seeing for the first time the sinister old storey-and-a-half house with its blank staring dormer windows looking over the cul-de-sac. Old Manson Voot and his sons lived there. No man crossed their path.

'I'm going to report to the traffic cop,' said Miriam. 'Right now.'

'Miriam,' pleaded Sam. 'Think. Where is this gunna get you? Just trouble for everybody.'

'Well,' said Miriam. 'I'll tell you what would get me somewhere. That twenty quid your black missus robbed me of. And I think the same from McGhee and the others. It's payday tomorrow and you all pass it over and go without your grog for a change.'

'McGhee's got nothing,' cried Sam.

'Well, he can raise it from old Mr Fixit. Anyway he must have something to see him through the slack season. I've never seen him short of a dollar. It's forty bucks each or I'll speak out. I'll say I didn't hear about the crash till afterwards, but I saw you blokes do him in. You meet me right here tomorrow night or up I go to Cop Larkman. He'll jump for joy. And as for that Beaumont-Foster with his royalties from that bogus carburettor, his money had better be there too. And Entwistle told Jack he makes big money on that slipe master. Just you tell your mates. It's fork up or else I'll go right ahead and tell the police McGhee was driving a dead man.'

'Miriam,' said Sam imploringly, 'we've got to live through this winter. I have to take a job where I can get it.'

'Right here on the bridge tomorrow night. Say eight o'clock,' said Miriam inexorably. 'Now I'll crawl into my hole with Jack snoring his drunken head off. Don't forget: eight o'clock.' She was gone.

Sam leaned against the parapet, his back to the salvage van, the wrecked truck, the station, the sprawling empire of the Freezing Works, and stared up river towards the viaduct at Bad Dog Bend where the Wainongoro joined the Kurikino, the *Wainongoro*, the Snoring Water. Here the pa had been built. Further out, Sam had been born in a cottage now tumbledown with the windows shuttered up and full of hay bales. Out there in the back country the wind sighed in the electric power wires and the roads were long and narrow and grey. Out there grew the lonesome pine.

Out there — how Sam longed to be back on the land! His father had died of pneumonia contracted when he had been drenched tending a bloat-stricken herd. His mother had sold the farmlet. For a while they had lived at Mrs Richardson's boarding-house on Eastwind Quay past where the Breens lived, until she too had passed away. His beloved mother! She had taken him so proudly to his dancing lessons in Harrowville. Her eyes were in the street lamps of the town on the hill, reflected in the water below. Sometimes in his more wretched moments he thought she looked down upon him from the clouds in the sky.

He always shut his ears to the baaing of the lambs in their pens. Heavy hearted, he had struggled on, turning more and more to booze. Then his grandmother had died. Sue with her dusky heart-shaped face with its islands of freckles had made him a new life. And now Miriam held him in the hollow of her hand.

He realised that forty dollars was cheap, but he knew enough about blackmail to know it would go on. True, her grip would weaken with every day she failed to approach authority, but a word to Jack meant trouble with the Voots. And that was nearly as bad.

Sick at heart he set off back to the cottage. The sight that greeted him when he had wearily ascended the steps stupefied him. Sue stood biting her nails and staring at the roof that was sagging nearly to the level of the veranda.

'My God!' he exclaimed. 'What happened? An earthquake?'

'The place is wrecked,' Sue gabbled. She grabbed Sam's arm. 'And I'd be raped if I hadn't clouted him with a bottle of the brew. The chimney's down. Andy told us a wind could blow it over but we kept on putting off fixing it. Voot kicked in the door and the windows are smashed. I tell you the place is wrecked. The boys are inside trying to jack up the roof. They had to go round the back to get in.'

Hands appeared beneath the iron. A voice shouted, 'Give us a lift, will yuh?'

They all heaved and the roof rose. McGhee shoved the kitchen table on its end under it.

'That'll hold it,' he grunted. 'Well, it should.'

They lowered the rusty iron on the top of the up-ended table. Sue and Sam ducked in and, being careful not to fall through the broken flooring, they all entered the doorless, windowless, tableless, kitchen. Sue subsided in a chair and began to cry. Her hair was over her face, her frock torn and her leg bleeding. She massaged her throat.

'He nearly did me in,' she babbled.

'Well, we can't tell no one,' said McGhee. 'He nearly mowed us down coming down the hill. Then he flaked on the bridge. We went up to him. The rest Henderson knows. He came to and grabbed my arm. All you have to remember is he was all over the road coming down the hill. Y'know, Sam, I don't think it's worth the money to try and fix this place up. Winter's coming and you can't live here. But you can try and sell the section.'

'Don't cry, darling,' said Sam soothingly. 'That awful business is cleared up. We'll rent a place somewhere.' In his heart a voice muttered, 'What with?' He knew he couldn't tell her about Miriam Breen. Sue was at breaking point now.

Having smoothed Sue's hair back and kissed her, he went to the cupboard and brought out some bottles of home-brew. He filled five glasses, but Sue just turned her head away when he offered her one. Sam drank it. Then his own.

'What a night!' he said.

'You can say that again,' said Entwistle. 'But our worries are over. I still think you did that, McGhee. I reckon there's method in your madness. Cheers.'

He picked up a glass from the floor. So did McGhee and the Remittance Man. Sam refilled his. Entwistle drank and pulled a face.

'Say what you like, it gives you a rosy glow. I reckon it's twenty per cent,' Sam said.

'Listen,' whispered Entwistle. 'Is that rain?'

Drips of water began to fall into the room.

'Looks like that chimney's buggered the roof,' said Sam. 'That's the finish. Always did have some leaks in the bedroom. Now we're swamped out in here.'

Entwistle stood up. 'I'm hitting the track. Got no coat. There's nothing we can talk about.'

'Just adhere to our story,' said Beaumont-Foster. 'Or rather McGhee's brilliant story.'

Entwistle shrugged. 'Well, Sam, sorry you're in this mess, but there's nothing we can do tonight. One thing, we haven't got "you know what" hanging over us. As Basil said, just stick to our yarn. If they want to know who was walking next to who we just can't remember.'

Sam knew he could have followed them out and disrupted their complacency, but he had just sunk into a chair. Drips were falling faster now.

Tomorrow would have to do.

## Chapter Twelve

Sam and Sue were used to three leaks in the bedroom, but had the bed strategically placed. They tipped it back in the same spot. A leg snapped off.

'What next?' groaned Sam. He propped a corner of the bed frame on a chair. The bed was a little uneven but at least you could stretch out on it.

There was no lower pane left in the double-hung window, but there was no wind, only steady rain which grew heavier through the night. The smell of the river and the cooked offal smell which lingered over the town when the pressure was lifted off the congestors was strong in the room.

Sam sat on the side of the bed with a bottle of brew. He had often proved it was a good anaesthetic. He also took a mogadon tablet to calm his nerves and two sodium seconal capsules for sleep. Sue rambled on for a while about Voot being just an animal and Spud being a cunning devil and then she fell asleep. Sam had schooled her carefully to know nothing about it. He tried to shut the thought of Miriam Breen out of his head. In the end the tablets and capsules washed down with the strong beer brought to him a feeling of bliss. The boys would think up something. Sam was glad he had gone to the doctor about his shakes and jumps, and his phobia that always working at a temperature below zero would thicken his blood and he would drop dead like Brendon O'Keefe and Jim Harris.

'No "Jim Harris" tonight,' he thought as he stubbed out his cigarette. It was a private joke between Sue and him. Jim Harris had once said, 'Now what's the first thing a man does after a naughty? Reach for a smoke.' After love-making Sue and Sam always smoked a 'Jim Harris'. But Jim Harris had smoked his last cigarette. He had hit the deck working right alongside Sam.

Sam had developed a nasty habit of suddenly stamping his foot and twitching his head: it was for all the world as if he were going to have a stroke. Or for that matter drop dead. Nobody who suddenly passed out had time to tell people what it felt like. Sam had found out the only cure was eight or nine glasses of beer with a double-headed whisky jammed in, to feel at ease and not care. He found it impossible to even eat a sandwich at 'Smoko' without jerking his head and stamping his feet. He began to take two bottles of his home-made beer to work in his lunch bag, an old school bag. The necks protruded at each end and had earned him the nickname of 'The Guns of Navarone'. He drank the beer furtively out of a cup. He had next reached the stage of hiding pint bottles of overproof commercial beer in the cistern of one of the lavatories. Finally, he had gone to Doctor Maddison, but the various tranquillisers they had tried had not taken the place of alcohol — which was not, as the doctor pointed out, 'on Social Security'. In fact, the doctor had hinted that he should cut alcohol right out; Sam had argued that the nerves had come first and that without a drink he had little fun in his life. He had to have relief from his frightening attacks of nerves. The doctor had raised his hands against Sam's protests.

'Try it out, there *is* more in life. You are an unfortunate that booze has got the better of. The cause is the cure, and the cure is the cause. It's a vicious circle.'

Mogadon and anatensol three times a day had done much to calm him, but real peace came to him with his sleeping draught. Along with his seconal he took rauwiloid for blood pressure. 'Just nervous hypertension,' the doctor told him. 'You'll have to get rid of this silly idea something's wrong with you.' Sam wanted to know what caused him to have blood pressure.

'Just part of your make-up, I suppose.'

Sam had often wondered why the army had rejected him. He wondered now if this was the third reason. He knew about his flat feet and his albumen of the kidneys which Doctor Maddison found he still had.

'Flush out your kidneys more. Drink more water.'

Sam realised he had just had a joke handed to him on a plate. By leaving out the 'water' he could say to his cronies in the 'Brian Boru', 'Now *I'm* here on doctor's orders. Not like you alkies. I often wonder what that thing was that got me booted out of the army.' With Sam it was always 'booted out' not 'turned down'. 'Probably something the only known cure for is going out rooty-tooting every night.'

Sam joined Sue in slumberland.

## Chapter Thirteen

Jack Breen, an overcoat over his underclothes, was sitting at the table in the kitchen with a flagon of New Zealand wine in front of him. Fortified to thirty-nine percent, it was the cheapest alcoholic drink procurable.

When Miriam entered she got herself a glass and poured a drink.

'What's the celebration about?' asked Breen. He had dissipation written all over his face and his eyes looked sleepy though he appeared to be sober. 'What the devil was that crash? It woke me up.'

'One of Voot's trucks hit the railcar. Jack Voot was killed.'

'He was what?' said Breen. 'He wouldn't do a crazy thing like that. Anyway what was he doing at this end of town as late as this?'

'Spud McGhee was driving,' Miriam told him.

'Spud McGhee,' cried Breen. 'What was wrong with Jack? Boozed I suppose. But I've never seen Jack when he couldn't handle a truck.'

'There's more to it than meets the eye,' said Miriam. 'I don't know the full strength of it but I do know something — Jack wasn't killed in the smash-up. Jamieson and his gang smashed flagons on him and kicked him and they killed him. Then they stuck him in the truck. He was supposed to end up in the river, but the truck went on to the bridge. That's when McGhee took over. I don't know what he was going to do exactly but that traffic cop fellow, Henderson, came along. No doubt about it, McGhee deliberately let the railcar hit them. He stopped on the line and then jumped out.'

'Is this fair dinkum?' said Breen, completely amazed.

'Fair dinkum. But you mustn't tell anyone. I've hung it on Sam Jamieson for forty dollars tomorrow night. And forty each from the others. That's a hundred and sixty dollars. Eighty quid in real money. And they should be good for more for me to keep my mouth shut.'

'I can't believe it,' said Breen. 'What was the fight over?'

'Sam's bitch of a wife reckons Jack raped her. Isn't that a laugh? They must have just had a row or something to make her come out yelling she'd been raped. Voot must have been on with her on the quiet.'

Breen shook his head as if the whole affair was too much for him. He poured out a fresh drink. Miriam drank her own, poured another, and then went and got a plain biscuit out of a tin in the cupboard.

'Well, I'll go to hell,' Jack said. They sat in silence for some time and then he said, 'It should be worth more than a mouldy eighty quid for us to shut our traps.'

'The trouble is they just haven't got it. If I don't tell the police, say tomorrow, they're going to believe them, not me.'

After Breen had mused for a few more moments, he said, 'Tell me everything about it.'

She told him in detail, but omitting the kiss with Sam on the hill.

'The Voots would kill them if they knew about this,' Breen shook his head. 'We'll get more money out of them all right even if it is too late to tell the cops. You can tell Jamieson and Co. if they don't fork up some more you're going to tell the Voots. Everybody knows they're a nasty crowd. I don't know anybody that isn't scared of them.'

When they had drunk some more sherry they decided to go to bed. The bed looked like a battlefield of blankets and sheets.

'I've got an idea,' Jack said suddenly. He had thrown his overcoat over a chair and was just in his underclothes. Miriam was straightening out the bedclothes.

'What?'

'Sam's section. That's a big chunk of land. There must be three building sites on it. We could raise a loan. We could collect rent instead of paying every week for this old dump. We could live in one of the houses.'

Miriam stared at him. 'But people will smell a rat. He wouldn't just give it to you.'

'The cottage isn't worth a damn. The section's overgrown to blazes. I could get the Voot's front-end loader buckshee and clean the whole place up.'

It was such an exciting idea they went back to the kitchen to talk it over. Breen put on his overcoat again and his worn-out slippers.

'He'll have to put up with it,' he said. 'We can just tell people we're paying him off. They'd give him ten years at least if they find out about tonight. I'll be with you tomorrow night and give him the story. I don't know who handles his affairs, but it's almost bound to be Tomblinson. That other firm have only been here about eighteen months. Jamieson can sign it over to me and just say it's a private transaction. You and your eighty quid! Just chicken feed. This is real money.'

'You really think he'll come across,' Miriam worried. 'After all it's only my one word against their four.'

'We can make it two. Say I came to meet you tonight and we both saw this scrap. I tell you, we've got him over a barrel.'

'Gee, but I hope you're right. And we can still get a quid or two off the others. Jack, we might be on the way up at last.'

'Well, I can't see how he can slide out of it as long as we get it over and done with quick. We'll meet him on the bridge tomorrow night and the next day it'll be all over. Bound to be a bit of red tape but it's simple and straight forward enough. Jamieson has come to a private agreement with me to hand over the property. That's all there is to it.'

Over sherry and biscuits they discussed it from all angles.

## Chapter Fourteen

It was the most melancholy awakening of Sam's life, which is saying something. Water had flowed under the door leading to the kitchen and the bedroom floor was awash. He put his socks and boots on in bed. Fortunately he had slept in his underclothes and he managed to haul on two pairs of trousers, his own and the thick pair issued by the company to freezing workers, before standing in half an inch of water and donning shirt, jersey and jacket.

The ruined kitchen swimming in water was a depressing sight. Sam drank a bottle of beer.

'No breakfast,' he told Sue. 'And no sandwiches for "smoko".'

He took his tranquillisers. He knew he had some beer in his locker.

'I'll go to the canteen for a bite. Probably have a meal there dinnertime too. Don't get too downhearted. We'll find a way out of this, somehow.'

'Jesus,' said Sue. 'Sammy, we'll have to go to Bad Dog Bend Pa or rent a room or something.'

'Not going back to no mat,' said Sam determinedly. 'It's what they're all waiting for. You better see what's around the town to rent.'

'Pay rent? It's tough enough in the slack season as it is.'

'Murdoch as good as said I could be a brushhand for him. You have a gander around.'

It was still raining steadily. Macintosh-clad, Sam crossed the bridge with a leaden heart.

Beaumont-Foster reading from a list on the wall broke the news.

'Well, the season terminates for us today. Only the foreman, Jeromson and a couple of oldies left.'

'Come along with me, Basil, I've got something to tell you you're not going to like.' In a corner he told him about Miriam Breen.

'We're in the cart, man,' he concluded.

'You can say that again,' said the Remittance Man. 'This can mean a stretch unless we fork up. There actually is a Beaumont-Foster carburettor y'know, but between you and me no one in their right mind would buy one. I think my pater in England has the only known one in existence. It takes a thankful of gas to go round the block. Well forty dollars won't kill us. Jail would.'

'Yes, but will it stop at that?'

'The longer we can stall her off the bettah. Holey smoke! What a worry?'

Just before 'smoko', the sergeant, a ball of importance, found Sam's gang stacking cartons of veal fillets. When they knocked off work a statement would be required from all of them.

'I'll come up about half-past three,' said Sam. 'Damned if I'm working after I get my pay cheque. I'll say you have to see me.'

'I also,' said Beaumont-Foster, 'will leave in Sam's company.'

'Bring McGhee and Entwistle,' said the sergeant.

When he had gone, Sam said, 'Not promoted to permanents again. That means no holiday pay. And there's been no overtime. It's jobs for us this winter, my boy.'

'Grim thought as it is,' nodded the Remittance man, 'the fact will have to be faced. I have some prospect, hazy as it is, of temporary employment with the Railway Department.'

'And I gotta chance of being a brush hand,' said Sam. 'I've done some painting you know.'

'If I can't land this job,' said Beaumont-Foster, 'I will, to employ a colloquialism, "shoot through" — that is if the Breen creature leaves us the price of a fare — to some address unknown. Think as I do, I can see no option but to pay and smile. With my hut money deducted I can't foresee much indulgence in the convivial pint.'

'And I'm going to end up paying rent,' growled Sam.

After 'smoko' Sam ran the risk of slipping away from the gang. Using the age-old excuse of appearing to be on some mission, he strode briskly, a quarter-filled sack of skids and gambols over his shoulder, along the siding, stepping over the bright blotches of blood with the hovering blow-flies outside the 'glory hole'. Over the fellmongery doors someone had scrawled, SO YOU WERE IN BELSEN, HUH? Higher up was inscribed: I PISS ON TORIES.

He had expected to find Entwistle standing at the bend of one of the slipe masters, the machines which had replaced the outcast but fabulously paid gang of men whose job had been to save the precious strands of wool after maggots had devoured the adhering meat. (There had been a separate row of seats provided for them at the cinema because of the smell these patrons exuded.) All sorts of stories had been told about these men. One was that they were so hardened to the filth and stench they had even placed bets on maggots racing. But now their place of employment was deserted and the concrete troughs were used for the soaking of bobby-calf skins.

Entwistle had a reasonably cushy job. He was obliged to watch the steam-gauge of his slipe master, put up with the roar of the machinery, and sort out and grade the wool which fell on his bench. This wool was thrown into baskets. Chunks of wool-denuded meat were tossed into a barrow and, at intervals wheeled to the 'glory hole'. Entwistle had also become hardened, to some extent, and if a sheep or lamb's head was expelled from the machine he rescued it and, with the help of a butcher friend, saved the brains which were a delicacy.

What puzzled Sam was that there was no sign of anyone at all. No one around the washers; no one at the paint table; no one on the 'bull-wagons' which transported the treated skins to the wool-pullers. The absence of these latter men Sam was prepared for, because they invariably knocked off early. It was obvious that men were still on the job from the carts loaded with skins that had to be hauled to the 'thrower on' at one end of the paint table. The trimmers who lined the table, even the foreman who supervised the spraying of the skins, were gone.

That 'smoko' was over Sam knew full well, so he could see no future in trudging up the stairs to where the men had their refreshment.

Then men began to flock in from the stock-yards. Among them was a pale-face Entwistle.

'What's going on, Tinny?' Sam asked.

'Oh hell!' said Entwistle. 'I just feel sick in the guts. The mentality of some people has got me licked. And to think these are the guys I have to work with! Some prize prick found a small hole in the wall through which you could see the lambs going along the line getting their throats cut. I wouldn't have gone out and stood in the queue if I'd had an inkling of what it was all about. You'd think it was a Punch and Judy show or something the way the whole bunch lined up. The foreman's just rounding them up now. I wish to Christ I'd worked in an office, anything. I ask you what pleasure can it give people to peek through a hole in the wall and watch lambs getting their throats slit? No, Sammy, you haven't got a bottle on you, have you? God, I feel like a bracer. I like to get my feet under the table just like anyone else, I guess, but these bastards are like guys sitting around a death chamber, giggling and eating pies.'

A man wandered up on his way back to his job and said, 'Get a good look-see, Tinny? Boy, that was the best view I've ever had. To think I bin working here all these years and I didn't know there was that hole in the wall.'

'Better get cracking,' Entwistle said, looking at the floor in a disgusted way, 'Johnny's back on the job.'

Sure enough the foreman had scrambled back on the paint table. He had his own stationary platform. The table itself worked in much the same manner as a revolving staircase.

'But, did you see …?' The man began, but Entwistle interrupted him.

'Piss off. I saw my share. If I don't get back and watch my steam pressure I'll blow the whole works up and every man Jack here. Might be a good thing too.'

The foreman shouted out, 'Back to your jobs. You're only trying to stagger out the day so you can get on overtime. C'mon the lot of you. You'd think you'd never seen a sheep killed before.'

Sam and Entwistle wandered moodily back to the slipe masters.

'What brings you over, Sam?'

He was acquainted with the sorry news and duly dumbfounded. Sam also informed him he was required to make a statement to the police.

'Should be knocking off just after four. I'll come up. That bitch! Just when I thought we were in the clear. We'll have to see Spud.'

'In the dinner-hour,' said Sam. 'God! I hope he's in his hut and hasn't gone fishing.'

'He'll be there. That guy's slipping lately. Doesn't seem himself.'

Sam drank the bottle of beer in his locker, purchased a ham sandwich at the canteen for lunch and made his way, accompanied by Beaumont-Foster, to McGhee's hut. Number thirteen, he thought; sure is an unlucky number.

The rain had ceased. The door of the hut was half-open. McGhee and Doc Colclough were crouched over a chessboard. There were few pieces left on either side and it was obviously the end game.

'Come in,' said McGhee. 'Park on the bed. I've got this game sewn up.'

'That's what you think,' said Doc Colclough. 'I've got a shot or two to fire. Might mate you yet.'

Doc Colclough was in charge of the Red Cross Department at the Works. Once in private practice, he had suffered a nervous breakdown and prescribed hard manual work for himself. Gradually his qualifications had leaked out and he had been prevailed upon to undertake his present post.

He moved a white bishop.

McGhee moved his king.

After long consideration the doctor moved his rook.

McGhee promptly pushed a pawn into the doctor's home line. He took it off the board and replaced it with a black knight captured earlier.

'Checkmate.'

The doctor stared for a long time and then said, 'Well, I'll be damned! I was sure you would queen that pawn. A queen would have missed me. No, you've got me. That turning it into a knight really put me in a cleft stick. You must have been working for that the last six moves. When you covered that rank with the rook before, I should have seen it coming. You know, you're the last guy I would have thought, to look at, could play chess — and yet every game we have had you outwit me in some crafty way.'

'I like to figure things out,' McGhee said modestly.

# Chapter Fifteen

Sam and Beaumont-Foster told the foreman they were wanted to make a statement about the railcar accident and asked to get away after 'smoko'?

'Can't see why not,' said the foreman. 'You're paid right up to date so you better go out through the stockyards so Grimshaw won't see you.'

They were paid at afternoon 'smoko'. They promptly tore open their wage envelopes.

'For crying out loud!' said Sam. 'Only thirty-eight bucks. I'll have to add to it to pay my whack.'

The Remittance Man with more tax and his rent, had less. He groaned.

They went through the stock-yards and behind the canteen to McGhee's hut. The three of them then left for town in raincoats though only a drizzle persisted. Sam ducked up to the cottage and was glad to find Sue out. Explaining why he needed a few dollars out of the tin in the dressing-table drawer on payday would have been awkward.

They walked in silence although McGhee did say, 'They'll try and trap us I suppose. Just stick to our simple story. If they try anything funny like who was next to who we just can't remember.'

Half-way up the hill McGhee halted and asked if they minded waiting a minute. He seemed to be in pain. After a few minutes he said, 'Just heartburn. C'mon.'

For once they passed the 'Brian Boru'. They had decided to get it over and done with. At the police station they were seated in a side room. They glimpsed a stranger whom they took to be a detective from Harrowville, Constable Mellow and Henderson. McGhee was taken first into the sergeant's office. Here Constable Mellow two-fingered his statement on the typewriter.

Entwistle was ushered into the side room by the stranger. Then arrived two men who by their conversation were railroad men. One by one the statements were taken and then each was sent on his way. The four freezing workers, inevitably, met at the 'Brian Boru'.

'Feel like sitting down,' said McGhee. 'Let's grab that table in the corner before the place fills up.'

Equipped with jugs they took seats around a corner table. Softly they compared notes. Everything seemed in order.

Although he pushed his money across, McGhee was the only one who made no trip to the bar to have the jugs replenished. They all gathered the impression he was feeling out of sorts. He said little, seemed sunk in gloomy thoughts. He surprised them once by saying, 'Y'know I've done everything. I bin at the works thirty-five years. Just living alone in a hut. Couldn't find a sheila with a white walking stick and dark glasses. I know I'm a freak. I've killed cows and bulls, pigs and little lambs what never done me no harm. You might as well say I've lived on blood and death. It wouldn't stick in my gizzard none to finish this Breen bitch off.'

'Oh don't talk that way,' said Sam. 'She's asked for it sure enough but then there would be some questions asked. Forty dollars hits hard but with a bit of luck we're out of it.'

'Her story becomes less plausible with the passage of time,' put in the Remittance Man. 'I can see no way out of paying this first payment. Have we got it?'

They had.

Sam put one hundred and sixty dollars in his pocket. 'God, this hurts,' he said. 'I'll be after Murdoch about the job first thing tomorrow. Wonder if Sue found a flat or something.'

Entwistle went out and returned with fish and chips. At last it was a quarter to eight.

'Well, zero hour,' said Sam. 'What's the odds the slut walks back to join us?'

'Well,' said Beaumont-Foster, 'if she does, our best move is to play broke. Not that we're far off it. Entwistle's still kept on, but we three'll be living on the smell of an oily rag.'

'I got reason not to give a damn,' said McGhee. 'But you'll hear about that one day soon. On your way, Sam. We'll be waiting here.'

Sam finished his drink and left. There was a light in the cottage and he wondered just how miserable Sue was. At least she knew nothing of their plight, even if only for the time being. Sam knew he would have to account for his wages somehow. Sue would stand by him, he had no doubt. The thought of leaving her while he spent years behind bars horrified him. Entwistle and Beaumont-Foster had both spoken of 'shooting through' but Sam reflected this would get them nowhere. The law had a long arm.

Miriam was on the bridge sure enough — but so was Jack. He moved straight up close to Sam who could smell the sherry. Breen was already drunk.

'God help you if you hadn't turned up,' said Jack Breen malevolently. 'We were on our way to spill the beans. Got the dough?'

Wordlessly Sam handed it over.

'A hundred and sixty dollars.' Sam looked at Breen stuffing the notes in his pocket.

'We're all down to a few cents,' he said.

'So are we,' grumbled Breen. 'Shovellin' gravel all day for a crust. What do you think the Voots would think about this?'

'Hey,' said Sam. 'That's part of the deal. We pay up and you shut up.'

'For this chicken feed?' said Breen. 'Tomorrow you and me are going to town. We'll go to whoever handles your affairs and transfer that section of yours to me. We'll say it's a private deal. You'll have to rent a place. There's good money at the Works and you can afford it. Others do. That Sue of yours can do some housework for people like Miriam has to do and stop playing ladies. Now who does handle your business and your property?'

'Tomblinson,' mumbled Sam. 'Be he knows damn well I wouldn't give it away.'

'I told you it was a private deal. You can do what you like with your own land. For all he knows, you might owe me money or something. Anyway we'll just say we've come to a private arrangement. We'll meet in the boozer. Go over to Tomblinson and get that section signed over. Don't matter what he thinks. I could be paying you off or something. All he has to do is arrange the transfer. Don't get any bright ideas. Just face it. If Miriam and I see Larkman and tell him what really happened you're a gonner.'

'It's four words to one,' quavered Sam.

'Two,' grinned Breen. 'I walked up to meet the wife last night and we both saw what happened. It's a serious business if we let it out, and it means the Voots will know too.'

'I wouldn't be in your shoes, Sam,' said Miriam.

'Let's go to the pub,' said Breen. 'I'll ring Tomblinson tonight and make an appointment to get this legally signed over. I'll let you know what he says and we'll meet up at the pub just before.

They walked up the hill; Sam, following on the narrow footpath. He was ruined.

When they arrived at Sam's gate, he said, 'I'll duck across and get my last dollar.'

'Don't you bring that bitch Sue,' said Miriam. 'I'll scratch her eyes out. Tell her to get busy and find somewhere to live.'

Sue was in bed with a magazine. She looked a picture of misery. 'Oh Sam,' she cried. 'Where you been? I had a pie in town. There's a flat over the café but do you know what they want? Eight dollars week. I think I might be able to get a job in the cafe. One of the girls is leaving. We'll manage all right but, hell, this is awful. The floor's flooded and just imagine a wind springing up. I'm freezing right now.' She shrugged down deeper in the coat around her shoulders.

'I've got to go up town and see Murdoch about this painting job.' Sam lied. 'The gun went off today. I'll be back as quick as I can, Sue. Cheer up.'

'Cheer up,' echoed Sue bitterly.

Sam tramped up the hill with his spirits at their lowest ebb. He rejoined his friends at the table. Breen came out of the Ladies and Escorts bar. He said to Sam, 'I've rung Tomblinson. Two o'clock will suit him fine. You be here about ten to two.'

'What was that all about?' Entwistle asked. 'Don't tell me she's brought that bastard in on the deal?'

'It's got me bamboozled, but she has,' Sam said. 'And am I up the creek without a paddle! He wants me to sign the section over to him. That leaves me high and dry. Tomorrow at two I'm meeting them in here, and then we're going over to Tomblinson's office to sign it over. Otherwise he and that confounded Miriam are going to the police. I'll just have to come to heel. I'm bust now except if I can land a job. We'll be living from hand to mouth. It looks like Sue'll end up working too.'

'Ye Gods,' said Beaumont-Foster. 'The unscrupulous blackmailing rascal.'

'The sod,' said Entwistle.

McGhee appeared on the point of passing a remark when he doubled over his glass.

'You crook, Spud?' Entwistle said.

'No, I'm right,' said McGhee, recovering. 'So you are out in the cold. It's Mrs Jamieson I'm thinking of and you saving my life that day when, poor blind bugger that I am, I nearly walked off the wharf. If you hadn't grabbed me that day ten years ago I was a gone coon.'

'Oh shucks,' said Sam, amazed that McGhee who had never spoken of the incident should now bring it up.

'Probably been just as well if you'd let me go,' said McGhee. 'Life's just one damned day after another. Look, I know you blokes think I'm crazy but I've had bad news today. I think Doc Colclough let me win that last game and it *was* my last game.'

'I feel you have indulged not wisely but too well to say such things,' said the Remittance Man. 'I'm no expert at chess but it appeared you are a remarkable player. Apparently your last move was a masterpiece.'

'I'd like my last move to be knighting a pawn on the Breens. Then I'd die happy.'

'Don't talk about dying,' said Sam. 'I'm a long way from dead yet and that goes for all of us. We may be in a position to tell them to get stuffed if they come at us again for dough. O.K. so I'm doing my section. Now is it likely I'd pass that over for nothing? Everyone knows the Breens are on the bones of their backsides. If I come across with that section that'll prove they're blackmailers and blackmail is a serious offence. In other words if we go they'll go too. Stall them. I'll have done in everything, but worse things have happened at sea.'

'Worse things do happen at sea. And at Kurikino too. You might as well know I won't be at the Works next season.'

'Not another job?' said Sam.

'I got a date with the old man with the scythe,' said McGhee. 'I'm not frightened of dying but there's different ways of setting about it. I'm not jumping for joy over the verdict on the specimens Doc Colclough sent away. He told me today. Malignant.'

'What are you talking about?' asked Entwistle.

'You jokers talking about shooting through,' said McGhee. 'But they'll get you wherever you go. Now I'm shooting through to somewhere where the Marshal's got no jurisdiction.'

'Crumbs,' said Entwistle. 'Now you've caught the big word disease off Bas. Longest word I know's corrugated iron.'

'Don't talk about iron,' said Sam. 'Makes me think of my poor old roof. Now look here, Spud, just what are you getting at? What's all this crap about kicking the bucket? You look good to me. Just let's forget the Breens.'

'Where are you gunna live?' said Spud.

'Sue's talking about some flat or other.'

McGhee appeared lost in meditation. Then he said, 'You'll have to shift tomorrow. Got much gear?'

'Some wedding presents. Just the usual, blankets, sheets, pots and pans. It'll take care of itself.'

'I kin get the old man's Dodge,' said McGhee. 'Listen. I gotta plan to kid the Breens a bit and you might end up owning that section yet. All you have to do is what I say. I'll come around about one o'clock and I want you to load some gear into the Dodge.'

'There's no need for that, Spud. Thanks for the offer.'

'You want to keep that section, don't you? Then you do what I say. I gotta plan. You know something? I'd make a good undertaker. I'm the last man to let you down.'

'That's more in keeping with your old wisecracking self,' said Beaumont-Foster.

'I still gotta date with a hospital and morphia,' said McGhee.

'I don't follow you. What is this rubbish?'

'I wish it was rubbish,' said McGhee. 'Still a bit of fishing left to do. Well, you might as well know.' He had his back to the crowded bar. He looked over his shoulder. Then he began to undo his shirt in front. He looked around again and then stood. He pulled up his singlet. Just in the region of his navel was what seemed to be a discharging boil.

'What the hell?' said Entwistle. 'It's a boil.'

'Not according to Doc Colclough and he's an M.D. He's been in touch with the people that know. Ever heard of cancer?' He rearranged his clothes and sat down. 'That's what it is, fellows. I asked him what the chances are and to tell me man to man. He said, three months.'

'Oh, to blazes!' said Entwistle. 'These quacks don't know everything. You just get ideas. Every time I go to bed I think I oughta wash my feet in case they find me dead.'

'Yes, he could be wrong,' brooded Sam.

''Fraid not,' said McGhee. 'Mind you I'm not saying these quacks don't make mistakes and I'm not saying they do, but it's getting a bit on the painful side.'

They sat in silence for a long time.

Beaumont-Foster suddenly quoted, 'Let us drink until the horrors come lest sober we go mad.'

It seemed the best move.

## Chapter Sixteen

Again they were inflicted with Amos Blennerhasset's ten o'clock voice. 'Time gentlemen, please. Home to bed and into mum or something.'

On slightly rocking feet they emerged on the 'Strip'.

'Ai am conscious of a certain feeling of well-being. Ai feel a desire to do well to mai fellow man,' the Remittance Man announced. 'Could this possibly be construed as a degree of inebriation?'

'Night air sure hits a guy,' observed Entwistle.

'Well,' Sam said. 'Can't ask you to my shack tonight. Hell, a wind is starting to blow up too. Hope it doesn't get any worse.'

'It'll blow before long,' said McGhee. 'Winter's just coming around the corner. But don't forget, Sam. Round up your gear for a shift. I want you to do this to suit my plan.'

'But —' began Sam.

'But me no buts.'

'If I pack,' said Sam. 'It may as well be for real. Perhaps I had better go across to the cafe and find out if I can finalise on this flat of Sue's. I suppose that's the place she meant. There's flats upstairs, I know.'

'No need tonight,' said McGhee. 'I just want you to do what I say. And that does mean packing for real. Try to understand this is part of a plan to slip the Breens up. Now, I'm saying no more. I'm going down to Dad's for the night. He'll still be tinkering around with something. Now you just be ready with your bits and pieces down by the gate about one tomorrow. See you, fellows.'

He set off towards the shop of 'Mr Fixit'.

'Poor old Spud,' said Entwistle. 'I thought he was a bit down in the mouth lately.'

'Looks like he's copped it awright,' said Sam.

'Dreadful fate,' murmured the Remittance Man. 'Truly there is no rhyme or reason in this world. Good clean living fellow just like us. Chain smoking and half-swozzled every night. There ain't no justice.'

McGhee had been correct in prophesying his father would be tinkering with something or other. This time he was peering at an old typewriter on his bench. He was surrounded by dismantled bicycles, both pedal and motor propelled. Even a little old Austin Seven had been driven into the shop through the double doors. Its motor hung by chains from the rafters. A pit had been dug in the floor of the shop. McGhee circled around it. His father looked up but said nothing. He poked around in the works of the typewriter with a screwdriver. 'Damned if I don't get this thing working yet,' he growled.

McGhee sat on a box. 'Stop here tonight?'

'Your bed's still there.'

'Mr Fixit' kept on picking away. There was a sheet of paper in the machine. 'Mr Fixit' tapped a few keys.

'Can I have the Dodge for an hour or so tomorrow?'

'Yep.'

'Is she going all right?'

'Battery might be a bit flat but she should fire with a crank. She'll need some gas.'

'What's that old bus worth?'

'Money won't buy it.'

'Look Dad,' said McGhee. 'I'd feel happier if I hired the car off you. It's way back, twenty-seven model. Can't be worth much.'

'Not selling, not hiring, you can have a loan of it though. Where you going anyway?'

'I'm going to the hospital,' lied McGhee. 'Booked in for a check over. I haven't been too flash lately.'

His father grunted.

McGhee pulled out his wallet. 'Will you look after this for me? There's about sixty dollars in it. Meant to stick it in the Post Office but didn't find time.'

'Leave it in your room.'

'O.K. I'll head there now and have a lay down. Had a few at the local tonight.'

'You ought to leave that stuff alone.'

'Can't just work all the time. Now don't forget that wallet in my room. I'll leave it there. See you in the morning.'

Sam, pyjama clad, sitting on the side of the bed with a bottle of home-brew in front of him and his feet on a magazine to keep them dry, was saying to Sue, 'Well, we might think we got troubles but you don't have to look far to find someone worse off. McGhee's riddled with cancer.'

In this exaggeration he actually hit the nail on the head. McGhee had been X-rayed at the hospital and the verdict was bad.

'This can't be right,' said Sue.

'Fraid it is,' said Sam. 'Showed us a mess on his belly like a boil tonight. Apparently Doc Colclough says it's malig something.'

'Well they can do miracles today,' Sue said. 'There's this cobalt treatment, for one thing.'

'Well, don't say nothing,' said Sam. 'Don't let on you know. Sue, what's the story on this flat?'

'It's above O'Brien's cafe. It's furnished. Two rooms, share the laundry and the toilet. It hasn't got bedding or pots or pans but there's a bed, table and chairs. It's not bad for eight dollars when you think it over and I'm almost sure I can get a job in the kitchen. Personally, I reckon we'd be better off back with Manu Te Kiri, but if you don't want it well you don't want it.'

'Seems to me people are right when they say Maori people head back to the mat,' Sam said, rolling a cigarette. 'It's just like Parkinson saying to me no matter what you drink and how you live it up you always end up with water. But no mat for me.'

'We'll need our mattress and sheets and blankets and pillows if we take this flat,' said Sue, knowing when she was beaten.

'O.K. I hope you're sure you can get it. McGhee's coming in his old man's car to help us shift. We've got to round up everything we need.'

'Is this dinkum?' said Sue. She sat up in bed. 'Boy, am I excited! If we can land jobs we'll be better off than we were. You can sell the section.'

Sam grimaced. He compromised. 'Sue I didn't tell you 'cause I thought you were miserable enough. Miriam Breen was on the hill and she saw us beat up Voot last night. She knows the score. She's dragged Jack in and they've blackmailed the lot of us for our wages this week. All we've got's a few dollars in that drawer.'

'She what?' exclaimed Sue.

'It's too big a risk letting them go to the police. Our story might stand up but I think a few inquiries and we'd be gone. Sue, I'd die if they shut me up and that's what ud happen for a cert.'

'I can't believe it,' muttered Sue.

Sam told her in detail, but omitting the transfer of the section, how the Breens had them with their backs to the wall.

After cursing the Breens from stem to stern she said, 'Well, if we can hang on for a month or two we'll be jake. They can't even tell the Voots then. We'll be safe in our flat with jobs. Still, it's a worry.'

'It's a worry awright. We'll just have to go with McGhee. This place won't see another winter out. You know what the weather can get like. Wind, rain, hail, the lot. No, we might as well face it. There's not much to slam together, is there? We won't need this bed and that worm-eaten old dresser.'

'Sam,' said Sue. 'I haven't been able to sleep. I'm going to get up and potter around packing anything we need now. A bit of toast for breakfast'll see us through. Sam, I'm so excited I just couldn't lie there any longer. Give us a mouthful, knock me up a cigarette and I'll get cracking. Let's see. Pots, pans, cups, glasses, the radiogram, that smoker's companion, plates. I'll pack things into any old box I can find. We'll grab the toaster after breakfast. There's the broom and the mop too. Some towels. In an hour we'll be as good as on our way.'

'I've taken my pills,' said Sam. 'But I'll lug things down to the gate tomorrow.'

'Don't you worry about me,' said Sue. 'I'm only too happy not to sit around that table that isn't there any more. It just seems like things might come right. You can't spend your life in one place, and I've said nothing, but I've been mighty lonely and I know every bump on Tiddly Tom's Hill. We'll never clean up this section, but we can sell it. Gee Sam! we might get one of these mini cars. We could be on the way, bad as things look. We'll leave the broken bed there, a better one's in the flat.'

She padded out to the kitchen.

Sam, already foggy with drink, let the seconal take over.

## Chapter Seventeen

At ten past ten that night Jack Breen, full of sherry, was having trouble with the front steps of the 'Brian Boru'. Twice he had nearly fallen. Miriam had rescued a flagon of sherry and it was now under her arm and not his. With her other arm, she supported him. Another man had him firmly around the waist. At last he was down the three concrete steps. Miriam and he, swaying and stumbling, began to walk.

'Pish far,' mumbled Breen. 'Drunk barsh. Getsh cab. Kin afford it now.'

'You'll have to lean on the wall while I ring from the phone box. I nearly rang one from the pub. I wonder if I ducked around the back I'd catch Blennerhasset.'

'Gis suck,' hissed Breen beginning to slide down the wall. 'Need sherry.'

'Wait till we're home,' soothed Miriam. 'We can celebrate then.'

'Too right we can cerrebrate. Too right. Flog off that section easy. No more scratching for a dollar.'

'Shsh,' said Miriam.

A Voot truck was coming out of the alley from the backyard.

A stocky figure with massive shoulders climbed out. 'Having trouble?' asked Joe Voot.

'I dunno how I'm gunna get Jack home,' said Miriam. 'He's been on the plonk.'

'Easy,' replied Joe Voot. He picked up Breen in a fireman's hoist. 'Go round the front and open the front door.'

He lumped Breen into the offside front seat. 'You'll have to sit on his lap, Miriam.'

The truck moved off.

'Got a bottle of sherry here,' she said. 'come in and have a spot, Joe.'

'Now, I just might do that.'

'All that land,' mumbled Breen as they reached the foot of the hill. 'I'll borrow a bulldozer and root that muck out. Reckon there's three building sites there.

Miriam, perched on his lap, tried to nudge him into silence.

'That's Jamieson's land,' said Voot as they turned on to the bridge.

'Not after tomorrer,' slurred Breen. 'All mine. Got the wood on Jamieson. He's comin' across with the section. He and Spud McGhee fixed Jack between them. Spud finished it off.'

Miriam was nudging back desperately.

'What's all this?' asked Voot.

Instead of crossing the tracks and turning left on the Eastwind Quay he braked to a standstill. On the right the road turned into wasteland where stood the little station. Here was the siding to the sprawling empire of the Freezing Works, the 'Eagle' as the men called it — the network of roads and ramps and loading-bays, workers' huts, storage sheds, stock-yards, the wharf, cranes, freight wagons and the great slaughterhouse itself with its towering chimney stack.

'Oh, he's drunk,' gabbled Miriam. 'Let's get him in the sack. Sure don't know how we'd uh got home tonight without you.'

'Yeah, but what does he mean they fixed Jack?'

'Why was Spud driving, eh?' dribbled Breen. 'Because your brother was dead, thas why.'

His head slumped between Miriam's shoulders. He was half asleep but the damage was done.

'So,' said Joe Voot softly.

'Come on in for a spot, Joe,' said Miriam, her brain awhirl. 'What did you stop here for? We live on Eastwind Quay as you know.'

'I'll skip the drink. I'll run you home and then I should just catch McGhee at the huts. I've got news for him and it's all bad.'

He drove off and took them home. Effortlessly he carried Breen into the house. Miriam opened doors for him and he threw Breen on to the bed.

He looked savage. 'If I can't get the truth out of McGhee I'll be back,' he said dangerously.

'Oh let's have a drink,' said Miriam. 'He's drunk and doesn't know what he's talking about.'

'No drink, I've got a date with McGhee. Jack was my young brother. I'll beat the truth out of that bastard.'

After he had stamped out, Miriam looked at her husband in disgust. Sherry, she thought, that's sherry for you. Damn and blast all fools. However, this thought did not stop her going into the kitchen and pouring out a drink for herself.

Breen was sprawled in the middle of the bed. Miriam went through his pockets in search of the blackmail money. She found it. She lay in the darkness of the spare room wondering how she could tell him he must have lost it. She had hidden it on top of the wardrobe.

For along time she was unable to sleep. The idiot, she thought. If I'd only kept it to myself! Now the Voots know. Joe'll beat the truth out of McGhee and the others. Then they'll go to the police. There goes our dream of Sam's section.

# Chapter Eighteen

Joe Voot's truck with the Breens aboard passed Entwistle and Beaumont-Foster as they lurched down the hill back to the compound.

On the bridge a Chevrolet car pulled in alongside of them. The driver, a Maori who threw the skins on the fellmongery paint-table where the skins were trimmed and sprayed with sodium sulphate, called out, 'Hey Tin-whistle, the Eagle shat today. We're grogging on regardless. Party in Johnny Whakaroa's bach. We got a keg in the back. Hop in.'

'Why not?' said Entwistle. 'Come on, Bas.'

They climbed in the back with the keg for company. They turned right and then off along a track through the wasteland. Here a disused railway carriage had been converted into a dwelling. Whakaroa was a railroad man, a ganger. Far from being the stalwart bullying type one would have expected, he was a smallish, mild mannered, well educated man who let riff-raff make use of his home. Anything for a quiet life seemed to be his guiding maxim. If you put a glass in his hand, he emptied it.

The three men who had been huddled in the front of the old sedan carried the keg into the carriage, to be greeted with shouts and cheers. Entwistle and Beaumont-Foster followed.

It was a very old type of carriage, with seats the full length. At one end the seats had been cut away by some bush-carpenter to allow living quarters. There was a bed, table, chairs and a small kerosene cooker. Lamps hung from the ceiling. The place reeked of beer, tobacco and dried fish, presumably shark. On the floor were fish-heads and the shells of mussels.

The beer was poured off into a bucket. An enamel mug was dipped in the bucket time and again. It seemed as if there were a shortage of containers. Two or three mugs appeared to be doing the rounds. Beaumont-Foster extracted the butt of a cigarette from his mug and drank politely.

Entwistle declined. 'I'm heading for the huts. Tired.'

'I shall accompany you,' said the Remittance Man.

They left the carriage.

A short burly figure crossed the blazing headlamps of a stationary truck. Joe Voot seized both men by their collars and shook them.

'Where's McGhee?' he snarled. 'He's not in his hut. I'm finding him and wringing the truth out of him about young Jack. And I'm getting the guts of what Breen was hinting at tonight if it's the last thing I do. Then, when I've half killed this bastard, I'm heading for Jamieson's. For all I know you guys might be on the list too ... You're as thick as thieves. Now is McGhee in at that party?'

'No, he's at his Dad's,' blurted out Entwistle, nearly choked by the grip around his neck.

'Is he now?' said Voot viciously. 'Well, I'm not losing sight of you two prize apes. Get in the truck. Maybe McGhee doesn't know it, but he's got visitors.'

For the second time that night three people packed into the cab of Voot's truck.

'He isn't, you'know,' said Beaumont-Foster calmly.

Voot had just been letting in the clutch. He declutched again. 'He isn't what?' he demanded. He was simmering with rage.

'Entwistle was mistaken. I assure you he was quite convinced that McGhee was at his father's place. As it happens, I know differently.'

'Where is he, then?'

'Fishing off the wharf. He distinctly told me he was catching the incoming tide tonight.'

'Did he? Well, I'll incoming tide him. He'll think all his birthdays have come at once. Get out, but don't try to bolt or I'll murder you both.'

They hopped down. Entwistle knew he should never have spoken, but failed to see how a wild goose chase could do more than delay the inevitable.

Across a disused side-line and the siding and then the main line they approached the wharf through piles of sleepers, oil drums and spools of wire littering a yard.

The old wharf was empty. The *Kahu*, a boat belonging to Grimshaw himself, was moored up close. The black water of the river swirled and slapped around the piers.

Voot went half-way along the wharf. He came back. 'He's not here.'

'He may be on the boat,' said the Remittance Man. 'I accompanied him on a similar expedition and we fished from the boat.'

Voot went to the edge of the wharf.

'McGhee,' he roared.

Only the swirl and slap of the water answered him. Beaumont-Foster put the flat of his foot on the small of Voot's back and pushed. Voot went over the edge and the sound of him striking against the *Kahu* was violent.

'Jesus!' exclaimed Entwistle. 'Can he swim?'

'I can only trust he's stunned,' panted Beaumont-Foster.

Entwistle knelt down to peer over the edge.

'No sign of him?' queried the Remittance Man anxiously.

After a while Entwistle said, 'No, no sign. With luck he'll drown.'

'And that means,' said the Remittance Man, 'Ai have joined the firm of McGhee and Co., Eliminators of the Ungoldly. Unorthodox methods employed, but success guaranteed.'

'I only hope we can get away with it,' grunted Entwistle.

The two men lit cigarettes. Sounds of the party in the bach drifted to their ears.

'In case of his undesirable return,' explained Beaumont-Foster, picking up a small rusting anchor, a three-pronged claw with shaft and chain, lying on the wharf.

'Good move,' said Entwistle. 'You're knighting your pawns, or whatever McGhee would say, tonight. You get behind him and let him have it. Then we'll pitch him in again. They might figure he split his skull on the rail of the boat.'

'That's what I hope *did* happen,' said Beaumont-Foster.

'But what the hell was he doing here in the first place? asked Entwistle. 'I'm afraid they're going to chase this up.'

'You know what gave me this inspiration?' said Beaumont-Foster. 'Voot's fishing bag in the cab of his truck. That green canvas one. It looked full of gear, lines, hooks, the lot. By the odour it exuded I would hazard, at a guess, bait too. Still we can check. We'll get it and chuck it on the deck of the *Kahu*. We'll turn out the lights on the truck. Voot's a bit stewed and jumps after his bag he has tossed on the deck. What fisherman hasn't done it? But he misses his footing and is claimed by the waters of the Kurikino. *Exeunt* the old firm of We, Us and Co. singing and dancing.'

'Well,' said Entwistle. 'We're sure knocking off these here Voots like salted peanuts.'

When they had chain-smoked a further two cigarettes, Beaumont-Foster put down the anchor and, his jocularity prompted no longer by tension but relief, said, 'Well, here's a ship coming down the harbour and not a whore in the house.'

They lit another cigarette.

'Let's get back to the huts and talk it over,' said Entwistle. 'We'll switch off Voot's lights and chuck that fishing bag on the deck.

In the Remittance Man's hut Entwistle sighed. 'I wish we had a drink. I'm a nervous wreck. Anyway, it looks as if Joe Voot's a gonner. I can't see any way of saving Sam's section. Spud reckons he's got an idea, but what it can be I can't imagine. Poor old Spud! Fancy having cancer. Well, an operation might fix it. But I can't see any operation fixing the Breens.'

'I can,' said Beaumont-Foster, running a finger from ear to ear across his throat.

'Well,' said Entwistle, 'there's thousands of throats getting cut every day at the Works and those poor little blighters don't mean no harm to nobody.'

'Truly,' said Beaumont-Foster. 'Our whole environment is one of death. By death we live, by death we die.'

'Sam's section,' brooded Entwistle. 'No, there's no way of Sam not paying the price for us all. If that Miriam Breen says a word there'll be trouble and big trouble. They're bound to believe her.'

'I can't get over finishing up Joe Voot,' said the Remittance Man. 'He was in a mood to kill McGhee.'

'I should never have said where he was,' said Entwistle. 'But he was choking me.'

'He would have tracked him down anyway,' said the Remittance Man. 'Well, at least that problem is over. But I'm afraid Sam's section is doomed. One word from the Breens to the law and our troubles will begin in earnest. My heart bleeds for Sam but there is nothing we can do.'

'Our only hope is McGhee,' said Entwistle. 'God alone knows what goes on under that spark-plug cap.'

'If you ask me,' said the Remittance Man. 'God wears one himself.'

## Chapter Nineteen

After a slice of buttered toast, a glass of milk for Sue and a bottle of home-brew for Sam, they made countless journeys up and down the steps until everything they thought they could conceivably need in their new quarters was down by the gate. There were even the last few bottles of Sam's home-brew, the washing machine and the preserving pan he used in the making. What *was* McGhee's plan? Sam wondered.

'We'll never get all this junk into the old Dodge,' he said, surveying the collection on the footpath.

But McGhee had thought of this. Attached to the rear of the old touring car was a trailer. He turned up just before one. A very hung-over Beaumont-Foster and Entwistle had just joined Sam and Sue. Entwistle was still on the payroll, but had played sick, a piece of acting which had not involved much pretence.

'Voot gets planted today,' said Entwistle.

'Dust thou art to dust returnest,' commented the Remittance Man. 'We cannot find sufficient hypocrisy in our hearts to attend the ceremony. We shall imbibe quietly in the "Brian Boru".'

'What a balls up!' said Entwistle. Did he or did he not wink at Sam over Sue's shoulder. 'Jack getting buried and them dragging the river for Joe. Heard tell they've got a helicopter coming in on the job. They found his fishing bag on the *Kahu*. Musta fallen in. Yet he spent the evening in the pub. Decided to fish the incoming tide I s'pose, and lost his footing on the boat. Or fell between the *Kahu* and the wharf when he jumped. His truck was there, close by. Now what do the Voots do? Go to Jack's funeral or hunt for Joe. Us, we do neither.'

Sue turned around to stare at Entwistle. Like Sam and McGhee she was dumbfounded.

'Joe Voot?' said McGhee. 'You trying to tell me he went fishing with that bellyful of beer?'

'I'm telling you just that,' said Entwistle. 'And his body hasn't turned up yet.'

'And we shall not be participating in the search,' said Beaumont-Foster.

'Well, I'll be stuffed,' said Sam. 'Sorry, Sue.'

'Joe Voot,' she said disbelievingly. 'First Jack Voot, now Joe. Hell's teeth!'

'Oh well,' said McGhee. 'Nothing we can do. He's not the first nor the last to drown.'

'How true,' said Beaumont-Foster, shaking his head sorrowfully. 'Many brave hearts are asleep in the deep.'

'Climb in,' said McGhee.

Even with the trailer there was little room left in the back seat of the Dodge.

McGhee said, 'Now it's important for Sam and Mrs Jamieson to sit in the back seat of the Dodge. You can squat on that mattress. Tinny and Bas can get in the front. I'll give them a ride up. When we pick the Breens up I want them in front.' He went around and cranked the car.

They all walked into the hotel together. The Breens were waiting for them. They looked uneasily at each other.

Apart from the barman they were the only people in the bar. They had five-ounce glasses of beer in front of them. The barman was leaning against the shelves.

'Oh well,' said the barman. 'In a way I can understand it. Nothing like fresh fish after beer. I've gone fishing myself to catch the tide when I've had a few beers. Wouldn't have given tuppence for bed.'

'Well,' said Miriam. 'It looks as if the fish have got him instead. Of all the crazy ideas. We had a bottle and I was only too ready to make supper. Nothing dangerous about opening a tin of herrings if he had a craving for fish. Well, we can only wait for news.'

She had turned so that she was addressing Sam and his friends as well as the barman.

'It's just too bad,' said Sam.

'It's a bastard,' said the barman. 'The night right after Jack Voot had copped it too. He's getting buried today. Hear you were driving, Spud.'

'Yeah,' McGhee replied. 'But he came to and grabbed my arm. My foot skidded off the brake pedal. The railcar was right on top of us. Christ alone knows how I got out. Should be my funeral too, by rights. Let's have a round of drinks.'

'Things are sure happening around old Kuri,' said the barman. 'Jack Voot, Joe Voot. Makes a man scared he might be next.'

Miriam started violently and paled as the sergeant and a stranger — the tall man in the dark suit the men had figured out as being a detective from Harrowville when they had been interviewed at the police station — walked in.

Apart from a quick glance the newcomers ignored the man.

'This is Mr and Mrs Breen,' said the sergeant and introduced Detective Hayward from Harrowville. The detective just nodded.

'Just felt I couldn't hang around that river,' said Miriam. 'And we've got some business over at Tomblinson's with Sam at two o'clock. Got an appointment.'

'I saw you coming in here,' said the sergeant. 'Now we want a statement from you both about everything concerned with this fishing. How long will this business take? When can you be at the police station?'

'Should be able to make it by half past two,' said Miriam. 'Perhaps a few minutes after.'

'Make it half-past three,' said the sergeant, consulting the stranger who nodded with a glance. 'Detective Hayward wants to inspect the scene of the fatality. Getting sick and tired of Kurikino. Two deaths in two nights. There's something fishy about it.'

'Certainly is,' said McGhee. 'He went fishing and he was drunk.'

The sergeant ignored him. He said to Miriam Breen, 'Half-past three then at the police station.'

The two big men left.

When they had finished the round of drinks, McGhee rubbed his hands. 'Well, let's get weaving.'

'But it's only twenty to two,' protested Miriam. 'Anyway, what've you got to do with this? It's just between Sam and us.'

'You'll see,' said McGhee. 'C'mon.'

'C'mon back,' Entwistle called after them. 'Something we'd like to discuss.'

Sam, Sue, and the Breens surveyed the laden trailer.

'I'm leaving Sue at her new residence,' said McGhee. 'Then I'll drop you off at Tomblinson's. At least you can give a hand to unload. Hop in the back, Sam and Mrs Jamieson. You two can climb in the front with me.'

They crowded into the old Dodge. McGhee cranked it again.

'What a junk heap,' sneered Miriam.

'I'm not saying it'll serve its purpose and I'm not saying it won't,' said McGhee as the car moved off. 'But it could.'

'The flat's above O'Brien's,' said Sue as they went past the cafeteria.'

'You leave it to me,' said McGhee. 'We're heading to Bad Dog Bend. We'll make other arrangements later.'

'We'll be late for Tomblinson's,' said Breen angrily. 'And we've got to make this statement later.'

'No, you won't be late. It's only a short trip. We'll make it awright.'

At the Wainongoro Road they turned off the Harrowville highway. It was a winding road higher over the river. Soon they arrived at the pa. It was the first time Sam had been there since he and Sue had so briefly parted.

'I'll speak to Manu', cried Sue in great excitement. She sprang out of the car.

'Take it easy,' said Miriam. 'You might have a miscarriage. Be a pity for O'Keefe to leave no family.'

But Sue was on her way to the whare of Manu Te Kiri.

'I tell you I've proved that's a lie,' shouted Sam furiously. 'Aren't you satisfied with ruining me?'

A fat Maori woman had appeared in the whare doorway. She pointed towards the large building which was the meeting house and kitchen. Behind it drifted smoke from driftwood fires. Sue went over and entered the meeting house waving for the others to follow her.

Soon she emerged with huge Manu and they went to an empty whare. McGhee bounced up to them in the old car.

'Good to know you're back with us,' said Manu, and to the others, 'Tena koa — How do you do?'

'It's empty except for a table and some chairs. So load your gear in.'

They entered the musty whare, each carrying some article. It was one large room. The table was big.

'Whatta you gunna call him?' said Miriam to Sue. 'Brendon?'

'I'll tell you something,' retorted Sue. 'It might be a girl but we're not calling it Miriam.'

The last thing Sam and Sue carried in, an end each, was the mattress. They laid it down in front of the open fireplace.

'I'll gather up some wood and get a fire going. Dry the place out,' she said. 'Look, there's stacks of kai over in the kitchen. What do you have to go back to town for? You'll have to come back on the Freezing Works bus.'

'It's just something I have to do,' Sam answered evasively.

It was harder to get away than he had imagined. Quite a few of the older Maoris had followed Manu and were busy rubbing noses with Sue and himself.

'Cut out this rigmarole,' snapped Miriam. 'It's just on two o'clock. Let's get moving. Rattle your dags, McGhee.'

McGhee unshackled the trailer from the ball on the back of the Dodge.

'We'll make better time,' he said. 'I'll pick it up when I bring Sam back. Incidentally, it's McKenzie's trailer. Get in the back, Sam. You two climb in front with me. Now don't panic. We're as good as there. We'll be away with a hiss and a roar.'

'Probably blow up,' Miriam said, scowling at McGhee cranking.

Watched by a curious crowd they moved off.

Amiria Te Kiri and Sue plucked armfuls of driftwood from stacks behind the kitchen. They lit the fire in the whare.

'Let's hear a record. There's a three-point plug over there,' said Amiria. She put on one of Sam's old favourites, Woody Hermann and his orchestra playing 'Dupree Blues'.

'Beauty,' pronounced Amiria. She turned it over and the fire crackled to the strains of 'Calliope Blues'.

'One thing I am going to do,' said Sue. 'I'm going to roll a spill of paper. Hold it in the fire and light a cigarette. That's how I'm going to light all my fags from now on. If you light a smoke that way it tastes better than if you use a match. Don't ask me why. It's just one of those things.'

They adjourned to the kitchen. Sue helped herself to a kumara floating in a curried eel stew. Afterwards she helped herself to mutton-flap in an unthickened onion stew. When the sizzling of a steak on the red hot oven ceased and the meat had been brought to the table by a Maori, Sue listened closely and could hear quite clearly the sound of the Wainongoro where it joined the Kurikino on its last lap to the sea. Sue knew that at night with the driftwood fire glowing, the swirl of the water would lull them to sleep. The *Wainongoro!* The snoring waters! My home, she thought, and, by God, when Sam wakes up beside the fire with no distance to fall to the floor and no bus to catch he'll be glad to call it his home too.

## Chapter Twenty

The side curtains of the old tourer flapped. Inset in them, the panes of celluloid were yellow and cracked. The view ahead was obscured by the head and shoulders of the Breens and what passed for shoulders with McGhee, his pine cone of a head with the spark-plug cap. The only view of the magnificent scenery Sam could get was by slewing around and looking through a back window.

What the devil was this plan of McGhee's? he puzzled. Surely nothing so infantile as being late for Tomblinson. McGhee was driving slowly enough, heaven knew!

On their left towered a bank smothered in bracken and fern. Here and there the roots of pines and macrocarpa trees had broken through the cliff. The needles of these trees were thick on the bracken and fern. On the right was a straight fall of almost one hundred feet into the river gorge. It seemed to Sam that the Dodge just fitted, but he knew there must be feet to spare or the double-wheeled big Voot trucks would never have made the grade and the corners without toppling. And Jack Voot was being buried right now! Sam knew it was the kick to the Adam's apple that had finished him but he felt no guilt. He had walked in fear of the brute too long. The Voots were notorious for exacting vengeance, all huge men. Except Syd, but he was generally regarded as one of the most evil of the family. Well, Jack was gone and apparently Joe too.

Suddenly Sam had an inspiration. Manu! He was the undisputed leader. The Voots' income would be hit hard if Manu shut them out and they were denied access rights to the quarry. He was Manu's cousin by marriage: surely he could be protected.

Feeling much happier, he remembered the last ride over this road in the taxi. Since then he had known happiness. Even without his section he could live on at the pa. The mattress in front of the fireplace had looked inviting. Even if he only thought of it as a holiday in the slack season. It rankled with Sam that he was not on the permanent staff, but now he reflected there was no need to catch a bus in the morning. He could eat kumara and corn and karaka berries done in the hangi overnight. Sam had seen hangis being prepared — whole beasts lowered on to the red-hot stones, covered with watered sacks and then the hole shovelled in. It was delicious meat.

And the bread, home baked, was like cake. The butter, also home churned, would be on the long tables in pie dishes. The tea would be in pots like gallon tins.

And then he could fish the rivers instead of slaving in the freezer with every minute seeming an hour. No rent to pay. The old Maori asked little from life, simple food; they were God's children. Like the seagulls, thought Sam, mother earth and the rivers were their bounty.

What, Sam reflected, had he worked for all these years? Or rather for whom? Amos Blennerhasset? Well, he would make his own beer.

His cottage and his section were gone unless McGhee in his mysterious mind had dreamed up a miracle.

No eight dollars a week rent. He had always sworn that Sue would never go back to the mat, but what alternative was there? Her obvious delight was his consolation.

For that matter, if only McGhee would think of something, he could sell the section himself and Sue and he could own a Mini to travel to and from Bad Dog Bend. He had never entertained the thought while the cottage had been habitable, but now ... Gee they could run up to Harrowville some afternoons!

Through the back window Sam regarded the high opposite bank of the river. It was bush clad. They were nearing the Devil's Elbow now, the sharpest bend on the road.

McGhee brought the car to a standstill.

'What the dickens now?' said Jack Breen. 'Should be helping look for Joe. They'll wonder where the deuce I am. But Tomblinson first with Sam Jamieson, eh? Sign over quick. I suppose there'll be the usual red tape. But it's simple. You're signing the property over to me because I did you a good turn. No need to elaborate. It should be straightforward. Now get this heap of nuts and bolts into gear.'

'The back wheel's creaking,' said McGhee. He turned around to Sam. 'Sounds to me like a stud's worked loose. Do us a favour, would you, and walk along beside and listen? I don't want to lose a wheel going round the "Elbow".'

To Sam's surprise, he winked. To his further surprise, he reached over and shook Sam's hand briefly. 'That's a boy, Sam, I'll crawl along in low gear. I'll knight a pawn here. Tell McKenzie where the trailer is.'

Sam climbed out and walked beside the slowly moving car.

'Can't hear nothing, Spud,' he shouted.

He began to run as the car sped up going up through the gears.

'Hang on, hang on.'

But McGhee sped up, the Dodge making no effort to turn at the 'Elbow'.

Sam stopped dead as the old car tore away the flimsy fence and somersaulted down down into the gorge.

He began to run. Only the rear wheels and the spare on the back were visible above the grey-green water.

'Spud!' he spluttered. That it was deliberate was all too clear. Spud McGhee had cut the Gordian knot. No knife, no morphia, no pain, no cobalt, no Breens.

For the Breens Sam felt nothing, but it dawned on him now the extent of his affection for McGhee. The long days at work, the evenings around the bar and around the table — Spud. Poor Spud!

It sounded like an epitaph. In a way it was.

A Voot truck with a new driver at the wheel pulled up.

'They went over,' said Sam. 'Their number's up.'

'Jesus!' said the truck driver.

He joined Sam at the edge of the ravine.

'I've taken Jack Voot's job, I've had the breeze up going over this road to and from the quarry. This sure doesn't make me feel any happier. How come you weren't in the car?'

'It's a long story,' said Sam. 'Soon as you hit town tell the police. I'm the only witness. They'll find me at Bad Dog Bend pa.'

'Who was in the car?'

'The Breens and Spud McGhee. He was driving.'

'Jack Breen drives for us too. Now he's drowned too. And is it the same McGhee that hit the railcar with Jack Voot?"

'Yeah,' said Sam. 'I saw that too. Well, wherever they're gone, heaven or hell, they can thrash it out there. Cop Larkman can only scratch his head; everybody's dead. Now you tell the police.'

'Sure will,' said the man climbing back into his truck.

Sam took a last look over the cliff.

Empty saddles in the old corral, he thought. He shook his head slowly. 'Dead men tell no tales,' he lipped.

Slowly he began his journey back, back to his pallet on the floor.

*Whakamutunga*

# Dick Seddon's Great Dive
## Ian Wedde

## 1    Backyard Ocean

He knelt in the black sand. Each wave sucked trenches beneath his knees. He began to sink and be buried. He lunged under the next one. The wave poured into his nostrils. He came up blind, his balls aching. He'd been turned around. A wave ground him into the dark. He felt his limbs stretched and drawn away. At one moment he saw the night sky and the stars, incredibly clear, but below him. Then they whirled upward and a sound with the mass of an immense wing or horizon slammed against his forehead. He felt the tortoiseshell bracelet torn from his wrist. It was as though his hand had gone.

Moments later he was floating quite gently. He'd passed beyond the fury of the breaking waves and now rose and sank slowly, turning over and over. He no longer had any sensation of struggling. He seemed to have left his body which he now watched calmly as it thrust its limbs out this way and that, jerkily as a child, as though the viscous medium in which it was trying to move had become thin, then a muffled vacuum, finally a space he seemed to pass through ... through some vanishing point at the back of his neck.

## 2

'Bring me some *shapely* shells,' she'd once said to him as he left for the beach.
Because I'm built for comfort
I aint ... built for speed
he was singing. He'd come back with four or five empty ice-cream tubs.
'It's all that's left.'
Wind and more wind. He wanted to gape, to retch. To get out of himself, how could that be done? It was as though he could have hung over the worn railing of the jetty, shoved a finger into his throat, and gasped out the cramped bile of energy which so occupied his time that the world and the friends in it were seen through a kind of veil, that their voices speaking came to him dully, from a distance, and he had to catch at them as they drifted or flew past, bending all his concentration and will to

accomplish a simple response to a simple greeting.

'Well, hello ...'

'Uh ... (who are you?) ...'

Though sometimes he heard his own voice, plausible and intense ...'That's not what I mean ...'

Ah, why did he have to explain so much? Couldn't he settle for anything?

The planks of the jetty were furrowed and scarred down their length. Here and there long splinters had lifted off the surface of the timber, but even these were worn and smooth, soft-looking. The structure was so solid, so resilient, so used! At the end where boats came to fill up with diesel the wood was soaked in dark oil, the broken ends and joints looked to have been charred ... yet even here, where the jetty had been battered and shaken through years of storms, where the slick poison of the oil had seeped and seeped into the grain of the planks and washed around the greeny standing timbers at the waterline, where the wood had the dead sodden appearance of the slimy apple boxes which washed up from time to time on the beach below the boathouse — even here the boards sprang beneath his weight and gave off a ringing sound when he stamped on them with all the angry force of his body.

Spray from the waves flew into his face. Along the shoreline the water had been stirred up into an ochre broth which matched the scars of slips along the peninsula. But the channel was still blue, like the swept sky, and crowded with speeding whitecaps. He turned his back into the wind, feeling it shove him suddenly towards the lee side of the jetty and almost lift him off his feet, ballooning his coat and trousers, whipping his hair forward around his face. He grunted, turning sideways, catching at the rail. The whole structure was alive, the rail quivered under his hand, the planks bucked against his feet. All at once he laughed, opening his mouth wide. The wind drove sideways between the nerves of his teeth, pushing one cheek out. By opening and closing the apertures of his lips and throat he could alter the pitch of the sound the wind made in him. It yawed and wailed, in his head ... he wondered if it could be heard *out there* as well: sensational, flashy ... bringing one hand against his groin, stretching the other out as though to grasp the neck of a guitar, going into a crouch, stamping one foot, miming some crude ferocious chops, opening and closing his lips and throat for the wind to sound in ...

He could see her at the shore end of the jetty: white face and dark blue jersey. He strutted towards her along the wet planks, lifting the guitar high, his eyes fixed on the audience, then crouching again over his narrow big-knuckled fingers, one boot sole sliding on to the wahwah pedal, laying that sultry wail over the notes. He kept his eye on her: 'How's the people tonight?' He saw the white flash of her teeth there in the distance. 'Solid,' he answered himself. 'Those chicks gonna leave some wet seats behind. ...'

Woohah!

... lifting the guitar high, eyes fixed on the audience so far down there, the pale mark of her face with the smile just showing, and the wind rushing into him like a giant respirator!

# 3

She's sitting alone in his room, bent forward over a table on which she's placed paper and pencils ... done this with sad precision, the neatness of someone who's determined to see something through. Her attitude's that of a woman listening.

It's summer, but cool, here in Port Chalmers, where a breeze from the south is moving the sappy broadleaf outside her window: the only window in the room, which she faces across the table and the blank paper, and which might be the only perspective she has on the world.

Out there the shiny evergreen moves in cool sunlight, also a few ngaio bushes, and some broom which, having been sprayed recently by the council, now has on it a drab olive patina of death. These plants grow from a scruffy clay bank haunted by neighbourhood cats which either doze among the shadows or else stalk blackbirds and thrushes in the undergrowth. Occasionally children slide and scramble down. Above the plants and the bank the chimneys of two houses can be seen. At this time of year there's no smoke. The top half of the window frames telephone wires, cloud, sky. That's her world. From time to time footsteps or a car pass through it. There are changes of light.

She keeps the window closed. It's an old-fashioned sash window. In order to raise it she'd have to bend forward, grasp two handles set at pelvis level in the window frame, and slide the frame upward in its grooves. This action would push her belly forward, arch her back, tip her chin up ... her hands, at the top of her stretch, would be level with her head ... the whole action would resemble that of a woman drawing a sweater or nightdress up over her head. Then she'd be standing naked in front of an uncurtained window opening on to a street.

Or else we can imagine her in morning sunlight, stretching naked in front of the same window. It's late morning, she wants to break the last sacs of sleep in her spine and shoulders. It's a gesture to admire. For someone to admire, for example a lover.

When she looks up from the paper on the table her own reflection in the window faces her, its back turned to what she sees through it: the world, her world, its earth, planets, creatures, sky ... its season, its voyeurs.

The empty paper isn't an invitation, it's an imperative. The attitude of a woman listening changes to that of a woman talking. Soon the pencils are blunt, the paper scattered over the table. In the window the reflection ignores not only the world, it ignores her as well. It never so much as glances at her. The light shifts. When she gets up and goes out she doesn't look at, through the window, at all ... she goes out.

Sooner or later she'll almost get up and lift the reflection over her head and stand there as though for the eyes of a lover, in air and sunlight ...

If I reconstruct his life for you it's going to have to be done like this. There's a line in his life which runs from south to north, from north to south, along which he was strung out like one of the strings of his neglected instrument. In the north he was Howlin' Wolf or Willie Dixon ... out of sight in the ponga grove below Beck's place, twelve-bar blues for the cicadas ...

Woo Hoo-oo
Smokestack lightnin'

In the south it was *He Ain't Give Ya None* … 'I got messed up around somewhere …': right at the edge …

It always seemed the wrong way around to me until I found myself, in the effort of trying to discover him, stretched tight between those same poles. He'd always had an obsession with the way things got divided along that line: North and South Viet Nam, North and South Korea, North America and Chile, Northern Ireland and the Republic, the silk millionaires of Milan or Como in northern Italy and the destitute south of that country. It was typical of him to bulwark a cheap idea with this kind of data. He collected it. He loved to quote the lines I taught him from a poem by Pablo Neruda, lines which have slipped in already without my even thinking about them: *You come from the destitute south,* and then at the end: *That is why I have singled you out to be my companion.* He'd say that the demarcations were never drawn by the people involved. That I know to be true now. Now that he's dead and I can't go to him and say *Tell me,* now that I have to involve my own imagination in what has the inexplicable (if you don't get it, tough shit) meaning of myth, I find he was often right and I knew it, *then* … but I was too proud to admit it.

I have had to learn the simplest things
last. Which made for difficulties.

Stop quoting at me, he'd say. Who are these people, do I know them. It's you I want to hear. It's you.

She stops. There's a commotion outside the window. Her friend Ingrid's coming back from the shops, pushing the baby in a pram. The dog's jumped up and knocked a bag from the end of the pram. Groceries roll into the road … Ingrid yelling Fuck off! the baby howling with fright. A neighbour runs out to help. Then the little cavalcade goes out of sight, out of the window space, Ingrid's narrow hands reaching forward to soothe the baby. Kate continues to see the colour of Ingrid's hair in the blond light among the leaves out there … everything can be slowed up in that world … its visitors linger …

In a way it was as though we never moved, as though he never left, as though I never remained behind … except now … except that now I understand more about it. He was trying to keep some kind of balance and this had come to have a geographical equivalent. And it also explains why he should be Howlin' Wolf in the harder north, and some kind of paranoid brinksman in the gentler south. His whole life was an elaborate mesh of checks and balances. If he'd found it was necessary to move up and down the country the way he did, then you can imagine the kinds of fantastic migrations he must have been compelled to undertake in his own head.

I know too that among the reasons for his leaving as he did was a desire that I shouldn't be hurt by him. I could always say to myself or to others, 'We had a quarrel, he's pissed off again to cool down.' Well, he tried: 'I'm not dependable,' he said.

I can say more than that. I can say that he loved me. *You come from the destitute south ... that is why I have singled you out to be my companion.* ... I remember the occasions he came back into the room where I was after he'd been away, and all I'd say would be, like, 'Oh hello, welcome *home* ...' And all the while my heart would be pounding so hard I was afraid he'd see it, and it wouldn't be until we got to bed that I'd let go ... which he could explain to himself in terms of my being a good fuck. The same thing probably happened to him the length of the country; not a single really open loving embrace, not a single unguarded welcome. He was often a prick. But what's on my mind now, like the sound of him picking out a twelve-bar blues in another room, is the thought that *that* may have been what he was looking for: a home. If I'd welcomed him as my heart now tells me I should have, he mightn't have gone out to Bethell's that night and drowned himself, since I know that's what he did.

And so I've got to set out, strung tight as he was, to try to find out if it was so, if I killed him, the only man I ever really loved, much as I must have seemed to resemble the other small cool assassins he knew.

He was right: we are split north from south, and the line isn't drawn by anyone involved. Perhaps if I find out enough about him, I'll find out who draws the lines. That would have been the kind of remark he'd have made. He used to talk of 'Them', until I got mad. I believe in Them now. I'd like to know who they are. Between us, jointly, we killed Chink.

Outside the light's shifted, it's deserted, but she doesn't look up, she goes straight out, leaving the door to bang wide open behind her, rattling the sash window in its frame.

# 4   The P.O.W. Snapshot

His 'Prisoner of War' photograph: that was his name for it. He was what's called a war baby.

'Listen, I'd like to tell you about myself, but I'm only allowed to tell you my name rank and serial number. That's the regulation *you* made, remember?'

Well, well ...

He said without much bitterness but at the same time without pity, in a strangely flat tone, that the only thing that ever really happened to his father was the war, that the small precious human events which followed became non-events, that his father's youth and the new love for his young wife 'were rendered down into base metal in the furnaces of the war' ... Kate hearing these words which seemed rehearsed, wondered if he was putting her on, but he wasn't ... that by virtue of a strange alchemy, the catalysis of the R.S.A., the horrors of his father's active service were transformed into a kind of gold standard against which the ordinary currency of his life was measured ... all those things he'd desperately longed for during the war ... these, this currency, was propped up by that standard, was found lacking by it. 'That gold was bad metal ... won, like the South African gold which crutches the present currencies of the West, by slave labour.' ... Kate again wanting to laugh, not just because she was stoned, but because he was like a parody, accomplished and deliberate ... ah, but of whom?

'My Dad once said to me: You think you're a bad sort, do you? You think you've been around? Well lemme tell you *I've done worse things than you!*'

The old man was incoherent, shaking, but that was what he wanted to tell his son: he, the old soldier, 'had the edge on him' still, had one or two 'up his sleeve', had done *worse* things than he, for Christ's sake! Chink didn't think of himself as bad. But somehow strength, danger, achievement and badness were mixed up in his father's mind ... ('*machismo*' ... 'supercock', Beck would say, allowing his lips to part just far enough to reveal the gap where his left eye tooth had once been ... a smile he reserved for 'special cases').

The old man thought his son was threatening him, flaunting his shiftless life, making fun of him. It was sad. He was deathly ill, he felt there was no time to lose: he was about to blurt out some confession, some act he'd kept a secret for years and years, to begin with because he was ashamed of it but later because the secret was something which warmed him, something which, like the war, was a grotesquely nostalgic antidote to what seemed to him to be the unremarkableness of his life, which was now about to end. He stood in his woollen dressing-gown, holding the back of the armchair, his face turning purple with the effort to breathe.

'Now listen young feller ...'

Chink's mother came back into the room. His father's confession sank again to wherever it had lain all those years. The lids dropped a little on his glaring eyes, his head dropped. His wife half carried him back to his bed. He would die with the weight of his secret to take him down among his comrades. Chink couldn't even have held his arm down the passage to the bedroom. There he stood, listening to his father's breath going away. *His shadow before me ...*

'A romantic, in a sense ... That's it, Kate: sibling rivalry. And for what? For who'd been *worse*, that's what ...' He laughed loudly. Ha ha! a demonstration qualitatively less malicious than Beck's 'special case' smile ... but then, it was Chink's father, and he was dead ...

He'd been telling her about the last showdown, the 'terminal quarrel'. She'd only just met him. She wondered if he'd inherited his father's urge to confess. But then, she'd started it. *I've done worse things than you.* That sentence was on his mind: some time he had to do, something he had to see finished. It touched her, in just the right place, at just the right time: she was doing some time of her own, in her own way.

'Is it so funny?'

'Is what so funny?'

'Your father's death.'

'Ah ... remember the photograph?'

Earlier on he'd produced it, but without rhetorical flourishes and without any apparent irony, from the inside compartment of a battered wallet where he evidently kept it as a talisman of some sort, though not a public one, since he had to grope clumsily with two fingers into this odorous sanctum, finally managing to draw the snapshot out between the forceps of his fingers, handing it across to her: a gesture she was stirred by to recognize as special.

Much later, almost three years later, he gave her the snapshot. He was going away 'again'.

'You might at least give me a photo,' she said. He allowed the sarcasm to sail past, not granting it even the smallest alteration of his expression. For the second time in three years he forcepsed out 'the P.O.W. snapshot' and passed it to her. She still has it: the only surviving likeness.

Battered and yellow, the photograph shows a small boy in shorts, awkward-looking, his feet in closed sandals turned inward at the toes, staring with an expression of mixed worry and distraction at something just to the side of the camera. One imagines his mother standing there saying 'Smile!' while his father aims the lens at the child's head and shouts 'Stand up straight!'

Behind him is a suburban back garden: on his left a dark paling fence, probably creosoted, with what looks like a passion fruit vine at the far end on a wire trellis. Directly behind him the perspective is abruptly halted by the back garden and brick kitchen wall of another house. You know it's the kitchen wall because of the kind of long window which goes above the sink unit. You have the feeling that a neighbour is watching the proceedings from this window.

On the boy's right hand side the photograph stops at a neutral edge broken by the protruding lower half of a deck chair and by the upper branches of a small feathery tree, probably a kowhai. It's summer: the boy is wearing a short-sleeved shirt, the light is bright and hot and humid, the deck chair is aimed at the sun, its shadow squats invisibly beneath it.

Somehow you know it's the week-end. The little boy looks penned up. He's probably close to tears. His rather thin arms hang at his sides, but stiffly, as though they too have been told to keep still. His fringe of hair has been plastered down and across his forehead, which even at his age (about five, you guess) is high and square and adult-looking, and without a backward slope towards the hair line, so that his eyes look unnaturally large and exposed, though rather lidless, without the protection of a ridge of browbone, as though the sockets are flush with the oddly flat planes of his cheek bones.

His nickname naturally was Chink ... bestowed, so he claimed, within the first week of primary school, though it sounds too sophisticated for five-year-olds ... somehow it's not a connexion you'd make without having the nickname there already, though once you had it it seemed obvious. Kate guesses it was probably used by the family.

She can imagine the scene at that first day at school: the little shy boy answering the teacher's question about his name: 'Chink'. The bright room fills with laughter. *Chink, Chink*! He bursts into tears. Then the young teacher attempts to comfort him.

'We know that's not his real name, now don't we children ...'

So not only did he answer the first question wrongly, but the name which stuck was by far the strangest and funniest in the school.

How much do we make of this? Not too much ... Kate, face to face with the melancholy, funny image of 'the P.O.W. snapshot', struggles against a procession of associations. But it's real all the same. Because from the very start, possibly even before this first day at school for all Kate knew, he became used to feeling separate.

Instead of retreating, however, his lidless pale eyes learned the habit of staring unblinkingly, sometimes almost without expression, at the person he was talking to, at the countryside, at crowds of people.

She sometimes longed to give him expression. The first time they made love she felt as though her cheeks were puffed out with some kind of pressure coming into her, some kind of breath. Then she looked at him. His face was blank. All at once the mask split slowly. 'Kate!' he shouted. 'Kate, Kate!' The beautiful smile remained there. It was comical. She'll never forget it. And she'll never forget the mask of his face before the smile broke it. It was like a glimpse of a world in which we're able to see the truth behind the cosmetic of gesture ... ape-skull, dog-skull, sheep-skull ... some split-second animal reflex just slipping from the face of the person who's been holding our arm or ruffling our hair, who's just kissed us on the lips.

'Listen, I'd like to tell you about myself, but I'm only allowed to tell you my name rank and serial number. That's the regulation *you* made, remember?'

Before he left school he already had a reputation, based entirely at first on his stare but later, because of the provocations of that stare, earned otherwise, for being tough, unafraid. His neutrality was a taunt. What had once seemed to be shyness came to look like precocious incuriosity. He was punished for insolence. By degrees he began to fit the definition he'd passively caused others to make of him. When he was twenty he spent one bad year at university in Auckland. He got into fights with drunks who thought they detected in his stare some kind of disgust or curiosity.

Yet women liked him. They believed him to be gentler than men did. Perhaps fear was the reason for this also. Kate doesn't really know, and can't stop to think, except of insolence and gentleness: the defined and the natural. Whichever way round it is. Oh, she needed the insolence too, or came to ...

'Tell me about yourself, Chink.'

'Listen, I'd like to tell you about myself but I'm only allowed to tell you my name rank and serial number. That's the regulation *you* made, remember?'

'Hey, Chink, this is a party, I only met you today, don't get heavy. I liked the way you told that burglary story. *That's* what I mean ...'

'What about what *I* mean? It's easy to be cool, sweetheart.'

His voice had gone flat. He stirred as though to move away. A pang of fear and longing entered her. On impulse she struggled towards him, on her knees, put her arms around his shoulders and kissed him on the side of his neck. He remained still under her mouth and hands. His long hair had a feral smell.

'Ah Chink, I'm sorry. I didn't mean to put you down. Go on, tell me about yourself. I'll *listen*, whatever you mean ...'

He sat motionless. Then his face was split by that odd hinged smile. He began to laugh, throwing his head back. His throat was white and stubbly.

'The Story of my Life. First I'll show you a picture of a prisoner of war ...'

Chink, the teller of parables, the bullshit artist ...

And now she's looking at 'the P.O.W. snapshot' in front of her as though she half expects it to utter something, a cry or words ... a miracle ...

# 5

It was a dark night, no moon, late autumn. He was cold and tired. He walked up the silent street hoping it wasn't going to rain before he got inside. His shadow passed him. It stretched out as though trying to break free, fell back behind him and then passed him again and again as he walked along beneath the street lamps. The rhythm of its movement and of his own feet drew him forward: the automatic compulsion of a work chant, of a route march, a pit saw. Wearily he amused himself with these imaginings. He decided on the work chant and began inventing African words for it: *Hai hai hai B'wana hai hai hai B'wana* ... His shadow advanced like the shadow of the overseer who was approaching him from behind. He awaited the lash. One day he'd rise up, they would rise up, he and his work mates, and chanting rhythmically would break with their mattocks the earth of the overseer's grave ...

A strange dim hush of sound filled the street: deep freeze units, people breathing in sleep, his ... Was he imagining it? There was a morepork and then two cats. The morepork continued for some time, unhurried, monotonous. The cats stopped moaning when they saw him. One of them suddenly ran across the road, its body elongated. The other followed. They disappeared into a dark garden. He strained to hear the breathing of the street but a slight breeze began to move the leaves of evergreens and shrubs. He turned up his collar, more for the sake of the gesture than for shelter, and changed hands on his holdall. He felt a sudden temptation to walk in the middle of the road, and did so. It seemed extraordinarily clean, the pavements too with their rinsed gutters and sharp-edged concrete curbing. If he chanted his work song the whole street would come alight and alive. Picture windows on the street front would light up, families of two, three or four would stand in the windows looking out at him, like advertisements for pyjamas or oil-fired heating, silent and motionless, smiling. He whistled instead

> If y' see ma
> littl' red rooster
> oh please ...

The breeze increased, blowing up the street from behind him, parting his hair across the crown of his head, suddenly scattering a few big drops of rain, *smack*, on the asphalt. He turned the corner out of the wind and into the quiet of shelter ... into his own street.

'His own street' ... its familiarity, even at night, even after long absence, filled him with an ache of loneliness. As a child he'd never thought of it as going anywhere: it was open-ended but static, and he'd never had any sense of movement until he'd turned out of it. And he'd never returned by way of it. He was 'home' the moment he came round the corner, into the street. At that point all journeys had ceased.

He'd once scraped a charred stick along a neighbour's white-painted paling fence, from one end to the other, *dah dah dah dadadadadadrrrrrrruuup!* digging that vibration which passed through elbow and shoulder to the shaken cavities of his skull and to his eyes jumping out of focus, the loud machine-gun rattle of the stick over the corrugations of the fence. The irregular charcoal line on the white paint had made a satisfying horizon, a dislocation of the ordered planes of the street. He'd been about to scrape the stick back in the other direction when the neighbour had run out screaming. Under the eyes of both neighbour ('Boys will be boys ...') and father ('... respect for property ...') he'd had to wash the fence with a cloth and a galvanized bucket of soapy water, on his knees on the pavement, smearing the dish-cloth through his father's shadow on the fence.

*Hai hai ...*

The fence was still there, still white. The rain began to bucket down, sluicing along the gutters, but he didn't run the last yards to the door of the house, because he was footsore and tired, because of the old half-remembered inhibition ... because he didn't know what to say when he got there.

> hai hai hai B'wana
> if y' see ma
> littl' red rooster
> oh please ...

... his mind, skidding in weary grooves, was stuck with not much more than that. It made about as much sense as the phrases he'd been rehearsing. Either way, he was going to fuck up.

The rain had soaked his hair and thighs: one of those sudden Auckland squalls. It stopped as immediately as it had come. He stood outside the gate of the dark house, put his bag down carefully and pushed the drenched hair back off his face and over his collar, wringing it behind his neck. Two empty milkbottles stood on the pavement below the letterbox. He picked up the bag and skirting the bottles opened the gate quietly and went up the neat concrete squares of the path. The night was once again still, the silence accentuated by the dripping of wet foliage, earth kisses of sinking wet. He trod carefully on the balls of his feet. It was pitch dark away from the street lamps, but he moved surely, by instinct and memory. Nothing had ever changed, nothing would have changed. There were no obstacles in his father's garden.

He went up the steps to the porch and put his bag down on the mat by the front door. He found he'd stopped breathing, in the effort to be quiet.

'Shit ...' He went back down the steps and around the side of the house.

His father's bedroom window was open a few notches. Chink stood beneath it, in the perfume of the lavender bush, listening. This time he had no doubts, didn't have to strain to hear the breathing. His father's breath seemed the loudest thing he'd heard since he'd begun the walk through the neighbourhood. He realized he'd been listening for it from the first moment he'd begun that walk, even from the moment he'd left the south to hitch north.

*The old man's sick, the overseer's sick.*

Chink stood in the dark beneath the window, head bowed, in an attitude of submission. Inside the house an old man lay in drenched painful sleep, labouring for breath.

The image of the youthful pyjama advertisement families in their pictures windows came to him. They gazed silently, with set smiles, at the dark street. Not a single old man among them to share their intimate and guaranteed comfort, only an old man's son walking alone in the middle of the road. Standing outside his father's window.

His mother's telegram had said 'Father ill.' It hasn't said come, but Chink had assumed that, had assumed the implication of a last chance to see his father. Standing in the damp cool darkness by the lavender bush, listening to his father's breath inside the house, Chink thought 'Why isn't he in hospital?' and realized that it had never occurred to him to wonder whether his father had asked to see him, whether he mightn't be *waiting for that* ... Oh Jesus Christ. He stood with his head dipping towards the medicinal odour of lavender. He couldn't believe that, but he should've thought of it. It wasn't impossible. How could he face it, such a scene, at this time? He should've done it himself, long ago, before it came to this ... some kind of trite tearjerker. A death bed scene, Jesus. And if his father didn't know he was coming, he now thought, that was worse, though it was what he'd assumed all along.

Ah, get on with it. He was helping his father to breathe, keeping to that rhythm. How hard it was.

He was here. Go inside, see him.

But he stood anyway, calming himself. He picked a sprig of lavender and crushed it, to smell. It seemed a violent odour. Rain fell again suddenly, rattling against the stiff karaka leaves above his head. Then it stopped, as suddenly. He heard his father breathing. Go inside, see him, *your Dad*. Fuck your vanity.

As he turned and went back towards the corner of the house he heard the milk delivery truck clattering further up the street. It must be nearly dawn, a late dawn, being autumn and cloudy. The sound of clashing milk crates opened up his sense of the space he was in. Stepping past the house corner, he stepped clear also of the difficult suffocation of night and his father's breath. He was still holding the lavender in his hand, once again a familiar smell. He stood under the dripping eave of the house, out of sight of the road, not wishing to seem a strange figure, an intruder, in the dim garden. Yes, the first weak light of day showed spaces between shrubs. Beyond the garden, in the grey higher air above the road, the street lamps were now greenish.

How often it was like this, calmness or a decision coming as the sense of a space opening out with dawn: partial, weary, leaving a certain measure to be guessed. How far to the gate? You knew, really. The uncertainty wasn't important. You could walk to the gate in the dark, in any case, without stumbling, if you had to. You had memory and instinct. There were no obstacles. And how often, for him, it happened at this time, literally dawn, a mysterious coincidence. Which way did it work? Was it the dawn, out there, that calmed him? It seemed rather that his action of coming to a decision, that interior part of it — *that* created a new day, drew it up out of the suffocation of darkness and confusion. Then there was light, a large space he inhabited, other people in it also. *He* did that. Nothing was given to him. He had to do it, to make a day for himself to live in, to live. A space, to live. Distance, to pass through. Having not slept all night, he would suddenly be exhausted and would go in and sleep for hours, whether there was a job he should be at or not. After dawn, nothing mattered. Nothing else, that is.

The milk truck reached the gate of his father's house. The milkman was whistling loudly and tunelessly: *a few of my favourite things, these are a few* ... Chink stood till the truck had gone, till it had turned the far corner, a long wait.

Then he went to the porch and picked up his bag and walked to the gate. To hell with it. What did it matter. He opened the gate towards himself. Let's go.

The milkman had left the two full bottles right in the centre of the space. The toes of his boots were against them. He'd almost kicked them over. There he stood. Then he bent down and picked the bottles up, awkwardly, with his free hand. He was wet through. What did it matter, after all. Carrying the bottles and his bag, he turned around and went back up the path again to the front door, and rang the bell.

There he stood again, waiting again. He could hear his heart: *hai hai hai B'wana.* Breaking the earth.

# 6

When he came in that Friday night from Beck's place he was so bent that for a long time he didn't notice anything. It was summer, his father was dead. For some time he'd found he preferred to be alone. But now he wondered why he'd come home, why he was alone, why he should've wished to be alone, how long he *had* been alone.

'Whatta mausoleum, Jesus ...'

Then as he was about to go to bed, not even bothering to take his clothes off, he saw a muddy footprint on the sheet, and the window above the bed swinging open.

'Hey ...'

It was about two in the morning. His watch face spoke out clear and serene. Somehow it seemed impossible at that hour, unravelled as he was, to deduce 'I've been burgled'. Gargled, ogled. Icicle, tricycle, bicycle. It was a *word*, was all it was.

'Someone's *done* this to me!'

Yeah, it was true. Sighing, he checked the flat by rote, counting its contents out under his breath. The furniture lay k.o'd upon the carpet. He (she? they?) didn't take the table/the chairs/the refrigerator, etcetera.

He zeroed in. Twenty dollars had gone from the cigarette box on the stereo lid, but nothing else (he scrabbled and counted) though there were signs that the thief (the *what?*) had poached himself an egg: the last one of a carton of half-a-dozen had gone, and there were breadcrumbs by the loaf where he remembered having cleared up scrupulously before going out that evening: filth of a forgotten week, dishes socks and bottles. What a time to choose! The pan in which the egg had been cooked lay tidily full of water with floating white bits in the sink. Very cool, he thought. An anal thief.

Then it occurred to him that it must've been a friend ('Yes yes!'). But a friend would've left a note, something ('Yes yes!') especially since twenty dollars wasn't chickenshit ...

He sat in the main room of the flat and noticed all at once the mess! Drawers had been opened and left so, the profligate contents of the bookshelves had been pulled out. The wreckage rushed towards him across the carpet. Had he done that or the, ah, thief?

By now it was about three in the morning. Not instinctively, but for some deep reason, though not without hesitation (he closed his eyes to consider) he put his boots on and went out to the road and kicked the bike alive. His head now felt fairly clear. He rode quickly down to the Newmarket police station. He rang the bell. No one came. A cruise car was parked outside, the blue lamp by the front door was on. He rang again, long bursts, holding his finger down.

'Why, Chink ...!'

'Hello Mum. How's Dad ...?'

Still there was no answer. There was a moral in this somewhere.

'Uh ... 'scuse me ...'

He walked around to the back feeling a flutter of panic and laughter in his stomach. His balls ducking for cover. He shook one of the windows.

'What kinda trip is this?'

He went back to the bike and started it. The streets were deserted, there was no traffic, not even through Newmarket. He chugged past a succession of red lights, leaving the bike in top gear and letting the revs drop right down ... sensing the light turn to green behind him ... feeling invisible, insubstantial, adrift. The highest 'vehicular density' in the Southern Hemisphere ... 'Oh yeah?' ... Where was everybody? The Stranger rides into town.

Then he thought of the new central police station, the skyscraper! And swung the bike fast up Carlton Gore and towards the centre of town. He was aware that he shouldn't be going fast ... might ride out of himself ... sense the signals turning green *back there*, too late ... but he felt a sudden mad confidence: here's the wronged citizen on his way to redress, yeah!

He opened the bike up along Symonds Street and swooped left down the hill past the Maori Wars memorial statue. *Through War They Won The Peace We Know* ... Pax Britannica was lost in the shade of the pohutukawas. He imagined her: voluptuous, paralytic, one arm locked upward, petrified foliage dripping from her free hand, a breasted *sadhu* ...

The traffic lights by the town hall turned green as though for him. 'Thanks.' He had a sense of inhabiting himself again. He negotiated the island at speed and then cut back and cruised slowly up the hill to the central police station.

It was all lit up, like Christmas, floor after floor, slender and cold. At first he wandered into the garage. There was no sign of anyone ('Whooohooo ...'). Squad cars were parked in rows under the dim lighting. He walked among them. They were useless, lacklustre, vapid. His boots echoed. There seemed to be no need to tread quietly.

After this he walked straight into the main building through a sprung inside door which sighed and closed behind him. The corridors were fluorescent-lit, deserted, filled with his loud footsteps. He walked past rows of doors towards the vanishing point of a corridor and came to a lift well. He went up floor by floor. It was all deserted. The glaring perspectives of the corridors receded in front of his feet. Vanishing points. He expected at any moment to meet a procession of men with bulging fish-eye-lens faces tramping 'without motion' towards him under the fluorescent tubes. Nothing of the sort happened. He hurried. When he got back to the second floor his vertigo left him.

All at once he saw the night desk off to one side of the main complex. There was a long counter inside a glass room with a swinging glass door. Pushing his unclear reflection aside he walked through to the sergeant behind the counter. There were three or four men in the room, spaced out among the hooded typewriters and telephones, behind the polished surface of the counter.

'I want to report an icicle.'

The sergeant, a tired man whose head was flat as though moulded by his cap, looked at him from his chair.

'What can we do for you?'

'I've been burgled,' said Chink, looking at the top of the sergeant's head. He was sure he'd spoken. He'd suddenly thought, 'What the fuck am I doing here?' He wanted to tell the sergeant that the whole station was open, that he'd walked around inside it for twenty minutes, that this seemed weird. He leaned against the counter. The room with the night desk was so bright!

'What time?'

The question skidded past him.

'What time did you notice the offence?' The sergeant repeated the question, a bored mutter, reaching sloppily across his desk for a notepad, not looking at Chink.

'At about two o'clock,' said Chink. He felt suddenly that he'd got it all wrong, that he was about to make an address. He stood up straight, smoothed his hair. The men in the room were looking towards him.

'What address?'

'Birdwood Crescent in Parnell,' said Chink crisply. He gave the number. His mind snapped into focus.

'You were out?'

'Yes.'

'Have you been drinking?'

'No.'

'All right,' said the sergeant. 'Go home and wait. I'll get a car to come round. Don't move anything. There's been a thief working the neighbourhood. You're about the tenth. Was your place locked?'

'He came in through a window.'

'You should know better,' said the sergeant, dialling a number with his pencil. He yawned and massaged his eyes, and rubbed the sad crown of his head. Chink heard him talking to a car: 'Meee maaaa mumm ...'

'They'll be there in about ten minutes,' said the sergeant. 'Do you have transport?'

'Yes.'

'Are you all right?'

'I'm fine,' said Chink. 'I'm tired, that's all.'

He'd remembered what was in the flat: some caps of mescaline, some caps of amyl nitrite. They were in a dispirin bottle in the living-room. Like the debris on the floor of the flat, the bottle rushed towards him. The sergeant still had the telephone in his hand.

'You'd better get back and let the C.I.B. in,' said the sergeant. 'They'll probably be waiting for you.'

'Rightoh,' said Chink. 'Thanks very much.'

He bowed, something like that, ran out. His wild reflection. At first he couldn't find the bike. Then he remembered it was around the other side of the building, at the top of the hill. He forced himself to walk to it. He *knew* he'd left the door of the flat open. He hurtled back across Grafton bridge and through the dark Domain, under an amazing summer night-sky, if only he'd known it, pulling up outside the flat at the exact moment the squad car, red light off, stopped on the other side of the crescent. A flashlight probed from the front window of the car at the number on the letter box. Chink bounded across the road.

'This is it, this is the burglary, I'll open the door, just got back from the station, gotta take a leak.'

'Calm down,' an invisible man in the car. 'Don't get excited and don't touch anything, we'll be right in.'

'Fine,' said Chink. 'I'll just take a leak.'

He walked back across the road, taking small steps, then opened the unlocked door, snatched up the dispirin bottle, flew through the lit flat to the bathroom. Shove it under the bath? He'd poached an egg, why shouldn't he have a piss? Have had a piss? They might want to look around in here. Ah shit ... The mescaline caps floated on the surface of the water when he threw them into the lavatory. He shook the amyls into his palm ... 'Fuck it!' ... cracking caps under his nose, snorting hard ... the reek of cheesy football socks. He heard the D's come into the main room of the flat. He three the remaining caps into the dunny and pulled the chain. The objects swirled and disappeared. He opened the window and flapped his arms, then washed under the hot tap, scalding his hands. He dried them and fumbled at the catch of the door. His fingers were shaking. He felt terrific. He put his hands on his knees, bent, and breathed deeply. Blood strutted finely through his body. He opened the door and went into the room where the police were.

'Sorry,' he said. 'I must've got a bit excited.'

There were three plain-clothes men in the room. They were looking at books and things on the floor. Oh, he'd got it wrong, quite wrong.

'Have you been at a party?' said one of the men.

'Yeah,' Chink rubbing his hands, 'but pretty quiet, you know, we were playing chess. Then I got back here, I didn't notice anything at first, then I saw a footprint on the bed, I thought it must've been a friend, he'd poached an egg. But any friend would leave a note, something, so I thought I'd better get on to it quickly otherwise I wouldn't have bothered ... what's it, nearly four o'clock, hell I seem to've been riding about for hours ...'

'Yes,' said the D. 'Could you show us where the entry was made?'

Serious these fellers.

Chink led the procession into the bedroom. The window was swinging open, summer night coming in, the muddy footprint was on the bed *right* next to the pillow. He resisted with difficulty an urge to wave his arm at the ludicrous evidence. The whole thing could have begun again, from the beginning, any number of times: Footprint, the K.O., the Egg, Britannica's Paralysis, Fourth-dimensional Christmas in the Cop Shop, nostalgic half-remembered Bikie Heart Stimulant, 'Ah those were the days ... almost as it used to be ...'

But he hadn't got back there, after all. He'd got it wrong. Now he was The Guide. Why had he wished to be alone? Why had ...

He stood humbly to one side repressing his commentary while one of the men opened a small case and began to dust for fingerprints. In Chink's experience the powder they used was black, but this stuff was white ... another joke? 'They're planting me.' It lay however like old dust on the cigarette box, the window-sill, the books on the floor. He hadn't got back there at all ...

Then the D asked to have Chink's print. A small panic. He almost said, 'You have it already, it's a black one.'

'We have to know what's yours and what isn't.'

'Oh yas ...'

'D'you read all this?' Holding up a copy of the *Connoisseur's Handbook of Marijuana*, one of *Cowboy Kate* (black holster a-swing by her creamy buttocks), and one of *Supercock* ... a quick selection.

'No,' said Chink. 'They belong to a friend, I've just got the loan of the flat until he wants it back, he's from the university ...'

'You're not a student?'

'No.' Chink sweating.

'I see.' The D takes details: it all goes in a book. 'But you'll be around for a while? You're not pushing off soon?'

'No.' Chink, meek 'n' mild. *Yes yes yes!* was what he almost said, as though to confess.

'Because we'll need to be able to get in touch with you if we find anything. This man's been working the area, if it's the same one. The prints will tell. Meanwhile, take your boots off before you get into bed, it might avoid confusion especially yours.'

'I did ...!' Chink, faint and stunned by the possibility that ...

'It was a joke,' said the D. 'Night-night, sweet dreams.'

Finally they left.

'God ...' He waited for an hour, crouched over his tumbling puppy-dog heart, peering past the curtain of the front window from time to time, then rode back round to Beck's place as dawn came up.

The party had finished. Chink made some tea and sat in the cluttered kitchen sifting data. It didn't make much sense. There was a growing racket, half sleepy half quarrelsome, of birds outside in the garden. He opened the curtains and sat drinking the tea from an enamel mug, looking out at the trees in the early daylight.

'Ah me.'

It was still and clear. An occasional car accelerated past the front of the house. He found a packet of cigarettes on top of the refrigerator and sat smoking, sipping the tea without milk or sugar. The house was very quiet. He hoped that someone would wake up soon and come to the kitchen. It was a good story.

'A funny thing happened to me ...'

Then he yawned till his jaw cracked. There were more cars outside now. His eyelids felt raw. Energy drained suddenly from him. I'll tell someone about it later, he thought, and went out into the garden to piss.

There was some broken glass by the kitchen door. He remembered why he'd left. No one had been rolled or cut or raped, but that wasn't the point ...

What is, *young feller* ...?

'Ah ...'

His mouth tasted bad. He shook the drops from his prick, yawning, stretching his back till it clicked. Why had he been so long alone? It was now full daylight. The early clamour of the birds had died away. I'll have a sleep, he thought, and went back into the house. He encountered a sour after-party smell as he opened the kitchen door. I should go home. Then he thought, *To that?*

He opened the door to the living-room. Some effort had been made to clear away the mess. Bottles were crowded into a corner, there was a cardboard carton filled with butts and other rubbish in the centre of the floor. The windows were open but the curtains hung motionless across them in the still air. At least the room wasn't stuffy. He went towards the sofa, saw someone on it covered with a tartan blanket, but was by this time too tired to explore further in the house. He took a cushion off a chair, put it in a corner, laid his head on it, and sailed instantly out of himself. The lights changing to green ... *back there* ...

That was how Kate saw him when she woke up later in the morning. ... And now, looking through her window, she doesn't see light among the leaves, the blond of Ingrid's hair where the leaves are stirring ... it's another summer altogether, filtered northern sunshine heavy in the corners of the room which is already growing hot, beams of glare shooting through gaps in the motionless curtains, iridescent patches and stripes of heat burning on the walls, a sour night-time exhalation beginning to gather in the silent house, waiting for the moment when the windows and curtains will be flung open ... The key ring with the ignition key of the bike is pushed on to the index finger of his right hand, which lies palm-up on the carpet. The hand's large and white, its fingers curled in sleep. There's a tortoiseshell bracelet on his wrist. The other hand's stuck under the waist band of his jeans. His legs are thrown down in front of him, with the scuffed toes of his boots turned out. His head's rolled off the cushion and is hanging to one side, on to his left shoulder, towards her. His nose has been running.

'Oh fuck ...'

It was the quiet head who'd sat with Beck most of the night, talking and smoking Beck's shit, who'd left about the time Beck started getting mad. Why was he back? He'd struck her as heavy. But he'd been making Beck laugh.

'He's bad news Kate, but fucking incredible lemme tell you, doesn't need anybody, quite insane, a real survivor. He'll be around for a while. His old man's just died, something shitty was going on there, cut off his power for a while. Chink's I mean. He's got someone's flat in Parnell, and their bike. People treat him like that.'

'Is he gay?'

'I tried him once.' Beck screaming laughter through his nose. 'It was soon after I'd met him, at Jan's place. I really dug him ... he had nowhere to stay ... he came back here with me ... the place was full of the usual creeps ... he said never mind, he'd find a place to crash somewhere else. I said he could share my bed. He said okay. I went and had a shower, you know, that bridal night feeling. When I got back to the room he was *asleep*, on the bed. I lay awake all night, what was left of it, wondering whether to wake him up and throw him out, or just kill him where he lay. I was so strung out! Finally I jacked off on his head. When he woke up in the morning I ripped into him ... said I knew about cockteasers like him ... that I didn't hold down a fucking awful lucrative job just to keep closets and jerks like him off the street, and he could get out. His expression never changed. He yawned and put a hand up to scratch his head, whereupon of course,' Beck screaming laughter again, 'he felt some glup in his hair. Can you imagine! You've seen him, he's big and strong. He brought his fingers down slowly. His expression still didn't change. Well, I was jumping around the room by this stage expecting to get my face smashed. But what d'you think happened? What d'you think? He just said, "Why weren't you straight with me, man? Why didn't you tell me?" So of course I said I did tell him, but that I didn't think I had to go through the alphabet. I mean, I thought he was *educated*. I mean, I thought he was telling *me*, for that matter. And then I realized what he'd said. I went hot and cold. "So you mean it's all right, you were just tired," I said. "Yeah, I was tired," he said, "but no, it's not all right, it's not my bag, but if you'd been straight with me I wouldn't have stayed with you and strung you out." Then he just got up, had a shower, washed his hair with my shampoo, thanked me for letting him crash, *apologized* again, and left, just like that! I couldn't believe it.' Beck pushed his serious beaky face close to her. It wasn't often he took off his masks. 'Is that naïve, or what? Or selfish? Or just very cool? I still don't know what he was doing to me. I can't shake the feeling it was deliberate. Lemme tell you Kate, he's weird. I can't sort him out. I mean, we're good friends now, I see him a lot when he's here, but he's kind of abstract, you know? If I ever made it with Chink I'd feel as though I'd been with something not quite human ... ugh ... he doesn't turn me on any more, but I like his mind, as they say ... ha ha. ... Mind you, women really dig him, perhaps if you tried him you'd find a human being, not that I'd recommend it ... one of these days he's gonna throw the switch. I wouldn't like to be the one he takes along ...'

So now she lay there on the sofa staring at this Chink. Beck talked as though she should've known the name. Well, so he was hot shit. He didn't look so good just at the moment. She decided he might be considerate enough, or blocked enough, to rate silent thanks, which was unusual at Beck's place. Beck's boarders were usually long on vanity and short on patience. That night one of them had pinched her sleeping-bag.

*Well, let's go.* She lay for a while looking at him. Beck was *afraid* of him. She'd never imagined Beck could be afraid of anyone. 'What have I got to lose?' he'd say.

'My *innothenthe*?' Singing, 'Give me your, dir-ty luurve ...', flashing his eye-tooth gap. Yet Chink robbed him of something, had robbed him. He must be blocked out of his mind to lie like that, she thought. He sprawled there as though he wanted to push his space to its limits. ... She was sitting with her legs drawn up under the blanket. She thought that most people enter sleep for protection: they draw their space around themselves. They curl themselves over their bellies, their soft parts. But this big pale hood was in occupation. His defencelessness was a kind of contempt.

Then he yelled, a whinny. She was just feeling about on the floor for her dress. *Oh shit*. She pulled the dress over her head. This looked like the time to get out. She struggled with raised arms to get the dress down. When her head pushed clear she saw him staring at her. He'd sat up. She jerked the material over her hips and legs. Too late. His teeth were set and he looked ill, or afraid.

'The Stranger ...' His lips had barely moved. He's mad, he's really fucked, she thought. Let's go. He was staring and staring. It was like talking to someone who looked at the bridge of your nose. There was a warp somewhere in his perceptions, the matching surfaces failing to come together, sliding out of alignment. C'mon, let's go. She needed to remind herself. Let's go, let's go. Please. She recognized a kind of helplessness immobilizing her. When she moved she would already have admitted defeat.

His stare suddenly fell full upon her, his eyes meeting hers as though for the first time. She saw him slump a little.

'Are you all right?' Well, no point in being original at such moments.

'What's your name?'

'I'm Kate.'

She waited. He was still staring. His gaze retained some insolence.

'Your name's Chink, isn't it?'

'I'm The Guide ...' His voice was quiet, rather arch. She was thinking, What a prick.

'Um, Kate. Sorry to bother you. I was having a dream. Last night was pretty weird y'see, I ...' He stopped, shrugged. It was as though he had something to tell her but couldn't be bothered finding the words. Or was he being polite? She was thinking, What about an apology for the intrusion. For your eyeful of me.

'I thought you were tripping or something,' she said.

'Oh no ...'

'I hope it wasn't a bad dream.'

'Familiar enough. And a waking vision to wake to.' He yawned then sat up and blew his nose into a dirty red handkerchief.

A compliment, well. ... She was even grateful, as he tossed it out.

'Well, see you,' she said. She was going to have a shower.

'Now Kate, be fair ...' He'd spoken finally in what she took to be his ordinary voice. She'd almost heard the gears changing somewhere, a shrill whine of effort cut off ... labouring torque giving way to a disengaged freefall ... He stood up and opened the curtains, flung them to either side of himself. It was a beautiful day. Late morning sunshine filled the big room. He stood rattling the keys against his palm, looking out.

'I want to have a shower,' she said.

'Lemme get you breakfast.'

'I want to have a goddamn *shower*.'

He was craning his neck to look out past the corner of the window, towards the street. 'Okay, I'll wait for you here.' He turned around at the same time as she stood up. He was leaning against the window frame, waiting, his eyes calmly meeting hers. She found herself grinning with the puzzled effort of avoiding his quiet insolence.

'But all I need is a cup of tea ...' It even *sounded* like a surrender. Why was she giving in when his insistence was so formless, so calm? He was smiling, an odd hinged opening of his face. His eyes simply waited, on her. There seemed to be no gesture she could make to break free of the assumption his manner implied.

'Is that all, a cup of tea?' His smile was beginning to split his head clear in half. She shrugged, flung her hands out.

'Yes, for Christ's sake!'

'Listen Kate, I've got a much better idea than that,' he said. 'Let's go out somewhere. I've got the loan of a bike. Let's go out and have breakfast somewhere. For Chrissake, whatta day! Let's get out of here before ...'

'Before the rest get up?'

'Yes, yes!'

He was laughing. She'd given in, she didn't know why. It was a relief. He pushed himself clear of the window frame and cocked his heavy head at her.

'Oh, all right,' she said.

'Okay, Kate ...'

Somehow he'd sensed her desire to get out of the stale house, right out of it, into the sunlight, out there. For a moment she pondered this package deal. He stood there by the open window, smiling, jiggling the key of the bike. Had he simply passed on his desire to get out? It didn't matter. Yeah, let's go. Saturday mornings at Beck's were usually lazy and bored: records, dope, half-hearted excursions as far as the park or a beach ... an inertia storing up irritations for the evening and the party.

Remembering this change of heart, she pauses, looks up. In the window her leafy reflection looks back at her. She's smiling. *Let's go ...*

'Come on, Kate.'

She had the shower. Chink had splashed water on his face. His long hair, which he fastened with a rubber band for riding, was damp by his ears. He drove quite slowly, heading for the harbour bridge. When they got to Victoria Park he stopped and took off his pea coat. There were games of cricket going on in the middle distance, beyond the dry shade of the trees bordering the park. It was a day of glassy clarity, less humid than usual, small high puffs of cloud appearing and disappearing. Heatwaves rose from the asphalt. Some ice-cream wrappers had already collected in the dusty gutter along the park, where sparrows were wrangling and fluffing out their wings.

Summer Saturday: hot, blue, and light beating like a pulse against the white concrete of the motorway overpass, against the glaring forecourt of the service station back up the road, out of which cars accelerated towards the North Shore beaches, passing Kate and Chink, filled with children and bright colours ... a kind of ferocity of purpose against which, or rather between which and the soporific games of cricket on the other side. Chink's leisurely act of removing his jacket and folding it over the petrol tank of the bike was a perfect cipher of freedom and pleasure: 'This is our pace, there's as much time as we choose to take.'

They reached the top of the bridge and could see the great yellow crane the Japanese engineers had floated all the way to the Waitemata ... imagine it in mid-ocean, that absurd beautiful garish machine breaking the horizon, making it finite, whichever way you turned. That was what she imagined, that day. Chink dipped the bike a little towards the centre of the road, a genuflexion ... 'Moby Dick,' he said ... and then they swooped over the vertigo in her stomach and down the long shimmering ramp towards the Shore, the family station wagons still zipping past on their right. Beyond them up the harbour were anarchic clusters of becalmed yachts, and beyond them, islands, olive green and then blue, leading out to an unnatural horizon, slashed, as in a child's drawing, across the whole bright perspective. Below the bridge on their left the houses were also like toys.

Is it 'memory' that plays these tricks? Some sort of current account, where you can make withdrawals so long as you also pay in? She's thinking of value, but not like that. Some memories seem to her like gifts. But others subtract from her when she receives them ... some kind of negative power, destruction. ... That Saturday, as she remembers it, is clear and simple, 'childishly' so. To come to her now, it's had to pass through the filters of three confused years. It's emerged brightly, strangely without sound, but full of motion and light and colour, the sense of a body stretching itself in a space which gives it room and time, a dreamlike sense of relaxation, dreamlike transport. How can there be anything left? Anything which hasn't lodged with the other litter and grit against the interstices of those difficult filters ... no doubt that's it: what she has, however trashy, is also refined. A defence. It's like the question, 'What else could I have done?' Choices are for the present, or the future: that *now* we keep waiting for ... or hauling in, like kids fishing, too hopeful to sit out the time until the actual tug of the present on the line tells us we're in luck ... The past is litter, pure gold. There's no further reduction to make, except destruction.

In the south once, on a stormy day, Chink had a long discussion with a young poet they'd gone to see. It was at the same house Kate's staying in now, though when she remembers it it seems elsewhere.

It had been raining for days, and blowing from the south. Everyone was on edge. They'd been discussing the problems of a mutual friend, drinking wine. Chink said, after a good deal of wrangling, and with sudden ferocity, that you learned nothing from the past, because there was no such thing, because any decisions you made had never been made before. Then Curtis said some lines from one of his poems.

> Last year's emotions
> jack off at the bottom of the garden
> it is better so
> what we go forward on is solid with their solitude

He was drunk, sententious. It had been a boring conversation. The room was stuffy, and stale with coal smoke. The lines sounded crude and easy to her. Yet it seemed that

Curtis and Chink agreed. But Chink sat morosely, looking out the window. The rain had stopped and a wash of sunlight flowed over the scrubby expanse of a hill opposite the house.

'That's not what I meant,' Chink said. Then he stood up and asked Kate if she'd like to go for a walk. They went abruptly out, leaving Curtis poking at the fire.

'Why did you put Curtis down?' she asked. They were labouring up a steep hill to the flagstaff above the docks. Chink was leaning forward into the slope. She couldn't see his face.

'Never mind,' he muttered. Then, after a pause, he added, 'I just thought it was a nasty poem — what does he know about such things, sitting in front of his fire?'

'But he's been through some heavy shit.'

'That's what I mean,' said Chink.

He stopped. They'd reached the top of the hill. Below them was the ferrous-red and black asphalt clutter of the little port, the cranes and derricks motionless and deserted, the sea grey. The wind whipped round them.

'That's what I mean,' said Chink again. 'I mean, Curtis just forgets it. He doesn't have any of it with him. Anything that happened once that mattered remains present, right? But he just shovels it all back behind himself. Yeah, you don't learn, you're changed, that's all. Oh, no doubt he's waded through as much shit as the rest of us. But look how clean he is at the end of it! Doesn't look as though he's been through a single change ... doesn't look as though he's had to change his mind *once* since he was on the tit!' Chink stood staring down into the cold silent basin of the port. 'I sounded like him then,' he said.

Then he began to walk down the other side of the hill. 'Let's get over to the back beach.'

They scrambled down the muddy path to the road which ran around the perimeter of the township's peninsula, along the channel. Here the sea was a dirty colour, except where the main current was flushing it clear. The tide was running in against the wind, pushing up white horses and spray. She was stumbling after Chink, wanting to say, 'You're wrong about Curtis, if you can think that about him then you can think it about me, and you're wrong ... it's possible to be born again.' But the wind was driving into her face.

But he'd started running, had leapt out on to a narrow jetty and was flying down it above the turbulent water. She watched in terror. She thought, He's going to jump ... It must have been the abandon with which he flung himself along the planks, towards the platform at the end. But when he got there he stood facing up the channel into the wind. Then he turned and started back. She could see how the wind shoved at him. He began to mime a guitar player, dancing towards her, opening and shutting his mouth. When he reached her they grabbed each other. His face was freezing. They hugged tightly, pummelling each other's backs and shoulders, in the lee side of a shed, hearing the water smacking under the jetty, the wind slashing among the trees. She kissed him again and again, pulling his cold face against hers, thinking, You're wrong, oh Chink you're wrong, none of that matters, this is what matters ...

But on that summer Saturday in Auckland there was no wind but the warm resistance of the air to the motorbike, and no past either, none that they shared, and no shelter needed, and no more limitation of the time they had than that absurd blue horizon, which would last as long as the day did.

They went and had lunch with some friends of Chink's who lived on the cliff at the end of Stanley Point. It was a familiar neighbourhood for Kate. She'd wished never to see it again. She had the strangest feeling, as it became clear which way Chink was going, that none of this was accidental.

'I used to live round here once,' she said into his ear, expecting him to turn his head quickly to reply, 'I know.' But he didn't say anything. When he steered into the street she still thought of as 'our street', she found that the bike was sailing her past familiar shop fronts, houses, trees, and it wasn't taking her *back there* at all ... none of it was worth a pinch of shit!

'Well, well ...'

When they got to his friends' house, Chink was welcomed with pleasure ('Hello stranger ...') as though he'd been expected. She didn't mind. The woman of the house, who was beautiful though no longer young, examined Chink with the proprietary eyes of a lover.

'What've you been up to?'

'Apologising,' he said. For some reason she found this funny. And Kate got her first taste of the legend: the woman's gaze leaving Chink, and seeming to break against Kate's young body: 'I name thee ...' It was a pleasure of a kind, to be credited with such a role ... to be credited with the power to play it.

Chink told them about the burglary, making a good story of it. It was the first time she'd heard him speak at any length, having only watched him at Beck's. She could see why Beck appreciated him. But there was no point interrupting him. When he'd told the story he was quiet again, lolling against the wall. It was as though he'd come all the way over to tell his friends the story of the burglary. The woman's eyes flicked at Kate, sorting out the fact that she hadn't been there at the time. They were all a little drunk. Then Chink suddenly said, 'Gotta go.' Kate saw the woman hug Chink goodbye, and quickly bunt her lean pelvis in against him. Then she was waving and smiling as Chink started the bike.

'Come and see us again soon ... you too ...'

They went back to the comical shambles of his borrowed flat and she helped him clear up. She was chattering on about how good it was to be in Auckland again. Then they had a coffee. She realized how tired he looked. It was about four o'clock.

'You look fucked,' she said. 'You'd better crash.'

'Do you want a ride back to Beck's?'

'No, I'll walk.'

'Come and have a meal later, then.'

'All right.'

'I'll meet you in Tony's in Khartoum Place at seven.'

She let herself out. He was wearily dragging off his boots and all at once burst into laughter and threw the boots at the wall.

She didn't go back to Beck's. She walked up to the Domain and wandered around, drank a Fanta. A wedding party was having its photograph taken by the duckpond. Children who didn't belong kept barging in on the scene, trying to get closer to the ducks, to give them bread. Then she sat in the late sun, on the grass, until it was time to set out to meet Chink.

The cars and children were leaving. They were packing up the games of cricket down there. She longed for the place to be deserted. The road which wound through the park was filled with traffic travelling in both directions. It was impossible to imagine where it might all be going, or coming from. It was like blood, a small section of a kind of endless reticulation, a maze, a mystery, within which there was an endless motion, utterly inscrutable ... yes, and if you tried to make sense of it, you'd go crazy. The lines of traffic were so unbroken that after a while their motion seemed almost to cease: she was looking at a snake-like scintillation, a flicker of stasis. She had the sense of occupying some kind of pivot or fulcrum. The city sounds which reached her seemed to tip past the point of perception where she could hear them. They became a kind of silence. She felt herself poised above a mystery, in a precarious balance. That woman on the Shore came suddenly to mind. She found herself laughing at the memory of the woman's eyes. How easy appearances were, and deceptions! How much the woman had assumed. All the same it had been pleasant, being cast in that role.

It was getting late. She stood up, brushing dry grass from her clothes. Below her the snake of traffic was once again in motion, and its noise reached her loud and clear. She went down and joined the flow.

She walked downtown across Grafton Bridge. Some Indian couples were going slowly in the same direction. She felt happy, and loose and graceful, like the slender young Indian women in their lovely saris, though beside them, she thought, she must look clumsy and eager. In Albert Park as she went through a few people were still lying about. The sounds of Saturday night traffic in the city rose towards her, muffled by distance and trees, but more it seemed by the warm evening air, filled with the perfumes of hot grass and flowers in the park.

She remembers that she took her sandals off and dipped her feet in the cool fountain, shuffling them dry on the grass, before going on down through the dim, verbena and rosemary scented paths under the trees, towards Khartoum Place.

They had dinner in the small crowded restaurant, then went up to the Kiwi. There was another party at Beck's. The noise and crush in the bar were frightful.

'I'm sick of his cynicism.'

'But it's only a manner ...' She wondered whether she should let on that Beck had told her the story about himself and Chink. She found it impossible to guess how he might react ... and thinking back now, while a cool summer rain storm drenches the green broadleaf outside the window and distorts her reflection in the glass, she finds she can't guess, even now, whether that piece of his past mattered enough to him for him to keep present, in that weird grab-bag of knowledge he contrived to lug around like Bunyan's Christian's burden, like some obscene fleshy encrustment ... the mask slipping ... the flicker of animal reflex. ... And *me*: did he remember *me*, did I matter?

'He loved me, he loved me ...'

The words surprise her into looking up: her reflection in the window is sad, its outlines warped by trickling rain: that static glitter of destruction, where time's arrested, where the process goes on and on and on, *there*, without change. Shaking her head, closing her eyes to her reflection.

It was Chink who wanted to go to the party, and in spite of what she'd said, she didn't want to go near it. Chink wasn't being kind to her, as dear Beck had to be, with his lectures on the evils of mandrax and on what he called 'the need to strike the rock with your staff': meaning get on with it ... have faith. Chink had no advice for her.

The bar was the usual zoo. They left before it closed. Of course they went to Beck's. Hardly anyone had turned up. Beck jogged through the main room with a tape-recorder.

'Had a full day?' He glared at Kate. 'Come with me, I've got a beauty.'

'D'you want to go?' Chink asked, but then went up the stairs anyway. She followed him into Beck's room. Beck was jumping around arranging things.

'This here's an experiment.' He fixed up the machine next to a boy sitting on the bed. 'And this is Julian, he's a poet or should I say another poet.'

They said hello. Beck turned out all the lights but one over his desk. He began to roll some joints there. The rest of them were sitting like a school class on the bed.

'Julian,' said Beck with magisterial air, 'doesn't believe in rational discourse. He believes that poetry's what comes naturally. So we're gonna have a go.'

The boy was very skinny with long red hair. He had a young white face. He was no match for Beck. They smoked a log. Beck was jumping around the room 'setting up the experiment', chattering away, something about 'Man is not a fly.'

'Everybody relax!' Beck switched on the tape-recorder. 'Now this is gonna come naturally,' he said.

The boy was smashed. He smiled and nodded.

'All right,' said Beck, 'what happens is the first thing you say, the first thing that comes into your head's the first line of a poem. But I'll tell you when you've hit it. Then you go on and say a poem beginning with that first line.'

'I've got a shitty cold,' said the boy.

'Cancel that,' said Beck.

'I've bought a car.'

'Cancel that.'

'It's spring.'

'Cancel that!'

'The broadbeans burst into flower?'

'Cancel that!'

'My lady's pregnant.'

'Uh huh?'

'She's reading Thomas Hardy and others.'

'Not bad. Go on. *Synthesize*, fellah.'

'A pregnant woman discovers the meaning of fiction.'

'Very good ...'

The boy suddenly cracked up. He rolled around on the bed laughing.

'All right, here it is:

> A pregnant woman discovers the meaning of fiction
> for the first time. What incredible
> feats of the imagination reveal themselves to her:
> e.g. *he* peddles *his* wife in the cattle market
> another lovely lady gets around
> shooting prize athletes with silver bullets.
> She browses over the books in her big blue dress.
> She is beautiful. She has never read
> this much fiction before.
> She has never understood so much.

'Well,' said Beck, and shot smoke from his nose, 'you got a really good first line but you blew the rest. Why couldn't you let the thing follow itself through?'

'Fuck you,' said the boy sleepily. 'You do better.'

'Let's see what you can make of those other shitty lines. What was the first one? Actually "shitty" something ...'

'I've got a shitty cold?'

'Yes, I've got a shitty cold. Let's see what you can do with that.'

'Okay. I've got a shitty cold.' The boy paused. 'Are you serious?' he said. 'That's not poetry.'

'Not yet it isn't.'

'Let's see,' said the boy dreamily.

> I've got a shitty cold. Out at sea
> the steamers' smokestacks tootle.
> South America's just over there
> where the Andes fondles divine nether parts.
> You can also blow your nose in them.

They were both rolling around laughing.

'Right, next was ...'

'I've bought a car,' said the boy.

'Go to it,' Beck looking the other way.

> I've bought a car
> oh no Joplin
> not even Bobby Magee
> history will make no distinction
> let the dealer look at your teeth lady
> this boy's buying older and older cars
> to get Janis back
> time is only consumer goods
> is only as good as the use you make of it
> that's what the man said
> when he sold me this Mercedes Benz

'"O Lord won't you buy me ... a Mercedes Benz,"' sang Chink in a Janis Joplin falsetto.

'Shut up Chink,' said Beck. 'You can be prima donna some other time. What's the penultimate, "It's spring"? Oh shit, what kind of treatment can you give that?'

> It's spring.
> Prove it.
> O my cock's flowered
> in the sun which
> accompanied her
> down the
> steps.

Then Julian sat back. 'I'm too spaced for this wee exercise,' he said.

Beck's face was white, as white as the boy's, in the dim room.

'Unsatisfactory class of students these days,' said Beck.

'Knock it off, Beck,' said Chink.

'Speak when you're spoken to,' said Beck. 'Buy Kate a ticket for your trip. Meanwhile me and Julian are gonna stay inside, we're conducting an experiment ... What's your last chance, Julian?'

'The broadbeans burst into flower.' He really wanted to get out, it was obvious. He jumped to his feet and shouted.

> The broadbeans burst into flower
> Us broads have been thirsting for hours
> Broad inna beam but first by the powers
> The orb's been lost in tough hours ...

'Oh fuck,' he said. He went out and slammed the door.

'The rest of you can go too, you bore me stiff,' said Beck.

The tape was still revolving on the machine. Chink reached over and turned it off. They went to the door. She looked back. Beck was shaking his head, as though about to cry.

'See you later, old Beck,' she said.

'All right ... that little shit ... I should've raped him with my broadbean.' He began to laugh, still shaking his head.

They descended majestically into the roar of the party. They didn't need Beck any more, bless him ... All at once she felt launched, felt that woman's champagne gaze break like a cool benediction on her skin, which rose in gooseflesh where Chink touched her to turn the corner of the stairs.

She kissed his neck. He told her enough to give them some kind of common past. The day's simplicity was lost. It no longer mattered. The order of things no longer mattered.

'Do you want to come back?'

They smiled at each other. They were transparent. Her heart was banging.

'It might be more peaceful than here.'

'Might be.' His face opened: that smile. 'All right,' he said. 'Let's go, Kate the Kate.'

Beck was shaking his head at her. He drew a thin finger across his throat. She didn't care. She could strike the rock with her staff.

Chink had taken a couple of Beck's joints. They smoked one outside in the garden. The noise of the party came to them like a soundtrack of a cheap film about a war. The sound of John McLaughlin's guitar pitched up from time to time out of the roar of voices, like a general who can't make himself heard. He's babbling retreat, and the army's attacking, or vice versa. Nerve warfare. ... Near them under the trees two girls were quarrelling. She heard one of them say, '... and now you ...'

They rode away from it all like survivors. It wasn't even very late, just around midnight. They sailed through the streets. She leaned her cheek on the back of Chink's old coat and sang:

> O Lord won't you buy me
> A Mercedes Benz ...

... and leans her cheek against the back of her hand, in this room where the light's fading again: the familiar coda of these days, a metric which is beginning to wind her up towards some gesture ... Though there are days like this one, when she gets up quietly and goes down to the other end of the house, towards the sounds of lives being lived there: the summer light of Ingrid's hair, the baby, Curtis ... these friends within whose circle she feels adrift, like an empty boat on a calm green lake ... But her friends don't know the words.

> O Lord won't you buy me
> A Mercedes Benz
> My friends are all dead
> I must make amends

# 7 Badedas Bath

Chink opened the door and went in ahead of her: taking possession. Someone's cleaned up, she thought. The afternoon had backed off. She thought of the people in it as 'him' and 'her'. Their voices had gone flat, the metallic squawk of memory, like Julian's voice on the tape-recorder. Or like the city sounds which tipped past her into silence, in the park. The most vivid surviving fragment was that of the girl's voice saying, bitterly, '... and now you ...'

The words that came out of her were huge, they filled her mouth, blocking her tongue. She wondered if he could hear them. He was at the far end of the room, turning on the record-player.

Then everything stopped. It had been nothing to do with her. She'd been brought to where she was meant to be ... as though she were about to emerge, there in Chink's borrowed flat, shedding the last disguise, lifting it from herself ... Oh she couldn't even speak. At the same time a vacuum was rising inside her. It seemed to be choking her. She saw Chink turn around. Her arms rose in front of her. Then he disappeared. Her eyes had closed. Tears were pouring down her cheeks. He'd crossed the room and was holding her. She could feel her arms going around him. He was huge and somehow light.

She was sitting on the sofa and Chink was kneeling in front of her. She began to cry, sobbing and gasping, and fell forward against him, to put her arms around him, her face against his neck. He held her gently, dipping his mouth on to her shoulder.

All at once she saw what she'd done. She saw herself holding out her arms like that: 'Come to me!' How absurd, how fucking stupid!

'Hey c'mon, take it easy, take it easy ...'

But it just kept winding out of her, like a siren ... oh oh oh oh oh ... The feeling was *shapely* ... She was aware of its limits as she was aware of the limits of her body. She could see her forearm around Chink's shoulder, and she rubbed her lips across it, feeling the small hairs. Then she pressed her mouth back against his neck. She thought that if she let go of him the feeling would go. He was still holding her gently. She found she was trying to say 'Thank you' and the thought of this made her laugh even harder. She wanted to say the shape of her feeling to him. It seemed that almost anything she said would do.

Then Chink pushed her back against the sofa. The instant quiet was like a blow. Chink was kneeling in front of her, his hands on her knees. She heard Howlin' Wolf on the record-player, solid and familiar: '... because I'm built for comfort ... I ain't built for speed ...'

'Well,' said Chink. 'You *are* a strange lady. Are you okay?'

'I'm sorry.'

She watched him walk away down the room and into the kitchen. On impulse she got up and began to rearrange things. She pushed some of the chairs around. She was doing this very seriously, with a feeling of sensible purpose. It seemed necessary to bring the room 'up to date'.

Chink came out of the kitchen with two cups.

'For Christ's sake ...' He stood in the kitchen door holding the cups. She was laughing. For the first time she felt that something depended on her. She sat down.

'D'you wanna go back to Beck's?' She tugged at his hand. Coffee slopped on to the carpet. He leant carefully over her.

'No I don't,' she said. 'I'm a bit stoned and I've had a hard time. That seems over now. I wanted to bring the room up to date, that's all. It's not complicated.'

He slumped down opposite her.

'Listen,' he said as though he'd made a decision, 'don't depend on me too much, that's what I mean. I'm not dependable.'

'I'm gonna have a bath,' she said.

The area he was getting into was unnecessary ... she refused it. He was still staring at her, with something furious in his expression, drawing pale bones up to the skin. But it was like stepping out of a two-dimensional world into one with depth, a real horizon: Chink in his chair, there. She was glad he wasn't just kind. There seemed to be plenty of time ... a space as dreamlike as the summer harbour.

'I'm going to have a bath,' she said again, but didn't move: she stared at him, he stared back.

Then Chink suddenly strained his eyes wide. He shot himself with two fingers under his left ear. Then he closed his eyes. He still looked white and weary. He was sitting sprawled in an armchair, his legs stretched out, his chin on his chest, occupying all the space there was.

It was a big old-fashioned bath with lion's-paw legs. The taps had neat porcelain buttons in their tops with 'Hot' and 'Cold'. She decided to fill the bath right up. While it was running she looked into the cupboard above the basin. There was some *Badedas* there, so she put it in the water when the bath was full. The water turned green. Then she looked at her face in the mirror. Her eyes were red and there were salty trails on her cheeks. She took her clothes off and looked in the mirror again, from different angles. She thought she'd got thin over the past weeks. But it made her breasts look better. She felt contented and orderly. She picked her clothes up and folded them on a chair. Then she made sure there was soap by the bath. She took a big loofah off a hook on the wall, and dropped it in. She weighed herself. She was a stone less than when Dave had left.

Then she got into the bath and lay flat with just her head out. The water came up almost to the edge. It was deep enough for her to feel suspended in. Her limbs hung, a warped and tender green. Steam had condensed on the white walls of the room, leaving trails, like my face, she thought: skinny, face like a bathroom wall. She ducked her head under and came up rubbing her hair. When she opened her eyes Chink was standing there with a towel.

'What's that green?'

'*Badedas* ... it was in your cupboard.' She lay still, looking up at him.

'I never thought of it,' he said. He dropped the towel on a chair and left.

Because she was in the bath she began to soap herself, automatically. *Not dependable* ... she tried the words in her head. Chink had had enough of her after all, 'a neurotic cunt'.

Then the door swung open. There was no one there.

'Goddamn draught.'

But two-thirds of the way up the edge of the door a single finger appeared, creeping around, testing the way as though blind. A second finger appeared, and a whole hand.

'Come in!' she shouted. 'Come in! Little hand, come on in! Come to Mama! I thought you were never going to come.'

The hand grasped the edge of the door. She was watching it, tense with glee like a child, when some distance below the hand she saw the end of Chink's erect prick creeping slowly into sight like a great cyclamen, an orchid, a corsage being offered shyly at the girl's door ... Holy shit! He was mad ...

'Bring your vulgar friend too,' she shouted.

Chink walked in, grinning. It was as though he was surfing towards her. She was screaming with laughter. He reached behind her and pulled the plug out. She'd sat with her back against the taps so she could see the door. Put it in lights. She had the feeling she'd been directed in some obscure theatrical game.

When some water had drained Chink put the plug back then gently pushed her head forward and began to soap her back. She rested her forehead on her raised knees.

'What a long back you have, like a real amphibian,' he said. He massaged between her shoulders and neck, then pushed his soapy hands slowly under her arms, passed them over her breasts. She let her weight rest on her forehead and closed her eyes. He held her gently, touching her nipples with the outsides of his thumbs. Then he took his hands away and lifted water with them to pour over her back. She sat up and turned her head. When she opened her eyes his prick was there.

'Hello, "friend" ...'

His fingers closed her ears ... she heard sea. Chink's muffled voice: 'Well, now Kate ...' She kissed his prick again, touching the side of it with her tongue, and closed her lips over it. It filled her mouth as the words had done earlier. It was as though it was the word she'd needed.

At night, now, she can hear Curtis and Ingrid making love ... and just at the moment she can hear them all living, *con moto*, there at the other end of the house, and the radio on, as though the sounds of their life have been set to tawdry music, for her benefit. ... She blocks her ears ... and closes her eyes, as she closed them then, her mouth at work on this message, her arms reaching awkwardly up out of the bath to hold him ...

Then Chink had taken his hands from her ears. He just moved away and got into the bath, his cock breaking surface like some kind of sea snake. They were sitting staring at each other again. She again had the sense of being directed in some game.

'Well,' he said. 'How are you Kate?' He was smiling. She just nodded, reached out to touch his face. He sat with his arms resting along the sides of the bath. 'You look fine to me,' he said. She nodded again. 'Right,' he said.

He soaped himself, whistling, smiling at her.

'You see me now in my element. I'm invulnerable.' Then he got quickly out, dried himself, cleaned his teeth, and left.

When she went into the bedroom she got another shock: the scene was 'set', all the corny paraphernalia ... a big candle had been lit, and incense, and Chink was sitting grinning on the bed, starting off the last of Beck's joints.

'Why, hello ...' She minced towards him, oopedoop. A game two can play, called 'Things happen after a Badedas Bath' ...

'Things happen after a Badedas Bath ...'

'What a long and lovely girl,' he said, with the same curious inflexion he'd given the words when he first spoke to her, from the living-room floor of Beck's place.

She sat beside him on the bed.

'Nice place you have here.'

'It's comfortable.'

Their bodies touched at thigh and shoulder. They smoked the log in silence, their fingers making the small journey back and forth, smelling each other's breath in the smoke, beginning to turn together until their shoulders no longer touched, until they were almost face to face, until she hooked one leg over one of his ... and then they did turn together, at last, with a shared groan, the hot roach dropped to the floor, the friend taken into Kate's upstretched fork ...

'Things happen after a Badedas Bath ...' She had time to whisper it, the name of the game. Then she forgot about it, the whole routine. Ah dear stranger, dear friend. There was that moment of doubt, when depth and time seemed to flatten out, when she saw his face like a mask. Then it broke. His comical smile and shout ('Kate, Kate!') were different from the comedy of the hand, the friend, the anxious lover, the Badedas commercial ... they weren't part of any game. He lay panting. Hey, strange man, that was lovely. That was a relief.

She was lying looking at him. He was very strongly made, but his body was almost hairless, except for a thin line which grew from his groin to a point just below his chest. His shoulders were broad but rather stooping. This gave him an appearance of menace at such times as he was standing still, in the corner of a room, for instance. *I've missed you, Kate.* His hair was long and black and straight. It was sawn off roughly across his brow, which increased the impression of immobility. All day the summer rain's been tapping at the broadleaf out there. When he smiled his face seemed to split in a straight line. When he laughed it was as though a hinge in his head had dropped: the bottom half of his face fell. His eyes were flat and exposed, set wide apart, grey. He could open them until they seemed to turn red at the edges. When he was angry all that could be seen of them was a wet glint, very bright. His hands were large and quite rough from the work he'd done. But the fingers were long and slender nevertheless. Playing a guitar made his hands look almost feminine, because the bunches of muscle in his palms were drawn inward, so that the whole hand matched the length and slenderness of the fingers. *If you wanna know something you have to ask the right question. It's like you have to know the answer already. So much time gets wasted.* Although his ribs showed, he didn't look skinny, because his arms were heavy and strong, and also because he had a thick waist. He claimed this was from swimming, which he'd done competitively. He kept very clean shaven. His chest and shoulders bore the scars of adolescent acne, as did his cheeks, though you tended not to notice this because of the general heaviness of his face. His feet turned inward ('swimming'), his legs were very long. His feet were ugly, with bunched toes, perhaps because he always wore boots. From behind he looked slender, though heavy across the shoulders. This may have been because, below the muscular waist, his buttocks and legs were skinny. *Hey Kate, tell the boss to blow it out his arse. This offer can't last.* There was a strange disproportion about him, and yet he was 'beautiful': his shapeliness was somehow simple and modest. He once said the same about her. *We were made for each other: watch this ...* She guesses it was because she's tall and dark with large breasts, and thin legs which embarrass her into preferring trousers. Lying face to face with their feet stretched out, her toes would come to the beginning of his instep. All day rain and dim humid light. Impossible to tell what time it is. When they placed their faces together his mouth was lower than hers, by the width of a lip, so that he could hold her lower lip between his while she held his upper one. Their eyes were level, though his were further apart. *I've missed you Kate.* His skin was very white, Celtic she thought. He hadn't been in the sun at all that summer.

How much of this she learned that night! She studied him, as though to remember.

Anything she learned later, like his hands playing a guitar, was made to fit that first lesson.

Now it seems to her that she studied him because of those precarious moments, during which a brand new certainty was shaken and shaken. Because we're not dependable. In such a short time she'd passed through release, to dependence, to a different equilibrium (she believed) whose balance was maintained by such brief moments as that of Chink's exquisite smile ... the simple sufficiency of his gentleness. At such moments, she thought, we transcend the inertia that attracts pain as surely as an open wound attracts flies. If only we can remember those moments, and at the same time keep the wound covered with whatever dressing or cosmetic we have, then we'll make it to the next zenith, the next miraculous smile, the next lesson. If it finishes now, she thought, that'll be no more or less than I expected from the start. At any rate I'll remember.

It was as though she heard two voices in the room: Julian saying, 'She has never understood so much', and the weeping girl in the dark garden '... and now you ...'

So she turned towards him again. He was lying on his back, his eyelids drooping, looking sideways at her.

'How'd you like to come south with me Kate, the day after tomorrow? We could have a good trip. Let's get out of here. Let's really get out of here.'

*At any rate I'll remember. If it finishes now.* In hope the mind closes, blinks and closes, like the eyelids of a lover. 'Oh let it happen.' And sometimes you can't open your eyes, even if you want to.

In the morning they put some gear on the train for Dunedin. Chink stored his friend's bike at Beck's place. Beck wasn't home so Kate left a long note: '... off to strike the rock ...'

The day after, Monday, they began hitching south, in the rain.

It's rained all day, however much day there's been.

It was that simple. The lesson learned and as soon occluded, to be relearned and ('let it happen') obscured, ignored, thrust aside, again and again: *faith's gorgeous frail galleon*, as Beck had said once, sailing his thin hands through an imaginary languid ocean.

'All right,' she said casually, closing her eyes. 'I'll come, I was thinking of heading off soon anyway.'

She'd given in. It was a relief.

And silently, 'Yes, yes, oh Chink, we could have a good trip. Let's really get out of here ...'

*Let's get the fuck out of here!*

# 8

Choose a date: 1860. Some things have happened, some haven't, and some are in progress. It's incredible how many men have wandered New Zealand keeping meticulous notebooks and sketchbooks. These men are often soldiers, others are surveyors or priests. They travel because they have to. There's no point asking if this compulsion's enforced by powers outside themselves, or by some inner power of their own. Are they functions or causes? Even a century and more later it's impossible to measure the proportions.

But looking at these sketches, the painstaking and oppressive detail of them, the omniscience of the light in which their subjects were seen, we sense the *certainty* of the men who made them. Though the conditions under which they were made must often have been anything but leisurely, they seem nonetheless to be leisurely. They're the products of an expansive faith. They measure time in expansive units. What they conceal are the small units: the time lag between the axe striking the tree and the sound reaching the other side of the valley ... the man falling, the sound of the musket ... the crack of the bullock cart's axle and the beasts wrenched to their knees in the river crossing ... the coughing of a Maori child with measles. They don't so much ignore such a scale as subsume it.

How different this freedom is from Chink's line of need, his exact and claustrophobic dedication ... Oh, he knew lots about some things ...

At this moment, in her sunny room, Kate's picking her way through a strange assortment of photographs and reproductions Chink had got together.

Delivering stores on the Waipa River near Ngaruawahia *circa* 1910 ... for'ard on the flatbottomed steam barge is a large winch. The boat's got almost no freeboard. The wheel's roughly amidships, where sacks of wheat and flour are piled. A plank's been laid from gunwale to bank. In the background are Lombardy poplars whose scale seems incongruous at first: then you realize that they're still young. There are also some macrocarpa, likewise well-established but young. A road runs past a small farmhouse. In the background is dense bush on hills, possibly Taupiri, the sacred mountain.

Here's Dick Seddon's Great Dive. They're waiting for him to come up. 'He stayed under 5 mins. A record!' It's on the Waikato River, at a Ngaruawahia Regatta. A willow shades a crowd of Maoris on the bank. On the river in the distance is a large canoe. Up close are two boats, the steam boat from which Seddon has dived, and a smaller boat with a brass band in it. Everyone is looking at the calm surface of the river, waiting. ... In the foreground is a large Maori with a black band on his left arm. On the back of this photograph Chink has scribbled *Te Waiorongo: the tranquil and peaceful waters*.

Ngaruawahia 1864: here's The Delta, in a lithograph by G Pulman of Auckland. The Key shows King's Palace, King's Tomb, House of Parliament. The note reads: *Most of the natives' huts are back about half-a-mile towards the bush*. To which Chink had added, *Inspection by request*. There are conical military tents. In the background the Waipa River has a wee canoe on it. In the foreground men in military uniform are getting out of a rowboat on the banks of the Waikato. The Delta is like the prow of a canoe, the jutting bows of a galleon. The flagpole, whose power was widely understood, is situated like a mast. Thus the Royal Compound sails faithfully into Kate's present, with Chink aboard ...

Here are two early photographs: *The Tomb of Te Wherowhero* and *The Whare of*

*Te Wherowhero*. The tomb is incongruous, built of weatherboard, set among scruffy bracken, on rough clay, the size of a big dog-kennel ... Kate remembers a portrait of the King, Potatau Te Wherowhero, by George French Angas: a tough kind face, hair fierce and curly as though to suggest energy, impatience, intellect, a large *kuru* in his left ear, heavy *moko*, sitting at ease in a blanket, probably on the selfsame Delta ... By the tomb stands a soldier: a Guide? The *whare's* also got soldiers around it, in ill-fitting uniforms ... some kind of Palace Guard? The proud wretchedness of it strikes her now. She remembers Chink's anger ...

In 1910 Simmelhag's Delta Hotel was the same grand building it is now. Then its proprietor was an Irishman, R Ryan. Its spacious upstairs rooms opened on to the impressive balcony. Its chimneys were built in two kinds of brick, for contrast. Its other decorations were solid and on a grand scale. In the photograph Chink kept, Maoris sit and lounge in the sun around the downstairs walls ...

A man was doing animal imitations at one end of the bar. The room was filled with tuis, dogs, cows. Outside the rain pelted down, the dull sound of a great hidden dynamo. There was a pool table at the far end of the room, and a blackboard with two names chalked up.

'D'you play pool?'

'If Paul Newman was a woman I'd be The Hustler.'

Chink took off his wet pea coat and put it with the bags, then walked down the room and wrote his name on the blackboard: *Chink*. Any questions. Under it he added *Kate the Newman*. He bought a jug at the bar and came back grinning, head falling apart.

A drunk man in a green cardigan caught at his arm. Beer slopped from the jug on to the floor. Chink performed a small arabesque, clutching the jug in both hands. He bent over the man. They appeared to be conferring together. Then Chink filled the man's glass.

'Rightoh mate.'

Because of the rain the room was about half full. Many of the drinkers were off the road repair gang. The animal man made a farting sound with his mouth: 'That was a student.' Chink took no notice, pulling his hair back and wringing at it.

'Gesundheit, Kate.'

'Sweet dreams, Chink.'

*Clink*: to Faith's Galleon ...

Every mile south he gets higher and quieter and crazier. His head's ripping right round. That's not a smile, its ...

'D'you know how I feel?' she said.

'Like two big tits on a pole.'

'No, listen. The other day I was walking up Queen Street. One of those Christian revivalists stopped me. He was outside John Courts, really weedy, wearing a suit and one of those Texan string ties. Behind him was a display window full of undressed manikins like a lot of scalded naked women in body stockings. He was really insistent. Young lady, young lady! The setting was so weird that I stopped. Then he asked if I'd been born again. He was staring at me like you do sometimes ...

'Yeah ...'

'No, shut up. It was obvious he didn't care that I was a woman. He hadn't noticed all those obscene mannikins behind him. I mean he'd chosen a piss-poor spot for his pitch. He stared at me and asked if I'd been *born* again. Usually I'd have said something smart, or walked on. But this time it was different. I was taller than him, but he was really intense. I heard myself saying, Yes, yes, I've been born again. His face lit up like a beacon. God bless you! He said. God bless you! God bless you! — about six times. Then I walked away. It really knocked me out. I really felt as though I *had* been born again. I even felt grateful to him. He really had power ... when I looked back, he'd gone.'

'Yes?'

'Don't things ever happen to you like that, Chink? You wonder if they were real. Yet they had this terrific feeling of purpose. It's as though you needed to invent them, as a kind of lever, to get yourself over ...'

Now why didn't that story get across ...

'Do you want to travel, Kate?'

'You mean overseas?'

'I mean Lake Chad, the Atlas Mountains, ultimately other universes ... There's plenty of time ...'

'I've never had the bread. I almost got to Wales once ...'

'*Wales?*'

'... But I've been tied down this way and that.'

'That's not what I mean. Like the feeling you're getting somewhere. Like right now, ah ... I'm in Marrakesh! I'm in Xanadhu!'

'Can I come?'

She'd been rehearsing her story about the revivalist. It's unlikely that considerations of trust occurred to him. To be straight, *no more name rank and serial number*, and to announce that you're *not dependable*, to crow like that: *I'm in Xanadhu!* ... what kind of vanity was at work here? She felt her heart sink.

'I'm talking about dreams, Kate. That's a habit of mine. Didn't you say Sweet dreams just now? I even met you in one, right? Here we are. It's Xanadhu, its amazing ...'

But the magic had gone: the room with its loud creatures, the sanctuary. She was going south, a direction she'd only recently escaped. Why? It was no part of any plan she had. It had nothing to do with her. She remembered Beck slicing a finger across his jugular. She thought, Go back to Auckland, Kate. It was as though Chink had addressed her, as though this was his first serious advice: You want to trust me? Okay: fuck off ...

His neutral face dips to his glass. He's stitched his comic head together. He puts a cigarette in his mouth. He watches her in silence: another staring session. Who are you. That's not a question.

She was going to stand up ... 'I'm sorry' ... walk back on to the road north. He wouldn't dream of her, even for the time it would take him to step out the door and continue in the opposite direction. He'd left everything. She could feel her legs preparing to stand. Goodbye lay like a morning-after taste on her tongue ...

Then Chink's eyes flicked right past her.

'Our names are up, Kate Hustler Newman.'

'Hey whatsyername ...'

'That's us.' He lofted one arm in the air. 'Come on Kate.' He stood up and leaned over the table and kissed her. 'We'll clean them up. We're quits now, no more name rank and serial number, okay?'

It was a kind of trial: paws running, running to charge his generator ... a maze to thread for her reward: Chink. She had the choice. She'd been given it.

Meanwhile he'd walked to the other end of the room where the pool table was.

You arrogant shit ...

He was chalking the end of a cue: efficient flicks of his wrist. The other two men watched her walk over. Hey, lookit this ...

'This is Kate Newman,' said Chink, 'the best pool player in the Pacific.'

'Chink, couldn't we ...'

'C'mon now Kate, you can't back out. We can beat them.'

The men were watching. They were drunk, friendly, scornful. One of them was the man in the green cardigan. Chink whistled and looked along his cue. She didn't want to play this fucking game.

'Right.' Chink wasn't going to break his stride. He rested the butt of his cue on the floor and grinned at the two men.

'What d'you want on?' asked green cardigan.

'A dollar?'

'Shee-it!'

'Rightoh,' said green cardigan.

Chink bought a jug. His head was dropping open again. He padded around the table between shots, whistling between his teeth. 'Distraction!' shouted someone. He played with panache, shooting quickly, filling the glasses. 'We're pretty good Kate ... gotta look after the brass ...'

They cleaned the men up. They played two more games and won. The opposition earnestly sliced shots round the table.

'Double or quits,' said green cardigan. He spat on his hands. There were four dollars up, counting the original one Chink had put in.

'Nothing in,' said Chink. 'Just double or quits on this, I'll make this a kitty, fair enough?'

'Fair enough,' said green cardigan. His companion was paying not playing.

'You're mad,' he said. 'This bloke's a cracker.'

'This time,' said green cardigan. 'Who wants to be rich?'

But they won again. Green cardigan handed over another four dollars. Chink took his own out, put another on the bar, held the remaining six in his hand.

'Anyone going south?'

'Smart bugger aren't you,' said the barman. 'There's more like you in the other bar. They look as though they could do with a few bob.'

Chink pulled his coat on in the shelter of the porch, flicking the collar up round his hyena grin.

'Hang on,' he said. 'I'll see what I can do with these people in here.'

'I'm not coming, Chink. You treat me as if I were just tagging along. What kind of stuff was that you were putting on in there? You were laughing at that guy in the green cardigan. You could see how pissed he was, and you kept tipping it into him.'

'I could've lost.'

'You didn't.'

'*We* didn't. Anyway it looks as though I have.'

'Chink stop playing games with me. No more name rank and serial number, remember?'

'So you'll come?'

'I don't know what to do. I never know whether you're playing a game with me or what. Even that night at your place.'

He was very pale. She saw his eyes, like that, wet glints.

'Why should I wish to prove anything to *you*, dear lady? What makes you think I'd want to turn it on for you? "That night at my place" ... what night? I'm not the boy next door. I'm not fucking Santa Claus either ...'

'All right then you bastard, just fuck off! You're full of shit ...' She was shouting in his face, crying with rage. The road behind him was slick with rain.

'Suit yourself ...'


Chink, love ... Just who are we always putting down? *Visionaries*? I sometimes hear my own voice, bitchy, like the woman who lived over the road when I was married to Dave. She used to abuse her kids, on and on. All they were doing was building some kind of secret place in the macrocarpa hedge.

Chink was a dreamer. Do we call him a visionary? Here we are, surrounded by the sea. The horizons are so endless we can almost meet ourselves setting out: endless possibility. ... What is there to talk over?

It was Chink who showed me the horizon out from Seacliff or Karitane, in the south. I'd looked at it before, often enough. But never *seen* it. When the day was hot with haze gathering in the distance, the line between sea and sky disappeared, so that the planes of the horizontal perspective curved upward into the vertical, into the milky blue dome of the sky, and back to horizontal, and over your head: a glaring wave of space and distance, within which you felt exhilarated, robbed of the simplest certainties: what was up and what was down, how to balance, how to *keep on* in a straight line ...

That day Chink demonstrated it: a swooping motion of his arms in front of himself and upward, plunging them finally over his head, and down to cradle it and clasp the back of his neck, his forearms and elbows pressed to the sides of his skull and sticking up like wings.

'The vanishing point is the back of your neck, or else within you,' he said mockingly from between the wings of his elbows, standing on the high cliff edge as though to chuck himself out like a dark ugly bird above the rocks and foam of the shoreline. 'So why kid yourself that physical motion's the most important part of journeying?'

He gave a flap with his elbows and began to walk backwards from the cliff across the paddock.

'I'm not moving,' he shouted. 'But *it* is!

Then he tripped and fell on his arse, laughing and laughing.

I suppose I became irritated with Chink and put him down as I continue to even now because in my heart I was sure he'd never in fact move gracefully out and away, leaving *us*.

Yet I suppose I had some kind of intuition early on of what his wandering up and down the country meant, and saw that those barely perceived migrations of mind and spirit which were the real, the massive correlative of the main trunk road — saw that those almost invisible migrations were substituting for something.

To the casual observer his life must have seemed an endless series of repetitive grubby excursions, campings, borrowings, ripoffs, bad deals, specious survival techniques. To those who subscribed to the cult of Chink, he was 'on the road': free and spaced, a gypsy freak. But those closest to him could see that Ngaruawahia was Marrakesh, Xanadhu.

I could see that. Or I suppose I could. But it made me angry. I sensed how exclusive it was: *Can I come?* I sensed that you didn't get invited ... but that you had to 'make a decision', as the revivalists say, all the same.

That woman over the road knew what her kids were up to. She knew that the macrocarpa hedge was Xanadhu, for example: the city of endless possibility. Yet she screeched at the kids. Of course there were also practical reasons: perhaps she longed for peace ...

But why couldn't I accept the endless possibility of Chink's vision? I stood there as he turned and went casually into the lounge bar. I had no real intention of leaving. Perhaps he guessed that ... he was vain enough.

I signed up for the trip by default. I didn't make any decision. It just wasn't within my power, at the time. I was in some kind of current. From time to time I'd get my head up, every few months, and then I'd be swept on.

Well, pick up on the company. A few ghosts here.

'Goodness me ... why hello ...'

It was Andrew who'd worked as a model: Vance Vivian slacks, grainy advertisements on the dull newsprint of the daily newspapers, a shit-eating smile on glossy Jaegger swimwear handouts, end-of-season specials at Keans Jeans. ... His likeness arrived unsolicited in your letter box. Years ago he'd collected rent from a house in Mount Eden left to him by his mother. Kate had had a room there when she was at training college and university. They all said Andrew was a bit of a dealer.

A month after moving in she'd got her *entrée* to that world. The narcs who busted the place pretended to be surprised to find her there.

'What are *you* doing here, sweetie?'

A really straight little arrow ... but that didn't prevent them from tipping her drawers out on the bed, pulling the carpet up, riffling through her Stage One textbooks. While the D's did the house she sat with her flatmates in the kitchen. Sure enough there was a little stash of acid under the stairs. None of them knew anything about it.

'Now what about visitors ... who comes here?'

'There's nobody, just us.'

'Now Kate, surely you realize how important this is. There must be someone you remember. We need your help. ... These people must be taught a lesson. You don't have anything to be afraid of. We know it's nothing to do with you ...'

'Nobody, there's nobody ...'

It was all true. But when Andrew got off the charge she felt as though she'd contributed. Some of the others moved out. She stayed.

'Now Kate here, she's not just a pretty face ...' Andrew's sarcasm was wary. She was on the inside. Thank you, officer: it's a whole new world, all right.

'... what about it, Kate? You'd really dig Sydney ...'

'Pick up for Andrew? For fuck's sake!' It was her new friend, 'Auntie Beck'. 'Listen, that bastard would've planted his own old mother. Four days in King's Cross ... far out. ... What'll you do there? You don't think Andrew's connexion's gonna show you around, do you? Ah Katie, I can just see you, eating another bag of prawns, going to the zoo, going to the pictures, and all you want to do really is take the deal back and say you want to forget it and go home ... only you don't know where to take it, because it was a girl you met by arrangement somewhere, and you haven't seen her again and you're not likely to ... So you carry your stash back through.

'Purpose of visit?'

'Holiday.'

'Four-day return concession?'

'Yes.'

'Have a good time?'

'Yes ... a good break before finals ...'

'I dunno, students these days ... your parents shouted you, did they?'

'Ah ... For Christ's sake Kate! And then here you are back again, say, you've been scared shitless, only you pretend it was "really far out", and you see Andrew getting around in a brand new van ... You know what he calls you? "Suzy Creamcheese" ... yeah, that's right ...'

And now here he was again. He was wearing a black Stetson with a peacock feather, white billowy trousers ... she forgets.

'If it isn't Kate!'

'How are you, Andrew ... it's been a long time.'

'Certainly has ...' He lifts his hat: his hair's cropped close. 'Three years ... yes they finally did it.' The Sportswear Smile, that wincing of the lips, his eyes avoiding something, or waiting for the glare of the studio lights ...

The other two she'd never seen before. One of them was older than the rest, about forty. She didn't catch his name. She got the impression he'd just chucked his job, and perhaps more than that. She lingers over the memory of him, wanting to sort him into some special category, but he won't keep still ... there's something about his resolute loneliness ...

Then there was the third, 'Californian John'. How did his hair get so blond, his denims so clean?

'Has this much time passed?'

Then she thought back to herself as a student in Andrew's house ... 'Jesus ...' Now she struggles to recognize herself at the Ngaruawahia pub. Is she that much wiser? 'I don't suppose I learned the simplest things last, or first.'

John was marching off up the road towards the bridge over the Waikato.

'I saw something, man ...'

They followed, in the rain. He was leaning over the bridge, looking at the ceremonial canoes moored there by the bank a little way up river, where the Turangawaewae *marae* was. He whistled in admiration.

'Lookit that,' he said. 'Look at *those*, those are Maori canoes, man.'

He held a hand out above the water: some kind of obscure salutation. The rain was pissing down and he had no coat on. There he stood, his shirt turning pink and transparent with wet, reverently shaking his head, one hand stuck out above the parapet of the bridge.

'Ah shit ...' Andrew sprinted back to the pub. The silent teacher followed him. Chink flashed Kate an enormous grin of derision. Then he began a lengthy address to John: the Huntly Line ... Bishop Hadfield ... the King Movement ... Waitangi. He was holding the American by the arm.

'Is that right, man, is that right?'

Chink frogmarched him across to the other side of the bridge and pointed downstream.

'It used to be there, on the Delta. There used to be a flagpole. The Delta sailed into the heart of this country. Now there's a fucking band rotunda, see?'

He frogmarched him back, John's tippytoeing feet trying to manage some sort of resistance. But he didn't stand a chance.

'... the first King was Potatau Te Wherowhero, he was a good man. His descendant Te Puea Herangi died not so long ago. The pallbearers represented all the ancestral canoes, *canoes*, right? — all except the Host Canoe, Tainui. They carried the coffin out of the gates, there ... When Te Wherowhero died his tomb was a little wooden hutch: that's what you *saw*, like you're seeing those canoes. But there was more to it than that, buddy ... now listen ...'

Chink was holding him by the upper arm: Kate could see John beginning to try and pull away. 'The night when the spirit leaves this world's called Te Pokumea, the vertiginous night, and it's carried off on Te Auterena, the steady current, which joins Te Aukumea, the dragging current at the beginning of Te Potekitea, the hidden night ...'

'Hey, man ...'

'... shut up and fucking well listen, you might learn something. ... When the soul's been prepared in Tiritiri o matangi it's ready to go on the last stage of its journey ...'

John now listened sadly, rain running off his beard. Some men had come down to the canoes and seemed to be preparing to move them. They were wearing bright yellow oilskins. Their shouts came downstream through the sound of the rain. Back up the road outside the pub Andrew began honking the horn of the kombie.

'... the spirit's conducted to Te Waiorongo, the tranquil and peaceful waters, where purification rites're performed before admittance to the temple of Rangiatea, the splendour of the heavens ...'

Chink had let go of the American's arm. Obviously he was putting the American on. Obviously he was serious. Kate couldn't measure the proportions. The rain was so heavy it was splashing from the road back up on to their legs. Upstream the men were shouting as they baled the canoes out with bright ice-cream buckets. She looked back down the river. What had been the Delta, that prow with its flagpole mast, was obscured by rain. Chink's voice droned on and on. She heard the American say, 'Okay man, now that's it, all right ...' and Chink, 'One more thing, mister.' He quoted the inscription on the Maori Wars memorial, corner Wakefield and Symonds Streets in Auckland: something about 'the friendly Maoris who gave their lives for the country during the New Zealand Wars 1845–1872: Through War They Won The Peace We Know.'

'How about *that*,' said Chink. He was hanging on to the American's arm again. John was about to hit him.

'Rightoh friend, school's out now,' Chink said, and the American ran back up the road, his back showing pink through his shirt.

Chink was doubled up with laughter. 'Ain't he a one,' imitating John's accent.

'You're a bastard. Where did you get all that stuff from? Was it for real?'

'Ah, I know what I'm talking about!' He was screaming with laughter. There they stood, laughing into each other's faces, under the rain which was pelting steadily down on them, the *marae*, the men with the canoes, the cars hissing by on the highway — a kind of difficult benediction.

'We've crossed the Huntly Line!' shouted Chink. 'We're out of range! Let's go, let's get it on! Fuck you all, white trash!'

And he went hopping up the side of the road, big dark awkward spider man, towards Andrew's kombie.

'Hai hai hai!

There was Chink in the front seat with Andrew.

'The ten o'clock ferry ...'

'Awright ...'

Officer's quarters ... The back of Chink's blue pea jacket was turned towards her. Rain drove against the windscreen. In the back of the van there were only mattresses, too low to see out the windows.

It was what's called O.P.: Officer Potential, the ability to make decisions in spite of others. John kept jamming cassettes into a player and turning the volume up. The officers had their heads together, they were making decisions. John took his wet shirt off. His skin was crawling with gooseflesh.

From time to time he'd pop up and look out the window: the barn, the town, the geese, the forest. Mezzanine sections of the landscape flicked past.

The quiet one closed his sad eyes. Ah, memories ...

A fun trip ...

'Hey, captain!'

Outside was the gloomy pine forest south of Tokoroa. It was dark in the van.

Chink's face when he turned to answer was indistinct.

'Do you want to stop for a pee?'

She mouthed at him, *I'm sick of this*.

'Can't hear ...'

She waved him away. The din in the decrepit van as it wound through steep sections was shaking her vision to a blur. Andrew tossed over a bag with a chillum and hash. Ah yes ... the whole routine. Yeah yeah. Keep them quiet. Up front the quarter-deck was doing speed, little pills. She'd just as soon have stopped right there. The back of that dark blue pea coat was beginning to tremble with velocity, laughter ...

Well, fuck it ...

At least John was quiet, chills racing over his immaculate Californian skin. She thought that he wore his origins like a Diners' Club seal of recommendation. That was one to tell Chink when she got the chance.

*The Doors*, over and over: 'This is the end. Beautiful Friend, I hate to set you free ...'. Nah nah nah. Dave had dug it. This had always struck her as a joke ... if you believed that custom and passion overlapped too rarely in a life already made short by the conventions of the times ... Claustrophobia! That was it. That was it again and again! A joke. 'I'll ne-ver, look-in, to-your, eyes, a-gain ...' And that life: little Jane, *Jane Mortimer Hamden* it said on the forms, which made it easier because the full name was so much one of those conventions. All that.

*But he smells like the bin*. The lino on the corridors, over-heated wards, the folding chairs, the needle, the green wrap-around smock bending over, 'There she goes now ...' All those smells: the lingering horrible formaldehyde smell of dissection, the smell of those little wads of cotton wool they dab you with before and after injections. It's like her friend Marie, a Czech Jewess who survived the Nazi camps and came here. She's a specialist teacher for deaf kids. One day an assistant mixed instant pudding for the kids to finger-paint with. They found Marie retching in the corridor. *You can't use food like that.*

The place where they taught the simplest things. It was ...

But all at once it was as though her memory tore free somewhere. Some kind of gap opened up. She was thinking of Marie roasting a marinated leg of lamb: the good astringencies of rosemary and garlic, and hot potato pancakes. Somehow Chink had stepped between her and that other memory.

The van was grinding through the dark stretches of highway approaching Taupo. Kate lay back staring at Chink's head where he sat up front rapping with Andrew.

'Marrakesh ... Xanadhu ...'

Ah, it was good at last! She struggled up to the front on her knees and leaned over the seat. The van was accelerating slowly on to the highway over the hill into Taupo. The rain had stopped. Clear of the forest, you could see how a steady wind was sweeping clouds from the sky. As the top of the hill crept towards them they all craned their necks. Then they were over.

The lake stretched into the distance in the pearly light of approaching dusk. At the southern end, hard-edged in that clear glow, the volcano was sending a plume of steam or snow-spume skywards from its cone. As they descended, the exhaust pipe rattling and farting, she leaned closer to Chink's ear, inhaling again that feral odour of his hair, placing her lips against the smooth skin behind his jaw, touching her tongue there.

'It's okay, for just another Atlas Mountain,' she whispered.

'Yeah, right,' he said. 'Right, it's really not bad ... in fact it's terrific! Can you dig the eternal snow? The Sahara's just over there! Rightoh Kate ... you ski down to the desert, then east a bit, then south across the burning sands. Day after day, 'brackish water', mana from heaven. And then ... one day ... there it is! Ah, you say, another mirage. So you go on putting one foot in front of the other, trying to unstick your tongue from the roof of your mouth. You rub your eyes. It's still there: Lake Chad! Trees, monkeys ... and lotus flowers in the lake. Cool jade water ... egrets and flamingoes. You come over the top of a dune, there it is! That's an amazing mirage! Look! It's got buffaloes splashing about in the water ... it's got a canoe with a fisherman ... it's got a little jetty with a store and a sign advertising beer from Strassbourg ... and you're actually walking into the mirage, you've stumbled along the jetty, you've pulled off your stinking clothes, you've toppled into the cool water, and now you're sitting on the end of the jetty at a little table, in the evening breeze, watching the sun set over Lake Chad, drinking Alsacian beer and eating a smoked-beef sandwich with slices of gherkin, running your finger through the frost outside your glass!' Chink's voice rose towards a scream. 'And you're thinking, "This isn't real! This is a mirage, man, but with mirages like this who needs the facts?" Lemme tell you, I'm gonna stay in this mirage. It's mine! Bring me another beer, also some fruit.' Chink mimed wiping juice off his chin, then he threw rinds into the lake. 'I like it here!'

'Far out,' said Andrew.

'Phew,' said Chink. 'What d'you say, Kate ... are you coming this time?'

They stopped at De Brett's hot springs. The small pool was greenish with sulphur and so hot Kate felt the blood pressing out against her skull, a pulse like the one in a baby's fontanelle. Her legs were stockings filled with sand.

'Well lookit that, that's a *real* Californian dick, "man" ...' Chink held out his own for inspection, free hand raised in mock salutation.

The main pool was cooler. Chink's heavy torso slid through the water, the lights around the pool catching the muscles of his back. Kate was wearing his T-shirt. The man who came out of the ticket booth with a whistle had a greedy expression. When she smacked her lips and waggled her tongue at him he went red and began shouting.

'Drop dead,' said Andrew.

'What a country,' the American kept saying as they climbed back up the hill. 'Oh wow, what a country, can you believe it?'

'We should kill him now, he's so heavy he'd sink,' Chink whispered.

'What about cutting off his Diners' Club Seal of Recommendation?'

'Now, you're just the bitch for the job ...'

They bought fish and chips and drove on. She couldn't eat. Chink had done a lot of Andrew's speed and was now yakking to him about The Doors. '... Jim Morrison's grave in the *Cimetière Père Lachaise* in Paris has more flowers on it than any other in the graveyard. Can you imagine little girls in white dresses with ribbons in their hair coming with bouquets, day after day? They let go of their mothers' hands and run to the graveside. Under the turf's this big dumb vulgar cock ...'

It was as though his voice was drawn away from her by an invisible tendon. It seemed to lope off, ahead of her, into distance and darkness. It was as though she was going to sleep not after one day, but three. It was as though she was going to sleep for the first time in her life. It was peaceful and foreign, like a graveyard in Paris. *Père Lachaise,* the name of a wise confessor.

'... they don't know what's happened to them,' said Chink's voice as it disappeared. 'The mothers don't know ...'

They veer in the dark, rise and fall. Then the headlights dragging them up a slope rising before them. They seem to be pivoting about his dark heavy head. She can't see his face, his back's turned to her, shoulders drawn up, turning with the heavy vehicle. Andrew has crawled into the back, is curled up with his knees under his chin. The American's asleep in the front next to Chink. 'I'm not dependable.' The way he has to hold his arms and shoulders to drive, is so solid and quiet. That's a strange thought, 'quiet'. Yet it is quiet and peaceful. In *Père Lachaise* they let go of their mothers' hands and run to the graveside. One of his shoulders lifts, his huge head rest on it, he's grappling across himself. Then he shakes a cigarette out of the packet: flare of a match, the American's mouth gaping where he leans against the opposite side of the cab. Chink opens the window to fling the match out. The wind blows his hair about, the sound of the engine enters. Who'll carry her inside? The bed will be there, she won't have to do anything, head lolling against ...

'Home James and don't spare the horses.'

'Shhh. ...' Legs and arms like stockings filled with sand. Someone's feet on the gravel driveway ...

'Open the door will you.' They let go of their mothers' hands and run to the graveside. A snake comes out of his flies, flat-headed, bloated with heat. It sinks its fangs into her, its tongue flickers to swab her skin, a flood of slow honey, she jerks and shudders. *This is the end, Beautiful Friend, the end.* ... Not Dave, the smell of pickled frogs. What a joke!

*Little Janie is very happy now, we all get on well over here. I don't think things would ever have worked out as they were. Now at least we're both free. I feel I've done that much for you ...* Ah, fuck off, shut up! That for comfort. There's none. The other for King Snake. The other for Chink.

His head hangs there above his shoulders. Being driven, being carried in. The darkness is motionless. They rock and rise in it, they turn and turn about his head.

*... write c/o the Biology Dept Australian National University, if you want to ...*

That, formaldehyde.

'Look at her, will you? Ah ...'

'Home James ...'

# 9     Killing the Fish

Chink: Once I went fishing in a small river south of Te Kuiti. There were good pools. It was getting towards sunset. Everything was right, beautiful ... the day, the place, how I felt, and there were fish rising everywhere. But I wasn't catching anything. So I reeled in. I watched the sun sinking and I just sat and thought. It was so quiet! I sat very still, and I really went down ... you know how you can. I watched the sun hit the top of the clay bluff at the other side of the gully, and I thought.

Yeah ...

The sun got behind the bluff. I was still sitting there. There was nothing but a red line at the top of the bluff: 'the gap between the worlds', remember? That you can go through, if you have the guts.

Then I got up and checked the line in, without looking, just flopped the fly on to the surface. And I hooked the biggest fish of my life. It was enormous, man, a monster! I played it and played it, running about a hundred yards down the bank, dodging through the manuka and the gorse, jumping over rocks, Jesus! 'You beautiful big fucker! Come on darling, come on come on!' — stuff like that. I could feel its life in the line, its strength, its fear, everything; it was like I was plugged into it, it was so close it was part of me.

And then I fucking killed it. Of course. I landed it and killed it! Ah ...

*Chink snaps his fingers, his eyes shut.*

That's how it is. You kill the fish every time. You kill a bit of yourself too. Like Einstein sitting in his chair, and then: 'Hey everything's powerful!' Oh ho. Yes, right. But he killed the fish ... he *had* to. Like Newton seeing that the sun was the Philosopher's Stone: 'Ow. Oh, I see ...' He killed the fish. He blew it. You can say the truth's *in* this thing ... in its flaw ... but the thing itself's a dead fish. Soon it will stink. Because you've stopped the motion. If it was right, then you'd never know ... you'd never see it ... because its continuous. So you kill the fish every time. You never know ... you never *will* know ...

But listen, what matters is being in the place, the fish rising, sunset, and your own head like a deep pool. Then standing up and casting like you didn't even think about it. You gotta take these risks, otherwise where are you? It's a price you pay.

Up till then it's beautiful, it's amazing ... Up to and including that cast: beautiful, phew ...

*Chink flops back in his chair.*

He said he'd suddenly thought, 'Yeah, I could be a musician!' That was before he went fishing that day.

'In the light of present material,' letting the phrase drift into silence. You never arrive. You never leave. There's no centre.

And yet you had a purpose: you came to fish. And so ...

'Yeah, I could be a musician!'

Well, why aren't you, sonny boy?

'Who could hang on for long with that kind of tension?' This is what she's thinking, now.

*I have had to learn the simplest ...*

'Who are these people! It's you ...'

... sometimes she's conscious of remembering with so much care that the love the care comes from must seem like an insult. There are problems she's always been on the outside of. Her mother used to talk about them. But Kate never imagined they'd matter much to her. How much should she tell? (How much does she remember?)

The movement, the *transport*, of the care with which she wanted to be with Chink faltered when he told her too much. It was as though he was putting her down.

'Let's do it by numbers, lady ...' When he was angry his face was blank. It often seemed to her that he *had* to win arguments, and that she had to let him. The process was as automatic as: *My cup runneth over:* waste, dilution: killing the fish. But not happiness, simple sufficiency, Chink smiling: his face an invitation.

What did reveal something about him was his father's shadow falling on the white palings in front of him, through which he slowly wiped the cloth, with a dull sense of the significance of what he was doing. The significance gained form as he grew up with the memory of this moment. The form was passed to her in what Chick said, reminiscing. It made no difference how many removes there are between her and what she remembers. She has to follow these circles back, or around. She has to go over it again and again, and then again. She has to invent the whole thing. Turning, as though to look at him again, and finding him watching her with half-closed eyes:

'Let's go, Kate. What d'you say?'

And it comes up out of her, immediately, as though she's dropped to her knees in front of you and sobbed out:

'Listen. I want to talk to you, I want to tell you!'

# 10  Yellow

Today the first cicada then warm rain tracking on ngaio bushes, the blackbirds in them. Yesterday I was happy. I painted the shed doors yellow: a homage to the hills, their gorse, then barberry, then kowhai, and broom, and now delicate lupin flowers around the sea's edge, and the ragwort just starting: that yellow, yellow! the colour of Hymen, of marriages (I was taught) but I think a sacred colour: spring, piss, and sulphur ... exorcism of winter. Near Bethell's in the north is a place I've been back to where pohutukawas like old elephants have sunk together to their knees, where in early spring the kowhai bend with yellow flowers. It was too early for many cicadas when I was there first. Instead tui and blackbirds and some wood pigeons had gorged themselves all day on kowhai flowers: dead drunk they gurgled among the branches, above the elephants, above Chink and me in the grass ... Too early for cicadas then, but they were there when I went back, and today there was one, here in the south, cracking and vibrating until the rain came. It's not the same. Something has changed, a season, something ... In that grove where elephants lie down their blood will burst out every year. But these hillsides march into the sea. The lupins hang out marriage bunting on the shore, they turn their pods down like thumbs ...

# 11

I feel like some tedious drunk at a party: starting *right* at the beginning, I mean this is the first time I've addressed you 'to your face'. There's some kind of compulsion.

My name's Kate. I'm not yet thirty. I'm tall and big boned. My skin's olive. My hair's black, straight, and cut short. My eyes are blue. I wear glasses to read and at the pictures. I've never been fat but I seem to be getting leaner as time goes on. I'm going to be one of those tall stringy old women who look as though they could survive forever like strips of biltong. My armpits, which Chink used to call 'tartubs', leak dark licks and curls. I shave my legs. My top lip has 'an Italian bloom', Chink used to say, 'like a Blackboy peach'. My mouth's very wide. I have one gold tooth (my father's idea — my practical mother objected). My nose is delicate and straight with pale nostrils. My eyebrows are also fine, though very wide and dark. My forehead, which is usually covered by my fringe of hair isn't high like Chink's was. My ears aren't delicate but you don't notice them because they're very close to my head. Chink's ears were what's called 'lugs': they had no lobes. My lobes are long, sensitive and downy. Blemishes: a large mole below my navel. Two similar moles, one high on my left cheek and the other just below my left collarbone, might be regarded as assets. I suppose an appendix scar counts as a blemish.

I guess I've described myself in a man's terms, as though through a man's eyes. (Chink's eyes.) Am I real to myself only as Chink saw me? I can't change the way I am. What I might wish to be is simply part of that. *You* think it out.

When I'm up I'm crazy, when I'm down I wish I was dead. But I don't like the grey areas.

Since having Janie I've used a coil but I resent it, it's an intrusion I can't change. I sometimes long for the world to open and suck me in and pour into me at the same time. I mean everything you do has some restraint attached to it. The nearest I ever got to that dream of abandon was having the baby. I loved that. I was reborn. I could feel every nerve and muscle in my body doing something about it and every bit of my head too. I fought against the mask they wanted to put on me at the last minute to help my breathing.

Then back came the restraints: Dave complaining that he thought it was time the baby was weaned. This was at six months. So I weaned her. I could have gone on for another year. I resented that so much I lost sight of the fact that it was my fault: I should have stuck to my intentions. And after that fucking with Dave was often hopeless: it was as though he was doing that according to a manual as well.

This is getting very confidential. But you can see why it was so important when the world stopped that night at Chink's flat.

I'm a young woman, Kate, not yet thirty. It's as though I can start any time. I've got enough energy for most of my friends put together. But I carry on in the same old way. The voice which you can't hear but which I hear calling and calling to the world, or announcing *I'm in Xanadhu!* saying *I'm going!* shouting *Let's get it on!* Shouting *Kate Kate Kate!* — I fob it off with temporizing promises.

And he's dead.

And yet I do feel as though I could begin now!

Poor Wedding Guest. You're probably feeling this way Chink must have sometimes: *Oh Christ, now what's this …*

I'm the youngest of a large family. I have five brothers. None of them lives in New Zealand. Three are in England, one doctor and two engineers. One is a marine biologist in California. The oldest, James, my favourite, has ended up as a teacher with the British Council in Teheran. He never married. All the rest have kids. We're a large successful scattered middle-class family. My father was a lawyer. He was killed in a car accident when I was fourteen. I didn't really miss him. When I think of him I remember his voice: a commanding bass. But he drank too much. I remember my mother shouting one day that when he died all his ambitions would seem as useful as a painful pee in a rusty bucket, to which he replied that he couldn't be held responsible for the poor quality of the receptacle but, by Christ, he could vouch for the quality of the piss.

I loved my mother. It's her I resemble, in some ways. She was Welsh, a compulsive singer, with a large primitive feeling for family, but given to a brand of sarcasm which only my father could match and beat. Quite often the whole family was caught in the crossfire. We tended, as children, to be mawkishly well behaved, but with secret lives.

I lived with my mother in Dunedin until I left school. I was *dux*. Then she insisted that I go north to university in Auckland. Something had got to me during my last year at school, some kind of boredom, or indifference. I didn't even sit some of the scholarship papers.

'You need to get out now before you're bored with being young,' my mother said with a certain flat inflexion she reserved for such shit-stirring comments. So, with some difficulty, she arranged for me to go north, on a teacher-trainee's bursary. She was right. I perked up. I had a good time. I also missed her. I found her conversation had spoiled me though at home I'd wanted to get out, away from it.

She told me not to come home for the short holidays. When I did come home for the first long summer vacation she pestered me with questions. Naturally I said it was fine. She'd had it all in letters. I added detail. She was enthusiastic. I couldn't make sense of the tone of her interrogation. Then she told me she was going back to Wales, to her family, a brother, and that she might stay 'for some time'. I noticed that she'd been dying her hair and I suddenly imagined it grey. I saw how the skin under her chin had loosened, how the angular lines of her body had become brittle, how her nails chipped easily, how tired and restless her eyes had become, how she coughed over the cigarettes she smoked from early in the morning. I suddenly realized that she'd been lonely since my father died. It had never occurred to me before! Except as a formula, that is.

At the funeral, which had been characteristically matter-of-fact, her tears had embarrassed me. Afterwards she'd launched herself ferociously back into the ordinary business of work and life, sitting smoking at the kitchen table with her markbook and piles of assignments, drinking endless cups of tea, pressing books on me which I didn't want to read — I remember Piaget — and referring always to 'your father' but never calling him by his name, which was James, like my favourite brother. None of *them*, incidentally, had attended the funeral.

When she said that, that she was going back to 'her family', I felt a terrible loneliness open in front of me, like the door of a derelict house. Her choice of phrase was hasty rather than cruel. But it hurt. And in spite of my brash answers to her questions I had no idea what I wanted to do. I'd been answering the way I sensed she wanted me to. I realized I'd be alone: there'd be no other 'family'. But I saw at the same time how she looked, how lonely *she* was. So when my mouth opened to protest, there was a pause like an actor waiting for a cue, and then I said, 'How wonderful', something like that. I think she heard the pause. She began to cry. When I'd finished my training, she said, she'd shout me a trip over to see her in Wales. If she hadn't come home by then. But she died two years later of bronchial pneumonia, when I was in my final year, when I'd just met Dave, when I was pregnant.

Bang. Reality. One of my mother's favourite phrases was 'come down like a ton of bricks'. She used to smack her lips over it, as though she relished something that definite and material. A favourite put-down expression was 'shillyshally'. She made the word limp and whine.

That was our family. We all insisted too much on independence, or had that insistence thrust upon us. How much I really loved my mother I didn't find out until I was in deep trouble. Then I felt her absence as something far worse than the lack of furniture and light in that derelict house of loneliness. I felt it as the loss of a kind of energy which I could have drawn on till I had the power to march into the house, illuminate it, fill it with loud voices and used objects, objects which would have the confidence, the material affection, of those chewed pencils she'd left lying around our place in Dunedin.

The trouble came soon enough. I'll spare you the worst of it, Wedding Guest, though I wouldn't have some weeks ago. If I feel like dedicating this brief reckoning to my mother it's because her power has seemed recently to become available at last. And not too late. That's the wonder of it, that feeling.

And dedicate it also to Chink. Darling Chink. Blessing you also frees me.

Yes, I know: *The Rime of the Ancient Mariner*. The patters that matter are the ones we're given, not the ones we impose. They emerge, the patterns emerge, that's all.

That's why I say I don't give a fuck whether you believe in Chink or not, or in me. Why do you think the Guest stayed? We all have to talk to ourselves sometimes. My father had the habit of baling people up at parties. I remember as a child listening to his insistent bass, from the top of the stairs. Among my mother's nicknames for him were 'Mariner' and sometimes 'Marinated'.

Xanadhu and the Mariner ... familiar as my mother's chewed pencils. And then a part of Chink's code. Do you expect me to avoid this?

The doctor said in as many words, 'You're pregnant.' The telegram said in as many words, 'You're motherless.' Somehow neither message was a surprise. The doctor merely put his signature to my certainty. He made it possible for me to think of a future: from a preoccupation with the certainty that I was pregnant, where my imagination was working at close range, I raised my eyes, increased the perspective, and saw a baby. There was a clear moment in which I said to myself, 'It's a girl, she's Jane, she's like me, she's like my mother.' Then I went home. One of my flatmates was waiting. She frogmarched me into the kitchen, sat me down at the kitchen table, and put a cup of tea in front of me. Her earnestness, which I'd misunderstood, made me laugh.

'I'm only pregnant,' I said. 'It's not the end of the world!' Something in me was singing like a power transformer, a high whine of energy, nearly hysteria. I was clinging in my mind to that clear vision of a little girl, called Jane.

It wasn't that, she said. There had been a telegram phoned through from Wales.

But somehow the fact of *that*, though I understood it, was unable to jar my vision of a daughter like me, like my mother. The telegram belonged to a process the major part of which I'd understood and accepted in a flash, and even with joy. Raising my eyes, I'd seen small dark Jane. I could neither lower them again, nor turn back to see my mother where she lay dead.

I'd been taken over. My present contained all the distance I was capable of covering just then. It was as though I thought, 'I'm the mother.' I didn't feel guilty or heartless. It did occur to me that no one stood between *me* and death: that I was next in line. But then I thought of Jane: the positions, their equivalents, seemed unchanged.

It was three years before I mourned my mother. It's taken another three to get me to where I am: the house lighting up, the voices coming back.

All that was in mid-summer. Dave and I got married the first week in March. With friends we rode over on the Devonport ferry across the windy harbour, and got drunk in the Devonport pub. I was only about two months pregnant.

The flat we lived in was half an old house above the Naval Base. The garden had run wild. I used to lie in one hot corner of it, behind some hibiscus bushes, sunning my nipples and belly. In winter I studied hard. I used to catch the ferry over to the city every day. At one stage, I used to spew over the stern. I gained a perverse kind of pleasure from this, I gave up smoking, stopped turning on, had no desire to drink, studied my diet, wanted to fuck a lot, and with Dave went nightly through a comical rigmarole of breathing exercises.

In October when I sat my exams I was nine months pregnant. It suited me. I wore hot yellow, my favourite colour. I wore extravagant trinkets and 'gauds' (a word I favoured then). I enjoyed dressing up this way. During exams, when I felt lousy and uncomfortable, I had to be escorted out frequently to pee. My picture even appeared in the paper: large Byzantine eyes, the blue of them darkened. I was riding really high. The climax was the birth of Jane: like bursting with joy. It was as though we'd all been taken in hand.

When I stood at the window of the hospital to watch for Dave coming to visit, my milk would dribble onto my feet. He, pale with overwork, would gaze at me with a kind of apprehension. His expression seemed to say, 'I've got more than I bargained for.' I didn't like the cigarette stains on his fingers, the smears and dust on his glasses. I was proud of my power, my new-felt beauty, my stature.

Beck despised Dave and went out of his way to bait him. When I was around he ignored him. He loved Jane and would play with her for hours. Finally Dave reported some sour comments Beck had made. I hadn't realized that Beck had been doing this behind my back. When I accused him of it he replied that he saw no reason to apologise for what he did 'outside my house' … Dave also lived a large part of his time away from me. He offered this comment blandly but I knew him well enough to guess that he was needling me. So I was angry. For revenge I told Dave about the conversation. So he lost *his* temper. (He seldom did.) We were having breakfast. Jane, who was one year old, was emptying the contents of a kitchen cupboard on the floor. Dave dumped his breakfast in the sink, breaking a plate, kicked the mess on the floor out of the way and left the house. I found myself despising the petulance of his gestures. That day he went to find Beck, had a row, told him not to come near our place again. By this stage I was really angry. Beck was *my* friend. I rang him and told him to come any time he liked. I was sick of an accumulation of proscriptions and irritations in my life. I suppose I was looking for a way back to the sense of stature I'd had when Jane was born. That had frayed, worn thin, become grubby, had been lost or thrown away, and there was no replacement.

One afternoon Beck came round. Janie was asleep but due to wake soon. I was sunbathing in my usual spot, reading. I heard Beck call out from the back steps. 'I'm down here,' I shouted. It was too hot to move. He'd brought some dope for me. We were sampling it when I heard the baby on the porch wake up. I knew she'd play happily for a few minutes. I didn't worry. Then I heard Dave: 'Hey, Kate!' Janie began to wail. Left alone she'd have been fine for a while. I made a point of leaving her for a few minutes before picking her up. Dave came through the bushes. We were turning on. The baby was crying. I didn't have any clothes on. Beck had been told to keep away. Dave stood there taking it in, then he went away and was gone for two days. I found out he'd stayed with a girl who worked in the university library.

When he got back we made up. He'd realized that the ingredients of the situation didn't mean anything. Yet it was at this point that the real crisis occurred. Because I was glad to see him back, because I felt guilty, for lots of confused reasons, I found myself saying, 'Anyway, Beck's a turd burgler, you know that.'

Immediately I looked at my husband with hatred. He'd made me say that. Characteristically he didn't notice this look. He was happy to have the affair sorted out. I doubt if it seemed to him to be a victory: he didn't think like that. But I did. I felt crushed. Before long I was despising the way he'd 'gone to weep on that girl's shoulder', and at the same time grinding my teeth with jealousy of her … far worse jealousy than I ever felt over Chink's women, of whom I was even somewhat proud.

How that mill does grind. It's so monotonous, so obvious, and it never stops. You talk yourself into something, you feel guilty about it, that makes you feel resentful, you blame the person you've wronged for getting the whole process started. The bigger the display of self-righteousness, the greater the culpability is likely to be. It's as though we believe that if we keep the mill going it will manufacture truth. We become shrill. We develop techniques of sarcasm and irony. The millstones rumble and squeal, our lies are given back to us, dusty nourishment. This is the bread *no one* can do without. This is our K-ration, our survival kit. When you are starving and there is food within reach, you don't go breaking your teeth on stones. That's it.

We moved south since Dave had to spend some time with the medical school in Dunedin. I bought a car and took a part-time teaching job at Kaikorai Valley High School. Janie was two and a bit. The car and a downpayment on a house had used up the rest of my inheritance money. But I was working. Dave was getting a Master's Bursary. There was family benefit. I had some quick love affairs which made me suffer in the usual ways but which I enjoyed, for the confidence they gave me. I don't really know what Dave thought. His calmness was sometimes like indifference. I suspected his kindness of being secretly spiteful. He said he wanted more children. I said I didn't.

For a time my claustrophobia left me alone. Then, as our routine became familiar again, it returned. I wasn't sleeping. I was often tearful. The psychiatrist my doctor referred me to prescribed mandrax, made wisecracks about behaviour patterns in young married women, quoted James K. Baxter's lines about young delinquent bags, wanted to interview Dave about our sex life (what sex life?) and extracted from me some kind of screwy rave about my mother. What I'd tried to say was that she would have cut through the bullshit. He accused me of saying that I felt I'd failed her. This performance disgusted me. Perhaps he was right: perhaps I'd come to him starving and he'd offered me a stone. I 'snapped out of it', which may have been the shrink's intention for all I know. At the time I thought he was brutal, unsympathetic and cynical. I didn't go back, except to renew my prescription. Quite often I found I was breaking through the mesh of claustrophobia: making gestures I enjoyed, which filled me with hope.

Jane, at two and a half or so, had become difficult to feed. It was mid-winter. To warm up after shopping one freezing Friday evening I'd gone to the pub with some friends. Janie was in the car. We all drank a couple of quick whiskies. Then I went home and made dinner. Dave was exhausted. I felt marvellous. But as soon as we sat down in the kitchen to eat, Janie started whining. 'Leave her alone,' said Dave. 'She'll eat when she's hungry.' He bent his head to his plate. He smelled faintly of formaldehyde. Jane was grizzling away, keeping one eye on me. I couldn't stand it. I picked up her bowl and dumped it on her head. The food splashed all over her face, all over the floor. Then I picked up her glass of milk, *chocolate* milk, and poured that over her head too. We faced each other. She opened her mouth to yell. But the sight of her was comical that I started laughing loudly. That was miraculous: she also screamed with laughter, licking at the horrible mess as it trickled down her face. It was an inspired gesture, it was *honest*, and we were friends, we understood each other.

Then I saw Dave's weary arms reach in as though from the edge of a frame and scoop Janie up and out of the picture, her mouth frozen upon that wonderful laughter. He was *coping*. He bathed her while I sat there at the table. Then, calming and without a word, he came back and cleaned up the floor. Ah, for Christ's sake! — what was a little mess for once! Why hadn't he entered into the spirit of the thing? Hadn't he seen what it meant? For *me*? Having broken for a moment through the net I felt as though something was now forcing my head down and back through it and closing the gap. My nose my eyes my throat were clogged with dust, it was dark, I was being crushed. 'Why did you have to spoil it?' But although the question had seemed simple at first, it began to grow, until I could no longer ask it. I couldn't get it out. It was like retching dryly on nothing.

My 'breakdown'. By the year's end we'd separated. I was still under observation. At the end of the summer Dave went to Australia on his scholarship. He took Jane. I didn't argue. There was no point. I couldn't look after her and I couldn't stand the sight of him. I heard that his girl-friend from the library in Auckland had gone to join him. I didn't care.

By the following spring I'd pulled myself together (let's put that in quotation marks: 'pulled myself together') for long enough to get discharged, let the house through the university housing officer, sell my car. (I stopped 'shillyshallying'.) I did this with the grim concentration of someone threading a needle with shaky fingers.

Then I flew up to Auckland to stay with Beck. I had plenty of money for several months, apart from what Dave was sending. So I planned to rest, really rest, have a good time, do nothing. Then I thought I'd 'review the situation'.

Beck threw all my mandies down a storm drain and spent a week abusing me. He took Dave's side. And then he lifted his wings like a bright gaudy little bantam hen, and I scuttled in.

And there was Chink ... sprawled out ... his nose running ...

A little more yet, Wedding Guest.

I want to ask you a question. That makes you real enough. I mean, I'm expecting an answer.

If I gave you three guesses at what my question is, what would you say? Let *me* guess at those:

1. Do I think my case is so different that it compels you to stay and listen?

2. Do I believe I can expiate (which sounds like spit) by sitting here going through all this?

3. Do I believe it's not too late? Or that by starting again I can exclude what's happened?

Give up. For once I'm going to surprise you. *Those* questions stink of formaldehyde. But don't fret, the smell no longer bothers me.

Here's my question. (Here's my stone.)

*How do you like my tone?*

(Hey, listen to that. It's a song, it's a wee number!)

Yeah, how do you like my song, you *cunt*. Chink would've eaten you alive. Smile, for fuck's sake! It's a wedding not a funeral.

Here I've sat for days, looking out the window at the same 'slice of life', like a section Dave might have mounted on a slide and looked at through a microscope. You can't imagine how familiar it is.

If I'm beginning to get the hang of you, then it follows that I've got a fair idea about myself. If that world-section is familiar to me, then I must be on similar terms with myself. It's got to be reciprocal. Sometimes I've written to your dictation. Sometimes that's made me want to scream.

Who are you, Wedding Guest? We killed Chink, remember? You're Them.

Only that procession there behind you, over your shoulder, is a wedding. When I get up and go out, you'll follow. When your back's no longer turned, Wedding Guest, I too will have joined the procession.

# 12 Home James

The day was grey, a promise of brightness in the south. There he stood, hands shoved into the old pea coat, gritty dockside wind blowing into his eyes.

The others hadn't been able to get a ticket for the kombie. Poor Californian John has said he'd 'come with you ...'

'Get fucked,' Chink and John parting on very bad terms.

So that lot drove off to have breakfast at the railway station, and Chink and Kate boarded the ferry and sat in the stern, arms round each other.

'Anyway,' said Chink, 'Andrew's jumping probation.'

Traffic ground past on the multipetal overpasses. It occurred to Kate that these structures would be beautiful without the traffic, which continued non-stop, slewing and backfiring into the ramps leading off to Murphy Street, Aotea Wharf ... the heads of the truck drivers could just be seen in the cabs of their vehicles above the concrete balustrades ... the purposeful set of their necks as they turned the trucks on to the ramps reminded Kate of the long night drive.

> They let go of their mothers' hands
> Home James & don't
> Spare the horses

... meat, paper, wool, fire extinguishers ... onions, and there go some 'day old chicks'.

Below the ramps was a rusty confusion of railway lines. A suburban unit went past, dingy splendid crimson. The windy air, whipping around grey cranes and derricks, was harsh with exhaust fumes, diesel, and the penetrating astringency of the harbour: not quite an open sea smell, since it retained something cloacal ... the air would also clear in the south ... closing his eyes against the grit, the leaden glare of low mid-morning light, 'Let's get out of here, let's really get out of here!"

The *Acapulco Maru*, Japanese, was unloading immense coils of steel cable: an ugly battered ship held tenderly against the wharf buffers ... the image has stuck with Kate, the same class of memories as that of Chink's mime at the back beach.

But the blackbacks lined up along the edge of the wharf, the decks of the ferry swarming with children — these must have reminded her of the Devonport Ferry, because she began to tell Chink about the first year with Jane. If he was surprised to hear about this 'other life', he didn't show it. He sat as though expecting one of the *Acapulco Maru's* coils of steel to drop on his head. As she talked he looked out towards the harbour mouth where a wedge of blue sky was slowly splitting the dark cloud that also covered the city. Kate was saying how she'd begun to do weaving that year: something she could stop and start, as the baby allowed her. She found she was good at it. She had a gift for improvisation.

'Crafty,' Chink with a hideous grin. 'The young mother ...'

At this moment the ferry began to move away from the wharf, towards open sea, the wedge of light: out into the blue. The nasty maverick smile struck on Chink's face.

'Here we go, lady ...' Taking Kate's hand, lifting his chin from the collar of his coat, he stalked to the bows and stood there until the ferry cleared the heads. It was choppy, but the sky was blue, the air clear ...

'... distance, wow ...'

It was the end of the summer holidays, the ferry was packed. Finally he stretched out on a vinyl squab in the cafeteria, surrounded by families getting a late breakfast. Kate leaned over and kissed him.

'Home James, don't spare the horses.'

'Don't spare the horse,' he cracked.

She had breakfast: juice, eggs, bacon, the whole shebang. She sat at the opposite end of the cafeteria from where Chink was sleeping: sat there, sometimes with a fork half way to her mouth, staring at him. '... they let go of their mother's hands ...'

Then she wandered about the boat. She expected to meet someone she knew. But there was no one else, not even a face which made her turn for a second look.

Later she had a beer in the bar, and read the paper, which was full of disasters. 'What am I crossing to, what am I leaving behind ...?' Around her, over the throb of the engines, fragments of talk were tossed to and fro, as though by the pitching of the ship in the open straits. The voices were insisting, insisting. Some of the men looked over at her: a tall dark girl, white-faced, a red bandanna tied around her throat, playing with the cigarettes she lit one after the other.

Then the boat steadied: it had entered the Sounds. Steep scrubby land slid by, and small islands and neat bays blazing with pohutukawa flowers. Through the window of the crowded cafeteria she could see Chink lying as before, with his old pea coat on, the shabby toes of his boots turned out, his head rolled over sideways, one hand stuck right down in his crutch.

He appeared at her side, his hair wet where he'd splashed his face in the washroom, at the moment the ferry was about to berth at Picton.

Blue sky, breeze, small craft in the Picton Sound: 'Pumpkin weather,' said Chink, pulling off his coat. Yet the air had an alpine clarity, a dry snap to it, *distance*. They ambled down from the terminus towards the esplanade.

'Well lookit that, never seen *that* before ...'

In front of them was an immense concrete vulva ... oh really? When you walked around it, it turned out to be a concrete whale, made into a slide ... but the children appeared to be slipping down between the labia of a gigantic snatch. Well *that* was worth watching for a while, in the authentic zesty summer holiday air sun and sea breeze. It was hard to know which was worse: a whale flensed and laid open down its backbone, or that puffy quim ... and zimmm! here comes little Terence with his shorts rucked up ... Chink: 'Imagine health stamps ...'

Chink came up with that words 'flense': turned out he knew something about whaling in the Straits and Sounds, and also about seals along the coast below the

Seaward Kaikouras. He told her about an old man he'd met who at fourteen had first gone out in a chaser, oar and sail against the rip in Tory channel, had become a harpooner, now had an elbow blown up like a balloon with old bone splinters. He regretted the rarity of whales 'these days' not for *their* sake but because duck shooting didn't measure up 'as a sport'.

'Did you know Errol Flynn's chauffeur came from Picton? ... How can you *settle* for less? I mean it's a matter of scale all the time, it's dead simple. ... Everyone's hooked on some scale ... give them something too small or too big and they freak out ...'

Chink's 'am I serious' routine. ... Meanwhile Kate imagined the old harpooner fucking a whale ... or a yellow Japanese crane in the ocean south of Java ... astraddle it with a tin hat on and a rivet gun in his hands ... 'Here it comes, red hot from an old-timer!'

'... the word like "flense" for what they do to seals is "flat" ... they "flat" them ... bit like running over possums with a logging truck: all that's left is skin and fur ...'

He'd never seen that kiddies' slide before, without Kate would never have stepped far enough off the asphalt of the road from the terminus to confront that ambiguous totem, but would have kept on at least as far as Kaikoura.

At about three in the afternoon they checked into a hotel, selected on the merits of its name: Terminus. In the public bar a loud pool school was in action. Through from the bar at the reception desk, Chink helpfully enunciated Kate's name.

'Yes, Mr and Mrs ahem Hemmedin ...'

And investigated the room for wallboard. It was high, intact. Potty and Gideon's Bible in a cabinet by the bed.

'Amazing ...'

Down the corridor, an immense bath.

'Amazing, amazing ...'

They went out: fish and chips, a swim, a couple of jugs in the bar (no game of pool). Upstairs with a huge bag of Bon Chretien pears and a jar of wine. It was just getting dark. Greenish scalding water thundered into the old-fashioned bath. Then sitting up in bed, eating pears, sipping at the wine, Chink read from the Gideon's:

> ... I praised the dead which are already dead more than the living which are yet alive.
> Yea, better is he than both they, which hath not been, who hath not seen the evil work that is done under the sun.
> Again, I considered all travail, and every right work, that for this a man is envied of his neighbour. This is also vanity and vexation of spirit.
> The fool foldeth his hands together, and eateth his own flesh.
> Better is an handful with quietness, than both hands full with travail and vexation of spirit.

'Phew, dig that ...'

And:

Two are better than one; because they have a good reward for their labour ...

Yeah ... and put the sunny Bond Chretiens on the floor and lights out ...

Easy to imagine that, as time passes, so do the connexions that memories hang on. But it's the memories that atrophy, shrink to fine points of focus, while the connexions, the bonds, get tougher, and longer, and lit by a concentrated dreamlike glare, a scrutinizing light whose purpose seems to be the destruction or at least the weakening of those surreal embraces, but whose actual effect is to temper and reinforce clutchings, spans, couplings, hair-fine parabolic filaments of 'meaning', until the whole intricate structure locks into some kind of equilibrium, and hardens there, until it resembles a gorgeous electronic circuit, in which links matter more than points of stasis, because it's important for the power to *continue*, no matter how it may be modified en route ... and what you want to be reassured about, is that the juice goes in one end, and comes out at the other ...

So that the memory becomes a power-grid: power-links between points of meaninglessness. So long as you don't get in there with a bomb, or don't shoot your way to the Master Switch and throw it to 'off', so long as you keep that whole circuit bathed in that hardening inward glare, then your power's always going to be *present*. Throw the switch, and you're left with an exquisite map of microscopic dots of rubbish: resting places but no travellers ... towns but no roads ... you used to know how to crochet (you remember the word 'crochet') ... you used to know where your sister lived (you remember her name) ...

Kate has seen them like that: their circuits like tinkling chandeliers which have gone out.

In her ear, like a cicada, is that phrase: 'the meaning of fiction' ... Julian, white-faced and red-haired, crows' feet at the corners of his young eyes, is her personal demon. But she likes him. She imagines him playing with his child.

Opposite her, in the window, the Wedding Guest looks back. She's no longer worried about motives ... she's no longer in any particular hurry ...

'Well now.'

Kate addresses her, watches her lips whisper, '*Well*, now ...'

... along the road a trail of Bon Chretien cores, on verges or chucked over fences into blond paddocks, and later just out of reach of surf, all of them loud with wasps drinking the saliva of Kate or Chink, Kate and Chink, as well as sweet pear juice. And somewhere along the way, the empty wine carafe dumped in a forty-four gallon drum rubbish-bin by some beach. A lot of rides, Chink always asking to be let out again. After dark, a cabin at Kaikoura ...

That's what Kate's got. She didn't even see the wasps. That's how it is.

Next day Chink shook her awake, pulled off the pink candlewick bedspread and the rayon sheet.

'These Norfolk Pines are the southernmost Norfolk Pines in the world, a tip for The Guide please, ta.'

His shoulders were straight. He was pointing like a dog. He promenaded south under the nitty pines, marginally successful transplants only, even in this temperate enclave: he and Kate were getting into different latitudes, where the 'Philip's Planisphere' (showing the Principle Stars visible for Every Hour in the Year) for lats. 30's–40's which Kate had bought on a whim a week or so ago in Auckland, was going to be unreadable, unless you knew your way around well enough to make the necessary connections by guesswork. Anyway, had they been able to see the stars in the morning sky, which had a pearly membrane of high cloud stretched across it, and lower down long streamers across the indigo buttresses of the Seaward Kaikouras, they'd have noticed Capricorn rising and chasing Scorpio westwards: Chink being a Capricorn and Kate a Scorpio, information they've already traded, as a formality. The morning will be spent under sensual Capricorn, while Scorpio slips down behind the barricades in the west. Capricorn rising ... by late afternoon Scorpio will be down. Capricorn dropping fast. Come darkness, Kate and Chink will look up at the Pleiades, a tender cluster above the western horizon, and Aldebaran blazing in Taurus. They will leapfrog up the firmament, through Orion to Canis Major, right overhead, just out of range of the scimitar of the Milky Way which, on this night, will sweep in an arc up and through the centre of the sky. ... Meanwhile the Norfolk Pines stand along the sea marge like burnt-out rockets At their bases, from dessicated grass, some bright marigolds grow. There's no one else about yet. Towards the western end of the esplanade is an explosion of geraniums ... Chink and Kate move on to the beach, a steep ramp of smooth pebbles. The sea bangs the stones around, even though the day is calm and still. Then the beach gives way to rocks. They clamber back up to the road. An oystercatcher, Pinnochio-nose (who's lying?) is fretting down there among the pools, orange beak flashing this way and that against the grey and buff rocks. Other flashes, of light, are breaking through above the cloud streamers against the mountains which Chink and Kate see as they turn to look back across the wide grey bay: there are green pendants on the slopes. A fishing boat is riding at anchor out in the bay. It has a square old-fashioned deck house, high bows. It moves with an odd jerking motion, the bows dipping down the angle of the anchor chain. Ahead of them, past a pale clutter of pumice along the seashore, they can see the sheds and jetty of the fishing company. Even though the high cloud is beginning to break up, the light is still glaring and low, throwing bright fragments into relief: marigolds, geraniums, the beaks and feet of seabirds, the far-off glass port holes of the fishing boat, green gems at the mountains' throats ... A sudden ricochet of light off the tin roof of the fishery sends a shatter of reflections among the windows of cars around the buildings. Then the cloudy retina closes again ... the scene remains as though photographed: foreshortened, clear, birds hung in still air ... and something has happened to your eyes: having trapped that detonation of light they stare back past white cataracts ... In the doorway of Virgo Fisheries Ltd lolls a man with such an eye, nacreous disc at its centre. Behind him fish are slapped on slabs ... white rubber aprons and smears of blood ... the quick flicking of knives ... while a transistor radio emits the squawks of a commercial breakfast programme.

'Gidday.'

'How are ya.'

The man flicks his cigarette butt out on the asphalt and turns back inside.

Gulls fight over fish-heads floating below some concrete steps where the high tide mark shows at a greeny line of slime and weed. There are triangular orange trickles of oxide below iron rings in the concrete pier. Some rowboats have been pulled up on to the dock. Cloudy rainwater and fish-scales wash over the base boards.

The cloud is really lifting now, the membrane getting thinner, tearing here and there. The atmosphere is heavy. There is no sea wind. In the dusty stands of weed along the gravel road where Kate and Chink are walking the insects are starting up: 'Wit wit wit'. Under this is a persistent harsh continuo: the vibrations seem to strike at the *inside* of some deep part of their ears. The sea now resembles molten lead. Two grey herons cast perfect reflections on slick sand. Chink and Kate walk past a fishing boat beached for refitting. It's being painted bright yellow. Lower down are uncompleted brush strokes of red lead. Along the side of the road is a dry waste of thistle and tussock, grey with pumice dust.

They come to a flat moonscape of rock where the road ends. Here the planes and surfaces are smooth and extend on all sides with shallow catchments of water which reflect light. The rock, wrinkled in soft folds like the skin of some great beast, has a silvery patina. Limpets cling to this skin like warts. Chink and Kate walk across it, past bladderweed and kelp embracing smooth white stones. The beast-skin gives way to such stones, these to a clanking volcanic rubble and a dark sea marge where lizards flick and shuffle into shadow. The lizards seem oily, yet they move with dry precision: *flick, flick*, like their tongues. In the dark crannies where the sea is washing the kelp glistens as though oily ... stirring in the shallows and clefts of rock.

Then the grey is swept away by sunlight. The cloud membrane has torn right across. High puffs of cirrus trot over blue sky. Heat bounces off the rock. Bumblebees stagger by, inept formations of shags make it to shit-splattered rocks where they spread their wings to the sun. Thistle, low thorn bushes and flax begin cracking and popping with heat.

Her eyes have gone nacreous, they're shining blindly with tears like the mother-of-pearl eyes of a watchful guardian, her glass cage of memory is jangling, the Wedding Guest opposite her is shaking her head and whispering, 'Oh fuck, oh fuck ...'

That distance! She's really feeling it ... on that barbaric rind of coast: Chink's scale, the spaces he's hooked on: nothing less than that transparent blue distance, into which the mind pours out, like an estuary into the sea ...

'Can I come with you?' She senses some kind of progression from her Badedas bath to the Pacific skyline! Now, there's a weird one! So all at once she's laughing and laughing. She's *free* ...

At this point Chink has stopped. A deep sound comes from low in his chest.

'What is it?' Like a child deep into some game, she's ready to believe anything.

He's staring ahead, past a pagoda-shaped rock formation on the edge of a stagnant inlet. Beyond this murky water is a small hillock. It's chalky, shaped like a shoulder blade, a dry scuff of tussock at its base, its upper edge scalloped sharp by wind. Beyond it the coast, precipitous and darkened with cloud above the ranges, recedes into the heat haze, a bare escarpment shining here and there where sunlight breaks through. Above the cloudy ranges the sky is a bleached-out blue, and below, where the deeper colours of the sea show among brown and white ribs and snags of rock, there's a flickering show of light, like thousands of jostling candles in some temple or procession.

'Hey, what is it?'

They skirt around the shoulder blade. Once their ears have got used to the sound of the waves and have dismissed it, the silence is trancelike. Not even birds.

'What is it, where are we going?'

She inhales a hot waft of something rank and feral, so sudden it shocks her, like a loud clap of noise by her ear. Birds scream upwards from the jagged rock formations ahead: terns and blackbacks, red insides of gaping beaks.

'Ah the darlings, the darlings!' Chink has stopped again, his face broken by a helpless grin of such release as she's only seen when he's making love ... Thinking he means the birds she looks up but he seizes her head and jerks it down, pointing her gaze at the gnarled confusion of rocks ahead.

And there they are: the seals, at ease on the jagged rocks: lithe plump flanks ... eyes large and dark and lovely, long lashed, tranquil pools ... yawning with satisfaction, a flipper scratching at buff pelt ... tender muzzles. Kate can see them everywhere, lolling on their stomachs or sides, or else propped up, small heads in the air, catching the sun and the breeze.

Some of those near-at-hand heave themselves in fright to the sea, and slide in. At once their grace is miraculous: shrugging off gravity like water over their shoulders, they turn to look back, sleek heads snouting up, huffing sea from their nostrils, and then dive away again, unthreatened, corkscrewing sideways with flippers slapping the surface of the water, browsing through dark kelp and bladderweed along the sides of the rocks, through the surge and backsuck of the swell, across rip-currents at the mouths of deep clefts, and from time to time driving on their tails up out of the water for long enough to shake a spray of sea from their pelts.

Kate and Chink sit for a couple of hours. After a while the seals ignore them.

'That,' jerking his thumb at the shoulder blade hill, 'is like a totem for me ... the face of it that looks north ... it marks a place ...'

He stops to watch a seal levering itself up on to the rock. Its slick pelt dries quickly to a light matt brown. It yawns and scratches, closing its eyes. Around it is a filthy litter of dry weed, rocks stained brown, urinous pools. Chink laughs, a sound like a seal bark. They go back the way they've come. They eat oranges, chocolate, cheese in the grass under the escarpment ... Capricorn rising ...

... it's all beginning to fade into the coast: somewhere along the maze of her memory the whole morning has slipped back into those dark clefts, their flashes of pink, and flicks of lizards, and glossy seals. It's as though Chink has a pelt, a lubricious sheen. Her sense of the importance of it all is fluent, moving with grace under language. Then it has to get up, like the seal that interrupted Chink: up into the light, among the slovenly wrack ...

In the distance people are pygmies: a thin clank of voices. They stumble painfully over the rocks. In our own element we're inept.

Chink and Kate are swimming. The cavalcade passes by, aware that these swimmers are naked. The voices fade around the point. Chink dives, shaking his white arse in the air. Brown fingers of rock stretch into the sea. A diver appears around one of them, comes ashore and flaps up the beach in black wetsuit and flippers, with a creaking bag of crayfish. They hadn't seen his stash near their clothes. Wordlessly he re-enters. Fins of Beast brush her legs ... Chink in greeny water floats on his back ...

Then they're on the clifftop in dry tussock, under the noon sun. They've sucked all the oranges, their skin is dry with salt. Through her eyelids she sees red.

'Close my ears.'

Her long thighs comply, his voice speaks in her belly.

'This is Dick Seddon's Great Drive: he stayed under 5 mins. A record!' Lizards under rocks, dark weed in sea crannies, pinkish hydras and polyps. He's telling her a story. 'In the palace of the King of the Sea ... the changes are either incredibly fast or else so slow you don't know about them. Some creatures metabolize oxygen, others have learned to slow their heartbeats down to one or two pulses an hour. Others have developed alternative systems ... tubes reaching to the surface ... portable survival kits ... But elegance is common to all ... even the immense cocoons and sealed suits of armour favoured by some denizens have grace. It's something ... to do with movement which is slowed down until no superfluity is possible ... But the loveliest are the butterfly fish which flutter in slow motion through the halls ... awakening reckless thoughts of laughter ...'

... shoulders off the ground, clutching his head, his ears uncovered and her cries pouring into them, gulls flipping on hot convections up past the cliff edge. Then he's come up, seal smell on his breath. Bam. That's it. Wow ... Looking sideways through the noon sunlight she sees a sheep looking back, its jaws grinding patiently sideways. It's too much ...

'You're cheap 'n' nasty,' she says. 'You're trash, you're ...'

The socks he pulls on over his white knobbly feet are full of holes. As they're walking back around the coast he says, out of the blue, 'Remember Te Waiorongo?'

She does now: 'the tranquil and peaceful waters'. She remembers Californian John black with rain on the Ngaruawahia bridge, the darkness over the desert road. *Home James* ... She has the impression, lost in the glass maze of her memory with its Bon Chretien cores yellow with wasps, its voyeur sheep, its sensual rind of coast, that the whole of that journey was a movement out into space and light: out into Chink's scale of things, driving behind that blue wedge of sky beyond the Wellington heads, on to pumpkin sunshine, beyond that again to the Kaikoura Bay, noon light and heat, the horizon from that clifftop, on and out ...

They hitched on south. Late in the afternoon they were dropped at Cheviot where a show was in progress. Voices on the p.a. system: 'Now in the ring Mark Pate on ...'

Chink: Did you hear *Willie-th-Pimp*?

'... (on Winnie-the-Pooh) ... would all those who have fleeces veges ecksetra in the shed please remove them ... would all Lions serving as stewards at the cocktail party ... Winnie-the-Pooh has been scratched ...'

... smell of ripe horseshit, horses farting and flapping their leathery nostrils, *prphapahgh*, and those young country women standing fist on hip, with small children in white shirts and jodhpurs, and all of them with such *confidence*: they stood by their landrovers, putting empty beer bottles back into chilly bins.

The showground was in a bowl cradled by hills. Chink found it hard to separate land shapes from the shapes of women and horses: they way sleek light struck the blond hillsides ... He moved as though followed by a spotlight through the twitching brilliance in the leaves of trees, among these people who looked at him with something like scorn. The evening sunshine gathered like a cloying mist through which he appeared to wade, a smile slipping in and out of his expression: an identification card he flashed on demand.

'Isn't this unbelievable, Kate?'

Tomato sauce from a hotdog ran over his chin. The quartered-orange sections of a garish merry-go-round canopy whirled. They drank beer at a bar set up where men sat around on haybales. Chink's face was red from the day's sun, the grin was opening his head.

But the sun was on the blond rim of hills. They went back to the road to get a ride. They were dropped a few miles further on, by the Hurunui River. The sun had set. They had pears, chocolate. There was water in the river. The sky was clear, the stars bright. They climbed a fence, scrambled down through dark willows. Above them, as they lay dizzily on the grass, the stars whirled. As this motion ceased, as the light poured down to them, as they began to hear the night sounds of the river and of sheep on the other side of it, it was as though that impenetrable indigo thickly sown with stars backed off, slewed out and away from them, leaving the stars hanging in a void, leaving Kate and Chink hanging there ... 'the splendour of the heavens': the Temple of Rangiatea ...

'What a trip ...'

... falling asleep among the stars ...

She stops. Opposite her the Wedding Guest's mouth is open. She's got this far. She's followed that movement out. She's remembered how space opened in front of them.

But something slams down. Along the circuitry of her memory, in its glass halls, she finds herself baulking at a figure, the face of a man. She imagines, in rapid succession, a coil of dark steel dropping from the *Acapulco Maru*'s sling, bright water turning leaden, windscreen wipers clearing spaces on streaming glass, the figure of a man, the figure of a man driving ...

He was a worker for the Tussock Board. The inside of his battered Ford, which he drove at breakneck speed towards Christchurch, has a low stink of solitariness: muttonfat, boots, tobacco. In the back seat, chucked into one corner, was a stained tartan rug and an N.A.C. flightbag with a tie hanging out where the zip was broken. Here Kate sat, wincing as he cornered. Chink sat in front. From time to time the man turned to Chink and made some comment. He spoke unemphatically. His voice was dry and carried effortlessly over the noise of the car and the rain. The third of his profile which Kate could see from behind had an ironic repose. He leaned into the corner against the car's door, his casualness concealing the skill with which he drove. His eyes were slightly hooded, sardonic, his nose hawkish. He was dark with sun and wind. The large hand with which he steered seemed hardly to grip the wheel. It rested there, vibrating, a cigarette held at the base of index and middle fingers.

The only thing she can remember him saying was, 'It's not a bad life.' As he said this, half-turning towards Chink who was looking straight ahead through the windscreen, the eye that Kate could see from the back seat wrinkled up at the corner, his mouth tightened with a dry smile. The car slewed through a ramp of gravel on to the long straights of the plains approaching Christchurch, the man's cigarette flew in a shower of sparks down the side of the car, a spray of rain landed on her cheek before he wound the window up again with a crude wrenching motion of his right. He and Chink were of a size, their shoulders similarly broad and hunched. As she dozed for the rest of the trip Kate often confused them, imaging that Chink was driving again ... 'Home James ...'

She remembers nothing more about the journey south.

'I mean, *what changes?*'

It goes on, in the old family way. In a sense it's beautiful.

Here she was today thinking and looking out her window, her world-section waving its gentle edges out there where the ragwort in the hill paddocks is waving its yellow banners for the end of summer ... she's changing, the procession is passing, she's entering upon the rigours of another season ... everything is waving to her ...

She was thinking about Kaikoura. She was dying for a long fuck in the sunshine. She was thinking that Ingrid's okay and the bay's lovely but Curtis is a drag — oh, he's kind, he's terrific, but he's a pissoff!

'Chink, you were never unctuous, thank god for that, nor was dear Beck.'

And she was thinking, 'When I've finished this I'll get a relief teaching job and save some money and go and see Janie in Canberra. She's nearly six!'

'If I could only see *you* again Chink. You poor old bastard.'

Then in came Curtis. When their eyes met she must've had fuck written all over her face. He'd brought her a cup of tea. There he stood with it. It dawned on her that he'd been dying to make it with her for weeks. He was obviously right there now. She stood up before he could put the tea on the table, went past him out the door.

'Must go to the grot.'

She sat for some minutes, shaking.

Because that leap's dumped her without her will and without her having thought of it, down, just less than three years after that trip through Kaikoura.

It was winter, the last of Chink's life, and the worst. He'd been away for months. She was living in Dunedin. She had a barmaid's job at the Gardens. She'd made up her mind that Chink had gone for good this time. No one had heard of him since he'd left. The job was lousy, it was cold. She was on the verge of pissing off north to the Bay of Islands.

Then Chink came back. This time he had a car and plenty of money. He'd changed. His face was pudgy, he'd turned into a real lush, and he had a collection of fancy gear: some O-tincture, some coke all got up in caps, likewise smack, prescription ritalin ... and three *cases* of Ribena black currant concentrate. The car was a second-hand '69 Jaguar. It had a cassette player in it.

She was behind the lounge bar thinking, 'Fuck this, I'll go tomorrow, I'll *fly*.' She bent down to take some glasses out of the rack. When she looked up Chink was sitting at the bar in front of her.

'I'll have a helicopter …' The old hardness of his eyes was dimmed by the plumpness surrounding them, the violet lush's bags. Some humour had gone too.

She left that night. But after a day or two it wasn't much use. Sometimes Chink didn't even stay with her. He was getting around with a neat character called Stu, a photographer. They egged each other on. Chink was drunk half the time and blocked out of his mind the rest. Kate felt as though she were tagging along. She didn't know what was the matter. When she suggested going north, Chink was silent. One night he fucked her as though it was an assault, groaning words which she couldn't understand. Afterwards he wept, secretly, blundering out of the room. Her nose was bleeding, the knuckle of one finger had turned blue and puffy by morning. Once or twice in town she saw him avoid her in the street.

Stu said he wanted to photograph her. That night as the three of them were walking home, Chink, with a long swing of his arm, flung a half-full tequila bottle through one of the second-storey windows of the university science block. Someone shouted. They all ran. When she got home neither Chink or Stu was there. The sound of them coming in late in the morning woke her. She heard them go into the living-room down the passage. It was the day for the photographs. She had a shower then went down to where they were.

They were standing in the centre of the room, facing each other, in the act of passing a whisky bottle: Dimple Haig, Chink's favourite. They both had a hand on the bottle as she came in: it was as though they were in the process of sealing some pact. It was dark in the room, a yawn of space, away from the low winter sun which by early afternoon was off the house altogether. From habit she switched on the light which hung directly above them. It increased the impression of a set piece. Then Stu tipped the bottle up and took a big swallow.

'Take a hit,' he said. 'It's gonna be cold as hell.'

The whisky dried her mouth, burned her stomach, but tasted bland. Chink pulled a wool hat on. Beneath it his white face was heavy and sullen. A stipple of flush beneath his eyes told her he was drunk. Stu shoved the bottle into a bag with the camera gear. Then he followed Chink out.

A queue of anonymous days, as dim as the claustrophobic winter spaces of the house, leaned into her from behind as she approached the daylight. Turning back against this pressure to switch off the light she imagined she saw, like a television ghost, the outlines of the two men with a hand each on the whisky bottle as though each drank to himself in a mirror: a drunk in a derelict house. Their last sentence, which she hadn't heard, hung there. Had it concerned her? Chink's silence told her yes. Then she switched on the light and turned with the tide and walked outside to Stu's car.

He and Chink were in the front seat. The camera bag was in the back. Kate climbed in next to it. She hadn't had breakfast. Chink sat motionless, the wool hat pushed low on his brow, his hands stuck into the pockets of his old blue pea coat. His shoulders drawn up to his ears, staring ahead through the windscreen with the bored expression of a sailor surveying the bleak dockside of some coastal port. It was like a second-rate impersonation.

'… and now you …' She'd remember the phrase.

After they'd driven some way along the Port Chalmers road Chink said, 'Pass the bottle.' He took a swallow and sat with the bottle between his knees. The stink of the tannery at Sawyer's Bay entered the car as they passed.

'Look up there!' Between Mount Cargill and the misty continuing range a ragged frond of blue sky was waving in from the valley to the north. 'It'll be fine over the hill,' Stu said. 'For fuck's sake cheer up.'

The shabby main street of Port was cold and deserted. While Stu went into a milkbar to buy cigarettes Chink and Kate sat silently in the car. Some proscription hung between them. Even if she'd wanted to she couldn't have reached forward, a gesture made familiar by repletion and travel, to touch his head or neck, breathe his tender hair smell.

'What about the Atlas Mountains?' She was going to say it, 'Wha' … wha' … wha' …', sadness shaking her lips until she whimpered. But an unloaded timber truck gunned past on its way up from the wharf. Then Stu got back into the car with chocolate fish. Chink shook his head. Kate pushed hers into her mouth, swallowed her words. The cheap mush seemed no more tasteless than the whisky.

Looking back as they wound up the hill west of the port she could see a motionless line of nappies hung out along the back of Curtis's place. Then they turned up into low freezing cloud, to cross the range.

On the other side it was clear and dazzling. In the distance the foothills beyond Palmerston showed sharp with snow. There was a dirty mush of snow along the side of the road where the sun had reached, and where it hadn't the hoar still lay brightly. The sea below was brilliantly faceted, blue and silver.

'Yeah, look at it!' Even Chink sat up straighter and tipped the bottle again, in salutation.

There was ice in the shaded corners. As Stu crept down the steep incline towards the coast, the back of the car seemed to lift off the road and shake and then slide sickeningly away from them. Vomit rose in her throat.

'Please stop, I feel sick.'

'We're almost there,' said Chink, and wound his window down. The icy air struck her violently. She cried out and retched, grabbing for a handkerchief. Stu skidded to the side of the road. She spewed out the door. Through a blur of tears she saw Chink sitting without turning. He tipped the bottle, looked out at the shining panorama. Stu stood some way off. When she'd finished he came around the car with a clean handkerchief. Chink lit a cigarette and sat waiting.

How she feared and hated the dragon-patience with which he guarded his hoard of torments. She didn't even know what they were: he'd never been straight about them.

When you go to someone for help, what happens? Ah, admit it. There it is: the shit on your shoes, the wound in your hide, the tear in your eye. You say, 'Help me.' The reply you get is, 'No, *you* help *me*.' Then begins a bargaining over who needs help the most, over whose puncture is more serious. That's what happens. Yet it works, as often as not: a resistance, a reef on which the leaking hull of your pain can break up and sink at last, as Kate's might have, or Chink's, that day ... gone down as though beneath the dazzling tinsel and azure meniscus of the sea, the glaring horizon.

Ice had set in the Purakanui inlet. There were no birds in the estuary, but crowds of them were wheeling above the long spit dividing the estuary and lagoon from the sea.

'I've seen them crashing into that stuff, that slush, sometimes it kills even big birds,' said Stu.

The ruts in the road were frozen solid. The cold in the sand of the track struck through Kate's boots. Here, in the overgrown path where the sun never came in winter, the frost crystals were so large and distinct they might have been the elaborate constructs of a science of cold: they were unreal, like models, and yet so perfect that they alone, out of the entire surrounding jumble of weed and branch and rock, seemed not be superfluous.

From the cliff to the left of the track hung ragged rows of icicles. The excavation of the small old quarry was filled with thick ice: when Stu jumped on it it cracked like a gunshot, a twenty-foot greenish fracture whipped out through the surface. The sand at the beach was also frozen: it was possible to cut it to a hard edge. This Chink did, using the large Green River butcher's knife he'd brought in his mussel kit.

Kate's boots were rubber so she walked out into the water and bent to scoop sea into her mouth. It was too shallow to be clear but she welcomed the grit and harshness of it.

Stu had walked on towards the bluff at the western side of the beach, over which was the other small beach he'd decided to use.

They were all spaced out widely in the cold brassy air: Stu, bent under his camera bag, about to disappear behind some rocks below the clay bluff, Chink carving sullenly in the frozen sand just beyond the opening of the path through the bare lupin and elderberry, and Kate pacing eastwards along the waterline, clutching under her coat the hand numbed by the water. There was no sound except sea. Even the wheeling gulls in the distance above the sandspit were silent, or else what small breeze there was blew their cries away.

She walked on for a hundred yards. Turning to look back she could see Chink, crouched in the sand at the western end of the beach. He could have been a child playing by itself, and so used to solitude that it's peopled its world for itself, and can talk all afternoon with these allies.

As she walked back he grew. She abandoned the image which had entered her mind: of picking up and hugging a solitary child, no bigger than Janie aged six, covering her serious face with kisses ...

He didn't look up as she walked past him towards the bluff. The frozen sand around him was carved into an intricate maze of sharp-edged rectangular walls and boxes. Pressing with rapt concentration on the back of the blade, he began to cut an extension, pausing for a moment to flick his tortoiseshell bracelet up out of the way.

On the other side Stu had collected a pile of driftwood and made an enormous fire. He stood panting by it, the bottle of Dimple cradled in his arms. He was squinting at the rock face. The low shadows of the early afternoon sun struck into it.

'It's perfect!'

'Phew, pick up on David Bailey.' She had a drink and stood by the fire. In the distance, out to sea beyond Warrington, tiny fishing boats could be seen in the clear focus of the air. They too were unreal, like a child's toys. As she looked out towards them across the crystalline glare of the water her eyes seemed to yaw on that surface, as the car had done on the dark ice of the hill. Stu was standing in silence, fiddling with his wristwatch. She sensed the mute presence of the sentence she'd missed: some pact, some kind of desolate mirror image. She felt sick again. There was a thin high whine of silence in her ears, a sound like cicadas. For a moment she hesitated, her nostrils tightening against that odour, suddenly hot with more than the heat of the fire, with some stifling nauseous access of energy which rose under her ribs, pressing her throat. She was about to raise her hand to shatter that shrill screen of silence like a pane of glass whose insistent faults blur any vision. The day's clarity, the piercing focus of the cold air, seemed themselves to be that desperate filter obscuring what was near-at-hand. Though the light might lead out to infinity and so back again, that too was an illusion. It all was. *Break it.* She raised her hand, raised the sentence, a heavy instrument, to break the pane: 'What did Chink say ...?'

She didn't say it. She stepped out of the heat of the fire, taking the scarf from her head with her raised hand, feeling the blood drop like mercury in her heart. The sweat was cold on her top lip, her forehead.

'Let's get it on.'

Real despair is impersonal. It seems finally to have no object. Chink, carving his labyrinth in icy sand, was as distant as the fishing boats being offered on their burnished tray, where her eyes slewed towards the bulge of the horizon.

But the energy which had fed her sickness had gone. She watched as Stu checked his gear. Then she took her clothes off and posed or walked or bent as he directed, feeling no cold, but getting into her overcoat from time to time and standing by the fire, sipping from the bottle. Soon she was drunk, dazed with heat and cold. Stu moved quickly and surely following some instinct. She stood with one leg propped high on a rock, the other knee turned outward, her head and torso bent as far back as she could get them. Stu was photographing from just beyond her foot, shooting along the length of her leg.

'Hey this is getting a bit tawdry.'

'Hang on sweetheart.'

From under her brows she could see the beach beyond, upside down ... and Chink come over the bluff and walk around the headland with his mussel kit. She turned, pressing her arms to the weathered rocks, hearing the shutter click and click beside her. She huddled by the fire in the overcoat, one breast and one leg carefully exposed.

Then it was enough. He passed the bottle over. She was shaking, the tears were running down her cheeks. She stood facing the headland where Chink had gone. Stu's cold hand pushed the coat aside and touched her breast.

'Why don't you dump Chink, the bastard's driving you mad.'

*That was it.* She saw them again in the centre of the room, in a formal attitude of agreement. In the derelict house. When she looked at Stu his face was doggish with desire. Passed over, passed on, like some used item. She pushed his hand aside and gathering the flapping overcoat around herself ran down the beach. The blurred pane broke. The near-at-hand rushed towards her, her feet struck against the shell-studded rocks of the headland. Slipping and clutching she got around. There was Chink, standing at the end of the outcrop, staring at some point far across the bay. At his feet brown sluggish kelp, green water. The mussel kit lay full beside him. She couldn't get a word out. When she was close he heard her and turned slowly, as though out of a vision. Then he ran forward and gathered her up, like a child, pulling her coat shut, pulling her against him.

'You fucking bastard ... oh Chink, oh Chink ...'

Then he took his wool hat off and pulled it over her ears and led her to shelter by the cliff.

'Shush ... hey, little one ...'

When she could speak properly she asked for a cigarette. He lit it and she got it, shaking, up to her mouth. The pain in her feet was agonizing. His eyes, for the first time since she'd known him, were openly overflowing with tears. He talked on and on.

'It's almost spring, we're past the solstice.'

'Can I come,' she kept saying. 'Can I come?'

... while his big hands, purple with cold, rubbed clumsily at her arms and shoulders, touched her cut feet, while he stared with those lidless tearful eyes into her face.

She was thinking, 'Perhaps this time he won't go away.' And looking out through eyes closing like a lover's, at the tiny fishing boats on their sea of brass: Beck's frail gorgeous galleons of faith.

# 13

If I get to know 'the material' well enough, I've kept thinking, then some sort of order will emerge. But that's been a kind of half lie.

I know it so well already that it's all present. Sometimes I can't remember the sequence in which things happened. I keep looking for something outside it all: a bad habit my mother taught me. But her endless supply of quotations would fizz like hard metal dropped in acid. Mine are downers: I grind them between my teeth and feel my sad blood thicken and relax ...

1.  '... what I give to all I withhold from each' (Reb Bunam)
2.  'You come from' etc. (You know the one)
3.  'O sightless tides / What blossom blows to you from spring hillsides?' (Currow)
4.  (Wait for it:) 'This fabulous shadow only the sea keeps' (Crane)

What a dreary little anthology. For a while sentences used to jump out of books at me. It was like seeing 'evidence' or 'clues' or 'material' everywhere. I picked up a book of Crane's poems, I saw that line, I shut the book, I began to cry.

It's like that little bastard Julian that Beck picked up so long ago: 'A pregnant woman discovers the meaning of fiction' ... *that* shot straight through the filter and lodged like some shrill implant just by my ear.

In fact I don't know how to get into this. I feel like writing at the top of a fresh page: SUICIDE! I mean, this is a serious matter. But I sit looking out the window at the ngaio, and listening to the cicadas, and how do I remember Chink? With love ... that is what's risen to the surface.

'You selfcentred heartless bitch.' Say it, then.

When I cry these days it's no longer for myself. It's as though its because there's sunlight among the kapuka and the ngaio, or rain ... blackbirds, or a cicada. I don't understand it. But the moment leads me out.

I always thought there were three kinds of suicide: suicide committed out of complete despair; suicide committed to regain love; and suicide committed with reason not feeling. The first kind, I thought, was meant to succeed but often didn't. The second kind, the saddest, wasn't meant to succeed. The last kind was meant to succeed and usually did.

That's bullshit. It doesn't work, there's no place for chink in it. For him to have a place in it, he'd have to permit it to fit him from the outside. But Chink's death emerged from within, as far as the unseen side of the skin of the whole of his body, and if we have auras then as far as the limits of his aura, and if we have astral bodies then as far as his astral body travelled from the body that held me in its arms at night. It didn't describe him, it created him.

It's impossible for me to imagine Chink's death without also imagining landscape and music. Yet neither exist. The landscape isn't a setting: his death creates it, as he moves towards that moment when death will compete its creation of him. After that moment of his death, the landscape ceases to exist. If I was to go back to Bethell's now, right down to the bit called O'Neill's, as I couldn't such a short time ago, it wouldn't be the place where he died. It would just be Bethell's beach.

And the music isn't an accompaniment to his death, but has gone forever, though when I imagine it it's close to the pitch of 'killing the fish'.

So those of you who doubt that Chink committed suicide are only playing with stencils, colouring-in-by-numbers, identikit. Your doubts are irrelevant. Even if Chink did not, in your terms, decide to do away with himself (let's drag all the stencils out of the cupboard), even if he did go out to Bethell's (alone?) and drown 'accidentally' having dropped a tab (alone?), it makes no difference. It was the shape he was taking. And how can you surrender to something which by-passes or subsumes the will just as surely as love can subsume reason? (Why didn't I dump Chink?) You stop the clock. You say, 'At *this* moment it happened. Its meaning is *here*.' You describe what you've stopped: a dead fish: Chink, on a trip, caught in the black surf. Meanwhile the 'truth' continues, breaking and reforming like the lines of phosphorescence in those dark breakers that dumped your only evidence into some fissure in the rocks.

What if you'd been able to make out a big smile on your evidence? Yeah, that would have been 'open to interpretation' too:

'What a way to go!'

*That's* obscene, not my light heart. You'll learn nothing from the black sand and rips of Bethell's, no matter how long you spend walking up and down the tide line.

'Look at that undertow ... that's how it would happen.'

So what? It *did* happen. That's it.

And you won't learn anything from your memory of Chink picking out a twelve bar blues in the clump of nikau palms at the bottom of the section of Beck's bach. Go and have a holiday there and see how much time you spend thinking of Chink, and how much your surroundings remind you of him. You'll get stoned, you'll trip, you'll swim, you'll eat mussels and rock cod, you'll sleep, fuck, laugh, talk. You won't drown. Your 'description' won't *mean* anything. Every so often the conversation will reach out, touch Chink: 'Do you remember ...?' It will be very gentle. You'll feel guilty because you're thinking of him so little. Well, don't feel guilty. Don't let it spoil your holiday.

How can I explain it? I don't mean to absolve myself. An order has emerged, that's all, and it's happened in spite of my struggle to work to a design.

I suppose the design was *I am to blame.* I suppose it was a kind of vanity. But what's emerged isn't like that at all. I began to realize it a while back.

It's all moving. I'm beginning to move with it. I don't understand, but I accept it. And so here I sit, your 'selfcentred heartless bitch', looking out through the open window at the broadleaf and the ngaio ... clear late summer sunshine, and a cicada, yeah! ... a cicada playing the blues!

# 14   Heartsease

"Listen Supercock I'm gonna give you a definition.' (Beck letting Chink have it, back up in Auckland again, the spring before his last, yellow kowhai weather, blue distance weather.) '... now listen: your trouble is Darwinian paranoia, a paranoia of biological necessity, a paranoia of practical genetics: the idea is that one cock can get around numerous women for purposes of procreation and so most men are, practically speaking, in terms of the survival of our species, redundant, unless we regard them as drones, suicide-soldiers, slaves. It's the women we can't cut down on, right Kate? ... huh ... all right, but this is the origin of what Kate calls 'male chauvinism' though I bet she's never thought about it. First: deep down most men know they're irrelevant unless they can prove themselves to be good studs and all that. Second: so they come on *machismo* but it's a sad sham and it destroys them as people. Third: they struggle to retain the power they know they don't deserve, they use this power in sexist programmes, phew, listen to *me*, they emphasize the symbols of maleness rather than its functions, since function and symbol are usually contradictory. Result: like, here's Chink with cock written all over him, yards of it, but he's got no children and all his other kinds of vital energies are directed inwards, not outwards into the species to educate it or reproduce it or protect it. Analysis: he's really a human dildo, a eunuch with a strapon, he's impotent, he's a self fucker ... Listen, all supercocks are really at an infantile stage of development, they wanna get back into the amniotic fluids, they wanna drown in their own come, they wanna be absorbed back into the process they can only guess at when they're fucking. Meanwhile the lady looks on patiently, and gets her kicks, or more likely gets hurt, and sometimes wonders why the stupid bastard has to go through all those changes, why he goes limp like a wee macaroni the moment she suggests he's letting her down, or not getting her up ... what a merry-go-round, Jesus! So if you wanna get off the merry-go-round you go gay: it's practical and sensible apart from anything else like fun, not that I could tell *you* that. ... Well, what are you, señor Prick, Chink suh, B'wana, do you have brains in your balls, are you a dildo, or are you a *kamikaze* fucker, dying to die, to get back, to be started over again ...?'

Of course Beck was putting Chink on. On this occasion Chink slowly unzipped his fly, took his cock out and held it across the palm of his hand.

'You're probably quite right, Auntie.' He was grinning straight into Beck's face. Then he tickled it 'under the chin' until it began jerkily to stand up.

'Stand up when Teacher comes into the room.'

But she's also thinking, 'Old Beck had a hunch ...'

They were walking from Waitakere station over the hill to Bethell's beach (not Beck, he'd gone on in a car with friends to the bach he shared down by the river), just Chink and Kate, ambling through dust while minahs chopped in and out from the sides of the road in front of them, flicking white wedge tails. Chink was singing:

> Some folks built like this
> Some folks built like that
> But the way I'm built
> Don't you call me fat
> Because I'm built for comfort
> I ain't built for speed
> But I got every thing
> Oh that a good girl need

Somewhere, over towards cleared ground, the magpies sounded like grand pianos with squeaky castors being wheeled around the hills ... a concert was in preparation, some kind of spectacular, something vulgar to remember it all by ...

From Eden Park the Waitakere ranges had been visible, purple in the distance. They'd been at cricket with Beck. He'd shouted, 'Stick it right uppim!' *Nok*: a cap had flown in the air, the ball had bumped under the grandstand. Beck: 'You beauty!'

'Stick it right up him,' she said, as they walked along. 'I don't want to spend the whole time out there listening to you two eating each other's hearts, doing your routines. I've been through that.'

'Right.'

> Because I'm built for comfort
> I ain't built for speed

he sang, down in the sunny ponga grove below Beck's bach. Everything was terrific. The cicadas were beginning to twang and scrape away.

'Bring us a few really shapely shells,' she said one day as he was off for a walk.

He brought some empty ice-cream tubs.

'It's all that's left.'

His smile was sunny, malicious: 'Woo-hoo-oo': Wolf howlin'.

One day they walked back along the valley and turned up the hill by the chicken farm. It's the light she remembers again, and the lizards in the dry toitoi debris by the roadside. Coming over the crest of the hill, they see a dry vista of manuka and yellowish clearings, bright flashes of old bush in the gullies. Then the valley opens out south-west to the roar of the sea, to a sky sandwich: to chow on a sky sandwich, to get cloud sauce on your chin, to share a slice with a friend ... they like that kind of appetite, smacking their lips over space ... they like to think that if blue is distance and yellow is where they're drunk with being, then they might live in a green space ...

*Wait, what's this ...*

She's tracking some bright filament. She follows herself and Chink into an old grove of pohutukawas. Orchids grow in the deep cusps and bowls of these trees which she thinks resemble elephants. There's a gaudy play of light in the stiff leaves of baby nikaus, down there among the old trunks: points of yellow and green fire. The trunks are grey and wrinkled. The light soaks into this, but blazes in new leaves. They climb through manuka, delicate black filigree above their heads, scurf of lichen and dry bark on the boles. A bird seems to say 'Chink, Chiii–iiink': his head turns that way. Wind in the branches sounds like the sea: they're underwater, held in the flickering light of a wave. Bellbirds and tui among kowhai flowers sound like ships' bells filtered by sea and distance. *The light, the light* ... she's been here before, it's as familiar as anything she knows about him. From the crest of the hill, jutting like the bows of an immense galleon out into the valley, preparing to launch itself across the plug of ironsand in the valley's mouth, they look west at blue, at space, at sky sandwich, at the sea's thin white line of foam. Behind them, below them, the birds gong and warble among yellow, the fire ... above their heads the minute black latticework of dry manuka twigs ... above that the blue northern sky ...

'*That's it*, that blue!'

It's raining. In the window her reflection watches her lips move. She says, 'I'm going crazy!' There's the Wedding Guest telling her she's going crazy. 'Hey, stop it!' (Hey, stop it!)

But she can't laugh. Her face has gone stiff. She's got something. She opens her eyes and writes:

1. he's green, he's got blue, it's distance, to approach her he's got to subtract blue from himself, he's got to change what he has into what he's diminished by, his power's reversed, he gets the Tasman instead of the Pacific.
2. she's yellow, she hasn't got blue distance, to approach him she's got to add blue to herself, she's got to change what she lacks into what she's augmented by, her impotence is diminished, but she reduces his scale.

'She gets a fucking Badedas bath ...!'

Yeah: she's increased, he's diminished. She's alive, he's dead. How neat.

'I'm crazy.'

The door bangs open where she runs out and through the house to Ingrid and the baby playing with empty preserving jars in the yard. The yellow shed doors are open in the sunlight. Yellow ragwort is glaring on the hillside opposite.

Comforting Kate as she cries in her arms, Ingrid watches the baby at the same time to see if it's frightened, and tries to understand what Kate's repeating, over and over: 'I'm yellow, I'm yellow, I'm crazy ...' She doesn't understand it, how could she? And Kate's been so much better ...

From the grove they walk downhill through shadow, in a primeval agglomeration of trunks, leafmould, the haphazard bright regeneration of pongas. In the raupo swamp at the bottom of the valley there's a simmer of wind in flax, toitoi, bullrush. The bullrushes resemble bees' legs laden with pollen.

Beyond the immense dam, the plug of ironsand in the valley's mouth, there's a lake, Lake Wainamu.

Chink: 'Lake Chad ...'

Grass stalks blown from their fixed points in circles and arcs on the dark sand make delicate relief lithographs, maps of mazes, of ways into the interior. The sand burns like glass.

Chink: 'Follow me.'

A white butterfly flickers above the sand in the distance, like a loose white robe, a burnouse.

The Guide: '...'.

The water is green and cool. Ducks clap and panic. Then it's quiet again.

They've made it. They've got there. They're drinking beer, eating smoked beef sandwiches. Their feet dabble through the dream surface of the lake.

They all play the following game except Beck who says he doesn't dig the symbolism.

Down towards the beach, where the river spreads into the sand, there's a deep cave in the cliff. The game is to get blocked and go there at night. There are ten of them altogether. They draw lots for which one will go right into the cave then turn off the torch. This one has to take up a position anywhere along the floor of the cave, which goes straight back into the hill. The remainder of the players outside draw lots for the order in which they'll run at full speed into the blackness. At any moment they expect to smash into solid rock. Their legs fail. Then those who are in there already pressed against the walls of the cave or lying awaiting on the floor, put out their hands. Or they all pounce on the victim.

Everyone becomes hysterical with laughter.

Only three people are able to run very far in. Clink's one of them. He flies through the blackness yelling wildly, grazes himself on the wall he runs into. Where he comes to a stop shouting 'Ow!' is a small ledge with a sick penguin sheltering on it. He says he could smell it when he stopped, something fetid, he could hear its difficult breathing. In torchlight it's revealed, a sad bird, puffed up defensively, one round eye filled with maggots.

When the torch is off and everyone's been quiet for a while, the glow worms light up along the ceiling of the cave, as though the scale of the universe has been reduced until stars press down on your head.

'Te Pokumea ...'

Outside, where Beck sits warming himself over a joint, the stars recede again to their proper perspective.

In daylight the river is sluggish. There's an oily sheen on the water from the swamp, orange tongues of iron oxide by the stream, bright mica in the sand. ... The universe is tipped up. You grind stars under your feet. Space is solid, it shifts and sucks just enough to slow you down. Running into distance (chasing a frisbee), your feet bog, you expect to smash your face into rock, to be crushed.

Lifting your eyes to the horizon, you experience salvation. You are poured out. You sense how that 'barrier' recedes forever.

You're not moving. But *it* is.


The north end of Bethell's beach, the part called O'Neill's, has pohutukawas with white trunks hugging the slopes behind the dunes. Standing in the sea are crude bulwarks and dragons' teeth of composite rock: fiercely dense firings of scoria, clay, iron, shell. In stormy weather gobs of yellow foam whirl inland. The sea boils in jagged fissures. In fine weather a haze of salt spray hangs in the air. Ripcurrents drive crooked lines of waves against the rocks. You can see what might happen.


'Chink, who's this Stranger?'

Chink's wet head jerked towards her. There was a patch of black sand on one cheek, like a contusion.

'Sorry,' she said. 'It's just that you've mentioned him or her once or twice as though I should know.'

He rubbed at the sand on his face. Then he rolled over. His belly was black with it. He scratched at it with one finger then lifted more and lazily dumped it on his belly and thighs.

'It's not important,' he said. He sat up and looked down the beach. 'It's just a fancy of mine. Or it could be like that guy over there on the rocks. Could be anyone. It depends.'

'The fisherman there?'

'Yeah, the fisherman, why not ...?'

At the far end of the beach (they were all at O'Neill's) a man was fishing from the rocks with an enormous rod, standing motionless and patient above the water which crashed below him. Kate hadn't noticed him before. Through the thin haze of spray and heat he appeared unreal, and with that hypnotic immobility of all patient fishermen. But she couldn't see why Chink should have singled him out, unless it was because the man singled himself out by being the only person with purpose on the beach.

But Chink appeared to be satisfied with his explanation. Or else the question didn't interest him. He stood up and sauntered into the water and when he was deep enough plunged under a breaker, reappearing seconds later with a shake of his head. Then he swam out some yards with his strong easy stroke, ducking the waves, and bodysurfed back in. He did this several times. Then he walked back. The solitary fisherman was also coming towards them along the tidemark. He and Chink met in front of her and dipped their heads in greeting: that familiar all-purpose male greeting.

'You want to watch it,' said the fisherman courteously. 'The tide's going out.'

'Yeah,' said Chink. 'Not much good for fishing either.'

The fisherman walked on, a short sun-darkened middle-aged man, with a wet sugar-bag over one shoulder, wearing white plastic sandals. As he got further away all that could be clearly seen of him through the haze was the dogged tread of the white sandals.

'So the Stranger's a chartered accountant who in retirement follows a lone romantic streak.'

Chink grinned, licking salt off his chin. 'That'd do,' he said. '"I was a chartered accountant until I discovered my romantic streak."'

'"I was a romantic until I was discovered by a chartered accountant."'

They went lazily through a few more changes in the little word game. But Chink's eyes followed the distant tread of the fisherman's sandals as he walked away from them with that solitary patient purpose through the heat haze, stopping once or twice to shift the big rod case to the other hand, the dark sugar-bag to the other shoulder.

# 15   Dynamite

The most he could do any more was hold a match to her cigarette. The cigarette was shaking so much because her hand was shaking that much. He had to follow the cigarette with the match like a turret gunner in a war movie taking a bead on the enemy. He kept getting metaphors like that: avoiding the issue? the 'saving grace of humour'? So, laugh.

There seemed to be a tremor just behind her eyes. It spread to her hand, to the jumping cigarette. His match jumped after it, soundlessly. Its movement said 'Duh duh duh duh duh', a children's matinée. One moment her eyes filled with tears which the tremor shook out on to her cheeks. Then the eyes closed. Then she laughed, she couldn't stop laughing. She shook with laughter. They were completely smashed a lot of the time. At least he was finally quit of his ferocious vanity (he invented the term himself). Dynamite! But was left with a bankrupt compassion (that was his too).

She walked along one side of the street. It wasn't raining, it had snowed and thawed, the air was clear, sunlight tinkled on to the rinsed pavements, small funicular gondolas of water drops hung along telephone lines. She could barely raise her eyes from the asphalt. He observed her from the other side of the street. He thought: 'If I call out she'll step out under a car.' Later it occurred to him that he could have crossed to her. (At that stage his vanity still had him by the throat.) He went into a newsagent's and bought a newspaper then went and had coffee. The Stockholm Conference on the environment was equivocating grandly. Banality. Dynamite! It seemed like a good day to be in the country up Central, but he couldn't imagine what he'd do there by himself. Park the car and drink, look at the Old Man Range, do some snow, ha ha. He wondered where she was going when he saw her on the other side of the road.

He felt very gentle. It seemed to him he felt great compassion. Only later did he realize it was vanity. When his pride and assurance were destroyed his compassion shrank, or at least his ability to articulate it did. Hah! Who are these people. She was always on about her fucking mother these days and it made her talk *like that*. She knelt in front of the heater, taking off her clothes. He pressed his lips to the crown of her head, her dark crown. She seemed so vulnerable! How our compassion flatters us. He made love to her gently and slowly, not wanting her to be alone that night, single that night, or ever, not wanting to leave her body. She trembled, turning her head from side to side on the pillow. He could see her teeth in the darkness. With despair he felt his prick shrinking. He held her, motionless, close to him. He shrank and left her. She slept huddled against him, breathing on his neck. He lay awake most of the night. In the morning he kissed her forehead and talked to her.

Whenever he sat in a room alone, or with her, which was now seldom, or even with a crowd, the Stranger entered. He was mostly quiet these days. He simply leaned in a corner and watched, with an expression of mild amusement, as she moved her cigarette towards his match. Sooner or later the Stranger would sigh: 'You see? Why pretend? You can't win. Look at her. Look at you. Look at the record. Try and imagine the future. Why not be honest? Compassion's a kind of vanity. It makes you feel good. It's an excuse for manipulating others. Don't you feel a shit when you know you've done that? Look at your record, brother. Your own need's the dragon that traps the princess that calls for the knight that kills you that has a need that becomes a dragon that traps the princess. ... Why not get out? There's no future in that system, only repetition. You don't need it. It doesn't need you. What I have to offer isn't even terrifying.

Dynamite!

Another time he bent her hand back and butted her in the face with his forehead. He wanted to hear something resist and break. Everything was so fucking passive! It was like being smothered.

But at least he was finally quit of his 'ferocious vanity'.

And with it, of a good part of his ability to 'articulate compassion'.

Those were the words he thought. Their stupid formality made him furious. But he persisted in the same vein. It was like a language she'd taught him. Along with a lot of other stuff. Now that he had, to a large extent, 'lost all interest in self', the most he could do anymore was hold a match to her cigarette. O yeah! In a corner of the room, paring his fingernails, the Stranger smiled his patient lopsided salesman's smile and raised one shoulder: 'Now you took like an intelligent fellow. Take my advice, brother.'

He bought a Fender Telecaster guitar: '... plugged into his Twin Reverb amp and very gently thumbed his machine. It responded like a crack of thunder ...' That was the advertisement. He couldn't get one beautiful lick out of it.

He'd though, 'I could be a musician ...'

Uh uh. No.


It was the clearest day for weeks: blue and sharp, cold, the sun bright, the far horizon where sea and sky met milky with brightness, the near horizon where pinewood and sky met bristling and hard-edged with black pine tops. In places where the sun hadn't reached the road, grass, leaves, was a thick hoar of frost. The upright crystals jostled each other on the surface of a leaf, like nerve endings, he imagined, somehow erogenous, frozen, a second's tastelessness on the tongue.

She leaned against weatherbeaten rocks having her photograph taken while he knelt in the sun at the end of the outcrop tearing clusters of mussels from the rough stone and stuffing them into a kit. He was going to cook them in beer and butter. He was pissed. He had no appetite. He tugged mechanically at the blue shells. The icy sea rushed in and out below his fingers. In summer the kelp would be chrome yellow. Now its thick fronds and broad muscled limbs were a dark brown, like seals.

Further offshore a few fishing boats were spaced haphazardly between sea and sky. Killing the fish. He imagined fish crowding into their nets, the soundless panic and agony, the net filled with scales resembling a dragon. Reality is a lattice, a net. It's the spaces that count. It's the spaces that trap you. There's no escape. Or ...

'That's right, brother,' said the Stranger. 'That would be the natural way. How you envied the seals! You could get back there. Just think of it: in your element at last! And the Pacific: peace, brother, peace ...'

'Do you have a cigarette?' she whispered.

He gave her one and lit it. Duh duh duh duh duh. What a day! Clear light! *The favourite lost by a neck*. In the net, strangling. Dynamite, dynamite!

'Listen,' he said, 'it's gonna be okay so don't *you* worry. What a day! We're almost past the solstice. It's almost spring! Look at the horizon, all the way to South America, the Pacific, Kate, the Pacific ...'

'*Can I come?*'

# 16

Leaving Dunedin early, a blur of long roads, driving in and out of rain. Then it began to clear. Imperceptibly his muscles began to relax. But he had to keep driving. He kept the cassette going. Gradually he sank back against the seat, began to look around himself as he drove. He slowed up.

'What a boring road,' he said aloud. He'd travelled it more times than he could remember. The banality of his thought was a comfort.

'Still, it's spring,' he said. That was another one. He laughed for a while. He tried a few more: 'Look at the lambs!' 'I much prefer hilly country.' 'We're averaging about forty.'

And out of Christchurch. His time had these big gaps in it. He took a swallow of Dimple, dropped a dexie down after it. Yes, it *was* spring, getting into it. Something inside him was pushing like a green spear of narcissus or common daffodil under the cold clod of his confusion. He could feel a gap opening up, and a perfume rising through him and passing from his nostrils to envelop him: clarity, softness …

Happiness?

In any case, Waikuku, a name, a bearing, evidence that he was moving. The sense of motion. It had become rare. He began to prepare his brief.

On the banks of Saltwater Creek the willows were tipped with ochre and yellow feathers of growth. And on.

On the western side of the road were stands of old gaunt gums, skin hanging in tatters. The swampy flats seemed almost to extend to the foothills, these to the mountains, hinted at but real, promising more: green, brown, blue, white: the receding colours were like a code: the message left him dazed.

And on: lupin, gorse, the heaps and gnawed corrugations of old dunes. He ticked off Kowhai Stream. West: a solitary cherry tree in blossom. East: a familiar scramble of lupin. The speeding leisurely car divided the universe up its spine. East and west fell away, marking exact divisions.

Amberley, another bearing: wide green empty verges, 'Arthur Burke' used cars, 'Bell Farm Machinery Ltd', a stunning orange sign with navy blue lettering. And on.

He looked west, where the sun tended, and saw an old calm derelict house but with a clothes line propped up with manuka poles in the paddock and a solitary pink shirt hanging on it.

Also west the railway line and on that a solitary man in blue dungarees with a shovel on a jigger, gradually falling back behind the speeding car, looking neither to left nor right, neither east nor west. Chink acknowledged his presence with a long glance in the rear vision mirror.

Then to the west was the old Amberley Lime Company's wooden building drying and grey without paint by the railway line, leaning its chute over.

On the roadsigns, magpies. Against the green before the brown, blue, white — against that spring extravagance glossy black Angus yearlings strolled. This was west.

And on. The Hurunui River. Yes …

And then before Cheviot, west: the first hit of the snow white Seaward Kaikouras, those mountains! whose purity froze and woke him, a vivid rush of sensation to the head.

Then the Jed River. Then Cheviot.

The light was losing out. Five forty-five in the evening when the gap opened up, the 'gap between the worlds', a bright space between the firmament and the mountain tops, and lower down, wedges of light in the foothills, like steps, leading up to that slowly closing doorway. Chink averted his eyes. He looked at the lambs. And then east, at the oriental cosmetic of the gashed and worn hills, the sexual shadow.

'I'm sorry Kate.'

His sadness wasn't painful. He'd have said that he was happy. The green flower had broken through his heart. But still he said to himself, 'I'm sorry Kate.'

And on. The Waiau River, Parnassus! no less! The familiar jokes were okay. Soon it was dark.

He woke cramped in Picton the next morning, and looked east. On the hillside above where he'd parked was a rich yeasty frenzy of yellow wattle flowers. Kate's favourite colour. He got out of the back seat stretching and pissed carelessly by the car. Kate's favourite colour again. It was a beautiful morning. He was as good as there. That speeding cleavage of the universe had been sutured. Deep down he remembered. Deep down he felt how that division (west: the glaring threshold — east: the sexual shadow) had passed through him and through his confusion: how the spring flower had pushed out.

He breathed deeply. The air was sweet: blossom and sea.

'Shit, lookit that wattle!' he said aloud.

His brief was complete.

So: early in spring he'd gone north, alone, in the car. Later he'd knelt in the black sand, in the warm night surf of Bethell's. There had been no horizon out from O'Neill's. The stars had been twittering like birds or cicadas: 'Chiii–iiink ...'

'Te Aukumea ...'

Moments before the wave had taken him it had occurred to him that he was in the wrong ocean! The fucking Tasman! The backyard ocean! A Badedas Bath! He'd opened his mouth to laugh and the wave had poured into him like nothing, like a great rift, like a great space, one he could pass through ...

This is how *she* sees it.

She's packing ... just enough to carry ... room for presents for her dark daughter on the other side of the Tasman.

Curtis drives her to the airport. He's sweating, close to tears. She kisses him because she's grateful, because he's good. There's no time to care how he interprets the warmth of her lips. Her aircraft tosses itself up into the blue.

# Te Kaihau/The Windeater
## Keri Hulme

*Lies & Reflections*

There is
a sandbank somewhere at the end of  Earth where ocean stops and welkin stops
and the winds of the world come to rest. They are chancy beings, like their cousins
the Fates, and prone to sudden inhuman boisterousness — which stands to reason;
they have never claimed to be human. Indeed, they affect to despise us and almost
anything to do with us. Someone got under their guard though, once. They became
aunties.

I thought I'd begin like this rather than by saying, I was born and now I'm dying.
That's so commonplace, and we know everybody does it. What I want to do is lay
before you the unusual and irrational bits from my life because they may make a
pattern in retrospect and, besides, they are the only bits that make sense to me right
now.

For instance, I made the mistake of asking my granny on *her* deathbed whether her
best story was true. Her best story went like this:

> 'There I was, not quite sixteen and your mother just due to come into the
> world and all alone, because your grand-dad had gone across the river with
> a barefoot horse and the river had flooded and he couldn't get back. I was
> greatly in pain and terrified that I wouldn't be able to help myself and maybe
> the babe would die before it lived ... at the worst moment, when it felt like
> your mother was going to be jammed in me forever and I could do nothing
> about it except sweat and scream, at that moment there was a light. Now,
> you must understand that we didn't have the electricity and it had been early
> afternoon when I began to labour and my labour had gone on deep into
> the night; I had lit no lamps and the range had long gone out. Today I'd say
> someone switched a light on: then, I thought the moon had come to visit. As
> well as the light, there was a sweet low voice, a man's voice, saying "Not to
> worry, girlie, she'll be right."'

My granny would shake her head in wonder at this point.

> 'How did he *know*, the man with gentle hands? That it'd be your mother
> coming into the world and not some boy-child? Anyway, my pain all went

away and your mother came smiling into life. And I saw that the light in
the room came from the glory round the man and though he said he was a
horse-doctor, I knew him for one of the Lordly Folk and wasn't this proved
when the shawl he gave the baby for a welcoming gift melted away when
she turned a year old?'

Well, I never had an answer for that question, never having seen the shawl (or
much of my mother for that matter). I grew up curious about granny's story though,
because she never had another like it — just dour little morals ill-disguised as tales.
So, I asked her on her deathbed, was it true? Lordly Folk and shining faces and that?
And she frowned, and whispered huskily, 'What would you tell your man when he
came home distraught and found you cleaned and peaceful and the baby wrapped
in a silken shawl? What would you tell anyone? The terrible truth?' Then she sniffed,
and died.

That has always been my trouble, you see. I have always asked the wrong
questions and I have always got answers. Now I would ask her, Did he have redbrown
skin faintly luminous, like the moon shining through a carnelian? Were his eyes so
black that you only saw the lightning crackling in them? Was there some small thing
malformed about him, a finger too many or a discolouration of skin?

It is four decades too late to ask her anything. You could try a question in the next
couple of hours, though.

## Behind Every Wayward Action Stands a Wayward Angel

I was a plump happy baby. I smiled at my unsmiling mother and chuckled wetly
and merrily when she cried. I smiled at everybody, I smiled at the whole world. I
thought life was a whole lot of fun. It was just as well I got smiling over and done with
then.

The first thing I remember is something everyone says I shouldn't, because I was
too young — eleven months old and just starting to walk. Nobody was keeping an eye
on me out in my playpen on the lawn, nobody thought they needed to keep an eye
on me. My mother was in the kitchen or wash-house, keening to herself (probably);
my Dad was knackering another unfortunate horse (probably), and my granny hadn't
come to live with us yet.

Now, the lawn was comfortably warm and I was chewing happily through an
earthworm. I remember, vividly, the gritty brownish insides and the moist pink skin
and the wriggle. Suddenly, there was a shadow and two cool redbrown hands and
a marvellous trustworthy voice (you bet your life eleven-month-old babies know a
trustworthy voice when they hear one) saying 'Ka kite te taniwha, e pepe?'

Well, that meant buggerall to me but I drooled earthworm charmingly and nodded
hard, indicating I was all ready to go or whatever. All I recall next is strong gentle dark
arms carrying me through the sunshine, bringing me to a waterlit place. 'Titiro!'

Can water both sink and burgeon at the same time? It was waterspout and
whirlpool, a great green helix of live water, anaconda parading through its own
massive and vibrantly-splendid coils, spooling and rising and falling, spooling and

rising and melding.

'He taniwha, ne?'

said the beautiful trustworthy voice, just before the gentle arms opened and dropped me in.

## Looking Like a Looking Glass

I don't remember anything else until I was ten or so. The rest of my childhood might as well have never happened. I am told that I stopped smiling. I grew into a large overly-toothy blundering child who lurched through life inviting adult snarls and blows until a teacher discovered I was legally blind.

Whoa back. Legally blind is not at all the same as the real thing. While I was an eye-cripple, unable to recognise people or hills or my own hands at the end of my arms, as soon as I got glasses I could see, more or less; I could make out what adults meant when they maundered on about birds or views (or lightbulbs, for that matter). While it was a nice surprise to discover such things at the age of seven, it had two curious effects on the way I looked at the world. One was, I never quite believed what I saw.

For instance, if I look in a mirror I see someone of average height and twice average weight with cloudy no-colour eyes and pale brown skin. As for my hair:

Granny: 'Your mother had fine silky seal-brown hair and I had fine silky seal-brown hair so where did those corkscrew red things come from?'

(Give her her due, she never looked at my father when she said this, who had fine silky coal-black hair anyway.)

But the person in the mirror isn't me as I *know* me. Many people have this feeling. If you look in mirrors, reflections is all you see ... true, but my feeling carries beyond mirrors. I look at a mountain I have looked at a thousand times before and think, Did that peak always look like that? Wasn't it a little sharper last time? And hasn't that bluff shifted slightly to the south?

The second effect of the belated discovery of short-sightedness was this: I know what I see (I think) but I'm quite prepared to acknowledge and believe someone else sees the same thing very differently — and that a third party sees something else again. Seeing is not necessarily believing: seeing is a matter of faith in sight.

If you look in mirrors, you might see someone else.

## Moonshickered

The house we lived in (until my granny died there, and my Dad and me moved out) was old. It mumbled to itself on dark nights. There were places on the back verandah that were dangerous for even a child to walk on, and none of the doors would shut because the joists and rafters had sagged. Outside, there was a garden as old as the house, and as well looked after. In fact, telling where the garden ended and the scramble of bush and swamp began was difficult. Two things helped: whoever had planted the garden had loved redhot pokers, and a rough perimeter of them resurfaced each spring; close to the creek, was an orchard, unpruned and lichenous but still producing fruit. A child told not to go into the bush could find helpful patterns of apples and pears, rotten or ripe, defining boundaries. A child was frequently told not to go into the bush. Granny did not like the bush. Maybe it arose from the fact that my grand-dad had wandered away into it and never reappeared. Maybe it was because she had spent most of her life helping to hack farms from the bush, and she thought it resented her, and hers. Whatever the reason, my granny had unpleasant ways of ensuring a child did what it was told, so I was grateful to the orchard and the kniphofia. Particularly to the former one memorable evening.

I was eleven and had been in the bush all day (I'll tell you why later). Come moonrise, I knew I was late getting home and that my granny would have searched the garden. I knew she would be waiting. I knew my Dad wouldn't be home.

Thinking back, from the vantage point of 30 years on, it was an uneasy light. There was the red hugeness of the moon swelling above the trees. There was the rotten-ripe air of the evening. There was my fraught state of mind. So the boy standing in the shadows swishing a stick through the air and matching its whistle with his own may not have necessarily been there (except I saw him plain as in daylight). I remember him as tall, with broad shoulders arrowing down to a slender waist, and I remember thinking it was the hunter's moon that made his hair and eyes both so black and so bright, and his skin so palpably red.

I looked warily at him and he tossed the stick to me and whistled, and tossed an apple to me and whistled, and I frowned at both for a moment until, in some atavistic corner of my brain, a thought formed, an old old thought.

Next moment I was excitedly gathering a skirtful of grub-rich apples, and *next* moment, hurrying home.

Incidentally, 'unthinking' is the only word I know to describe that state of atavistic *knowing*, but 'moonshickered' fits pretty well what happened next.

When my granny said coldly from the back verandah, 'Well madam, where have we been and how are we going to explain it?' I giggled. I sat down ten feet away and fitted an apple to the stick and flicked it and it sped with bruising force to spatter squashily all over granny. Her howl of outrage was matched by my squealing laughter, her movement towards me by two more speedy apples. I kept up a barrage of apples and laughter and she retreated into the house.

O that cider smell fizzing in my nostrils! And laughter rising in pitch to become ululation as twenty thousand wild and battle-happy ancestors rose out of their dark and joined me hurling apples and jigging under the bloody moon.

When Dad came home, there were shattered windows and apple splatters and smears everywhere and his mother-in-law cowering pale-faced and shaking inside and his maenad daughter raging redfaced and shrieking with laughter outside.

My granny and I declared a truce thereafter.

The old old thought I had was called 'atlatl', but that's not as helpful as 'moonshickered' is it?

## Jokes of Gods and Whims of Ancestors

My granny finally died when I was 18. She took a long time about it. She had a stroke (unfortunately she was making porridge at the time and dropped onto our coal range) (Dad found her) (I found Dad) that disabled her from doing everything a human does, except talk. There was another question I asked her on her deathbed: Where do you come from? 'I'm a Celt,' she replied with an ancient and unknowable pride.

Well, her accent was odd, could've been Irish or Scots or maybe anything else. All in all, she didn't tell me much at all. (Of course, now I'd know to ask who her mother was, who her father was ...)

My Dad wasn't much help with the matter of ancestry either. When asked about his mother-in-law to wit his wife to wit my mother, he said, 'Dunno much except the old bloke came from Cornwall.'

It was a bit tender to approach my Dad on the subject as to where *he* came from, who *his* parents were, because he'd been brought up in an orphanage. He knew he was part-Maori (so did Granny, who made sour snide little comments about that), and at some time during his orphanage years he'd been taught the language. He didn't tell it to me — or rather, he told an infinitesimal amount to me.

Because when as a 13-year-old, newly gone to high school, I finally plucked up courage to ask him, 'Dad um, about your Maori side, our Maori side, *my* Maori side ...?' he smiled tightly and said, and wrote down for me so I couldn't mistake the answers to my questions Who are you and Where do You come from?

'Ko Pakatewhainau te iwi, no Wheatewhakaawi.'

I made the mistake of saying that out loud out proud at school.

## All the Smiling Faces Lonely People Keep on Walls

Photographs make up a large part of some people's lives. They will grin at old photos, weep before portraits, relive days so long ago they are turned sepia and curly at the corners. They keep their friends on the mantelpiece and their relatives in albums that would smell musty, only the leaves are turned so very often they smell of sweat and finger-grease and tears.

They prefer to talk to pictures because you can make the perfect answers back.

That doesn't quite apply to my father.

He is largely a silent man and I think I have conveyed that he couldn't care less about dead family. I think he loved my mother (who left him just after I was rescued from seeing the taniwha). I know he loves *me* which is not as reassuring as it might ordinarily be.

You see, he is a knacker, a horse butcher. Somebody has got to do the job, sure. My father is, I understand (never having seen him at work), gentle and dispassionate and thoroughly efficient. No horse, I understand, ever goes terrified to its death in my father's yard; no owner of a horse has ever made a complaint about the way my father treats the dead horses he sometimes has to collect. In fact most of them hand him photographs of their beasts in their heyday, ears pricked forward, eyes liquidly ashine and alert.

If the owners of the horses he kills, or retrieves, don't give him a photograph, he takes one himself before the creatures are dead or are seen to be dead. He lives in two rooms above his knackery. The walls of the rooms are covered with many thousand photographs of horses. He is surrounded by horses, equine sad looks, equine glad looks, equine sighs and equine laughs.

My father loves horses much more than he does humans but I rather hope he will put my photo in some small spare space soon.

## An Episode of Bagmoths

I spent as much time in the bush as I could as a child because I was looking for rare insects, maybe ones no-one had ever found before. O the sadness when I found one ...

Now, when you're very shortsighted, you only see what is immediately in front of your nose. I early became aware of things that writhed oozily or scuttled away on a fringe of legs. When I learned to read, I read voraciously — but only about insects. They were my fascination and comfort and path to future fame (I thought).

We have many splendid and curious small creatures, from giraffe-weevils to astelia moths. There is such a range with so many bizarrely-beautiful life-cycles, that I should have grown up into a happy-ever-after entomologist.

I was 12, I had a collection of moths that would make a lepidopterist sweat with pleasure but it lacked something that, while not in itself a rarity, was very rare in an undamaged state.

Are you familiar with the work of an Australian cartoonist, Mary Leunig? Her art is generally macabrely, bitterly, funny, but there is one where the humour is relatively gentle. It shows a young male moth with gaudy wings standing by a suitcase and looking at his watch. On the wall behind him is a skinny bagmoth case — his own. There is also a fat wriggling case — the woman, of course, late as usual in getting ready you think, and grin before turning to the next page. The real joke is that the woman in this case will never finish getting dressed because female bagmoths remain forever in their cocoons. They are wingless grub-like creatures: to pull one out of its silken home is to kill it.

Male bagmoths pupate and emerge winged and ready for action. There is one slight problem. Bagmoths tend to live way apart from each other, munching their way through the bush, dragging their cases behind them. As in everything else, the race is to the swift — first come, first serve so to speak — so off flutters the male in feverish haste, battering himself against twigs and branchlets and ruining himself as far as I was concerned. The only thing to do was to make a collection of bagmoths, hope there was a male among them, and anaesthetise it as soon as it came into the world.

I scoured the bush for bagmoths and found a thousand and 33. I converted my wardrobe into a bagmothery and reaped manuka by the armload to feed them. They all reached maturity and *none* of them turned into beings with wings. At least, not the proper Oeceticus omnivorous wings.

I was looking at them disconsolately one afternoon, one thousand and 33 fat bagmoths hauling their homes around as they got stuck into fresh sprays of manuka, or snoozing, the mouths of their cocoons drawn shut. And suddenly, I saw it. One cocoon was contorting into s-shaped bends. It was wriggling frantically. Bagmoths did not do this in my experience, even when attacked by parasitic wasps. A male moth was hatching, late but at last!

I took off my glasses and leaned eagerly close to the switching case. In one hand I had a killing bottle. Any moment now ... something began to emerge from the bottom of the bagmoth case, very slowly at first but then with awful swiftness. Insect legs, insect abdomen, glorious? red! wings and a tiny head. With teeth. It looked like a human head. With human teeth. It was grinning at me, its minute black eyes viciously bright. The grin lasted a very long second. Then the thing dived powerfully into the air and sped past my goggling eyes out through the door and away.

I didn't touch or look at or even think about an insect in any entomological sense ever again.

Incidentally, if you're wondering how bagmoths female and male get it together in real life, why not keep a couple and see? Hurry, though. There's not much time left.

## Never the Same Wind Twice

There's only one thing I've ever discovered since, that I enjoy as much as I enjoyed the world of insects and believe you me, I've tried more than a few things.

It's breathing.

Ordinary day-to-day breathing is fine, having the charm of novelty inasmuch as every lungful is slightly different, and deep breathing alright for some situations, and meditational breathing okay if you like meditation, but what I am talking about is the awareness of breathing.

Some mornings I'd wake up very early and grin with delight as I drew in that first conscious chestful of air. It tasted better in my lungs than wine ever tasted on my tongue. It was ecstasy, it was *sweet,* air soughing in and all my little alveoli singing away with joy and oxygen-energy coursing through every space and particle of me. I could feel my heart in its cardiac sac swell and float, held down only by ropes of veins ... it flutters against those ties, wanting to soar in free air as a great luminous pulsing living balloon ... hey! grab another breath! This time'll do it!

You've heard skylarks duelling for space, each pegging his own sky-claim with frantic song, making a chestburst effort to keep every other dueller fenced out as they quest higher and higher into the blue yonder? Sometimes I'd feel like their song on ordinary everyday air.

I *love* breathing. Damn, but am I going to do it hard when I stop.

## Granny's Revenge

I cried just after my granny died, not for her though (she was far better dead by that stage, and I hadn't liked her much while she was alive). Remember I said the old lady had spent most of her life helping hack farms from the bush? Well, we had always understood that each new farm had just about paid for the last one, and that when my grandfather was lost to the bush, my granny was left destitute. But no: she had twenty thousand pounds squirrelled away and she left it all to me. My Dad grinned faintly when he learned that. He gave me good advice. 'Buy a small house and invest the rest girl,' and then he shifted quite happily into the loft rooms of his knackery. I did what he said, bought a solid little house on the edge of town, right on the beach, and put the rest away to work for me. If I lived fairly frugally, I'd never have to work for it.

Boy, the old lady must have hated me a lot. She'd obviously never forgotten those apples.

## The Early Sown Skulls

We were one hell of a gang on the beach.

There was Elias, who lived closest to me, quarter of a mile away, bright and gay and very knowledgeable about drugs. He was discreet but indefatigable in the pursuit of new lovers. There was Pinky and Molly and Chris, an oddly-sexed trio who were indefatigable in pursuit of each other but rather liked others to watch. There was me, independent and alone and indefatigable in pursuit of any boy or man who would help me explore more of myself as a woman.

Don't yawn like that. I'm not going to tell you any of what went on except to say that I learned a lot about myself and others and enjoyed most of the learning very much for the three happy years it went on. At least, I think I did. What with the drink and the smoke and capsules that Elias handed round with gay abandon, I can't remember much of the detail.

I do remember the young pothead who staggered to our bonfire one night, drawn by The Smoke amongst all the other.

'Could smell it a mile away,' he husks, and coughs throatily. He's a stocky youth with an oddly-gaunt face, and raggedy-black hair. The firelight dances on his bare chest and shoulders, on his teeth as the joint passes to him and he smiles slowly, 'maaan, that's so sweet,' cupping his hands round its ember end. He sucks and sucks and sucks, an inhalation into the deeps of his belly down below his belly down past his horny bare soles maybe, and the joint grows ash and shrinks and shrinks to a sickly stickily-yellow roach that he finally takes away from his lamprey suck and looks at admiringly. An nth of an inch left, just nippable by nail, bong fodder only. Without breathing out, not seeming to be breath-holding, not even looking distended round the cheeks or chest or eyes, he passes the thing on. Pinky was next, and dropped it, and we couldn't find it in the sand.

The young pothead smiles his gaunt slow smile at us, and it seems to have too many teeth now. None of us grin too widely back. As I recall, he never did breathe that toke out.

By the by, Elias and Pinky and Molly and Chris lived long happy lives by the standards of a couple of centuries ago.

## The Beach Arab

When I didn't know what I know now, I said that the Beach Arab was pothead's cousin. I was only half-joking, for while he was tall and thin (but full in the face), he had a similar slow smile and the same raggedy black hair. He never wore anything but denim shorts and his skin was a rich reddish brown. If you were on the beach, you generally heard him before you saw him because he played a fat little flute made of bone whenever he was alone. He came shyly to our bonfires at first, always eating whatever food was handed round with his fingers, even when it was a salmon mousse the fastidious Elias had made one March evening. He came less shyly as time wore on and he came to know Elias, then Chris and Molly, and lastly, me. Soon after that, I left the beach forever — but that's a story to come.

He had a strange sense of humour, the Beach Arab (no, he never told us a name).

There was one afternoon I recall in bright detail: three American tourists had invaded our bonfire and were talking loudly, heartily, amusing themselves with the local natives. We were quiescent under more sherry and smoke than usual, smiling dreamily and politely at them when their words gonged more harshly than ordinarily at us. The Beach Arab trailed in, a little after the voice of his flute.

And presently one of the Yanks said gushily, 'And what do you Mayories eat?' Chris who was Danish from Dannevirke looked at Elias whose parents both came from England, and Elias looked at Pinky, a strident Glaswegian, and Pinky in turn stared in astonishment at Molly who blushed all over her Coast Irish face. She didn't look at me, and while I was thinking out loud 'Uuhhh ...' (what the hell did my father ever eat that was different, except horse?, and that didn't seem too Maori to me), the Beach Arab smiled and bowed and swept off a rock and away scuttled a small crab and the Beach Arab dived on it and put it in his mouth, chewing and smiling while the Americans gasped and went Mygahd Dan do you *see* that? and the little legs (half of them) tweedled on his lips until he swallowed the first bit and sucked them in.

They deserved it. I mean, did you ever see a brickred Maori? Okay okay okay, so did I, so have I.

## Birds of a Feather

It was a three-quarter moon, waxing, that night. We lay together just beyond the rim of the firelight, listening to the others talk. Later, when they had gone, the Beach Arab played his bone flute: rather, he talked into it and the words came out intelligible music. His round face looked both very dark and very oriental under the moon.

After we had made love, I smiled at that moon. I had a house; I had the kind of life that suited me down to the ground, and I didn't have to work to enjoy it; I had friends who were warm good fun, and here I lay satiate, gently held by a young man's strong arms, gently held by a lover. I went happily to sleep and dreamed of taniwha.

When I awoke at sunrise, he was gone, but not far. There he was, down by the sea's edge, naked, washing himself. I ran gaily down to help.

I remember thinking, I must have something on my contact lenses, he can't have feathers on it.

I remember saying, hesitantly, 'hey that looks like fun?' but then his upright ure wilted and the shining bronze-green feathers tucked themselves down tidily round it.

I remember looking at the flat silver sea, watching the water suddenly shiver under a passing breeze.

I remember his smile, o yes. I had seen that same smile on too many different faces, a whole flock of them.

I remember running home and locking my door and *never* going onto the beach again.

Funny thing though: I don't remember feathers on it under the three-quarter moon.

## Home Is Where The Heart Is

My solid little house has four rooms; bedroom, wash-house, kitchen and livingroom. For three years I kept it immaculate. For the next ten years I — grew things. Don't get me wrong: it was comfortable enough. I had some pet slime moulds in the wash-house and a live & let live policy with any other agents of decay. There were umbrella toadstools on a dishcloth that I recall fondly, and something phosphorous in a bedroom corner that I never touched. Once a month, when the local liquor store delivered my crate of gin, I gathered up all of the tins I had strewn around, put them neatly into rubbish bags and left them out for whoever takes such things away. Someone did. Just as someone delivered the tinned food I ordered.

I'd've kept on that way until my liver gave out except for a series of accidents.

## Dry Horrors

About four one morning I awoke with a throat-aching thirst. This was usual and so was my remedy, stumble out to the kitchen and get water in a glass and gulp it. After the second gulp, I remembered something.

Now, I'd had contact lenses for 12 years, ever since long-ago Elias suggested they'd be a better idea than glasses. He was so right: I had got to love rain, and swimming was fun; steam, whether from showers or just-opened ovens or body-heat, was no longer a blinding hazard, and I never once sat on my lenses.

I'd just swallowed them, though.

Remember breaking your lens-case yesterday? Remember putting your lenses into that glass just before you stumbled off to bed? Yeah, you remember alright.

I thought about an emetic.

I thought again.

I whimpered until dawn.

In desperation, I rang my father. He sort of snuffled. 'Um well,' he said, seemingly unsurprised to hear from me for the first time in two years and with such a subject too, 'yeah well. Flax'll make you run, y'know. You can always stop it afterwards with little koromiko leaves.'

I wasn't sure whether he meant to use the koromiko as a cork and I wasn't going to ask.

'I'm not scrabbling round in my own shit,' I said shortly.

'You could always have a good meal of, say, scallops, to make it easier?' He openly snorted.

Conversation between a knacker and a drunkard isn't an easy matter, even when they're father and daughter. He did promise to take me to my optician's however, and three hours later, there he was, spruce and grinning on my doorstep. He sniffed a little at the fungal smell and looked sideways at my puffy face and gin-bloated body. He always did think people should go to hell in their own handbasket however, so made no comment at all, merely guided me into a taxi and out into the optician's and back home again.

'Take care,' he said then, and that was the last I've seen of him. You'll gather we weren't ever close. I should have been born a doomed filly.

Until my new lenses arrived, I lived back in the world of blurs. I couldn't go outside because I couldn't see who or what was coming — and for the first time in a decade, I wanted to go outside. Being returned to a condition of childhood had the odd effect of making me, well, not a child, but in some way renewed. The half-empty crate of gin was left untouched while I engaged in warfare with heat (you ever tried to pour boiling water from a jug you can't see into a cup you can't see?) and retaught myself to see with my fingers.

When the new lenses arrived, I put them in and realised immediately that was a mistake.

They melted into my eyes and I could see perfectly but not only what I wanted to see.

## They Have Made the Moon a Skull Who Was my Lady

It is three sober days and nights later. I am walking back to the cleansed house under a thin frail fingernail edge of moon. I am breathing deeply and with joy for the first time for years and frankly don't care if there are creatures with feathered penises in this world.

There are two people swaying together at the bus-stop. She is short and stocky, almost squat, and she is tall and heavily-built and they are twined. The stocky one is muttering. They have made the moon a skull now, walking on it, she is a skull now, while the tall one is singing sadly about some lady lost, some lady gone, and the words run eerily together, mutter and song. As I tiptoe past, they stop singing and muttering and stare at me. Their eyes glow.

I look hastily away and see that the grinning moon really is a skull, the fingernail edge a highlight on her bare jawbone.

## They Have Exits And Entrances Galore

Someone or something has started using my print as a getaway route.

It is a reproduction of George O'Brien's *Dunedin Harbour From Flagstaff Hill* and every so often, just as I've stopped looking at it, a particle of intense light swoops into the water past the wharf on the lefthand side of the picture. Three seagulls flying in an isosceles triangle mark the spot.

The oval 19th century print doesn't bat an eyelid at this intrusion, not even when a similar (identical?) light sears *out* of the water (aft of the steam vessel making its way across the harbour).

There! I caught one out of the corner of my eye doing it again!

## The Constancy of Roads

I discovered today that, during my ten years self-immurement, my optician's clinic had burned down and she had shifted to the North Island. I had walked down to the clinic, my courage screwed to breaking point, to have her test my strange new eyes.

Walking back, I can't find the bus-stop.

## Denying the Mouse

I can hear it. Every night for the last week.

Clink of chopsticks on foodbowl as it creepytoes across seeking morsels, leftovers, bits I've missed. Everything gets gnawed by its tiny defiling teeth.

I've left out tasty poisons for it, in neat dishes. One night I heard it chuckle over my latest cunning trap.

The experts advise setting baits in its own run. How? Mouseruns are the most secretive of paths. They go winding in and out of my walls with no sign, not even an exit hole. Entrances in deep shadows, exits elsewhere.

I can't believe I have a mouse problem. For one thing, in all the years of sloth and mould, neither rats nor mice showed up. Why should my bleached clean house draw them? For another, the thing is way too smart, and there was that chuckle. Maybe a mouseman? A minute anthropomorph, complete with basket of pottery droppings to scatter or stick in strategic places — what better way to disguise your predations than under the guise of another pest? and somehow, I can't see him/her/it raising narrow buttocks and squeezing out an instant turd. Nah, a little factory where they manufactured guises in silence.

In my walls.

Come out! I know you're there. If I can only see you once, I won't kill. I won't even try to kill you. I'll stop setting traps and I'll put out little dishes of good food. Come on, play fair.

Tonight there are two of them, and I can hear their thin voices singing 'We'll Meet Again.'

## Even Barnacles Have a Swimming Phase

I had a choice; stay, and drink myself to death, or, leave and try and find a heart somewhere else.

There was an eager buyer for my house the first day I put it on the market. He was an ordinary-looking fellow, thin and pale with nondescript hair, so I let him have it for five times the price I had paid for it.

His smile lit up his mirrored shades.

## Next Time, Leave it Lying There

At first, I spent a lot of time on the Cook Strait ferries. It was soothing, watching the waves from the safety of the deck, and I liked the food. I stayed one night in Picton, the next in Wellington, and I could have gone on living like that for the rest of my time except I got noticed after the first year, and turned into a celebrity after the second.

I gave in and bought a motor-home and set off round the North Island first, never staying more than one night in any place. I had no pictures and the van was mouse-proof and I never looked for bus stops or at moons.

I did pick up hitch-hikers — I liked to talk and there is something wrong about telling stories to your own ears.

I had been driving around for a year when I picked it up.

There was a young weary man slumped at the side of the road. He lifted his head and gave me a tired one-sided smile when I stopped. He didn't say anything while I talked, just stayed with his head bent, long felted rastafarian dreads swaying as we sped round corners. I thought one side of his head looked ... odd, as though the skull was slightly dented and the skin darker and oilier there, but he was quiet and tired with none of the jolty energy or lightning smiles that I knew and dreaded. He didn't say a word until I said, 'Taumarunui, mate, I'm stopping here,' when he said 'Ta, mate,' and slipped out the door before I'd pulled to a stop. Tired he might have been, judging by his bent head and the way he sloped in his seat, but he was exceptionally agile. He did a speedy little dance as he hit the road, never a slip or a stumble, and then trudged slowly, heavily away. The van spun up a small whirlwind as I drove into the town.

## It's Better Never than Late

Nemesis shouldn't look like this.

Forearms on the table, head on clenched fists, I study the thing.

It lies in a pool of light, in the one-eyed glare of the lamp.

It looks like a slender rectangular tube.

It is a dull leaden colour, but is partly wrapped in what looks like finely-plaited sennit.

The sennit is darkly gold and ends in a snood as though it were hook.

It is three inches long and half an inch wide and half an inch high.

It weighs nearly forty pounds.

I *know* that is impossible.

When I picked it up off the seat it felt warm. I swung round to look for the young rasta but he wasn't anywhere around of course.

It is now very cold. A thin splay of ice crystals creeps out all around it.

I touch it with a tentative finger. A shining bead leaks out, bleeds out, like freshmelted solder or particularly viscous mercury. It lies there, glaring up at me.

The finger I touched it with aches.

After a while, I pour myself a gin. Then I pour myself another gin.

In the morning, there are little silver words on the table.

WHAT IS RAISED WILL BE SUNK.

And the tube is snugly ensconced in my aching left hand and I cannot let it go.

## Mules Are Stubborn Creatures

I caught up with him many many months and miles later, on a marae in the far north.

He was lolling next to a very old woman and he hadn't bothered to change any of his shape. He knew I'd get to him when the time was ripe and he was ready.

I stood cradling my hand which had become inhumanly swollen. He stares openly at me and I stare openly back. For all his illdoing he is utterly beautiful, red and black and white perfection.

He is smiling at me and his smile is without pity.

I ask without words, How do I get rid of it? and he answers without moving a muscle, Go to Rotorua and find the pool that bears my name. It will come off in the pool.

'That will kill me!'

and he shrugs, still smiling.

The elder snuffles round her cigarette, unruly shreds of tobacco leaking out in a fan. She grates, 'It's all for the best, dear' and grins, an eldritch mahogany unsuitable grin.

There's a pigeon beside her with bright black eyes.

'They often come to me dear,' she says hoarsely, 'though they never admit they're lonely,' and a strong wind from the east came up and spun her and the bird away.

## The Tantalising Maze

Is there ever a real answer to anything or a true end to any story?

I hope you realise I tried so hard to stay away from the boiling mud of Rotorua but the strongest of people would be daunted by a fortypound weight clenched forever in one hand.

Yes, I tried cutting my hand off. Whatever the sinker is made of, it is impermeable and has grown all through my arm.

Yes, I tried taking my hand to every doctor and quack under the sun, but they couldn't see anything or feel anything.

It all boils down to this: there are things quite outside humanity and we can't do battle with them. We have to leave it to their own kind to bring them to heel.

Doubtless they will, if they feel we and the world are worth it.

Would you like to know the brightest dream I had of the future? (No, you wouldn't like to know the other ones at all.)

## Never Trust a Dreamer Who Can Also Tell Stories

'Give me that bottle. This one's gone dry.

I've been out picking cockles. It's spring tide. They dig themselves down to normal level but the water leaves them exposed early. When you walk over the mudflat, you see them clamping shells, squirting water in bepuzzlement. I have two kit of cockles — I know, that don't mean much to you. All I know is that two kit give you a feed and enough left over to swim in apple vinegar, put in the cool place for tomorrow.

I think sometimes of those squirts. A watercry of help. Dismay. Horror. When you pour them out of the kit into the pan, they don't make a noise, not like mussels. They sik and hiss and squeak sometimes. Cockles just lie there and die in the steam. Only some don't. Obstinate. You get this feeling when you finally crack the shells that they hoped their shutness would save them. It doesn't. Of course. Crack them on that stone.

I like my cockles raw. Smack two shells together, like cracking walnuts. The weaker always gives. That's sweet, living meat. Or, just steam them open, the flesh not burnt, just lushly half-cooked. Add a sauce. Vinegar if you're feeling harsh. Or a mix of rootginger (did you see the big lilies blooming up on the hill as you came through the big swamp?) and garlic and soy. We still get the soy from Dunedin. The people of heaven never quite left there. Just as well, eh? There'd be none left otherwise. Add some sherry — now, that cask I have comes from Nelson, they got a rich crop there. I swap my bulks for that sherry. And the wine of course. Have some more.

Anyway, you got this sauce, sherry and ginger, garlic and soy, and you dip the nearly-dead not-cooked meat into it, and eat.

O it's sweet.

I almost wouldn't mind someone eating me, like that, did they it with appreciation, like that.

My glass?

O, there's one here can mould glass. Blows it. Makes fires and breath and silica sand to a magic. Containers. Jewellery. A weapon or two. My glass. That's her over there, squatting next to the hunter with the copper earrings. Drift we call her. Lightning we call him. I'm translating, of course.

Anyway, momentarily, and we can eat the cockles I picked. Friend, you'll understand if I say I'm a little surprised to see you here bare? I mean nothing coarse. Yes, that's the old worm ... you'll know that worm eh! Eh, the times the creature has coursed the worm. The last season I saw you was Thunderstorms. Seven cycles ago.

Here in the simple seaward hills, we don't take note of more than a year-name. But you know that of course. It's not that we pride ourselves on ignorance. No-one but a fool does. Just, our way is working up more bones, lapping our own fat cover, growing our own strength. Eating and growing. Us. Basic.

Yes, bare is maybe a wronging word.

I see in your silence your woundedness showing.

Look, when you walk round in your metal skin someone sooner or later is going to think, Ah hah! Flesh *and* cooking pan. That's the way we are round here and you've been on expeditions enough to learn that. We don't think your armour protection or superiority. We skewer.

Taking that metal hide off isn't trust though. Trade for trade is what every thing is. You didn't leave us that worm, for nothing. Your skin's not off, for nothing.

Well, you know better than to misunderstand the savagery and viciousness of us children, heh?

I'm sorry for all the smoke, the cavern is new and unfiltered yet. Nah, it's no special fire, just a joy-thing for this night. Night comes, we must have shelter. Sometimes a fire too. Smile against it, but you wouldn't be out there either, in your suit or out of it. It's wilder than us, night, and too many things tramping around with a taste for soft meat.

Metalmaster, I can ask you bent questions. You come from Cityrace. Can you answer this? Lately I have these night-thoughts. Whatever the Singers tell, I don't think we've changed. Did we ever love each other? Say the Singers. Me, I think we're just the same as we always were, humans, cockles.

A pity you're bare. It's so nice, cracking shells.

Have that bottle, there's wet enough in it, yet.'

## I Mean, It Probably Was a Dream

That's all it was. Ten minutes of talk, our kind of language yet not our talk. Sitting in a dark smoky place, with a lot of people around chatting their not-our-language and gnawing things. Sitting in somebody else's head and knowing they were terribly afraid. Sitting in their head and listening to a skinny old man ramble on about how he liked cockles. Wishing his eyes weren't so shiny, weren't so black, and especially wishing I couldn't see what all the other black-eyed people were chewing on.

If it was a dream, the future is going to be way worse than the past.

I don't like thinking that today is the high crest of humanity; tomorrow, we all fall down.

## The Jewelled Frame

It's funny, trying to encapsulate your own life. As I said at the beginning, it's only the peculiar bits that make any kind of sense, but I am disappointed in my hope of them also making a pattern.

What I seem to have created for you is an old spiderweb, the kind that is a gallery of past feasts. Here an emerald shard of manuka beetle, there the plundered silken hold of a wolf spider's egg-case; some delicate purple-blue, powdery blue tussock butterfly wings interspersed between the coarse and glassy remnants of blowflies, and in this broken corner, kept as ruby as in their strident heyday by some nasty arcane skill, the little lights of cicada eyes …

What is missing, what is needed to make sense of it all, is the spider.


## If You Can Raise Up Islands, You Can Push Them Down Again

I know exactly what is going to happen when I drop the sinker in the boiling pool.

There will be a few indescribable seconds of passing between consciousness and nothingness but that doesn't worry me.

The body will drift down, down, and the snooded sinker will slide down further and faster. Some time later, it will reach the place where the crustal plate is tender and touchy and then, like a good little bomb, it will shed its protective skin and be what it is, a seed of antimatter.

And just before the fish shatters into an archipelago, the incandescent cloud will roar helterskelter over Auckland and boil all the northern sea to a frenzy. And all along the line, the volcanoes will gout and the wild tsunamis rear up and speed in huge glassy walls over every innocent island there is. And the canoe will rock and most of it slide under the waves.

Unless my Dad is killing a horse at the time, he will probably be looking at a picture of his vanished daughter and wondering why he can't yet decently take it down and leave the room to the laughing horses.


## A Question for the Spider at the Heart of Matter

Who made the fatal mistake?

There was a childhood spent fishing up islands and wasting Granny's fiery nails. Snickering over Tuna's dirty jokes and then massacreeing Tuna in a dirty-joke way. Putting stutters in the sun's path, battering down a star's pride, because it was a way to make the world happy. But then you wanted to play saviour and there is *no* fury like a saviour scorned.

Your fury was an impotent sputtering for so long; you were reduced to small deadly jokes. Then, I think, you learned to fly from mind to mind and time to time as easily as you formerly flew from man to bird and back again. After that, it was an easy jump into another world altogether where you could play at large again.

There was this troublesome reminder here and now though, a splinter that irked. Maybe you would have been content to let the matter rest, let the Old Lady keep what you had unwisely made available for her to take.

Somebody offended your pride so much that you made a sinker where before you'd made a hook, that you made lucky me over to find it.

Who?

249

## The Windeater

There isn't such a word, eh. There's a lot of us around though.

I came across the term as a gift, if you like, a sort of found gift. For instance, you break up a perfectly respectable word, happily married in all its component parts: you know it means several things, like a loafer or a braggart. Or a woman who takes part in certain rites. Or it can mean the acquisition of property without any return being made, as well as a spell that is cast to punish somebody behaving in such an unmannerly fashion. That's when it's a whole unbroken word, but if you split it, a power leaks out and becomes a woman trying to make sense of her self and her living and her world.

Which all goes to show the charming naivety of us humans. Sense of a world indeed!

> Now, ask me anything you like because
> my hand is getting too heavy and
> in another second,
> I'll be gone.

# The Transfer Station
## Russell Haley

### OUT ON THE COAST

My old man told me once that there used to be nothing except a dirt road out from the city to this coast and you drove through native bush most of the way. I don't know. It's hard to imagine. The station at the end of the wharf seems to have been at the bay for ever. It certainly looks old enough to have been here in his time.

I took a walk under the piles the other day and there's no missing the way the concrete is being scoured by the tides. Then, of course, some of the stuff from the station doesn't stay down in the rift. Things come knocking in on a spring tide. If you look at those black dunes to the south-west and remember the prevailing wind then you can see that the station is right in the eye of a natural sand-blaster. Leave a car out on the wharf for a year and it'd be stripped back to bright metal.

There have been a lot of changes since Dad's time and some of them I can't abide. Like the language that most of the youngsters can speak from the cradle. I'll listen to it — you can't help doing that — but I'll be damned if I'll learn it except for bits I can't avoid. Those two girls now at the other end of the bar — they're chattering on and they run our way of speaking into the other so quickly you can hardly follow them. I'll go to my grave using my own tongue and be buggered to what you hear all around you.

From the feel of things they didn't get the poles down deep enough when they built this café. A convoy of those big red Meltimi Company trucks just went by on their way to the station and my glass nearly tipped over. What a waste of good grog that would've been. Whisky tastes the same as it always used to and that's one thing I can't complain about, except the price.

It would be good if you could still go out on the point near O'Neills and catch even a rock cod. But the fish got scarce years back. First they were hard to find and then if you did hook one it came in with open sores or growths and you either tapped it with a priest or threw it back. They can lie themselves blue in the face but everyone knows it's the pipes.

I like the music in these places. You don't have to think much when it's coming out of the walls. I've known it louder than this and even though it's their stuff the kids don't seem to pay much attention to it. They can listen and talk and watch all at the same time.

Jesus! That was a big yellow bastard. They're the Échelle trucks and you have to say their name right if you phone to complain that their vehicles are breaking up the road with the weight they carry. In summer you get nearly as much dust flying on the highway as on the clay road behind my crib. Well, they don't take much notice even if you make the effort to sound like them. One December I got a water-cart out from the Forestry to damp down the back road but the next day it was just as bad. The only relief you have from all this traffic is during statutories or feast days and I'm half fooling myself when I say that because that's when the kids usually get out here on their bikes.

Everyone knows the stories about them but they don't seem to care. Three were drowned here last summer. Can you imagine swimming in that sea? Their bodies were swept fifty miles north but the big news was that they'd come to the bay in a stolen car.

It was headlines everywhere, of course, when that old joker rode for days from the backblocks when he'd been given the bad word. I mean they even heard about that one overseas. It was on the BBC World Service. You wouldn't have thought that an old bloke like that would have known how to find the transfer station, never mind ride his horse all the way down here. Well, you probably know the rest. Take your pick of the two endings. One where he puts his spurs in and they both jump into the rams before the supervisors can pull the switch. Or the other where he dismounts and puts the stunner to the gelding's head. He's so close to the edge that when the horse falls it carries him in.

But people aren't really concerned. That was a three-day wonder but with the kids it's happening all the time. Not a word from the radio and they're buried in small print in the paper unless they can find something special to hang the story on.

God, it's peculiar how that happens. There's a bump and a lurch and I'm back here at the table but I've been off Christ knows where and for how long. I talked to the two girls with the albino hair and they bought me another drink. They called me Dad. Oh they were having a bit of a laugh too but it was all good-natured. They'd been waiting for their friends but they gave up after the police came in and checked their IDs. They were all right, the girls I mean, and they weren't in trouble but they left soon after.

I dreamed about them, very fast and clear, when I went off. In my mind they'd each had a front tooth knocked out so they had small plates. It was all very funny in the dream and we were laughing because somehow they'd got them mixed up and they had to exchange right here in the bar. Then I was looking more closely at the girl nearest to me and I could see right through the lens of her eye.

When I was a kid I went to a pool once and a man had to take off his artificial leg to go swimming. Anyway, it's the colour of the plastic I remember more than anything. And that was how it looked in the chamber inside Glory's head. That was her name. In there it was this ... pinky-brown shade and there were lines of small holes where the different pieces of her head were stitched together.

After Glory and Chantal bought me the whisky I offered them a bed at my place. All above board and in another room from me. They looked as though they needed a decent place to sleep. How can I explain it? Those girls wouldn't have been much more than eighteen but they seemed to have already worn themselves out. Except for talking. But I asked them what they wanted to do with their lives, which is a stupid question to put to anyone that young. It was when they first came to my table and I was a bit lost for something to say. Everything except yesterday is ancient history to them and the day before today, they let me know, was probably even more boring than this one. But I said it and they laughed so loud with their heads back I could see right inside their mouths. Maybe it was that that set the dream off.

'We want to get out of it,' they told me and that wasn't much of a puzzle. I thought they meant with smack or coke or the pills they empty into something sweet and thick like Drambuie.

It was only later that I saw they might have meant *really* out of it like the old bloke with his horse. That's no mystery either. I understood them. You need something and they've got nothing. When it comes to it, all I've got is a bit of history, if you like. The crib, the garden, Helen's persimmon tree, memories of my old man. It doesn't add up to much but it seems to be enough. For them, everything's been spoiled from the beginning. Lights-out factories so there's no work. All the rest. The hot pipes in the sea. The station at the end of this wharf where you see near-new stuff pouring down into the rams and they're things you've never had a hope of owning.

Chantal had a rough tattoo on her left arm. It was a heart with a dagger through it and drops of blood. Then round the top in a kind of scroll it said: R.I.P. Kat. I asked her what it meant and she told me it was for a friend who went into the jaws off the back of her boyfriend's 1200cc Yamaha.

'She got out of it,' Chantal said.


I usually try to hang on in the café until at least midnight. That leaves me less time of dark to get through. I'm an early riser. Another reason for staying late is that there aren't as many trucks around then. It's only a ten-minute walk to my bach but during the two day-shifts the road's a stream of vehicles. Midnight to eight is the closest thing to a lull. God knows why but even the robot factories seem to slow down in those hours. So waste disposal gets less urgent. Anyway, it means I can get home without seeing more than a couple of big trucks.

After the girls left I felt low and nursed my drink. The barman had other notions since I was the last customer.

'Come on, Pop,' he said, 'dépêche-toi.'

He's got a black streak of hair across his bare scalp and his hands are always busy. I can't stand waiters who keep wiping your table. Not only that — he's a familiar bugger. I've never given him permission to talk to me like that. Some people start to treat you like a kid when they think you can't control your bladder any more.

The Coleman is always burning in my crib after dusk. It makes me feel as though there's something to come home to. I leave it on when I'm sleeping. That way if I peg out without ever knowing it, some other bugger might wonder why I've got the lantern on in daylight. I've got a horror of not being found. They can do what they want with me as long as they are there reasonably soon. As far as I'm concerned, they can wheel me along the wharf in a barrow and throw me down the slot. You're not there to know it, are you? And that's why the girls and their young mates go on about getting out. You're not there any more. It's only the getting that's bad. They choose such painful ways of going about it. I mean they really knock themselves around and that makes me want to weep for them. But, once it's done, it's all chemistry and physics from then on.

The point of all this is that when I got home, lights burning, Glory and Chantal were waiting for me in the house.

'You ought to change your key place,' Glory said.

'If I did you wouldn't be here, warm and cosy.'

'It might not be us next time.'

'I'll think about that one when it comes. Now I've got no money but there's home brew in the back shed.'

'You'll do,' Chantal said.

'Those arseholes never came,' Glory said. 'Did you mean it about a bed?'

'It was a dinkum offer. Still is.'

'Shall we condescend, Madame?' Chantal made a face at her mate.

'If the piss is good,' Glory told her friend.

There's no faulting my beer if you pour it with a steady hand. By the time we'd got through half a dozen the girls were roaring with laughter and I've got to admit I was smiling more than usual. During those couple of hours I really got to like those two youngsters. I thought I understood them. It seemed to me that maybe there wasn't such a big gap between us as I'd thought back in the café. Not that I made advances of any kind. They were young enough to be my granddaughters. In a way I wished they were. Both of them swore like troopers and tipped my grog back much faster than I could. It was an evening to remember. Nothing like that had happened to me in donkey's years.

And that's it. They both tumbled into the spare double bed that I don't use any more. In the morning they cooked up some breakfast and woke me with a cup of tea. They'd put sugar in it but never mind. I hadn't shaved, of course, and I knew my breath would have been pretty horrible with all the whisky and beer, but they gave me a hug and a kiss.

I suppose they went back to town. Any of those Meltimi or Échelle drivers would have picked them up. I go to the Pure Light Café but I haven't seen them since. And this is the thing. This is the thing that buggers me up. I come back home to the lamp shining in the bach and there's no one there, even though I leave the key under the same stone. I come home and the crib's as quiet as the transfer station on a maintenance day and I wonder if those two young girls have got out of it. Because you see while we were drinking my beer there seemed to be some point to it all. We sang songs and swore and they insulted each other all in a lovely happy way and the next morning they left.

As far as I know they might be dead somewhere in an empty house and no one has found them yet. It's one of the reasons, I think I told you, why I leave my Coleman on through the night.

# THE QUARRY

My most frequent dreams are about this coast. There's always something different just around the corner. You come round the side of a hill and the world you know is joined without a seam to something else. You're in a familiar room with solid furniture but the walls are fluttering shadows and shifting in and out across that border, which isn't a division, is the bush. Sometimes your parents speak to you abruptly and you watch them talk and know that they are dead.

It was my job to make tea on a morning and if someone asked me what were the best times we had towards the end I'd probably tell them it was sitting in bed with Helen and drinking that first cup of tea of the day. Anyway, I'd go through my dreams and she'd encourage me with the odd word or two. Funny, she didn't dream much herself. Or she didn't choose to talk about them.

Well, all that's in the past except I keep on having the same kind of dream. One when Helen was alive was where was lying up in the ironsand dunes. There are places where the wind and salt give the surface a hard crust. Walking around up there is how I imagine it's like to make your way across snow, even though the sand is black and gets hot enough to burn you in summer. There'd be the same break and plunge through, the feeling that you could disappear at any moment.

There was this trapdoor I pushed to one side and then I could look all the way down to the centre of the dune. Warm air moved past my face.

'What did you see?' Helen asked.

I'm still not sure if you really do see anything in dreams. I think that sometimes you change what you know or what you hear back into sight. There was a kind of *reluctance* in what was there to become visible.

'Lines of smooth trees growing on their sides,' I told her.

That wasn't it even though it was the almost-picture I had in my head.

'The roots were sprouting from the trunks and twisting down through the sand.'

Last night the weather was disturbed. The wind must have shifted round so it was coming from the east and it helped to carry away the rumbling noise from the transfer station. My crib was moving and creaking and on the roof the wind found a loose sheet of tin. It must have been vibrating against a couple of sprung leadheads because it sounded as though someone was trying to drill through the corrugated iron.

I get on comfortably enough in the bach but it still throws these surprises at me. It's as sound as a bell three hundred and sixty-four days in the year and then some combination of wind and rain will discover a leak. I climbed up there this morning and I'll be damned if I can find any loose tin.

So it was obviously the weather that gave me a restless night. It was one of those where you don't fully wake up but you know you're not sleeping and something halfway between an idea and a dream takes hold and you can't shake it off. I was lifting and moving stuff but I wasn't sure what it could be or why I had to get it out of the way. Then finally I slid down deeper and I was back in the old quarry with my father.

The gravel works must have supplied all the metal they needed in the beginning when they built the road out here from the city. I'm talking about the pick-and-shovel days when my grandfather was a young man.

You can still find the quarry if you know where to look for the turn-off up the highway. There's a dirt road with an entrance nearly hidden behind the manuka. It's on the south side.

I hadn't thought of it until now but the machinery out there must have been like a small early version of the mills and rams in the transfer station. There's a timber and sheet-metal tower where the crushing went on. A high ramp came from the face and small tipper-trucks moved along this on a narrow-gauge track. The rock was fed in by gravity.

There isn't much left of the plant and equipment now. Over the years the place has been stripped and vandalised. What I remember about it as a kid is that everything was covered in grey dust. For miles before you got there the bush looked as though it might be growing on the moon. Pools of standing water looked thick enough to walk on. When it rained, you expected everything to petrify with a brittle skin. The dust covered the workers' cars and got into their clothes and changed their faces. They looked like dead men and they scared me witless. Yes, it was still going when I was a boy and I saw it.

In the dream Dad was talking about something else. We could have been back in our house on the edge of the harbour.

'You can try as hard as you like but someone always leaves the door open.' He said this as though he was distressed about a recent event. Then he cuffed me hard on the back of my head.

Everything stopped in the quarry and I knew that they were going to detonate the charges. There was half a hill in front of us. Dad touched me on my arm and then he slid down through a fissure in the ground. I didn't see this but I knew he'd done it.

Puffs of grey smoke came from the cliff face. A cloud blew outwards and even though it surrounded me, I could breathe easily. I walked forward slowly and the hill had gone. There was a rocky path that led to a small platform with an iron railing. Out at sea large ships with white sails were coming to anchor in the bay here. It was like it used to be before the transfer station.

As I started to wake up, I could hear a pack of dogs barking and snarling as though they'd caught something to feed on.

I realise that there would be plenty of people who'd say it's me who has a sheet loose for bothering to remember a dream like that. But you see my father died, oh, more than twenty years ago. I was very fond of him and my mother who went just before him. And Helen and I were ... well, we were very close. The only time I hear them is in dreams. I've listened for them as hard as I can in other ways. Day and night I've gone out somewhere quiet and I've waited, keeping as still as possible.

You get some pretty odd ideas at times like that. There was one evening when I walked north along the beach and crossed the saddleback. I went so far that eventually the station was just a dull throb. There seemed to be nothing else alive out there except for me and a night bird calling from the tea-tree beyond the first slope of dunes. I waited and listened and that was it. Probably I was standing watching the sea lift and fall for more than an hour and I didn't hear the faintest whisper from anyone. Not a murmur. There never has been. It's not that their voices are drowned in the rattle of the bush or the turning of the sea. They've been absolutely silenced.

It was when I heard *nothing,* listened all that time to silence, that another thought swept over me. I once knew an old joker who'd been struck by lightning when he was out for a walk in tussock country. He was hit by a bolt and he survived. I remember asking him what it felt like. He was a funny old bugger and he'd told the story a few times.

'It was like nothing on earth,' he said. 'There was a white blaze in my head but it felt like ice. I was turning in circles in this cold white room and then there was nothing else in the world.'

I suppose I felt a bit like that old bloke as I stood out there in the dark. I'd been listening for my parents or Helen and then it suddenly came to me how many *other* people had died in the whole history of the earth. Billions of men, women and children have lived and worked and died. At least as many, I'd guess, as all the stars I could see on one sweep of the sky.

The world is like that station there at the end of the wharf. For millions of years it's been grinding us up and pouring us back as dust. And not one single person ever seems to have broken through that silence one way or another.

All those voices. All the thinking that living creatures have ever made and yet the smallest wave turning over on the beach made more noise than this gathered up dead. That's what I thought on O'Neills Beach over the saddleback. How completely empty the universe is with a great soundless gale of nothingness blowing right through it.

No wonder we dream. We'd kill ourselves if we didn't.

Even that isn't much of a consolation, though. Dreaming I mean. When you think about my father going on about an open door you can make almost anything you want of it. What I'm saying is that if there is a door in a dream then *it* is *you* and it's also you on either side of it. Open it or slam it closed and it all amounts to the same thing. Except that it makes you feel that there's a mystery going on and you don't know everything.

A man would be a fool to claim that any of this is a discovery. Helen knew about the silence long before I did. I think she understood those dreams of mine too. You see, I know it back to front around here. There are the dunes to the south-west. Here's our crib with the useless dying forest of radiata behind. I'm familiar with the whole landscape and it's not hiding anything. It *isn't* any different around the bluff.

If I could make my dreams happen in another way then I'd get them to take things away. The transfer station could turn into fog overnight. Then the pipes we can't see but everyone knows they're pouring hot stuff out into the sea from them. If I could order my dreams around I'd get them to return this place to how it was when my grandfather first came here. Same dunes. Same big sea. But none of this. None of this machinery and poison. And there used to be all the fish you could eat and when you hooked them they weren't sick with this disease that flays them alive.

Helen was more clear-sighted than I'll ever be. I can't imagine her dreaming of white ships sailing into the bay and there being no station out there filling the rift in the sea bed with all the city's heavy trash. Helen always said this coast was ruined. But she also knew that there was nowhere else to go. This is what we've got. There's nothing else around the corner.

When I had to flag down a truck to take us into the city at the end there, we'd already done all our talking about living and leaving. She wanted me to scatter her ashes here and I've done that. But it was while she was alive that she wanted that to happen. So she could see it in advance. To know where the last of her would touch the ground. She had no time for mysteries. Right at the end her mind was absolutely clear and she knew that everything she'd had up to then was all that she'd got.

But I dream about her. I dream about my old father and my mother. And that's all I've got except for wind and rain — this sun and silence.

## THE PREACHER

You must have seen the Preacher. He turned up here on the coast about ten years ago and he didn't look as bad then as he does now. In fact he was a neat and tidy joker and we didn't realise at first that he was living rough. He stopped shaving and it wasn't too long before we knew he never washed because he's pretty hard to get close to, especially in summer. He doesn't listen to you either but at first he did. At least you could pass the time of day with him. Funny accent, though. We couldn't work out where he came from.

He was wearing one of those long oilskin parkas the first time I saw him and right from the start he had his supermarket trolley. He's a kind of mobile landmark now.

You get parties of foreign engineers and scientists being taken around the transfer station and the thing they want to photograph is the Preacher pushing all his worldly goods down the wharf in that rusted-out trolley. It doesn't pay to look too closely at what he's got in there. There are skips filled with quite useful stuff waiting to be racked out to the station and tipped into the jaws. Often there's clothing and furniture. I once heard one of the operators saying that the only thing the station didn't take was hospital waste and human remains. The bastard was laughing as he said it.

But any number of old washing machines, whiteware of all sorts, even computers and other modern-looking gear all find their way out along the line and end up compressed to next to nothing and pushed into the rift in the sea bed.

The Preacher doesn't collect that kind of stuff. Somehow the things he puts in the trolley all seem to be absolutely useless to man or beast.

Anyway, that shopping trolley. The Preacher has worn the metal wheels right down so he's now running on one or, at the best, one and a half castors. It's a hell of a balancing act for him as he shoves the thing around from one end of the wharf to the other and back again. Or around to the café across the main road from the station. So his plastic bottles, rags, packets of newspapers and those nameless things all have to be carefully loaded.

The Preacher is pretty much a creature of habit. Well, maybe that's not the best phrase for how he behaves. It's more of a mania really. He heads in this direction down the wharf on a morning and then he either hangs around the Pure Light Café or heads out up the highway for half the day. On an evening he makes for his hidey-hole at the station. The one that all the operators know about. Whichever way he's going it's a long push and he's looking straight into the sun each way. The bits of his face that you can see are burned the colour of mahogany.

Then there's his nickname, of course. They say he was one of those charismatics in the city. The story is that he had a wife but she ran off with another bloke. And that was it. The Preacher gave up everything because he couldn't get his wife to come back to him and he couldn't find his tongue any more in the pulpit.

There are plenty of other tales about him. The fellows at the station are supposed to strip him down once a year because he never takes a stitch off. Then they hose him clean and dress him in fresh clobber they've saved from the skips. But if all that is true, why haven't they managed to find him a new trolley?

The time we had our bit of a tussle he was out in front of the Pure Light and he was definitely stroppier in those days.

'Are you corrupted?' He said this without so much as a blink of a greeting.

'No more than you,' I told him. I started to walk away. It was getting close to noon and I fancied a drink.

"Don't you want to be saved?"

'No,' I said. 'No, I bloody don't.'

'You're lying,' he said. 'Everyone wants to be saved.'

'Right now I'd rather have a whisky. I'll shout you one as well if you like.'

He hung around outside the window and eventually he buggered off. And what is the point I was trying to make? I seem to have forgotten. But maybe it's this. I really meant what I told him. Oh, not the business about the drink. I'm talking about the religious stuff. You see if I thought there was even the smallest grain of truth in what those people say, I don't think I could go on. I'll tell you why.

The morning that Helen felt really bad I flagged down a Meltimi truck right outside the front gate here. We always had our own bits of the garden and for months she'd been letting hers go. She didn't say much but it was obvious her back was giving her a lot of pain. Helen was never one to complain. In fact she once said to me, but not in a nasty way mind you, that if ever she did tell me something was wrong like a headache or a sore throat then the next day I'd got something worse.

But there was no keeping things hidden that morning. I'd never seen anyone that colour before. She was like that rough newsprint they use now and it seemed to hurt her even to speak.

We never did get the telephone put on in this bach and when the new power lines went down to the bay we let that go too. So we've always used Colemans for light and the primus for cooking. Helen and I were probably the last people in the country to run a fridge on kerosene.

The Pure Light Café, down where the beach used to be, is open twenty-four hours in summer and eight till eleven the rest of the year and of course they've got the phone. I asked Helen if I should dodge down there and call an ambulance from the city. She knew and I knew that it might be half a day before one got here. We're only twenty-five miles from the GPO but that's how it's gone since they made it a private service. They'd probably argue they'd need to pick up four people to justify a trip out here or they'd charge more than we could afford. They might never come at all after promising.

So I stood at the edge of the highway outside our place and I waved down the first red truck that came by empty from the transfer station. The driver was a decent joker, one of ours, and he helped me to get Helen up and into the cab. There was a bench seat behind the driver's and she could lie down.

He was one of those young fellows who's old before his time if you know what I mean. Too many smokes and too much beer. And what with all the hydraulics on those big trucks I don't suppose you get any more exercise driving one of them than you would running a family car. So he was wearing his belt low and there was more skin showing on his head than on mine. But he was a nice enough young bloke. I saw him reach out for his smokes and then he looked at Helen in the mirror and he changed his mind.

'Where'd you reckon?'

'It would have to be the Women's.'

'I used to come out here as a kid,' he said as he went through the gears.

The Ministry took out most of the bends on the old road when they built the highway but it's still a climb until you're running through the catchment area.

'You been out here long? In your bach?'

'When we moved out here we were still driving on the left.'

'Jeez!'

But he knew something about the coast, I'll say that for him. He told me about how he used to come fishing with his old man. Quite often they'd take home a bag of mussels and a couple of snapper maybe. Perhaps he was older than I thought.

Anyway, talking about those days set us both off remembering and we seemed to reach the hospital in no time. He parked right in front of those doors that open and shut by photo-electric. Then he helped me all the way in with Helen until a nurse told us where she could lie down.

I started going through my pockets and then I felt ashamed of even the thought when he put his hand on my arm.

'Give us a cup of tea when I'm on the four to twelve. I hope your wife's better soon.'

With that he was off. I don't even know his name.

In some ways you have to consider yourself lucky, even if you can't see it at the time. We were covered for the hospital under the old scheme. They at least had the decency to keep that going. But of course I'd just walked out of the house as I stood. I had a few coins in my pocket but nowhere near enough to find a place to board while I waited.

They operated the next day and Helen seemed to get better once she was over the anaesthetic. She was well enough to ask me how I was managing.

'I'm putting up at a mission for the time being.'

She gave me one of her looks. If she'd been completely well, she'd have wormed it out of me. Instead, Helen let me know that she knew and that she wasn't going to fret about it for the present.

'And you're growing a beard again.'

'Cover up some of the lines.'

'You still look lovely to me,' my wife said.

I don't know any man who could stand that. Oh Christ, I don't mean I was embarrassed. I was filled with guilt that I hadn't said the same kind of thing to her every day of our lives. And now I knew it was too late.

There was a young nurse who gave me cups of tea. A porter used to keep a meal for me now and again. After the first couple of nights no one seemed too concerned if I dozed off in the waiting room.

'You won't sell up and move, will you?'

We'd thought about it over the last years and then we realised that with the station there it would be impossible to get rid of the place. All we could do was close the door and walk away. But where would we have gone? So when Helen asked me that she must have slipped back to a time when we had a chance. Before the transfer station knocked the value off everything around here.

'No, I'll be hanging on,' I told her.

'Good,' she said. 'Because I can see myself there.'

One of the things I can still hear Helen telling me is not to be morbid but there are some things that have to be said. Because I *can't* see her here. We lived in this crib for all those years. I've only to walk out the back and there's the persimmon tree she planted and her garden running to seed.

But I can't see her. I can't talk to her. There's a silence that's so empty you don't even try to get an answer back from it. And this is the mad thing. Sometimes when I think about that absolute silence I get this huge surge of ... excitement. Please don't get me wrong. What I mean is that I'm looking forward to being *nothing*. I'm not rejoicing that Helen can't be found. I miss her more than I could ever say. All the words we have are too small and used up. It *isn't* excitement, though that's heading close. No. Joy is the only word that'll do. I'm filled with joy when I think of not being here.

So that's what I meant when I told the Preacher that I wasn't interested in being saved. I meant that I already was — but in my own way. Anyway, it was something like that I was trying to say.

# EVEN THE DOGS

You can take the old forestry road from out the back of my crib and if you didn't know any better you might think you'd managed to get away from the transfer station. What I mean by that is you can't see the installation for the ironsand dunes. And the sound of the jaws and the diesels on the highway gets mixed in with the pounding of the surf. But if you live here you can never forget what they've done to this place.

The experts have been out here looking at the trees. Taking needles and little snips of bark. There's no doubt that miles of radiata are dying and most of the pohutukawa on the coast are looking sick but they reckon they can't work out why. They're still trying to blame the possums. But not one of them thought to come and ask me or any of the other oldies who've tucked themselves away in baches and humpies around here.

As far as I'm concerned, it couldn't be any simpler: the station is poisoning the land. Around here used to be the last bit of unspoiled country west of the city. The region's natural playground is what the Authority once called it and in the old days that meant you'd see trampers moving through the bush and people could still enjoy a walk on the miles of beaches.

I've always had the feeling that trees listen through their roots and talk with their leaves. So what's the story they're getting and telling? I'll tell you. It's move over, your time's gone! The reason I think that is because it's how we feel here. Those of us who have managed to hang on.

We're all past it and I don't mind saying it. My old man was from another world and I saw part of what he knew.

Those government scientists couldn't find an answer if it had four legs and ran up to them barking. Because who built the highway out here? Who constructed the transfer station and the pipes where they run hot waste out to sea? They think you're only half there if you ask simple questions. And all you need to know is who is the wharfinger. Who claims they own this place? Well, I'll give it to you in two words — the Government. They are the ones who are killing the coast.

I'd rather not talk about it. Things like that get me too worked up. But I set off the other day to do something ordinary and simple and everything that's wrong about this place suddenly hit me all over again.

It was time for me to go scrounging for more firewood. The forestry begins right behind my bach but it's as clean as a whistle nearby. I've picked out everything from under the trees. So I set off up the back road with my hessian bag.

There's two ways of thinking about gathering cones and kindling. You can pick the stuff up as you go and then when your sack is full you turn back. I'm not sure that I'm too keen on this way, except when it's raining or maybe with a big south-westerly blowing. And the other method of going about this, of course, is to enjoy your walk and go as far as you feel. On the way back you do your collecting. Almost always you end up carrying your load a lot further but who gives a bugger on a good day.

Anyway, I was out strolling with an empty bag and I noticed a new bach off the road a little and squatting in a dip in the land. It was put together with sheets of rusted corrugated iron and pieces of wood from packing cases. You could read the stencilled writing on one bit of pine. Something had been shipped out from Marseilles. Roof tiles probably. Whoever built the humpy could have found a use for some of those. He'd gone to the trouble of fetching nikau fronds from the nearest patch of bush so he had some sort of roof over his head. Though I've never seen anyone around here who's been able to thatch well enough to keep the rain out.

Looking at that place I have to admit that I felt a twinge of excitement as well as regret. Regret for two reasons. Another humpy meant that someone else had been driven out from the city for one cause or another. No pension, a lost ID, anything. And I like my solitude. But I know I'm also a contradictory bugger. The excitement came from thinking about meeting someone new.

When I took a sniff round there, it was closed up and silent. The door was tied with a bit of wire. I wouldn't have dreamed of going in, even if I did peer through a rough window made from a scrap of transparent plastic.

He was fixed up in a pretty ragtag and bobtail way. There were some apple cases, a primus, a bed of lashed poles and sacking. Poor sod, I thought, I've got a spare room with a real double bed and my crib looked like a palace beside this. He didn't seem to have a battery radio either and that's something I couldn't understand. You can go into any of the skips lined up waiting for the station tipper and find half a dozen thrown away. They're sealed, of course, but if you crack them open carefully you can take out the dead longlife and put in a couple of new cells.

Just a bit further up the road I saw my new neighbour. At least I assumed this must be him. He had a dog and they were coming slowly towards me. It was one of those huskies. They're about the same size as Alsatians but their coats are black and white — thick as well. But the most unusual thing about them is their eyes. They're blue but that doesn't really say it. The colour of copper sulphate crystals is the closest I can get to that shade. Like blue ice lit up from behind.

This one was very old. He dragged his back paws but his eyes still made me feel uneasy. I mean they look at you as though *you* had to explain yourself. When he got closer, I could see that the black had turned to grey and his mouth hung slack. But he was still the sort of dog where you felt you'd better let him sniff you over slowly.

And the old joker? Not much different from me, I suppose. Someone who'd got smaller inside his skin. But he had a big white moustache that was yellow in the middle. I guessed he still rolled his own.

'Morning,' I said. 'Not a bad sort of day.'

'Oui, pas mal, Monsieur.'

I walked on and started to keep my eyes open for fallen wood and pine cones. The excitement I'd felt earlier had gone. In fact I felt disappointed. Finding out that the new neighbour wasn't one of our own turned my mind to all those other things I'd rather not think about.

That evening I opened a can for my dinner and found it was haricot beans. The local superette has a bin of specials where the labels have come off. The tins cost next to nothing but you take pot luck. I once had chocolate pudding three nights in a row.

I listened to our news while I waited for the beans to warm up. Another car filled with kids had gone off the point. That's not too far from here but further south. The road goes nowhere else except to the lookout and you can park twenty cars there. At the edge there's a tanalised fence and then a sheer drop to the sea.

Sometimes when a vehicle has gone over, the bodies have been found a hundred miles north. If we could still fish on this coast you could imagine what that would do but it's under a permanent ban anyway.

There are times when I think that the station out here is like a big candle and the kids are moths. If they're not racing down to the wharf on the highway then they're going at that fence on the lookout at a hundred and twenty k's and seeing how close they can get before braking.

I suppose I sound as though I don't care. The truth is I don't dare let myself feel. I'm not ready to slide over the edge into the jaws and if I allowed myself to think, if I let those feelings wash over me, then I'd probably jump. I'd go with them.

As it is, sleep is the nearest I ever get to disappearing. Only *this* night I had a dream and it was so real it woke me up.

I was walking along the dirt road with the old bloke and his dog. He was talking away and the dog was answering back. There he was with his mouth drooping in a big sulk. And then I had one of those flashes you get in dreams when you know that you're dreaming and I realised that not only was the dog talking but he was using the old man's language.

'Je suis un peu patraque,' he said. The poor old fellow was tired and feeling out of sorts and he didn't want to be on this walk. What he fancied was to be lying on his heap of sacks in the crib.

I'd no sooner taken all this in when I had another turn. It makes you think that dreams are made more like onions than stories because here was another layer. I knew *I* was dreaming in that language.

I never use it if it can be avoided. But it's obvious I know more than I let on, even to myself.

Judging from the way the night felt, all this was at about three in the morning. Tea is supposed to keep you awake just as much as coffee but I find that a cup in the night will send me off again. So I got up and set the kettle on the primus. I had to have a piss so I put on my overcoat and went outside.

There's one thing you can say — they haven't managed to fuck the stars up yet. My god, you could see millions that night. I remember thinking what a hell of a big show it was and all for nothing. Some people say that they can see a design in all that but I find purpose is harder to believe in than chance. Even when the very worst happens, chance isn't against you — it's indifferent. With purpose you end up having to believe that there's a meaning in every catastrophe, every cancer, each horrible death. No, there's no design. And in all our secret hearts I think everyone knows it.

That was it for the rest of the night. I drank my tea and fell asleep. If there were any more dreams then they disappeared the moment I woke up. So what would have happened to the one about the speaking dog, I wonder, if somehow my mind had been able to smooth over the disturbance and let sleep continue? Is that blue-eyed beast swimming through my darkness and *still* talking?

The thing is, I don't know whether he and his master are alive or dead. I went up the same road yesterday. This time I'd started to fill my sack on the way. Don't ask me why. The weather was decent enough.

There was nothing in that little hollow in the land except the sheets of tin lying flat and sifted over them was a thin layer of ash. I turned and went home to my crib.

Nothing would have persuaded me to check under those pieces of corrugated iron. I didn't want to know. There are some things you just shut your mind to. As I said before, if you didn't do that you'd be ready to roll over the edge. That's how it is around here.

## ASH

Of course I'm a bit drunk. And I've only had two, maybe three, off the top shelf. Ask the joker behind the bar if you really want to know. But it isn't just the whisky talking. There are days when all I have to do is look at a clock or a calendar and I can't think straight. You know the arm of land with the black dunes over there? South-west. Across the bay from the transfer station. Well, that's what set me off tonight. You look through your window and you see something that's been there all the time? I was having a smoke at home before I came down here. Yeah, it was those two girls I met in this bar that started me rolling my own again. All I did was touch the ash off on the edge of the tin. I was in my kitchen and I looked up and there was the station and across the water light was still catching the tops of the ironsand dunes. Do you know what I mean? There's me sitting and thinking nothing. The station's grinding up anything they can feed it with and pumping it into the sea. And the dunes were blown from a volcano hundreds of miles down south and thousands of years ago. Millions maybe. It rocked me, I'll tell you, how you can be in your own place, quite still and empty, and then you're thinking about ash and time and everything that's gone. So I decided to come down to this café and have a couple of drinks. It was the way everything connected up when I looked out through the window of my bach. You see, Helen asked me to do one last thing for her — like the volcano hundreds of miles down south and thousands of years ago. She said once she wanted to be able to see herself here and that meant bringing her back to where we had spent most of our lives. It was only a small cardboard box and the wind was strong enough to take her away from me but at that time I couldn't think of that dry ash as her. Then it was nearly done, except I couldn't just let the last go. I'm not saying what I did. So that's it. Ash, I mean. It's falling all over the world for everyone. That's what I was thinking when I looked at those black dunes which I must have seen every day of my life for the last forty or more years. Even the earth throws up its hands and scatters its own. And some days all you can do about it is have a drink or two. I'll tell you something else. If I couldn't do this — sit in a bar and talk about the things I've been thinking about — then I'd be done with it. As quietly as possible and without any fuss but I'd do it just the same. I've felt like that for a long time. But even then there's still a puzzle. Not the ash and the wind and the comings and goings and millions of years passing and those we love dying. It's being here and *going on*. That's what I'll never work out. Because it's something more than having a drink and a smoke and finding someone to talk to. It's going on when the earth has opened up and there's ash falling all over the world and tomorrow will be just the same as it has been today. That's the real mystery.

## LUPINS

Those manuka walking-sticks all looked much the same to me but Helen made a different one every year. There are still some healthy patches of bush south of here and Helen went looking where there were old canopy trees like puriri. In those places the tea-tree would be reaching for light so it grew tall and thin with no side branches and just a tuft of leaves on top. Maybe it was kanuka she used. Anyway, it was easy enough for her to cut a straight length of the right thickness — about twice the girth of my thumb.

I never did find out what happened to the old sticks. It wasn't something I thought about. But there should have been dozens around the bach or in the lean-to and there's nothing much else in there other than my bottles of home brew.

Once she had a perfect bit of wood she trimmed the ends with a small saw she kept just for that purpose. She always used to borrow my old Opinel knife to scrape off the strings of dead bark.

It was funny watching her choosing which end would fit in the palm of her hand and which she'd use to prod the ground or slash at plants she didn't like. Helen would always take a swipe at the kerosene tree that has been running wild along this coast since I was a boy. Even the fallout from the transfer station doesn't seem to affect that weed or the privet. Though there's no point in whacking at the stuff with a stick. Like a lot of things around here they're invaders. You've got to dig them right out or poison them.

She'd stand under her persimmon tree round behind our crib and balance this length of manuka on her finger to decide which way up or down it would go. When she knew which was the top end she used to sand it until it was round and smooth. You'd think with all that work she'd keep a decent stick for years. But no. Something about them wore out. And it wasn't that the timber had gone dry or dead.

Helen always preserved her sticks, for the year they were in use, with a mixture of raw linseed, malt vinegar and meths. If you've got any furniture that hasn't been varnished then that concoction of Helen's is the stuff to use on it. You've got to shake it up well.

But why didn't I think of it before? What she did with the old sticks, I mean. Why are there gaps like that which you want to fill in later but can't.

In a way they were part of herself, I suppose. Everywhere we went — on the beach, up the dunes to the south or the north, in the bush — Helen's stick always went with her. Something of Helen must have got down into that wood and it was strong enough for her not to want to leave them lying around for anyone else to use. Not even me.

Only once, as far as I remember, did she forget one of them when we'd had an evening down at the Pure Light Café on the edge of the bay near the transfer station. She was drinking white rum and I was on my usual whisky.

Well, we got home and then things blew up. I tried to calm her down but I said the wrong thing. I told her it was only a piece of tea-tree and we could get it in the morning.

'I'll have to go back,' Helen said.

'They'll be closed. You know we were the last out through the doors.'

'I don't care. We'll wake them up.'

The couple that ran the place then lived on the premises. You have to, of course. It's only forty or fifty minutes to the city on the highway but in summer the bar is open all hours.

I've never got used to walking down to the bay since the traffic increased so much. Why they didn't make footpaths when they built the road I'll never know but I expect they thought that most of the locals would give up in disgust when the transfer station began working. Most of them have. It's all truck drivers and youngsters down at the café these days.

But off we set. Meltimi and Échelle are the two biggest disposal companies but even their trucks aren't so frequent after midnight so only a couple of heavies passed us. Those diesels draw so much wind you feel as though they're sucking you into the road when they go by.

There were no lights on in the café and when I dodged around the side there wasn't a sign of life from the Salerre couple. They must have fallen into bed the minute they locked up after us.

'They're already asleep,' I told Helen.

'I don't give a bugger,' Helen said. 'Go and wake them up.'

'Do it yourself,' I said. 'You're the one that wants the bloody thing back.'

She looked at me for no longer than a second and didn't say a word but then, quicker than I could stop her, she banged her elbow through the pane of glass closest to the door lock.

I was still wishing that I hadn't spoken to her in that angry way when she slipped her hand in and opened the door.

So that was how Helen rescued one of her walking-sticks. When the time of the year came around to make another, that one disappeared and joined all its mates. I don't know. At one time I thought she might be planting them somewhere in the bush and had put so much of herself into them that they'd taken root and sprouted. It's all nonsense, of course. I've covered every square yard of where we used to walk and there's no magic ring of manuka sprung up anywhere.

But you know a good stick isn't to be sneered at. There have been a few times recently when one might have come in handy, like when our Prime Minister came here on a flying visit during the last election. He didn't give a damn about us locals. There were far more votes for him at the transfer station where their jobs depend on garbage.

The week before he came here I heard him on the radio. If you hadn't known already then you could soon have worked out that there was an election due. Troadec was using our language. I won't say he was speaking it. He'll never get rid of that accent of his but you could make out what he was saying.

It's funny as well. That was supposed to be a news item so why did he get so much uninterrupted time? Nobody seems to ask questions like that any more. He talked about equality and economics and defence. But mostly about defence and how much safer we were now that we had powerful allies who were also our blood kinsmen. I can't bear to think about him. It was his people who started putting out hot waste through the station. I blame him for the fact that we can't swim in our own sea here or catch a fish. I hold him responsible for Helen's disease. So yes, I'd have liked a club in my hand when he was driven down the wharf after visiting the station. I'd have felt good putting a pole through his window and giving him a good clout.


Not that it would help. Nothing does. Not even dreaming which used to give me a sense that she was still here. I was with her again last night.

*Helen had her new stick.* She swung it at the dusty grass that grew at the side of the forestry road.

'No rainbows,' she said.

We were walking northwards and came to the place where the dirt track turns into a sandy path. The air was hazy with the blown mist from the breakers over the ridge on our left. Ahead of us the pines skirted the dunes and stretched back inland for as far as you could see. Many of the trees were dying but there had been no gales lately to bring the dead ones down. We could get out of the pines by following the path up into the low black sandhills. Helen pointed with her stick and that's the way we went.

It began to change around then. The dream. Lupins had grown over the trail and we crushed them underfoot as we tried to get through to a clear space. The smell coming from the broken stems was all wrong. It was the chemical scent of dead ants. There were dark blue bees circling among the flowers but the lupins were also in pod. I watched one break open and the black seeds spilled all around us.

Helen slashed at the plants but her stick caught in among them and it was flung off to one side. Then she stopped moving and was suddenly very calm.

'I'll be out of here first thing in the morning.'

I expected her to say something else to me but that was it and she was farther away than I thought.


There was a time when I used to believe that dreaming of the dead was the last true connection we had with them. It could be right. But I also used to think that being able to dream of them was the only way you could keep *yourself* going. After my dream about the lupins I'm not so sure. If you know even in your sleep that they are dead, then what possible consolation is there?

I'd rather go out in the bush and find a nice tall stem of manuka. You can cut a stick with an ordinary knife just like Helen did. You chop away using the blade like a small axe. One cut down at a forty-five-degree angle and then one up to meet the first. You circle the stem. When you take it home and trim it up the tea-tree will make you one of the hardest and most enduring walking-sticks you can get.

What you do with something like that is up to you. When this year's gone maybe I'll know what Helen did with hers.

# MEMORIAL

I've only just started to put everything together. Even now I'm not sure if this is in the right order or not. But I was standing in my kitchen this morning making a cup of tea and I *knew* I'd seen Glory and Chantal before. What I mean is that the night I put those two girls up and we drank most of my home brew wasn't the first time we'd come across each other. I'd been with them at their friend's wake without really knowing it.

I'd drawn a kettle of water but the primus was acting up a bit. There was enough pressure but the stove didn't seem to be making its usual noise and the flame was uneven around the burner. It was yellow on one side as well.

Helen had managed to lose the pricker years before so I was going to have to fiddle with the thin-nosed pliers and a fine sewing needle. When you clear the jet with something makeshift like this you have to be careful to keep the needle straight as you prod, otherwise you can snap the end off and then the hole is blocked for good.

That worked all right. I put the kettle back on. Then I realised that the primus sounded much the same as it had before. What was different was that the transfer station wasn't working down in the bay. Everything sounded unusual. There were blackbirds arguing in the garden out the back, *pinking* away at each other. They were claiming territory as usual, I suppose, but their notes were shriller, as though they'd just arrived from a foreign country. The roof was starting to warm up in the sun and beginning to shift. I'd nearly forgotten the noise the iron makes when it eases itself like that.

You can be driven half mad by the din from a factory or a mill and then when it closes down you discover that you've got used to it. There's something missing. But you feel the station more than hear it. The vibration comes up through your bones and into your ears from inside. When you do notice it out there it's like something big and alive coming towards you, only somehow it's got itself tethered for the moment.

I was putting the pliers away when the sleeve of my dressing-gown caught my cup and down it went. It's one of those special glass ones like they use in the café and it didn't break when it hit the floorboards. Of course it was that small mishap which took me back to a particular evening at the Pure Light Café. I was in the middle of something and from where I was sitting at my usual table it could have been a party.

The couple that owned the place then were called Boennec. We never got on first name terms but that's no surprise. I'll be damned if I can ever think of them as belonging here. Especially when they try to make you feel inferior because you still use your own language. They were just the bone-necked pair to me. I was glad when they went. The new bloke is one of them as well and too familiar but he doesn't make my skin crawl like they did.

Anyway, they'd opened up the Grange Bar which is that tanalised pine building behind the Pure Light. It's really nothing more than a drinking shed and I wouldn't normally go in there. Surprisingly enough, people still come out here in droves in the warm weather and that's when they throw the Grange open.

So it must have been summer. Between November and March is the closest I can pin it. By the time I called in at the Pure Light there were cars and bikes parked all along the front and there was a band trying out its instruments inside. The station was working, of course, and lines of badbins were moving backwards and forwards along the wharf. There was a stiff south-westerly blowing too so the surf was crashing on what's left of the beach and in among the piles of the wharf and the station. You could tell we were in for a noisy evening.

Someone of my age ought to have had more sense. There was plenty of beer back at my crib but I enjoy something harder now and again. I probably thought — one good drink and then home to bed. I can't remember but I imagine that'd be right.

Boennec and his wife had extra staff on in the Grange but even so I sat for a long time at my table in the small bar. The double doors were open behind me so the music the group was playing came pouring through. There seemed to be a lot of speeches and announcements in between too but there was so much electrical howling and volume on their gear that I didn't take a great deal in.

When Boennec finally came to serve me I asked him for a double. God knows when he might be by my table again. He could see I was alone but he brought me two glasses of whisky and a carafe of water. I can't explain why but that set things off badly for me. All I had to do was pour one glass into another and I'd have my double. So it can't have been that. It must have been the language thing.

Youngsters were arriving all the time. You'd hear their brakes outside and then they'd tramp through the small bar in their heavy boots to get to the Grange. They didn't look happy at all and by now I'd started to think that it wasn't an ordinary party going on next door.

Nobody took much notice of me, least of all the owner and his wife. They were going flat out in the booze barn pulling in as much coin as they could while things were sweet. You can bet there was a lot of short-changing happening at the same time. One young girl asked me for a light as she headed out for a spell. I started to explain that I didn't smoke any more but she shook her head and walked off. She had that white powdery make-up on and she'd been crying.

Boennec was behind the bar but I couldn't catch his eye. I got up and looked through the french doors. The band was playing on a small stage they'd set up at the far end. They had the biggest speakers I'd ever seen and a young bloke was crouching in the hollow space inside one of them. He had his eyes closed and his mouth open. He could have been shouting or singing because his throat was moving.

I hated to do it but Boennec had turned something on in my head with his two glasses. I went to the bar and asked for what I'd wanted before. But I used some of his language.

'Double whisky,' I sand, 'mais un verre this time.'

'I understand.'

'Why didn't you know what I meant before?'

'Pardon?'

'You heard what I said.'

'I think perhaps I will not serve you, Monsieur.' Boennec turned and pointed to the notice on his wall about preventing public drunkenness.

That was when I was going to reach across the bar and hit him. I felt a hand on my arm and I swung away from whoever had a hold on me. When I'd got a bit of space I could see it was one of the young fellows from the Grange room. I'd noticed him earlier. A long time back he'd lost an eye. From the shape of the scars it looked to me as though a broken bottle had been used on him.

'What are you after?' He gave me a funny sort of grin.

'I was drinking Scotch earlier.'

The young bloke said something very fast and drinks were served to both of us on the counter top. I had my double in the one glass.

'Bring it through,' he said and I went with him into the other room and sat at his table.

After I'd thanked him he told me his name. He was called Ray but up to losing his eye most of his friends called him Sting. He'd been back, mostly, to Ray for the last couple of years.

'You know why I gave you a hand?'

'Because you hate those arseholes as much as I do?'

Ray laughed and nodded. 'But there's something else as well.'

He waited and I took a drink of my whisky.

'You're ... unusual,' he said.

'I'm old. That's about it.'

'No. You saw me earlier and you just looked. It's those who turn away or pretend there's nothing that get me. So you're different.'

'What's the party for?' I asked after a while. I knew by now it wasn't that but I didn't know what else to call it.

'We're sending off a friend of ours.'

The only reason we were able to talk was that the band had packed it in for the time being. Most of the windows were open and mosquitoes were drifting in on the night air. The cigarette smoke didn't seem to put them off. Nor the other stuff. When Ray shoved his packet and lighter across the table to me I lit up a smoke as well. I hadn't done that for years and I wondered why I'd ever stopped. Something is going to get you for sure.

'How old was your friend?'

'Don't know,' Ray said. 'Hardly knew her. But she was one of our crowd, you know.'

I was thinking it was about time to leave. Ray was a nice enough fellow but we hadn't got much to say to each other. But a young woman got up on the stage and plugged in her guitar. Two others joined her and without any preliminaries they went off into a song about their friend which lasted twenty minutes or more. I couldn't move but it wasn't politeness that kept me there. God knows what it was but they really said something to me. I thought of Helen and all the time we'd had together and how I'd made myself *not* feel when she died.

When the song came to an end the two singers just stepped down from the stage. The one with the guitar adjusted the mike.

'We all know what we're going to do now and I don't think there's anyone out there who'll stop us.'

Right around the room people were standing up and finishing off their drinks. Some were crushing out their cigarettes while others were lighting fresh ones. I had that hot feeling under my ribs that you get before something really important happens. But I had no idea what was going on. There was no hurry but people were moving out through the double doors.

'Come on!' Ray put his hand under my arm.

'Where are we going?'

'To the transfer station,' he said.

Ray had a big ancient Holden with a ding in every single panel but it started first go.

'Wind your window down,' he said. 'It'll be up to you to throw the flowers.'

I turned to look at the box of roses on the back seat. They must have cost him a bomb.

'Like that,' I wanted to know, 'or out of their wrappings?'

'Just as they are.'

The first cars were already making their turn onto the station's wharf. They were going left but no one in front of us signalled. There was a long interval between each bump over the expansion joints.

Someone must have got into a panic at the station. You'd think that when they saw the convoy the guards or engineers, whoever was in charge of security, would have banged on all the floodlights. It was after midnight and the place was already dimmed down for the quiet shift. I was watching the line of vehicles ahead on the long straight stretch of the wharf when all the lights went out under the canopy of the transfer station.

You could feel the pulse now of the crushers and rams and then the first of our cars must have begun to slow as it ran alongside the length of the pit. Their brake lights flashed and for an instant you could make out a few details — steel walkways, pipes running everywhere, a curved wall that might have been the side of a turbine. The crushing zone was a black ravine.

There was a line of crawling cars now and passengers reached out of their windows to throw flowers into the jaws. We were under the canopy as well and the noise from all our engines was louder than the station's machinery. The sound was reflecting off all those hard surfaces but I still thought I could hear the workers yelling.

Ray shouted too as he slammed on his brakes. The Ford immediately in front of us had come to a complete halt. I had the box of roses in my hand and I could have thrown them from there but I sat paralysed. The rear doors of the Falcon opened and two young women stepped out onto the concrete. They both had white hair and pale faces. In that dazzling light from our headlamps their lips were the colour of blood. Together they crossed the small distance to the edge of the pit and looked down.

I don't know why but seeing those two standing there made me feel worse than I had when the trio sang their song back in the bar. If they'd thrown flowers like the others I might not have felt so bad but they seemed to have nothing in their hands. To be honest I had my teeth clenched tight and I'd stopped breathing because part of me was saying they might jump. Right at that moment all the station lights came back on.

They looked around as though they'd forgotten where they were and they held their hands over the edge and each let something fall. To this day I'm not sure what it was they'd brought to the station. It could have been a letter they'd written. I've though about this a lot since that instant in my kitchen when I remembered them. Those two young women might have been dropping photographs of their friend into the jaws.

Then we were moving again. We'd nearly reached where we had to turn away before Ray got through to me. I was still sitting there with the box of roses.

'We're not coming out here again,' Ray was shouting. 'Do it now!'

I thought that would be the end of it. Ray knew where I lived because I'd told him about the bach but he didn't slow at the end of the wharf. He swung the Holden back towards the Pure Light.

'What about the flics?' There's no cops at the bay but those fellows at the station would have been bound to call the police out from the city.

'If they come,' Ray said, 'it'll take them another half-hour, forty minutes. And what have we done?'

'I dunno,' I told him. 'Caused a disturbance, I suppose.'

Ray just laughed. He parked the car and we walked back towards the café. The band must have been in one of the first vehicles to go through the station. They were warming up again in the big bar.

'Or they could throw up a roadblock and stop you all on your way home.'

'Listen,' Ray said. 'Friends die. And those fuckers aren't going to stop us seeing them off in our own way.'

I had to agree with him. We sat at our old table and Ray wouldn't let me buy the next round of drinks. I thought about Helen and what it had been like to scatter her ashes when all that was over and I had to admire what those youngsters had done.

How do you even begin to try to say what can hardly be said? Something went out of the air of that big bar and something else came back in. I heard a glass break. Someone laughed. The drummer said this had to be their last number but it went on and on. The kid who'd crouched in the front of one of the speakers was singing now and you could hear him. Some of the others were dancing in a cleared space. They knocked into each other and when they staggered they held each other up. I knew then how much younger they all were than me. Most of them were laughing or smiling. Couples were touching and kissing and the wake had turned into a party.

I looked across the table at Ray and he nodded. There were no shadows on his face. He turned to watch the band and his scarred side was nearest to me. I saw what a good-looking bloke he was. He was more than that. He was handsome.

A young woman in a sleeveless black jerkin was standing by our table. She picked up Ray's glass and drank from it. Her white arms were covered in scrawled tatts. She held out her arms to me.

'Come on. You can do it.'

We danced together. I never knew her name but we danced and we stood without talking for just a moment when the music stopped.

And this is the part I can't work out. This is the thing I haven't got straight. There was no police raid. No arrests up the highway as far as I could tell form listening to the radio the next day. Somehow I got back to my crib. I don't know whether I walked or Ray drove me. The Boennec couple shot through at the end of that summer. I never saw any of those young people again. Or at least I didn't think I had until I was making my pot of tea this morning and having trouble with the primus. It was then that I remembered Glory and Chantal.

Why it didn't click the night they stayed here in the bach I don't know. I'd met them at the Pure Light when there weren't many people there and we got talking. They told me a friend of theirs had been killed and I still didn't make any connection. We've all got a death somewhere and Helen's swamped most of my feelings about what had happened to others.

But we had a good time talking and drinking my beer. They slept in our old bed and I dossed down as usual on the couch. As a rule I don't have much to do with young people. Well, the truth is I more or less keep myself to myself. I pass the time of day with the fellow who runs the store. One of the engineers at the station has a word with me now and again. The new barkeeper at the Pure Light is a bit more friendly than Boennec even if he is a familiar prick.

After the wake, though, I felt differently about the youngsters who came out here on their bikes or in their old cars. No matter how tough they look in those leather jackets and jeans they're just as fragile as you or me. They die just as easily. Maybe even easier because they don't give a shit about their lives. That's crazy, isn't it? They care more about their friends than they do about themselves. I don't avoid the kids now, though. On that night when we all drove up the wharf to the station I felt that I'd joined them somehow.

So this morning when the idea went through my mind that I'd met Glory and Chantal before, I believed I knew who they were. I'm almost certain that they were the two who got out of the Falcon and dropped something, whatever it was — letters or photographs — down into the jaws of the transfer station.

I wish I'd thought of that the night they stayed with me. Ray is still on my mind and so is that young woman I danced with. I'd even quite like to hear that group playing again.

But what I really think about is this. I'd like to look for them in the city. There's a couple of Meltimi drivers who wave if they see me at the side of the highway. One of them might give me a lift into town. Then again, there are millions now in the city and I only know three first names.

It's a crazy idea, isn't it? Up until this morning I thought I'd be stuck out here at the coast for ever. When Helen died, it seemed all I could do was to come back home. She planted the trees out the back. That was her garden. I scattered her ashes at the top of the ironsand dunes.

And this morning the station stopped working for an hour or so. It's going again now and the noise is all mixed up with the wind and the sea. But I've had a breathing space and I can't see any reason why I shouldn't move on.

It's late now but tomorrow I might just get out on the highway and thumb down one of those big red Meltimi trucks.

## THE PERSIMMON TREE

There was a hard blow in the night and the wind took most of the dead leaves off Helen's tree. I huddled down under my blankets and thought about what the garden would look like in the morning, the ground scattered with soft fruit and most of it would have those dark powdery blemishes. The persimmons look as though they've been dusted with the pollen off paspalum grass. It was years before I could eat the things and I only tried them at first to please Helen.

It's funny how you think in the night. I could see the brittle tree and my wife climbing up through the branches. Then *I* was falling and hit the ground and my heart was going so hard I thought it would burst.

This place can still look beautiful at night. I had to get up and make tea. When it was brewed I put on my old army coat and carried my mug outside. There was no traffic and when I leaned against the wall of the cottage I was sheltered from the wind. I didn't go round the back. For some reason I couldn't make myself walk the short distance to look at her garden and her tree.

The sound of the mills in the transfer station usually reaches my crib but the noise was being pushed away by the wind. There was enough starlight to see every blade of grass on the strip of front lawn. It seemed almost worthwhile living here.

When I walked round the back of the bach in the morning to look at the persimmon tree it was just as I'd imagined it would be. There was a litter of twigs underneath it and most of the fallen fruit was useless. We'd had a good season and in spite of the blustery weather last night there were clusters of persimmons on some of the stronger wood.

In the daytime, no matter how hard I tried, I couldn't remember how Helen looked as she weeded the garden, as she talked to me at breakfast. I mean I couldn't see her *moving*. All I seemed to have in my head were those still photographs.

So how was it that a girl I never knew kept coming into my mind? She's dressed in leather and she's sitting on the pillion of one of those big bikes. I see the motorcycle flip over and slide into the jaws in a shower of sparks but at that moment I shut things off. She and her boyfriend aren't going in with the bike. There's just one machine falling into the rams of a bigger one. The two kids have disappeared.

There was a time in the late morning when I was standing at the gate. I don't know how long I'd been looking at my crib and the top of the tree behind the tin roof. The sky was a clean swept blue and off to the side where the radiata begins it was dark. At the very topmost of the tree a few persimmons had survived the wind. They were like small suns. They shifted and blurred and then came sharp again.

Then it was as though I was back in the middle of the night. Something happened without my forcing it. I saw the cottage door open and Helen waved me in for smoko. That was it. It came and went. The place was so empty. I had to turn the battery radio on.

You don't catch me down at the Pure Light Café talking about old times and what a paradise the coast used to be. Even my old man couldn't remember when this place was untouched. In his time there was a fair-sized settlement here and most of the weekend cottages were close to the dirt road. So you can say it's been quite a few years since it was an unspoiled wilderness.

When Dad was a young larrikin he and all his mates used to race up and down the tideline in their old stripped cars. It was a normal Sunday outing for families to drive ten miles up the beach for a picnic. Before all the pines went in you'd often get a whiff of exhaust smell on a bush walk.

But there's a difference between a bit of human activity and what's happened here since the station went in. I don't mind the highway and the noise so much. What I can't stand is that the sea isn't fit to fish in any more and that inside this bach there's another kind of silence even when the rams and mills are crushing and grinding half a mile down the road. It's the quietness of photographs I can't bear. And it's not being able to get that girl and that bike out of my mind that would drive me away from here if there were anywhere else I could go.

No, it's a bugger of a place down here on the coast now but there's nothing I can do about it. You see it's too late to move back to the city because the worst of the city came here. What I wish is that the youngsters weren't so hard on themselves. So many of them come here and don't go home again. If they had homes to go to.

When the Government built the highway they had to buy and bulldoze most of the baches. Ours was set well back so we escaped. But almost all of the old residents were pushed out years ago. The shop and the café would close down tomorrow if it weren't for the truck drivers and the operators at the transfer station. I can't bear what's happened to this place but now I couldn't live here if that monster shut down. And whatever I've said I don't think I could live anywhere else.

If only they weren't putting hot waste into the sea through their pipes. If only I could go fishing again. Helen and I lived in the city before we bought the crib. We learned to put up with the noise and dirt and I could live with that now if they could make the sea clean again. And if the kids didn't come out to the coast to die.

It's night and the wind has come up again. I turned in hours ago but I've been lying here thinking. Something seems to have changed and I don't know why. Before I came to bed I had a look at myself in the mirror. I saw how old I was and it was so funny I cracked up laughing at myself.

'What does it matter?' I said to myself in the glass. 'Why on earth should you give a shit about anything?'

Well, I do and I don't, if you know what I mean. I always was a contradictory sod. I do care about them because they're young. I don't care about myself any more.

So I've been lying here sorting things out slowly. I saw Helen move today. She wasn't just a still photograph. And the girl. I can make her walk away from the jaws. You can do anything inside your head. The girl is climbing the tree. Helen is wearing black leather.

But I know it won't be that way when I wake up in the morning. You can make anything happen in your mind. The trouble is, that's where it stays. Just like me and the transfer station at the end of the wharf in the mouth of the bay.

# CARLTON

This must be one of the smallest big cities in the world. There are still a few of the old-time pubs left in the centre and if you're looking for two people in a million you need only try a few bars if they're someone special like those two girls. I found a room in a boarding house near the hospital so I could walk in to most of the places where the kids do their drinking. I'd only been here a couple of days when I met someone who knew Glory and Chantal.

The house where I was staying has been around for a hundred years. The weatherboards had once been painted blue and at the back there was a long sagging balcony that looked out over the gully where the motorways roar with traffic day and night.

When the house was first built as a mansion it was perched on the edge of a valley that was dark green with native bush and a creek ran down there among the tree ferns and nikau. When they built the péage connections the Ministry had to move the oldest graveyard in the city. I've always thought that when the bulldozers first went in and started turning over that ground they were making a connection they didn't intend but once it was made it could never be undone. The highway and death were linked before they laid the first lane.

The girl was called Kerry and she was suspicious of me at first. It should have been obvious that I wasn't trying to pick her up or that I wasn't a flic. Too old for both but I suppose she might have thought I was an informer. So I had to tell her all about the wake for Glory and Chantal's friend which had happened out at the coast months back. She'd heard about that so she got a bit easier with me.

I'd bought a jug and we were drinking beer.

'So why are you looking for them?'

It's hard to give someone a straight answer when you've not been able to work it out properly for yourself. I took another drink of beer and bludged one of her cigarettes.

'I'd just like to talk to them again.'

Kerry shrugged her shoulders and blew smoke at the ceiling. It looked as though she wasn't going to tell me anything.

'I've no idea where they are.' Then she shouted across the room at a friend of hers.

She picked up her cigarettes and lighter and shoved them in the top pocket of her denim jacket.

'I wasn't going to kill myself or anything like that,' I told her, 'but I'd given up, if you know what I mean ... before they came and stayed at my bach.'

I was telling Kerry all this in a rush and I didn't even think about what I was saying.

'They went on about getting out of it just like their friend had but I couldn't stand the thought of that happening to them when they were so young. I liked them and we had a good evening together. It didn't come suddenly but after that night I found that, well, I hadn't given in after all. So I wanted to see them again to tell them about going on. About not getting out of it.'

Kerry stood up to go. Her friend had been waiting by the door for her all the time I'd been talking.

'The last time I heard they were in a house called Carlton over near the park. I don't think they're there any more, but.'

It was too late to do anything that evening so I set off the next morning to look for Glory and Chantal's house. It was a sunny day and for the first time since I'd hitched a ride in from the coast I thought that the city wasn't such a bad place to be.

I'd had a look at a street map before I left the boarding house and I'd found a Carlton Road that ran alongside the edge of the park. Starlings sat on the power lines and the road was so hot that passing cars sounded as though they were driving over a thin film of water. I went into a corner dairy and bought an ice cream. I hadn't done that for more than thirty years.

Carlton still had an intact glass name plate with gold lettering but as soon as I saw the house I knew that I wasn't going to find the girls there. You can feel the life even in a derelict house if people are squatting in it. And a place that's as orderly as you like goes wrong very quickly if it's not lived in. There's no way this makes any sense but I knew that my crib would look all right when I returned because I *meant* to go home. If I'd walked out on it for good then was forced back, I'd find it starting to decay.

This big old two-storeyed house was dying. I looked at it from the gate in the high tecoma hedge and it was obvious that the piles had gone. Carlton was leaning to one side and the weatherboards had sprung away from each other and split. The whole structure probably rested on scoria which, by chance and convenience, the builders of that time used for foundations. If there wasn't a block where they needed it they'd stick a puriri log in the earth.

Most of the windows had been smashed and the front door was open. In front there was the frame of a motorcycle that was almost hidden under a thick web of kikuyu grass and near the front steps there was one of those concrete double sink units from a wash-house. Something glittered in the dark water in one of the sinks and a goldfish broke the surface and then disappeared again. I suppose it was surviving on mosquito larvae.

I was trespassing but I didn't care. The wide hall was scattered with newspapers and broken glass and the doors that led off it had hasps and staples nailed to the frames and architraves. But nothing was padlocked.

The communal kitchen was at the end of the hall. When I went in, the walls flickered in the way your vision goes when a migraine headache is about to start. But there was nothing wrong with my eyes. The room was seething with cockroaches which had skittered for cover as I opened the door. In one corner there was a fridge that had been painted red. The gas stove was choked with grease. I backed out into the hall and left the kitchen to the vermin.

Glory's room was upstairs. Her name was spray-painted on the door and when I went in you could feel a different atmosphere. The place was untidy but it wasn't dirty. The sun was streaming in through the window and it made a big patch of warm light on the threadbare carpet.

I wasn't tired but I sat down for a while in an armchair. Glory had left some of her concert posters pinned to the walls.

It would have been a nice comfortable room when she was there. The single bed still had a flock mattress on it and the cast-iron fireplace has been black-leaded at some time. The surround had all its original tiles in place. On the mantelshelf there was a jar filled with drooping sprays of swan plant.

This wasn't a dream. I know I go on about them a lot but this wasn't a dream. As I sat there a monarch butterfly flitted slowly a across the room towards the window. It settled on the pane and its wings closed and then stretched. I'd never noticed before how their diagonal markings lead up towards the head and make a soft dark arrow. The monarch shook its orange and black wings in the sun.

I tried to open the window without disturbing the butterfly but the sash was jammed. So I put my finger on the warm glass and then moved it back slowly towards its head. The monarch crawled onto my finger and clung there.

It seemed to take me a long time to get downstairs and out into the open.

They lay their eggs on the swan plant, those monarchs, and their caterpillars will eat voraciously before they change and hang on the bare stems in their small green lanterns. I suppose Glory must have looked after the plant in her room. She would have watched those strange gold-flecked green capsules and waited for the butterflies to emerge. Instead it was me who saw one of them.

I stood in Carlton's overgrown front garden and held out my hand. The monarch lifted away from my finger and danced in the air.

Wherever they are, I hope that Glory and Chantal have a good life. As I stood there in that wilderness of thorn-apple and privet I knew that I wouldn't be trying any more to find those two girls. They'd gone off and I'd done what I could and that was it. I had to let them go.

As for me, well, I'll be back at the coast the next day or the day after and then it will just be a matter of getting by. And that seems to be enough for the time being.

# The Halcyon Summer
## Witi Ihimaera

*Once there was a nest, floating on the sea at summer solstice, and happy voices to charm the wind. The nest is gone now, drifting away on the tides. But somewhere, somewhere must surely float scattered straws, even just a single straw, which I may light upon.*

# 1

It was the year that Sir Apirana Ngata died. That summer the children's grandparents decided to go to the Empire games in Auckland. Tama was the eldest — an important eleven-year-old — and had two sisters, Kara and Mere. It was decided that the children would stay with their great-aunt, Nani Puti, while their parents were away.

'What about the land troubles?' their father asked their mother.

'The kids will be all right,' their mother answered.

The children had never been to Nani Puti's — all they knew was that it was way up the Coast somewhere, past Ruatoria.

'I'm coming with you,' Tama said to his father.

'No, you have to look after your sisters,' his mother responded.

'Then *you* go with them,' he answered.

He tried to pinch her but she only pushed him away. 'Just as well you're going up there,' she laughed. 'Nani Puti will sort you out.' But as a bribe — only if they were good children, mind — his mother said she would bring back some toys: a red clockwork train for Tama and a doll each for Kara and Mere. That decided the matter.

One morning, while the children were still asleep, their mother got up and packed a small brown suitcase with the clothes she thought they would need: a few shirts, shorts and a pair of sandals for Tama and some cotton frocks for his sisters.

'You kids won't need much,' she said. 'It's summer and it gets hot at Nani's place. Most of the kids up there run around with no clothes on anyway.'

At that remark the children started to kick up a big fuss because they were very shy and didn't relish the idea of showing their bottoms and you-know-whats to strangers.

'Oh, don't be silly,' their mother told them. You won't have to take your clothes off if you don't want to.'

Tama wasn't too sure about that either.

The children had to take a nap in the morning — they always took a nap if they were going anywhere, even to the two o'clock pictures at the Majestic. But they couldn't sleep. The thought of being deserted by their parents, and of being taken against their will to a strange relative's place in the strange country, frightened them.

When their mother found them awake she was very cross. 'It's about time you got to know your relations,' she said. 'You kids are growing up proper little Pakehas. And your Nani is always asking me if she's ever going to see you before she dies. Don't you want to see her?'

Tama was not feeling very respectful and would have answered 'No,' if he'd been able to get away with it. This Nani sounded alarming — she was very old for one thing, being sixty, and had white hair and tattoos on her chin. How she ever managed to get married to Uncle Pani and have twelve children was beyond his comprehension. Not only that, but the whole family had names longer than Tama's mother, which with Turirumanareti something-or-other, and they spoke only in Maori. How would he be able to talk to them? Thank goodness he had been to Scouts, and Kara had learned some sign language from Janet, the Pakeha girl next door, who was a Brownie. But Tama still didn't like the idea of going — it was all Maoris up the Coast, no Pakehas, and he and his sisters were used to Pakehas. Furthermore, Maoris wore only grass skirts and probably never even wore pyjamas to bed, and he knew that was rude.

'You kids are going and that's it,' their mother said. Nani Puti is expecting you.'

At that, the children knew their fate was sealed, because it was impolite not to go to someone's place when they were expecting you; just like the time when Allan invited Tama to his birthday party and his mother got cross when he hadn't turned up.

So after their nap the children's father put their suitcases in the car and yelled out to them to hurry up as he didn't have all day — both he and their mother acted as if they couldn't wait to get rid of the children. Mere started to cry and was given a lolly. Tama and Kara told their mother not to forget the toys. Then the children all hopped in the front with their father and waved.

'Goodbye, Mummy.' They hoped that she would change her mind and take them up to Auckland too — but she didn't. Instead she fluttered her hand.

'Look after your sisters,' she cried out to Tama, and went into the house.

Tama wondered if they would ever see her again.

The children slept most of the way to Nani's place. The heat from the Ford always made them sleepy. But most of all they hoped that when they woke up they'd find that leaving home had just been a bad dream. It wasn't a dream though, because every now and then Tama would make a small crack in his eyes and look out and watch as Gisborne went past, then Wainui, and then Whangara. At Tolaga Bay their father stopped to refill the car with petrol. He bought some orange penny suckers for Tama and Kara because they had pointed out that Mere had been given one. At the shop Tama saw a newspaper billboard: *Trouble Deepens On The Coast: Arson Suspected.* For a while after that they sat quietly licking their suckers and watching the hills ahead. Then Tama realised that Mere had been given another sucker at Tolaga Bay and that wasn't fair either because it meant that she had had two and he and Kara had only one. But their father wouldn't stop the car gain. He said it was a long way to Nani's place and he was in a hurry.

Sometimes the children sang songs because their father liked them singing as he was driving. He said it helped keep him awake. Shortly afterwards the children stopped singing, but their father remained awake. It seemed as if years went past before they reached Tokomaru Bay. That was the furthest away from Gisborne they had ever been. They watched silently as the township slid past and they fell off the edge of the world.

The children must have been asleep for a long time — Tama having his usual dream about being chased by a giant green caterpillar — because when the car gave a big bump it was night.

'Where are we, Daddy?' Tama asked.

'Almost at Nani's place,' he answered. 'Hop out and open the gate.'

Tama peered out and saw the gate like a big white X. The gate didn't have a latch, just a piece of wire wound round and round a batten, but he managed to get it untangled and the gate swung open. When he returned to the car Kara and Mere were awake, and they all sat clutching each other and watching the headlights bobbing along the rough muddy track like a drunken man. Then all of a sudden Mere screamed. The track had disappeared and the car was at the edge of a cliff. Far below the sea thundered against the rocks, white-tipped and angry — hiss, roar, crash, boom — and on a small spit of sand shone the lights of Nani's place.

'Here we are,' their father said.

Mere started to cry again.

'Oooh, don't leave us here, Daddy,' Kara said.

'Bob, is that you?' a voice yelled, using their father's European name.

Their father yelled back.

'Hang on a minute,' the voice said.

The children looked down to the house and saw a man putting on his gumboots in the light of the doorway. He shouted in a strange language and a smaller shadow appeared from inside with a tilley lamp. The man took the lamp, and the children watched, mesmerised, as it glided along the beach and started to climb the cliff. They heard the man huffing and puffing and swearing when he slipped, and they clutched each other even tighter because he sounded just like the fee-fi-fo-fum man. Then he was there and although he didn't look like a giant, you could never tell. With him were some other children wearing pyjamas tucked into shoes — and one of the boys must have had two left feet.

'Tena koe, Bob,' the man said.

He shook their father's hand and, when Tama gravely extended his, shook that too.

'Here, give that suitcase to Albert,' he said.

But Tama shook his head. He didn't want to give their clothes away, just in case — the clothes might get thrown away and, with only one set of clothes left, what would they wear on washing day? The man laughed.

'Okay, boy,' he said. 'Well, let's all go down to the whare. Your Nani's been waiting for you all day.'

The children followed the man down the cliff, just like little billygoats trying to get over the bridge before the troll got them. The man looked at them and he and their father laughed. So did the other children — and Tama knew that they thought he and his sisters were sissies. Tama wanted to box them all.

Then they reached the whare. Tama bent down to take off his shoes.

'E tama!' the man said. 'Leave them on!'

But Tama shook his head vigorously — he knew that Maoris were like people from Japan and taking your shoes off was a sacred custom.

Suddenly the light seemed to go out and a big mountain was standing there.

'Tena koutou, mokopuna,' Nani Puti said. She couldn't have seen Tama's outstretched hand because she grabbed him tight and squashed him against her and kissed him all funny because she hadn't put her teeth in. Then she held him away, so as to get a good look, and mumbled something in Maori and English.

'You kids look like June,' she said, referring to the their mother's European name.

She pressed noses with their father — which Tama knew was the way Maoris kissed, just like the Eskimos — and then began to growl because they had arrived so late.

'Only ghosts arrive at night,' she said.

Ghosts? But she must have forgiven their father because she was soon speaking flat out in Maori and giving him playful smacks.

Tama observed Nani Puti carefully. She wasn't exactly the oldest woman he had ever seen but she must have come close. Her hair was certainly as white as he had expected. As for the moko, it was rather pretty really once you realised that is was supposed to be there and not to be rubbed off every night. Nani Puti must have known Tama was staring, because suddenly she stared right back, crossed her eyes and did a pukana. Kara got alarmed — even more so when Nani Puti mumbled, 'You kids are too skinny. Doesn't June feed these kids, Bob? We'll soon put the beef on them.'

Kara stared at the big black pot on the open fire. She had visions of herself sitting in it with an apple in her mouth just to sweeten her up. But then one of the girls went to the pot, opened the lid, and the pot was already full of stew.

Nani Puti gave a blessing on the food, and the children sat with their father eating the stew. The hadn't realised how hungry they were and ate everything — potatoes, mutton chops and some funny stuff which was seaweed.

'May I have a knife and fork please?' Tama asked.

The other children had laughed out loud at his accent and, when he started to eat, copied his movements. They were mocking him, and Tama didn't like that. What embarrassed him most, though, was that his father forgot his manners and started eating with his fingers. Tama well knew that could lead to the end of civilisation. Every now and then the other children would giggle and put their hands over their faces, look at Tama and his sisters, and giggle again. Tama decided to ignore them and to listen to what the adults were saying. The only trouble was that his father, Nanny Puti and Uncle Pani were talking mainly in Maori, and only a few sentences made any sense to Tama.

'It's good to know you've got support,' his father said.

'We may have lost the case in court,' Nani Puti answered, 'but no one's going to move us off.'

Uncle Pani laughed and Tama thought he saw him motion to a corner of the room where there was a rifle.

By that time Tama had been able to put names to his cousins' faces, so that when, after tea, Nani Puti called to Grace, Lizzie and Sally to do the dishes he knew who they were. Grace was the eldest girl — she must have been eighteen — and when she moved she did so knowing how good she looked. Sally had short hair and was growing her chest. Lizzie was around Tama's own age and looked like a boy. Dutifully, Tama and his sisters asked if they could help — and the boy cousins fell about themselves at the thought of Tama doing the dishes. Tamihana was the big brother — he must have been about twenty and surely weighed ten tons. George came next, then Albert, Hone, Sid and Kopua. Phew! Two other brothers had already left home and were working on a local farm. Baby Emere was crawling on the floor. All these names to remember. But even more confusing was that the cousins with the European names also had Maori names and vice versa. Just as well, Tama felt, he had got good marks at school for memorising words in spelling.

'Well, I had better start heading back,' their father said.

Mere had fallen asleep and had been taken to bed. Kara was crying and Tama felt like crying as well. He didn't like the idea of staying here at all. He and Kara walked with their father to the car. Their father kissed them.

'Be good,' he said.

'You will come back to get us, won't you?' Kara cried.

'Of course,' he answered.

'When?' Kara wailed.

'Soon,' he replied.

He stepped in the Ford, started the motor, swung the car around — and the children were left there, standing with Nani Puti. Insects buzzed and flitted in the lamplight.

That night Tama was very weepy. Nani Puti had said, 'Why don't you bunk in with the other boys?' but he had said no. Tama had never slept with anybody else before. The trouble was that this got him off to a bad start with the boys, who then had to sleep in two beds while he slept in the third by himself — and that only made him feel lonelier than ever.

After all the lamps had been turned down, Tama heard the saddest sound in the world. His sister Mere had woken up and was calling:

'Mummy? Mummmmeeeeeeee.'

Tama got up and went to her. 'We just have to be brave about it,' he said. 'We have to be brave little Indians.' He kissed her and went back to his own bed. Just as he lay down he saw Nani Puti — she had heard Mere too. Nani Puti had a candle in her hand and it floated into Mere's room and floated out again. This time Mere was in Nani's arms.

'Shhhh, shhh,' Nani said to Mere. She began to sing a Maori lullaby. The song was so comforting, sounding like something floating on the sea. Then it began to drift out beyond the point where Tama could follow it, and he fell asleep.

# 2

The next morning Tama was woken by angry voices outside the bedroom window. He looked out and saw that a policeman was standing there, leaning over Nani Puti. The policeman's face was swollen and red.

'You tell Pani,' he said, 'the next warning will be the last.'

The policeman strode back to his car.

Tama jumped out of bed and hurriedly got dressed. He called through the wall, 'Kara, are you there?' There was no answer so Tama crept slowly into the room to take a look. Kara was gone, but there was Mere, playing by the fire. Tama ran to give her a hug and that was when Nani Puti returned.

'Morena, sleepyhead!' Nani said. 'You must have had good dreams, eh?'

Tama nodded, 'Yes, thank you.'

'My moko, you're June's kid all right,' Nani laughed. 'You hungry for some breakfast? Grace! Come and get some kai for this kid.'

Tama felt a little ashamed about that, and when Grace appeared he said, 'I'm sorry, Grace.' He just didn't like the idea of her always being in the kitchen like Cinderella. Then Tama asked, 'What did the policeman want, Nani?'

A flicker crossed Nani Puti's face. 'What policeman!' she laughed. 'No policeman has been here.'

While he was eating his breakfast Tama looked around the room. In the daytime everything looked smaller — how ever did Nani and Uncle manage to live with all their children in such a small house! It was even smaller than the one the Old Lady in the Shoe lived in. Gosh! There were just three bedrooms and this big room for eating and living in. The room was very plain with hardly any furniture except the table, two long forms, a settee in the corner, a few extra chairs, a cupboard for crockery, a wireless set and a small tin food safe. On one wall was a picture of the King. On a second was a colour magazine picture of Tyrone Power in *Blood and Sand* — Grace's boyfriend was supposed to look like that but handsomer. Just above the table was a photo of the whole family. Tama couldn't see Emere though, and when he pointed this out to Nani she laughed and said, 'Emere's there!' But Tama still couldn't see her so Nani pointed to her stomach, and Tama thought she was rude. Streamers from last Christmas were strung among the rafters. Hanging from the middle was a long sticky flypaper spattered with dead flies. On the mantelpiece above the fire was a piece of newspaper which had been cut into jaggedy patterns. Every now and then the wind would go *whoosh* in the chimney. Outside was the constant swish, swish, swish of the sea.

Nani Puti went out the back door, and Tama saw Kara playing with Sally and Lizzie. Tama felt she had forsaken him — and Mere too — and Kara made it worse by running in and laughing.

'So you're up at last.'

When she went to sit by him Tama pinched her hard. Her eyes brimmed with tears and she ran out again. Tama didn't know what to do. He had finished his breakfast but he couldn't really go out and skip over a rope with *girls*. Not only that, but Grace was wanting to clear up. 'You should go outside,' Grace said. 'The boys are somewhere out there.'

Tama stepped out into the light. He had to shade his eyes from the sun. He saw Hone, Sid and Kopua just beyond the back fence. He walked over to them. 'Hullo,' he said.

They pretended to ignore him and then Sid answered, 'Why, *hullo*, in a put-on hoity-toity manner.

Kopua jabbed Sid with an elbow and, looking up at Tama, said, 'You must have had a good sleep, cousin.'

But before Tama could reply, Sid interrupted, 'Yeah, especially since he didn't have to sleep with any of his stink —' and Sid pinched his nostrils sarcastically '— cousins.'

Kopua again came to the rescue, saying, 'Easy, Sid. He's just a townie —' and he turned to Tama '— aren't you, Tama?'

But Sid didn't want to let it go. He stood up and shoved Tama so hard that Tama fell to the ground. 'Think you're better than us, eh? Just because you live in the town. Just because you speak all la-di-da …'

Tama felt the heat of humiliation on his face and he rushed at Sid, arms up and ready and fists bunched. He'd had a few boxing lessons at school and was rather proud of his prowess.

'Hey,' Sid said, pushing Tama away. But Tama's blood was up and he got a few lucky hits in. However, any betting man would have placed more money on Sid, who was not only taller and heavier but more experienced. With a great sense of shock and pain, Tama found himself floored with a bloody nose.

'You — you — rotter!' Tama cried. And he launched himself at Sid again. This time there was no option for Sid but to knock his cousin down for the full count.

When Tama came around he found himself next to the outside pump by the horse trough. Kopua had a wet rag and was cleaning the blood from Tama's nose. He looked at Tama's left eye and whistled. 'That's going to come up a real beauty.'

Tama was still so humiliated that he pushed Kopua away.

'Hey,' Kopua yelled. 'What's up with *you* then! If you want to fight the lot of us, that's fine. But it will be better for *you* if we're friends. Okay?'

Tama shrugged his shoulders.

'Gee,' Kopua sighed, 'you're a hard fella all right. Come on.' He jerked his head to Tama. 'I said *come on*, willya! You don't want to stick around here so that your sisters can see you got beat, do you?'

Kopua started to walk away and then, like a jackrabbit, he charged up a tall hill. 'Yahoooo!'

By the time Tama caught up with him, Kopua was already sitting at the top, chewing a piece of grass. Tama had cooled down a lot by then, the humiliation receding — and then he forgot all about that when he saw Nani Puti's house below.

'Your house!' Tama gasped. The sea appeared to be ready to snatch it with blue fingers. 'It's almost in the sea!'

'You *are* a townie!' Kopua laughed. 'Can't you tell a high tide when you see one? You want to come here in the winter time — we turn into a boat then!'

Tama felt awed. There seemed such grand *insolence* in the sight of that small tin shack — for it really was just rusting corrugated iron — sitting there for all the world like King Canute daring the waves to come any further.

'Don't you get afraid?' Tama asked.

'What of?'

'The sea of course!'

Kopua was surprised. 'Why should we?' he asked. 'It's only sometimes that our little toes get wet.' The twinkle in his eyes was a dead giveaway that he was teasing. Then Kopua stood up and pointed out to sea. 'Look over there, Tama!'

Tama shaded his eyes and saw a small rowboat bobbing like a broken straw on the glistening ocean. 'Is that Uncle and Tamihana?' Tama asked. Kopua nodded and said:

'They're getting us some crayfish for tonight.'

Tama looked again, puzzled. 'But they haven't got fishing rods,' he said. Kopua laughed again.

'Gee, don't you learn anything at that townie school of yours?'

Suddenly Tama saw a *flash* from the house. Nani Puti was there and she had a mirror in her hand.

'Huh?' Kopua said.

There was an answering *flash* from the rowboat.

'Mum must want Dad to come in early,' Kopua continued. 'Something must be up.'

The boys were silent a while and then:

'How long have you lived here?' Tama asked.

'All our lives,' Kopua replied.

'Do you think you'll ever move?'

'What for? You don't understand, eh cuz. Didn't your mother ever tell you that she's from here? And that her mother was from here? In the old days there was a big Maori pa, right where our house is. It used to guard the whole Coast. It's famous.' Kopua puffed the words up with pride. 'And all the land —' Kopua described a large generous circle '— that you can see once belonged to us. Now, only this —' Kopua pointed down at the beach '— is left. The pa is gone, the land is gone, but our house and we are still here. And Mum's the big chief here. She'll never leave. Even if people are trying to get us out.'

Tama wanted to know more but Kopua appeared to want to go.

'Come on,' Kopua said.

'No, I don't want to go back to your house yet,' Tama answered.

'That shiner's still gonna shine even at night,' Kopua said. 'Okay, there's still lots to show you.'

Together the two boys walked along the cliff, with Kopua pointing out all the landmarks — where the canoes used to be launched from, where the kumara pits once were, the palisades, the urupa — and Tama began to hear ancient voices calling from the land and to feel an absurd sense of exhilaration, of belonging, of *this* history being *his* legacy, of *this* place being *his* place. He felt cross that his mother had not told him all this herself.

'She probably did,' Kopua said. 'You probably didn't listen!'

Which might have been true, because Tama had always been more interested in the Celts and the Romans. But come to think of it, Nani Puti could have been a Maori Boadicea, yes, *and* Mummy too.

By that time it was mid afternoon.

'I have to milk the cows,' Kopua said.

The two boys returned to the house. Kopua went to bring in the cows and Tama helped bail them up.

'What do you do at school?' Kopua asked from between the depths of Blackie's udder.

'I'm in form one,' Tama answered.

'So am I' said Kopua.

Squirt, squirt, went the milk in the bucket.

'Oh,' Tama responded, because Kopua was at least thirteen to his eleven.

'And what are you going to do when you grow up?' Kopua asked.

Tama didn't want to answer, because if he opened his mouth the smell of the cow bail would get in and it was *atrocious*. 'A teacher,' he said quickly. How come Kopua didn't expire from the odour?

'You have to have a lot of brains to be that,' Kopua said. 'I think I'll be a racing-car driver. Brrmmm, brrrmmmm.' He began to fantasize on the cow's udder and Blackie glared at him as if to say, *Well if you drive your car like you pull my teats the only trophy you'll ever win is* — and she presented him with a cowpat.

For the rest of the afternoon Tama tried to hide his damaged nose and his black eye. But Mere had screamed and Kara had always wanted to be a nurse — and she asked Nani Puti if she could have some bandages and chloroform.

'Your uncle will have something to say about this when he gets home,' Nani said at dinner.

Sid shifted uneasily on the form.

But any displeasure of Uncle's was nothing compared to Tama's discomfort and, in the end, he just *had* to ask: Nani, may I use your toilet?'

Nani smiled and said:

'It's outside.'

This was exactly what he had been dreading.

'Hone will show you, otherwise you might fall in.'

This was even worse.

Tama put on his shoes and followed Hone to a tin shed at the end of a long track. Hone shone the torch inside. 'I'll wait here,' he said.

'Oh no,' Tama answered, 'I'll be quite all right.'

'Oh yeah?'

Hone shone the torch to the top of the shed where a big black spider was.

'All right then,' Tama conceded. He dropped his trousers and just managed to sit down in time before Hone shone the torch accidentally on purpose in the direction of his you-know-what.

'Oops,' Hone said.

He did it again. Tama wished the shed had a door on it. He felt so shy sitting there in full view of his cousin, the house and the whole *world*.

'Pass me a comic,' Hone said.

Tama reached down to the wooden boards and threw him a tattered western.

'Do you read comics?' Hone asked.

'Our mother doesn't let us,' Tama said.

'Gee,' Hone responded in a hushed voice, as if a world without comics was too awful to contemplate. 'What do you read then?' he asked.

'Oh classics,' Tama said, trying to brush it all off, 'like Rudyard Kipling and H. Rider Haggard. Have you read *She*?'

Hone rustled his comic. 'Phew,' he said. *'No wonder.'*

For a while there was silence.

'I've finished now,' Tama said, dressing quickly.

'Just in time,' Hone answered. He shone the torch on the black spider. There it was, dangling right over Tama's head. Mere won't like *that*, Tama thought.

When Tama and Hone returned to the house they found that Uncle Pani had arrived back from town.

'Sid's for it now,' Kopua whispered as Tama walked in. And, sure enough, there was Sid, looking as if it was high noon and the hangman had come to Dodge City. But Uncle was mean and waited until the girls were in bed and there was just himself, Nani Puti and the boys in the big room. Then:

'Come here,' he said to Tama.

Uncle inspected the black eye. 'Who did it?' he asked.

Tama gulped. 'It was Blackie,' he said. *Please forgive me Blackie, you can kick me hard tomorrow morning.*

Uncle snorted and turned to Nani Puti, who was trying very hard not to laugh.

'Listen to the boy,' Uncle said to her. 'Did you know that Blackie could kick as high as Ginger Rogers?'

'Oh, it's true, Uncle,' Tama went on earnestly, 'honest Indian.'

Then Uncle frowned and said:

'Bring the Bible, Puti.'

Next minute, there it was, the Word of the Lord, right in front of him.

'Now swear,' Uncle said.

And Tama thought, *Our Father which art in Heaven, I can't tell on my cousin, you won't send me to hell will you?* He closed his eyes, took and deep breath and — Uncle Pani took the Bible away. 'Nothing is worth telling a lie for, boy,' Uncle said. He looked keenly at Tama, but all that Tama could hear was the Hallelujah Chorus because he had been saved.

'Yes, Uncle,' Tama said meekly.

The Uncle turned to the boys and said:

'All right, Kopua, go outside and get the biggest branch you can find. I know it was you.'

By his time Nani Puti was red with mirth — just as well she had taken out her teeth. And it was then that Sid stepped forward.

'I'll go,' he said.

'Well, make it a big branch,' Uncle told him. 'You should know better than to pick on a boy younger than you.'

Later that night Sid told Tama that Tama was *okay* for not squealing on him.

'We'll be mates, eh?' Sid said, and they shook on it.

When they were getting ready for bed Tama asked if they could bunk together. But before getting into bed Tama walked into the girls' bedroom to check on Kara and Mere — they were both fast asleep. On his way back he saw the light still on in Nani's bedroom.

'So how long have we got?' he heard Nanny ask.

'Maori Affairs is appealing the decision for us,' Uncle said.

'I was born here,' Nani replied, 'and I am not going to die anywhere but right *here.*'

Her voice was as eternal and as strong as the sea. Mere didn't cry that night.

# 3

Tama was horrified to find his cousin Kopua hauling him up from sleep at five o'clock.

'The cows,' Kopua said.

'Do you get up this early every morning?' Tama asked.

Kopua nodded, and Tama shuddered and was glad that in the town milk got delivered by the milkman. On their return from milking, Tama saw that Grace and Sally were also up, preparing breakfast. Grace was very beautiful — all dishevelled and untidy, but somehow attractive. Tamihana was awake too and dressed. Sounds of morning prayers came from Nani's and Uncle's room. The rest of the household was still asleep. Then Nanny came in and:

'Morena, moko,' she said. 'Kei te pehea to moe? Kei te pai?'

Tama looked at her curiously and he saw a shadow cross her face.

'You don't know, eh?' she asked.

'I beg your pardon, Nani?' Tama responded.

'You don't know your Nani's language,' Nani said.

'I know some French,' Tama said helpfully. 'Parlez-vous francais?'

Nani smiled at him, a small smile which was only just there. Then Uncle Pani came in and started ordering everybody around. 'You want to come out with me?' he asked Tama.

'In the rowboat? Oh, yes please,' Tama responded.

Nani went to remonstrate, but Uncle said to her:

'Oh, we'll just go to the Point and back. Not far. Just for the morning.'

And Nani nodded that was all right then. 'I want to take the mokos to the reef later,' she said.

Tama went with Uncle Pani and Tamihana to the boat. The sea was like glass that had just been shined by the sun and polished by the wind. 'I've never been in a rowboat before,' he said.

'No?' Uncle asked, amazed. 'Gee, what do you do in the town!' He and Tama sat in the boat — and Tamihana pushed it out on the sea and jumped in with them. Uncle Pani took up the oars and rowed with a strong, easy rhythm. Sometimes Tamihana took over. Once Tama offered, but all he could do was make the rowboat go round and round in circles.

'Never mind, Tama,' Uncle laughed. 'Your Uncle's too heavy for you. Boy, you wouldn't have been any good in the old days.'

'I beg your pardon, Uncle?' Tama asked, not understanding.

'This was the Maori life, Tama.' Uncle replied. 'The men did the fishing and the women cooked the fish.' But Uncle Pani was wise enough to see that he had hurt Tama.

'Times change, moko,' he said. 'These days, the person who fishes with the brains is sometimes more successful than the one who fishes with the hands.'

The rowboat reached the first marker where the crayfish pots were waiting to be brought up. Tamihana began to pull up the line and, far down, Tama could see the wire cage coming up. The crayfish pot broke the surface, and Tamihana reached in and grabbed the crayfish. Tama thought he was very brave, because the crayfish were very fierce, waving their legs in the air and going click click *click*. Tamihana threw one at Tama's feet and he yelled, almost upsetting the boat.

'Just as well it wasn't a mouse,' Uncle laughed, 'otherwise you would have got on the seat and we would have been *over*.'

The seagulls thought it was funny too because they crackled and cawed and chuckled and squealed overhead.

For the rest of the morning Uncle and Tamihana rowed from one marker to the next, bringing up the crays, and while they were doing so, Uncle Pani reminisced about the old days. Up until that time Tama had thought that Uncle Pani was just, well, Uncle *Pani*. He hadn't realised that Uncle had been so handsome, so strong, so sought-after, such a fantastic rider of horses, the best athlete on the Coast, the greatest fullback that Ruatoria had ever seen and such an all-round sportsman.

'If it wasn't for me getting those two tries, drop-kicking that goal from halfway in the last five minutes and then going over again right on the whistle, the Coast would have lost,' he said. Tama's eyes were so wide with amazement that he didn't see Tamihana put his finger up to test the strength of the wind. 'That's why your Nani fell in love with me, Tama, right on the spot. She had to queue up for me though, I wasn't an easy catch, they were all after me, Maori and Pakeha girls alike. But I let her come first because she was the only one who was not after my *money*.'

At that, Tamihana let out a snort. 'Gee, Dad, dream on.'

But that enabled Tama to ask:

'Uncle, why do we call you Uncle, and Nani, Nani?'

Uncle Pani looked hurt. 'You mean you can't see how old your Nani is and how young and gorgeous-looking I am?' he asked.

Tama didn't want to offend his Uncle so he didn't answer.

'She was sure lucky getting me,' Uncle sighed. 'If I had known she was waiting in the bushes to lead me astray ...' He tsk-tsked to himself. 'Tama, watch out for these Coast women,' he said. 'They're dynamite.' He grew reflective and looked back at the house, floating there on its spit of sand. 'But if you find a woman like her, Tama, you *grab* her, boy. You grab her and hold her so *tight* she can't get away. She's the one who keeps us all together. Keeps the land together. Not just for our family but all our whanau. Your mother and you too. She's the one.' He took off his hat in a salute. 'Then he looked out to sea. 'E hoa, looks like you're out of luck today.'

'Why, Uncle?'

Uncle Pani smiled mysteriously. 'Usually a white shark appears. It's our kaitiaki. Our protector. I haven't seen it for a while. Perhaps next time.'

By the time the rowboat returned to shore it was filled with seething, clicking crayfish. Uncle and Tamihana took most of the catch on the truck to Ruatoria. Kara came running to Tama, dressed in her frilly swimsuit, crying:

'Come on, Tama, Nani's taking us down to the beach!'

Behind her, Tama could see Mere jumping up and down — she had a bucket and spade in her hand. Nanny and the others were watching their antics as if they were creatures from another planet; they went to the sea just about every day and couldn't see what the fuss was about. There they were, all dressed in holey shirts and old black football shorts, and there were the city cousins all decked out like Christmas.

'All right, all right,' Nani said to Kara, trying to calm down Kara's boisterous glee. 'But work first and then swim.'

'Work?'

'You want to eat tonight, don't you?' Nani asked. Haven't you kids ever ... You *do* know what pipis and pupus are? How about kinas? *What!* What the blimmin' heck does your mother feed you, you poor mokos!'

With that, Nani yelled instructions to Grace and Sid and then, like Boadicea, she led the way to the reef.

The reef was about a mile away and so isolated that the seagulls were outraged at this invasion of shouting children. *How dare you, how dare you!* they shrieked from the blue vault of sky. Unheeding, the town children ran on while the country cousins followed with the sugarbags and kits for the shellfish.

'Come on, Nani!' the town children cried.

The old woman only nodded her head, hoping that the gods of this place would understand that this was a new generation which knew nothing of the old ways and traditions, and she said to the gods:

'Be forgiving, e Tangaroa, of the ways of the innocent.'

As if to reassure her, a bright blue kingfisher scooped across the inlet, flashing its reflection across the water.

'Oh look, Nani, look!' the children cried.

Then they were at the reef and the old woman issued instructions. The town children thought it was such fun and not like work at all. They had to pair up — Tama with Sid, Kara with Sally, Grace with Mere, Kopua with Hone, and Nanny with Lizzie

— and with Emere slung on her back, wasn't that just sweet? Then out they went to gather dinner.

Tama was wearing shoes to protect his feet from the sharp reef. Sid gave Tama a sack to hold. He reached into the water, underneath a ledge and *tugged*.

'This is paua,' he said. In his hand Sid had a big shell and inside was a long black piece of rubber. 'You have to be quick, because if the paua knows you're going to grab him he sticks tight to the rock. Then you have to use a knife to get him off. You try.'

Tama put his hand under the ledge and his face screwed up — what if there were an electric eel there or a giant clam? 'Oouchh,' Tama yelled. 'There's something prickly down there.'

Sid laughed. He grabbed underneath and pulled out a brown spiky ball; it looked like it would be good at puncturing tyres. 'This is a kina,' Sid said. 'We eat this too ...'

Which was just the thing that Tama was afraid he would say.

Once the first sack was filled, the two boys hauled it back to Nani Puti.

'To Tangaroa goes the first of the catch,' she said, and she took some of the shellfish to a deep pool and returned them to the sea.

'Why did she do that?' Tama asked Sid later.

'It is always done,' Sid responded. 'Tangaroa is the Sea God. He gives us blessings. So this is our way of thanking him.'

It didn't take the boys long to fill their second sack. Sid did most of the work. Tama had to use the knife. But that didn't matter to Tama because he was feeling so happy and elated — and he just didn't know why. Perhaps it was the whole excitement of not having to go to a grocery store and get food but actually diving for it yourself. Or maybe it had to do with a growing sense of belonging — and of being accepted — by his cousins. Or perhaps it was because work brought with it a sense of achievement — as if he was doing something worthwhile. Perhaps, perhaps — and as he worked, he became more entranced by the reef and more akin with it. And his Nani, watching from afar knew what was happening and thanked Tangaroa for his *communion*.

'Kua mutu!' Nani Puti said. 'We have enough! Work is over! Now you kids can have a good swim and cool off.'

She sat on the beach watching for a while and she felt so glad June had sent the mokos up to her. That was the only way the whanau would keep together. She heard Kara scream and saw that she had caught a baby octopus — or the other way around.

'Why don't you put it back?' Nanny said.

Kara's eyes were large. 'Can Grace do it, Nani?' Kara asked. The ... the mother octopus might be out there.'

Nani Puti glanced over to Mere, and there she was, building a sandcastle and looking for all the world as if she was on a beach at Brighton. *What future lies in store for you, my moko Pakeha?* Nani Puti asked herself. *What future lies ahead for us all?* And then Tama was there, shaking himself like a little puppy.

'You having a good time?' Nani Puti asked.

'Oh yes, thank you, Nani,' Tama answered.

'Would you like to sit and korero with your nani?' she asked.

Tama nodded his head vigorously. 'Uh huh.' He sat down with her and both of them were looking at the reef and the sea. And the minutes went by but not a word was spoken between them, and yet Tama felt as if they had been talking for *ages*. What about? Why, sea and sky of course, earth and ocean, man and land, sea and land, man and man, kinsman with kinswoman, kin with kin.

'All your bones are here,' Nani Puti said, and Tama felt a great sense of *completeness* in her words, and he was falling through the blue well of the sky. 'No matter where you go in your life this is your home. No matter what you do with your life, these are your people. Whenever you need us, all you have to do is call. And whenever you are needed, you must come. Do you understand?'

'Yes, I understand, Nani.' Tama nodded.

In that mood of absolute enchantment the kingfisher came again, skimming its royal colour across the water.

The next days drifted past like a dream. Tama and his sisters grew strong and brown under Nani Puti's dictum — work first, then you can play later. It was therefore with a sense of surprise that the children received the postcard from their mother. They had been riding horses — or 'hortheth' as Mere would have lisped — all afternoon and having bareback races with their cousins along the beach. Far off, Nani Puti had appeared waving her apron. As soon as they saw their mother, the cousins did a conjuring trick and disappeared into thin air — how were Tama, Kara and Mere to know that the horses belonged to the Pakeha neighbour, Mr Hewitt?

'Don't you worry,' Nani told Tama. 'I know you kids got left holding the bag.'

She handed the postcard over to Tama and set off with a big branch to find their cousins. *Dear Tama, Kara and Mere,* Mum had written, *Daddy and I have arrived in Auckland. We are missing our babies very much. Tama, I hope you are looking after your sisters. Kara, you do as Nani says. Mere, are you being a good girl? We will be back soon. Love Mummy. XXXXXXX*

'Have Mummy and Daddy been away a week already?' Kara asked.

'Just about,' Tama said.

The children were a little disconsolate at dinner that evening — and matters were made worse when Uncle Pani told Mere she could cook her very own crayfish. Until that time Mere had quite happily eaten everything served up to her including crays. But when she popped a 'Mere-thized baby crayfith' into the boiling pot with her own pudgy hands and heard it scream she felt like a murderer. 'Put crayfith back!' she said, pointing at the sea. 'Put back, Uncle!' She drummed her fists against her chest. From then on she refused to eat crayfish, using her well-known complaint that 'my bottomth thtuck' — which was her way of saying she was full or had constipation. However, everybody brightened up when Nani said that she and Uncle had business with Maori Affairs (Nani didn't seem to be very happy about it though) and that all the family would be going to Ruatoria the next day.

'Can we go to the pictures?' Sid asked anxiously.

'The two o'clock and the eight o'clock?' Grace chimed in because she wanted to see her boyfriend, and night-time made him more daring.

'You kids are given an inch ...' Nanny sighed. 'Oh, all right. But I don't want dirty kids to shame me. So, bath-time!'

While the girls were doing the dishes Tama went with the boys to the wash-house, where they filled the copper and lit the fire beneath it. When the water was boiling they stood in a row and swung buckets down the line from the wash-house to the whare, where the bath was.

'Quick! Let's get in now,' Sid hissed.

But Nani saw him. 'Hey! You boys let Grace and the girls go first,' she yelled. 'You make the water too dirty with your patotoi feet.'

'Yes,' Grace continued. 'We don't want Kopua's kutus floating in our water.'

So the boys had to put on their clothes again and wait until the girls had finished.

There was something in the very idea of a 'bath' that always brought the lady out in Grace. She emerged from her usual place in the kitchen in a long pink robe and towel turban, positively t-rrr-ipping on her toes to the bath. Following behind her came Sally, Lizzie, Kara and Mere like adoring acolytes holding the scrubbing brush, shampoo and Sunlight soap which Grace would apply to her hair, face and person. This was no longer the Grace who tucked her dress into her pants when playing touch rugby with her brothers, nor the sister who yelled endearments like 'Hoi, kina head' or 'Gedoudahere, tutae face.' This was some other more divine creation. Anybody looking on and listening as she slipped into the bath would have thought this was Cleopatra swimming in asses' milk rather than in a rusty tub with a candle on the rim. Surrounded by the smaller girls — all in awe of voluptuous curves — Grace would sigh, 'Make more bubbles dahlings,' or 'Mmmm, more shampoo, sweetnesses,' or 'Oooo, just a little softer with the soap, babies.' And as they ministered to her she would let them in on the secrets of How To Be Seductive or What To Do If He Wants To Go All The Way. And if she ever heard the irritated yells of her brother, 'Hurry up, Grace!' or the *thump* as a cowpat hit the roof, she simply sighed. There was a big difference between brothers and MEN.

Was it all worth it? Oh yes, for to see Grace transfigured by soap and water, gilded by the moon, queening it across the paddock and around the cowpats was to witness ... a vision. Not only that, but one knew that one was only seeing part of the miracle. The full miracle would only be apparent after Grace had carefully plucked her eyebrows all off (and replaced them with black pencil ones), lipsticked her lips pink on the outside and deep red inside (to make them look narrower) and applied hair rollers (to substitute her straight hair with a style that approximated to the latest rage). For now, though, this glimpse of the Serpent of the Nile, Ruatoria-style, preparing to go by barge to meet a hick-town Mark Antony the next day, was sufficient.

Once the girls had finished their toilette the boys emptied the bath and refilled it — Have a bath in girls' water? No fear! They were just about to hop in for the second time when Nani Puti and Uncle Pani came out. 'You boys last,' Nani Puti said.

Oh, the boys were so angry because had they known that Mum would pinch their water, they wouldn't have filled the bath to the brim. But finally it was their turn after all — and there was Tama, for the first time in his life, taking a bath with other people. Initially, he was embarrassed about being in the middle with Sid, Hone and Kopua, especially since they were always dropping the soap.

'Oops,' they would say as they hunted for it and ended up with a handful of you-know-what. The splashed each other too. But very soon Tama forgot about his inhibitions.

'Oops,' he said as he searched for the soap.

The next morning, after breakfast, Tama and the boys were the first to get dressed and to be waiting on the truck. There was a certain unspoken protocol to all this, as if it was expected that the boys should wait the longest. Five minutes later Uncle Pani arrived in tie, sports jacket and hat, followed another five minutes after by the smaller girls and Emere. Fifteen minutes passed until Nani Puti appeared.

'Oh …' The little girls sighed on cue at the sight of Nani in coat and hat, stockings and white Minnie Mouse shoes, putting on her gloves and trying not to look too self-conscious in the unaccustomed elegance. Head down and still fussing about her seams, she was handed into the cab — an act reserved for occasions like this — by a gallant and proud Uncle Pani. Ten minutes after that one of the girls was despatched to tell Cleopatra to shake a leg, returning to say, 'She's almost there — wherever 'there' was.

Then, just before everybody's patience exploded, she appeared – Grace, the eldest girl and apple of everybody's eye, wobbling on red high heels and dressed to kill.

Not for our Grace a simple dress and a few accessories. Oh no, this kid knew she wasn't going to get to town for another couple of weeks, so she was making the most of it. Her hair was positively rolling in curls. The dress was lime green and the neckline was as low as Grace thought she could get away with. There must have been at least five petticoats to flounce that dress out as far as it went. Not only that, but the dress was surely five sizes too small — and knew it. And why wear only one bangle and necklace when you have a whole drawer full?

'Come on, Grace,' Nani Puti said.

Lost in a vision of her own beauty, jangling like a cowbell and walking as knock-kneed as a pukeko, Grace swayed and dipped and staggered toward the truck. Eyes never glittered as green-shadowed as hers, lips were never as luscious or greasy red, and if there was too much powder, don't forget that it had to last the whole day. Only one problem remained: all she had to do was make sure that her beauty would not be destroyed by the dust on the way to Ruatoria.

Tama didn't have much time to appreciate Ruatoria because it was almost two o'clock — Nani Puti having stopped at a few relations' places on the way to take shopping lists to town — when they arrived. The movie was a double feature, hooray, with Audie Murphy in the first one and …

'Oh,' Grace screamed, 'Rory Calhoun!'

But while his cousins were jumping up and down, waiting for their picture money, Tama and Kara exchanged puzzled glances — was this *it*? This one main street with a few shops, picture theatre and hotel? Where was the *rest*?

'Here you are, mokos,' Nani said. She gave Tama, Kara and Mere five shillings each and Tama said:

'But Nani, we haven't got any change.'

'No, this is for being good mokos,' Nani answered. 'But don't forget it has to last the whole day.'

Tama had never seen so much money.

'Hurry up!' his cousins were saying, 'otherwise the picture will have started before we get there.'

Before they knew it, Tama, Kara and Mere found themselves being whisked off by their cousins, leaving Nani and Uncle standing in the dust.

'Come back to the truck after the pictures,' Nani called. She was biting her lips nervously and ruining her lipstick. By then Grace had got the tickets at the movie house and shooed them in, hissing:

'I don't want to see any of you till afterwards. And if you want to go to the lav, Lizzie, you find it yourself.'

With that, and in a flurry of hugging and screaming, Grace joined up with her friends and went into a huddle over The One And Only Subject: BOYS. Grace's boyfriend was already inside — it wasn't done for boyfriends to wait; apart from which, he would have to buy the girl her ticket, and he wasn't that dumb.

'Come on,' Kopua said, rolling his eyes.

Inside, mayhem was in power. The rules of the game were that the little children should go down the front where they could be pelted with peanuts and jellybeans — so off went Kara, Mere and other others. The big boys, who grudgingly allowed younger boys like Tama and Kopua to join them, all sat at the back. The middle territory was for the females of the attached and hoping-to-be attached variety — there they could be looked over or boasted about by the boys behind. Naturally Grace made a wonderful entrance, cracking gum and wobbling her way down the aisle with her friends. Without looking back, she hissed to one of them, *crack*:

'Where is he?' *crack*.

'On the left side,' *crack*, 'over there!' her friend responded.

The first feature was called *Adventure Island* and Tama fell in love with the red-headed lady in it — Rhonda Fleming. He was amazed how vocal everybody was, cheering, hissing, booing, offering advice like, 'He's just behind you,' or 'Hurry up and *kiss* her.' They cheered again and again, and threw peanuts everywhere.

During all of this, Grace and her boyfriend sat staring at each other through the gloom (that was her, wasn't it, the one in green?) but not moving towards each other. That would look too forward. No, this was reserved for intermission. At that stage Grace was supposed somehow to be standing at the doors, her hand dangling somewhere in reach, so that — just before the lights went out — her boyfriend could grab it and haul her inside. Once that was accomplished, it was up to the boyfriend to show the goggle-eyed younger boys like Tama how to woo a girl, and up to Grace to make sure he left at least six cherries on her neck to prove he'd been there. As far as Tama could make out, the main object was to plant your lips on hers to stop her breathing, and when she was faint for lack of air, you started to move your hands downward. If you were lucky, despite her struggles, you got as far as the belt — but no further, buster. (The girls always relied on the brevity of the second feature to save them from a fate worse that you-know-what.) Watching all this, as well as the picture, it was no wonder that Tama was in a state of shock when the lights went back on. As for Grace, she had *triumphed* and there she sat in absolute adoration of her beloved. Nor did it matter that her hair, lipstick, eye-shadow, powder and eyebrows had been totally obliterated — she had *Prevailed*.

'Eeee, Grace!' Kopua said pointing at her neck, which looked like a vampire had attacked it.

Grace stared at Kopua as if he was a creature from another planet. 'Oh, go squeeze yourself,' *crack*, 'Pimple-face,' *crack*, she said.

Afterwards, Grace, Tamihana and George went off with boyfriend and girlfriends, and the rest of the children raced to the local shop, where they bought dinner — a pie, softdrink and doughnut each.

'Wasn't it neat when …' the young boys said to each other, reliving the two movies they had seen.

'Yeah, boy!'

As for Tama, he was still trying to recover. Then, remembering that they were to meet Nani and Uncle at the truck, they raced back. The truck was there, with the baby Emere sleeping in the cab, but Nani and Uncle were nowhere to be seen.

'They're in the pub,' Hone said, jerking his head at a large building, which shook with singing, boozing and laughing. 'But they'll be out by six.'

The children walked around a while with Kopua introducing Tama and his sisters to the locals. Tama decided that Ruatoria wasn't so bad. It was kind of like Dodge City or a sleepy Mexican town south of the Texas border, with the roughest, toughest, meanest, most colourful coyotes this side of Tombstone, *yup*. People still rode horses into town and swaggered in and out of the local cantina.

Then it was six o'clock and people began to burst out of the hotel, clutching crates of beer and each other.

'Here they come,' Kopua said.

Tama couldn't see Nani Puti or Uncle Pani, and while he was looking in the crowd somebody grabbed him. A bloated face peered into his and an overpowering smell of beer and stale sweat enveloped him.

'Keeoraa morgor, waz za pitcha kapai? Wherez za kidz —'

Before he could prevent it, the figure lurched forward toward Kara and Mere, who both screamed.

'Wazza madda, morgors? Iz only meee,' the face said.

Then Uncle Pani was there to rescue them. 'Hey, you haurangi moll,' he said as he grabbed her and pulled her away.

Were it not for the Minnie Mouse shoes, Tama would not have recognised Nani Puti at all. She looked like some huge macabre cray which had been scalded in hot boiling water and was still screaming. Her eyes were red and bulging and her face was hanging in ugly scarlet folds down her neck. Her hair was straggly and the hairline was thick with foam-like perspiration.

'Yezzzz,' Nani Puti said, 'iz only your Nanneee …' She went to lean on the truck and fell over. 'Fuggen hell,' she swore, 'Blimmen hell.' And she laughed and laughed in a horrible unfunny way, her lips blubbering and her eyes streaming with tears, just sitting there in the dust in her nice dress and coat. Uncle Pani went to pick her up and his voice was angry.

'Hey, *Mum*, snap out of it,' and he swore under his breath. 'Lizzie!' he called. '*Lizzie!* Come and take your damn mother to the lav.'

And Lizzie said, 'Oooo,' and wrinkled her nose as she and Uncle helped Nani over to the public toilet.

It had all happened so quickly that Tama was still bewildered. He felt that the real Nani Puti had been stolen away and a false Nani Puti had been put in her place. Kara came to him, shivering. 'I don't like Nani Puti like this, Tama,' she said.

Mere was still snivelling with fright. Uncle Pani returned and saw their fear. 'Don't worry kids. Your Nani will be right as rain.' He bent down to Mere's level and kissed her. Then, standing, he addressed Tama man to man. 'Your Nanny was never able to hold her beer, and I couldn't stop her. She just wanted to drink her troubles away.'

*Troubles?*

'We've had some bad news, boy.'

Lizzie returned with Nani, who was looking much better. Even so, Uncle gathered everybody and told them he was taking Mum home but he had spoken to Auntie Trixie and she was going to the eight o'clock pictures, so she could bring them home afterward. The cousins were glad about that but Tama said:

'I think Kara, Mere and I will come back with you. Mere's just about asleep anyway and Mummy wouldn't like it if we didn't look after her.'

'Okay, Tama,' Uncle said. 'Well you kids get in the back then.'

Tama, Kara and Mere waved goodbye to their cousins and as the truck trundled out of Ruatoria they huddled beneath the blankets. Night fell quickly and very soon Uncle had to switch on the headlights. Tama wondered whether they were the only ones alive in the whole wide world. Nani Puti was sick three times, and at every *heave* Uncle would say:

'That's it, dear. Get it all out and you'll feel better.'

As heavy as Nani must have been, Uncle carried her from the truck into the whare when they got home.

Swish, *swish*, went the sea.

'Help me with your Nani,' Uncle asked Tama when he had lit a candle and put Nani on the bed.

Tama took off her hat and shoes, and while Uncle lifted Nani up he removed her coat and Kara took off her skirt. Nani flopped down in her petticoat. Mere got a flannel and cleaned her face. 'There,' Mere said.

That night Kara and Mere came to sleep with Tama. They were upset because adults were supposed to be strong. Yet Nani kept on crying and crying as if her heart was breaking. She must have known the children were still awake, because she called out to them.

'Yes, Nani?' they said as they stood at the doorway.

She was sitting up in bed having a cup of tea. When she saw them her face screwed up. 'I'm sorry, mokos.'

'You don't have to be sorry, Nani,' Kara answered. 'You're big enough to do exactly what you like!'

'We can't be brave little Indianth all the time,' Mere added.

Nani smiled wanly. She kissed the three children on their foreheads. Just before they all left the room she shot Tama a piercing, smouldering glance.

'Never trust the Pakeha, Tama, never,' she said. 'And when you get older, you learn all you can about the Pakeha law so that you can use it against him.'

The flame from the candle flickered, almost faltered, casting strange shadows on the walls.

Nani Puti recovered quickly and the next day no mention was made of her drunkenness. Tama's cousins had had a wonderful night.

'You would have loved the movie,' Kopua said.

As for Grace, she resumed her usual stance as Cinderella in the kitchen, dreaming of the next time her boyfriend would be able to attack her neck.

So the summer resumed, day after day, as if it was everlasting — a long glorious hot halcyon summer. Tama and his sisters continued to work in the mornings and play with their cousins in those joyous afternoons. Sometimes Tama would go out in the rowboat with his Uncle and, recalling an earlier occasion, he asked:

'Uncle, do you think we'll see the shark today?'

Uncle looked toward the horizon, seeking a disturbance in the ocean. 'Something must be wrong. It loves to come and scratch itself on our dinghy.'

Nothing but the sea ever glistening.

More and more, Tama found himself wanting to wander alone around the hills and bays. He would run to the top of the hill overlooking the whare and look across the beach which was so much part of his cousins' lives. He envied them their living here, in this seeming timeless place, and would close his eyes hoping to imprint it all on his retina. To see Nani Puti sitting on her doorstep in the sun made him grin with happiness. To watch Uncle and Tamihana bobbing in the ocean made him want to be a fisherman like they were. And the cup of his contentment would begin to bubble over, and he would run back down the hill to be with his sisters and cousins.

At the same time, despite the kingfisher days of forever sun, Tama began to notice that little things were going wrong — like, for instance, the long absence of the pet shark. Out of the corner of his eye, he would see a cliff face crumbling, or a stone falling into the sea, or a dead fish floating on the surface of the sea. The rowboat sprang a leak one day, and later Hone made a small gash in his leg with a fishhook. Nani Puti herself was cut by a broken bottle in the sand. Just little things — but both Nani and Uncle saw them also and seemed powerless to stop them happening. Something was out there, something, somewhere, some *thing*. Then the policeman arrived a second time, bearing a government letter and was it Tama's imagination or had Uncle Pani picked up his rifle and ordered the policeman away? After that, Nani and Uncle seemed to grow older and darker before Tama's eyes, and he realized how vulnerable and how unprotected they were against the ills of the world.

In this mood of disquiet, with the edges of the world crumbling away, Tama found himself returning again and again to the sanctuary of the reef. He wanted to *know*, but know what? And just as he tried to memorise the landscape he did the same with the reef. In his own helpless schoolboyish way he would measure out the distances between one prominent feature and the next — six paces to the pool with the seahorse, five strokes across to the next with the baby octopus — as if it were all going to disappear. He would watch the ocean and wish the pet shark to appear, as if such a supernatural event would stop what was happening and make it all right again. He read desperation in the normally routine prayers that Nani and Uncle intoned morning and evening. When they started to leave the children for long periods, travelling from marae to marae throughout the Coast, Tama wanted to know why. And then, when Maori kinsmen began to gather with greater frequency at the whare, debating and shouting through the stomach of the night, he wanted to join them. But his Uncle would say:

'Don't you worry, moko. This is for your Nani and me to sort out.'

Yes, it might all have been just his imagination — like the morning, just before dawn, when he felt the compulsion to visit the reef. He was running along the beach where there was so much earth and so much sky that he could have fallen into it all. Suddenly he heard a sound, a seagull calling. He looked out to sea. He had to shade his eyes because the sun was rising. There, framed in that golden aureole of light, bobbing on the blood-red sea, Tama thought he saw the rowboat. Nani Puti and Uncle Pani were in it. Nani was standing in the boat, dressed in black, and she was singing a Maori lament. It sounded like a farewell song to someone, as sad as Snow White's dying. The next day more kinsmen arrived. From then on, they began to stay.

The solstice came to an end. One morning when the sea was sparkling, a car appeared on the cliff. Waving to Tama, Kara and Mere from far away were their parents. The children were overjoyed to see their parents, who looked bronzed and happy and — like gods really. When Kara told their mother about all the adventures they had been on she laughed.

'I told you you'd like it at Nani's place,' she said.

Tama watched his parents with growing discomfort because they seemed unaware of what was happening, really *happening*. His parents had brought gifts for Nani and Uncle, who accepted them politely, and for the cousins — Grace gave a scream of delight at the new H-line dress that their mother had brought back from Auckland. And the thought came to Tama that his parents and his family were foolish people because they were so privileged that they could never see beyond themselves.

'We'd better go,' Tama's mother said. 'Nani and Uncle look like they're having a meeting.'

Only then did their father understand. He talked to their mother and she stared around her — and her eyes brimmed with tears. She went up to Nani Puti.

'How *dare* you,' their mother said. 'How *dare* you think that we would come and go just like that. We — I — my children — have as much right as you over this place. And *you* were going to let me walk in and out again without telling me? Don't you *dare* do this to me. Ever again.'

Nani Puti and their mother began to cry on each other's shoulders, and Nani Puti was firm.

'You would only get in the way, June,' she said.

'When do you expect the police to come?' their mother cried.

'In two days' time, but *sshhh*, we don't want to upset the mokos.'

Their father appeared to be arranging something with Uncle Pani about returning with their mother as soon as was possible. Uncle Pani showed their father how well oiled the rifle was. Their father looked grim and almost afraid.

'Okay, children,' their mother said. 'Time for us to go. Say goodbye to your Nani and your cousins.'

Suddenly Tama didn't want to go at all. He felt a sense of panic, as if the caterpillar train of his nightmares was catching up on him. Something was happening at the edge of childhood. It was just around the corner and, whatever it was, it would forever change all their lives.

'Nani? Uncle!' Tama cried.

But his Nani and Uncle and cousins were gently shepherding him, his sisters and parents along, away from the house and past the tent encampments of the kinsmen. Before Tama knew it, they were all standing beside the car.

'Goodbye, my cousins,' Tama cried. 'Goodbye, Uncle. Nani, goodbye ...'

Nani gave a sudden hoarse cry, as if she were in deep pain. The ocean flowed from her as she grabbed Tama again and again.

'Never forget, my moko,' she said, 'never ever forget.'

Tama threw his arms around her. 'No, Nani, I'll never *never* forget. Honest Indian, Nani, honest.'

Tama, Kara and Mere crowded the back window waving and waving and waving. And, when there was enough spit in his mouth to make the words, Tama whispered:

'Oh, Mummy, oh, Daddy, it was the *best* summer I've ever had. Ever.'

For some reason his vision became all blurry as if, after the long summer, rain had finally come to the Coast.

*Once there was a nest, floating on the sea, at the edge of childhood. Then it was gone, its straws scattered across the waves. And I have been a kingfisher searching, always searching.*

# Frames
## Mike Johnson

Politics overwhelms us; remember Neruda, 'one morning the bonfires / leapt out of the earth / devouring human beings.' *Devorando seres*, as they say in dry Castile or Barcelona with its orthopaedic shops. It's a short hop from Barcelona to Algiers, Algiers to Tel Aviv. In our grandfathers' day they took twenty thousand of our young men, the best and worst, and consigned their bodies to the leaping bonfires of places like Verdun and Passchendaele. Pretty much a whole generation for our small country; pretty much a clean sweep. 'A wave of pride / and knives!'

Politics overwhelms us, and it's hard to forget Neruda, or Lorca under the ground, even here, in paradise, surrounded by tall, quiet pongas roasting in the cicada sizzle, in a world where Algiers and Tel Aviv exist only by report, and Verdun and Passchendaele belong to the litany of history. There's a radio somewhere playing a slow, mournful version of 'Po Kare Kare Ana', by a revamped, reissued Howard Morrison, reminding me that it's Waitangi Day tomorrow, the day the Maori chiefs gave away their *rangatiratanga*, their sacred authority, believing they were being guaranteed it.

That's why I love Neruda, who can reclaim the personal from the political without losing the force of either, who can make his claim upon the body of love and weep the blood of children. I envy him this facility, this fluid concourse with compassion — the King Midas of poetry, Marquez called him.

Eleanor plays on the trampoline. From where I'm sitting I can see her, rising up into my line of vision and back out again, grinning at me cheekily, knowing I'm supposed to be working. What she doesn't know is that I'm thinking of her mother, whom she resembles more every day, wondering how to introduce her, weighing the balance of narrative perspectives, feeling out the words in front of me, wondering when I'll start writing.

I cannot go unaided on this expedition. I need my Neruda around me, my Tarot pack wrapped in silk, coffee, and Eleanor's figure rising and falling in the background. I need the murmur of angry voices, pious voices, on the radio. The treaty has not been honoured. Of course. Our public complaints are our private sorrows; in five years Auckland will have shanty towns; events have outflanked the lyric; Salman Rushdie sees out his first year as fugitive. I ring him up. 'Salman,' I say to him, 'I want to salvage something from this mess, what shall I do?' 'If you want to be famous, pull the beard of Allah,' Rushdie advises me. 'Does Allah have a beard?' I ask him. There is a short pause before his voice echoes around the world, 'Most assuredly. I've never doubted that.'

Hearing Salman say this, I take heart.

I have decided to call your mother Monika, Eleanor, and address this to you. How I imagine you will be in ten years' time.

It was seeing your eyes that brought about this shift in focus, and the name Monika came to me for reasons of my own, as a private joke. You were rising and falling on the trampoline, laughing, and your eyes were suddenly the colour of the Aegean, the Mediterranean; the same colour as Monika's eyes. These tricks of light are always being played on writers, on mothers and fathers, anyone who brings out a few old photographs to shuffle through. I shuffle through mine now, looking for one of Monika as she was then, when her eyes looked like yours. I bring these out to supplement Neruda and the Tarot deck. It's a superstitious concoction I'm after here, something to redeem the past and pull it from the hat in a puff of smoke: the treaty is not a fraud, the earth has not been swallowed by a hungry dragon. The personal is possible. Out of the mess we salvage a few personal effects and place them in a suitcase. Ring a few friends. Here's a passport, water-stained, full of visas; it's passed through its last border. Here's a woollen cushion-cover spun and woven by nuns in Muslim Algeria, in a small town call Ghardaia, where the famous rugs are made. Here's a photograph of Monika showing the colour of her eyes, the same as yours. That'd be Greece, 1976, another island.

You'll know the Neruda poem: 'Light wraps you in its mortal flame.' He speaks of 'the old propellers of twilight'; *las viejas hélices del crepúsculo*. It sounds better in Spanish. How good he is at sadness, the old master! The shaded twilight tones, *crepusculo* and politics. 'And the blood of the children ran through the streets / without fuss, like children's blood.' Monika's eyes darkened in the bright, sharp, ultraviolet salted light of our homeland.

I pause at a shot taken just last year. You were jumping on the trampoline then also; you're in mid-air, your hair standing out. That moment surely recalls this one. Monika and I are sitting as if someone is about to take our photograph. For the record; for history. I've taken my dark glasses off for the occasion and can be seen squinting into the light, thinking of politics. Monika's hand on the couch is pure archaeology. The camera sees it all and notices nothing. This is not a valley of stones, but a valley of honeysuckle and green. Our posing here begs the question, for our relation is as formal and oblique as is required of the divorced. Ten years pass in a shuttered instant. History is as glass; the treaty is back to being a good honest fraud once more, and everything we came back to this country for is right in front of us. Happy families.

Somebody said that our land is too young to have fully formed ley lines. Such a land is like the body of a child. In Europe the ley lines are clogged with the fatty deposits of industrialism, the sclerosis of civilisation. And between the two lies the huge round of the ocean, the bulk of the continents. We are separated from our history as by that round of ocean. There is a slow erasure that brings in its wake a starless quiet to the traveller; I go there with Neruda and Lorca to reminisce, to run backwards through lines I've only half forgotten.

'Memory is a literary event,' I murmur, staring down at the keyboard, tracing the lines of a poem on my palm. 'And the blood of children ran through the streets without fuss.'

You spring on the trampoline and I sit here pretending to write, watching you and thinking about the nineties; Neruda would have understood this time of sadness and the death of trees. He would have stood weeping in valleys of bitter rain, dunked his verse in dead oceans, spread his heart across driftnets and crepuscular hopes. It is my conceit to feel he might have loved the stark radiance of our half of the southern sky in the Age of Plagues. Is he so far away from us now, this Neruda? He is just across the curve, on the same latitude of ocean, a parallel descent. In the end, politics overwhelmed him. The fall of Allende broke his heart.

For Monika read grace and beauty. I can put off the moment of having to start writing by flicking through the deck, looking for the right card for her, trying to get that side of it clear. I choose the Queen of Cups, Waite deck, high Rosicrucian style. She sits on her throne staring into her ornate chalice. Around her feet laps water as blue as the Aegean. She is robed in memory and desire, contemplative but self-involved. The Queen of the Throne of the Waters. The power of reception and reflection. She is not so much the queen of history but its dreamer; this symbol of her not so much an idea as a memory. Monika has that elegance, that self-involvement, that capacity to be immersed in her pose. I've seen it in you too when you act the adult.

I can see it in this one; Monika's wearing a long, flowing dress. That must be Spain, 1974. Formentera. Another island. I'm squinting again. On that island, unlike this one, the landscape has overwhelmed its history, subdued its inhabitants to a small, insular people with dark, walnut skin. The inhabitants, history tells, are descendants of those witches and wizards dumped there by the inquisition to die for lack of water. But the witches and wizards survived and with their witchery and wizardry built huge cisterns to catch enough winter rain to last through the dry season. The combination of light and ochre rock on the bare plateau of La Mola makes for an hallucinatory realism. The photograph just about gets it, with Monika looking like a flower growing out of the rock, the Queen of the Throne of the Waters.

That third person in the photograph is Juliet de Bairacli Levy, the famous herbalist and animal doctor, who lived on La Mola with her two Afghan hounds. She hated the hippies because of their drugs, telling me that any substance that widened the pupils of the eye permitted the soul to escape by that route from the body. As parts of the soul escape, holes appear in the aura and the organism becomes open to illness and death. She did her best to cure me of my penchant for mushrooms and cactus, and once saved Monika's life by stopping an infection with a herbal poultice. She was a witch whose soul found affinity with the spirits of the original inhabitants, the wise ones who built the cisterns and planted the fig. Unfortunately her beloved Afghans did not find favour with the descendants of those wise ones: taciturn, dwarfish farmers who, afraid for their sheep, began to shoot at the dogs.

'They're only chasing rabbits,' she told us.

When she left La Mola she put a curse upon the place, saying some great evil resided there and that the hippies would all die of diarrhoea and hepatitis.

That fourth person, standing on the rock beside the Queen of the Throne of the Waters is a genuine ghost, Klaus or Werner or someone, the German who threw himself into one of those cisterns, either by accident or design or a spoon-cooked infusion of both. Probably a terrorist, somebody said, a Baader-Meinhof escapee; but then, all Germans were Baader-Meinhof escapees in those days, everybody was on the run from politics. Everybody was big on paranoia.

There is a fifth person not in the shot; the son of a very famous person. I'll call him Isaac, and he has one immortal line I have to make room for within the blinkered field of the narrative. Isaac is not in the shot because he made sure he was not in it, made sure he was never in any photograph. Crippled from the waist down, he lived in a darkened room of a whitewashed cottage with a large-eyed Catalan girl called Pilar, lying stranded on a bed or sitting in his wheelchair consuming hash and wine, listening to Bloody Dylan, as he called him. We can date that year to Bloody Dylan's seventies epic, *Blood on the Tracks*. When I met Isaac for the first time he was listening to the first song on this album, pounding his fist against the side of his wheelchair. *Now I'm goin' back again, I've got to get to her somehow / All the people we used to know, they're an illusion to me now / Some are mathematicians, some are carpenters' wives / Don't know how all that started, don't know what they're doin' with their lives.*

He repeated this verse aloud in a sarcastic voice when the track finished. 'Bloody Dylan never worked down a mine and had fifty ton of rock fall on his legs,' he said vociferously in a very cultured English accent.

'And what were you doing down a mine?' I wanted to know.

'I was a conscientious objector in the Second World War.'

'He was very drunk last night,' Pilar said quietly. 'He smoke and drink all the time.'

'I've lived here fifteen years,' he told me. 'I know this Fascist Spain as well as my own mother. I want to hear that Bloody Dylan song again. I want to hear that verse about Rimbaud dealing slaves. Rimbaud lived in exile most of his life, you know.'

A few weeks later, around midnight, the doors of Bar Miguel swung open and Isaac entered in a panic, pushing his chair along by the wheels.

'Franco!' he screamed. 'Franco ...'

There was a sudden silence. Miguel himself stood behind the bar by the radio, which was playing military music, his face frozen.

Isaac flung out his arms.

'*Franco ha muerto!*' he screamed. It was his moment in Bar Miguel, his immortal line that brought the news to La Mola.

All the Argentineans without passports started clapping.

I digress, but it's always like this before the writing begins; the evasions and the indulgences. Perhaps a second cup of coffee, a few more moments of quiet observation of my daughter on the trampoline, that's you at eight, looking like your mother. Tomorrow our temporary, unelected Prime Minister, Geoffrey Palmer, will deliver a speech on the meaning of the Treaty of Waitangi. It will be a very predictable speech, I could write it myself for him, if I had the time. I can hear the empty phrases now, ringing in my ear over the shouts of protesters ... *mutual co-operation ... historical opportunity ... hard work ... vision of the future ...*

There's another photograph here somewhere, of what our vision of the future means. Monika, posing on a rock by the sea, Venus-in-a-halfshell position. The rock on which she's standing, probably somewhere around the Kaikoura coast, is covered with the embedded, empty shells of rock oysters. There's a right and a wrong way to take rock oysters off a rock. The correct way, the hardest way, is dig the whole oyster off, leaving the rock clear for a new generation of oysters. The incorrect way is the easier way, just to lever off the top shell, take the meat and leave the inner shell embedded; no new rock oyster can take root there, or ever will be able to take root until someone prises the old shells off.

There's nothing but distraction. I go to put the photo from Formentera aside as possibly useful, along with the Kaikoura shot, when I remember something that was not to be a part of the narrative. A violation sudden and incomprehensible. Monika was raped on that island, by a Catalan who waved money under her nose then took her to his place and raped her at knife-point. I have always felt that rape is that kind of crime in which our most private agonies, and the dreams of the powerless, meet our public dread, our collective horror. We wanted to go to the police, but everybody advised us against it.

'Go to the police, and she get raped again, by police,' Pilar told us.

Take a bus from Skikda or Annaba on the African Mediterranean coast and travel directly south, you pass through a rich coastal plain as fair and wooded as anything in Europe, you pass over the peaks of the *Atlas Saharien* into an increasingly denuded landscape. Finally all plants vanish but thyme, which in turn gives way to a rocky moonscape. Several hours into this granitescape and a strange creature appears on the horizon, a large curved slug, pale and smooth against the weathered rock. A sand dune. Soon there is nothing but dunes, austere and sensual, and several hours into the dunes you come to the doomed town of El Oued, where they have one modern hotel with high-quality tap fittings and no water. If you want a bath an attendant will bring you water in a bucket from the swimming pool.

I've got two shots, one shows me bargaining with the traders for fresh and succulent dates, the arches of El Oued's market in the background; the other shows Monika looking hot and abstracted with Pierre standing to one side. Looking at the queasy Pierre, I realise that this is not El Oued, this background, but Annaba. That uninteresting building behind them is the Lycée Moubarek El Mili. Pierre and I have just dropped by to pick Monika up after work in Pierre's beloved Citroën; after the demands of teaching, her face is still finding its familiar shape.

I could carry this on by finding a card for Pierre and opening up a spread for him.

that wouldn't take long. Here he is, a knight riding through the desert on his black charger, his robe decorated with salamanders. The Lord of Flame and Lightning, Crowley says. The desert is of course, North Africa, his place of banishment from Paris; the black charger is his Citroen, which stood for all that he once had. The salamanders are the gremlins of the world all taking a little piece out of his flesh. He's full speed there under the jagged sky. Seventy kilometres an hour in second gear.

*Y a lo exterior regresan las cosas en ti ocultas.* 'And the things that hide in you come out again.' That line goes with the photograph of Monika and Pierre. Some things stay hidden, some things only photographs bring out. A moment's disarray, perhaps; a memory that passes over the face of being snapped, close as a shag's wing to sea tip. 'I come to speak for your dead mouths,' Neruda says, and Rushdie concurs. The mouths of the dead are full of prayers, he tells me.

Seeing Pierre, so unmistakably French, makes me think about this act of writing coming up, this careful re-creation the cicadas set ticking. Like a public speaker, like Pierre himself, I must appear in correct dress, speak in the proper register which is, as Neruda correctly guessed, the register of dead mouths. Which, in turn, is why literary nostalgia marks the fiction of the nineties; Victorian novels, picaresque novels, Georgian novels, Gothic novels, twenty-first-century novels. Literature becomes one great fancy dress party, verisimilitude of costume the object.

I was going to write a novel or at least some extended fiction with Pierre as the central character. A Parisian architect living in Algeria in declining circumstances; an ideal fictional creation, it would be; ready made. With his oversized raincoat, his grubby shirts and his Latinate English, a wife ill in Paris and a junkie daughter living in Istanbul, forced to move to Algeria and take a job beneath his talents, Pierre appeared at our door with his lines already learned, his costume immaculate, his posture perfected. Pierre, in search of a mistress. Pierre, rather plump, his jowls trembling, behind the wheel of his Citroën.

We got plenty of laughs out of Pierre.

His decline proceeded in appropriately delineated stages. At first he had a good hotel room at the Hôtel de la Paix. There was a view over Annaba and the necessarily sparkling Mediterranean. Pierre could sprawl on his balcony, which was decorated with plump European masonry, and look out wistfully across this sparkling Mediterranean towards Europe, where his dreams were all of Paris with its wide boulevards and elegant cafés under striped awnings; white wine that sparkled like foam; statuesque whores with their black stockings and dyed hair. And history. And culture. He liked to call Annaba by its old French name, Bône, and when he said it, a lilt entered his voice, a note of grandeur. A touch of colonial class.

But with that peremptory suddenness with which change announces itself, he was moved by a polite but implacable staff out of his suite into a tiny room no bigger than a closet. A room with one iron bed and no windows. King Hussein was coming with a large entourage. They would need many rooms. The whole hotel. So Pierre moved to the Hôtel de la Gare, not quite up to the standard of the Hôtel de la Paix, with no balcony or plump masonry.

From then on the movement was towards the threadbare and disreputable, the events of his life assuming a lurid, fictional quality. This is Lawrence Durrell country (almost), where I could lie around smoking hashish and dream of vast literary projects. An *Algerian Quartet* with Pierre as its mysterious central character. An Algerian *Thousand and One Nights* with the Queen of Cups as Scheherazade. Algeria, near enough to Durrell country for the dubious and the shady, like Pierre, to find a brief niche; for an expatriate Frenchman to form a *liaison* with a Bulgarian agronomist who wasn't supposed to be fraternising with the locals, especially the corrupt, bourgeois French. She was a tall, dark woman with amazingly serene eyes. It was a cloak-and-dagger romance with hurried meetings and fast getaways in Pierre's Citroën.

Eventually politics overwhelmed them. Like a proper Frenchman, Pierre lay in his seedy hotel room and dreamed of love. Somebody started following the agronomist. The Citroën became very conspicuous. Pierre took on the shabby appearance of a hunted man, a man with forked eyes. They came to lunch one day so that Pierre could introduce us. We sat under the spreading bougainvillaea drinking expensive French wine and discussing the deteriorating state of affairs in North Africa.

'I am here,' Pierre said, spearing a piece of asparagus, 'back in 1960, during the war of independence. Things were different then.' I knew he was thinking of his employers, Algerians, who took every opportunity to do him down.

They left suddenly, halfway through the meal, Pierre's knife and fork clattering onto the table. I'd had enough wine to have become interested in the latest developments in agronomy in Bulgaria when, abruptly, Monika and I were left alone at the table facing four meals and four half-drunk glasses of wine. (I lie, Pierre's was empty.)

'Bloody old Pierre,' Monika said and laughed mirthlessly, leaning back in her chair.

'I wonder what role he played here, during the war,' I said thoughtfully, narrowing my eyes. My vast literary project took a new turn; Pierre was being hunted as a war criminal by a fanatical Muslim sect secretly backed by the Bulgarian government.

The light was falling all around us. It jangled off the plates and the glasses; a strong mellow light that brought out the colour in everything.

'Bloody old Pierre,' Monika said again, looking around the table.

As befitting any character of such fiction, Pierre took to consorting in the evenings with seedy criminal types. Those who hung out in the run-down cafés that littered the backstreets and alleys of Annaba, clandestinely drinking wine. He couldn't stay in his hotel room at night, he told us. It was far too depressing. Already his writer, I pictured him in his dingy room, somewhat overweight, lying sweating on his narrow bed, twisting and turning in an effort to feel comfortable in the body. During this phase he was always sweating.

The agronomist disappeared, one day simply failing to turn up for an assignation. There was something very predictable about it, he told us, very mundane. At any moment anyone might disappear in a place like this; it wouldn't pay to make inquiries. A Gallic shrug of the shoulders. A suggestion of pain and hurt around the mouth. I perceived then, in literary terms, that a broken heart, or something approaching it, was an essential way-station on Pierre's downward path. An essential ingredient of a Poor Pierre syndrome that gave a helplessness to his shrugs and justified the bottle of wine

(French, if he could get it) purchased from marginal acquaintances to take back to his room for comfort.

It was then that he produced the sick wife in Paris with more apologetic shrugs, a reluctant conjurer of all the right elements of disaster. She was to visit soon. When I thought about it, I saw that a sick wife in Paris (with the nature of the illness made properly vague) was fitting, inevitable even. With his every shrug he lifted his past up and down on his shoulders. Why hadn't I thought of it in the first place? She would have a high-rise apartment in one of these new areas of standard urban development, her life one of monotony and illness. This sick wife was part of a larger package, including the daughter on drugs in Istanbul who would become a major character in the *Algerian Quartet*; she would practise a sort of — the details were not clear — soporific abstraction from the plot, providing a new and surprising angle on the action in my Durellian gameplan. Character, Durrell counseled, is a function of landscape.

This sick wife came and stayed and went away again. He brought her to see us and she sat in frozen immobility, staring out towards the sound of the sea. Her face reminded me of the worn-away concrete visage of the cat/lion that stood by our door, features scoured to the indistinguishable. When I saw how long it took her to get her cup from the table to her lips, I got some inkling of what this 'illness' might be. There's many a slip between cup and lip, I thought, watching the slow, trembling ascent; and she is passing through each one of them, each possible slip, each lapful of hot tea the way a sleepwalker would ascend a staircase with no railings in some Escher diagram. I guessed Valium, or something stronger. Voluntary exile.

Pierre spoke about her and in front of her in English, which she couldn't understand. When he laughed she moved her head up and down like a marionette.

Of course, photographs are a distraction; history is a distraction; the narrative must burrow off into the past, seeking connections, something to share. We can still get a laugh out of Pierre. We have to go back fifteen years to get it, to a time when there was no you to bounce on the trampoline, no separation behind us, no broken treaty, no savagery and disillusionment; and the sadness of Neruda belonged to others. *Llevo en mano la paloma que duerme reclinada en la semilla*, 'I carry in my hand the dove that sleeps recumbent in the seed.'

In the light of this it's not surprising Pierre comes to represent something metaphorical. He lends himself to notions of the transitory, the entropic. Algeria, itself a symbol of French defeat, a hotel room with its Albert Camus view. A man with a body like a battered suitcase and a portable past; Pierre the disposable memory. Not so much a person as a walking syndrome. And a little of his angst rubs across on us, even now.

Pierre himself was not insensible to the symbolic weight of his position; that aspect was all a part of the lament. It helped bring out the sweat, the unease. In the end he shot through, as we knew he would, harried by the authorities on account of his Citroën, which was all that remained of his Paris status now both wife and agronomist were gone. *Do you have a proper permit for the vehicle? How long have you had it in the country, monsieur? May we have a look at your work permit, again, please? We're terribly sorry but you will have to take this car out of the country. Why? Because the stamp in your passport covering the vehicle has expired. Surely you are aware that such permits only last six months. No* (an eloquent shrug), *it cannot be stamped in Annaba. Why? No office for such a stamping exists; no such stamp exists except at the borders. It is a border stamp. It's really very simple, monsieur. The permit has expired. No amount of protestations or sweating will make any difference. Special permission? There might be a chance if you go to Algiers, to the Minister of the Interior, but of course you can't take your car there. Why? Because* (a touch of impatience) *your vehicle has no permit. It is an illegal vehicle, in fact. Illegal vehicles get impounded, surely monsieur knows that. Anyway, Tunisia is only two hundred miles away. Already there is a lot to pay.*

*Monsieur.*

To begin with I thought he'd be an ideal subject for fiction and that my *Algerian Quartet* would grow, as it were, out of the cuffs of his shabby shirts. Scenes would spring up out of his characteristic mannerisms; but when I came to do the writing I realised I had made a mistake. I had fondly imagined, in the fondness of golden Mediterranean evenings, that he would more or less write his own part. The landscape was already there, I didn't have to imagine it: the dingy backstreets, the smoke-stained coffee houses, the drug parlours, poverty in all its public vulnerability; Pierre, in true Durrellian fashion, an extension of that background. Part of the light and shade on Avenue de la Révolution. Through these streets his curved-nosed Citroën would glide as through a made-to-order dream. But in the writing, what writing there was, I discovered a peculiar and irritating feature of Pierre's personality: he was already fictionalised.

He could not take a second layer of fictionalising. There was no way of presenting him without having him seem to step straight from the pages of a Sartre or Camus story. 'I eat,' he once told us, lamenting his weight, 'to compensate for the mediocrity of life'; a line I couldn't fit into any dialogue or have come out sounding less than contrived. He fitted the bill perfectly. Too perfectly. It is conceivable that Pierre had read it somewhere, filing it away for use at an appropriate moment. A life that lampoons art as grossly as Pierre's makes for gross art. Eventually I came to see him as a caricature, a half-realised literary fragment in a long, drab overcoat with a round, sweating face. He would stand in front of me as I paused over the page, his passport in his hand, pointing to the expired vehicle permit, his jowls quivering with indignation.

*Illegal vehicles get impounded. Surely monsieur knows that.*

*Already there is a lot to pay.*

The moment in the hammam; there has to be room for it. Stories are built on the fiction of moments, character on the fiction of self, but it is the body that fascinates. Form, line and feel. While we can forget everything else if we try, it's hard to forget the body.

In the cool of the evening Monika steps up into the hammam. It's a good way to see her, in those few moments of rich, mellow light, walking up the ancient stone steps, looking forward to getting really clean for the first time in days, already feeling something of that easy sensuality of a clean body.

A woman meets her at the entrance-way and stares at her for a few moments before gesturing her through a door; she finds herself in a grotto full of nooks and stone caves hung with patches of steam and littered about with the naked bodies of women, twenty or thirty of all shapes and sizes. Warm water runs across shallow pools in the floor where more women lie, allowing the water to trickle across their bodies. As soon as Monika enters they fall silent with one accord, as if everyone had been watching the door at the same moment. All heads turn in her direction.

She turns to her guide, who, without looking at her, shows her where she might place her clothes. Then Monika understands. French women never come here. They clean their bodies in the privacy of their own bathrooms, even if bellboys have to run back and forward with buckets of water from the swimming pool, rather than display their Christian bodies to the Muslims. Most of these bathers will never have seen a naked foreign woman.

Suddenly very self-conscious indeed, she removed her long skirt and light jacket, leaving on her knickers and a brief top.

The silence intensifies. No one says anything as Monika places her skirt and jacket on the rack indicated, no one's face reveals anything except that of a pretty young woman just past puberty who holds her hand up to her mouth. There's no way she's going to step out of her last bits without everybody seeing.

Turning, she faces them. It is too late for any other course, already the damp heat is working on her skin, sending a trickle of moisture from her armpits down her sides, flushing her skin of tiny grains of sand and prickling her breasts with beads of sweat. With unhurried movements she takes off her top and knickers and faces her audience, standing with her legs a little apart, her arms by her sides.

Standing there, showing herself to these silent women in that marble and sandstone grotto, she feels the political and historical weight of a women's nudity, its fact as flesh and fetish.

Here I am, her body says to them, meeting their stares in all its slender paleness, showing them the line of breast and thigh, buttock and back. Here I am, with all the usual aspects in the usual places. Just the same as you.

Maybe not so fat.

We must have jumped four years. The jacaranda and flame trees are in bloom. You can see them in the background along the Whakatane River. When this was taken we were walking along the old river course admiring the red and blue flowers, pushing you along in front of us, taking turns, watching the sky turn from pink to mauve and from mauve to violet. We were in the mood for taking photographs and remembering deserts. Now and then, a petal with its small freight of twilight would float poetically past, with you providing the gurgling baby noise behind. The trampoline was only a distant twinkle in your eye. We paused to look at the willows dragging at stagnant reflections, the way willows should. A poem arrived as a small, hollow feeling in the pit of my stomach. Algeria was very far away.

This moment had been lying in wait for Monika and me, for all three of us. It was there, even as we sat under the bougainvillaea drinking French wine and talking to

Pierre. I don't like the thought of time lying in wait, the notion of moments waiting to spring out at us from behind some ordinary action such as a walk by the river or on the beach. Since he's dead I can't ring Pablo Neruda and talk about it, but if I am very quiet I can hear his ghostly voice, whispering.

'What is this I'm feeling?' I whisper back. 'I feel like a child, abandoned. I'll never want to write these passages.'

'Cold flowerheads are raining over your heart,' Neruda's hushed reply comes. A cool, spidery voice. *'No es sino el paso de un dia hacia otro. It is only the passage of one day towards another.'*

He must be talking of datura, the moonflower. When I think of Neruda, Monika's face becomes a home of shadows. In the photograph, you are seen kicking restlessly in your pushchair. I remember a gull passing overhead, high up, crying, *alack! alack!*

'What was it I wanted?' I breathe back to him, holding the photograph with both hands, as if I'm going to rip it down the middle.

'To throw yourself like a dove of mourning and snow upon a body,' the whisper returns. 'That you might join your wolf steps to the steps of man.'

Thinking of this, I look at Monika. I could come no closer, approaching some hidden place she lived in her mind. I approached as a trespasser, a thief in the night. Although I stepped carefully choosing my words, I was in the place of stumbling with her. The poem enlarged the hollow in my abdomen.

*Alack! Alack!* Neruda was too close for comfort. Our memories could not hold us together. I wanted the poem to be mine.

Like Pierre and his manufactured French self, the willows are a temptation to false creation; they drag too authentically at the stagnant water. That's why they were planted, to do our weeping for us far from home. A dragonfly ignites the green scum. Something flickers across the glazed surface. The poem hides with you in the shadow.

For Monika, walking by the river bank, there was silence here, also, but it was not like the intense silence of the hammam, focused and socially charged; here it was the silence of the perpetual present; *las viejas hélices del crepescúlo*. The spin of light and emptiness. Neruda took the best lines.

> *The great roots of night*
> *Grow suddenly from your soul*
> *And things that hide in you come out again*
> *So that a blue and pallid people*
> *Your newly born, takes nourishment.*

Eleanor kicked at the water. A blue flame hovered over the marsh. A crack opened up in my chest; I wanted to decipher the calligraphy of branches on the water. Of course I did. The calligraphy of a moment in which love dies. For no particular reason, nor crime incurred. Just dies. Among the hanging willows and the gulls. I picked you up to calm you, tossing you up and down. Nothing had happened, but I was already living my future grief at being parted from you. I was living out a moment on a beach I hadn't yet seen. The same gull was working, high up, where there was still light. The poem was searching for a way through.

*Alack! Alack!*

*Mater dolorosa.* I have seen them on the beaches of Italy and Greece. The maenads who tore to pieces Pentheus. We see her face in storms, hear her voice call from valley to valley. The Empress. Note the open lotus in her right hand; a gown decorated with pomegranates. Her name is the Daughter of the Mighty Ones; 'that through which something passes', it says in my dictionary of the Tarot. 'Passage', 'transition', I write on a piece of paper. I make a paper dart and watch its nomad flight through the air.

*Mater dolorosa.* Words spoken out of the stars of love; the wisdom of understanding.

She who is also capable of terrible anger and awesome violence. Mother of earthquakes.

Out of her robes Monika stepped on the way from the kitchen to the bathroom, heading for your room. She passed into the hall, a grim line around her mouth. She is the seed in the darkness of night, it says here, love between mental complements, that which produces works of art or devours her children.

Bit by bit, the house had lost its neutrality. The kitchen had lost its neutrality. Eventually the bedroom started to take sides. The closet got in on the act, favouring her clothes over mine. We passed each other on the way from the kitchen to the bathroom, her going the other way, a poem sliding around inside my hand, her looking in the other direction.

We were trying to come to grips with it. The power of the mind and its complements, the card tells us. I had a copy of 'If you meet Buddha on the road, kill him', but gave it away because I hated the title. I still hate it. The poem was feeling its way toward my fingers, a tiny child of words. It didn't have any jacaranda blossoms of stagnant reflections, but Monika was in it. The gull survived.

Whakatane was there, outside the world of bathroom, kitchen and bedroom, drifting into the Pacific, crunching plates with South America. Treaties and betrayals. The strange language I didn't recognise on the street was Maori.

It was the time of the Springbok tour, politics was overwhelming us; we passed each other in the lounge heading for the bedroom, or the bedroom heading for the lounge, or the kitchen heading for the bathroom, trying to piece it together, loops of time, asking if we couldn't stay together after all, even while flying apart. We were flying apart with no sensation of flying apart, passing each other on the way to the bathroom or the bedroom, eyes averted, making coffee, smoking cigarettes, facing that the moment of decision had already passed, unnoticed and unrecorded, scratched on the face of some hour we let slip in the general letting slip of things. Maybe even in Athens or Algeria or Rome or Delhi. Some foreign place.

This was an un-mating dance full of silences and rapid, disconnected speech.

We were home. This was Aotearoa.

I told her I thought Pierre might be used obliquely in a shorter piece of fiction in which he would occur merely as an incidental, a stepping-stone on the way somewhere else. A fitting enough end for him. The only problem being I would have to change his character somewhat to make him plausible, an odd conundrum, but he would serve. At a pinch he would serve. He would sit beneath the bougainvillaea and have his moment of glory. Monika looked at me then as if she were seeing me for the first time. I saw the shock pass over her face. I wanted to shut myself away from a look like that, to hide in the bathroom or the bedroom. It is the hard look offered a stranger when they ask you for a light and you are living in a foreign land with an expired visa. I wanted to get up and put on the jug, clatter some cups (an oddly warm, human sound), put on a record, read a poem ('alone in the loneliness of this hour of the dead'), search out a cigarette. Get stoned. If you had not been asleep I'd have talked to you in jostling, infant syllables, just as I'm doing now.

Walking from the lounge into the kitchen, it struck me that I was as absurd as Pierre, walking back and forth, waking in the morning in windowless rooms head thick with last night's wine, waiting for light, waiting for nothing at all, not even the dog speech of morning, unnoticed and unrecorded, passing Monika in the kitchen, caught up in this thing we couldn't put down. Wanting to fill the moments between the other moments, thinking about flame trees and reflections, about making a quick getaway, teased by the fictional surface, the linking and weaving, not recognising her, passing her on the way to the kitchen or bedroom. 'I was alone like a tunnel,' the master says.

'The things that hide in you come out again.'

You were screaming your head off, red in the face; Monika was passing me as she went from the kitchen to your room, your bottle tucked under her arm.

In a few days Nelson Mandela will be released from a South African prison where he has been incarcerated for twenty-seven years for crimes against the state. It will only take him a moment, no longer than a second, to step from the shadow of the prison to the light of the street. A moment like any other.

Everywhere, it seems, power is in retreat. But politics is not. East Berliners now cart home pieces of the wall as souvenirs or sell them to foreigners. And what has happened to this naive, opportunistic capitalistic impulse? The state has taken it over and is running it as a monopoly, organising the sale and distribution of pieces of the Wall. Taken out of politics, they are just ordinary pieces of wall, within the narrative of politics, they are a testimony of some kind. Like splinters of wood from the Holy Cross. With politics and literature it is the same, everything becomes a testimony, and every thoughtless, foolish word evidence.

What can Mandela do but walk out of the prison and be swallowed by history? I sit here on Waiheke (another island) and think of the Springbok tour of '81 and a house in Whakatane that consisted of endless kitchens, halls and bedrooms in one restless, shuffle-through scene.

We have to live through the beach scene yet, I think with dread. Thank God I haven't started writing. Nothing's committed, nothing's irrevocable. In art, as in politics, everything needs to be centrally organised around a guiding principle. All for the sake of a democracy of ends every scene, every word, must pass before a bureaucracy of purpose where it is tested for fitness against stringent criteria. But in this loose moment before the writing begins, anything might happen, everything does happen. The Wall comes down. Mandela is released. The Communist Party of the Soviet Union dismantles itself. The dead are resurrected in Tiananmen Square. Ceausecsu gets back into his coffin and closes the lid. Monika and I wake up in the morning in the same bed with a child between us. A poem comes in from the cold. A house in Whakatane replicates itself through bedrooms, bathrooms and kitchens. Tribal elders wend their way to Waitangi, hoping for a miracle. A black man steps from the shadow of the prison into the streets. Another man sits at a blank page and tries to recall how a woman looked at him ten years ago; like politics, it seemed important at the time.

*

Like the traditional unquiet ghost, I return to the Whakatane house; whoever lives there now must sometimes feel my shadow passing over their skin, or pause a shade too long when a gull cries. At least I like to think of it that way. Once I reach the house, I pass through its endless kitchens (where radios are blurting a commentary of the first Springbok test), bathrooms and bedrooms to find myself sitting in my study, door shut, arm around my notebook the way I used to hold it at school when I would hide my large, dyslexic printing from prying eyes.

I'm sitting at my desk, my arm protectively around my notebook, hoarding the poem, saving it up for the page. I can sit this way for an hour with nothing passing through my head but the dazzle of time, whispering to myself in a strange tongue, juggling the pen against my teeth, holding the words open for the poem.

Yes, yes, it might work, this.

At the same time I note I am subconsciously following Monika around the house as she moves from the lounge to the bedroom to your room, ever turning the domestic wheel. I travel with her, see the rooms fold out in front of her and close in behind; I take your baby bottle from the jug and hold it against my wrist while the poem passes through me and whispers onto the page line by line. Eventually the bed gives a disgruntled squeak as Monika falls into it. The lamp on my desk throws a square of light onto the driveway and the hedge. I hear her restlessly turning the pages of a book. I wait for you to sleep and I smoke in the silence. I can't find the last line of the poem and begin searching for it along the bookcase, under the spare single bed, out the window in the oblong dark, behind the wardrobe, along the autobahns of Germany and the sparkle of the Mediterranean. This silence has a material, tangible quality, oozing from the artefacts in my room. One is a crystal I am assured has healing properties. Held to the light, it is a rock full of rooms.

On the shelf above my desk sit the peculiar 'rock roses' of Algeria, aggregates of sand that grow in a crystalline formation. We dug them up with our own hands from the sands of the Sahara. As I look at this fragment the last line of the poem comes to me. I bear it back to the page the way a child carries a glassful of water. When I arrive I find another last line already there, where it should be, written down. The last line so carefully carried to the page is superfluous; the line I was searching for, a chimera.

Europe is like a motorised museum. Passing through the Ruhr is like travelling through the ruins of a civilisation already ancient, already on a par with the carefully preserved ruins of the Romans. In Köln the venal splendour of the old Roman baths vie with the smokestacks of an industrial faith. Everything is greying and fading. Everything is being eaten away by smoke and acidity, and therefore everything belongs to one standard, past time. The time before this.

It is no longer a landscape we were driving through but a smokescape, a whirl of shifting particles through which can be glimpsed, at odd intervals, patches of forlorn countryside or huddled, red-bricked towns.

'Do you realise that is our ancestral homeland?' I gestured out the window. 'The Germanic heartland of the mind. Ha ha. This is where our roots go. Black Americans have to go to Africa to discover their source. We come here. Isn't it an intensely moving experience?'

Monika was looking out the window with a shocked look on her face. There was a grim set of her mouth I had never seen before.

'Did you know,' I said cheerfully, 'that more than ten per cent of German forests are dead? The exact percentage is not known. It could be twenty per cent by now. They're dying from acid rain. When the forest dies, the spirit dies. *Das Innenleben ist dann tort.* No more Hansel and Gretel. Soon the people will start to die.'

I stopped to take a photograph.

Although we were driving through one of the most densely populated areas of Europe, there was a vacated, empty feeling about the random slices of countryside we glimpsed, as if it had all been abruptly deserted with the smokestacks still smoking, the clocks still flicking from second to second, the elevators still sliding up and down inside office blocks and shopping complexes; a whole culture abandoned in mid-flight. A monstrous *Marie Celeste*. Everything here belonged to pre-history, post-history.

'I don't ever want to have children,' Monika said distinctly. 'I don't want them to grow up in a future that looks like this.'

There was a new grimness around her mouth. I'd go on seeing it, even when it wasn't there.

'Things are probably better in North Africa,' I said.

The smog swirled around us like confetti.

*Roma.* City of histories. It was a hot, windless day when they got the bus to Via Dei Fori Imperiali to have a look at the famous Colosseo. They began arguing as soon as they got off the bus.

Monika wanted to go through the Foro Romano (noble ruin) to the Via Dei Cerchi, down to the Piazza Di Porta Capena and back up to the Colosseo by way of Di S. Gregorio. Michael said that was a silly idea and that they should immediately look over the Colosseo, since it was right there in front of them. Then they could go to the Foro Romano, and, if they really felt like walking, they could get onto the Corso Vittorio Emanuel and walk up to the Citta del Vaticano. Michael had always wanted to see St Peter's.

They stood there sweating stubbornly and gazing at their tourist maps. Then Monika moved off, hips swinging defiantly, towards the Foro Romano, determined to make it alone despite the warnings about thieves, pickpockets and con-men. Michael turned his back (why should he care?) and walked over to the Colosseo, deciding to sit and wait for her or, better still, take off on his own somewhere and give her the fright she deserved. He had time to reflect on how obdurate her arse looked as she moved off down the Corso whatever-the-hell-it-was.

The smell of cats soon drove Michael out of the Colosseo and he decided to walk down the Via Di S. Gregorio to meet her. He got to the Piazza Di Porta Capena and looked up the Via Dei Cerchi, but she was nowhere to be seen. Somebody that looked like her turned off to the Circo Massimo. He walked around that monstrously baroque monument until he surprised a woman with a flared red dress and black shining hair, who was not Monika. She gave him a dark, lustrous look that probably didn't mean anything and walked away. Then he saw Monika standing by the Ponte Palatino so he made his way there, walking faster now. It's not love but panic that counts, he thought.

When he got to the river, with its dull, concreted banks, she was gone. Instead there was a Communist demonstration, calling for a more just and equitable society. Many people marched past, their faces flushed, shouting. There was colour everywhere and lots of red. A vehicle drove in front of them with the top down and a man with a loud-hailer haranguing the streets. Michael paused, entranced, remembering his own demonstration days in Cathedral Square protesting the Vietnam War. The last days of *the Holyoake years*, for God's sake. They would demonstrate then retire to the Gresham to drink and line up a partner for the night, preferably one still hot from protest. Everybody fucked after a protest, it was as natural as the second beer.

He stopped to light a cigarette and thought about it, suddenly dizzy from heat and slogans. A peculiar sense of exaltation took hold of him; his heart bumped unsteadily against his ribs, as they say in stories. His groin tingled. He had this vision of arriving back at the hotel on Via Vittorio and finding her gone. As simple as picking up a backpack. Suddenly small and grandly alone, he watched the tide of people washing back and forth over the bridge.

He had the sensation of waking as after a long, deep sleep, and wandered along the river around the Lungo-Tevere de Cenci with hardly a thought in his head, noticing nothing. He sat down at an open-air café to a *cappuccino* with the fantasy that all his money was gone, all his clothes were gone. Everything. No identity; to not remember who he was or where he came from. No job, no history, no past, no future. No country. If anyone asked him who he was he would tell them. 'I am a device,' he would say. 'A means for perpetuation from one moment to the following moment.' The coffee was heavy and sweet. He smoked rough, filterless Italian tobacco and the smoke burned his throat.

He walked on, hardly feeling the fall of his feet on the pavement. Past the bridges, the Ponte Garibaldi, the Ponte Sisto, the Ponte Mazzini and finally to the Ponte Vittorio Emanuel. In the distance he could see the S. Pietro in Vaticano, recognising the route they had tentatively mapped out.

Rome ballooned into a big city; beyond the tiny triangle they'd traced with their fingers lay a huge sprawl of streets in which they would never find each other. And beyond lay a world as full of cities as Rome was of streets. One moment of inattention and they were lost, quite lost; three or four years of relationship down the tubes of Via this or Corso del that. A frightening, exhilarating thought.

As he wandered along, hardly aware now where he was or to which part of town he was heading, he found he was in the course of his meditations as it were, following the person in front of him. A young woman in red plastic high-heeled shoes and hip-high jeans. As soon as he noticed this she became aware she was being followed and immediately sat down at an open-air café. He took the table next to hers and played the game of watching her while pretending to smoke and drink coffee. He had no particular reason for doing this, any more than a child does when it plays at not stepping on the cracks. Soon he became bold and ordered wine. He didn't order the wine for any purpose other than to get drunk and sit out the dazzle of the afternoon, *Vino tinto, per favore!*, and dream grandiose literary projects. A great hymn to beauty. A Roman trilogy. The woman had dark blonde hair and a suede jacket. Her whole outfit was neatly put together and he decided she'd do as a minor character. A walk-on, walk-off part. Maybe one line. One parting shot. Suddenly she turned to him. Her eyes glinted like polished greenstone. Contact lenses, he figured out later.

'Have you lost something, pal?' she said in a hard, American voice.

As departing obdurate arse, Monika comes off okay, but I don't give much for Michael's chances. He's neither the sort of hero I would have chosen nor does he have the name I'd have given myself, and I trust I can write him out in the first draft or so. Writers are supposed to have some sympathy for their characters, and this is not always feigned, but loyalty is another matter. Catch him walking slowly back to the hotel in Rome, knowing Monika will be there waiting for him; catch him sitting under the bougainvillaea in Annaba drinking illicit wine; catch him walking all night under the influence of mushrooms, following the full moon across the stone fields of La Mola; catch him anywhere and you'll find him letting this or that important thing slide. A missed opportunity there. A failure of nerve somewhere else. A chronic sense of unworthiness. Why should such a character have any claim on my loyalty, or demand special dispensation, especially when that character has no necessary case for admittance to the text, no automatic right of inclusion? I can see it's easy for the clean lines of a story to be muddied by a character like that; there are so many temptations. If I had been Michael, I would have handled that whole Roman incident quite differently. I would have got on a bus to somewhere, or a train to somewhere else and changed my whole life.

I wanted to recall Algeria. Soon the Mediterranean, Pierre, then Abdul Aziz, became an obsession; the sunlight on the sea at the Whakatane River mouth, the long, wild stretch of Piripai, made me nostalgic. Pablo Neruda made me nostalgic, being able to write the most shatteringly valedictory lines. Everything was saying farewell. The electric jug said farewell to the standard lamp and the standard lamp said farewell to his upmarket friend, the stereo.

Our home assumed the aspect of a busy motel. As all the chattels and domestic objects said their farewells, they became impersonal, retreating behind their functions. Meaning emptied out. Monika departed with you, and I no longer heard your child sounds around the place, just an echo of them in a toy left behind or a pile of nappies. Now the house was like my study, a tomb of words; already there was someone else. Michael was back in love, the world would never be the same.

Monika was gone. Alone, I moved from the kitchen to the lounge and up to your room. I stood at your empty cot for a time listening the way one does at a gravestone. I wanted to hear the sound of you, the breathing of you, the small, high noises children make in sleep. I was half expecting to hear the cry of a gull above the house: *alack! alack!* Your cot appeared to rock gently in the shadows. 'There I was without a face and it touched me,' Neruda said. I began to touch the secret body of my grief.

Poems were starting to come in rapid bursts. Each line was a painful awakening to words. Each word a tiny cold star on my palm. Love came up out of the lines to catch me in the chest. I threw myself into the wild Muehlenbeckia that grows along the Piripai dunes and watched the net of stars over Whale Island.

I sang chorus after chorus of 'Summertime' to the empty cot.

Michael checked his passport.

I've just found the Lord of the Waves and the Waters. He is a knight, wearing a winged helmet, riding over a desert towards the river and mountains. His arms are tattooed with red fish. At first I thought he might stand for Michael, the winged helmet being properly suggestive, but I quickly perceived Abdul Aziz was the man I was looking at. A stranger, sailor, man coming from far away: drugs, merchants of the same. A dreamer haunted in his vision.

Aziz came to me straight out of the Old Testament; an ordinary man, a postal clerk, with dark Bedouin eyes. A man whose loneliness had made him generous. Michael and Monika went down with hepatitis, and for seven weeks there was nothing to read in the house in English but the Bible. Too weary for modern, barbarous tongues, Michael made for the rich diversity of King James' English, reading the Old Testament through twice, lying on a rubber mat on top of an old door on a concrete floor.

Abdul Aziz arrived bearing clean, uncontaminated water. Michael and Monika gazed at one another through a yellow fog, just strong enough to crawl out the door into the sunlight. Aziz took them on a drive up into the hills where the air was cool and clear. Up there, Michael could drink mineral water and look weakly out towards Annaba on the coast, thinking of regeneration. He was weak but prepared, somehow independent. His encounter with severe illness, watching Monika's skeleton stretching out of her body like one of Isaiah's curses, had brought about not so much a change of nature, as it might in Victorian fiction, but a certain lessening of resistance to the facts. Soon they'd be leaving this cursed Barbary Coast and returning to New Zealand. He was prepared.

There is, he decided, in the human male of his culture at least, a long second adolescence which usually dissipates itself somewhere in middle age with some messy mid-life crisis; he was just thirty-two, he could avoid all that bullshit. He could work it out.

The afternoon quietened in mellowness. They sat alone outside the sleek, modern, whitewashed hotel and watched the blue wash of the sky darken to indigo, the scratching of the tall, native pines against it. He thought of the bulk of desert to the south. Aziz had himself a discreet beer and told them of his life. Born in the desert, he had spent many years in France, and he freely confessed that his job at the Annaba post office did not satisfy him.

As the light further mellowed and Aziz got started on his second beer, he showed them the scars on the inside of his arm where the French had tortured him during the war of independence. On that day, history caught up with him. Michael had never seen politics inscribed so clearly on a man's body; never seen such visible evidence of human impotence. Yet Aziz bore no bitterness towards the French; a typical coastal Algerian, he was as much French as Arabic. He demonstrated cheerfully with his own cigarette how they pushed the flowing tips of theirs into the flesh where the veins are. While he spoke of the incident he smoked several cigarettes. Michael thought of Pierre. Could the morbidly sensitive Frenchman have done something like this, been a torturer?

One could only look at the scars on the Arab's arm for so long before they became very ordinary, crepuscular blotches, Michael decided. He felt humbled by it all.

As the amber light settled in around them, Aziz tearfully admitted his life had been an empty one. The wings on his helmet I see as his aspirations, his frail destiny. Aspirations he nourished with no hope of fulfilment. He envied them, he confessed, for their easy mobility, their ability to travel. He would like to travel. To go to England was an old dream, inescapably the dream of a postal clerk in Annaba. England he associated with honour and courtesy, with courtly values. Michael tried to tell him about perfidious Albion and a land-grab masked by a fraudulent treaty. Aziz just shook his head. Fraudulent treaties were nothing to what the French were capable of. Like his own arm, the Algerian war was not so much a war as a series of atrocities.

Yes, give him travel. The Pacific! How he would love to see the Pacific! But behind this aspiration, deeper embedded in his loneliness and thirst, there was a yearning to enter that quasi-mystical state of union and love with a woman; to know what that blessed state was, denied him by the history and circumstances of his own marriage, his time and place.

Michael wanted to know the story of that marriage, but this called not just for another beer but a bottle of whisky, for, Aziz explained, it was the kind of story that could not emerge without one, and was therefore the kind of story he did not tell very often.

The bottle of whisky, Michael was given to understand, was some sort of literary device; both prop and prompter as required, the contents would empty as the story filled. Procuring it, however, involved some negotiation with shadowy figures, a lot of rapid speech in Arabic and the passing over of a considerable amount of money. Michael wondered how much this story had cost him, over the years.

He married a traditional Bedouin girl from the desert, from the tents, he said, as he ceremoniously opened the bottle and poured himself a tot. It was a real Bedouin wedding, held in a small town in the middle of the Sahara. He had only seen his bride once, briefly, at her house (she had been permitted to walk slowly past a doorway and back again), and, being young and completely ignorant, he approached his older brother on the morning of his wedding to ask what he should do that night. His brother was preparing to slaughter a goat for the coming nuptials. He'd marked the beast with a piece of red chalk and was looking for a bucket.

'Tie her up and take her by force,' his brother advised, placing the bucket underneath the goat's neck. 'The old women can fix it up in the morning.' This gnomic utterance filled him with dread. What would the old women fix? He'd heard tales of chicken blood on sheets, and of the men of the woman's family standing at the door of the bridal chamber, assessing from her cries of pain the virility of the groom. Afterwards, she would have to tell a woman in her family, an aunt or grandmother, how copious her husband's sperm was; reassurance on this point would bring smiles all around. A man with a plenitude of sperm would have a large, healthy family. If he wished, she could be circumcised, but that would cost him.

His brother's knife flashed in the sun. Before it landed the goat squinted up at Aziz, its pale eyes blank. Blood squirted into the bucket.

He was too terrified to ask advice from anyone else.

The wedding festivities were long and arduous with many flowery speeches from both families and much eating and dancing. During the ceremony his bride, of course, was so heavily veiled he could not see her face. Finally, in a state of nervous exhaustion and trembling with fear and dread, he was led to the small room the happy couple had been assigned for the night. He went through the door and closed it behind him, not before catching a glimpse of burnoused figures hovering nearby in the moonlight. These were in-laws, the brothers and cousins of his wife, who would wait silent and unmoving near the door. He knew now the stories were true — he had an hour or two at the most to prove his manhood.

Upon closing the door he found himself in almost a total darkness but for a glimmer of light that fell through a small high window. That meagre, silvery glow fell on a small, frightened face turned in his direction. She was no more than a child, pressed against the opposite wall.

He stood paralysed by the door.

'Help me,' he whispered across the room. 'I don't know what to do.'

At that point in the story Aziz stopped as if he didn't want to finish, making a great show of lighting his cigarette and checking the level of the whisky; but it was, I believe, more of a storyteller's dramatic pause than anything else. If this had been a nineteenth-century novel they were hearing, they might have been treated to a dissertation upon Bedouin morals and manners, or a detailed description of contemporary Arabic fashions.

'What happened next?' they urged him. 'What did you do?'

He gave a slow, sad smile and lifted the drink to his lips, taking a long draught before answering.

'I took her by force,' he answered simply.

Finding nothing with which to tie her down, the room containing only a bed, a table, and a pitcher of water, he turned to the small frightened face, able now to make out the slim body huddling into itself. As he approached, driven by the thought of the silent burnoused figures outside, she drew away, back along the wall, away from even the wan, diffuse light from the high window. Her timidity awoke in him a desperate rage. He stood in front of her, his body trembling. 'I don't know what to do,' he repeated. It was true he'd seen goats doing it, and dogs, but how could that help him now? Now that he was utterly subjugated, utterly humiliated?

She turned her face away from him, but her eyes stayed on his, huge and terrified. She was wearing a long gown, tied loosely at her neck and waist. Looking at the graceful line of her neck where it vanished into the gown, he thought of the goat his brother slew the day before, the hard, blank light that shone in its eyes the moment before its throat was cut, and a terrible rage burned in his hands. He stepped forward, and as he did so he felt the pressure of innumerable hands pushing him from behind. Male hands, the hands of her brothers, his and her father, his male ancestors, her male ancestors, all stood behind him grinning. *Take her by force.*

He took the gown and tore it apart in one fluent gesture, finding beneath the body of an adolescent girl, pale and shaking, opening up to his eyes in a swoon of terror.

Her helplessness, her passivity, enraged him still further. This holy wrath took over his body with hot hands. It was only then, he related sadly, in the grip of that violence, that he discovered his male instincts. In that fury, he said, his body knew what to do, which was first to beat her until she cried out. When her first cry rang out, a savage sense of triumph took hold of him and his erection became painfully swollen. He understood what it was her brothers wanted; it was to hear this very cry, this wailing evidence that she had been properly taken, properly subdued by her husband. These same brothers, who a few weeks ago would have cut throats, his included, to preserve the honour and the virginity of their sister, now, in spirit at least, filed into the room to watch silently from beneath their cowls as that same sister, pissing with fear, went down on her knees before her legitimate husband, who beat upon her with his open hands and with his fists. These same brothers now nodded with satisfaction to hear her cry of agony as he forced her open, taking her from behind as he'd seen animals do, blood running down her thighs. Let the women fuss with their sheets and spill the blood of the best layer in the brood; her cries, his tearing snorts, told them all they needed to know.

There was feasting and laughter long into the night.

Only rarely, he told us, did he ever have sexual intercourse with the woman he raped that night; once or twice, the same hurried terrified motions in a darkened room. The same rigid limbs and averted eyes. Living together with her as childless strangers in the same house. He had already taken us to that house. It was very Western and full of bric-a-brac. She occupied the kitchen and he the two back rooms. The lounge was their no-man's-land, where a heavy, ornate clock sat on the mantelpiece springing the hours. There was a dustless, uninhabited silence in that room.

In the silence that followed the story, while Aziz attended to the last of the whisky, Michael realised what position he and Monika occupied in the constellation of Aziz's feelings. They were the binary star of true love. The ideal couple, free to work together and travel the world. Free to love each other in that blessed state, unmaimed by history. He held them in his gaze with moist affection, nursing his whisky, turning his wounded profile towards the city.

But there was more than this. For Aziz one member of this binary star shone far brighter than the other, and that had to be Monika. He had told the story for Monika, for he nursed a deeper, more secret feeling. Such a man, Michael realised, would look into every woman's face for that true complement, for that possibility. For that dream.

Michael looked at Monika and her face was suffused with compassion, her eyes turned to Aziz. To have lived the way he has, Michael marvelled, the sustained desperation, and not just sit down one day and offer your bones to the sun.

*Allah Akbar! Allah Akbar!*


Before I start writing I know I'll have to ring my good friend, Mr Salman Rushdie, once more. When he finally comes to the phone he sounds exhausted. It must be very tiring, to be a famous writer on the run from the jihad. Or perhaps it's the thousands of miles of telephone network that had dehydrated his voice.

'I'm going to write a passage,' I tell him, 'which might be construed as highly critical of the Muslims. I'm a quiet, family man; I don't want to bring the jihad down on my neck. Or be a refugee in my own country.'

"Don't worry about it,' he advises. 'You can write what you like, they won't take any notice. You see, my crime was not so much writing a disrespectful novel — all good novels are disrespectful — but being an apostate. It says in the Holy Koran that an apostate must die. With an infidel it is different, the Holy Koran teaches some compassion for the infidel, who, after all, has never known the grace of Allah. For the apostate, no such compassion is possible, for the apostate has known the grace of Allah and either one of two things has happened. Either Allah rejected him or he rejected Allah. Effectively they both add up to a death warrant. So most apostates stay very quiet about it, the mosques are full of them, showing public observance.'

'Wasn't there something about a French singer?'

'A storm in a tea-cup. Listen,' his voice assumes a hoarse, hectoring tone, 'think of Paul Bowles. Now there's a writer who's been saying insidiously nasty things about the Muslims for years, hinting at things far worse than my innocent literary romping, and he lives on quietly in Morocco, respected and revered. Why doesn't the Heavy Brigade take out a contract on Paul Bowles? Simple, he's not an apostate. What are you writing? Is it a comedy? The danger in writing comedy is that some people have forgotten how to laugh. Their bodies have forgotten what to do.'

'Not so much a comedy,' I hedge. 'I haven't actually started writing yet, just a few notes on stray characters. I thought of more of a contemplative piece. A mood piece. Recollective. Some sort of split narrative would serve . . .'

'Forget it. Keep it simple. Say what you've got to say and get out while you still have your arse.'

'But, Salman, your own books are nothing like that, they are quite baroque.'

'So what? It's still good advice. I'm just a scapegoat.'

After talking to Salman it's difficult to settle to work once more, to sit at my desk. I know it's horrible for him but I can't help thinking that it must be very exciting also, that something like that would certainly take the boredom out of being a writer. And further, I can't help feeling that in some way he must revel in this. He must grin and grin and grin and grin.

I look over the brief array of photographs. The shot of Abdul Aziz is the poorest, a fuzzy beach scene in winter. Aziz is pointing out to sea so there's no clear view of his face. Of all of them I like the one taken last year, with you in the background on the trampoline. Michael and Monika, late period, *circa* 1988. Neruda lying casually on the table between, with my own first book, casually disassociated from the Neruda, on the couch where Monika is sitting.

The last photograph in this meagre bunch is best called a snapshot, one that unexpectedly worked. It's a beach scene, summer evening before the light goes, when the shadows are tall. Monika and you are walking up off the beach, your shadows leaning into each other. It's just Oneroa, with houses all around, but somehow the scene contrives to be isolated and somewhat desolate, with the jumble of dark rock behind. This is the much dreaded beach scene, and I immediately perceive that in narrative terms nothing happens at all. It's a non-moment. Three people go down for a walk on Oneroa beach and go home again. That'll knock their socks off. My publisher will give me three million dollars advance and I'll go into hiding before the storm breaks.

> It is the hour of departure, the cold hard hour
> Which night fastens to timetables.
> The rustling belt of the sea girdles the shore
> Cold stars arise, black birds migrate.

Michael was against the walk from the start. He hated finalities and hours of departure. Timetables. His first view of the beach, from the top of the steep path above, was an occasion for a sudden acute feeling for the temporary and contingent in life. The beach was, in one sense at least, like a vast waiting-room at some celestial airport or railway station, slowly emptying of people.

And that, he saw, was how they lived their lives, inhabiting them for a time, camping in their bodies, moving on, visiting their emotions only to take leave of them again. Ironically it was people like Pierre and Aziz, seemingly so much like characters from an exotic fiction or an arcane card pack, who fulfilled completely the terms of their existence, helpless and unprotected. Pierre, floundering in the general disintegration; Aziz, tracing the outline of his scars. But Monika and Michael were always in transit, living out of suitcases and wallets.

After all, they could always come home.

Michael walked to the edge of the sea and looked out towards South America. And this *was* home. The edge of the earth. This was where the snake swallowed its tail, right at the edge of the land. Beyond here, nothing, *wahi ngaro*. A little postmodern haiku had been erected by the Traffic Department to make this very statement:

NO TURNING
BEYOND
THIS POINT

Michael took it to heart and knew it was true. This was not just another foreign country, he had to convince himself of that. This walk on the beach was where it ended. He'd foreseen it some time ago, right down to the last detail. The way you ran on ahead, picking up bits of coloured glass long smoothed by the action of the sea. You wore a small, colourful little bag with mirrors sewn into it, and into this the bits of glass would go until it was filled. He foresaw it all, every detail.

Monika joined him, and looked out to sea. The tide was out and the beach was a gleaming, reflective expanse. Gulls walked stiffly away from their shadows. She stood to one side, strained and uneasy, staring out to where the horizon line was thickening, glancing back to the beach, our child, the sweep of the peninsula. She felt it too. The sense of composition and finality.

Our Eleanor trotted after the gulls, her arms outstretched. That's you at two and a half. The gulls did their stilted walk away from you, their bobbing shadows blurred and insubstantial on the wet sand. A few of them took off and flew low towards the waterline. Poems came and went like tricks of light. Michael waited for some kind of revelation. None was forthcoming. Monika walked across the sand to join you, to kneel by your side and look at your coloured glass. Together, you and she made a study of daughter and mother. She spoke quietly to you, showing you how the sun slanting over the water caused our shadows to grow into elongated caricatures of our motion. You ran and jumped, trying to catch up with your shadow.

Your shadow and hers merged into one when she picked you up, having overleapt themselves into symbols, having merged into a bulky creature with impossibly skinny legs. Daughter-in-mother.

Michael returned, as I do now, to the deceiving fictional connection, shadow and image, event and echo. He made a small joking remark to the effect that life was not fair. You put your head on Monika's shoulder. She replied stiffly that, on the contrary, it was very fair.

Everything was agreed although nothing had been said. You would go with your mother.

As they left the beach and began to wind up the zig-zag path to the top of the hill, Michael took you in his arms. He was walking upward against the terrific weight of the hill. Against the terrific frailty of his bones. The beach fell into a grey whisper behind them. He sang three verses of 'Summertime' to get to the top of the hill, where the sweep of the beach and cliff presented itself in solemn dignity. He was drowned in its nomenclature. The beach was filling up with shadow, the wet sand had lost its sheen and turned black.

'Let's go home,' Monika said. Already they were practised strangers.

When I look up from my notes and see the empty trampoline I feel an immediate sense of loss. Like every other object we might put into a fiction, it has accumulated emotional weight, a certain symbolic resonance. It must stand for childhood, of course, the perpetual weightlessness and movement. Now it is empty it becomes, by the same logic, more poignant than before; your childhood is nearly over and in a few short years you will be able to read these words. Thus the empty trampoline stands like a purified symbol I can't shake off. I remember my waiting over your cot, waiting for an absent child's cry.

Carefully I put away Neruda and the Tarot pack. I know they're not going to give me the kind of help I need. In the photograph this same yellow, Penguin Neruda sits on the table, where it's treated like an old, half-outgrown friend. Monika's hand lies on the couch like something discarded and left to age ten years. I put away the photographs too. Then look carefully at what I have left.

There is the past, composed of shiny fragments, faces without names and names whose addresses have been lost. Pierre and Aziz walk on to take their bows, glancing uneasily around. I peer down the Via del Corso towards the Piazza del Poppolo. I think of the last conversation Michael had with Monika. It was about his writing. He had risen from the table, she from the couch. You had stopped jumping on the trampoline and were running through the honeysuckle at the bottom of the valley. She was getting ready to take you and walk up to the road.

'I'm working on prose now,' Michael told her. 'It feels like prose, anyway.'

He rolled a smoke for them to share, the way they used to. 'I'm cutting down on my smoking,' he told her. 'I'm starving out the rat.'

'Do you ever write about us. I mean directly?' she asked, starting to put together your things.

'Hardly ever.'

'Why not?'

'It would almost be like cheating.' Michael gave his most literary shrug. 'Or plagiarising. Everything's there. The details, the myths, the settings, the emotions, the totalising impulse. Everything frozen as in amber.' I think of the milk that runs through jade. 'Like Pierre and Aziz we've lived our fictions.'

'Wouldn't that make it easier?'

'Or harder.' Michael drew on his cigarette. 'All we really have is frames.'

I'm glad he's said this, for now I know I have my title. The very first word.

'Frames?'

'The bit that goes around the outside.'

We both laughed.

I see the poem turning like a starfish, frame by frame. It's picking up speed. I was bending over and kissing you who cling too hard to me.

'Did you enjoy your bounce?'

You nodded fervently. Monika looked politely away. These bloody endings.

'Teddy's never going to die,' you said sombrely.

Michael wished you hadn't said that, not right at that moment; it totally ruined the naturalism of the whole thing, but that's why you said. And he had to agree; there is certain immortality to teddies.

The Howard Morrison song ends. He sang 'Po Kare Kare Ana' as if it was a lament.

I'm happy, now I have my title. I have my first and last line. Tomorrow I'll start writing.

# Pack of Lies
## Chad Taylor

### —ONE—

My hands are all bloody. They got blood on them when I wiped my head before and with the bang on my head — whatever it was, something blunt, it was hard, Christ, I gritted my teeth — it must be bleeding. It's warm and it smells. If I turned the lights on I could see exactly how bad it is but I'm not going to turn the lights on. Not just yet. Turning them on would mean trying to stand. I can't stand yet. Christ. Not just yet.

I think I am going into shock. I think I am, I can feel it. I'm pretty sure I am. I should just stand up and click the light switch now. Now. And see the blood in the mirror and know it's mine, when the bald lightbulbs snap on above the sink. I hug my knees lying sideways on the floor, sideways in the dark, waiting. My hands are sticky and warm. The taps are still on, running down the porcelain into the drain curling away.

I dropped the card. It was a nice card as birthday cards go. To A Girl Who Is Seven. It's lying on the floor somewhere, by the door where I dropped it. It felt light between my fingers and then slippery — sticky. To a girl who's bigger and brighter every day. Blue puppies in a basket of flowers. A Very Happy Birthday To A Girl Who Is Seven. Somewhere in the dark.

The phone receiver crackles, the woman with the sweet voice still talking, chattering away, saying the police will be there very very soon. It dropped the card. I want to stand up but I can't. I will. But not yet.

Numb. I can hardly feel my legs. I'm going all numb. There is no moon through the bare windows, the only lights are the stars. The phone receiver is saying, now can you just give me your name again?

Catrina Phillips, something-something road, something-something suburb. I've said it so many times I am starting to forget. When I was small I would whisper a new word over and over again until it stopped meaning anything. And I would say, Grandma, what does it mean? When I knew perfectly well. Over and over.

God. I'm going to throw up. I really am. I'm going to be sick. I huddle my knees to my lips and smell denim. Christ. I gritted my teeth, when it hit, something blunt it was, something hard. Now don't worry because we're sending a car, it was in the area and it's on it's way now, it will be there very soon. I lost the card, though. And she says: the card?

I meant to pay for it. Intended to. I picked it out and walked to the counter but the man was busy and I went to look at some books, and it wasn't until I was leaving that I realised the card was still in my hand. I stood at the front of the shop in the light of the electric eye with the doors wanting to close. If I went back inside and told them they wouldn't believe me. If I put it in my pocket and kept on walking I would be stealing it. I couldn't go either way. When I got home I wrote twenty on it. To A Girl Who's Twenty Seven.

We used to hop in front of the electric eye and watch the doors open and close.

I want my head to be alright. I hate anything when peoples' heads get hurt. Your brain is so soft, it can't take very much. You hear about kids who fall off their bike and that's it: dead. And then you hear things like the man who lived after getting a steel bar through his head. He was a steel worker, this Englishman, and it was on a building site.

Someone dropped a bar — a pike — about four feet long and it fell down two stories and went through the front half of his brain. He didn't even pass out. The skin grew over and he lived for another 10 years. But then at the end of his life he went quite crazy. I guess he just lost too many brain cells in the end. The thing with head injuries is that you never know. I want someone to get here so I can find out if I am going to be okay. I want to stand up and turn the lights on. But not just yet.

The doctors don't know either. Doctors find everything out by accident or because they are crazy themselves. There was a doctor who had his head cut open during the French Revolution. He bandaged it with a splint so it stayed open and never healed, and for the next four years he took samples of his own brain fluid. He did it by tying bits of sponge onto string and pulling them around the inside of his skull. He finally died when a knot in the string cut into the sac around his brain. That was the only thing that stopped him — he would have carried on dredging his head with a sponge forever, otherwise. That's a man of science for you — that's what medicine is. The only thing that stops them is dying, and when they die someone else wants to cut them up. Like they cut up murderers and prisoners for autopsies and medical schools. I mean, if they base all their research on what they cut out of insane people then how do they learn to treat normal people? They can't even treat old people. Old people get sat in a corner with dribble coming out of their mouth and they can't even speak. They piss into a tube and they die, they're vegetables. All they do is sit and look, stare out the window until they fall apart. Stare and wait for someone to come.

The curtains are pulled back and it's late and it's dark. The stars look thicker in the smog. And my head hurts, my mind aches and it's not fair. I bite my lip. The phone receiver is still talking. Talking and talking. And the traffic is going past. Even at this time of night it is the rush hour. My hair is starting to stick to the carpet. I pull myself closer against the corner of the wall, the damp edges of wallpaper and the skirting board speckled with fly dirt. The flat is so dirty. I should clean it really. You should always have it clean. You never know when someone is going to come round. Be on your best. And I would be, but my head hurts. I must have gritted my teeth and fallen down and covered my face with my hands. I don't even know. But they will tell me later. They will sort it out.

The water is running over the edge of the sink and seeping into the carpet. I can feel it creep under my head and shoulders, toward the telephone. It will be dangerous if it touches. A shock from the phone will kill you straight. When they first invented telephones it happened all the time. Women picked up the receiver wearing heavy gold earrings and the electricity jumped right out.

I have been in this flat forever, lying here, sitting in the dark, making cups of tea, ringing people up. There are a whole bunch of people I need to call but I'm not going to get round to it, I'm not going to get it done. I've got to clean first, do my hair, get tidied up. I bought this hat, a red straw hat. From a secondhand place. Fuck it won't even fit on my head now. It won't even go on. My ears are ringing and the phone is off the hook.

When the police lights arrive they make a lonely noise, tyres crunching on the empty driveway. I listen to the footsteps looking to see which flat it is and the radio and the inevitable knock on the door — if I could open the door it would already be open. Wouldn't it? They can't work that out.

They look through the window and they look back through the curtains. Please hurry. Really. Break a window. I don't mind. It belongs to the landlord anyway. So. Each person casts a dozen different shadows, overlapping.

I roll on my back, still holding my knees to my chest and call out: break the window. The shadows stiffen. PLEASE BREAK THE FUCKING WINDOW. I'm not going to yell help. They rattle the lock. Fuck, fuck, fuck. It's on a chain. IT'S ON A CHAIN. You think they could work it out. THE DOOR'S ON A FUCKING CHAIN. What do they want, a key under the mat? I can't get up to unlock the door. I don't want to try and stand just yet. PLEASE BREAK — fuck it. Alright. HELP.

Alright? Loud enough?

The door jumps off its hinges like it's been trained and the glass goes everywhere and then they are on me. They turn me over and examine my head and someone is calling for an ambulance, a stretcher, a doctor. They find a first aid kit and press cotton wool on my head. They wrap me in a blanket and say to keep still, but I'm not moving, I'm not going to try and stand up just yet. I want to stay where I am, curled up on the floor under the rug, in a warm corner with my head in my hands, the place where I got hit in my hands, where it hurt. I want someone to stroke my head. The policewoman says she will stroke my head. She puts rubber gloves on first.

# — TWO —

Traffic is passing on the road outside. All the nurses and patients and people visiting. There is a Bambina parked over by the trees. I used to drive one. I remember when I brought it I came in and everyone asked what I'd chosen and I said an Italian car, because the Italians were the best at Formula One racing.

When the Italians first started developing Formula One racing cars they made them all small, like they made all their other cars. Fiat made most of them. Anyway, there was nothing wrong with the small cars mechanically or design-wise — in fact many of them were as fast as the other competitors. But the Italian team never won any races.

They couldn't figure it out. They put the cars through tests and trial runs and they took the engines apart and put them back together again, but no one could find anything wrong with them. So the Fiat bosses flew in a German analyst and he went through their whole technique — design, construction, maintenance, everything. And the German guy realised what was wrong. The problem, see, wasn't the car at all — it was the driver. The Italians were really upset when he said it because that's like the most insulting thing you can say to an Italian man — that he can't drive. But when everyone had calmed down the German analyst explained: it's not that the drivers aren't good — it's just that they're *too big*.

The trick with racing car driving is that when he's the right size, the driver becomes the car's centre of gravity. A Formula One car is designed so that every time you take a corner the four wheels skid *around* the driver, like a top. If the driver is too big then everything goes out of whack and the car doesn't skid evenly. The front wheels skid a little more or the back wheels don't skid enough and you come out of the curve on the wrong angle. And then, once you're on the wrong angle, you lose your acceleration. When you jump the pedal the car doesn't go forward, it goes sideways. And that's where all your gas goes. You're slower on the track, you use more gas, you eat up the tyres, and you have to go into the pit stops more often. And that was why the Italians were losing races.

After the Italians thought about it, they paid the German analyst a whole lot of money and sent him home, and then they started looking for drivers who were the right size. In fact they didn't even care if they found people who were drivers — they just wanted someone the right height and weight, which, for the sort of cars they were making then, was around five feet. The racing team had posters printed and put up in every village in Italy, and they went on the radio, and Mussolini made speeches about it, and it became a sort of national search. They didn't want boys, of course, because boys can grow bigger. They only wanted short men.

They tested a lot of the men who applied, hundreds if not thousands, and they took at lot of them on the team, but the most famous was a man called Guiseppe Marchetti who stood four foot nine. The racing team chose him straight away because he was perfect — the right height, and he used to work as a taxi driver, which meant that he was pretty fast.

So this guy Marchetti became the world's shortest Formula One racer. All the other guys from the other teams laughed at him when he walked into the pits because he was tiny — the English driver was five eleven and the Germans were pretty big too. All the other teams were racing big cars at that time and so hadn't noticed the thing about the driver's weight so much. I guess once a car gets over a certain weight it doesn't matter if the driver is big or small. Certainly the Italians were the first ones to notice the anomaly.

Anyway, on his first race Marchetti just shot through and nobody could believe it. The race was held in the south of France and everyone was cheering like crazy for the French Renault driver, who stood five foot eight, but Marchetti passed him as if he was standing still and his Fiat engine was screaming because it was burning around so fast. After he crossed the finish line the engine actually started to catch fire but that didn't matter, he had won the race and he became the first Italian for years and years to do so. The crowd hoisted him up on their shoulders and carried him to the presentation stand. The mayor gave a speech but no one could hear it over the shouting, and then they asked Marchetti to say something but the microphone stand wouldn't fold down that far so he refused because he didn't want to be made fun of. Two big blonde women presented him with the trophy which was as tall as he was and after he took it the women lifted him up with one arm each, so his feet were dangling off the ground, and everyone was cheering and cheering.

Marchetti became like the best driver in Italy. He was the fastest and Fiat were making him the best engines they could, and they not only kept the Italian cars small but actually designed them around his body. They took plaster casts of him in the driver's seat and weighted them, for accuracy. The plaster casts sell for hundreds of thousands of dollars today — or lire, I guess, depending on whatever the exchange rate is.

He won all the Formula One races for six years, plus racing in a lot of other categories as well and winning them, and the Italian team became the most famous team, and Mussolini gave him a couple of medals. It was a joke at the time: every year Marchetti would win the Formula One, every year he would get another medal from Mussolini. He was a millionaire and as famous as a movie star. He married this incredibly beautiful fashion model and lived in a big house, but he went and raced all the time, and spent hours and hours with the mechanics, helping design the racing cars and stuff. I don't know if she minded that too much, but she wasn't perfectly happy with it.

Anyway. The other teams who raced in the Formula One were getting really frustrated with not winning, especially the Germans. Hitler had a whole lot of money in Formula One racing because he wanted the Germans to beat the world at everything, probably as practice for the war — so Germany could practice winning and everyone else could practice looking up to them, I guess, that was how Hitler thought. So the Mercedes team especially wanted to start winning. They did all this research into the Italian cars but couldn't come up with any answers until one day someone heard about the German analyst who had done work for the Italian team, and they called him up and he told them the secret was the driver's weight and size, and suddenly everything clicked.

That was in 1935 and for the next five years leading up to the Second World War, the Italians never won another Formula One race in that time. The Germans trained up drivers that were the right shape and size for their bigger, more powerful cars and beat everyone flat. Marchetti just about went crazy. And the Italian team started designing bigger cars, the same size as the Mercedes and the Porsches, and looking therefore for bigger drivers, and suddenly Marchetti was out of a job. They fired him in 1938 in favour of some other guy who was over six foot.

After the Italians dropped him, Marchetti said he was going to enter as a private competitor, but he couldn't find a sponsor. So he paid for everything himself and the cost was fantastic. He started drawing up designs for a new racing car — for street racing, because he could see that that was where the future of racing was. He designed it around his own body weight and height, because he still believed that a really good small car could go faster than a big one. But it was costing him a fortune to develop. He started by selling off his properties and his tools and even some of his trophies. In the end his wife left him and he couldn't keep up the payments to his mechanic and he went bankrupt — this was in 1939. He went back to driving a taxi in Rome. He drove really fast to get lots of fares but even that wasn't enough — the banks were going to put him in jail. So he sold the designs for his new car to Fiat, in May 1939. He was killed in the war, I read, but I think he killed himself really, because he had come so far and tasted what it was to be really great, and now he had nothing again, and he couldn't handle it.

Fiat just put the designs away and forgot about them. They only bought them to be kind to Marchetti, I think they felt they owed him. But in the sixties someone dusted off the designs and changed them a little bit here and there and started making them as a normal car, and that became the Bambina. It was perfect because it was so small, and everyone bought it for driving around cities in. But whoever took out the plans remembered Marchetti because they left his name on the car: just under the lid, the bonnet, when you lift it up, the word MARCHETTI has been stamped into the frame — no explanation or number or anything, nothing but the word caked in grime from the engine. Most people who buy Bambinas now wouldn't even know it's there, let alone what it means.

## — THREE —

'Catrina?' He holds out the card, puts it in my lap. 'Think this is yours.'

To A Girl Who Is Twenty-Seven. Yes.

'Your birthday, is it?'

No, my friend's. Babe's.

'How is the head feeling?'

Fine.

'Bill Howard. Do you remember, we …'

Yes. Not that I do really. All cops look the same.

'At the flat, that's right.' He holds his ID close so I can see without having to lean forward. He folds it back in the flap of his wallet and puts it in his breast pocket. Brown tweed and curly hair and big thick shoes. He sniffs. 'The nurses said you're a little tired. But I thought I'd come in and see how you were.'

The iron leg of the chair squeaks as he pulls it up. He holds his left fist in his right hand on the edge of the bed. He has big hands.

'Do you work with Babe?'

No. She works at the tenants' society. Our birthday's in the same month. But she looks older than me. Because she's taller. It was her party last night. I didn't have time to look for presents. I only got her the card. I turn it in my hand.

'Twenty-seven,' he says.

Yeah. They don't print cards with Happy 27th on them, though. I don't suppose women want to know. I guess it's different for guys.

He smiles. 'Not much different.'

Well.

'That was at the Astor …?'

Yeah. The Astor is sort of the student pub. Everyone goes there.

'Can I ask you some questions, Catrina?'

I don't know if I feel like it.

'Well, I've read your statement and there are some details I want to go over with you. I'd like to get some facts clear in my head, build up a picture. You know?'

I guess.

'Good. Now you haven't identified the person who attacked you …'

No.

'Did you see the person at all?'

No.

'Was there anyone outside the flat before you went in?'

No.

'You didn't see anyone?'

No.

'And no one followed you home?'

No.

'You were coming from university?'

Yes.

He nods. 'University. It's hard to get in these days. My daughter's finding that.'

I guess.

'What course are you doing?'

What do you want to know for?

'Just interested.' He smiles again. 'You don't have to tell me if you don't want to.'

The fluorescents are still burning, white lines reflected in the wide, red windows as the sun begins to rise.

Political studies.

He nods. 'I'd like to do something like that sometime. Later, maybe, adult education, something like that. When do you graduate?'

Well, I've got, shit, I have to count … a few more units in all. It always seems like there's a few more.

'Okay.' He opens his notebook. 'I have some statements here … We had a report.'

A police report?

'No, witness reports. Some people who say they saw you in the early evening, in the Ascot. They say you were having a drink with some other students, friends of yours. And you stayed for …' He flicks through the pages. 'Four or five rounds …?'

There were a lot of people drinking. Birthdays, you know.

'Of course. Drink much?'

No.

'One of our people spoke to someone who said that you were in a distressed state. The person says you were in the toilets — crying, is what they said.'

I don't think so.

'Are you sure?'

The truth is I was a little pissed off yesterday. I'd had a full day and I'd had to carry my books, and my back was sore. It all kind of builds up. All the little things do. It gets you down a bit.

He reaches into his jacket for a thick, dry fold of papers and spreads them flat on the sheet. 'I understand. So that's what you think this person saw?'

I guess so. I mean, I'm not that person, but it sounds like that to me.

'Okay.' He gives me a different look. Just a brief glance, as if he is having a new thought and there is a new problem. But that is only for a moment and afterwards he returns to the papers, which are neatly typed.

'We looked at the report on your injuries, and as you know we looked around the flat ...' He flicks through the pages. 'You had concussion. Swelling and bleeding around the side of the head ...' He stabs fat fingers at his temple. '... which implies being struck with a pointed object. Now, the front door of your flat opens into a polished wooden landing ...' The fat fingers make themselves onto a little corridor. '... which leads to a kitchenette. In the kitchenette is a stove. The corner of that stove is bloodied.' The fat fingers hang in mid-air. 'Do you remember falling on the stove, Catrina?'

Falling? No.

'Were you pushed against the stove?'

I don't know. My eyes itch. Maybe I was. I think ... I rub my nose with my unbandaged hand. I think maybe I could have been.

'How do you think that might have happened?'

I guess ... whoever it was ... gave me a shove. Hit me on the side of the head and I tried to stand up, to stay straight but I slipped.

'Slipped?'

My head's starting to hurt again.

'You're a very lucky girl.'

I don't fucking feel like it.

'Please Catrina. I'm not here to upset you.'

You fucking are. You fucking are upsetting me.

'Please calm down.'

I am fucking calmed down. I sit back and push the air out of the pillows and fold my arms and he waits, staring.

'Can you remember ...'

Why don't you go fuck yourself.

He takes a breath.

I sit still.

He stares and waits but I keep my mouth shut.

He lets out his breath.

'Okay'.

He sits back again.

'I have arguments like this with my daughter,' he smiles.

I bet.

'Catrina, do you know someone called Wayne Martin?'

What?

'Wayne Martin.' He flicks out a photo that doesn't look like him at all. 'Young guy, about 25 years old.'

I'm not …

'Catrina. This isn't helping anyone. Please be honest now. Do you know Wayne Martin?'

Yes. A long time ago. Before Babe.

'You go out with him?'

Not now.

'But you used to?'

Yes.

'How are things between him and you, now?'

We're … I look for the word. You can never phrase it when you want. Friends. We're friends, I guess.

'Good friends?'

Um. sort of.

'Catrina, about five minutes after you called in last night, one of our cars picked up Wayne Martin.'

Oh.

'Right in your neighbourhood, about two blocks away from your flat. Drunk. Now, that's not a coincidence, is it?'

What happened?

'He's helping us with our enquiries.'

Oh.

'Did he push you into the stove, Catrina? Across the floor?'

I don't remember.

'Could he have borrowed a spare key from you?'

I don't recall.

'Please try.'

I am.

'Catrina, this is hard for you to say, I realise that. You went out with him for a long time, didn't you? We understand the …' He reaches for the word. '… *conflict*. The problems. Conflict of interest. We don't blame you for that. You're not the one in trouble here. Wayne is the one in trouble. We've got him. We had him even before you were admitted to hosopital. One block away from the reported incident, intoxicated. Drunk and aggressive. We *knew* what had happened. *I* knew. But when *these* came in …' He shakes the witness reports. 'There were some bad things said about our procedure …'

I don't have anything against the police.

'I know you don't. I know that. And there are things said about you. The sort of things that upset you — but relax. Alright? That's what I'm here to tell you. I know now — we know — that's not the case.

'So. Just tell me now, very quietly. Just between you and me.' Big hairy jacket.

'No details, just what happened. Very simply. We can follow up the rest later. Did you argue? Were you seeing someone? He's a violent bloke …' Moles on his hands, scratches. 'You argued about … something? Were you drinking with him this evening? Did he invite himself round? You let him in, had a beer, few drinks, had an argument, something like that? Is that what happened? It looks that way to us.'

Yellow fingernails, smoker. First knuckles of his fingers smell.

'Did you argue,' he shrugs, 'on the way home …?'

I hold the pillow.

'All we need's a yes, Catrina.' He smiles. And we can deal with the rest.'

He'd go to jail.

'With his record? Yes, he would.' He taps the page with his pen. 'You'd be quite safe.'

He smiles. My head hurts. I try to say things but my head hurts. When he smiles his lips disappear beneath his moustache.

'You know, my girl's about as old as you.'

Hugging the pillow.

'My daughter. She's about your age.'

That's weird. What would it be like having a cop as a father? I think you would need a sister. One at least.

'We have enough to lay charges …'

I'm feeling so tired.

'Perhaps we could come and see you this afternoon. Or you could come into the station. For a fuller statement.'

The nurse said I wasn't allowed to get tired. I remember she said so.

'It's important we can act on this, Catrina. There's a lot of …'

Can you get the nurse to come in please? I'd like you to get the nurse to come in. I think I'm having a relapse or something.

His smile disappears.

'Alright.'

Can you get her now, please?

'Where do you think you'll be staying, Catrina?'

Could you get the nurse?

'Where, Catrina?'

With Babe.

'I'll give you a call.'

I don't remember her number.

'Is it listed?'

I'm not sure. I think I've got temporary amnesia or something.

Can you just get the nurse?

Through the window the sun is slowly rising above the trees and the kitchen people are starting to wheel in breakfast on wobbly trolleys. Officer Howard turns and walks out, his big shoes squeaking on the linoleum.

I didn't want to piss him off too much. He had big hands and big arms. I bet he could lift you right off the ground if he wanted. I stand the birthday card next to the bed, so I can see it from where I lie.

# — FOUR —

Babe has always been difficult about her birthday and now that she is having more of them it seems to be getting more difficult. I tried to talk her into the idea early because I figured the problem would only exacerbate itself but she said no, she still didn't feel like having a big fuss made over her on the day. I remember one time I invited her for a picnic on Mt Eden. She was really cagey about it. Finally she said she'd come if she could bring a friend and I said okay. I baked her a chocolate cake and bought champagne and remembered to bring the cutlery and a blanket and glasses wrapped in tea-towels. We arranged to meet on the summit around midday.

I was still waiting for her at 12.30. It was the middle of summer and really hot and my arms were aching from holding the hamper, but I figured she would show. At one o'clock I decided to go looking. It didn't take long to find her. She was down the side of the hill under the trees with her friend. In the shade. I just climbed back up to the top of the hill.

There were people riding horses around the hill, taking them up the slow road and then letting them climb down the rougher parts of the slope. There is a riding club around Mt Eden somewhere. My aunt rides there. She has ridden ever since she was a little girl.

She was brought up on a farm someplace and she and all her friends had horses, like children have bikes now, and they rode everywhere: to school and to visit each other and to go into town. One day my aunt's friend told her about a woman who read palms and they decided to go and see her. The palm-reader was about eighty and living by herself and she wouldn't read palms for money — she'd do it if you took her a packet of biscuits or some tea or something like that. She didn't like making money off it.

So my aunt and her friend, who was called Pip, rode over to the other side of the valley to meet this palm-reader. There were no proper roads then, only dirt tracks across the fields, and the ride took a couple of hours, which is a long time on horseback. When they got there the woman took them inside and sat them down and they gave her a packet of biscuits and a chocolate bar and they had tea together, and talked about nothing in particular. Pip and my aunt were really careful not to say anything which would give them away.

The woman did my aunt first. She spread my aunt's right hand out on the table and ran her fingertips along the lines and said, well, you live on a farm, and you've done this and this, and it all turned out to be true. Then she turned to my aunt's left hand and said you'll grow up in the city, and you'll marry a man who looks like such and such, but you won't stay together very long … and things like that. My aunt was very excited by it and a lot of the things since then have turned out to be true, they've happened, although she doesn't talk about that day very much.

When it was Pip's turn the woman read her right hand and got some things right although there were a few things wrong, but that was okay and Pip was really excited. When the woman turned to Pip's left hand she went quiet. She said nothing, only stared. And Pip said, what is it? And the woman said, I'll tell your fortune but not out loud, I'll write it down for you, and you mustn't read it here, you must read it when you get home. Pip got very excited. The woman wrote it down on a piece of notepaper and folded it and gave it to my aunt to carry saying, you mustn't give it to her until I've said. The girls left saying thank you, and mounted up and started riding.

It was getting towards the end of the day and they were both in a hurry to get home anyway, let alone to read the note and find out what the secret was, and they were excited as hell. After talking about it they decided 'home' meant anywhere on Pip's property so it would be safe to read it as soon as they reached the outskirts of the farm. They started the horses up to a gallop and headed back. They were about two miles away from the farm when Pip's horse caught its hoof in a ditch and threw her and cracked her head open on the hard summer ground. She was killed instantly.

My aunt rode back to the farm and got everyone and they came driving and riding and running out to where Pip lay but she was stone dead, of course, there was nothing they could do. They took my aunt home and she went into her room and lay on the bed. And then she remembered the palm-reader's note, much much later, and she took it out of her shirt and opened it up and it said, 'no future.'

I always wondered how the palm-reader felt when she read that. She must have known what was going to happen, if not specifically then in a general way, she must have figured it out. My aunt never said if she went back to the palm-reader. She only told me that story once, after she'd had a bit to drink, and when I asked her about it again she didn't really go into the details.

I watched the horses on the side of the hill for a long time and waited for Babe and her friend to turn up. When they did show I said I hadn't been waiting long. I looked at her and her friend drinking champagne and giggling and wondered what would happen next, if it would last until the following birthday or what. We lit the candles on the cake and watched them burn in the open air.

## — FIVE —

The buzzer rings muffled from the other end of the hall. My head throbs under my hat. Babe's house has not been painted in a long time and if you touch the weatherboards what colour remains peels off in parchment flakes. Wasps hang above the weeds. The garden here used to be really something. Whoever owned the house before grew the front trees into animal shapes — one was a duck and another was a dog. The back lawn was concreted over and everything in it was made of cement — flowers and fountains and gnomes and seals and pelicans. Babe was very proud of it. The tree-animals have pretty much lost their shape, now.

Babe opens the door in her kimono and blinks and doesn't say anything. I hold out the card. She looks at it, and then at me, and then takes the card and opens it with one hand against her breast and reads it slowly. She combs the hair back behind her ears with the card tip and folds her arms and leans on the door. She knew what it said anyway.

'Well,' she murmurs.

Didn't mean to get you out of bed.

'Wasn't even sleeping.'

I left without giving it to you. I thought you should have it.

'Thank you.'

I just came round. I thought you'd be having breakfast or something. The concrete steps are dirty. It is after ten.

'Well, you'd better come in, then.'

Sorry.

'S'okay.' She leads us down the hall, leaving me to shut the door.

'You had breakfast?'

Yeah.

She stands the card on the stove top and rubs her eyes and gives me a pink stare. 'Bet you haven't.'

I'm not hungry.

'That's not what I asked you.'

I know.

She goes through the fridge. The saucepans hang on black steel hooks and there is garlic on a string and the shelves are full of food. She always said she wanted a great kitchen and now she has it. She squints to read the carton label. 'Juice?'

What sort?

'Orange'.

Yes please.

'And breakfast?' She bends over the fridge again. 'You want cereal or shall I cook you something?' She takes eggs out of the tray. 'We've got bread.' She shuffles round in the cupboards. 'I bought it fresh. I'll cook you something.'

You don't need to.

'I don't mind,' She smiles. I watch the rug on the lounge floor while she cracks the eggs in a black iron pan. 'I was worried after you left.'

You don't have to worry.

'You want bacon?'

No thanks.

'Kidneys?'

Oh Jesus.

'You need some iron. You're getting anaemic.' She presses her thumb into my cheek. 'Look at that.'

Well I don't feel so good.

'Don't you?'

Is Brian up?

'At work already.' She wipes her nose. 'Toast. Yes?'

Babe.

'Yup ...'

Babe?

'What?'

Babe, I'm ...

'You're what?'

There's been some trouble.

'Where?'

Just something. It happened and …

'What d'you mean?'

She straightens up. I try to tell her but I can't.

'What sort of trouble?'

I wiggle behind the bench and wave my hands and stammer. I can't say it. I can't even begin. It's like trying to explain everything right from the beginning, all at once with no space for breath. You can't just explain one single thing. And that's why explaining is always a waste of time, always. I just take off my hat and it's there, under the straw.

'Oh my God. Trina. Trina? What happened?'

It takes me ages to talk.

'Trina? Shit. Jesus. What hit you? Who was it? Jesus.' She stares at the bloody bandage. 'Christ it's a mess. It's slipped.' She starts tucking it back in place. 'Jesus, Trina. Have you reported it? What …'

I spoke to the police.

'What happened?'

They said it's some guy, they've got some leads. And. I guess. And. That's …

'Oh honey.'

She asks me a whole lot of questions I can't answer and I start blubbering again so she stops and says, you can tell me after breakfast. I stand there looking stupid. I don't know whether to sit down or stand up. She leans across the counter and hugs me and I knock over my juice but it doesn't matter, neither of us go to wipe it up. I just lean with my face in her big shoulders. The orange juice runs off the bench. We hug for a long time.

I drink my coffee outside, with the animals. There are all kinds in the backyard. There is a seal and two big cats, and some penguins and a flamingo. They are so well made, cast in moulds. The moulds are worth a lot of money now, if you can find them. They used to be made at this factory in America, down in Texas. In the wide open plains. They had the patent for cement flamingos and they cornered the market. When lounge decoration stopped being fashionable they turned bankrupt, and nobody knows what happened to the moulds. And now cement flamingos are in fashion again, in some circles at least. Babe is going to tear the cement up soon and plant a real garden. But she has to keep the flamingo, I tell her, picking at its pink enamel, so her kids can ride on it.

'That's a good idea.' She takes up the greasy dish. 'More toast?'

No. I ate like a pig. Thank you.

She cleans up everything. I stretch out on the sun chair. The swing-frame squeaks when she sits down with fresh coffee and puts my head in her lap. The sky is flat and white. I remember this morning's sunrise, the light over the trees outside the hospital.

'Up on the hill,' Babe says. 'It's nice up there.' She strokes my hair. 'How're you feeling?'

That's what everyone asks.

'Well can you tell me?'

I don't feel like talking. I have kind of talked things out in my own mind. Breakfast was nice.

'Is there anything else you want?'

No.

'I want to change this dressing.'

The doctors said to keep it on.

'Just the outer bandage. It'll look nicer and you'll feel better.'

Okay.

She frowns looking down on me as she changes it. I press my finger on her forehead, between her eyes. She is going to get an old lady's forehead if she is not careful. You should rest more. We should go away. Do you want to go away? I'd like to. Just for a few days.

'Wish I could.'

If you wanted. I know this place. It's such a great place. It's terrific. We could stay a few nights there.

'Nice dream.'

It's not a dream. We could do it.

She gives me her patient smile. 'You did get a bang. Easy,' she says. 'Take it easy.'

But I can't stop. it just comes out. My face is a big red mess. I messed it up by getting hurt. With this, my head. Throbbing under the bandage. I didn't mean to get hurt. It was going to be a big surprise. We had it all organised, all of us. Everyone. It's going to be a big party and we were meant to be on our way this morning. I was meant to get you to go last night, that was the whole idea. We booked at this hotel. I'm the one who's meant to get you up there but all I do is start an argument and get put in hospital and fuck it all up. We booked ahead so we could all have a weekend there, just have some fun someplace for a couple of days, get pissed and muck around and say Happy Birthday babe — it was going to be a big surprise.

For a girl who's twenty-seven.

She looks at me with her mouth open.

'Oh baby.'

She puts both hands on my shoulders.

'Oh Trina. That's so...' She gives me a hug. 'Oh wow.' She has a smile as wide as a street. 'That's so amazing. You're wonderful. You haven't messed it ... oh Trina. Oh wow.'

I've ruined it, messed everything up, I've made a wreck of it. We're supposed to be driving down. We're supposed to be *there* by now.

'You haven't, you haven't, you haven't.'

I was supposed to be the one to get you down there and it wasn't like that would be hard, all I had to say was let's go away for the weekend and that would be it, I'd ask you last week and you'd say yes and everyone else'd do the rest. But I haven't had the chance to do anything. I left it all too late and then we start scrapping. And now I'm gonna have to ring everyone and say it's off and they'll be all organised to go and it'll be fucked, a write-off.

'Oh Trina. Don't ring anyone. Don't do a thing.'

Shit.

'Listen …'

I've fucked it up.

'Listen, Trina, listen — we'll go. We'll go and we won't say anything. I'm sorry. We've got to go. You've got to. Trina!'

Only if you want, if you really want.

'Oh wow. Of course I want to …'

She holds me by the shoulders and says, Catrina, *you've got to*. And she squeezes my hand, puts her fingers through mine and squeezes and hugs and lies laughing, stretched out in the grass at my feet.

## — SIX —

Where the motorway ends the traffic slows and bunches up at the first set of lights before the open road. The intersection runs between dry fields and vegetable stalls under green canvas. Babe leans on the wheel. 'Jesus my stomach,' she says. 'Full of rocks.' We creep forward when the lights turn red. At least it's sunny. Everyone's getting out of town for the weekend. 'Good thing you booked, huh?' Babe gives me a smile. 'You're so sweet.' Cradles her belly. 'Shit.' After the lights she pulls over by the vegetable stalls and cuts the engine. 'One of them must have a bathroom …' She throws me the keys and gets out and walks over toward the caravans.

I lean back and watch the trucks go by.

After a while she comes back with white plastic shopping bags stretched with the weight of things for dessert, things to eat on the way, things that were incredibly cheap — paw-paws and soft avocados and bananas. I offer to drive but she promises she's okay, and she does look better. She shuts the back and gets in, pushes her hair back behind her ear and rattles the column-shift. 'It takes a bit of getting used to,' she mutters. The petrol gauge says empty 'but ignore it. The whole thing's crap.' Babe scratches the windscreen. 'It didn't get a warrant. That's the pins — three hundred dollars. I mean where am I supposed to find that? I could've killed the guy.' So I spit on my finger and rub the ballpoint date out and turn the 10 into a 20 with a little work. It's a start anyway. She laughs. The traffic is moving pretty fast. She takes the birthday card off the dash and reads it while she steers.

'So when did you organise all this?'

Ages and ages ago. Everyone was talking about your birthday, doing something special. For the oldest.

'Was it your idea?'

It just sort of came up.

'I've never had a surprise party before. Are they gonna jump us when we get there, are they waiting?' She glances in the mirror. 'We might pass them going down.'

Yeah. You say if you start getting a headache.

'I'll be fine. I should be worrying about you.'

You've worried.

'And I'm the only one, it seems. Didn't the police ask anything?'

They asked about Wayne.

'That loser?'

They found his name in some file.

'He's a blot on your copybook, that guy.'

He wasn't so bad.

'He hit me once.'

What? Jesus.

'At one of the first parties you had there. We were talking and he just flared up. Sulky little bastard.' She looks in the mirror. 'At the big party. You had your new dress. We sat on the bed and read magazines. Do you remember? And just before the party ended I got up and went to the bathroom. There were only a few people left. Wayne and his mates were blocking the way to the bathroom. They wouldn't let me through. So I swore at them and they folded, of course — they fold when someone really stands up to them. But when I came out Wayne was there and he did his nut. Thoroughly. And he pushed me against the wall, with his fist. Stupid bastard. He went to hit me and I shouted and one of the others stopped him.' She strokes my cheeks. 'And then I came back to you.' She shakes her head. 'He took you for shit.'

It was Babe who said fuck him, you've got to go. And she said it really urgently, like there was a fire or something: *You've got to.* She held me and she promised, rocked me back and forth in the taxi back seat and when I started to count how many weeks' rent I had on my fingers, she locked her fingers through mine in a fist so instead of five fingers I had ten — she was going to pay half. What'd he say? she asked. Did he throw a shit?

She lent me her suitcase so I could pack my clothes, and when I got to the flat she gave me her study lamp. She came in holding it and said, You mustn't get behind. Which was like a joke because I was so far behind already. I'd done no work all year.

She wrote out all her notes for me in shorthand and made me cram nights — we sat on the bed and she pinched me every time I made a mistake. I ended up with C passes and Babe called it the luckiest day in my life. She told me to get straight to university, where they had internal assessment and course-work evaluation and a whole lot of other things your harder-working best friend could help you with, as well as a cafeteria you could sit in all day. And that sounded wonderful, that sounded like perfection.

We used to sunbathe in her back yard. She took everything off and sat under the lawn umbrella and wondered aloud if the sun would fade her tattoo. She has a great tattoo, an ankh — on her tailbone. The artist who did it liked her so much he said I'll throw in a nipple for free so she got her tit-ring done. I didn't have anything on my body. When I joined her in the sun the neighbours complained, as if we had exceeded our nudist quota or something. The grass was clean and cut short. The squared blades left a pattern on your skin when you rolled over.

In the kitchen we ate old sausage rolls and meat pies and white bread rolls with marmalade and flat beer. We watched TV in the lounge and left grass stains on the carpet. We de-stocked the grog cupboard and worked our way through the cocktail guide.

Her bedroom was upstairs. In the last hours of the day sunlight fell across the grammar homework pinned up on the wall: lists of *Learn By Monday* and *Memorise!* She kept Polaroids filed under the glass top of her dresser and shoes on a white wire rack at the bottom of her wardrobe. I remember lying on the quilt with the my chin in my hands while she tickled my back, and I would envy her winklepickers. My clothes were such as mess. I swapped: her gold slingbacks for my denim jacket, her bustier for my Docs.

Babe had lots of looks but gradually she got stuck in the sixties, with hairspray and long dresses and fingernails and eyeliner. She became a more intense version of women who demonstrate whiteware products on television, taller with longer, darker hair and tighter wool suits and pointier shoes. I didn't have any money to buy clothes then. It was the first time I'd admitted it to anyone. Babe felt sorry for me and took me out shoplifting.

She talked me into it. She borrowed my big overcoat and made me wear her raincoat even though it hadn't rained all day and we went into Woolworths and she said okay, what's something you like and I said I'd changed my mind again, I didn't want to do it. She said, go ahead, but I was getting sweaty and my hands were shaking and I was too nervous so she said okay, well, get us some pick and mix then, and then she wandered off. I started to bag sweets when one of the staff came up to me and I jumped about a mile but all he said was, please use the scoops provided and not your hands, and I smiled and said sorry and he said that's okay. I finished and paid for the sweets, counted the change out loud. Babe wasn't around so I went outside holding the docket in front of me, and waited on the street and she came out a little later and said well, let's go home then. I offered her the sweets but she said not now — she kept her hands in her pockets. We walked to the bus stop around the corner and as we got behind the building she stopped and opened her coat and an electric frypan fell out. In it's box. And she had stockings and T-shirts and socks and some men's business shirts and some perfume.

We ate the pick and mix at night, in bed. We got zits in the morning, and squeezed them for each other. And then she would do my makeup. She did it every morning for a year.

She plucked my eyebrows and gave me cats' eyes, rouged my cheeks, powdered my nose, made my mouth go from big and red to small and black, drew lines on my face, made me grow my eyebrows back, rimmed my mouth with lip-liner, ran around my eye with pencils, pierced my ears, shaved the sides of my head, shaved my neck, plaited my hair when it grew back, gave me dreadlocks and dyed them from red to black to blonde to three-day-old-vomit yellow. And the said part never washed out or sat flat or returned to its natural skin colour. Once she drew all over me with a mapping pen and I nearly fainted in the shower trying to scrub it off. She read how Mary Quant had her pussy dyed green and shaved into a love-heart and I held my legs up in the air while she took to me with nail scissors.

We got invited to parties where we didn't know anyone. We stole wine from the kitchen and drank it outside sitting on car bonnets with stereos thumping. Babe necked with strangers and I threw up in the bushes. We scored lifts from people who thought her clothes were weird and I was some kind of freak beneath the makeup and paint. We shared hangovers and breakfasts. We made toast and cut it into triangles and took it back to eat in bed. If I had left an extra ridge of jam dripping off my slice after buttering it I would let Babe lick the corner. I watched her tongue licking the burnt crust. Burnt because whatever I try to cook ends up burnt. But when Babe made toast it came out golden brown and white in the middle. Perfect toast, always.

And I could say, come back to my place. And with the lights off we could manage something, achieve a certain grace, because that's the difference between a big house and a small one. In a big house it is a long walk from the lounge to the bedroom — but in a small place all it takes is a nudge. All you have to do is lean across and shut your eyes. You don't have to say a word. The next morning you can cook breakfast and carry it back to bed before it gets cold. You never have to put clothes on to answer the phone — you can spend the whole day naked if you want because there are no hallways or stairs or a backyard. Two voices can fill up a whole house.

I press my face against the cold glass window to watch the car's shadow jumping and shrinking against hills and sidings. I trace my finger on the car window, on the Standards Authority branding. The Standards Authority branding tells me the window is safe, the car is safe, the road is safe and nothing can possibly go wrong. I rest my cheek against the cold smooth glass. Babe is a great driver. Normally I am nervous in cars but when she drives I feel like curling up and going straight to sleep.

The landscape flashes by.

## — SEVEN —

'You awake?'

We are the only ones on the road. The car rumbles like its big old engine is bored, with nothing to overtake. The fuel gauge says empty.

Sure I am. She rubs my neck.

'Lazybones.'

I'm tired. I went to sleep in the sun. How far is it?

'Not far. What's this place like, anyway? Are you allowed to tell me? Or is that part of the deal?'

It's a great place.

'Well it has to be right. It's for my birthday.'

I know it will be. The rooms are huge and you can fit six people in a bed and the baths are a proper depth and the hot water is endless because it's thermal, it comes up from the ground. There's colour TV with cable channels and a video channel that plays soft-porn at four in the morning. The tables in the dining room are covered with starched white cloths. The foyer walls are plastered with flags — racing pennants and screenprinted native birds and visitors' business cards. They have this duck pond out the back, ringed with ferns and a garden of rocks and pebbles and it's lit up at night in blue and red and yellow, and the ducks go to sleep in the different colours, tuck their beaks under their wings.

Babe smiles. 'Sounds classy.'

Hey, I know what it *is*, but they do everything for you and there's plenty of it and that's what motels are about.

'Motel? I thought you said it was a hotel.'

No, I said motel. Is there any difference? Playing with the radio, we are just out of range of the city stations. Do you still have your tattoo?

'Of course I do.'

Are you going to keep it forever?

'They fade, eventually. The ink spreads as it grows through the new skin.'

So one day it won't be there.

'It'll be softer, but it will be there. Smudged.' She frowns. 'What's this place called?'

The Mirage.

'Is it new?'

I went there three years ago and it was old then. I don't think they've changed a thing. They can't afford to. How many people come and stay at a place out here? We count the billboards and gas stations, the old diesel pumps and single post boxes at the end of long dirt driveways. I used to wonder what it would be like growing up in a place like this, with no one around. The only people who come to stay at places like this are people from town, because they don't really know what it's like. Stuck out there without TV.

'Oh come on.'

I know. But I … feel that. Out here.

'It's quiet at night. You can see all the stars.'

I like hearing people around.

'I know what you mean.'

Do you ever get scared, driving by yourself?

'When?'

At night. Do you think bad things are going to happen if you stop?

The sun glares on the dash.

'I don't like stopping at night unless I have to. I read about enough cases as it is.' She shakes her head. 'A friend of mine at work got stopped and beaten up really badly.'

I saw a programme about this woman who was driving at night through some place in Britain and it was the time, a few years ago, there'd been these killings, women had been killed. They'd been murdered at the scene of road accidents when they stopped to help. Well this night, she was driving and saw an accident up ahead, on the road, and a man was waving her down. He was limping. He was waving for her to stop. So she thought, he's hurt, I'd better pull over, she slowed the car down. But as she got to the side of the road he ran for the driver's door and pulled it open and grabbed her and he was covered in blood. And she just screamed and hit the accelerator but he held on, grabbed her shoulders and held until he fell away. He rolled on the road, yelling. And there was an ambulance coming so she waved it over, and the ambulance stopped and she ran over to it and called the driver, and the driver got out and stuck a scalpel into her throat. The driver was the killer. Because he was in uniform he could always get drivers to stop.

'Huh.' She smiles. 'I haven't heard that one.'

People are always intimidated by uniforms. They always do what someone in uniform tells them. That's why it's so easy to impersonate doctors and policemen. People see the uniform and they stop thinking. Once you look right people believe everything you say.

If you don't, pretending is impossible. Like, Spencer Tracy was always too short and if they didn't get that right, the whole picture was ruined. He had to wear clogs all the time. For every scene where he kissed a woman they cut big bits of wood and taped them to the bottom of his shoes, so he could reach. Otherwise he couldn't get up there. That's why in portraits, the woman is always sitting down — if she's taller than the man then the whole thing looks ridiculous.

There was that actress, the German one, who was six foot three. Her husband was another actor — he was famous and the studio got her to marry him for the publicity and so she could get citizenship. But she hated him because he was only five foot something and they looked ridiculous together, when they went out to openings. She ended up stabbing him when he tried to use a dildo on her. And then she committed suicide. Their daughter saw the whole thing.

Japanese actors hardly ever commit suicide. It's to do with their training: they're taught not to respect it. In the Kabuki, everything is so dressed up it doesn't matter if you're short — it's all makeup and masks, that's the tradition. And there's hardly anything on stage, just the actors and a few props. Have you ever seen it? It's so beautiful, just a screen and masks and a single room and all these people watching in the blue light, watching and appreciating and saying nothing.

'That's what I mean about the peace and quiet,' Babe says. 'Living out here. You could just watch. Brian and I were thinking about finding a place out in the country. He doesn't mind the drive and I'm not going to be working so … I don't know. Maybe it's something we'll do.'

There is a goat run along the side of the road, a rusted shed and a long wire hung with rags.

'Which way do we go here?' Babe asks, pointing at the intersection. 'Is it a left or a right?'

It was a long time ago. I don't even remember this part. I think one way is long and the other way is a little shorter, but not by much. I think you can go either way. You might as well.

Babe stops at the Give Way for a little while, the engine idling, and then the wheel turns slowly in her hands.

## — EIGHT —

At the Mirage the curtains are drawn over the ranch sliders and the sign lights are burning in the afternoon sun, bright wires beneath VACANCIES HOT TUBS SKY ELECTRIC BLANKETS. Apart from a dirty ute and white painted lines the gravel carpark is empty. We probably passed everyone on the way down and didn't even see them. It's like that when you drive for a long time, your mind wanders and you stop recognising stuff. Babe stretches her legs. The duckpond will still be out back, behind the main building, you'll see it at night when they turn the spots on. The bushes are waiting to be cut back after summer and the wooden railings are bone-dry.

I walk along to the booking office and hit the buzzer, which pisses off the manager but he wasn't looking up or anything, he was watching a rugby game in the office with his back to me and I feel stupid waiting for ages for people to turn round. He is skinny with a funny haircut and he talks down to me like I'm a little girl. I tell him about the booking but he doesn't remember, he hasn't even written it down and he starts making a fuss about it. He goes on and on like someone's grandmother, fuck. Babe starts to come in but I promise to sort it out. She goes back and waits by the car. The manager is starting up a real argument. There is a crutch leaning on the desk, I think he's a bit funny or something. I explain again more slowly and he finally lets me have a room — when it was mine in the first place anyway. Christ. But then it is more expensive that it was going to be so I have to use Babe's cheque, which is really embarrassing and then he starts hassling her about ID and credit and stuff, it's terrible. I start to argue and he says well go somewhere else if you want, they'll require the same ID. So we sign but I think his attitude really sucks and I'm gonna complain about it later. Although I don't know who you complain to about managers.

He gives us cabin five, right at the end with a brass camel on the doorknob, and Babe watches him walk back to the office. 'What's wrong with his leg?' she says holding back the curtains. 'He looks really weird.'

I reckon it's artificial. He has big shoulder muscles — see? — like he's used to pushing himself around in a wheelchair all day. Babe nods.

Everything is smaller than it was last time, they've put in false ceilings or something. But the décor is the same and they still have the same paintings, the camel train leaving tracks in the desert near the bathroom and the black Japanese fishing boats in the sunset above the bed. They're such cool paintings. If I painted it would be paintings like that.

'Will a whole surprise party fit in here?' Babe wonders, opening and shutting the cupboards. 'I mean if we only want to sit around and talk... These tea-bags are really old. Did we bring tea-bags?' I didn't bring anything. She rinses two dishes and starts stacking them with fruit. 'We'd better go out and get something. Is there a dairy round here?'

I don't remember.

Babe shakes her hair loose. 'We'll have to get some things. Otherwise there'll be nothing to eat. Okay? Come on.'

I'm tired.

'Come on, there's a place down the road.'

Can we drive?

'No, we're going to walk, it's five minutes away.'

It's cold.

'Borrow my jacket.'

She throws me her leather coat, cut bum-length like an army coat. It's beautiful. The leather is cold at first but it gets warmer.

The dairy windows are covered with chipped paint signs and something yellow is dripping down the back of the refrigerator. The woman behind the counters says hello when we come in and starts talking to Babe as if they are old friends. Babe buys two big bottles of Coke and a covered dish of dip. I think the dip looks too old. 'Well you don't have to eat it,' she says. 'Choose a chocolate bar.' We choose about five between us.

Babe makes the woman go out back for fresh cheese. I spin the wire book racks. In between faded paperbacks there are rows of old unread magazines — *True Romance Fiction, Flying Saucer, True Detective Stories*. I really like the *Hot Couples* magazine, I like the readers' forum. Babe says the letters are made up but they all seem different to me, I guess they must be written by the same person, but it's impossible isn't it? I mean this one here is about chicken drumsticks, would you think that up? I think it'd be easier to do it and then write about it afterwards than to think it up sitting at a desk in an air-conditioned office.

'Come on, they make it up — you know they do. Look at these contributing editors.' She runs her finger down the names. 'They don't actually edit anything — they're the ones who write the letters.'

There are about fifty contributing editors. Well, I guess they do write it. There are so many of them. But if all the contributing editors sit in the same office together, like what do they talk about? Do they have group discussions about what things they're going to put into the letters or do they make it up separately? And what does this guy, the supervising editor do? Does he go round the desks every morning and say we'd like a little more cocksucking this month, or breasts are definitely last year's thing. And if he does police what everyone else is writing, who tells him what to do? Does he have research done or does he just put in the sort of sex he likes himself? Is it possible for a contributing editor to go too far? Would you get fired for being too dirty, or not dirty enough? I can imagine you getting fired for being too decent about it. And whereas most companies have really flirtatious office parties I think the *Hot Couples* office parties would be really civil and everyone would go home separately. It's hard to imagine the home life. If the kids were off school they couldn't exactly come to work with you.

And what if someone who reads the magazine *does* write a letter in about sleeping with their schoolteacher or something, what then? Do the contributing editors add little bits to it to make it more dirty or do they take the dirty bits out? Do they reject it because it isn't in their style? See what I mean? When you think about it, it's kind of more likely that people just write in about sleeping with their schoolteacher and a whole bunch of contributing editors do the work of checking the spelling and withholding names and addresses by request.

'Shall we get bread?' Babe wonders. 'They've got wholemeal.'

She isn't even listening. The shopkeeper is straightening the chip packets. I slip the magazine down the front of my jeans and walk out into the fresh air and leave Babe to choose whatever she wants. The roadside grass grows through dead wood and tyres.

The manager is waiting on the deck in his socks, his curls tangled.

'Call for you,' he says. 'Before'.

Who was it?

'A guy ... Howard.' He unfolds a tiny square of paper into two, then four, then eight, and squints at his own writing.

Really?

'Says please call back.' He holds it out. 'City number.'

Thanks.

'Says it's urgent.'

The paper is damp in my palm.

'You can use the office phone. Call direct.'

I'll take care of it.

'Sure? He said you *have* to ring back.'

Thank you.

'Okay.'

The flyscreen bangs shut behind him.

Babe catches up behind me. I drop it on the gravel. What sort of bread did you end up getting, anyway?

The manager watches us all the way to our cabin. He sits on the other side of the mesh at the wide, bare desk, his crutch leaning against the wall. He's such an old perve. He winked at me before.

## — NINE —

I flop on the bed and tug my boots off, wiggle my toes in the socks with the holes in them. We should clean up, but we're hardly dirty. When I find the remote there is a Marilyn Monroe movie on, the one where she's in love with the two guys in drag. The only extra channel is showing football.

I love those old movies that finish with the big swell of music and someone riding off into the sunset with THE END, a real whizz-bang finale and the audience claps and it's all over. All of Marilyn Monroe's movies are like that. I guess her life was like that too. It must have been amazing being her and then leaving behind all those secrets, all the stuff she wasn't meant to know — the stuff about the Black Dahlia murders and Jack Ruby and being on the inside with all the Kennedy brothers and the mafia and the CIA.

'I read an excellent book on the CIA,' Babe says. She lies on her stomach with a bag of chips and we talk and eat all through the movie, like she tells me some more stuff about the Kennedy assassination that I didn't know, how Lee Harvey Oswald was short-sighted and not even a very good shot.

354

'In all the photos of him as a young man he's wearing glasses — but in all the later photos that the CIA released to the press they couldn't have him wearing glasses because people wouldn't believe that someone with glasses could be a crack marksman and kill a president. So they had all the photographs retouched, and they went through all his family photo albums and tore out all the photos of him wearing glasses and destroyed the negatives so there were none left. Which is a shame because with glasses on Lee Harvey Oswald looked a little bit like James Dean — he looked really fragile and vulnerable. Normally' — she makes pointy shapes with her fingers — 'he wore these cute little horn-rims.'

Babe talks some more about Lee Harvey Oswald, how you can tell that photo of him holding the rifle and the socialist newspaper was faked because the shadows on his nose go in a different direction to the shadows cast by his body. 'And that's the thing about Lyndon Johnson, too, a lot of his photos were faked to make it look like he was taller than he really was. In order to secure the Texan vote.'

On the TV Marilyn is playing the ukelele and she sounds better than the whole orchestra put together and she's going to marry the millionaire, which I think becomes the sequel. I thought it was really incredible how no one ever went digging for more after she died, no one ever sorted through the clues. My favourite photograph of Marilyn Monroe is that one of her taken at a press conference. She's sitting wearing a short dress in the middle of all these journalists and the men are all laughing and looking really excited and she's smiling for the camera and it looks like a normal photograph until you realise she's not wearing any panties. It's a very famous photo because it was originally printed in newspapers and magazines without anyone noticing. You can look at the photo for ages and not see her cunt. You have to want to see it before you can.

*

'No sign of anyone yet.'

Babe lets the curtains fall.

'What time is it?'

Not late.

The sun went down quick, dropped behind the hills leaving the hotel sign lonely and bright. Further down the road is a gas station and a block of shops and a takeaways all lit up by floods, and a line of utes and dirty cars and trail bikes. The air is cold. There is only news on TV, and on the other channel is football.

'Do you thing they know where to find it?'

I'm sure they do. Relax.

She stares out through the curtains. 'It's dark.'

I used to work nights at the Easter Show: Thursday nights at the candyfloss stall. I wound sugar on dirty blonde sticks. It was as dark as it is now. The gates had started to close and the lights around the ferris wheel were switching off and the PA was telling families to go home but come back tomorrow as they crossed the grass, stepping over crushed cups and cold batter hot-dogs. My job was to shut the booth and take apart the candyfloss machine and scrape the nozzles clean of dried pink sugar. But this night I hadn't even started because I was too busy watching Wayne standing by the shooting gallery.

Wayne was waiting for the stall owners to finish bolting up the cover boards. And then one of the stallholders said something about me, made a joke out loud, and that was it, Wayne dropped everything and whacked them. He went for them both. They didn't even see it coming, he beat the shit out of them, slapping their heads against the boards and left them lying. But he still came over to give me the panda. He introduced himself and I stared at his swollen face. No one ever got into a fight because of me before. It was just so fucking amazing I couldn't believe it. He said maybe we could go to a movie or something. I said that would be good. He recited my phone number and said he wouldn't forget it and walked off. The panda felt sticky in the dark. Big John.

He picked me up most days after school. His car was a rusty heap of shit with a chrome exhaust down one side. It did not have a warrant or registration or hubcaps or tyre-tread. It did have a re-bored engine block and a hand-brake. The clutch was hair-trigger: you started it by rolling down hills or by pushing and the first revs sounded like backfires piled on top of each other. It broke every written and unwritten school rule of young female conduct just being parked opposite the gates. Five minutes before the bell rang it was surrounded by six hundred giggling classmates. It was a car that gave you hickies if you so much looked at it. When we overtook the bus Big John throttled back for a moment to let the other girls see his decorated knuckles reaching under my skirt, squeezing. And better yet his car stopped outside the same gates the following morning, my creaking passenger door yawned open, my eyes were red and my skirt wasn't pressed. Because Big John and I had sex. Nights of sex, bad sex, fucking, sucking sex, screaming kick the walls and dig-your-nails-in sex. My friends stayed behind for music lessons while we drove home and stuck our tongues in everything. When he dropped me off in the morning I ached.

Summer that year was the hottest on record, two degrees higher per day on average. We kept the curtains drawn and the windows shut all day. We made cinnamon toast and then sat down to watch TV and there was a western on. I loved westerns. And this one starred John Wayne and I looked up at Wayne and said – Big John. He didn't say anything. By the end of the week everyone was calling him Big John. That's when his nickname stuck — in the heat.

There is a noise from outside.

'Someone's coming,' Babe says. The car stops and the engine stops and there is talking and laughing and the doors slam as people get out. Their weight shakes the board steps leading up to the office. There are couple of them and they sound drunk. They belt on the office door. They're gonna wake the guy up. Fuck, he deserves to be woken up.

'Listen …' And she stops to count the vehicles following – three in all crunching loose metal and slamming their doors. The lights are coming on in the reception office but his time and the funny man with the curly hair is telling everyone to be quiet over the noise.

Babe drags on the cigarette. Her eyes are shining in the weak light.

'It's them.' She starts to smile.

They are all drunk and talking and roaming along the balcony walkway and arguing with the manager about the price of the rooms and laughing about how late they are and blaming the weather and the drive down. Music swells from the car tape decks when they open the doors. Babe slides off the bed and straightens her shirt.

'Should we go to the door? Or should we wait? Am I allowed to know? I don't know what to do. Am I supposed to be asleep?'

They are all crowding into the office now, giggling. She walks to the window and peeks out the curtain, her shoulders hunched. 'It's so dark. I can hardly see them.' She pushes the curtains aside more. 'How many did you invite? There's about twenty people.' She presses her nose against the glass. 'Trina there's …' She stays with her face against the glass. 'There's …' She shades her reflection with her hand. 'The cars are all new. Did they rent cars? They …'

She lifts her hand higher. She stares out the window at the booking office and watches the people packed into it, the people spilling out, the people she doesn't know. Just strangers.

Some of them are Japanese I think. Babe looks at them one by one to be sure, shading her reflection with her hand. Someone taps on the glass and she lets the curtains fall. She finds herself an orange in the fruitbowl and runs over its skin with her fingertip. The tip of her cigarette glows in the dim room.

'It wasn't them. Did you think it was?'

I thought it might have been.

'You looked surprised.'

Did I?

She slowly peels the orange over the bench. She holds the cigarette in her mouth. It looks bloody awful, you cigarette hanging out like that. It looks sloppy.

'Is there something you're not telling me?' she asks, softly.

What do you mean?

'It's just that you had that look on your face that you get sometimes.'

What look?

She breaks the orange open with her thumbs. 'They are coming, aren't they? Everyone is meeting us here for my party, right?'

We did talk about it.

'Did you?'

We said how it would be nice to get away for the weekend. We thought about booking a whole lot of places, and I suggested here, and I thought it would be good. Because I really think you need to take a break from things. You're working all the time and we hardly see you, none of us do. And soon you won't feel like travelling, and then you'll have everything else to deal with …

I thought it would be good. I had it all planned. The others were interested. I did tell them. The do know. I mean, we're going to have a good time. We always find stuff to do. We always have. I think we'll have a great time. Regardless.

The orange on the plate has gone. Babe watches me. He hands are folded in her lap.

I thought it would be good.

She switches off the lights and goes into the bathroom. I can hear the shower running. I could get up and turn on the lights but I don't feel like it, not just yet. I sit in the dark wondering if I should open the window so all the cigarette smoke has somewhere to go.

## — TEN —

When I was a kid, I used to dream. Once I had the flu and my fever was so high I could only half-sleep in bed. I dozed propped up with pillows. When I opened my eyes the room was dark and there was a man waiting for me at the end of the bed dressed in a monk's cloak with a hood over his head. I didn't know who he was, his face was hidden by the darkness and the brown cloth. I was so afraid I wanted to scream but my throat was swollen and I could barely breathe let alone call out. All I could do was sit up holding the sheets to my neck and watching him. Finally he held out a little stainless steel measuring cup and gestured for me to take it. He was there to give it to me. I shook my head because I thought it contained poison. He didn't say anything, just gently held the phial closer. I tried sitting and waiting but I was too nervous and finally I gave in and drank it. All it turned out to be was medicine, the sweet stuff with alcohol in it that I liked. After I finished the man nodded and sat with his hands resting in his lap, and I fell asleep. When I woke up for real he was gone and my fever was worse than before, it was raging.

When I woke up Babe was sitting at the bottom of the bed, her chin in her hands. The refrigerator hums. I am warm in the bed and my mouth is dry. The clock says one in the morning.

'You were so sound asleep.' Babe says. 'Your face was perfectly still.'

Was I?

She nods. 'Do you want some tea? She doesn't look angry. 'I made some.'

So I sit up, white with one sugar thanks. She nods at the plastic cup. 'I was worried there weren't going to be enough.'

Yes.

'I really thought it was the manager. I thought he'd just forgotten ...'

Is there any chocolate left?

'A bit.' She pushes the silver paper in her lap, picking up the scraps with her licked fingertip.

The manager has freckles, liver spots. The Boston strangler had freckles — he covered them with women's makeup when he went out, he was so embarrassed. Pancake. He killed because he hated his skin — he hated women's skin, the feel of it. He strangled wearing leather gloves. And he only killed women who were fair-skinned. Did you know that?

Babe relaxes, she lets her shoulders fall forward.

'Why did you say everyone was coming?'

I thought they would.

'You didn't, really.'

I did. We talked about it. I thought there was going to be a party. And then all the way down here I was thinking to myself, thinking you know, those guys probably aren't gonna come. They must be busy or something, they forgot. It's typical, right? They never turn up.

'They came to your party last year.'

That was a great party. We hired a place and had a sound system and a proper bar and I got so drunk. I had to sit outside throwing up for half of it. Babe sat with me.

'You were really sick.'

I was okay.

'Shall we go back tomorrow?'

No. I don't want to go back to town. Not just yet.

I tuck my feet under her soft curves thickened by sheets. Her hair is so long it comes down past her waist.

'You should grow yours.' She stares slow. 'You've got beautiful hair.'

She used to put waves in it with curlers and a hairdryer. She would tease it up, spray it. And it went stiffer when it had a colour through it.

'It used to take hours. God.'

I loved that. I loved when she did my hair. She used to do it with highlights and shaved up the sides, mohican.

'I thought you hated it.'

No. I loved when you made me blonde.

'It looked strange.'

No, it was great.

'Was it?' Babe smiles. When you leant over the sink with the hot water running forward, your eyes red and itching.

Do my hair, Babe.

'It's a bit late.'

It's barely one o'clock. We'd still be getting ready to go out at one, still be putting on the finishing touches. She complains she hasn't brought anything with her, but I have. I slide it out from under the bed.

'Is that my makeup case?' She snaps the locks open. 'God. It's my old case. You kept it.'

I still use the eye shadows.

'You do not, you never wear makeup. Trina. Wow.'

She goes through the colours and brushes and pencil stubs. I kept it. It's the sort of thing you never throw out because it might come in useful. You never know when you're gonna get dressed up. I need to pee, excuse me a sec. The cold porcelain seat. Maybe I should grow my hair. When I hold it up it looks good in the mirror … like that. But it gets stupid and fluffy. There's sleep in my eyes after only maybe an hour. Cold water running.

Babe is still sitting on the bed when I go back, the pots and trays spread out on the sheets. Aren't they great? All the colours. This one's nice, this one's great. But it's not as dark. And this one. Do my makeup, Babe. Please? We could go out.

'Where to, the gas station?'

Do my makeup.

'Your face is dirty.'

I washed it. I'll wash it again.

'I'm tired.'

Do my makeup.

'Trina.'

Please.

'Well … You'll have to take it off again.'

I don't mind.

She clicks on the bedside lamp. I want to lie down, which isn't the proper way but I'm tired, so she makes me lie with the light right between my eyes. She squeezes a tiny sponge in her fist.

'How do you want this? Heavy? It's just gonna make a mess …'

There are false eyelashes here, you know. Okay. This stuff is so black.

'Well, it's practically black. It's dried … there's some stuff down the end … There's some other stuff — this stuff — that's fresh. Look, it's still fresh. Smell? Okay. Look up … at the top of the bed … Good and the other … Okay. Now look down.'

Her breath smells of chocolate. Her hand is heavy with the small wet brushes, pressing my eyeballs through their lids. She purses her lips to blow dust off jars. I lie in the pillow feeling my face wet and tighten into a new shape, heavy and dark with a small sharp jaw, and my eyes tickle with the new lashes and my nose tingles, my whole face feels like jewellery, like I shouldn't move it too fast and Babe rattles in the box, goes through containers, gets tissues from the bathroom. Can I open my eyes yet?

'Not yet.'

When can I look?

'Not till I've finished.'

When will you be finished?

'Ages and ages.' She steadies her fingers on my cheek so she can draw a straight line. 'Now be still.'

\*

'… I had this workman once. Just a young guy. He was putting drains in along the fence, in the property next door. We watched them from the window …'

You and who else?

'Just a friend. We watched them and picked them because he was the youngest. He was still a virgin. He said he wasn't but he was so nervous he had to be.'

Did you sleep together?

'I sucked him off. On the kitchen table. He squealed. Like a little pig. He tried to ring later but we hung up. It was just for fun.' Babe turns my face in the light, her pencil following the eyelid curve. 'Just something you do, you know?'

How many men have you slept with?

'Lost count.'

Really?

'No,' She smiles. 'I remember.'

How many?

'Enough.'

I've hardly slept with any.

'Crap.' She slaps my ear. 'You are in a mood. Other side ...'

I can see the lightbulbs with my eyes shut, shining through the red skin. There haven't been so many, really.

Being stroked wakes up the skin on my face. Makeup reminds you. Each layer highlights what's missing, what's been. Someone see you made up and thinks, she's pretty, but you know what went into it and it doesn't feel pretty at all. That's why people become different after makeup — their face changing reminds them of who they are. Your face is retraced along the lines of what you've been through and the lines lead back to who you are now.

'I never thought of it like that.'

I bet you did.

'I don't think that much about it.' My face feels like warm mud. Babe is busy concentrating. I think this is the first time I have seen her so content. She is always happy when she is doing something for people, like making them breakfast or combing their hair or doing their face. She's such a mother. She's going to be a great mother. She's going to run after her kid all the time and be one of those mothers who never puts their kids down. I can see it. She combs my hair back behind my ears and touches up my nose again. She shows me how to hold my mouth so she can trace the upper lip. The lipstick smells like old wax. She's going to do this for her daughter someday, she'll be doing her makeup all the time. She blows dust off the curling tongs and plugs them into the socket.

\*

'There.' Babe sits back. 'You look amazing.'

Do I?

'You really do.'

Can I get up?

'Sure. You got a cigarette?'

Is it dry? I thought you said you were going to give up.

'I earned it, I'm tired.' She goes through my packet and lights one and pulls on it and squints at her work. 'Your eyes are still a bit sticky, don't open them too much. Here.' She finds a pocket mirror. 'Look.'

Wow.

'You like it?'

It's how I used to do it.

'Careful, don't touch.'

It's so thick. I look fifty years old and a millionaire.

'Now you can take it off and go to bed,' she laughs.

I'm never going to take it off.

Babe sits holding her eyebrow pencil. In the mirror I look older and sharper. I look drawn with a hand steadier than mine, eyebrows black, eyelines black, lips black, hair black. Babe slides off the bed and straightens her shirt, and goes to wash her hands. Face white, hands white, teeth white, nails white. Babe watches me from the bathroom mirror and smiles.

## — ELEVEN —

A long time ago I remember looking in the mirror and wondering how it reflected. The only thing on the back was dark red paint which I didn't believe could reflect anything. I liked how you could tilt the mirror and knock your reflection off its feet.

Once Babe made me up like this and we went dancing. It was late and a Saturday and everything was full, and we ended up in some dive at the top of town sharing a table with these Russian sailors. They were into dancing and bought us drinks constantly so after a few hours we were pretty spinny and in a good mood. Babe was off somewhere. I wasn't used to that, I was used to being with her. One of them said I've got something if you want, come downstairs, and I went with him into the street out back and we had half each. For a long time nothing happened, and then it didn't seem to matter how long time took, how long we waited.

It was the Russian guy's last night here and he started telling me how he didn't want to go back home. He came from a town in the north of Russia where they make all the rods for nuclear reactors. They mine the uranium up in the mountains and bring it down to this particular place and make it into rods which are then shipped out in big cement containers to all the power plants in Russia. This guy was in charge of checking the concrete containers. He said in the seventies, when Russia had lots of money, the containers were made very carefully but now the government was trying to get by with less and made containers using as little cement as possible. He said the containers were now no thicker than his finger and often they were cracked or open at one side because the panels of cement hadn't been poured correctly. He said the whole town was radioactive now, everyone was sick with it. He said he went back to visit his girlfriend and she looked 20 years older than him. She looked like a stranger.

I remember he had bad teeth and he was proud of his fillings. He pulled his lip out with his fingers to show me all the metal in his teeth. Dental work is very expensive in Russia but everyone from his town had good dental work — they made fillings out of the old uranium. He said his whole mouth was radioactive, just a little bit. He said, kiss me and see what happens. Afterwards I went inside the ladies room and looked at myself in the mirror and it was like a different person staring back.

When the Christians kept people prisoner in the Crusades they would put masks on them in jail so that no one could tell who the prisoners were. That way you couldn't complain to the authorities if there was someone in jail who you knew and had been improperly arrested, and you couldn't know who was being held where if you wanted to storm the prison and release them. When the prisoners were released and their masks taken off they would have forgotten what they looked like. And when the prisoners' families came to collect them, they wouldn't recognise each other. Usually the prisoners' wives would have taken up with someone else, which makes you wonder how much they needed to be married in the first place.

They also invented chastity belts for the Crusades. I don't think they really worked. I spent a long time trying to work it out and I can't see really how you can manage to shit and piss when you're wearing steel pants, let alone have your period. even if they only have a hoop and a belt it's still pretty inconvenient, and I think anyone with a lock on their stomach every night and day for three years would start to figure a way of picking it. There was one queen who worried about her husband so much she lost weight and the thing just fell off. She stepped out of it and had a good time for three years. It wasn't that she had a lot of lovers but she had a lot of friends and she could do all the things she wasn't supposed to do by herself, like reading and riding and hanging round taverns and stuff. Then when her husband wrote to say he was returning she tried to get her chastity belt back on and found she'd become too fat to slip into it again, on account of all the mead and cakes and ale. And so she really started to worry then, and of course went off her food and lost weight and just managed to get the thing back on before the king got back. But even if that hadn't happened I think she should have been able to figure her way out of it if she really wanted to.

## — TWELVE —

Babe is cupping herself in her fingers, measuring her reflection. Soon she will ripen to a pear curve. She turns on her heel to imagine the shape she will be — she lifts her chin a little. The curve of her neck and her gentle shoulders, the tiny black stem of a gap between her thighs. The tattoo shimmers on her tailbone. She smiles as I bump past and sit knocked-kneed to pee. She toys with the tiny snick of gold in her nipple, tipping it on a finger's end.

It's not real gold, is it?

'Eighteen carat.'

Have you taken it out before?

'Not for a while. It's grown in and got infected.'

Youch.

'Only slightly. It was sore when it first got done and it hurt for months after that, every time I touched it. I thought I'd really done it, ruined something. Your body remembers.' I look worried and she rolls her eyes. 'If you can't handle it …'

It's better if I wash my hands first.

'You're not taking out my appendix or anything.'

I don't want to leave a scar.

'It's only a little hole.'

I read about a woman who let old mascara cake up so much that a chip of it scarred her retina. They fix eyes with lasers now, heat-stitch them. Under local anaesthetic. But that must give you a headache. I got a headache even after the x-ray.

'Medicine.' She sniffs. 'It's so bad for you.'

During the French revolution old ladies used to take boys into theatre boxes and jerk them off and rub the come into their faces because come makes the skin tight, with all the minerals. It made them look young for the evening. But you can't do that now. I mean, you could if you'd both had blood tests and were married to someone. But then you wouldn't need to take someone to the theatre to do it, if you were married. They don't even have theatre boxes now. You'd have to do it at the pictures.

She laughs. She looks at us side by side in the mirror, our toes touching. 'Your skin's so smooth.' She dabs at my eyelids. 'You look beautiful.'

I used to wear makeup like this all the time.

'I know.'

I used to wear it in summer, thick foundation and I remember sweating through it, it was like wallpaper paste. This summer felt as if was raining even when there were no clouds. The rain would come and you'd think, thank God, the weather's broken, and then it would go away again — and humidity would be worse than ever. It came out in lumps. When I went to the doctor he said it was tomatoes but it wasn't tomatoes at all. I was allergic to the whole weather, to the air.

'Lead in the air and the power lines and processed food. It's poisonous. You shouldn't live in the city. I don't know how you do it. And now people breaking in.'

I know.

'Well ...?' She touches my shoulder.

Okay.

She tears off some tissues like it's going to bleed buckets.

'It's not. Don't be such a child.' She sits on the formica sink-top, leaning back under the single light. I wash my hands anyway and hold her nipple. The ring moves but only slightly, there is a piece of flesh around it, half-coloured like the moon on a fingernail. I lick my thumb to soften the skin, thinking I could maybe push it back with something.

The rose-bruise, grey veins feathered outwards, a pool's ripple.

In the makeup box is a nail file with a flat edge for pushing back cuticles. I think it will do. See?

'That looks fine.'

I'll try.

'Ow ...'

Is that hurting?

'It's okay. Ow.'

It's gonna hurt.

'Just do it quickly before it hurts.'

I press with the metal edge, and the nipple flesh pops back along the ring and a dot of blood appears and swells before a break appears in the metal and I can twist the ring apart into a C-shape and it comes away. Babe lets her breath out and presses the tissue against her nipple. I drop the ring on the side of the sink. It nearly falls but I catch it. It nearly falls down the drain and is lost forever.

Her eyes are watering like it really smarts. I dab her with warm water until there is nothing there. She's laughing because it hurt. And then I kiss it, the coarse dark skin under my lips shuddering in the fluorescent light. And I wait.

Babe does nothing, leaning back against herself in the mirror, closing her eyes to my mouth on her nipple, the gentle sucking and my hands in the small of her back holding her close.

Babe's mouth against the glass, thinking to herself, long slow licks.

'Catrina ...'

Her palms lift me away and smooth my temples and she picks up the hairbrush and combs my hair. She licks my eyebrows flat and gives me her t-shirt and walks me back to bed with her arm over my shoulder. She falls asleep holding my hand and saying nothing.

*

The bathroom light is burning in the mirror.

Babe.

My makeup is sticking to the pillow.

Babe?

I shin the bedside table and the dead heater hisses. The curtains feel damp from the rain, cool to touch. As I stand they bump my legs in the breeze, moved by the empty night air.

The sun is still a long way away, underneath the hills. My face is dark in the window glass, the makeup thick. The Japanese are partying next door, singing karaoke, drinking and talking, jet lag I guess. Their room lights shine through the rain.

Adults never go to sleep when they should. When kids get tired they drop down anywhere and shut their eyes — they're either running or unconscious. The older you get the more you find yourself stuck in between. You stay awake because there's something to do or someone to talk to, and when you do get to bed you dream or don't sleep because you're worried, and in the morning you're still tired but have to get up anyway. You end up halfway between day and night and not enjoying either.

The older I got, the less I slept. I would get up after bedtime to watch television through the crack in the lounge door. Everyone knew I was doing it but they let me stay there. They figured I'd fall asleep sooner or later but I didn't, I stayed and watched programmes for hours through a half-inch gap. When I got to watch the whole screen it was never as good. The gap made everyone look so tall on the black and white, tall and skinny and beautiful.

# — THIRTEEN —

First thing in the morning, Babe wakes up and runs to the bathroom to vomit.

Do you want anything?

I can get you anything.

She hunches over the toilet, retching, her cheeks red. Sick on her hair hangs in strands.

She asks me not to stroke her back, so I stop.

We did talk about the surprise party. We did. It was gonna be something like this. Some place. Okay? It was going to be like this.

It felt right.

Oh God.

We can go home soon if you want. We can go home now after breakfast.

You're so pale.

If you want a doctor the manager can call one, I'm sure. I can't believe you're like this every morning. Well, I can't. Not without a party the night before, right?

She goes back to bed and pulls the sheets up around her neck.

I wring out a hot flannel and wipe her face.

That's cool, isn't it? That feels good. Pressed on your face. I love a hot flannel. My grandmother used to wipe my face with a hot flannel. When she was alone she used to cry. I didn't know what to do about it. For a long time I thought it was something I'd done. It never occurred that she would get upset over someone other than me. She was so professional when she spoke with other people. Hearing her chat with the grocer was like listening to a stranger, she was so collected. I forget his name. He moved away after a time but she never got sentimental over it. Other people never rattled her.

It was a long time ago.

Are you feeling better now?

You should sleep.

I'm sorry Babe.

I'll clean everything.

*

The rain is spitting. I walk slowly in the fresh air. The dining room windows are steamed up. The people inside — the ones who arrived last night — are still shouting and laughing. The manager waves to me from the office.

'Another call,' he says. 'After midnight.'

Did it get you out of bed? I'm sorry.

'Told them to ring back.' He hands me the note. 'We don't put calls through that late. Who's up at that hour, eh?'

Yeah. Well. Thanks.

'You can come and use the office phone if you want.'

Maybe after breakfast.

'The number's there.'

I put the note in my pocket. Thanks.

'No problem. If they ring back …'

Actually, my friend's a bit sick this morning, so maybe you should hold our calls.

'Not well, is she?'

Just a cold. But if you take a message, that would be great.

He says he is happy to do that. The fly screen squeaks shut again. He watches me from behind the door. I pull up my collar and run across the gravel.

\*

'Theo.' He holds out his hand.

Hi.

'Pleased to meet you, Catrina.'

He wears a baseball cap and a hunting jacket. He has food caught in his gold front tooth. He goes through his jacket pockets. 'You want some chocolate?' he says. 'I got some chocolate here somewhere.'

Not before breakfast.

'So you girls been staying here long?'

We came in yesterday.

'Pretty formal for breakfast.'

My reflection sits on his shoulder, the smudged girl, false eyelashes and her hair teased, checkered tablecloths, people queuing on the food counter. He wonders:

'You from round here?'

My friend lives just over the hill.

'Is that so.'

Her family live there. She's from a farm, originally.

'And are you a farming girl?'

No. I'm from the city.

'But you're staying here.'

Her family's having this big family reunion at the farmhouse and they kind of ran out of beds.

'Don't like her parents, huh?'

It's not that.

'Don't like your choice in friends?'

What friends?

'You meeting someone here, right?' He runs his finger around his eye, pointing at my makeup. That makes me smile. You got it wrong.

'Have I?'

Yep.

'In that case … ' He tips his baseball cap. '… I do beg your pardon.'

Is that your home team? On your cap. Rams. What do they play?

'Football. You been to Los Angeles?'

Nup.

'Rams play for Los Angeles.'

His breath smells of beer. He waves his big red fingers at the Japanese guys. 'They all got them. But they're not from Los Angeles.'

But you're from Los Angeles.

'Nope.'

I thought you were.

'Not from Los Angeles.' He sucks in his top lip and leans over. 'So you're not waiting for anyone?'

No.

'Well that's good.'

Why's it good? He only smiles and jiggles his drink.

'You sure you don't want one?'

It's not even lunchtime.

'Hair of the dog.'

That bit you.

'What's that?'

Hair of the dog. That bit you. It's the saying.

'That's it. That's what I said.' He shakes the can. 'You got it.'

Did your breakfast take this long?

'Haven't had any. We've been at it all night. Sorry if we kept you up.'

You were pretty quiet.

'Quiet.' He looks pleased. 'Hard to believe.'

I heard singing.

'Karaoke.'

Did you sing?

'We all sang.'

You got in late enough.

'Guy at the desk wasn't too pleased.'

He's weird.

'D'you ski?'

Sorry …?

'Do you ski? You know.' He mimes holding poles. 'Snow.'

Oh. No.

'Great powder this season.'

Is that good?

'Oh yes. That's the best.'

Is that your friend?

'Which one?'

The one throwing up.

'Oh. A-ha ha. Pete.'

Everyone is shouting and pointing.

'Pete! PETE. A-ha ha. You're messing up the place. PETE.'

God.

'Pete, Pete?' Theo shrugs. 'He'll be okay in a second.'

He should be outside.

'Is he putting you off your breakfast?'

I don't even have my breakfast. I'm still waiting.

'Well he'll probably still be going when it arrives. A-ha ha a-ha.'

Wipes his nose with the back of his hand, Jesus.

'That's just a little joke. I was making a little joke there. A-ha.'

Yeah …

'You're a quiet one.'

What's that mean?

'Means you're quiet.'

Shouldn't you look after your friend …

'He's okay. So, you like my cap?'

It's okay.

'Well here. You have it.' He puts it on my head. 'S' big for ya. Lookit. You got a little head.' He snaps off a piece of chocolate. 'Sure you don't want some?'

*

Wayne was standing in the kitchen drinking from a baby bottle of scotch. There were two chocolate bars lying on the sideboard in their wrappers. He offered me some but I said no. He looked at me funny when I said it. I wanted to jump off and run into my room, then. But I didn't. I made myself sit there and tell him I wanted to move out. I tried to explain how I wanted to live by myself so we could go out with each other again — we could call each other up and meet in town for coffee and go to the movies and decide afterwards whose place to stay at. The cold bench was stinging my legs. We could leave clothes at each other's house by accident. It would be like a normal relationship, it'd be fun. Don't you think?

He spat at that, he said it was a stupid fucking idea. He yelled in my face. You're all the fucking same, he said. Fucking Lorraine and fucking Alison and fucking Sharona. And I said well it's your fault for going out with girls who were all song titles. He got really pissed off then, he started banging things. You're all the same, you all lie through your teeth, you're a liar like the rest of them. You're worse than them. You're *worse*. He stalked me around the house, yelling and punching walls. He smashed a whole lot of stuff, and that made it easier. I sat in the bedroom waiting for him to finish, listening to things coming off the shelves and crashing on the floor.

I thought about him with other people and that made me angry too. I stayed on that night. I slept by myself with the door locked. But I didn't stay angry. I thought saying goodbye to people you hate would be easy, but it's not. Saying goodbye to people you hate is hard because you know you're never going to see them again.

## — FOURTEEN —

Babe lets her speech slur, lets it roll out slowly, and looks at the Rams cap with sleepy eyes. Over at breakfast. This funny guy gave it to me. He's staying with his friends. Her cheek rests against the pillow, pink on the soft white. Are you feeling better?

'I'd love some melon.'

The fruit looks green but it is ripe on the inside. The pips slide from the flesh to leave a small wet crease. She chews slowly. Are you always so sick?

'Sometimes.'

I didn't think it was true. I thought it was only like that on TV.

Yeah. Sometimes …' She laughs. 'Don't look so worried.'

I think you should eat. I scoop her up some more on the spoon.

She holds it in her mouth, letting the juice run. 'It's so sweet,' she says.

I can get you something proper.

'No no.' She wipes her lips. 'This is the right thing.'

*

In the afternoon I get the pool key. She doesn't want to get out of bed but I make her come for a swim in the rain. It'll warm you up. Even just putting your feet in is enough. See? I want to splash in the water. She sits on the edge, shivering in a towel.

The cold has trapped the air in the valley like a fog. You can smell the log fires and car exhaust. The hills are almost invisible. The motel sign is bright against the road, flashing VACANCIES.

'What else did you and your friend talk about?'

We were just waiting for breakfast. It took ages. I had sausages and bacon and eggs and toast and coffee — everything.

'Your appetite's back.'

After the long drive. The air makes you hungry, maybe. She nods. Are you going to get in? You'll freeze. How's your tit?

'Swollen.' She cups it in one hand. 'Not because of you, though. You did a good job. You were gentle with it.'

Maybe I should go into the tattoo business.

'Yeah.' She drops the towel and steps into the water. 'Christ, it's hot.'

Only because you're cold. She eases onto the wooden seat. When she is under she takes my foot and starts rubbing it. I still get sprains — the bones click in and out. I can never be bothered getting it seen to. It's such a fuss. I hate doctors.

It's been quite a week, with your birthday and everything. All the fuss. Everywhere I go there's a fuss. I was thinking about next year — I thought I might go back and finish my course. Over the last few years … I missed the reading. And a degree might get me a better job. Do you think? I mean, I'm living so close to town, now. I could probably even manage the work myself … It feels really good when you rub just … there. By the heel.

If I owned this place I would be in the pool all the time. Bugger the guests. I can't believe that guy doesn't use the place. I don't think anyone does. Maybe it's got something to do with his leg. Maybe he fell in and burned himself. You know, when they first tapped into the spring. It's thermal, isn't it? That would cook your flesh right off.

Last time we came down here I bought one of those little jars of sand. You know the ones? The little test-tubes filled with layers of different coloured sands. Finally I opened it up and stirred them together.

The makeup sweats out of my pores. Do I look young again? I liked it messed up, I enjoyed looking like that. Babe wonders about that. She rubs my other foot. That feels so very good. 'Does it?' she says. She leans back against the rim, watching me splash around, her skin beneath the water.

## — FIFTEEN —

Theo's crowd are still going. That makes it over 24 hours. The light from the cabin shines through the curtains and the music thumps through the walls. I stare at the ceiling and consider going over. I have been asleep since dinner. The sheets are damp and my neck itches. Maybe I'm getting a cold. I feel like swimming again. I could lie in the pool all night.

*Hot Couples* is spread on the floor, the glossy pages wobbling in the party lights. There are men being jerked off and women arching their heads back and cocksucking and women being fucked. I read about the nymphomaniac who likes three men at a time, the man who likes fists up his arse, about warm wet cunts. I read all the things that fit in vaginas: takeaway chicken legs and champagne bottle necks and gloved fingers and boot heels. There are men who suck themselves off with vacuum cleaners. Boys are initiated by cleaning women and maids and maths tutors and au pairs and neighbours. Semen tastes sweet and warm and rich and bitter. All the cocks are enormous and the women stay wet forever. There is even a woman with tattoos — the tattooed lady.

As she sleeps, Babe's tattoo stares up at the wall, perched on her tailbone. When it was first finished I had to change the dressing for her — it bled until it scabbed and then later the scab fell off.

I once went out with a guy who was covered in tattoos. When he undressed he was black with them. But he never got any done on his hands or neck. He said that's the only place you can't get tattooed. If you have them on your face you get into fights all the time — just by someone looking at you. He got blood poisoning in the end and was put into hospital. And he was deficient in Vitamin D because the skin hidden under all the ink and scars didn't get any sun.

There was this murder case where the killers cut up a man and fed his body to the shark. Later the shark was caught by a fishermen and opened up and they found the victim's arm inside. They identified the arm by the tattoo on the bicep, and put the murderers in jail. I thought being in the stomach of a shark would eat away at your skin but evidently shark stomachs don't have a very high acidity. I guess they have a pretty low stress lifestyle when you think about it, floating in the water and eating whatever comes along. That is the way to be: big and hungry, and you just take whatever you want when you see it. You don't think twice about anything. And whatever you take, whoever it is, they wouldn't even see it coming.

The people in *Hot Couples* are still sucking and fucking, still stretched over poles and bars and steaming rods, hiked up and glistening and stroked red and moaning. They mutter and gasp and beg and throb. They fall to their knees and reach new heights of passion. They split their ripe peaches and buns and strawberry blonde bushes. I turn the pages one after the other in the dark, in my fingertips — one kiss after another, one tongue and one crack and one furrow.

*

'… Trina.'

She is breathing hard with her face down in the sheets. The panic in what she says has yet to harden. My hands are warm and her back is warm and her thighs spread like her swollen nipple. She tastes of clean salt.

'Trina stop it.'

Her hands are gradually getting a grip and her back straightens.

The strong parts are waking up, the difficult things, the reasons, the practical considerations, the legal aspects, the homework pinned to the wall in the sun.

'Trina stop.'

Do you remember in the sun, the grass? Wet after swimming practice and the bathroom mirror? You never have that feeling again.

She takes my wrists and she's big, she just twists right out from underneath.

I'm not going to cry. All I can do is lean forward and kiss her again. I'm not going to cry.

She fetches me one, hits me right in the face with her open hand and yells.

I catch the bedside lamp when I fall. It goes through the window and people come running.

The door jumps off its hinges and then they are on me.

*

The music is even louder inside. The cigarette smoke makes me cough. Theo and all them are still drunk and he still manages to get me down on the bed and carefully clean my head — the stitches have opened up and they hurt for the first time. All that fuss in the hospital and now, when I could really do with a hit of gas or pills or something, I'm stuck in a hotel room full of old songs and cigarettes and Rams caps. Theo hovers with a cotton wad. I think he is seeing double and trying to decide which one is me.

Later on I get up and sing, and everyone claps along. I sing:

Tall and tan and la la la lovely,

The girl from dum te dum goes something

And when she la te dum — everybody goes — Aah.

Theo laughs.

'You got a great voice.'

Have I?

'You should sing more.'

I don't know what to say. Should I?

'Of course you should.'

Then sing it with me.

He gets up and holds the microphone.

'Ready ... Go!'

Tan and tall and la la la lovely,

The girl from something or other goes walking.

Theo puts his arm around me and everyone claps.

Tan and tall and la la la lovely.

Everyone wants to know what happened to my head. It was a dog. There is a big black labrador that lives next door to me. It's lovely. No no, I *like* dogs. I like him. Bruno, his name is. Listen: this is how. I always play ball with this dog, we play fetch. He's lovely. I have this big children's ball and I throw it and Bruno brings it back every time. Well a few days ago, right, we were playing in the back yard. I was sitting in the sun with my hat over my face and I threw the ball and it went into the bushes. And Bruno didn't come back for ages. He was sniffing around in the bushes going crazy. So I went and helped him look. I was rooting around in the bushes — I still had my hat on, see — and I came up suddenly and he thought my head was the ball and he bit it. He was so sorry about it. He licked me for ages. He knew he'd hurt me and he didn't know what to do.

\*

Even after you have finished loving someone it is still nice to see them. When Wayne first came round he sat next to me on the couch for a long time and held my hand. It was uncomfortable sharing. My furniture is the wrong shape. When he kissed me it was short. Like a baby kiss. He didn't know what to do. I didn't know what I wanted either. We watched the gas burn in blue rows. He talked about staying but I said no, it's Babe's birthday and we're gonna meet for a drink. He looked down. Birthdays are important and you can't forget them. We're going up, me and the guys, all our varsity friends. You can come along if you want to. He knew he could. He said sorry when he left and I said, sorry for what? It could have been worse — if we'd argued, had a fight or something. And then he walked out. That was three nights ago. It seems longer.

## — SIXTEEN —

The bedroom glows in the red hum of the fan heater. Everyone else is playing cards in the next room, shouting and jeering. Theo talks about funny things. He lies with his hands clasped behind his head and his cap over his eyes.

'You sure you're feeling okay?' he asks.

Yeah.

'You sang great.'

I used to sing in the choir.

'Aah. That's nice.'

We had a choir at school  and I sang in the front row. I was one of the best. And then I strained myself and got sick. This ball of fluid swelled up in my throat, it was a cyst …

'A goitre?' He frowns.

That's what it was. It swelled up and almost stopped my breathing and I had to go into hospital. That was the week before my final exams. So I got aggregate scores and they weren't enough for my degree. I only got average scores. I needed higher.

'What really happened to your head? You've got a bad bang there.'

It's embarrassing.

'You don't have to tell me.'

I know. I was shopping, I was going out, carrying my groceries down the escalator. And I slipped. In the middle of the store, in front of everyone. I went face first into the doors.

'Jesus.'

They didn't break, but … they're strong glass. I just bruised it. I woke up lying in all my food. They wanted to call an ambulance — honest, I was going to die of embarrassment.

'That's pretty ugly,' he grins. 'Sorry. Not laughing at you.'

You should — it's funny. I laughed afterwards. Eventually.

'You've had quite a time. After your friend drinking like that …'

Babe doesn't drink that much.

'She drank enough to get up and push you pretty hard.'

She's kind of upset. In fact she's very upset. Some people were meant to come up this weekend but they didn't. It's her birthday. We had this party all arranged and they didn't come.

'What, and she's up here waiting?'

That's right. They're friends too.

'That's pretty shabby.'

Yeah.

He pushes his cap back and stares at the ceiling and then he looks over at me. He has a hard stare. Not angry, though. He stares as if he's looking for something small. 'Well, she shouldn't be by herself, you friend.'

I think she wants to be alone. Like Greta Garbo.

'She should get over here and unwind.'

She's fine, really.

'Are you scared?'

Of course I'm not scared. But …

'It's hard making up, I know that. But we should do it. You should try, at least.' He raises his eyebrows. 'A little humility. It's important. The world's a very selfish place.'

Come on.

'It is. I see it. I meet a lot of people. When I was going round Europe I had to look after myself all the time. Once I was on a bus, sitting with these young guys, locals. It was a hot day and they were sharing a can of soft drink and they offered me some.

Later I fell asleep, and when I woke up my pack was gone. The whole thing. Passport, money, everything. The police said the boys has slipped me an anaesthetic in the can. It's an old trick. I fell for it. I was totally ripped off. And that's what it's like. Everyone's out to get you. You should look after the people that aren't.'

I just don't think we should wake her up again.

'Well. Okay.' He rests back on the pillow. 'She's your friend.'

Yes.

'You known each other long?

Years and years. Where are those guys from?

'Oh we met up. Group booking, we got a discount. I never met them before.'

Not even Pete?

'Nah. I make friends fast. You have to — travelling.'

I guess we're friends, now.

'Guess so.'

I feel like more wine. I know I shouldn't but I feel like it. It's not having any effect at all. Maybe because the air is dry. You sweat out alcohol in dry air.

'Sure. Go ahead.'

Want some?

'I had enough.'

I know, but do you *want* some?

'Shit.' He grips my arm like he is testing to see if I am really there. 'You are a smart arse.'

I'll get the bottle.

Theo has the same painting hanging over the bed in his cabin, the Japanese fishing boats, red in the sunset. He doesn't want me to talk. His belt buckle comes from California, solid silver, beaten and drilled. His hands are big enough to pick me up, right off the ground. I didn't even dress properly. I've got my top and my jeans and he tugs them off and the only thing underneath is me, stretched out on the floor holding the wine bottle so it doesn't spill. I lie sideways on the floor, sideways in the dark, waiting. And he puts his hands under my head and cradles it like a grapefruit as he lifts me again, right off the ground like I weigh nothing at all, and the bed is narrow and the springs squeal and my hands reach up to the picture frame, spread on the sweating wallpaper and he asks what I want but I don't know. I say just more and he asks, like this, more of this, and I say yes, anything, just more and more and more of it.

*

The fan-heater stayed on all night. I open my mouth in the bathroom mirror. The back of my throat is raw from breathing.

'So it is …'

*It hurts.*

'Aww.'

His big arms go around me twice. Jesus. He can lift me — do you *mind?* — he can lift me off the floor.

'Gave you a sore throat. Are we still friends?'

Yes. I slept like a log.

'I noticed.'

I guess we missed out on the party.

'There'll be others.'

I bet there will.

'You should join us for lunch. The boys should be up about four. That's an early start for us.'

I think we're going this morning.

'Stay for the afternoon.'

She's — you taste funny — she's my lift.

'How'm I meant to taste?

I dunno.

'You're going to town, right? You can get a lift with us.'

I'd … better not.

'Well, think about it.'

I came up with Babe …

'Okay. But you're welcome to. Okay? We're planning on staying in the city until our flight leaves. Some nice hotel.'

Where you can throw up on the carpet.

'Uh-huh.'

## — SEVENTEEN —

The cabin curtains billow out like skirts. Babe is reading in the morning sun, the blankets around her feet. The picture hangs over her head. Junks in the sunset.

'Just something from work.' She flicks the pages. 'Not even interesting.'

I'm so tired.

'Was the party good?'

I sang.

'One of them came over and said hi.'

Oh.

'Some guy — Theo?'

I didn't know he came over.

'He said I shouldn't feel bad about what I did.'

That was nice of him.

'Nice. Sure.' She shrugs.

Do you want a glass of water? I'm going to have a glass of water. Jesus it's cold. What time is it?

'Come sit with me.'

I've got cramp.

'Slept crooked, huh?'

I don't why it is. I look at the empty bottom of the cup. I hate drinking from plastic. I like a glass. Plastic does make water taste different. They did a test on it once. It's something to do with the oxygen bubbles that sit on the bottom of the cup when you fill it.

'Here. Sit.'

She examines my cheek, then my head. 'The swelling's down.'

It doesn't feel swollen at all.

'What was it like over there?'

It was a good party.

'Sounded like it. Meet anyone?'

Lots of people.

She smooths the blankets.

'So what is it that I don't have to feel bad about?'

Pardon?

'Theo said I was forgiven, and I wondered: what was it exactly that I did?

I don't know. You'd have to ask him.

'Did you say something to him?'

No. We talked about lots of things, but not about you. He's been all over Europe and the States.

'Trina.'

I said you were pissed off about the birthday not happening.

'The birthday was never going to happen.' She bristles. 'You lied about the party. Did you tell him that?'

I stand the plastic cup on the bench. You don't have to snap. It wasn't like that.

'What'd you tell him?'

You still had your birthday. Look, you're older. See? Without any help. My head hurts. I want to sleep.

'Didn't you sleep last night?'

What d'you care?

'With Theo?'

Maybe.

'What'd you tell him, Trina?'

Does it matter?

'Of course it matters. It matters to me. I'm your friend. At least I'm supposed to be. I don't feel like it sometimes. You drag me around. You bring me up here. You say everyone's coming and they aren't. You — you ...' She throws up her hands. 'Last night!'

What about last night?

'I wonder what goes on in your head sometimes. I really fucking do.'

It doesn't matter.

'It does!'

I'm gonna go for a swim.

'You're not.'

I'm gonna get the key. Do you want to come? I feel like a swim.

'Trina I'm talking to you. I want to talk to you. I want you to talk to me.'

Is there a dry towel?

'What did you tell everyone about me?'

Nothing.

'What did you say?'

Babe stares. I can't find my towel. I look in my bag and underneath my bag and the bed. It takes forever to find. Maybe it isn't even worth going for a swim. You know how it is? You spend the whole night looking forward to something, and then when it comes to doing it, you don't want to.

Babe used to be a great swimmer, before. She took classes in it. Not that I went to classes. I wasn't going to be shouted at in front of everyone else. She showed me how that night, after the late class. I always forgot my towel. I remember having to go back into the changing rooms all the time. I left it at the gym and at home and at other people's places. In my locker. The smell of the changing rooms. Chlorine and piss and wet wood. My wet togs went mouldy. They squeaked on the bench as I sat down, squeezed out the water between my legs as I laid back with my eyes shut, waiting. The last locker doors banging shut with the lights off and waiting stretched out under the clothes hooks for the kisses and the stroking and the warm taste. Thinking, then, I don't want to go for a swim. Not just yet.

Theo swims, did I tell you? He has a stomach like a washboard, all the muscles. A real swimmer's body. He used to swim twenty lengths a day, a hangover from his college training. He was in a representative team. He could have gone for the Olympics, probably. He was that good. He shaved his body every day to cut down the drag and he clipped his hair short. But in the end he gave it up. He said he got sick of being in the water all the time, never lifting your head up. And I know what he means.

But there is nothing else to do. I have to go for a swim. It is either sit here and talk to you — her — or get into the water. And I like the water.

I shut the door behind me.

## — EIGHTEEN —

The pool steam cools along the timber fence. There is a jet of hot water just below the surface, playing with my hands.

I don't let Babe in at first, when she knocks. I sit and hope she will go away. Explaining is such a waste of time. She knocks again. I reach out and undo the latch and the door opens.

She is still dressed. But the seats are wet, the ground is wet, the walls are wet. I mean, what's the point? Why don't you just get in? Why not? She talks about getting her togs. I mean … Jesus. She looks at me. She steps out of her skirt and piles her things in a heap and climbs slowly into the water.

The steam rises in curls. The curls do not last long. They thin and become invisible. Babe rocks from one side to the other, dipping her round shoulders in the water, being careful her hair doesn't get wet.

'I didn't want to do anything this weekend. I wanted to stay in bed.'

That's almost what you have done.

'I drove.'

Yeah.

She cups her nipple in the water.

'Are there pools for the other cabins?'

No. But they have nicer showers.

'How are the rooms?'

Bigger. Bigger and better.

She looks down like she understands. Her feet play with mine. I don't feel like it.

'Rub your back?'

It isn't dirty.

'Come on,' she says quietly. 'Turn around.'

I turn my back on her and she comes forward and begins to knead my shoulders, the muscles, the joints, cracking under her fingertips. She has strong hands.

'Everything's hatching out.' She wipes down my spine. 'Being flushed.' My neck under her thumbs. 'Leaving your body.'

Everything aches. My legs ache, my tailbone. Do you feel a different part of you floating? With the baby?

'I hardly feel anything.'

Do you and Brian still do it?

She laughs. 'He's only just started speaking to me again.'

You can keep going until the eighth month.

'I know.'

There was this woman who got pregnant for a second time when she did it in the ninth.

'Trina.'

I read it.

Babe smiles. She kneads my arms, the biceps, elbows, wrists. I didn't even know I had muscles there. I thought it was only bone. Gristle.

'What you said last night — about lying on the grass.'

Nothing.

'You said …'

I meant, your back lawn.

'At Dad's.' She recalls. 'It's sold now. Subdivided. It was the last big lawn in the street.'

It makes me smile.

'What happened after you left the pub on Thursday?'

Rub my stomach. She turns me round and runs her hand across my belly. Slow circles.

I tell her.

I tell her about the walk home, being angry. I tell her about swearing when my key sticks in the lock. About slamming the door and my feet slipping and my head. Calling

111 and not being able to speak. Have you ever lost your voice? You open your mouth and no sound comes out. The receiver waiting in the darkness. Eventually the operator decided on the police. I didn't call them. I thought I needed an ambulance. I thought my brains were dripping out of my head.

She stares at me with dark, dark eyes. The jet nozzle shimmers.

'Did you tell them?'

They were really stupid.

'Did you tell them what you told me now?'

No.

'What did you tell everyone last night — at the party?'

I didn't tell them I love you.

She holds her hands around my waist.

I lean forward and close my eyes and kiss her. She offers her cheek.

Clean wind runs through the cabin. Everything is quiet and hung over. I could pack but I didn't bring anything. I run a comb through my hair so the water patters on the carpet. My head-cut has closed, nothing more that a pink scab. I comb my hair over what will become a scar.

The kitchen is dirty. The melon sits in the fridge with only one slice missing. The fruit is soft. When I move it from the bowl the mites float up. Ants stick in the juice. The fruit is extra-ripe, extra soft stage of its life, the last burst of sweetness before it turns rotten. We haven't even touched it.

I should leave a note but there's no pen and besides, Babe won't be surprised. She said she was going to do all the driving anyway. I will catch up with her later to explain. Maybe next weekend. Afterwards.

The manager watches me crossing the gravel carpark — he knows, the little prick. He probably peeks at the cabin windows. There was this guy once, in America, a serial killer who lived in a hotel. He used to trap the guests by …

Theo's cabin is empty.

All the cars have gone.

They said they were going to stay till four.

The next cabin is empty as well.

The beer cans are stuffed in a paper sack.

He said they were going to be there until four. He said come over for lunch. He was heavy on top. He put his arms round me and kissed me and lifted me off the floor.

The manager watches me walking back. He pushes the fly screen ajar and the dull metal squeaks.

'Left quarter of an hour ago,' he says.

He holds the fly screen open with one hand. It is a dirty screen, the aluminium flecked with white and grease and dirt.

Oh.

'I rang through their chit.' He holds the yellow paper. 'Credit card bounced.'

The yellow slip flutters in the wind. He turns it in his hand as if it's something he's caught and doesn't know what to do with.

He leans against the fly screen.

I'm sorry?

'Your other booking. The one I forgot.'

I never booked. They're not coming. They never were.

'Really.' He raises an eyebrow. 'So you've lost them.'

The fly-screen squeaks shut behind him. Trucks are going by on the road. The sky is hard and blue with nothing in it.

## — NINETEEN —

Babe is waiting in the cabin, sitting on the end of the bed, her cheeks red from the hot water. She has a towel wrapped around her. He hair is stuck down in strands and the black elastic band she wears is tight around her wrist. She stands up when I enter. She wipes her cheeks. I scrape my boots on the mat and walk over to the sink and pour a glass of water and drink it slowly, in one gulp.

Babe lets the towel drop and stands barefoot on the carpet. I take her in my mouth and put my hand around the small of her back and guide her, stepping backwards to the bed. She undresses me, first my top and then my jeans. We fall naked into the bed, into the open sheets, and my mouth fills with her smell, her taste, my lipstick.

\*

Sid Vicious and Nancy died after they OD'd together. When the police arrived the bodies were in a terrible condition. Normally it takes 24 hours before a body starts to rot, but Sid and Nancy started to rot straight away. The police said it was because they had taken so much heroin in the last few weeks. I think it was because they were so consumed by love that they were wasting away. All that killing themselves did was to get rid of the last thing that was left.

The curtains swell in the wind and the sunlight falls on the doormat.

We left the door open the whole time.

She laughs at that. You would always pick fights with him.

You were fighting when I left, standing on the doorstep and screaming at each other. He was screaming at me as well but I didn't look back. He was telling you to keep out of it but you wouldn't. Telling you to keep out of something is a good as an invitation. Like a birthday card is as good as telling you to stay away.

You kept on shouting at him while I was loading my stuff in the taxi. The taxi driver was going to leave because he thought there was going to be violence. He didn't want to get involved or have to appear as a witness because that would mean losing work. He was telling me all this and trying to make excuses while I stuffed five dollar bills into his hand to stop him driving away with my things. When we got in the back seat you put your fingers through mine and squeezed.

My flat has nothing in it now. It used to be full of junk. Clothes and shoes and empty bottles. At night it feels as if everyone has booked out without paying, graduated and driven away.

Suddenly we are the only ones left, Babe and I. She is in the pool and I am standing on the verandah holding a baseball cap that isn't mine and the paper sack is full of bottles and the chit has bounced. The clouds are low but we might as well still be sunbathing on her dad's lawn, or sitting at the end of the row at the pictures, or running out of the store, the doors opening at the command of the electric eye. I have sweated out the makeup but everything might as well be black and white and overdressed, I might as well be fifty or a millionaire and say that everyone did come up for the party after all. They should have come. They really missed something good. They probably wouldn't think it was something good — they'd probably be bored, and they'd say so. The others can be pretty cruel when they want to. They'd probably want to put a record on or change the channel or turn up the stereo until it thumped through the walls. But they did miss it, they missed something good, something amazing and rarely seen, like Marilyn Monroe's cunt in the newspaper photo — something you have to want to see before you can.

*

I could do a lot of things. I could clean up the mess in the room or make some phone calls or tell Detective Sergeant whoever or pick up the card and stand up and snap on the lights — I could do a lot of things. But not just yet. I don't feel like it just yet. I stand on the verandah for awhile, stand and listen to the trucks rumbling past, going back and forth, back and forth, back and forth, taking nothing nowhere and back again.

*

Babe is waiting in the cabin, sitting on the end of the bed. She is fully dressed. Her bag is by the door and her black leather coat lies across her knees. She stands up when I come in and wipes my cheeks. She goes to the sink and brings me a glass of water. She says, it's time to leave. I've had enough holiday. She picks up her bags. I drink the glass slowly, in one gulp, and stand it next to the empty bed.

# — TWENTY —

'There are these two drunks driving home, Frank and Joe, and Joe says, Frank, Frank, we're getting closer to town. And Frank says, How can you tell? And Joe says: 'cause we're hitting more people.'

That's terrible.

Babe leans over the wheel, laughing.

That is terrible.

'Come on, it's a joke.'

And you a lawyer.

'Solicitor,' Babe says, wiping the tears from her eyes.

The wheels slide on the gravel road.

'So those guys bounced a cheque.' Babe shakes her head. 'That's classic. Truly. The manager hassles us for credit ID but when the boys come in he lets them through, doesn't check, doesn't worry — and he gets done. Seventy percent …' she raises her finger '… seventy percent of people committing credit fraud in this country are male. But it's the women they ask for ID. It makes you — what are you eating?'

I made Babe pack the fruit, in plastic bags.

'You don't have to eat it.' She makes a face. 'It's half rotten.'

It's only soft. Besides. It'd be a waste.

'It hardly cost anything.'

It's nice. Try some. I hold up a spoonful of melon and she takes it in her mouth like it's a dog turd, keeping her eyes on the road all the time. Come on. Chew.

She swallows. 'It should be fresh.'

It's not that bad. Fruit's good for you. You can tell when it's off because it goes rotten. You can tell just how fruit is and this is okay.

'I'm sorry. I'm scratchy.' She looks at herself in the rear view mirror. 'I feel awful.'

You look okay.

'It's because I'm tired. I feel like I was up all weekend. And when I do sleep I get woken up by your friend knocking on the door to tell me I don't have to be sorry for something I haven't done in the first place.'

He was only being nice.

'He was being a jerk. It's typical, you know? Typical fucking American. Him and all his piss-head friends being so up themselves that …'

Have some more melon.

'I don't want any more.'

Come on.

She looks worried, chewing. Take it easy, will you? I smooth her head. You frown. You're going to get an old lady's forehead.

'Hey: pay attention. *I am* an old lady.'

No you're not.

'I am.' She drums the steering column. 'And soon I'm going to be a lot older.'

She is going to do all these things she has never done before. And she will leave so much behind, everything, it will peel back a shockwave.

'I'm worried about *what* I'm going to leave, you know? It's like having to move your entire house in one afternoon — I'm bound to forget the one thing I need, or leave something behind that's really important.'

You will take everything you need.

'And what about the other things?'

They'll follow.
'I hope so.'
They'll come running.

*

We pull over at one of the tourist places, a brown and white brick house done up with fake weatherboards and shuttered windows and a sign saying CAFE: MEAT PIES. She orders Devonshire teas while I sit by the window. Traffic runs past the wide glass, my reflection. The checkered tablecloth.

'Um! Cream!' She wipes her chin. 'And the jam's fresh.'

After this the tea tastes bitter.

'I'll have yours if you don't.'

No. I'll save you from it.

The scones are warm and the cream is freshly whipped. Pressed between your tongue and the roof of your mouth it becomes liquid again. And it is nice. It tastes good.

'You don't get teas this good in the city.'

Oh come on.

'You don't. They're served in the hotels but they keep them a little too long.'

Conoisseur.

'Frances at work — you know Frances — she and I go out for tea once a week and it's never as good as this.'

Another logging truck goes past.

'They're stripping the forests out here. Clear-felling.' She crumples her napkin. 'When they're finished all the forests are gonna be gone.'

They'll grow back.

'Not the same forests, the originals.'

Close enough.

We watch the window. Across the road is nothing but trees — no buildings or houses. Only shade and a black mud gutter and pine needles six inches thick, the colour of rust. Underneath them is warm, where the bugs live — centipedes and ants, hiding from the birds.

Do you like your work?

'Not all the time. But mostly.'

What things?

'I like … working with other people. Helping them. A lot of people can't afford legal advice. They don't even know what's appropriate to them — their situation. We help them, and that feels good.'

Will you stay there?

'The pay's not good. But …' She tips her head. 'The harder things get for me, the more it makes me appreciate that … other people have it harder.'

You'll end up working for free.

'I think I practically do now. Besides,' She pats her stomach. '… I'm stopping in six months anyway.'

Will you go back to work?

'Not straight off. Brian'll be working, so …'

So who'll look after things when you do?

'Friends, I suppose.' She pours more tea. 'Are you volunteering for the roster?'

I didn't say that.

Babe holds her cup with two hands, smiling.

She lets me drive the rest of the way. I stomp on the accelerator, gobbling the miles between us and home, racing the trucks. Anyone would think we were in a hurry to get back.

The rain is waiting. Babe parks down the driveway so I can get out my things — and the fruit. 'Throw it out!' she urges. But it's fine, really, and I carry it to the steps and then go back and lean in the window to say goodbye.

'So this was my birthday party,' she smiles.

Christ. I know. I'm sorry.

'It's okay.' She puts her hand on my neck. 'It was okay, it was fun.'

It wasn't fun really. It was a whole lot of noisy people in a hotel and a grumpy manager.

'Were you talking with him? Before we left. I saw …'

No. Not me.

'Oh.'

How're you feeling, your stomach …

'Good.'

I've made you late for work.

'I rang in sick.'

Did you? I can never do that by myself. I get a friend to do it for me. You know: hi, this is Catrina's flatmate and she's not feeling well …

'You should go flatting with someone again.'

I guess.

'You shouldn't be all by yourself.' Babe cups her breast, her nipple. And I put my hand on it lightly, feeling the swelling. She looks up, red-eyed from the late nights and the talking and the drive and maybe something else and smiles and squeezes my hand. I lean back and fold my arms. She backs the car up the driveway, her long hair hanging out the window. I stand in the rain and watch her drive away.

The flat is so stuffy I have to open the windows. The lounge window has been repaired and the room smells of fresh putty. The new pane is cleaner than the others. I guess I will have to clean them all, now. The police didn't clean up anything.

The people upstairs are banging around, arguing. I bet if I rang them up and complained — for a change — they'd still keep on doing it. They are arguing about tonight's dinner party: what to cook, who to invite. So it's going to get noisier but at least they'll stop shouting when their friends arrive. Because you never talk about anything with your friends — all you do is have a good time.

I feel like being by myself tonight. Here seems more peaceful than the motel, even though everything is still around you — the traffic and the buildings and the people upstairs. Being crowded isn't so bad. I like having things around me. I don't know what to do with the baseball cap. I put it on the bench for now.

The landlord came down, before. He's a neat sort of person. He's an architect. To build this place he collected junk from the wreckers' yards and turned all the bits into something else and painted it white. Like the pillars by the door, they're not pillars at all — they're drainpipes, stood on one end. I'd like to build my house that way. Take the bits people want and turn it into something surprising. People appreciate you doing that, at least they do when you point it out to them. Most of the time they don't even notice.

The drive has really worn me out. I should eat something, but I don't.

I sit in bed watching the gas flames, the sheets around my chin.

My main concern is that it's not much of an ending. People used to say to me, Catrina, why do you say all this? And I could give them a hundred reasons, as many reasons as you like. I could even make some reasons up. But the real reason is simple. I like the endings. I can't be bothered with the little ones, myself. I like the big ones and the look on people's faces when they're over. I like everything to end in wide screen colour with the music swelling up and the audience cheering and the picture saying THE END.

The gas flames whistle. Night is outside, on the cold side of the glass.

The phone messages are still folded in my jacket pocket, the squares of paper covered in the manager's scrawly writing. I put them on the floor by the bed. I will ring back tomorrow. Tomorrow first thing.

Good night from something-something city, something-something road. It's warm and it's dark. And there is no noise, and sleep is a nice place to be, but it could be better. You know? I could never have met Wayne and never left him. He could have just never existed. And Babe would never have met anyone else, either. She would have hundreds of clothes and shoes and change her look every day, like she used to. And she would be happier like that, she wouldn't be being sick in the mornings and worrying about her job and what's going to happen next, about forgetting things. I would really like to give you a story like that, really give it to you good, and at the end the camera would pull back to widescreen colour with the music swelling in your ears and the audience cheering and the last words would flash across the screen, THE END.

But in the meantime the gas flames burn soft, and paint the room blue, and that's the best I can manage. Even if it isn't, it will do for now.

Believe me.

# Biographical Notes

## Janet Frame (1924–2004)

Janet Frame, the most internationally renowned New Zealand writer since Katherine Mansfield, was born in Dunedin, the third of five children. Her father, George, was a railway worker, and her family made several moves in her early years before settling in Oamaru in 1930. Her mother, Lottie, wrote poetry and instilled a love of literature in her children. Frame has written extensively about the tragic circumstances of her early life (including the deaths of two of her sisters) in her three volumes of autobiography *To the Is-Land* (1982), *An Angel at My Table* (1984), and *The Envoy from Mirror City* (1985), subsequently collected into a single volume, *Janet Frame: An Autobiography* (1989) and made the basis of the film *An Angel at My Table* (1990) directed by Jane Campion.

After Waitaki Girls High School, Janet attended Dunedin Teachers Training College and Otago University (1943–44). She abandoned teaching and after illness became a voluntary patient at Seacliff Mental Hospital in 1947. Mistakenly diagnosed as schizophrenic she was a psychiatric patient for eight years, during which time she was regularly subjected to electric shock treatment. Frame published her first story in 1946 and eventually her first collection *The Lagoon: Stories* was published in 1951. After her release from hospital in 1954 Frame lived for a time with the writer Frank Sargeson in Takapuna on Auckland's North Shore where she wrote *Owls Do Cry* (1957). She lived abroad from 1956 to 1963, mostly in Ibiza and London. In London she wrote several novels including *Faces in the Water* (1961), *The Edge of the Alphabet* (1962) and *Scented Gardens for the Blind* (1963). Also in 1963 Frame published in the United States *The Reservoir: Stories and Sketches* and *Snowman Snowman: Fables and Fantasies*; a selection from these was published in the United Kingdom and New Zealand as *The Reservoir and other stories* (1966).

Frame returned to New Zealand after the death of her father in 1963. She published several more novels including *The Adaptable Man* (1965), *A State of Siege* (1966) and *The Rainbirds* (1968) — published in the United States as *Yellow Flowers in the Antipodean Room* (1969). In New Zealand, Frame lived first in Dunedin and in several other towns mostly in the North Island including Whangaparoa, Auckland, Stratford, Levin and Avondale; she eventually settled again in Dunedin in 1997 until her death in 2004. She travelled frequently to the United States in the 1960s and 1970s, often to writer's residencies, such as Yaddo. Her later novels were *Intensive Care* (1970),

*Daughter Buffalo* (1972), *Living in the Maniototo* (1979) and *The Carpathians* (1989). She published one collection of poetry *The Pocket Mirror* (1967), a children's book *Mona Minim and the Smell of the Sun* (1969), and a book of selected stories *You Are Now Entering the Human Heart* (1983), which included the first New Zealand publication of the novella, *Snowman, Snowman*. Numerous critical studies of Frame's work have been published. A biography, *Wrestling with the Angel: A life of Janet Frame* (Viking) by Michael King was published in 2000.

The source of the text included in this volume is *You Are Now Entering the Human Heart* (Victoria University Press, 1983).

## Maurice Shadbolt (1932–2004)

Maurice Shadbolt was born in Auckland and educated at Te Kuiti District High School, Avondale College and Auckland University College. He was a newspaper journalist and scriptwriter for the New Zealand National Film Unit before going to Europe in 1957, where he published a well-received first collection of stories *The New Zealanders* (1959). Back in New Zealand, where he eventually settled in Titirangi, Auckland, he published a further collection of stories *Summer Fires and Winter Country* (1963) and a book of three novellas *The Presence of Music* (1957). He returned to the novella for his last book of fiction *Dove on the Waters* (1996). Between 1965 and 1993 he published ten novels: *Among the Cinders* (1965), *This Summer's Dolphin* (1969), *An Ear of the Dragon* (1971), *Strangers and Journeys* (1972), *A Touch of Clay* (1974), *Danger Zone* (1975), *The Lovelock Version* (1980), *Season of the Jew* (1986), *Monday's Warriors* (1990), and *The House of Strife* (1993), the last three being a trilogy of historical novels about the New Zealand Wars of the nineteenth century. In addition to his novels Shadbolt wrote two autobiographical works, *One of Ben's* (1993) and *From the Edge of the Sky* (1999), the play *Once on Chunuk Bair* (1982), and several works of non-fiction including *New Zealand: Gift of the Sea* with photographs by Brian Brake (1963), *Love and Legend: Some Twentieth Century New Zealanders* (1976), and (again with Brake) *The Reader's Digest Guide to New Zealand* (1988). There are also two volumes of selected stories, *Figures in Light: Selected Stories* (1978), and *Selected Stories* (1998).

The source of the text used in this volume is *The Presence of Music: Three Novellas* (Cassell, 1957).

## Ronald Hugh Morrieson (1922–1972)

Ronald Hugh Morrieson was born and spent his whole life in the town of Hawera, South Taranaki. His father died when Morrieson was nine and he spent the rest of his life living at home with his mother and aunt. In his twenties and thirties he worked as a dance-band musician round South Taranaki, eventually in his forties giving up performing for music-teaching (piano and guitar) so he could concentrate on writing. His first two novels *The Scarecrow* (1963) and *Came a Hot Friday* (1964), published in Australia, received excellent reviews and attracted the attention of some well-known New Zealand writers including Maurice Shadbolt, Dick Scott, Frank Sargeson and C.K. Stead, who tried vainly to promote his reputation and arrest his disastrous alcoholic decline. His two later novels *Predicament* (1975) and *Pallet on the Floor* (1976) were published posthumously, having failed to attract a publisher in his lifetime. His only two short surviving stories 'Cross My Heart and Cut My Throat' and 'The Chimney' were also published posthumously. After his death Morrieson's early books were reissued and three of the novels were made into feature films. Sadly, his posthumous success proved the accuracy of his gloomy prediction to Maurice Shadbolt, 'I hope I'm not another one of these poor buggers who get discovered when they're dead.' Peter Simpson wrote a critical study of his work for Oxford University Press's 'New Zealand Writers and their Work' series, *Ronald Hugh Morrieson* (1982) and there is a biography by Julia Millen, *Ronald Hugh Morrieson: a biography* (1996).

The source of the text used in this volume is *Pallet on the Floor and two stories*, with an introduction by Peter Simpson (Penguin 1983).

## Ian Wedde (born 1946)

Ian Wedde was born in Blenheim and at the age of seven travelled abroad with his parents for eight years, living in East Pakistan (now Bangladesh) and the United Kingdom, where he attended boarding school. He returned to New Zealand at fifteen and was educated at Kings College and the University of Auckland (MA, 1968). After graduating he travelled extensively in the Middle East and Europe before returning to New Zealand in 1972. He lived first in Port Chalmers before moving to Wellington in 1975. Wedde began publishing poems and stories from the late 1960s. His first substantial collection of poems was *Made Over* (1974); other volumes include *Earthly: Sonnets for Carlos* (1975), *Spells for Coming Out* (1977), *Castaly* (1980), *Georgicon* (1984), *Tales of Gotham City* (1984), *Driving Into the Storm: Selected Poems* (1987), *Tendering* (1988), *The Drummer* (1993), and, after a gap of some years, *The Commonmplace Odes* (2002). *Dick Seddon's Great Dive* (1976), a novella, was later included in *The Shirt Factory and Other Stories* (1981). A major historical novel, *Symmes Hole* (1986), was followed by *Survival Arts* (1988). With Harvey McQueen, Wedde edited an important anthology *The Penguin Book of New Zealand Verse* (1985), and, with McQueen and Miriama Evans *The Penguin Book of Contemporary*

New Zealand Poetry (1989). Between 1983 and 1990 Wedde was art critic for the Evening Post (Wellington). He has curated a number of art exhibitions including Now See Here! Art, Language and Translation (with Gregory Burke, 1990) and Fomison: What Shall We tell Them? (1994). In 1994 he joined the staff of Te Papa Tongarewa/The Museum of New Zealand as Concept Leader Humanities, a position he held until 2004. A large selection of his critical writings was published as How to be Nowhere: Essays and Texts, 1971-1994 (1995); a further collection of essays, Making Ends Meet will be published in 2005. Now an independent writer and researcher, he is the Meridian Energy Katherine Mansfield Memorial Fellow in Menton, France, in 2005.

The source of the text used in this volume is The Shirt Factory and Other Stories (Victoria University Press, 1981).

## Keri Hulme (born 1947)

Keri Hulme was born in Christchurch, the eldest of a family of six children. Her father came from Lancashire stock, while her mother was a mixture of Orkney Scots and Maori (Kai Tahu, Kati Mamoe). She was educated at Aranui High School and spent holidays with her mother's extended family at Moeraki on the east coast of the South Island, the place she regards as her turangawaewae, 'the standing place of my heart'. She first came to notice as a writer by winning the Katherine Mansfield Award for her story 'Hooks and Feelers' in 1975; meanwhile she worked for over fifteen years on the novel which was eventually published as the bone people in 1984. Success at home for what is so far her only novel was followed by the unprecedented accolade (for a New Zealand writer) of the Booker Prize in 1985, which led to multiple translations and international attention. Hulme has also published two collections of poetry, The Silences Between (Moeraki Conversations) (1982) and Strands (1992). The generically ambiguous Lost Possessions (1985) is sometimes treated as a poetry collection, sometimes as an extended story. Hulme has published two volumes of stories, Te Kaihau/The Windeater (1986) and Stonefish (2004), and a work of non-fiction, Homeplaces: Three Coasts of the South Island (with photographs by Robin Morrison) (1989). She lives in the remote coastal settlement of Okarito in South Westland.

The text of Te Kaihau/The Windeater is taken from the collection of that name published by Victoria University Press in 1986.

## Russell Haley (born 1934)

Rusell Haley was born in Yorkshire. After two years National Service in the RAF (partly in Iraq), he emigrated to Australia in 1961 and then to New Zealand in 1966, graduating MA at the University of Auckland in 1970. He was part of the group which produced the journal *The Word is Freed* (1969–72), editing the last issue, *Freed at Last*, himself. Initially Haley focused on poetry, producing *The Walled Garden* (1972) and *On the Faultline* (1977). His first story collections were *The Sauna Bath Mysteries* (1978) and *Real Illusions* (1984). Haley's quotation from Salman Rushdie: 'I build imaginary countries and try to impose on them the ones that exist', might be applied to *The Transfer Station* (1989), a story sequence. Haley has published four novels, namely *The Settlement* (1986), *Beside Myself* (1990), *All Done with Mirrors* (1999) and *Tomorrow Tastes Better* (2001). He has also written a biography of the painter Pat Hanly, *Hanly: A New Zealand Artist* (1989), and edited with Susan Davis *The Penguin Book of Contemporary New Zealand Short Stories* (1989).

The text used here is taken from *A Spider-web Season and The Transfer Station* (Hazard Press, 2000).

## Witi Ihimaera (born 1944)

Witi Ihimaera was born in Gisborne of Te Atianga-a-Mahaki descent. His family marae is Rongopai in Waituhi near Gisborne. He attended various high schools and the University of Auckland, eventually completing his BA at Victoria University (Wellington). After working for the Post Office he became a diplomat from 1973 to 1989, including postings to Canberra, Washington and New York. His first book was *Pounamu, Pounamu* (1972), followed by two novels *Tangi* (1973) and *Whanau* (1974); a second volume of stories was *The New Net Goes Fishing* (1977). After the best part of a decade of silence he returned with *The Matriarch* (1986) and *The Whale Rider* (1987), later made into a successful film directed by Niki Caro (2002). Other novels are *Bulibasha: King of the Gypsies* (1994), *Nights in the Gardens of Spain* (1995), *The Dream Swimmer* (1997), *The Uncle's Story* (2000) and *Sky Dancer* (2003). Later story collections are *Dear Miss Mansfield* (1989), *Kingfisher Come Home: the complete Maori stories* (1995), and *Ihimaera: His Best Stories* (2003). Recently, Ihimaera has begun issuing substantially revised editions of his early works including *Pounamu, Pounamu* (2003) and *Whanau II* (2004). He has edited several anthologies of Maori writing including *Into the World of Light* (with D.S.Long, 1982), the five volume series *Te Ao Marama* (1992–96), and *Where's Waari?* (2000). His play *Woman Far Walking* was performed and published in 2000. He is professor of English at the University of Auckland with responsibility for the Creative Writing programme.

The text used here is taken from *Ihimaera: His Best Stories* (Reed, 2003)

# Mike Johnson (born 1947)

Mike Johnson was born in Christchurch and grew up in rural Canterbury. He graduated from the University of Canterbury in Political Science and spent the years 1972–80 travelling in Europe, Africa and Asia, and working as an English language teacher, before returning to settle on Waiheke Island. He has worked as a teacher, bookshop owner and more recently as a creative writing instructor. He has been active in environmental politics, twice standing for parliament for the Green Party. He has published four books of poetry: *The Palenquin Ropes* (1983), *From a Woman in Mount Eden Prison* (1984), *Standing Wave* (1985) and *Treasure Hunt* (1996). His works of fiction are: *Lear: the Shakespeare Company Plays Lear at Babylon* (1986), *Anti-Body Positive* (1988), *Lethal Dose* (1991), *Foreigners: Three Novellas* (1991), *Dumb Show* (1996), *Counterpoint* (2001), and *Stench* (2004). He currently teaches creative writing at the University of Auckland.

The text used here is taken from *Foreigners: Three Novellas* (Penguin, 1991).

# Chad Taylor (born 1964)

Chad Taylor was born and educated in Auckland, graduating with a BFA from the University of Auckland. He has written film scripts as well as fiction. He has published five works of fiction: *Pack of Lies* (1994), *Heaven* (1994), *The Man Who Wasn't Feeling Himself* (stories, 1995), *Shirker* (2000), and *Electric* (2003). Several of his novels have been translated into German, French and Italian. A feature film has been made of *Heaven* (Miramax, 1999), known in Europe as *The Paradise*. He was the literary fellow at the University of Auckland in 2003, and has contributed to the university's creative writing courses.

The text used here is taken from *Pack of Lies* (Hazard, 1994).

# Acknowledgements

The editor would like to thank the publishers of the following books in which the works listed first appeared or were printed.

Every effort has been made to locate copyright holders or their agents. The publisher would be interested to hear from any copyright holders who have not already been acknowledged.

Maurice Shadbolt, *Figures in Light* (1967) from *The Presence of Music: Three Novellas* (Cassell, 1967).

Ronald Hugh Morrieson, *Pallet on the Floor* (1976) [written 1971–72], from *Pallet on the Floor and Two Stories* (Penguin, 1983).

Ian Wedde, *Dick Seddon's Great Dive* (1976), from *The Shirt Factory and other stories* (Victoria University Press, 1981).

Janet Frame, *Snowman, Snowman* (1963), from *You Are Now Entering the Human Heart* (VUP, 1983).

Keri Hulme, *Te Kaihau The Wind Eater* (Victoria University Press, 1987).

Witi Ihimaera, *The Halcyon Summer* revised in *Ihimaera: His Best Stories* (Reed, 2003) from *Dear Miss Mansfield* (Viking, 1989).

Russell Haley, *The Transfer Station* (1989), from *A Spider Web Season & The Transfer Station* (Hazard, 2000).

Mike Johnson, *Frames* (1991), from *Foreigners* (Penguin, 1991).

Chad Taylor, *Pack of Lies* (Hazard, 1994).

# SEVEN NEW ZEALAND NOVELLAS

KATHERINE MANSFIELD

FRANK SARGESON

MAURICE DUGGAN

PATRICIA GRACE

ALBERT WENDT

PETER WELLS

ELIZABETH KNOX

EDITED BY PETER SIMPSON

Edited and with an introduction by Dr Peter Simpson, this anthology profiles the short novels of seven leading writers:

| | |
|---|---|
| Katherine Mansfield | *Prelude* |
| Frank Sargeson | *That Summer* |
| Maurice Duggan | *O'Leary's Orchard* |
| Patricia Grace | *Valley* |
| Albert Wendt | *Flying-fox in a Freedom Tree* |
| Peter Wells | *Of Memory and Desire* |
| Elizabeth Knox | *Pomare* |

*Seven New Zealand Novellas* was shortlisted for the Montana Book Awards 2004, reference and anthology section.

ISBN 0 7900 0896 3